Praise for *Warbreaker*

"Sanderson's heroines and heroes are outstanding—especially Vasher, whose special relationship with his sentient sword is both sardonic and sinister. The mysteries of life after death, of identity and destiny, of the politics of magic, are unveiled through three-dimensional characters. Not only has Sanderson drawn a freshly imagined world and its society, he has also given us a plot full of unexpected twists and turns. In subtle prose, notable for its quiet irony, Sanderson tells the story of two sisters and the god they are doomed to marry. **Anyone looking for a different and refreshing fantasy novel will be delighted.**"

—Michael Moorcock

"Chosen by the estate of the late Robert Jordan to complete the final volume in Jordan's mammoth Wheel of Time series, Sanderson again demonstrates his capacity for handling large and complex themes while creating believable characters. He also succeeds at building a unique fantasy environment in which color and *breath* are the basis for magic. This is **essential reading** for fantasy fans."

—*Library Journal* (starred review)

"This **very superior** stand-alone fantasy proves, among other things, that Sanderson was a good choice to complete the late Robert Jordan's Wheel of Time saga. Sanderson is clearly a master of large-scale stories, splendidly depicting worlds as well as strong female characters."   —*Booklist*

"A highly readable and compelling stand-alone volume from the acclaimed author of the Mistborn trilogy. As is to be expected, **the world-building is superb**, utilizing a thoroughly thought-out system of magic and religion. Highly recommended to fans of epic fantasy."

—*RT Book Reviews* (4½ Stars, Top Pick!)

Praise for Brandon Sanderson

"Always the best fantasy writers strike off on their own, and now their work is coming to the fore. . . . For instance, Brandon Sanderson's Mistborn trilogy is new but complete, so there's no waiting to get to the end of the story. The motley cast of talented misfits is trying to bring down a thousand-year empire (try to avoid thinking 'reich'), but the heroes discover to their dismay that as bad as the empire was, it was holding back something even worse.

"Or if you want to get in on the ground floor, look at Sanderson's newest hardcover, *Warbreaker*—a whole new magic system with Graustarkian intrigue at the highest level."   —Orson Scott Card

"Sanderson is an evil genius. There is simply no other way to describe what he's managed to pull off in this **transcendent** final volume in his Mistborn trilogy."
                              —*RT Book Reviews* (Gold Medal, Top Pick!)
                              on *The Hero of Ages*

"Sanderson's conclusion to [his] epic . . . resonates with all the elements of classic heroic fantasy, along with unusual forms of magic and strong, believable characters. Chosen to complete the late Robert Jordan's mammoth Wheel of Time series, Sanderson proves himself **a master storyteller** in his own right."
                              —*Library Journal* on *The Hero of Ages*

"A great epic fantasy . . . Fans of Terry Goodkind and Terry Brooks will find *The Well of Ascension* fulfilling, satisfying, and incredibly exciting."   —*SFRevu*

"Brandon Sanderson is the real thing—an exciting storyteller with a unique and powerful vision." —David Farland

Books by Brandon Sanderson

Warbreaker

THE MISTBORN TRILOGY
Mistborn: The Final Empire
The Well of Ascension
The Hero of Ages

Elantris

Alcatraz Versus the Evil Librarians
Alcatraz Versus the Scrivener's Bones
Alcatraz Versus the Knights of Crystallia

The Way of Kings

Warbreaker

Brandon Sanderson

TOR®
fantasy

A TOM DOHERTY ASSOCIATES BOOK
NEW YORK

For Emily,
who said yes

This is a work of fiction. All of the characters, organizations, and events portrayed in this novel are either products of the author's imagination or are used fictitiously.

WARBREAKER

Copyright © 2009 by Dragonsteel Entertainment, LLC.

Excerpt from *The Way of Kings* copyright © 2010 by Dragonsteel Entertainment, LLC.

Edited by Moshe Feder

Map by Shawn Boyles

A Tor Book
Published by Tom Doherty Associates, LLC
175 Fifth Avenue
New York, NY 10010

www.tor-forge.com

Tor® is a registered trademark of Tom Doherty Associates, LLC.

ISBN 978-0-7653-6003-8

First Edition: June 2009
First Mass Market Edition: April 2010

Printed in the United States of America

0   9   8   7   6   5   4   3   2   1

Contents

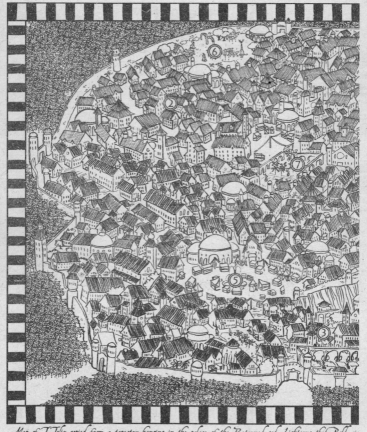

Map of T.Tolir copied from a tapestry hanging in the palace of the Returned god Lightsong the Bold, ci

T'TELIR

1 – THE COURT OF GODS
2 – THE HIGHLANDS
3 – LEMEX'S HOUSE
4 – DENTH'S SAFEHOUSE
5 – MARKET
6 – D'DENIR GARDEN
7 – CROSSROADS GARDEN

ca 327. This artistic representation of the city is not to scale, but is a useful reference of relative locations

Acknowledgments

Working on *Warbreaker* was an unusual process in some ways; you can read more about it on my website. Suffice it to say that I had a more varied pool of alpha readers than normally, many of whom I know primarily through their handles on my forums. I've tried to get everyone's names in here, but I'm sure I'm going to miss some. If you are one of those individuals, feel free to e-mail me, and we'll try to get you in future printings.

The first acknowledgment goes to my lovely wife, Emily Sanderson, whom I married while writing this book. This is the first novel of mine that she had a large hand in by giving me feedback and suggestions, and her help is greatly appreciated. Also, as always, my agent, Joshua Bilmes, and my editor, Moshe Feder, did an extremely large amount of work on this manuscript, taking it from the Second or Third Heightening to at least the Eighth.

At Tor, several people have gone well beyond their call of duty. The first is Dot Lin, my publicist, who has been particularly awesome to work with. Thanks, Dot! And, as always, the tireless efforts of Larry Yoder deserve a note, as well as the excellent work of Tor's art director genius, Irene Gallo. Dan Dos Santos did the cover art of this book, and I strongly suggest you check out his website and his other work, because I think he's one of the best in the business right now. Also, Paul Stevens deserves a word of thanks for being the in-house liaison for my books.

In the special thanks department, we have Joevans3, and Dreamking47, Louise Simard, Jeff Creer, Megan Kauffman, thelsdj, Megan Hutchins, Izzy Whiting, Janci Olds, Drew Olds, Karla Bennion, Eric James Stone, Dan Wells, Isaac Stewart, Ben Olsen, Greyhound, Demented Yam, D.Demille, Loryn, Kuntry Bumpken, Vadia, U-boat, Tjaeden, Dragon Fly, pterath, BarbaraJ, Shir Hasirim, Digitalbias, Spink Longfellow, amyface, Richard "Captain Goradel" Gordon, Swiggly, Dawn Cawley, Drerio, David B, Mi'chelle Trammel, Matthew R Carlin, Ollie Tabooger, John Palmer, Henrik Nyh, and the insoluble Peter Ahlstrom.

Prologue

It's funny, Vasher thought, *how many things begin with my getting thrown into prison.*

The guards laughed to one another, slamming the cell door shut with a clang. Vasher stood and dusted himself off, rolling his shoulder and wincing. While the bottom half of his cell door was solid wood, the top half was barred, and he could see the three guards open his large duffel and rifle through his possessions.

One of them noticed him watching. The guard was an oversized beast of a man with a shaved head and a dirty uniform that barely retained the bright yellow and blue coloring of the T'Telir city guard.

Bright colors, Vasher thought. *I'll have to get used to those again.* In any other nation, the vibrant blues and yellows would have been ridiculous on soldiers. This, however, was Hallandren: land of Returned gods, Lifeless servants, BioChromatic research, and—of course—color.

The large guard sauntered up to the cell door, leaving his friends to amuse themselves with Vasher's belongings. "They say you're pretty tough," the man said, sizing up Vasher.

Vasher did not respond.

"The bartender says you beat down some twenty men in the brawl." The guard rubbed his chin. "You don't look that tough to me. Either way, you should have known better than to strike a priest. The others, they'll spend a night locked up. You, though . . . you'll hang. Colorless fool."

Vasher turned away. His cell was functional, if unoriginal. A thin slit at the top of one wall let in light, the stone walls dripped with water and moss, and a pile of dirty straw decomposed in the corner.

"You ignoring me?" the guard asked, stepping closer to the door. The colors of his uniform brightened, as if he'd stepped into a stronger light. The change was slight. Vasher didn't have much Breath remaining, and so his aura didn't do much to the colors around him. The guard didn't notice the change in color—just as he hadn't noticed back in the bar, when he and his buddies had picked Vasher up off the floor and thrown him in their cart. Of course, the change was so slight to the unaided eye that it would have been nearly impossible to pick out.

"Here, now," said one of the men looking through Vasher's duffel. "What's *this*?" Vasher had always found it interesting that the men who watched dungeons tended to be as bad as, or worse than, the men they guarded. Perhaps that was deliberate. Society didn't seem to care if such men were outside the cells or in them, so long as they were kept away from more honest men.

Assuming that such a thing existed.

From Vasher's bag, a guard pulled free a long object wrapped in white linen. The man whistled as he unwrapped the cloth, revealing a long, thin-bladed sword in a silver sheath. The hilt was pure black. "Who do you suppose he stole *this* from?"

The lead guard eyed Vasher, likely wondering if Vasher was some kind of nobleman. Though Hallandren had no aristocracy, many neighboring kingdoms had their lords and ladies. Yet what lord would wear a drab brown cloak, ripped in several places? What lord would sport bruises from a bar fight, a half-grown beard, and boots worn from years of walking? The guard turned away, apparently convinced that Vasher was no lord.

He was right. And he was wrong.

"Let me see that," the lead guard said, taking the sword. He grunted, obviously surprised by its weight. He turned it about, noting the clasp that tied sheath to hilt, keeping the blade from being drawn. He undid the clasp.

The colors in the room deepened. They didn't grow brighter—not the way the guard's vest had when he approached Vasher. Instead, they grew *stronger*. Darker. Reds became maroon. Yellows hardened to gold. Blues approached navy.

"Be careful, friend," Vasher said softly, "that sword can be dangerous."

The guard looked up. All was still. Then the guard snorted and walked away from Vasher's cell, still carrying the sword. The other two followed, bearing Vasher's duffel, entering the guard room at the end of the hallway.

The door thumped shut. Vasher immediately knelt beside the patch of straw, selecting a handful of sturdy lengths. He pulled threads from his cloak—it was beginning to fray at the bottom—and tied the straw into the shape of a small person, perhaps three inches high, with bushy arms and legs. He plucked a hair from one of his eyebrows, set it against the straw figure's head, then reached into his boot and pulled out a brilliant red scarf.

Then Vasher Breathed.

It flowed out of him, puffing into the air, translucent yet radiant, like the color of oil on water in the sun. Vasher felt it leave: BioChromatic Breath, scholars called it. Most people just called it Breath. Each person had one. Or, at least, that was how it usually went. One person, one Breath.

Vasher had around fifty Breaths, just enough to reach the First Heightening. Having so few made him feel poor compared with what he'd once held, but many would consider fifty Breaths to be a great treasure. Unfortunately, even Awakening a small figure made from organic material—using a piece of his own body as a focus—drained away some half of his Breaths.

The little straw figure jerked, sucking in the Breath. In Vasher's hand, half of the brilliant red scarf faded to grey. Vasher leaned down—imagining what he wanted the figure to do—and completed the final step of the process as he gave the Command.

"Fetch keys," he said.

The straw figure stood and raised its single eyebrow toward Vasher.

Vasher pointed toward the guard room. From it, he heard sudden shouts of surprise.

Not much time, he thought.

The straw person ran along the floor, then jumped up, vaulting between the bars. Vasher pulled off his cloak and set it on the floor. It was the perfect shape of a person—marked with rips that matched the scars on Vasher's body, its hood cut with holes to match Vasher's eyes. The closer an object was to human shape and form, the fewer Breaths it took to Awaken.

Vasher leaned down, trying not to think of the days when he'd had enough Breaths to Awaken without regard for shape or focus. That had been a different time. Wincing, he pulled a tuft of hair from his head, then sprinkled it across the hood of the cloak.

Once again, he Breathed.

It took the rest of his Breath. With it gone—the cloak trembling, the scarf losing the rest of its color—Vasher felt . . . dimmer. Losing one's Breath was not fatal. Indeed, the extra Breaths Vasher used had once belonged to other people. Vasher didn't know who they were; he hadn't gathered these Breaths himself. They had been given to him. But, of course, that was the way it was always supposed to work. One could not take Breath by force.

Being void of Breath *did* change him. Colors didn't seem as bright. He couldn't *feel* the bustling people moving about in the city above, a connection he normally took for granted. It was the awareness all men had for others—that thing which whispered a warning, in the drowsiness of sleep, when someone entered the room. In Vasher, that sense had been magnified fifty times.

And now it was gone. Sucked into the cloak and the straw person, giving them power.

The cloak jerked. Vasher leaned down. "Protect me," he Commanded, and the cloak grew still. He stood, throwing it back on.

The straw figure returned to his window. It carried a large ring of keys. The figure's straw feet were stained red. The crimson blood seemed so dull to Vasher now.

He took the keys. "Thank you," he said. He always thanked them. He didn't know why, particularly considering what he did next. "Your Breath to mine," he commanded, touching the straw person's chest. The straw person immediately fell backward off the door—life draining from it—and Vasher got his Breath back. The familiar sense of awareness returned, the knowledge of connectedness, of *fitting*. He could only take the Breath back because he'd Awakened this creature himself—indeed, Awakenings of this sort were rarely permanent. He used his Breath like a reserve, doling it out, then recovering it.

Compared with what he had once held, twenty-five Breaths was a laughably small number. However, compared with nothing, it seemed infinite. He shivered in satisfaction.

The yells from the guard room died out. The dungeon fell still. He had to keep moving.

Vasher reached through the bars, using the keys to unlock his cell. He pushed the thick door open, rushing out into the hallway, leaving the straw figure discarded on the ground. He didn't walk to the guard room—and the exit beyond it—but instead turned south, penetrating deeper into the dungeon.

This was the most uncertain part of his plan. Finding a tavern that was frequented by priests of the Iridescent

Tones had been easy enough. Getting into a bar fight—
then striking one of those same priests—had been equally
simple. Hallandren took their religious figures very seriously, and Vasher had earned himself not the usual im-
prisonment in a local jail, but a trip to the God King's
dungeons.

Knowing the kind of men who tended to guard such
dungeons, he'd had a pretty good idea that they would try
to draw Nightblood. That had given him the diversion he'd
needed to get the keys.

But now came the unpredictable part.

Vasher stopped, Awakened cloak rustling. It was easy to
locate the cell he wanted, for around it a large patch of
stone had been drained of color, leaving both walls and
doors a dull grey. It was a place to imprison an Awakener,
for no color meant no Awakening. Vasher stepped up to
the door, looking through the bars. A man hung by his arms
from the ceiling, naked and chained. His color was vibrant
to Vasher's eyes, his skin a pure tan, his bruises brilliant
splashes of blue and violet.

The man was gagged. Another precaution. In order to
Awaken, the man would need three things: Breath, color,
and a Command. The harmonics and the hues, some called
it. The Iridescent Tones, the relationship between color and
sound. A Command had to be spoken clearly and firmly
in the Awakener's native language—any stuttering, any
mispronunciation, would invalidate the Awakening. The
Breath would be drawn out, but the object would be unable
to act.

Vasher used the prison keys to unlock the cell door, then
stepped inside. This man's aura made colors grow brighter
by sharp measure when they got close to him. Anyone
would be able to notice an aura that strong, though it was
much easier for someone who had reached the First Heightening.

It wasn't the strongest BioChromatic aura Vasher had

ever seen—those belonged to the Returned, known as gods here in Hallandren. Still, the prisoner's BioChroma was very impressive and much, much stronger than Vasher's own. The prisoner held a lot of Breaths. Hundreds upon hundreds of them.

The man swung in his bonds, studying Vasher, gagged lips bleeding from lack of water. Vasher hesitated only briefly, then reached up and pulled the gag free.

"You," the prisoner whispered, coughing slightly. "Are you here to free me?"

"No, Vahr," Vasher said quietly. "I'm here to kill you."

Vahr snorted. Captivity hadn't been easy on him. When Vasher had last seen Vahr, he'd been plump. Judging by his emaciated body, he'd been without food for some time now. The cuts, bruises, and burn marks on his flesh were fresh.

Both the torture and the haunted look in Vahr's bag-rimmed eyes bespoke a solemn truth. Breath could only be transferred by willing, intentional Command. That Command could, however, be encouraged.

"So," Vahr croaked, "you judge me, just like everyone else."

"Your failed rebellion is not my concern. I just want your Breath."

"You and the entire Hallandren court."

"Yes. But you're not going to give it to one of the Returned. You're going to give it to me. In exchange for killing you."

"Doesn't seem like much of a trade." There was a hardness—a void of emotion—in Vahr that Vasher had not seen the last time they had parted, years before.

Odd, Vasher thought, *that I should finally, after all of this time, find something in the man that I can identify with.*

Vasher kept a wary distance from Vahr. Now that the man's voice was free, he could Command. However, he was touching nothing except for the metal chains, and metal was very difficult to Awaken. It had never been alive, and it was far from the form of a man. Even during the height of his power, Vasher himself had only managed to Awaken metal on a few select occasions. Of course, some extremely powerful Awakeners could bring objects to life that they weren't touching, but that were in the sound of their voice. That, however, required the Ninth Heightening. Even Vahr didn't have *that* much Breath. In fact, Vasher knew of only one living person who did: the God King himself.

That meant Vasher was probably safe. Vahr contained a great wealth of Breath, but had nothing to Awaken. Vasher walked around the chained man, finding it very difficult to offer any sympathy. Vahr had earned his fate. Yet the priests would not let him die while he held so much Breath; if he died, it would be wasted. Gone. Irretrievable.

Not even the government of Hallandren—which had such strict laws about the buying and passing of Breath—could let such a treasure slip away. They wanted it badly enough to forestall the execution of even a high-profile criminal like Vahr. In retrospect, they would curse themselves for not leaving him better guarded.

But, then, Vasher had been waiting two years for an opportunity like this one.

"Well?" Vahr asked.

"Give me the Breath, Vahr," Vasher said, stepping forward.

Vahr snorted. "I doubt you have the skill of the God King's torturers, Vasher—and I've withstood them for two weeks now."

"You'd be surprised. But that doesn't matter. You *are* going to give me your Breath. You know you have only two choices. Give it to me, or give it to them."

Vahr hung by his wrists, rotating slowly. Silent.

"You don't have much time to consider," Vasher said. "Any moment now, someone is going to discover the dead guards outside. The alarm will be raised. I'll leave you, you *will* be tortured again, and you *will* eventually break. Then all the power you've gathered will go to the very people you vowed to destroy."

Vahr stared at the floor. Vasher let him hang for a few moments, and could see that the reality of the situation was clear to him. Finally, Vahr looked up at Vasher. "That . . . thing you bear. It's here, in the city?"

Vasher nodded.

"The screams I heard earlier? It caused them?"

Vasher nodded again.

"How long will you be in T'Telir?"

"For a time. A year, perhaps."

"Will you use it against them?"

"My goals are my own to know, Vahr. Will you take my deal or not? Quick death in exchange for those Breaths. I promise you this. Your enemies will *not* have them."

Vahr grew quiet. "It's yours," he finally whispered.

Vasher reached over, resting his hand on Vahr's forehead—careful not to let any part of his clothing touch the man's skin, lest Vahr draw forth color for Awakening.

Vahr didn't move. He looked numb. Then, just as Vasher began to worry that the prisoner had changed his mind, Vahr Breathed. The color drained from him. The beautiful Iridescence, the aura that had made him look majestic despite his wounds and chains. It flowed from his mouth, hanging in the air, shimmering like mist. Vasher drew it in, closing his eyes.

"My life to yours," Vahr Commanded, a hint of despair in his voice. "My Breath become yours."

The Breath flooded into Vasher, and everything became vibrant. His brown cloak now seemed deep and rich in color. The blood on the floor was intensely red, as if aflame. Even Vahr's skin seemed a masterpiece of color, the surface marked by deep black hairs, blue bruises, and sharp red cuts. It had been years since Vasher had felt such . . . *life.*

He gasped, falling to his knees as it overwhelmed him, and he had to drop a hand to the stone floor to keep himself from toppling over. *How did I live without this?*

He knew that his senses hadn't actually improved, yet he felt so much more alert. More aware of the beauty of sensation. When he touched the stone floor, he marveled at its roughness. And the sound of wind passing through the thin dungeon window up above. Had it always been that melodic? How could he not have noticed?

"Keep your part of the bargain," Vahr said. Vasher noted the tones in his voice, the beauty of each one, how close they were to harmonics. Vasher had gained perfect pitch. A gift for anyone who reached the Second Heightening. It would be good to have that again.

Vasher could, of course, have up to the Fifth Heightening at any time, if he wished. That would require certain sacrifices he wasn't willing to make. And so he forced himself to do it the old-fashioned way, by gathering Breaths from people like Vahr.

Vasher stood, then pulled out the colorless scarf he had used earlier. He tossed it over Vahr's shoulder, then Breathed.

He didn't bother making the scarf have human shape, didn't need to use a bit of his hair or skin for a focus— though he did have to draw the color from his shirt.

Vasher met Vahr's resigned eyes.

"Strangle things," Vasher Commanded, fingers touching the quivering scarf.

It twisted immediately, pulling away a large—yet now inconsequential—amount of Breath. The scarf quickly wrapped around Vahr's neck, tightening, choking him. Vahr didn't struggle or gasp; he simply watched Vasher with hatred until his eyes bulged and he died.

Hatred. Vasher had known enough of that in his time. He quietly reached up and recovered his Breath from the scarf, then left Vahr dangling in his cell. Vasher passed quietly through the prison, marveling at the color of the woods and the stones. After a few moments of walking, he noticed a new color in the hallway. Red.

He stepped around the pool of blood—which was seeping down the inclined dungeon floor—and moved into the guard room. The three guards lay dead. One of them sat in a chair. Nightblood, still mostly sheathed, had been rammed through the man's chest. About an inch of a dark black blade was visible beneath the silver sheath.

Vasher carefully slid the weapon fully back into its sheath. He did up the clasp.

I did very well today, a voice said in his mind.

Vasher didn't respond to the sword.

I killed them all, Nightblood continued. *Aren't you proud of me?*

Vasher picked up the weapon, accustomed to its unusual weight, and carried it in one hand. He recovered his duffel and slung it over his shoulder.

I knew you'd be impressed, Nightblood said, sounding satisfied.

1

THERE WERE GREAT advantages to being unimportant.

True, by many people's standards, Siri wasn't "unimportant." She was, after all, the daughter of a king. Fortunately, her father had four living children, and Siri—at seventeen years of age—was the youngest. Fafen, the daughter just older than Siri, had done the family duty and become a monk. Above Fafen was Ridger, the eldest son. He would inherit the throne.

And then there was Vivenna. Siri sighed as she walked down the path back to the city. Vivenna, the firstborn, was . . . well . . . Vivenna. Beautiful, poised, perfect in most every way. It was a good thing, too, considering the fact that she was betrothed to a god. Either way, Siri—as fourth child—was redundant. Vivenna and Ridger had to focus on their studies; Fafen had to do her work in the pastures and homes. Siri, however, could get away with being unimportant. That meant she could disappear into the wilderness for hours at a time.

People would notice, of course, and she *would* get into trouble. Yet even her father would have to admit that her disappearance hadn't caused much inconvenience. The city got along just fine without Siri—in fact, it tended to do a little better when she wasn't around.

Unimportance. To another, it might have been offensive. To Siri it was a blessing.

She smiled, walking into the city proper. She drew the inevitable stares. While Bevalis was technically the capital of Idris, it wasn't that big, and everyone knew her by sight.

Judging by the stories Siri had heard from passing ramble-men, her home was hardly even a village compared with the massive metropolises in other nations.

She liked it the way it was, even with the muddy streets, the thatched cottages, and the boring—yet sturdy—stone walls. Women chasing runaway geese, men pulling don-keys laden with spring seed, and children leading sheep on their way to pasture. A grand city in Xaka, Hudres, or even terrible Hallandren might have exotic sights, but it would be crowded with faceless, shouting, jostling crowds, and haughty noblemen. Not Siri's preference; she generally found even Bevalis to be a bit busy for her.

Still, she thought, looking down at her utilitarian grey dress, *I'll bet those cities have more colors. That's something I might like to see.*

Her hair wouldn't stand out so much there. As usual, the long locks had gone blond with joy while she'd been out in the fields. She concentrated, trying to rein them in, but she was only able to bring the color to a dull brown. As soon as she stopped focusing, her hair just went back to the way it had been. She'd never been very good at controlling it. Not like Vivenna.

As she continued through the town, a group of small fig-ures began trailing her. She smiled, pretending to ignore the children until one of them was brave enough to run forward and tug on her dress. Then she turned, smiling. They re-garded her with solemn faces. Idrian children were trained even at this age to avoid shameful outbursts of emotion. Aus-trin teachings said there was nothing wrong with feelings, but drawing attention to yourself with them was wrong.

Siri had never been very devout. It wasn't her fault, she reasoned, if Austre had made her with a distinct inability to obey. The children waited patiently until Siri reached into her apron and pulled out a couple of brightly colored flowers. The children's eyes opened wide, gazing at the vi-brant colors. Three of the flowers were blue, one yellow.

The flowers stood out starkly against the town's determined drabness. Other than what one could find in the skin and eyes of the people, there wasn't a drop of color in sight. Stones had been whitewashed, clothing bleached grey or tan. All to keep the color away.

For without color, there could be no Awakeners.

The girl who had tugged Siri's skirt finally took the flowers in one hand and dashed away with them, the other children following behind. Siri caught a look of disapproval in the eyes of several passing villagers. None of them confronted her, though. Being a princess—even an unimportant one—did have its perks.

She continued on toward the palace. It was a low, single-story building with a large, packed-earth courtyard. Siri avoided the crowds of haggling people at the front, rounding to the back and going in the kitchen entrance. Mab, the kitchen mistress, stopped singing as the door opened, then eyed Siri.

"Your father's been looking for you, child," Mab said, turning away and humming as she attacked a pile of onions.

"I suspect that he has." Siri walked over and sniffed at a pot, which bore the calm scent of boiling potatoes.

"Went to the hills again, didn't you? Skipped your tutorial sessions, I'll bet."

Siri smiled, then pulled out another of the bright yellow flowers, spinning it between two fingers.

Mab rolled her eyes. "And been corrupting the city youth again, I suspect. Honestly, girl, you should be beyond these things at your age. Your father will have words with you about shirking your responsibilities."

"I like words," Siri said. "And I always learn a few new ones when Father gets angry. I shouldn't neglect my education, now should I?"

Mab snorted, dicing some pickled cucumbers into the onions.

"Honestly, Mab," Siri said, twirling the flower, feeling

her hair shade a little bit red. "I don't see what the problem is. Austre made the flowers, right? He put the colors on them, so they can't be evil. I mean, we call him God of Colors, for heaven's sake."

"Flowers ain't evil," Mab said, adding something that looked like grass to her concoction, "assuming they're left where Austre put them. We shouldn't use Austre's beauty to make ourselves more important."

"A flower doesn't make me look more important."

"Oh?" Mab asked, adding the grass, cucumber, and onions to one of her boiling pots. She banged the side of the pot with the flat of her knife, listening, then nodded to herself and began fishing under the counter for more vegetables. "You tell me," she continued, voice muffled. "You really think walking through the city with a flower like that didn't draw attention to yourself?"

"That's only because the city is so drab. If there were a bit of color around, nobody would notice a flower."

Mab reappeared, hefting a box filled with various tubers. "You'd have us decorate the place like Hallandren? Maybe we should start inviting Awakeners into the city? How'd you like that? Some devil sucking the souls out of children, strangling people with their own clothing? Bringing men back from the grave, then using their dead bodies for cheap labor? Sacrificing women on their unholy altars?"

Siri felt her hair whiten slightly with anxiety. *Stop that!* she thought. The hair seemed to have a mind of its own, responding to gut feelings.

"That sacrificing-maidens part is only a story," Siri said. "They don't really do that."

"Stories come from somewhere."

"Yes, they come from old women sitting by the hearth in the winter. I don't think we need to be so frightened. The Hallandren will do what they want, which is fine by me, as long as they leave us alone."

Mab chopped tubers, not looking up.

"We've got the treaty, Mab," Siri said. "Father and Vivenna will make sure we're safe, and that will make the Hallandren leave us alone."

"And if they don't?"

"They will. You don't need to worry."

"They have better armies," Mab said, chopping, not looking up, "better steel, more food, and those . . . those *things.* It makes people worry. Maybe not *you,* but sensible folk."

The cook's words were hard to dismiss out of hand. Mab had a sense, a wisdom beyond her instinct for spices and broths. However, she *also* tended to fret. "You're worrying about nothing, Mab. You'll see."

"I'm just saying that this is a bad time for a royal princess to be running around with flowers, standin' out and inviting Austre's dislike."

Siri sighed. "Fine, then," she said, tossing her last flower into the stewpot. "Now we can all stand out together."

Mab froze, then rolled her eyes, chopping a root. "I assume that was a vanavel flower?"

"Of course," Siri said, sniffing at the steaming pot. "I know better than to ruin a good stew. And I still say you're overreacting."

Mab sniffed. "Here," she said, pulling out another knife. "Make yourself useful. There's roots that need choppin'."

"Shouldn't I report to my father?" Siri said, grabbing a gnarled vanavel root and beginning to chop.

"He'll just send you back here and make you work in the kitchens as a punishment," Mab said, banging the pot with her knife again. She firmly believed that she could judge when a dish was done by the way the pot rang.

"Austre help me if Father ever discovers I like it down here."

"You just like being close to the food," Mab said, fishing Siri's flower out of the stew, then tossing it aside. "Either way, you can't report to him. He's in conference with Yarda."

Siri gave no reaction—she simply continued to chop.

Her hair, however, grew blond with excitement. *Father's conferences with Yarda usually last hours,* she thought. *Not much point in simply sitting around, waiting for him to get done. . . .*

Mab turned to get something off the table, and before she looked back, Siri bolted out the door on her way toward the royal stables. Bare minutes later, she galloped away from the palace, wearing her favorite brown cloak, feeling an exhilarating thrill that sent her hair into a deep blond. A nice quick ride would be a good way to round out the day.

After all, her punishment was likely to be the same either way.

DEDELIN, KING OF Idris, set the letter down on his desk. He had stared at it long enough. It was time to decide whether or not to send his eldest daughter to her death.

Despite the advent of spring, his chamber was cold. Warmth was a rare thing in the Idris highlands; it was coveted and enjoyed, for it lingered only briefly each summer. The chambers were also stark. There was a beauty in simplicity. Even a king had no right to display arrogance by ostentation.

Dedelin stood up, looking out his window and into the courtyard. The palace was small by the world's standards—only a single story high, with a peaked wooden roof and squat stone walls. But it was large by Idrian standards, and it bordered on flamboyant. This could be forgiven, for the palace was also a meeting hall and center of operations for his entire kingdom.

The king could see General Yarda out of the corner of his eye. The burly man stood waiting, his hands clasped behind his back, his thick beard tied in three places. He was the only other person in the room.

Dedelin glanced back at the letter. The paper was a bright

pink, and the garish color stood out on his desk like a drop of blood in the snow. Pink was a color one would never see in Idris. In Hallandren, however—center of the world's dye industry—such tasteless hues were commonplace.

"Well, old friend?" Dedelin asked. "Do you have any advice for me?"

General Yarda shook his head. "War is coming, Your Majesty. I feel it in the winds and read it in the reports of our spies. Hallandren still considers us rebels, and our passes to the north are too tempting. They will attack."

"Then I shouldn't send her," Dedelin said, looking back out his window. The courtyard bustled with people in furs and cloaks coming to market.

"We can't stop the war, Your Majesty," Yarda said. "But . . . we can slow it."

Dedelin turned back.

Yarda stepped forward, speaking softly. "This is not a good time. Our troops still haven't recovered from those Vendis raids last fall, and with the fires in the granary this winter . . ." Yarda shook his head. "We *cannot* afford to get into a defensive war in the summer. Our best ally against the Hallandren is the snow. We can't let this conflict occur on their terms. If we do, we are dead."

The words all made sense.

"Your Majesty," Yarda said, "they are *waiting* for us to break the treaty as an excuse to attack. If we move first, they will strike."

"If we keep the treaty, they will *still* strike," Dedelin said.

"But later. Perhaps months later. You know how slow Hallandren politics are. If we keep the treaty, there will be debates and arguments. If those last until the snows, then we will have gained the time we need so badly."

It all made sense. Brutal, honest sense. All these years, Dedelin had stalled and watched as the Hallandren court grew more and more aggressive, more and more agitated.

Every year, voices called for an assault on the "rebel Idrians" living up in the highlands. Every year, those voices grew louder and more plentiful. Every year, Dedelin's placating and politics kept the armies away. He had hoped, perhaps, that the rebel leader Vahr and his Pahn Kahl dissidents would draw attention away from Idris, but Vahr had been captured, his so-called army dispersed. His actions had only served to make Hallandren more focused on its enemies.

The peace would not last. Not with Idris ripe, not with the trade routes worth so much. Not with the current crop of Hallandren gods, who seemed so much more erratic than their predecessors. He *knew* all of that. But he also knew that breaking the treaty would be foolish. When you were cast into the den of a beast, you did not provoke it to anger.

Yarda joined him beside the window, looking out, leaning one elbow against the side of the frame. He was a harsh man born of harsh winters. But he was also as good a man as Dedelin had ever known—a part of the king longed to marry Vivenna to the general's own son.

That was foolishness. Dedelin had always known this day would come. He'd crafted the treaty himself, and it demanded he send his daughter to marry the God King. The Hallandren needed a daughter of the royal blood to reintroduce the traditional bloodline into their monarchy. It was something the depraved and vainglorious people of the lowlands had long coveted, and only that specific clause in the treaty had saved Idris these twenty years.

That treaty had been the first official act of Dedelin's reign, negotiated furiously following his father's assassination. Dedelin gritted his teeth. How quickly he'd bowed before the whims of his enemies. Yet he would do it again; an Idrian monarch would do anything for his people. That was one big difference between Idris and Hallandren.

"If we send her, Yarda," Dedelin said, "we send her to her death."

"Maybe they won't harm her," Yarda finally said.

"You know better than that. The first thing they'll do when war comes is use her against me. This is *Hallandren*. They invite Awakeners into their palaces, for Austre's sake!"

Yarda fell silent. Finally, he shook his head. "Latest reports say their army has grown to include some forty thousand Lifeless."

Lord God of Colors, Dedelin thought, glancing at the letter again. Its language was simple. Vivenna's twenty-second birthday had come, and the terms of the treaty stipulated that Dedelin could wait no longer.

"Sending Vivenna is a poor plan, but it's our only plan," Yarda said. "With more time, I know I can bring the Tedradel to our cause—they've hated Hallandren since the Manywar. And perhaps I can find a way to rile Vahr's broken rebel faction in Hallandren itself. At the very least, we can build, gather supplies, live another year." Yarda turned to him. "If we don't send the Hallandren their princess, the war will be seen as our fault. Who will support us? They will demand to know why we refused to follow the treaty our own king wrote!"

"And if we do send them Vivenna, it will introduce the royal blood into their monarchy, and that will have an even *more* legitimate claim on the highlands!"

"Perhaps," Yarda said. "But if we both know they're going to attack anyway, then what do we care about their claim? At least this way, perhaps they will wait until an heir is born before the assault comes."

More time. The general always asked for more time. But what about when that time came at the cost of Dedelin's own child?

Yarda wouldn't hesitate to send one soldier to die if it would mean time enough to get the rest of his troops into better position to attack, Dedelin thought. *We are Idris. How can I ask anything less of my daughter than I'd demand of one of my troops?*

It was just that thinking of Vivenna in the God King's

arms, being forced to bear that creature's child . . . it nearly made his hair bleach with concern. That child would become a stillborn monster who would become the next Returned god of the Hallandren.

There is another way, a part of his mind whispered. *You don't have to send Vivenna. . . .*

A knock came at his door. Both he and Yarda turned, and Dedelin called for the visitor to enter. He should have been able to guess who it would be.

Vivenna stood in a quiet grey dress, looking so young to him still. Yet she was the perfect image of an Idrian woman—hair kept in a modest knot, no makeup to draw attention to the face. She was not timid or soft, like some noblewomen from the northern kingdoms. She was just composed. Composed, simple, hard, and capable. Idrian.

"You have been in here for several hours, Father," Vivenna said, bowing her head respectfully to Yarda. "The servants speak of a colorful envelope carried by the general when he entered. I believe I know what it contained."

Dedelin met her eyes, then waved for her to seat herself. She softly closed the door, then took one of the wooden chairs from the side of the room. Yarda remained standing, after the masculine fashion. Vivenna eyed the letter sitting on the desk. She was calm, her hair controlled and kept a respectful black. She was twice as devout as Dedelin, and—unlike her youngest sister—she never drew attention to herself with fits of emotion.

"I assume that I should prepare myself for departure, then," Vivenna said, hands in her lap.

Dedelin opened his mouth, but could find no objection. He glanced at Yarda, who just shook his head, resigned.

"I have prepared my entire life for this, Father," Vivenna said. "I am ready. Siri, however, will not take this well. She left on a ride an hour ago. I should depart the city before she gets back. That will avoid any potential scene she might make."

"Too late," Yarda said, grimacing and nodding toward the window. Just outside, people scattered in the courtyard as a figure galloped through the gates. She wore a deep brown cloak that bordered on being too colorful, and—of course—she had her hair down.

The hair was yellow.

Dedelin felt his rage and frustration growing. Only Siri could make him lose control, and—as if in ironic counterpoint to the source of his anger—he felt his hair change. To those watching, a few locks of hair on his head would have bled from black to red. It was the identifying mark of the royal family, who had fled to the Idris highlands at the climax of the Manywar. Others could hide their emotions. The royals, however, manifested what they felt in the very hair on their heads.

Vivenna watched him, pristine as always, and her poise gave him strength as he forced his hair to turn black again. It took more willpower than any common man could understand to control the treasonous Royal Locks. Dedelin wasn't sure how Vivenna managed it so well.

Poor girl never even had a childhood, he thought. From birth, Vivenna's life had been pointed toward this single event. His firstborn child, the girl who had always seemed like a part of himself. The girl who had always made him proud; the woman who had already earned the love and respect of her people. In his mind's eye he saw the queen she could become, stronger even than he. Someone who could guide them through the dark days ahead.

But only if she survived that long.

"I will prepare myself for the trip," Vivenna said, rising.

"No," Dedelin said.

Yarda and Vivenna both turned.

"Father," Vivenna said. "If we break this treaty, it will mean war. I am prepared to sacrifice for our people. You taught me that."

"You will *not* go," Dedelin said firmly, turning back

toward the window. Outside, Siri was laughing with one of the stablemen. Dedelin could hear her outburst even from a distance; her hair had turned a flame-colored red.

Lord God of Colors, forgive me, he thought. *What a terrible choice for a father to make. The treaty is specific: I must send the Hallandren my daughter when Vivenna reaches her twenty-second birthday. But it doesn't actually say* which *daughter I am required to send.*

If he didn't send Hallandren one of his daughters, they would attack immediately. If he sent the wrong one, they might be angered, but he knew they wouldn't attack. They would wait until they had an heir. That would gain Idris at least nine months.

And . . . , he thought, *if they were to try to use Vivenna against me, I know that I wouldn't be able to stop myself from giving in.* It was shameful to admit that fact, but in the end, it was what made the decision for him.

Dedelin turned back toward the room. "Vivenna, you will not go to wed the tyrant god of our enemies. I'm sending Siri in your place."

2

SIRI SAT, STUNNED, in a rattling carriage, her homeland growing more and more distant with each bump and shake.

Two days had passed, and she still didn't understand. This was supposed to be Vivenna's task. Everybody understood that. Idris had thrown a celebration on the day of Vivenna's birth. The king had started her classes from the day she could walk, training her in the ways of court life and politics. Fafen, the second daughter, had also taken the lessons in case Vivenna died before the day of the wedding. But not Siri. She'd been redundant. Unimportant.

No more.

She glanced out the window. Her father had sent the kingdom's nicest carriage—along with an honor guard of twenty soldiers—to bear her southward. That, combined with a steward and several serving boys, made for a procession as grand as Siri had ever seen. It bordered on ostentation, which might have thrilled her, had it not been bearing her away from Idris.

This isn't the way it's supposed to be, she thought. *This isn't the way* any *of it is supposed to happen!*

And yet it had.

Nothing made sense. The carriage bumped, but she just sat, numb. *At the very least,* she thought, *they could have let me ride horseback, rather than forcing me to sit in this carriage.* But that, unfortunately, wouldn't have been an appropriate way to enter Hallandren.

Hallandren.

She felt her hair bleach white with fear. She was being sent to *Hallandren,* a kingdom her people cursed with every second breath. She wouldn't see her father again for a long while, if ever. She wouldn't speak with Vivenna, or listen to the tutors, or be chided by Mab, or ride the royal horses, or go looking for flowers in the wilderness, or work in the kitchens. She'd . . .

Marry the God King. The terror of Hallandren, the monster that had never drawn a living breath. In Hallandren, his power was absolute. He could order an execution on a whim.

I'll be safe, though, won't I? she thought. *I'll be his wife. Wife. I'm getting married.*

Oh Austre, God of Colors . . . she thought, feeling sick. She curled up with her legs against her chest—her hair growing so white that it seemed to shine—and lay down on the seat of the carriage, not sure if the shaking she felt was her own trembling or the carriage continuing its inexorable path southward.

———— ❧ ————

"I THINK THAT you should reconsider your decision, Father," Vivenna said calmly, sitting decorously—as she'd been trained—with hands in her lap.

"I've considered and reconsidered, Vivenna," King Dedelin said, waving his hand. "My mind is made up."

"Siri is not suited to this task."

"She'll do fine," her father said, looking through some papers on his desk. "All she really needs to do is have a baby. I'm certain she's 'suited' to that task."

What then of my training? Vivenna thought. *Twenty-two years of preparation? What was that, if the only point in being sent was to provide a convenient womb?*

She kept her hair black, her voice solemn, her face calm. "Siri must be distraught," she said. "I don't think she's emotionally capable of dealing with this."

Her father looked up, his hair fading a bit red—the black bleeding away like paint running off a canvas. It showed his annoyance.

He's more upset by her departure than he's willing to admit.

"This is for the best for our people, Vivenna," he said, working—with obvious effort—to turn his hair black again. "If war comes, Idris will need you here."

"If war comes, what of Siri?"

Her father fell silent. "Perhaps it won't come," he finally said.

Austre . . . Vivenna thought with shock. *He doesn't believe that. He thinks he's sent her to her death.*

"I know what you are thinking," her father said, drawing her attention back to his eyes. So solemn. "How could I choose one over the other? How could I send Siri to die and leave you here to live? I didn't do it based on personal preference, no matter what people may think. I did what will be best for Idris when this war comes."

When this war comes. Vivenna looked up, meeting his eyes. "I was going to stop the war, Father. I was to be the God King's bride! I was going to speak with him, persuade him. I've been trained with the political knowledge, the understanding of customs, the—"

"Stop the war?" her father asked, cutting in. Only then did Vivenna realize how brash she must have sounded. She looked away.

"Vivenna, child," her father said. "There is no stopping this war. Only the promise of a daughter of the royal line kept them away this long, and sending Siri may buy us time. And . . . perhaps I've sent her to safety, even when war flares. Perhaps they will value her bloodline to the point that they leave her alive—a backup should the heir she bears pass away." He grew distant. "Yes," he continued, "perhaps it is not Siri we should be fearing for, but . . ."

But ourselves, Vivenna finished in her mind. She was not privy to all of her father's war planning, but she knew enough. War would not favor Idris. In a conflict with Hallandren, there was little chance they would win. It would be devastating for their people and their way of life.

"Father, I—"

"Please, Vivenna," he said quietly. "I cannot speak of this further. Go now. We will converse later."

Later. After Siri had traveled even farther away, after it would be much more difficult to bring her back. Yet Vivenna rose. She was obedient; it was the way she had been trained. That was one of the things that had always separated her from her sister.

She left her father's study, closing the door behind her, then walked through the wooden palace hallways, pretending that she didn't see the stares or hear the whispers. She made her way to her room—which was small and unadorned—and sat down on her bed, hands in her lap.

She didn't agree at all with her father's assessment. She *could* have done something. She was to have been the God King's bride. That would have given her influence in the court. Everyone knew that the God King himself was distant when it came to the politics of his nation, but surely his wife could have played a role in defending the interests of her people.

And her father had thrown that away?

He really must believe that there is nothing that can be done to stop the invasion. That turned sending Siri into simply another political maneuver to buy time. Just as Idris had been doing for decades. Either way, if the sacrifice of a royal daughter to the Hallandren was that important, then it still should have been Vivenna's place to go. It had always been *her* duty to prepare for marriage to the God King. Not Siri's, not Fafen's. Vivenna's.

In being saved, she didn't feel grateful. Nor did she feel that she would better serve Idris by staying in Bevalis. If her father died, Yarda would be far better suited to rule during wartime than Vivenna. Besides, Ridger—Vivenna's younger brother—had been groomed as heir for years.

She had been preserved for no reason. It seemed a punishment, in some ways. She'd listened, prepared, learned, and practiced. Everyone said that she was perfect. Why, then, wasn't she good enough to serve as intended?

She had no good answer for herself. She could only sit and fret, hands in her lap, and face the awful truth. Her purpose in life had been stolen and given to another. She was redundant now. Useless.

Unimportant.

⁓∞⁓

"WHAT WAS HE *thinking*!" Siri snapped, hanging half out the window of her carriage as it bounced along the earthen road. A young soldier marched beside the vehicle, looking uncomfortable in the afternoon light.

"I mean really," Siri said. "Sending *me* to marry the Hallandren king. That's silly, isn't it? Surely you've heard about the kinds of things I do. Wandering off when nobody's looking. Ignoring my lessons. I throw angry fits, for Color's sake!"

The guard glanced at her out of the corner of his eye, but otherwise gave no reaction. Siri didn't really care. She wasn't yelling at him so much as just *yelling*. She hung precariously from the window, feeling the wind play with her hair—long, red, straight—and stoking her anger. Fury kept her from weeping.

The green spring hills of the Idris highlands had slowly faded away as the days had passed. In fact, they were probably in Hallandren already—the border between the two kingdoms was vague, which wasn't surprising, considering that they'd been one nation up until the Manywar.

She eyed the poor guard—whose only way of dealing with a raving princess was to ignore her. Then she finally slumped back into the carriage. She shouldn't have treated him so, but, well, she'd just been sold off like some hunk of mutton—doomed by a document that had been written years before she'd even been born. If anyone had a right to a tantrum, it was Siri.

Maybe that's the reason for all of this, she thought, crossing her arms on the windowsill. *Maybe Father was tired of my tantrums, and just wanted to get rid of me.*

That seemed a little far-fetched. There were easier ways to deal with Siri—ways that didn't include sending her to represent Idris in a foreign court. Why, then? Did he really think she'd do a good job? That gave her pause. Then she considered how ridiculous it was. Her father wouldn't have assumed that she'd do a better job than Vivenna. Nobody did *anything* better than Vivenna.

Siri sighed, feeling her hair turn a pensive brown. At least the landscape was interesting, and in order to keep herself from feeling any more frustrated, she let it distract her for the moment. Hallandren was in the lowlands, a place of tropical forests and strange, colorful animals. Siri had heard the descriptions from ramblemen, and even confirmed their accounts in the occasional book she'd been forced to read. She'd thought she knew what to expect. Yet as the hills gave way to deep grasslands and then the trees finally began to crowd the road, Siri began to realize that there was something no tome or tale could adequately describe.

Colors.

In the highlands, flower patches were rare and unconnected, as if they understood how poorly they fit with Idrian philosophy. Here, they appeared to be everywhere. Tiny flowers grew in great blanketing swaths on the ground. Large, drooping pink blossoms hung from trees, like bundles of grapes, flowers growing practically on top of one another in a large cluster. Even the weeds had flowers. Siri would have picked some of them, if not for the way that the soldiers regarded them with hostility.

If I feel this anxious, she realized, *those guards must feel more so.* She wasn't the only one who had been sent away from family and friends. When would these men be allowed to return? Suddenly, she felt even more guilty for subjecting the young soldier to her outburst.

I'll send them back when I arrive, she thought. Then she immediately felt her hair grow white. Sending the men back would leave her alone in a city filled with Lifeless, Awakeners, and pagans.

Yet what good would twenty soldiers do her? Better that someone, at least, be allowed to return home.

❧

"ONE WOULD THINK that you would be happy," Fafen said. "After all, you no longer have to marry a tyrant."

Vivenna plopped a bruise-colored berry into her basket, then moved on to a different bush. Fafen worked on one nearby. She wore the white robes of a monk, her hair

completely shorn. Fafen was the middle sister in almost
every way—midway between Siri and Vivenna in height,
less proper than Vivenna, yet hardly as careless as Siri.
Fafen was a bit curvier than either of them, which had
caught the eyes of several young men in the village. However, the fact that they would have to become monks themselves if they wanted to marry her kept them in check. If
Fafen noticed how popular she was, she'd never shown it.
She'd made the decision to become a monk before her tenth
birthday, and her father had wholeheartedly approved.
Every noble or rich family was traditionally obligated to
provide one person to the monasteries. It was against the
Five Visions to be selfish, even with one's own blood.

The two sisters gathered berries that Fafen would later
distribute to those in need. The monk's fingers were dyed
slightly purple by the work. Vivenna wore gloves. That
much color on her hands would be unseemly.

"Yes," Fafen said, "I do think you're taking this all wrong.
Why, you act as if you *want* to go down and be married to
that Lifeless monster."

"He's not Lifeless," Vivenna said. "Susebron is Returned,
and there is a large difference."

"Yes, but he's a false god. Besides, everyone knows
what a terrible creature he is."

"But it was my *place* to go and marry him. That is who
I am, Fafen. Without it, I am nothing."

"Nonsense," Fafen said. "You'll inherit now, instead of
Ridger."

Thereby unsettling the order of things even further,
Vivenna thought. *What right do I have to take his place
from him?*

She allowed this aspect of the conversation to lapse,
however. She'd been arguing the point for several minutes
now, and it wouldn't be proper to continue. Proper. Rarely
before had Vivenna felt so frustrated at having to be proper.
Her emotions were growing rather . . . inconvenient.

"What of Siri?" she found herself saying. "You're happy that this happened to her?"

Fafen looked up, then frowned a little to herself. She had a tendency to avoid thinking things through unless she was confronted with them directly. Vivenna felt a little ashamed for making such a blunt comment, but with Fafen, there often wasn't any other way.

"You do have a point," Fafen said. "I don't see why *any- one* had to be sent."

"The treaty," Vivenna said. "It protects our people."

"Austre protects our people," Fafen said, moving on to another bush.

Will he protect Siri? Vivenna thought. Poor, innocent, capricious Siri. She'd never learned to control herself; she'd be eaten alive in the Hallandren Court of Gods. Siri wouldn't understand the politics, the backstabbing, the false faces and lies. She would also be forced to bear the next God King of Hallandren. Performing that duty was not something Vivenna had looked forward to. It would have been a sacrifice, yet it would have been *her* sacrifice, given willingly for the safety of her people.

Such thoughts continued to pester Vivenna as she and Fafen finished with the berry picking, then moved down the hillside back toward the village. Fafen, like all monks, dedicated all of her work to the good of the people. She watched flocks, harvested food, and cleaned houses for those who could not do it themselves.

Without a duty of her own, Vivenna had little purpose. And yet, as she considered it, there *was* someone who still needed her. Someone who had left a week before, teary-eyed and frightened, looking to her big sister with desperation.

Vivenna wasn't needed in Idris, whatever her father said. She was useless here. But she *did* know the people, cultures, and society of Hallandren. And—as she followed

Fafen onto the village road—an idea began to form in Vivenna's head.

One that was not, by any stretch of the imagination, proper.

3

L IGHTSONG DIDN'T REMEMBER dying.

His priests, however, assured him that his death had been extremely inspiring. Noble. Grand. Heroic. One did not Return unless one died in a way that exemplified the great virtues of human existence. That was why the Iridescent Tones sent the Returned back; they acted as examples, and gods, to the people who still lived.

Each god represented something. An ideal related to the heroic way in which they had died. Lightsong himself had died displaying extreme bravery. Or, at least, that was what his priests told him. Lightsong couldn't remember the event, just as he couldn't remember anything of his life before he became a god.

He groaned softly, unable to sleep any longer. He rolled over, feeling weak as he sat up in his majestic bed. Visions and memories pestered his mind, and he shook his head, trying to clear away the fog of sleep.

Servants entered, responding wordlessly to their god's needs. He was one of the younger divinities, for he'd Returned only five years before. There were some two dozen deities in the Court of Gods, and many were far more important—and far more politically savvy—than Lightsong. And above them all reigned Susebron, the God King of Hallandren.

Young though he was, he merited an enormous palace. He slept in a room draped with silks, dyed with bright reds and yellows. His palace held dozens of different chambers, all decorated and furnished according to his whims. Hundreds of servants and priests saw to his needs—whether he wanted them seen to or not.

All of this, he thought as he stood, *because I couldn't figure out how to die.* Standing made him just a bit dizzy. It was his feast day. He would lack strength until he ate.

Servants approached carrying brilliant red and gold robes. As they entered his aura, each servant—skin, hair, clothing, and garments—burst with exaggerated color. The saturated hues were far more resplendent than any dye or paint could produce. That was an effect of Lightsong's innate BioChroma: he had enough Breath to fill thousands of people. He saw little value in it. He couldn't use it to animate objects or corpses; he was a god, not an Awakener. He couldn't give—or even loan—his deific Breath away.

Well, except once. That would, however, kill him.

The servants continued their ministrations, draping him with gorgeous cloth. Lightsong was a good head and a half taller than anyone else in the room. He was also broad of shoulder, with a muscular physique that he didn't deserve, considering the amount of time he spent idle.

"Did you sleep well, Your Grace?" a voice asked.

Lightsong turned. Llarimar, his high priest, was a tall, portly man with spectacles and a calm demeanor. His hands were nearly hidden by the deep sleeves of his gold and red robe, and he carried a thick tome. Both robes and tome burst with color as they entered Lightsong's aura.

"I slept fantastically, Scoot," Lightsong said, yawning. "A night full of nightmares and obscure dreams, as always. Terribly restful."

The priest raised an eyebrow. "Scoot?"

"Yes," Lightsong said. "I've decided to give you a new

nickname. Scoot. Seems to fit you, the way you're always scooting around, poking into things."

"I am honored, Your Grace," Llarimar said, seating himself on a chair.

Colors, Lightsong thought. *Doesn't he ever get annoyed?*

Llarimar opened his tome. "Shall we begin?"

"If we must," Lightsong said. The servants finished tying ribbons, doing up clasps, and draping silks. Each bowed and retreated to a side of the room.

Llarimar picked up his quill. "What, then, do you remember of your dreams?"

"Oh, you know." Lightsong flopped back onto one of his couches, lounging. "Nothing really important."

Llarimar pursed his lips in displeasure. Other servants began to file in, bearing various dishes of food. Mundane, human food. As a Returned, Lightsong didn't really need to eat such things—they would not give him strength or banish his fatigue. They were just an indulgence. In a short time, he would dine on something far more . . . divine. It would give him strength enough to live for another week.

"Please try to remember the dreams, Your Grace," Llarimar said in his polite, yet firm, way. "No matter how unremarkable they may seem."

Lightsong sighed, looking up at the ceiling. It was painted with a mural, of course. This one depicted three fields enclosed by stone walls. It was a vision one of his predecessors had seen. Lightsong closed his eyes, trying to focus. "I . . . was walking along a beach," he said. "And a ship was leaving without me. I don't know where it was going."

Llarimar's pen began to scratch quickly. He was probably finding all kinds of symbolism in the memory. "Were there any colors?" the priest asked.

"The ship had a red sail," Lightsong said. "The sand was brown, of course, and the trees green. For some reason, I think the ocean water was red, like the ship."

Llarimar scribbled furiously—he always got excited when Lightsong remembered colors. Lightsong opened his eyes and stared up at the ceiling and its brightly colored fields. He reached over idly, plucking some cherries off a servant's plate.

Why should he begrudge the people his dreams? Even if he found divination foolish, he had no right to complain. He was remarkably fortunate. He had a deific Bio-Chromatic aura, a physique that any man would envy, and enough luxury for ten kings. Of all the people in the world, he had the least right to be difficult.

It was just that . . . well, he was probably the world's only god who didn't believe in his own religion.

"Was there anything else to the dream, Your Grace?" Llarimar asked, looking up from his book.

"You were there, Scoot."

Llarimar paused, paling just slightly. "I . . . was?"

Lightsong nodded. "You apologized for bothering me all the time and keeping me from my debauchery. Then you brought me a big bottle of wine and did a dance. It was really quite remarkable."

Llarimar regarded him with a flat stare.

Lightsong sighed. "No, there was nothing else. Just the boat. Even that is fading."

Llarimar nodded, rising and shooing back the servants—though, of course, they remained in the room, hovering with their plates of nuts, wine, and fruit, should any of it be wanted. "Shall we get on with it then, Your Grace?" Llarimar asked.

Lightsong sighed, then rose, exhausted. A servant scuttled forward to redo one of the clasps on his robe, which had come undone as he sat.

Lightsong fell into step beside Llarimar, towering at least a foot over the priest. The furniture and doorways, however, were built to fit Lightsong's increased size, so it was the servants and priests who seemed out of place. They passed from room to room, using no hallways. Hallways were for servants, and they ran in a square around the outside of the building. Lightsong walked on plush rugs from the northern nations, passing the finest pottery from across the Inner Sea. Each room was hung with paintings and gracefully calligraphed poems, created by Hallandren's finest artists.

At the center of the palace was a small, square room that deviated from the standard reds and golds of Lightsong's motif. This one was bright with ribbons of darker colors—deep blues, greens, and blood reds. Each was a true color, directly on hue, as only a person who had attained the Third Heightening could distinguish.

As Lightsong stepped into the room, the colors blazed to life. They became brighter, more intense, yet somehow remained dark. The maroon became a more true maroon, the navy a more powerful navy. Dark yet bright, a contrast only Breath could inspire.

In the center of the room was a child.

Why does it always have to be a child? Lightsong thought.

Llarimar and the servants waited. Lightsong stepped forward, and the little girl glanced to the side, where a couple of priests stood in red and gold robes. They nodded encouragingly. The girl looked back toward Lightsong, obviously nervous.

"Here now," Lightsong said, trying to sound encouraging. "There's nothing to fear."

And yet, the girl trembled.

Lecture after lecture—delivered by Llarimar, who had claimed that they were *not* lectures, for one did not lecture gods—drifted through Lightsong's head. There was nothing to fear from the Returned gods of the Hallandren. The gods were a blessing. They provided visions of the future, as well as leadership and wisdom. All they needed to subsist was one thing.

Breath.

Lightsong hesitated, but his weakness was coming to a head. He felt dizzy. Cursing himself quietly, he knelt down on one knee, taking the girl's face in his oversized hands. She began to cry, but she said the words, clear and distinct as she had been taught. "My life to yours. My Breath become yours."

Her Breath flowed out, puffing in the air. It traveled along Lightsong's arm—the touch was necessary—and he drew it in. His weakness vanished, the dizziness evaporated. Both were replaced with crisp clarity. He felt invigorated, revitalized, *alive*.

The girl grew dull. The color of her lips and eyes faded slightly. Her brown hair lost some of its luster; her cheeks became more bland.

It's nothing, he thought. *Most people say they can't even tell that their Breath is gone. She'll live a full life. Happy. Her family will be well paid for her sacrifice.*

And Lightsong would live for another week. His aura didn't grow stronger from Breath upon which he fed; that was another difference between a Returned and an Awakener. The latter were sometimes regarded as inferior, manmade approximations of the Returned.

Without a new Breath each week, Lightsong would die. Many Returned outside of Hallandren lived only eight days. Yet with a donated Breath a week, a Returned could continue to live, never aging, seeing visions at night which would supposedly provide divinations of the future. Hence the Court of the Gods, filled with its palaces, where gods could be nurtured, protected, and—most importantly—fed.

Priests hustled forward to lead the girl out of the room. *It is nothing to her,* Lightsong told himself again. *Nothing at all. . . .*

Her eyes met his as she left, and he could see that the twinkle was gone from them. She had become a Drab. A Dull, or a Faded One. A person without Breath. It would never grow back. The priests took her away.

Lightsong turned to Llarimar, feeling guilty at his sudden energy. "All right," he said. "Let's see the Offerings."

Llarimar raised an eyebrow over his bespectacled eyes. "You're accommodating all of a sudden."

I need to give something back, Lightsong thought. *Even if it's something useless.*

They passed through several more rooms of red and gold, most of which were perfectly square with doors on all four sides. Near the eastern side of the palace, they entered a long, thin room. It was completely white, something very unusual in Hallandren. The walls were lined with paintings and poems. The servants stayed outside; only Llarimar joined Lightsong as he stepped up to the first painting.

"Well?" Llarimar asked.

It was a pastoral painting of the jungle, with drooping palms and colorful flowers. There were some of these plants in the gardens around the Court of Gods, which was why Lightsong recognized them. He'd never actually been to the jungle—at least, not during this incarnation of his life.

"The painting is all right," Lightsong said. "Not my favorite. Makes me think of the outside. I wish I could visit."

Llarimar looked at him quizzically.

"What?" Lightsong said. "The court gets old sometimes."

"There isn't much wine in the forest, Your Grace."

"I could make some. Ferment . . . something."

"I'm sure," Llarimar said, nodding to one of his aides outside the room. The lesser priest scribbled down what Lightsong had said about the painting. Somewhere, there was a city patron who sought a blessing from Lightsong. It probably had to do with bravery—perhaps the patron was planning to propose marriage, or maybe he was a merchant about to sign a risky business deal. The priests would interpret Lightsong's opinion of the painting, then give the person an augury—either for good or for ill—along with the exact words Lightsong had said. Either way, the act of sending a painting to the god would gain the patron some measure of good fortune.

Supposedly.

Lightsong moved away from the painting. A lesser priest rushed forward, removing it. Most likely, the patron hadn't painted it himself, but had instead commissioned it. The better a painting was, the better a reaction it tended to get from the gods. One's future, it seemed, could be influenced by how much one could pay one's artist.

I shouldn't be so cynical, Lightsong thought. *Without this system, I'd have died five years ago.*

Five years ago he *had* died, even if he still didn't know what had killed him. Had it really been a heroic death? Perhaps nobody was allowed to talk about his former life because they didn't want anyone to know that Lightsong the Bold had actually died from a stomach cramp.

To the side, the lesser priest disappeared with the jungle painting. It would be burned. Such offerings were made specifically for the intended god, and only he—besides a few of his priests—was allowed to see them. Lightsong moved along to the next work of art on the wall. It was actually a poem, written in the artisans' script. The dots of color brightened as Lightsong approached. The Hallandren artisans' script was a specialized system of writing that wasn't based on form, but on color. Each colored dot represented a different sound in Hallandren's language. Combined with some double dots—one of each color—it created an alphabet that was a nightmare for the colorblind.

Few people in Hallandren would admit to having *that* particular ailment. At least, that was what Lightsong had heard. He wondered if the priests knew just how much their gods gossiped about the outside world.

The poem wasn't a very good one, obviously composed by a peasant who had then paid someone else to translate it to the artisans' script. The simple dots were a sign of this. True poets used more elaborate symbols, continuous lines that changed color or colorful glyphs that formed pictures. A lot could be done with symbols that could change shape without losing their meaning.

Getting the colors right was a delicate art, one that required the Third Heightening or better to perfect. That was the level of Breath at which a person gained the ability to sense perfect hues of color, just as the Second Heightening gave someone perfect pitch. Returned were of the Fifth Heightening. Lightsong didn't know what it was like to live without the ability to instantly recognize exact shades of color and sound. He could tell an ideal red from one that had been mixed with even one drop of white paint.

He gave the peasant's poem as good a review as he could, though he generally felt an impulse to be honest when he looked at Offerings. It seemed his duty, and for some reason it was one of the few things he took seriously.

They continued down the line, Lightsong giving reviews of the various paintings and poems. The wall was remarkably full this day. Was there a feast or celebration he hadn't heard about? By the time they neared the end of the line, Lightsong was tired of looking at art, though his body—fueled by the child's Breath—continued to feel strong and exhilarated.

He stopped before the final painting. It was an abstract work, a style that was growing more and more popular lately—particularly in paintings sent to him, since he'd given favorable reviews to others in the past. He almost gave this one a poor grade simply because of that. It was good to keep the priests guessing at what would please him, or so some of the gods said. Lightsong sensed that many of them were far more calculating in the way that they gave their reviews, intentionally adding cryptic meanings.

Lightsong didn't have the patience for such tricks, especially since all anyone ever really seemed to want from him was honesty. He gave this last painting the time it deserved. The canvas was thick with paint, every inch colored with large, fat strokes of the brush. The predominant hue was a deep red, almost a crimson, that Lightsong immediately knew was a red-blue mixture with a hint of black in it.

The lines of color overlapped, one atop another, almost in a progression. Kind of like . . . waves. Lightsong frowned. If he looked at it right, it looked like a sea. And could that be a ship in the center?

Vague impressions from his dream returned to him. A red sea. The ship, leaving.

I'm imagining things, he told himself. "Good color," he said. "Nice patterns. It puts me at peace, yet has a tension to it as well. I approve."

Llarimar seemed to like this response. He nodded as the lesser priest—who stood a distance away—recorded Lightsong's words.

"So," Lightsong said. "That's it, I assume?"

"Yes, Your Grace."

One duty left, he thought. Now that Offerings were done, it would be time to move on to the final—and least appealing—of his daily tasks. Petitions. He had to get through them before he could get to more important activities, like taking a nap.

Llarimar didn't lead the way toward the petition hall, however. He simply waved a lesser priest over, then began to flip through some pages on a clipboard.

"Well?" Lightsong asked.

"Well what, Your Grace?"

"Petitions."

Llarimar shook his head. "You aren't hearing petitions today, Your Grace. Remember?"

"No. I have *you* to remember things like that for me."

"Well, then," Llarimar said, flipping a page over, "consider it officially remembered that you have no petitions today. Your priests will be otherwise employed."

"They will?" Lightsong demanded. "Doing what?"

"Kneeling reverently in the courtyard, Your Grace. Our new queen arrives today."

Lightsong froze. *I really need to pay more attention to politics.* "Today?"

"Indeed, Your Grace. Our lord the God King will be married."

"So soon?"

"As soon as she arrives, Your Grace."

Interesting, Lightsong thought. *Susebron getting a wife.* The God King was the only one of the Returned who could marry. Returned couldn't produce children—save, of course, for the king, who had never drawn a breath as a living man. Lightsong had always found the distinction odd.

"Your Grace," Llarimar said. "We will need a Lifeless Command in order to arrange our troops on the field outside the city to welcome the queen."

Lightsong raised an eyebrow. "We plan to attack her?"

Llarimar gave him a stern look.

Lightsong chuckled. "Fledgling fruit," he said, giving up one of the Command phrases that would let others control the city's Lifeless. It wasn't the core Command, of course. The phrase he'd given to Llarimar would allow a person to control the Lifeless only in noncombat situations, and it would expire one day after its first use. Lightsong often thought that the convoluted system of Commands used to control the Lifeless was needlessly complex. However, being one of the four gods to hold Lifeless Commands *did* make him rather important at times.

The priests began to chat quietly about preparations. Lightsong waited, still thinking about Susebron and the impending wedding. He folded his arms and rested against the side of the doorway.

"Scoot?" he asked.

"Yes, Your Grace?"

"Did I have a wife? Before I died, I mean."

Llarimar hesitated. "You know I cannot speak of your life before your Return, Lightsong. Knowledge of your past won't do anyone any good."

Lightsong leaned his head back, resting it against the wall, looking up at the white ceiling. "I . . . remember a face, sometimes," he said softly. "A beautiful, youthful face. I think it might have been her."

The priests hushed.

"Inviting brown hair," Lightsong said. "Red lips, three shades shy of the seventh harmonic, with a deep beauty. Dark tan skin."

A priest scuttled forward with the red tome, and Llarimar started writing furiously. He didn't prompt Lightsong for more information, but simply took down the god's words as they came.

Lightsong fell silent, turning away from the men and their scribbling pens. *What does it matter?* he thought. *That life is gone. Instead, I get to be a god. Regardless of my belief in the religion itself, the perks are nice.*

He walked away, trailed by a retinue of servants and lesser priests who would see to his needs. Offerings done, dreams recorded, and petitions canceled, Lightsong was free to pursue his own activities.

He didn't return to his main chambers. Instead, he made his way out onto his patio deck and waved for a pavilion to be set up for him.

If a new queen was going to arrive today, he wanted to get a good look at her.

4

SIRI'S CARRIAGE ROLLED to a stop outside of T'Telir, capital of Hallandren. She stared out the window and realized something very, very intimidating: Her people had *no* idea what it meant to be ostentatious. Flowers weren't ostentatious. Twenty soldiers protecting a carriage was not ostentatious. Throwing a tantrum in public wasn't ostentatious.

The field of forty thousand soldiers, dressed in brilliant blue and gold, standing in perfect rows, spears raised high with blue tassels flapping in the wind . . . *that* was ostentatious. The twin line of cavalrymen atop enormous, thick-hoofed horses, both men and beasts draped with golden cloth that shimmered in the sun. *That* was ostentatious. The massive city, so large it made her mind numb to consider it, domes and spires and painted walls all competing to draw her attention. *That* was ostentatious.

She'd thought that she was prepared. The carriage had passed through cities as they'd made their way to T'Telir. She'd seen the painted houses, the bright colors and patterns. She'd stayed at inns with plush beds. She'd eaten foods mixed with spices that made her sneeze.

She hadn't been prepared for her reception at T'Telir. Not at all.

Blessed Lord of Colors . . . she thought.

Her soldiers pulled in tight around the carriage, as if wishing they could climb inside and hide from the overwhelming sight. T'Telir was built up against the shore of the Bright Sea, a large but landlocked body of water. She could see it in the distance, reflecting the sunlight, strikingly true to its name.

A figure in blue and silver rode up to her carriage. His deep robes weren't simple, like those the monks wore back in

Idris. These had massive, peaked shoulders that almost made the costume look like armor. He wore a matching headdress. That, combined with the brilliant colors and complex layers of the robes, made Siri's hair pale to an intimidated white.

The figure bowed. "Lady Sisirinah Royal," the man said in a deep voice, "I am Treledees, high priest of His Immortal Majesty, Susebron the Grand, Returned God and King of Hallandren. You will accept this token honor guard to guide you to the Court of Gods."

Token? Siri thought.

The priest didn't wait for a response; he just turned his horse and started back down the highway toward the city. Her carriage rolled after him, her soldiers marching uncomfortably around the vehicle. The jungle gave way to sporadic bunches of palm trees, and Siri was surprised to see how much sand was mixed with the soil. Her view of the landscape soon grew obstructed by the vast field of soldiers who stood at attention on either side of the road.

"Austre, God of Colors!" one of Siri's guards whispered. "They're Lifeless!"

Siri's hair—which had begun to drift to auburn—snapped back to fearful white. He was right. Under their colorful uniforms, the Hallandren troops were a dull grey. Their eyes, their skin, even their hair: all had been drained completely of color, leaving behind a monochrome.

Those can't be Lifeless! she thought. *They look like men!*

She'd imagined Lifeless as skeletal creatures, the flesh rotting and falling from the bones. They were, after all, men who had died, then been brought back to life as mindless soldiers. But these that she passed looked so human. There was nothing to distinguish them save for their lack of color and the stiff expressions on their faces. That, and the fact that they stood unnaturally motionless. No shuffling, no breathing, no quivers of muscle or limb. Even their eyes were still. They seemed like statues, particularly considering their grey skin.

And . . . I'm going to marry one of these things? Siri thought. But no, Returned were different from Lifeless, and both were different from Drabs, who were people who had lost their Breath. She could vaguely remember a time when someone back in her village had Returned. It had been nearly ten years back, and her father hadn't let her visit the man. She did recall that he'd been able to speak and interact with his family, even if he hadn't been able to remember them.

He'd died again a week later.

Eventually, her carriage passed through the ranks of Lifeless. The city walls were next; they were immense and daunting, yet they almost looked more artistic than functional. The wall's top was curved in massive half-circles, like rolling hills, and the rim was plated with a golden metal. The gates themselves were in the form of two twisting, lithe sea creatures who curved up in a massive archway. Siri passed through them, and the guard of Hallandren cavalrymen—who appeared to be living men—accompanied her.

She had always thought of Hallandren as a place of death. Her impressions were based on stories told by passing ramblemen or by old women at the winter hearth. They spoke of city walls built from skulls, then painted with sloppy, ugly streaks of color. She'd imagined the buildings inside splattered with different clashing hues. Obscene.

She'd been wrong. True, there *was* an arrogance to T'Telir. Each new wonder seemed as if it wanted to grab her attention and shake her about by her eyes. People lined the street—more people than Siri had seen in her entire life—crowding together to watch her carriage. If there were poor among them, Siri couldn't tell, for they all wore brightly colored clothing. Some did have more exaggerated outfits—probably merchants, since Hallandren was said to have no nobility beyond its gods—but even the simplest of clothing had a cheerful brightness to it.

Many of the painted buildings did clash, but none of it

was sloppy. There was a sense of craftsmanship and art to everything from the storefronts, to the people, to the statues of mighty soldiers that frequently stood on corners. It was terribly overwhelming. Garish. A vibrant, enthusiastic garishness. Siri found herself smiling—her hair turning a tentative blond—though she felt a headache coming on.

Maybe . . . maybe this is why Father sent me, Siri thought. *Training or no training, Vivenna would never have fit in here. But I've always been far too interested in color.*

Her father was a good king with good instincts. What if—after twenty years of raising and training Vivenna—he had come to the conclusion that she wasn't the right one to help Idris? Was that why, for the first time in their lives, Father had chosen Siri over Vivenna?

But, if that's true, what am I supposed to do? She knew that her people feared Hallandren would invade Idris, but she couldn't see her father sending one of his daughters if he believed war was close. Perhaps he hoped that she'd be able to help ease the tensions between the kingdoms?

That possibility only added to her anxiety. Duty was something unfamiliar to her, and not a little unsettling. Her father trusted her with the very fate and lives of their people. She couldn't run, escape, or hide.

Particularly from her own wedding.

As her hair twinged white with fear at what was coming, she diverted her attention to the city again. It wasn't hard to let it take her attention. It was enormous, sprawling like a tired beast curled around and over hills. As the carriage climbed the southern section of town, she could see—through gaps in the buildings—that the Bright Sea broke into a bay before the city. T'Telir curved around the bay, running right up to the water, forming a crescent shape. The city wall, then, only had to run in a half-circle, abutting the sea, keeping the city boxed in.

It didn't seem cramped. There was a lot of open space in the city—malls and gardens, large swaths of unused land.

Palms lined many of the streets and other foliage was common. Plus, with the cool breeze coming over the sea, the air was a lot more temperate than she had expected. The road led up to a seaside overlook within the city, a small plateau that had an excellent view. Except the entire plateau was surrounded by a large, obstructive wall. Siri watched with growing apprehension as the gates to this smaller city-within-a-city opened up to let the carriage, soldiers, and priests enter.

The common people stayed outside.

There was another wall inside, a barrier to keep anyone from seeing in through the gate. The procession turned left and rounded the blinding wall, entering the Hallandren Court of Gods: an enclosed, lawn-covered courtyard. Several dozen enormous mansions dominated the enclosure, each one painted a distinct color. At the far end of the court was a massive black structure, much taller than the other buildings.

The walled courtyard was quiet and still. Siri could see figures sitting on balconies, watching her carriage roll across the grass. In front of each of the palaces, a crew of men and women lay prostrate on the grass. The color of their clothing matched that of their building, but Siri spared little time to study them. Instead, she nervously peered at the large, black structure. It was pyramidal, formed of giant steplike blocks.

Black, she thought. *In a city of color.* Her hair paled even further. She suddenly wished she were more devout. She doubted Austre was all that pleased with her outbursts, and most days she even had trouble naming the Five Visions. But he'd watch over her for the sake of her people, wouldn't he?

The procession pulled to a stop at the base of the enormous triangular building. Siri looked up through the carriage window at the shelves and knobs at the summit, which made the architecture seem top-heavy. She felt as if the dark blocks would come tumbling down in an avalanche to bury her. The priest rode his horse back up to Siri's window. The cavalrymen waited quietly, the shuffling of their beasts the only sound in the massive, open courtyard.

"We have arrived, Vessel," the man said. "As soon as we enter the building, you will be prepared and taken to your husband."

"Husband?" Siri asked uncomfortably. "Won't there be a wedding ceremony?"

The priest smirked. "The God King does not need ceremonial justification. You became his wife the moment he desired it."

Siri shivered. "I was just hoping that maybe I could see him, before, you know . . ."

The priest shot her a harsh look. "The God King does not perform for your whims, woman. You are blessed above all others, for you will be allowed to touch him—if only at *his* discretion. Do not pretend that you are anything other than you are. You have come because he desires it, and you will obey. Otherwise, you will be put aside and another will be chosen in your place—which, I think, might bode unfavorably for your rebel friends in the highlands."

The priest turned his horse, then clopped his way toward a large stone ramp, leading up to the building. The carriage lurched into motion, and Siri was drawn toward her fate.

5

*T*HIS WILL COMPLICATE things, Vasher thought, standing in the shadows atop the wall that enclosed the Court of Gods.

What's wrong? Nightblood asked. *So the rebels actually sent a princess. Doesn't change your plans.*

Vasher waited, watching, as the new queen's carriage crept up the incline and disappeared into the palace's maw.

What? Nightblood demanded. Even after all of these years, the sword reacted like a child in many ways.

She'll be used, Vasher thought. *I doubt we'll be able to get through this without dealing with her.* He hadn't believed that the Idrians would actually send royal blood back to T'Telir. They'd given up a pawn of terrible value.

Vasher turned away from the court, wrapping his sandaled foot around one of the banners that ran down the outside of the wall. Then he released his Breath.

"Lower me," he Commanded.

The large tapestry—woven from wool threads—sucked hundreds of Breaths from him. It hadn't the form of a man, and it was massive in size, but Vasher now had enough Breath to spend in such extravagant Awakenings.

The tapestry twisted, a thing alive, and formed a hand, which picked Vasher up. As always, the Awakening tried to imitate the form of a human—looking closely at the twistings and undulations of the fabric, Vasher could see outlines of muscles and even veins. There was no need for them; the Breath animated the fabric, and no muscles were necessary for it to move.

The tapestry carefully carried Vasher down, pinching him by one shoulder, placing his feet on the street. "Your Breath to mine," Vasher Commanded. The large banner-tapestry lost its animate form immediately, life vanishing, and it fluttered back against the wall.

Some few people paused in the street, yet they were interested, not awed. This was T'Telir, home of the gods themselves. Men with upward of a thousand Breaths were uncommon, but not unheard of. The people gawked—as peasants in other kingdoms might pause to watch the carriage of a passing lord—but then they moved on with their daily activities.

The attention was unavoidable. Though Vasher still dressed in his usual outfit—ragged trousers, well-worn cloak despite the heat, a rope wrapped several times around his waist for a belt—he now caused colors to brighten dramatically when he was near. The change would be noticeable to normal people and blatantly obvious to those of the First Heightening.

His days of being able to hide and skulk were gone. He'd have to grow accustomed to being noticed again. That was one of the reasons he was glad to be in T'Telir. The city was large enough and filled with enough oddities—from Lifeless soldiers to Awakened objects serving everyday functions—that he probably wouldn't stand out *too* much.

Of course, that didn't take Nightblood into account. Vasher moved through the crowds, carrying the overly heavy sword in one hand, sheathed point nearly dragging on the ground behind him. Some people shied away from the sword immediately. Others watched it, eyes lingering far too long. Perhaps it was time to stuff Nightblood back in the pack.

Oh, no you don't, Nightblood said. *Don't even start thinking about that. I've been locked away for too long.*

What does it matter to you? Vasher thought.

I need fresh air, Nightblood said. *And sunlight.*

You're a sword, Vasher thought, *not a palm tree.*

Nightblood fell silent. He was smart enough to realize that he was not a person, but he didn't like being confronted with that fact. It tended to put him in a sullen mood. That suited Vasher just fine.

He made his way to a restaurant a few streets down from the Court of Gods. This was one thing he *had* missed about T'Telir: restaurants. In most cities, there were few dining options. If you intended to stay for a while, you hired a local woman to give you meals at her table. If you stayed a short time, you ate what your innkeeper gave you.

In T'Telir, however, the population was large enough—and rich enough—to support dedicated food providers. Restaurants still hadn't caught on in the rest of the world, but in T'Telir, they were commonplace. Vasher already had a booth reserved, and the waiter nodded him to the spot. Vasher settled himself, leaving Nightblood up against the wall.

The sword was stolen within a minute of his letting go of it.

Vasher ignored the thievery, thoughtful as the waiter brought him a warm cup of citrus tea. Vasher sipped at the sweetened liquid, sucking on the bit of rind, wondering why in the world a people who lived in a tropical lowland preferred heated teas. After a few minutes, his life sense warned him that he was being watched. Eventually, that same sense alerted him that someone was approaching. Vasher slipped his dagger from his belt with his free hand as he sipped.

The priest sat down opposite Vasher in the booth. He wore street clothing, rather than religious robes. However—perhaps unconsciously—he had still chosen to wear the white and green of his deity. Vasher slipped his dagger back into its sheath, masking the sound by taking a loud sip.

The priest, Bebid, looked about nervously. He had enough of a Breath aura to indicate that he'd reached the First Heightening. It was where most people—those who could afford to buy Breath—stopped. That much Breath would extend their lifespan by a good decade or so and give them an increased life sense. It would also let them see Breath auras and distinguish other Awakeners, and—in a pinch—let them do a little Awakening themselves. A decent trade for spending enough money to feed a peasant family for fifty years.

"Well?" Vasher asked.

Bebid actually jumped at the sound. Vasher sighed, closing his eyes. The priest was not accustomed to these kinds of clandestine meetings. He wouldn't have come at all, had Vasher not exerted certain . . . pressures on him.

Vasher opened his eyes, staring at the priest as the waiter arrived with two plates of spiced rice. Tektrees food was the restaurant's specialty—the Hallandren liked foreign spices as much as they liked odd colors. Vasher had placed the order earlier, along with a payment that would keep the surrounding booths empty.

"Well?" Vasher repeated.

"I . . ." Bebid said. "I don't know. I haven't been able to find out much."

Vasher regarded the man with a stern stare.

"You have to give me more time."

"Remember your indiscretions, friend," Vasher said, drinking the last of his tea, feeling a twinge of annoyance. "Wouldn't want news of those getting out, would we?" *Do we have to go through this* again?

Bebid was quiet for a time. "You don't know what you're asking, Vasher," he said, leaning in. "I'm a priest of Bright-vison the True. I can't betray my oaths!"

"Good thing I'm not asking you to."

"We're not supposed to release information about court politics."

"Bah," Vasher snapped. "Those Returned can't so much as *look* at one another without half of the city learning about it within the hour."

"Surely you're not implying—" Bebid said.

Vasher gritted his teeth, bending his spoon with his finger in annoyance. "*Enough,* Bebid! We both know that your oaths are all just part of the game." He leaned in. "And I *really* hate games."

Bebid paled and didn't touch his meal. Vasher eyed his spoon with annoyance, then bent it back, calming himself. He shoveled in a spoonful of rice, mouth burning from the spices. He'd didn't believe in letting food sit around uneaten— you never knew when you'd have to leave in a hurry.

"There have been . . . rumors," Bebid finally said. "This goes beyond simple court politics, Vasher—beyond games played between gods. This is something very real, and *very* quiet. Quiet enough that even observant priests only hear hints of it."

Vasher continued to eat.

"There is a faction of the court pushing to attack Idris," Bebid said. "Though I can't fathom why."

"Don't be an idiot," Vasher said, wishing he had more tea to wash down the rice. "We both know Hallandren has sound reasons to slaughter every person up in those highlands."

"Royals," Bebid said.

Vasher nodded. They were called rebels, but those "rebels" were the true Hallandren royal family. Mortal men though they might be, their bloodline was a challenge to the Court of Gods. Any good monarch knew that the first thing you did to stabilize your throne was execute anyone who had a better claim to it than you did. After that, it was usually a good idea to execute everyone who *thought* they might have claim.

"So," Vasher said. "You fight, Hallandren wins. What's the problem?"

"It's a bad idea, that's the problem," Bebid said. "A *terrible* idea. Kalad's Phantoms, man! Idris won't go easily, no matter what people in the court say. This won't be like squashing that fool Vahr. The Idrians have allies from across the mountains and the sympathies of dozens of kingdoms. What some are calling a 'simple quelling of rebel factions' could easily spin into another Manywar. Do you want that? Thousands upon thousands dead? Kingdoms falling to never rise again? All so we can grab a little bit of frozen land nobody really wants."

"The trade passes are valuable," Vasher noted.

Bebid snorted. "The Idrians aren't foolish enough to raise their tariffs *too* high. This isn't about money. It's about fear. People in the court talk about what *might* happen if the Idrians cut off the passes or what *may* happen if the Idrians let enemies slip through and besiege T'Telir. If this were about money, we'd never go to war. Hallandren thrives on its dye and textiles trade. You think that business would boom in war? We'd be lucky not to suffer a full economic collapse."

"And you assume that I care about Hallandren's economic well-being?" Vasher asked.

"Ah, yes," Bebid said dryly. "I forgot who I was talking to. What *do* you want, then? Tell me so we can get this over with."

"Tell me about the rebels," Vasher said, chewing on rice.

"The Idrians? We just talked—"

"Not them," Vasher said. "The ones in the city."

"They're unimportant now that Vahr is dead," the priest said with a wave of his hand. "Nobody knows who killed him, by the way. Probably the rebels themselves. Guess they didn't appreciate his getting himself captured, eh?"

Vasher said nothing.

"Is that all you want?" Bebid said impatiently.

"I need to contact the factions you mentioned," Vasher said. "The ones who are pushing for war against Idris."

"I won't help you enrage the—"

"Do *not* presume to tell me what to do, Bebid. Just give me the information you promised, and you can be free of all this."

"Vasher," Bebid said, leaning in even further. "I *can't* help. My lady isn't interested in these kinds of politics, and I move in the wrong circles."

Vasher ate some more, judging the man's sincerity. "All right. Who, then?"

Bebid relaxed, using his napkin to wipe his brow. "I don't know," he said. "Maybe one of Mercystar's priests? You could also try Bluefingers, I suppose."

"Bluefingers? That's an odd name for a god."

"Bluefingers isn't a god," Bebid said, chuckling. "That's just a nickname. He's the High Place steward, head of the scribes. He pretty much keeps the court running; if anyone knows anything about this faction, it will be him. Of course, he's so stiff and straight, you'll have a hard time breaking him."

"You'd be surprised," Vasher said, shoveling the last bit of rice into his mouth. "I got you, didn't I?"

"I suppose."

Vasher stood. "Pay the waiter when you leave," he said, grabbing his cloak off its peg and wandering out. He could feel a . . . darkness to his right. He walked down the street, then turned down an alley, where he found Nightblood—still sheathed—sticking from the chest of the thief who had stolen him. Another cutpurse lay dead on the alley floor.

Vasher pulled the sword free, then snapped the sheath closed—it had only been opened a fraction of an inch—and did up the clasp.

You lost your temper in there for a bit, Nightblood said with a chastising tone. *I thought you were going to work on that.*

Guess I'm relapsing, Vasher thought.

Nightblood paused. *I don't think you ever really un-lapsed in the first place.*

That's not a word, Vasher said, leaving the alley.

So? Nightblood said. *You're too worried about words. That priest—you spent all those words on him, then you just let him go. It's not really how I would have handled the situation.*

Yes, I know, Vasher said. *Your way would have involved making several more corpses.*

Well, I am a sword, Nightblood said with a mental huff. *Might as well stick to what you're good at. . . .*

———⟨⟩———

LIGHTSONG SAT ON his patio, watching his new queen's carriage pull up to the palace. "Well, this has been a pleasant day," he remarked to his high priest. A few cups of wine—along with some time to get past thinking about children deprived of their Breath—and he was beginning to feel more like his usual self.

"You're that happy to have a queen?" Llarimar asked.

"I'm that happy to have avoided petitions for the day thanks to her arrival. What do we know about her?"

"Not much, Your Grace," Llarimar said, standing beside Lightsong's chair and looking toward the God King's palace. "The Idrians surprised us by not sending the eldest daughter as planned. They sent the youngest in her stead."

"Interesting," Lightsong said, accepting another cup of wine from one of his servants.

"She's only seventeen years old," Llarimar said. "I can't imagine being married to the God King at her age."

"I can't imagine you being married to the God King at *any* age, Scoot," Lightsong said. Then he pointedly cringed. "Actually, yes I *can* imagine it, and the dress looks painfully inelegant on you. Make a note to have my imagination flogged for its insolence in showing me that particular sight."

"I'll put it in line right behind your sense of decorum, Your Grace," Llarimar said dryly.

"Don't be silly," Lightsong said, taking a sip of wine. "I haven't had one of *those* in years."

He leaned back, trying to decide what the Idrians were signaling by sending the wrong princess. Two potted palms waved in the wind, and Lightsong was distracted by the scent of salt on the incoming sea breeze. *I wonder if I sailed that sea once,* he thought. *A man of the ocean? Is that how I died? Is that why I dreamed of a ship?*

He could only vaguely remember that dream now. A red sea . . .

Fire. Death, killing, and battle. He was shocked as he suddenly remembered his dream in starker, more vivid detail. The sea had been red as it reflected the magnificent city of T'Telir, engulfed in flames. He could almost hear people crying out in pain, he could nearly hear . . . what? Soldiers marching and fighting in the streets?

Lightsong shook his head, trying to dispel the phantom memories. The ship he'd seen in his dream had been burning too, he now remembered. It didn't have to mean anything; everyone had nightmares. But it made him uncomfortable to know that *his* nightmares were seen as prophetic omens.

Llarimar was still standing beside Lightsong's chair, watching the God King's palace.

"Oh, sit down and stop looming over me," Lightsong said. "You're making the buzzards jealous."

Llarimar raised an eyebrow. "And which buzzards would those be, Your Grace?"

"The ones who keep pushing for us to go to war," Lightsong said, waving a hand.

The priest sat down on one of the patio's wooden recliners and relaxed as he sat, removing the bulky miter from his head. Underneath, Llarimar's dark hair was plastered to his head with sweat. He ran his hand through it. During the first few years, Llarimar had remained stiff and formal at all times. Eventually, however, Lightsong had worn him down. After all, Lightsong was the god. In his opinion, if he could lounge on the job, then so could his priests.

"I don't know, Your Grace," Llarimar said slowly, rubbing his chin. "I don't like this."

"The queen's arrival?" Lightsong asked.

Llarimar nodded. "We haven't had a queen in the court for some thirty years. I don't know how the factions will deal with her."

Lightsong rubbed his forehead. "Politics, Llarimar? You know I frown on such things."

Llarimar eyed him. "Your Grace, you are—by default—a politician."

"Don't remind me, please. I should very well like to extract myself from the situation. Do you think, perhaps, I could bribe one of the other gods to take control of my Lifeless Commands?"

"I doubt that would be wise," Llarimar said.

"It's all part of my master plan to ensure that I become

totally and redundantly useless to this city by the time I die. Again."

Llarimar cocked his head. "Redundantly useless?"

"Of course. Regular uselessness wouldn't be enough—I am, after all, a god." He took a handful of grapes from a servant's tray, still trying to dismiss his dream's disturbing images. They didn't mean anything. Just dreams.

Even so, he decided he would tell Llarimar about them the next morning. Perhaps Llarimar could use the dreams to help push for peace with Idris. Since old Dedelin hadn't sent his firstborn daughter, it would mean more debates in the court. More talk of war. This princess's arrival should have settled it, but he knew that the war hawks among the gods would not let the issue die.

"Still," Llarimar said, as if talking to himself. "They did send *someone*. That is a good sign, surely. An outright refusal would have meant war for certain."

"And whoever Certain is, I doubt we should have a war for him," Lightsong said idly, inspecting a grape. "War is, in my divine opinion, even worse than politics."

"Some say the two are the same, Your Grace."

"Nonsense. War is far worse. At least where politics is going on, there are usually nice hors d'oeuvres."

As usual, Llarimar ignored Lightsong's witty remarks. Lightsong would have been offended if he hadn't known there were three separate lesser priests standing at the back of the patio, recording his words, searching for wisdom and meaning within them.

"What will the Idrian rebels do now, do you think?" Llarimar asked.

"Here's the thing, Scoot," Lightsong said, leaning back, closing his eyes and feeling the sun on his face. "The Idrians don't consider themselves to be rebels. They're not sitting up in their hills, waiting for the day when they can return in triumph to Hallandren. This isn't their home anymore."

"Those peaks are hardly a kingdom."

"They're enough of a kingdom to control the area's best mineral deposits, four vital passes to the north, and the original royal line of the original Hallandren dynasty. They don't need us, my friend."

"And the talk of Idrian dissidents in the city, ones rousing the people against the Court of Gods?"

"Rumors only," Lightsong said. "Though, when I'm proven wrong and the underprivileged masses storm my palace and burn me at the stake, I'll be sure to inform them that you were right all along. You'll get the last laugh. Or . . . well, the last scream, since you'll probably be tied up beside me."

Llarimar sighed, and Lightsong opened his eyes to find the priest regarding him with a contemplative expression. The priest didn't chastise Lightsong for his levity. Llarimar just reached down, putting his headdress back on. He was the priest; Lightsong was the god. There would be no questioning of motives, no rebukes. If Lightsong gave an order, they would all do exactly as he said.

Sometimes, that terrified him.

But not this day. He was, instead, annoyed. The queen's arrival had somehow gotten him talking about politics—and the day had been going so well until then.

"More wine," Lightsong said, raising his cup.

"You can't get drunk, Your Grace," Llarimar noted. "Your body is immune to all toxins."

"I know," Lightsong said as a lesser servant filled his cup. "But trust me—I'm *quite* good at pretending."

6

SIRI STEPPED FROM the carriage. Immediately, dozens of servants in blue and silver swarmed around her, pulling her away. Siri turned, alarmed, looking back toward her soldiers. The men stepped forward, but Treledees held up his hand.

"The Vessel will go alone," the priest declared.

Siri felt a stab of fear. This was the time. "Return to Idris," she said to the men.

"But, my lady—" the lead soldier said.

"No," Siri said. "You can do nothing more for me here. Please, return and tell my father that I arrived safely."

The lead soldier glanced back at his men, uncertain. Siri didn't get to see if they obeyed or not, for the servants shuffled her around a corner into a long, black hallway. Siri tried not to show her fear. She'd come to the palace to be wed, and was determined to make a favorable impression on the God King. But she really was just terrified. Why hadn't she run? Why hadn't she wiggled out of this somehow? Why couldn't they have all just let her be?

There was no escape now. As the serving women led her down a corridor into the deep black palace, the last remnants of her former life disappeared behind her.

She was now alone.

Lamps with colored glass lined the walls. Siri was led through several twists and turns in the dark passages. She tried to remember her way back, but was soon hopelessly lost. The servants surrounded her like an honor guard; though all were female, they were of different ages. Each wore a blue cap, hair loose out the back, and they kept their eyes downcast. Their shimmering blue clothing was loose-fitting, even through the bust. Siri blushed at the low-cut fronts. In Idris, women kept even their necks covered.

The black corridor eventually opened into a much larger room. Siri hesitated in the doorway. While the stone walls of this room were black, they had been draped in silks of a deep maroon. In fact, *everything* in the room was maroon, from the carpeting, to the furniture, to the tubs—surrounded by tile—in the center of the room.

The servants began to pick at her clothing, undressing her. Siri jumped, swatting at a few hands, causing them to pause in surprise. Then they attacked with renewed vigor, and Siri realized that she didn't have a choice except to grit her teeth and bear the treatment. She raised her arms, letting the servants pull off her dress and underclothing, and felt her hair grow red as she blushed. At least the room was warm.

She shivered anyway. She was forced to stand, naked, as other servants approached, bearing measuring tapes. They poked and prodded, getting various measurements, including ones around Siri's waist, bust, shoulders, and hips. When that was finished, the women backed away, and the room fell still. The bath continued to steam in the center of the chamber. Several of the serving women gestured toward it.

Guess I'm allowed to wash myself, Siri thought with relief, walking up the tile steps. She stepped carefully into the massive tub, and was pleased at how warm the water was. She lowered herself into the water, letting herself relax just a fraction.

Soft splashes sounded behind her, and she spun. Several other serving women—these wearing brown—were climbing into the tub, fully clothed, holding washcloths and soap. Siri sighed, yielding herself to their care as they began to scrub vigorously at her body and hair. She closed her eyes, enduring the treatment with as much dignity as she could manage.

That left her time to think, which was not good. It only

allowed her to consider just what was happening to her. Her anxiety immediately returned.

The Lifeless weren't as bad as the stories, she thought, trying to reassure herself. *And the city colors are far more pleasant than I expected. Maybe . . . maybe the God King isn't as terrible as everyone says.*

"Ah, good," a voice said. "We're right on schedule. Perfect."

Siri froze. That was a *man's* voice. She snapped her eyes open to find an older man in brown robes standing beside the tub, writing something on a ledger. He was balding and had a round, pleasant face. A young boy stood next to him, bearing extra sheets of paper and a small jar of ink for the man to use in dipping his quill.

Siri screamed, startling several of her servants as she moved with a sudden splashing motion, covering herself with her arms.

The man with the ledger hesitated, looking down. "Is something wrong, Vessel?"

"I'm *bathing,*" she snapped.

"Yes," the man said. "I believe I can tell that."

"Well, why are you *watching*?"

The man cocked his head. "But I'm a royal servant, far beneath your station . . ." he said, then trailed off. "Ah, yes. Idrian sensibilities. I had forgotten. Ladies, please splash around, make some more bubbles in the bath."

The serving women did as asked, churning up an abundance of foam in the soapy water.

"There," the man said, turning back to his ledger. "I can't see a thing. Now, let us get on with this. It would not do to keep the God King waiting on his wedding day!"

Siri reluctantly allowed the bathing to continue, though she was careful to keep certain bits of anatomy well beneath the water. The women worked furiously, scrubbing so hard that Siri was half-afraid they'd rub her skin right off.

"As you might guess," the man said, "we're on a *very*

tight schedule. There's much to do, and I would like this all to go as smoothly as possible."

Siri frowned. "And . . . who exactly are you?"

The man glanced at her, causing her to duck down beneath the suds a little more. Her hair was as bright a red as it had ever been.

"My name is Havarseth, but everyone just calls me Bluefingers." He held up a hand and wiggled the fingers, which were all stained dark with blue ink from writing. "I am head scribe and steward to His Excellent Grace Susebron, God King of Hallandren. In simpler terms, I manage the palace attendants and oversee all servants in the Court of Gods."

He paused, eyeing her. "I also make certain that everyone stays on schedule and does what they are supposed to."

Some of the younger girls—wearing brown, like the ones bathing Siri—began bringing pitchers of water to the side of the tub, and the women used these to rinse Siri's hair. She turned about to let them, though she tried to keep a waterlogged eye on Bluefingers and his serving boy.

"Now," Bluefingers said. "The palace tailors are working very quickly on your gown. We had a good estimate of your size, but final measurements were necessary to complete the process. We should have the garment ready for you in a short time."

The serving women doused Siri's head again.

"There are some things we need to discuss," Bluefingers continued, voice distorted by the water in Siri's ears. "I presume you have been taught the proper method of treating His Immortal Majesty?"

Siri glanced at him, then looked away. She probably *had* been taught, but she didn't remember—and either way, she wasn't in a frame of mind to concentrate.

"Ah," Bluefingers said, apparently reading her expression. "Well then, this could be . . . interesting. Allow me to give you some suggestions."

Siri nodded.

"First, please understand that the God King's will is law. He needs no reason or justification for what he does. Your life, like all of our lives, is in his hands. Second, please understand that the God King does not speak with people such as you or me. You will not talk to him when you go to him. Do you understand?"

Siri spit out a bit of soapy water. "You mean I'm not even to be able to *speak* to my husband?"

"I'm afraid not," Bluefingers said. "None of us can."

"Then how does he make judgments and rulings?" she asked, wiping her eyes.

"The Council of Gods handles the kingdom's more mundane needs," Bluefingers explained. "The God King is above the day-to-day governance. When it *is* necessary for him to communicate, he gives his judgments to his priests, who then reveal them to the world."

Great, Siri thought.

"It is unconventional that you are allowed to touch him," Bluefingers continued. "Fathering a child is a necessary encumbrance for him. It is our job to present you in as pleasing a way as possible, and to avoid—at all costs—irritating him."

Austre, God of Colors, she thought. *What kind of creature is this?*

Bluefingers eyed her. "I know something of your temperament, Vessel," he said. "We have, of course, researched the children of the Idrian monarchy. Allow me to be a little more personal, and perhaps a little more direct, than I would prefer. If you speak directly to the God King, he will order you executed. Unlike your father, he is not a man of patience.

"I cannot stress this point enough. I realize that you are accustomed to being a very important person. Indeed, you still *are* that important—if not more so. You are far above myself and these others. However, as far as you are above us, the God King is even *farther* above you.

"His Immortal Majesty is . . . special. The doctrines teach that the earth itself is too base for him. He is one who achieved transcendence before he was even born, but then Returned to bring his people blessings and visions. You are being given a special trust. Please, do not betray it—and please, *please* do not provoke his anger. Do you understand?"

Siri nodded slowly, feeling her hair bleach back to white. She tried to steel herself, but what courage she could gather felt like a sham. No, she wasn't going to be able to stomach this creature as easily as the Lifeless or the city colors. His reputation in Idris wasn't exaggerated. In a short time, he was going to take her body and do with it as he wished. Part of her felt a rage at that—but it was the rage of frustration. The rage that came from knowing that something horrible was coming, and from being unable to do anything at all about it.

The serving women backed away from her, leaving her half-floating in the soapy water. One of the servants looked to Bluefingers and nodded her head in respect.

"Ah, finished are we?" he asked. "Excellent. You and your ladies are efficient, as always, Jlan. Let us proceed, then."

"Can't they speak?" Siri asked quietly.

"Of course they can," Bluefingers said. "But they are dedicated servants of His Immortal Majesty. During their hours of service, their duty is to be as useful as possible without being distracting. Now, if you'll continue . . ."

Siri stayed in the water, even when the silent women tried to pull her out. Bluefingers turned around with a sigh, putting his back to her. He reached over and turned the serving boy around as well.

Siri finally allowed herself to be led out of the bath. The wet women left her, walking into a side room—probably to change—and several others led Siri toward a smaller tub for rinsing. She stepped down into the water, which was much colder than the other bath, and gasped. The women motioned for her to dunk, and she cringed, but did so, cleaning off most of the soap. After that, there was a final, third tub. As Siri approached, shivering, she could smell strong floral scents coming from it.

"What's this?" Siri asked.

"Perfumed bath," Bluefingers said, still turned away. "If you prefer, you may have one of the palace masseuses rub perfume onto your body instead. I advise against that, however, considering time restraints. . . ."

Siri blushed, imagining anyone—male or female— rubbing her body with perfume. "This will be fine," she said, climbing down into the water. It was lukewarm, and the floral scents were so strong that she had to breathe through her mouth.

The women motioned downward, and—sighing—Siri dunked beneath the scented water. After that, she climbed out, and several women finally approached with fluffy towels. They began to pat Siri down, their touch as delicate and soft as the previous scrubbing had been hard. This took away some of the strong scent, for which Siri was glad. Other women approached with a deep blue robe, and she extended her arms, allowing them to put it on her, then tie it shut. "You may turn around," she told the steward.

"Excellent," Bluefingers said, doing so. He strode toward a door at the side of the room, waving for her. "Quickly, now. We still have much to do."

Siri and the serving women followed, leaving the maroon room for one that was decorated in bright yellows. It held a lot more furniture, no bath, and a large plush chair in the center of the room.

"His Majesty is associated with no single hue," Bluefingers said, waving to the bright colors of the room as the women led Siri to the plush chair. "He represents all colors and each of the Iridescent Tones. Therefore, each room is decorated with a different shade."

Siri sat, and the women began to work on her nails. Another tried to brush out the snarls that had come from the hearty washing. Siri frowned. "Just cut it off," she said.

They hesitated. "Vessel?" one asked.

"Cut off the hair," she said.

Bluefingers gave them permission, and a few snips later, her hair was in a bunch on the floor. Then Siri closed her eyes and focused.

She wasn't certain how she did it. The Royal Locks had always been part of her life; altering them was like moving any other muscle to her, if more difficult. In a few moments, she was able to get the hair to grow.

Several women gasped softly as the hair sprouted from Siri's head and moved down to her shoulders. Growing it made her feel hungry and tired, but it was better than letting the women fight snarls. Finished, she opened her eyes.

Bluefingers was watching her with an inquisitive expression, his ledger held loosely in his fingers. "That is . . . fascinating," he said. "The Royal Locks. We have waited quite some time for them to grace the palace again, Vessel. You can change the color at will?"

"Yes," Siri said. *Some of the time, at least.* "Is it too long?"

"Long hair is seen as a sign of beauty in Hallandren, my lady," Bluefingers said. "I know you keep it bound up in Idris, but here, flowing hair is favored by many of the women—particularly the goddesses."

Part of her wanted to keep the hair short just out of spite, but she was beginning to realize that such an attitude could get her killed in Hallandren. Instead, she closed her eyes and focused again. The hair had been shoulder length, but she extended it for several minutes, making it grow until it would reach all the way down her back once she stood.

Siri opened her eyes.

"Beautiful," one of the younger serving women whispered, then flushed, immediately returning to her work on Siri's toenails.

"Very nice," Bluefingers agreed. "I will leave you here—I have a few things to deal with—but will return shortly."

Siri nodded as he left, and several women moved in and began to apply makeup. Siri suffered it pensively, others still working on her nails and hair. This wasn't how she had imagined her wedding day. Marriage had always seemed distant to her, something that would only happen after spouses had been chosen for her siblings. When she'd been very young, in fact, she'd always said that she intended to raise horses instead of getting married.

She'd grown out of that, but a part of her felt a longing for such simple times. She *didn't* want to be married. Not yet. She still felt like a child, even if her body had become that of a woman. She wanted to play in the hills and pick flowers and tease her father. She wanted time to experience more of life before she was forced into the responsibilities of childbearing.

Fate had taken that opportunity away from her. Now she was faced by the imminent prospect of going to a man's bed. A man who wouldn't speak to her, and who wouldn't care who she was or what she wanted. She knew the physical requirements of what would be involved—she could thank Mab the cook for some candid discussions on that point—but emotionally, she just felt petrified. She wanted to run, hide, flee as far as she could.

Did all women feel this way, or was it only those who were being washed, primped, and sent to please a deity with the power to destroy nations?

Bluefingers eventually returned. Another person entered behind him, an elderly man in the blue and silver clothing Siri was beginning to associate with those who served the God King.

But . . . Bluefingers wears brown, Siri thought, frowning. *Why is that?*

"Ah, I see that my timing is perfect," Bluefingers said as the women finished. They retreated to the sides of the room, heads bowed.

Bluefingers nodded to the elderly man. "Vessel, this is

one of the palace healers. Before you are taken to the God King, you will need to be inspected to determine if you are a maiden and to ensure that you don't have certain diseases. It's really just a formality, but one that I'm afraid I must insist upon. In consideration of your bashfulness, I did not bring the young healer I had originally assigned to the job. I assume an older healer will make you more comfortable?"

Siri sighed, but nodded. Bluefingers gestured toward a padded table on the side of the room; then he and his serving boy turned around. Siri undid her robe and went to the table, lying down to continue what was proving to be the most embarrassing day of her life.

It will only get worse, she thought as the doctor did his examination.

Susebron, the God King. Awesome, terrible, holy, majestic. He had been stillborn, but had Returned. What did that do to a man? Would he even be human, or would he be some monster, terrible to behold? He was said to be eternal, but obviously his reign would end eventually, otherwise he wouldn't need an heir.

She shivered, wishing it could just be over with, but also grateful for anything that delayed matters for just a little longer, even something as humiliating as the doctor's prodding. That was soon done, however, and Siri quickly did up her robe again, standing.

"She is quite healthy," the healer said to Bluefingers. "And most likely still a maiden. She also has a very strong Breath."

Siri froze. How could he tell . . .

And then she saw it. She had to look very closely, but the yellow floor around the surgeon looked a tad too bright. She felt herself pale, though the nervousness had already made her hair as white as it went.

The doctor is an Awakener, she thought. *There is an Awakener here, in this room. And he touched me.*

She cringed, skin writhing. It was wrong to take the Breath from another person. It was the ultimate in arrogance, the complete opposite of Idris philosophy. Others in Hallandren simply wore bright colors to draw attention to themselves, but Awakeners . . . they stole the life from human beings, and used *that* to make themselves stand out.

The perverted use of Breath was one of the main reasons that the Royal line had moved to the highlands in the first place. Modern-day Hallandren existed on the basis of extorting the Breath of its people. Siri felt more naked now than she had when actually unclothed. What could this Awakener tell about her, because of his unnatural life force? Was he tempted to steal Siri's BioChroma? She tried to breathe as shallowly as possible, just in case.

Eventually, Bluefingers and the terrible doctor left the room. The women approached to undo her robe once again, some bearing undergarments.

He will be worse, she realized. *The king. He's not just an Awakener, he's Returned. He needs to suck the Breath from people in order to survive.*

Would he take away her Breath?

No, that won't happen, she told herself firmly. *He needs me to provide him with an heir of the royal line. He won't risk the child's safety. He'll leave me my Breath, if only until then.*

But . . . what would happen to her when she was no longer needed?

Her attention was drawn away from such thoughts as several serving women approached with a large bundle of cloth. A dress. No, a gown—a gorgeous gown of blue and silver. Focusing on it seemed better than thinking about what the God King would do with her once she bore him a son.

Siri waited quietly as the women put it on her. The fabric was amazingly soft on her skin, the velvet smooth as petals from a highland flower. As the women adjusted it on her, she noticed that—oddly—it laced up the side instead of the back. It had an extremely long train and sleeves that were so long that if she put her arms down at the sides, the cuffs hung a good foot below her hands. It took several minutes for the women to get the ties done up right, the folds situated correctly, and the train even behind her. *All this so that it can be taken off again in a few minutes,* Siri thought with a detached sense of cold irony as a woman approached with a mirror.

Siri froze.

Where had all that color come from? The delicately red cheeks, the mysteriously dark eyes, the blue on the top of her eyelids? The deep red lips, the almost glowing skin? The gown shone silver upon blue, bulky yet beautiful, with ripples of deep, velvet cloth.

It was like nothing she'd seen in Idris. It was more amazing, even, than the colors she'd seen on the people in the city. Staring at herself in the mirror, Siri was almost able to forget her worries. "Thank you," she whispered.

That must have been the right response, for the serving women smiled, glancing at each other. Two took her hands, moving much more respectfully now than when they'd first rushed her from the carriage. Siri strode with them, train rustling behind her, and the other women stayed behind. Siri turned, and the women curtsied to her one at a time, heads bowed.

The last two—the ones leading her—opened a door, then gently pushed her out into the hallway beyond. They closed the door, leaving her.

The hallway was of the deepest black. She'd almost forgotten how dark the stone walls of the palace were. The hallway was empty, save for Bluefingers, who stood waiting for her with his ledger. He smiled, bowing his head in respect. "The God King will be pleased, Vessel," he said. "We are exactly on time—the sun only just set."

Siri turned from Bluefingers. Directly across from her was a large, imposing door. It was plated entirely with gold. Four wall lamps shone without colored glass, and they reflected light off the gilded portal. She had no question as to who lay beyond such an impressive entrance.

"This is the God King's sleeping chamber," Bluefingers said. "Rather, *one* of his sleeping chambers. Now, my lady, you *must* hear this again. Do nothing to offend the king. You are here at *his* sufferance, and are here to see to *his* needs. Not mine, not your own, and not even that of our kingdom."

"I understand," she said quietly, heart beating faster and faster.

"Thank you," Bluefingers said. "It is time to present yourself. Enter the room, then remove your dress and underclothing. Bow yourself to the ground before the king's bed, touching your head to the floor. When he wishes for you to approach, he will knock on the side post, and you may look up. He will then wave you forward."

She nodded.

"Just . . . try not to touch him too much."

Siri frowned, clenching and unclenching her increasingly nervous hands. "How exactly am I going to manage *that*? We're going to have sex, aren't we?"

Bluefingers flushed. "Yes, I guess you are. This is new ground for me too, my lady. The God King . . . well, only a group of specially dedicated servants are supposed to touch him. My suggestion would be to avoid kissing him, caressing him, or doing anything else that might offend him. Simply let him do to you what he wishes, and you should be safe."

Siri took a deep breath, nodding.

"When you are finished," Bluefingers said, "the king will withdraw. Take the bed linens and burn them in the hearth. As the Vessel, you are the only one allowed to handle such things. Do you understand?"

"Yes," Siri said, growing increasingly anxious.

"Very well then," Bluefingers said, looking almost as nervous as she was. "Good luck." With that, he reached forward and pushed the door open.

Oh, Austre, God of Colors, she thought, heart pounding, hands sweating, growing numb.

Bluefingers pushed her lightly on the back, and she stepped into the room.

7

THE DOOR SHUT behind her.

A large fire growled in a hearth to her left, bringing a shifting orange light to the large room. The black walls seemed to draw in and absorb the illumination, making deep shadows at the edges of the room.

Siri stood quietly in her ornate velvet dress, heart thumping, brow sweating. To her right, she could make out a massive bed, with sheets and covers of black to match the rest of the room. The bed appeared unoccupied. Siri peered into the darkness, eyes adjusting.

The fire crackled, throwing a flicker of light across a large, thronelike chair sitting beside the bed. It was occupied by a figure wearing black, bathed in darkness. He watched her, eyes twinkling, unblinking in the firelight.

Siri gasped, casting her eyes downward, her heartbeat surging as she remembered Bluefingers's warnings. *Vivenna should be here instead of me,* Siri thought desperately. *I can't deal with this! Father was wrong to send me!*

She squeezed her eyes shut, her breathing coming more quickly. She worked shaking fingers and pulled nervously at the strings on the side of her dress. Her hands were slick with sweat. Was she taking too long to undress? Would he be angered? Would she be killed before even the first night was out?

Would she, perhaps, prefer that?

No, she thought with determination. *No. I need to do this. For Idris. For the fields and the children who took flowers from me. For my father and Mab and everyone else in the palace.*

She finally got the strings undone, and the gown fell away with surprising ease—she could now see that it had been constructed with that goal in mind. She dropped the dress to the floor, then paused, looking at her undershift. The white fabric was throwing out a spectrum of colors, like light bent by a prism. She regarded this with shock, wondering what was causing the strange effect.

It didn't matter. She was too nervous to think about that. Gritting her teeth, she forced herself to pull off her undershift, leaving her naked. She quickly knelt on the cold stone floor, curling up, heart thudding in her ears as she bowed with her forehead touching the floor.

The room fell silent save for the crackling hearth. The fire wasn't necessary in the Hallandren warmth, but she was glad for it, unclothed as she was.

She waited, hair pure white, arrogance and stubbornness discarded, naked in more than one way. This was where she ended up—this was where all her "independent" sense of freedom came to an end. No matter what she claimed or how she felt, in the end, she had to bow to authority. Just like anyone else.

She gritted her teeth, imagining the God King sitting there, watching her be subservient and naked before him. She hadn't seen much of him, other than to notice his size—he was a good foot taller than most other men she'd seen, and was wider of shoulders and more powerful of build as well. More significant than other, lesser men.

He was Returned.

In and of itself, being Returned wasn't a sin. After all, Returned came in Idris, too. The Hallandren people, however, kept the Returned alive, feeding them on the souls of peasants, tearing away the Breath of hundreds of people each year. . . .

Don't think of that, Siri told herself forcefully. Yet as she tried to clear her thoughts, the God King's eyes returned to her memory. Those black eyes, which had seemed to glow in the firelight. She could feel them on her still, watching her, as cold as the stones upon which she knelt.

The fire crackled. Bluefingers had said that the king would knock for her. What if she missed it? She didn't dare glance upward. She'd already met his gaze once, if by accident. She couldn't risk upsetting him further. She just continued to kneel in place, elbows on the ground, back beginning to ache.

Why doesn't he do something?

Was he displeased with her? Was she not as pretty as he'd desired, or was he angered that she'd met his eyes and then taken too long to undress? It would be particularly ironic if she offended him when trying so hard not to be her usual flippant self. Or was something else wrong? He had been promised the eldest daughter of the Idrian king, but had instead received Siri. Would he know the difference? Would he even care?

The minutes passed, the room growing darker as the fire consumed its logs.

He's toying with me, Siri thought. *Forcing me to wait on his whims.* Making her kneel in such an uncomfortable position was probably a message—one that showed who was in power. He would take her when *he* willed it, and not before.

Siri gritted her teeth as the time passed. How long had she been kneeling? An hour, maybe longer. And still, there wasn't a hint of sound—no knock, no cough, not even a shuffle from the God King. Perhaps it was a test to see how long she would remain as she was. Perhaps she was just reading too much into things. Either way, she forced herself to remain in place, shifting only when she absolutely had to.

Vivenna had the training. Vivenna had the poise and the refinement. But Siri, she had the stubbornness. One only had to look back at her history of repeatedly ignoring lessons and duties to appreciate that. With time, she'd even broken down her father. He'd started letting her do as she pleased, if only to save his own sanity.

And so she continued to wait—naked in the light of the coals—as the night wore on.

⸺◈⸺

FIREWORKS SPRAYED SPARKS upward in a fountain of light. Some fell close to where Lightsong was sitting, and these blazed with an extra, frenzied light until they died away.

He reclined on a couch in the open air, watching the display. Servants waited around him, complete with parasols, a portable bar, steaming and chilled towels to rub his face and hands should he feel the need, and a host of other luxuries that—to Lightsong—were simply commonplace.

He watched the fireworks with mild interest. The firemasters stood in a nervous cluster near his position. Beside them were a troop of minstrels that Lightsong had called for, but hadn't yet asked to perform. While there were always entertainers in the Court of Gods for the Returned to enjoy, this night—the wedding night of their God King—was even more extravagant.

Susebron wasn't in attendance himself, of course. Such festivities were beneath him. Lightsong glanced to the side, where the king's palace rose soberly above the court. Eventually, Lightsong just shook his head and turned his attention back to the courtyard. The palaces of the gods formed a ring, and each building had a patio below and a balcony above, both facing the central area. Lightsong sat a short distance from his patio, out amidst the lush grass of the expansive courtyard.

Another firefountain sprayed into the air, throwing

shadows across the courtyard. Lightsong sighed, accepting another fruit drink from a servant. The night was cool and pleasant, fit for a god. Or gods. Lightsong could see others set up in front of their palaces. Different groups of performers cluttered the sides of the courtyard, waiting for their chance to please one of the Returned.

The fountain ran low, and the firemasters looked toward him, smiling hopefully in the torchlight. Lightsong nodded with his best benevolent expression. "More fireworks," he said. "You have pleased me." This caused the three men to whisper in excitement and wave for their assistants.

As they set up, a familiar figure wandered into Lightsong's ring of torches. Llarimar wore his priestly robes, as always. Even when he was out in the city—which was where he should have been this night—he represented Lightsong and his priesthood.

"Scoot?" Lightsong asked, sitting up.

"Your Grace," Llarimar said, bowing. "Are you enjoying the festivities?"

"Certainly. You might say I'm positively in*fested*. But what are you doing here in the court? You should be out with your family."

"I just wanted to make certain everything was to your liking."

Lightsong rubbed his forehead. "You're giving me a headache, Scoot."

"You can't get headaches, Your Grace."

"So you're fond of telling me," Lightsong said. "I assume the revelry outside the Holy Prison is nearly as amazing as what we have here inside?"

Llarimar frowned at Lightsong's dismissive reference to the divine compound. "The party in the city is fantastic, Your Grace. T'Telir hasn't seen a festival this grand in decades."

"Then I repeat that you should be out enjoying it."

"I just—"

"Scoot," Lightsong said, giving the man a pointed look, "if there's *one* thing you can trust me to do competently on my own, it's enjoy myself. I will—I promise in all solemnity—have a ravishingly good time drinking to excess and watching these nice men light things on fire. Now go be with your family."

Llarimar paused, then stood, bowed, and withdrew.

That man, Lightsong thought, sipping his fruity drink, *takes his work far too seriously.*

The concept amused Lightsong, and he leaned back, enjoying the fireworks. However, he was soon distracted by the approach of someone else. Or, rather, one very important someone else leading a group of far less important someone elses. Lightsong sipped his drink again.

The newcomer was beautiful. She was a goddess, after all. Glossy black hair, pale skin, lushly curvaceous body. She wore far less clothing than Lightsong did, but that was typical of the court's goddesses. Her thin gown of green and silver silk was split on both sides, showing hips and thighs, and the neckline was draped so low that very little was left to the imagination.

Blushweaver the Beautiful, goddess of honesty.

This should be interesting, Lightsong thought, smiling to himself.

She was trailed by about thirty servants, not to mention her high priestess and six lesser priests. The firemasters grew excited, realizing that they now had not one, but two divine observers. Their apprentices scurried about in a flurry of motion, setting up another series of firefountains. A group of Blushweaver's servants rushed forward, carrying an ornate couch, which they set on the grass beside Lightsong.

Blushweaver lay down with customary lithe grace, crossing perfect legs and resting on her side in a seductive yet ladylike pose. The orientation left her able to watch the fireworks should she wish, but her attention was obviously focused on Lightsong.

"My dear Lightsong," she said as a servant approached with a bunch of grapes. "Aren't you even going to greet me?"

Here we go, Lightsong thought. "My dear Blushweaver," he said, setting aside his cup and lacing his fingers before him. "Why would I go and do something rude like that?"

"Rude?" she asked, amused.

"Of course. You obviously make quite a determined effort to draw attention to yourself—the details are magnificent, by the way. Is that makeup on your thighs?"

She smiled, biting into a grape. "It's a kind of paint. The designs were drawn by some of the most talented artists in my priesthood."

"My compliments to them," Lightsong said. "Regardless, you ask why I did not greet you. Well, let us assume that I had acted as you suggest I should. Upon your approach, you would have had me gush over you?"

"Naturally."

"You would have me point out how stunning you appear in that gown?"

"I wouldn't complain."

"Mention how your dazzling eyes glisten in the fireworks like burning embers?"

"That would be nice."

"Expound on how your lips are so perfectly red that they could leave any man breathless with wonder, yet drive him to compose the most brilliant of poetry each time he recalled the moment?"

"I'd be flattered for certain."

"And you claim you want these reactions from me?"

"I do."

"Well blast it, woman," Lightsong said, picking up his cup. "If I'm stunned, dazzled, and breathless, then how the hell am I supposed to *greet* you? By definition, won't I be struck dumb?"

She laughed. "Well, then, you've obviously found your tongue now."

"Surprisingly, it was in my mouth," he said. "I always forget to check there."

"But isn't that where it is expected to be?"

"My dear," he said, "haven't you known me long enough to realize that my tongue, of all things, rarely does what it is expected to do?"

Blushweaver smiled as the fireworks went off again. Within the auras of *two* gods, the sparks' colors grew quite powerful indeed. On the far side, some sparks fell to the ground too far from the Breath auras, and these looked dull and weak in comparison—as if their fire were so cool and insignificant that they could be picked up and tucked away.

Blushweaver turned from the display. "So you *do* find me beautiful?"

"Of course. Why, my dear, you're positively *rank* with beauty. You're literally part of the definition of the word— it's in your title somewhere, if I'm not mistaken."

"My dear Lightsong, *I* do believe that you're making sport of me."

"I never make fun of ladies, Blushweaver," Lightsong said, picking up his drink again. "Mocking a woman is like drinking too much wine. It may be fun for a short time, but the hangover is hell."

Blushweaver paused. "But we don't get hangovers, for we cannot get drunk."

"We can't?" Lightsong asked. "Then why the blazes am I drinking all of this wine?"

Blushweaver raised an eyebrow. "Sometimes, Lightsong," she finally said, "I'm not certain when you are being silly and when you're being serious."

"Well, I can help you with that one easily enough," he said. "If you *ever* conclude that I'm being serious, then you can be sure that you've been working too hard on the problem."

"I see," she said, twisting on her couch so that she was

facedown. She leaned on her elbows with breasts pushed up between them, fireworks playing off her exposed back and throwing colorful shadows between her arched shoulder blades. "So, then. You admit that I'm stunning and beautiful. Would you then care to retire from the festivities this evening? Find . . . other entertainments?"

Lightsong hesitated. Being unable to bear children didn't stop the gods from seeking intimacy, particularly with other Returned. In fact, from what Lightsong could guess, the impossibility of offspring only increased the laxness of the court in these matters. Many a god took mortal lovers—Blushweaver was known to have a few of her own among her priests. Dalliances with mortals were never seen as infidelity among the gods.

Blushweaver lounged on her couch, supple, inviting. Lightsong opened his mouth, but in his mind, he saw . . . her. The woman of his vision, the one from his dreams, the face he'd mentioned to Llarimar. Who was she?

Probably nothing. A flash from his former life, or perhaps simply an image crafted by his subconscious. Maybe even, as the priests claimed, some kind of prophetic symbol. That face shouldn't give him pause. Not when confronted with perfection.

"I . . . must decline," he found himself saying. "I need to watch the fireworks."

"Are they that much more fascinating than I?"

"Not at all. They simply seem far less likely to burn me."

She laughed at that. "Well, why don't we wait until they are through, then retire?"

"Alas," Lightsong said. "I still must decline. I am far too lazy."

"Too lazy for sex?" Blushweaver asked, rolling back onto her side and regarding him.

"I'm really quite indolent. A poor example of a god, as I keep telling my high priest. Nobody seems to listen to me, so I fear that I must continue to be diligent in proving my point. Dallying with you would, unfortunately, undermine the entire basis of my argument."

Blushweaver shook her head. "You confuse me sometimes, Lightsong. If it weren't for your reputation, I'd simply presume you to be shy. How could you have slept with Calmseer, but consistently ignore me?"

Calmseer was the last honorable Returned this city has known, Lightsong thought, sipping his drink. *Nobody left has a shred of her decency. Myself included.*

Blushweaver fell silent, watching the latest display from the firemasters. The show had grown progressively more ornate, and Lightsong was considering calling a halt, lest they use up all of their fireworks on him and not have any left should another god call upon them.

Blushweaver didn't make any move to return to her own palace grounds, and Lightsong said nothing further. He suspected that she hadn't come simply for verbal sparring, or even to try and bed him. Blushweaver always had her plans. In Lightsong's experience, there was more depth to the woman than her gaudy surface suggested.

Eventually, his hunch paid off. She turned from the fireworks, eyeing the dark palace of the God King. "We have a new queen."

"I noticed," Lightsong said. "Though, admittedly, only because I was reminded several times."

They fell silent.

"Have you no thoughts on the matter?" Blushweaver finally asked.

"I try to avoid having thoughts. They lead to other thoughts, and—if you're not careful—those lead to actions. Actions make you tired. I have this on rather good authority from someone who once read it in a book."

Blushweaver sighed. "You avoid thinking, you avoid me, you avoid effort . . . is there anything you *don't* avoid?"

"Breakfast."

Blushweaver didn't react to this, which Lightsong found

disappointing. She was too focused on the king's palace. Lightsong usually tried to ignore the large black building; he didn't like how it seemed to loom over him.

"Perhaps you should make an exception," Blushweaver said, "and give some thought to *this* particular situation. This queen means something."

Lightsong turned his cup around in his fingers. He knew that Blushweaver's priests were among those who called most strongly for war in the Court Assembly. He hadn't forgotten his phantom nightmare from earlier, the vision of T'Telir on fire. That image refused to fade from his mind. He never said anything for or against the idea of war. He just didn't want to be involved.

"We've had queens before," he finally said.

"Never one of the royal line," Blushweaver replied. "At least, there hasn't been one since the days of Kalad the Usurper."

Kalad. The man who had started the Manywar, the one who had used his knowledge of BioChromatic Breath to create a vast army of Lifeless and seize power in Hallandren. He had protected the kingdom with his armies, yet had shattered the kingdom as well by driving the royals into the highlands.

Now they were back. Or, at least, one of them was.

"This is a dangerous day, Lightsong," Blushweaver said quietly. "What happens if that woman bears a child who isn't Returned?"

"Impossible," Lightsong said.

"Oh? You are that confident?"

Lightsong nodded. "Of the Returned, only the God King can engender children, and they're always stillborn."

Blushweaver shook her head. "The only word we have for that is from the palace priests themselves. Yet I've heard of . . . discrepancies in the records. Even if we don't worry about those, there are plenty of other considerations. Why do we need a royal to 'legitimize' our throne? Isn't three hundred years of rule by the Court of Gods sufficient to make the kingdom legitimate?"

Lightsong didn't respond.

"This marriage implies that we still accept royal authority," Blushweaver said. "What happens if that king up in the highlands decides to take his lands back? What happens if that queen of ours in there has a child by another man? Who is the heir? Who rules?"

"The God King rules. Everyone knows that."

"He didn't rule three hundred years ago," Blushweaver said. "The royals did. Then, after them, Kalad did—and after him, Peacegiver. Change can happen quickly. By inviting that woman into our city, we may have initiated the end of Returned rule in Hallandren."

She fell silent, pensive. Lightsong studied the beautiful goddess. It had been fifteen years since her Return—which made her old, for a Returned. Old, wise, and incredibly crafty.

Blushweaver glanced at him. "I don't intend to find myself caught, surprised, like the royals were when Kalad seized their throne. Some of us are planning, Lightsong. You can join us, if you wish."

"Politics, my dear," he said with a sigh. "You know how I loathe it."

"You're the god of bravery. We could use your confidence."

"At this point, I'm only confident that I'll be of no use to you."

Her face stiffened as she tried not to show her frustration. Eventually, she sighed and stood, stretching, showing off her perfect figure once more. "You'll have to stand for something eventually, Lightsong," she said. "You're a god to these people."

"Not by choice, my dear."

She smiled, then bent down and kissed him softly. "Just consider what I said. You're a better man than you give yourself credit for being. You think I'd offer myself to just anyone?"

He hesitated, then frowned. "Actually . . . yes. I do."

She laughed, turning as her servants picked up her couch. "Oh, come now! There must be at least *three* of the other gods I wouldn't *think* of letting touch me. Enjoy the party, and do try to imagine what our king is doing to our legacy up there in his chambers right now." She glanced back at him. "Particularly if that imagining reminds you of what you just missed out on." She winked, then glided away.

Lightsong sat back on his couch, then dismissed the firemasters with words of praise. As the minstrels began to play, he tried to empty his mind of both Blushweaver's ominous words and the visions of war that had plagued his dreams.

He failed on both counts.

8

SIRI GROANED, ROLLING over. Her back hurt, her arms hurt, and her head hurt. In fact, she was so uncomfortable that she couldn't stay asleep, despite her fatigue. She sat up, holding her head.

She'd spent the night on the floor of the God King's bedchamber—sleeping, kind of. Sunlight poured into the room, reflecting off of the marble where the floor wasn't covered with rugs.

Black rugs, she thought, sitting in the middle of the rumpled blue dress, which she'd used as both blanket and pillow. *Black rugs on a black floor with black furniture. These Hallandren certainly know how to run with a motif.*

The God King wasn't in the room. Siri glanced toward

the oversized black leather chair where he'd spent much of the night. She hadn't noticed him leave.

She yawned, then rose, pulling her shift out of the wadded mound of dress and putting it on over her head. She pulled her hair out, flipping it behind her. Keeping it so long was going to take some getting used to. It fell down against her back, a contented blond in color.

She'd somehow survived the night untouched.

She walked on bare feet over to the leather chair, running her fingers along its smooth surface. She'd been less than respectful. She'd dozed off. She'd curled up and pulled her dress close. She'd even glanced over at the chair a few times. Not because of defiance or a disobedient heart; she'd simply been too drowsy to remember that she wasn't supposed to look at the God King. And he hadn't ordered her executed. Bluefingers had made her worry that the God King was volatile and quick to anger, yet if that was the case, then he had held his temper with her. What else was he going to do? The Hallandren had waited for decades to get a royal princess to marry into their line of God Kings. She smiled. *I do have some power.* He couldn't kill her—not until he had what he wanted.

It wasn't much, but it did give her a bit more confidence. She walked around the chair, noting its size. Everything in the room was built to be just a little too large, skewing her perspective, making her feel shorter than she was. She rested her hand on the arm of the chair, and found herself wondering why he hadn't decided to take her. What was wrong with her? Wasn't she desirable?

Foolish girl, she told herself, shaking her head and walking over to the still-undisturbed bed. *You spent most of the trip here worrying about what would happen on your wedding night, and then when nothing happens, you complain about that too?*

She knew she wasn't free. He would take her eventually—that was the point of the entire arrangement. But it hadn't happened last night. She smiled, yawning, then she climbed up into the bed and curled up under the covers, drifting off.

⎯⎯⎯∞∞∞⎯⎯⎯

THE NEXT TIME she woke was a great deal more pleasant than the previous one had been. Siri stretched, and then noticed something.

Her dress, which she'd left sitting in a heap on the floor, was gone. Also, the fire in the hearth had been rebuilt—though why that was necessary was beyond her. The day was warm, and she'd kicked off the covers as she'd slept.

I'm supposed to burn the sheets, she remembered. *That's the reason they stoked the fire.*

She sat up in her shift, alone in the black room. The servants and priests wouldn't know that she'd spent the entire night on the floor unless the God King had told someone. How likely would it be for a man of his power to speak with his priests about intimate details?

Slowly, Siri climbed out of bed and pulled the sheets free. She wadded them up, walked over, and threw them into the large hearth. Then she watched the flames. She still didn't know why the God King had left her alone. Until she knew, it was surely better to just let everyone assume that the marriage had been consummated.

After the sheets were done burning, Siri scanned the room, looking for something to wear. She found nothing. Sighing, she walked to the door, clothed only in her shift. She pulled it open, and jumped slightly. Two dozen serving women of varying ages knelt outside.

God of Colors! Siri thought. *How long have they been kneeling out here?* Suddenly, she didn't feel quite so indignant at being forced to wait upon the God King's whims.

The women stood up, heads bowed, and walked into the room. Siri backed up, cocking her head when she noticed that several of the women carried in large chests. *They're dressed in different colors from yesterday,* Siri thought. The cut was the same—divided skirts, like flowing trousers, topped with sleeveless blouses and small caps, their hair coming out the back. Instead of the blue and silver, the outfits were now yellow and copper.

The women opened the trunks, removing various layers of clothing. All were of bright colors, and each was of a different cut. The women spread them out on the floor before Siri, then settled back on their knees, waiting.

Siri hesitated. She'd grown up the daughter of a king, so she'd never lacked. Yet, life in Idris was austere. She'd owned five dresses, which had nearly been an extravagant number. One had been white, and the other four had been the same wan blue.

Being confronted by so many colors and options felt overwhelming. She tried to imagine how each would look on her. Many of them were dangerously low-cut, even more so than the shirts the serving women wore—and those were already scandalous by Idrian standards.

Finally, hesitantly, Siri pointed at one outfit. It was a dress in two pieces, red skirt and matching blouse. As Siri pointed, the serving women stood, some putting away the unchosen outfits, others walking over to carefully remove Siri's shift.

In a few minutes, Siri was dressed. She was embarrassed to find that—while the clothing fit her perfectly—the blouse was designed to reveal her midriff. Still, it wasn't as low-cut as the others, and the skirt went all the way down to her calves. The silky red material was far lighter than the thick wools and linen she was accustomed to wearing. The skirt flared and ruffled when she turned, and Siri couldn't be completely certain it wasn't sheer. Standing in it, she almost felt as naked as she'd been during the night.

That appears to be a recurring theme for me here, she thought wryly as the serving women backed away. Others approached with a stool, and she sat, waiting as the women cleaned her face and arms with a pleasantly warm cloth. When that was done, they reapplied her makeup, did her hair, then sprayed her with a few puffs of perfume.

When she opened her eyes—perfume misting down around her—Bluefingers was standing in the room. "Ah, excellent," he said, servant boy standing obediently behind with ink, quill, and paper. "You're up already."

Already? Siri thought. *It has to be well past noon!*

Bluefingers looked her over, nodded to himself, then glanced at the bed, obviously checking to see that the linens had been destroyed. "Well," he said. "I trust that your servants will see to your needs, Vessel." With that, he began to walk away with the anxious tread of a man who felt he had far too much to do.

"Wait!" Siri said, standing, jostling several of her serving women.

Bluefingers hesitated. "Vessel?"

Siri floundered, uncertain how to express what she was feeling. "Do you know . . . what I'm supposed to do?"

"Do, Vessel?" the scribe asked. "You mean, in regards to . . ." He glanced at the bed.

Siri flushed. "No, not that. I mean with my time. What are my duties? What is expected of me?"

"To provide an heir."

"Beyond that."

Bluefingers frowned. "I . . . well, to be honest, Vessel, I really don't know. I must say, your arrival has certainly caused a level of disruption in the Court of Gods."

In my life, too, she thought, flushing slightly, hair turning red.

"Not that you're to blame, of course," Bluefingers said quickly. "But then . . . well, I certainly wish I'd had more forewarning."

"More forewarning?" Siri asked. "This marriage was arranged by treaty over twenty years ago!"

"Yes, well, but nobody thought . . ." He trailed off.

"Ahem. Well, either way, we shall do our best to accommodate you here in the king's palace."

What was that? Siri thought. *Nobody thought . . . that the marriage would really happen? Why not? Did they assume that Idris wouldn't keep its part of the bargain?*

Regardless, he still hadn't answered her question. "Yes, but what am I supposed to *do*?" she said, sitting down on the stool again. "Am I to sit here in the palace and stare at the fire all day?"

Bluefingers chuckled. "Oh, Colors no! My lady, this is the Court of Gods! You'll find plenty to occupy you. Each day, performers are allowed to enter the court and display their talents for their deities. You may have any of these brought to you for a private performance."

"Ah," Siri said. "Can I, maybe, go horseback riding?"

Bluefingers rubbed his chin. "I suppose we could bring some horses into the court for you. Of course, we'd have to wait until the Wedding Jubilation is over."

"Wedding Jubilation?" she asked.

"You . . . don't know, then? Were you not prepared for any of this?"

Siri flushed.

"No offense intended, Vessel," Bluefingers said. "The Wedding Jubilation is a weeklong period in which we celebrate the God King's marriage. During that time, you are not to leave this palace. At the end of it, you will officially be presented to the Court of Gods."

"Oh," she said. "And after that, I can go out of the city?"

"Out of the city!" Bluefingers said. "Vessel, you can't leave the Court of Gods!"

"What?"

"You may not be a god yourself," Bluefingers continued. "But you're the wife of the God King. It would be far too dangerous to let you out. But do not fret—anything and everything you might request can be provided for you."

Except freedom, she thought, feeling a bit sick.

"I assure you, once the Wedding Jubilation is over, you will find little to complain about. Everything you could want is here: every type of indulgence, every luxury, every diversion."

Siri nodded numbly, still feeling trapped.

"Also," Bluefingers said, holding up an ink-stained finger. "If you wish, the Court Assembly meets to provide decisions to the people. Full assembly meets once a week, though daily there are smaller judgments to be made. You aren't to sit on the assembly itself, of course, but you will certainly be allowed to attend, once the Jubilation is over. If none of this suits you, you may request an artist of the God King's priesthood to attend you. His priests include devout and accomplished artists from all genres: music, painting, dance, poetry, sculpture, puppetry, play performance, sandpainting, or any of the lesser genres."

Siri blinked. *God of Colors!* she thought. *Even being idle is daunting here.* "But there isn't any of this that I'm *required* to attend?"

"No, I shouldn't think so," Bluefingers said. "Vessel, you look displeased."

"I . . ." How could she explain? Her entire life, she'd been expected to be something—and for most of her life she'd intentionally avoided being it. Now that was gone from her. She couldn't disobey lest she get herself killed and get Idris into a war. For once, she was willing to serve, to try and be obedient. But, ironically, there didn't seem to be anything for her to do. Except, of course, bear a child.

"Very well," she said with a sigh. "Where are my rooms? I'll go there and situate myself."

"Your rooms, Vessel?"

"Yes. I assume I'm not to reside in this chamber itself."

"No," Bluefingers said, chuckling. "The conception room? Of course not."

"Then where?" Siri asked.

"Vessel," Bluefingers said. "In a way, this entire palace

is yours. I don't see why you'd need specific rooms. Ask to eat, and your servants will set up a table. If you wish to rest, they will bring you a couch or a chair. Seek entertainment, and they will fetch performers for you."

Suddenly, the strange actions of her servants—simply bringing her an array of colors to choose from, then doing her makeup and hair right there—made more sense. "I see," she said, almost to herself. "And the soldiers I brought with me? Did they do as I commanded?"

"Yes, Vessel," Bluefingers said. "They left this morning. It was a wise decision; they are not dedicated servants of the Tones, and would not have been allowed to remain here in the court. They could do you no further service."

Siri nodded.

"Vessel, if I might be excused . . . ?" Bluefingers asked.

Siri nodded distractedly, and Bluefingers bustled away, leaving her to think about how terribly alone she was. *Can't focus on that,* she thought. Instead, she turned to one of her serving women—a younger one, about Siri's own age. "Well, that really doesn't tell me what to spend my time on, does it?"

The servant blushed quietly, bowing her head.

"I mean, there seems to be a lot to do, if I want," Siri said. "Maybe too much."

The girl bowed again.

That's going to get very annoying very quickly, Siri thought, gritting her teeth. Part of her wanted to do something shocking to get a reaction out of the servant, but she knew she was just being foolish. In fact, it seemed that many of her natural impulses and reactions wouldn't work here in Hallandren. So, to keep herself from doing something silly, Siri stood up, determined to examine her new home. She left the overly black room, poking her head out into the hallway. She turned back to her servants, who stood obediently in a line behind her.

"Is there any place I'm forbidden to go?" she asked.

The one she was addressing shook her head.

Fine, then, she thought. *I'd better not end up stumbling upon the God King in the bath.* She crossed the hallway, opened the door, then stepped into the yellow room she'd been in the day before. The chair and bench she'd used had been removed, replaced by a group of yellow couches. Siri raised an eyebrow, then walked through into the tub room beyond.

The tub was gone. She started. The room was the one she remembered, with the same red colorings. Yet, the sloped tile platforms with their inset tubs were gone. The entire contraption must have been portable, brought in for her bath, then removed.

They really can *transform any room,* she thought with amazement. *They must have chambers full of furniture, tubs, and drapings, each of a different color, waiting upon the whims of their god.*

Curious, she left the tubless room and moved in a random direction. Each room appeared to have four doors, one on each wall. Some rooms were larger than others. Some had windows to the outside, while others were in the middle of the palace. Each was a different color, yet it was still difficult to tell the difference between them. Endless rooms, pristine with their decorations following a single color's theme. Soon, she was hopelessly lost—but it didn't seem to matter. Every room was, in a way, the same as any other.

She turned to her servants. "I would like breakfast."

It happened far faster than Siri would have thought possible. Several of the women ducked out and returned with a stuffed green chair to match her current room. Siri sat down, waiting as a table, chairs, and finally food were produced as if out of nowhere. In less than fifteen minutes, she had a hot meal waiting for her.

Hesitantly, she picked up a fork and tried a bite. It wasn't until that moment that she realized how hungry she was. The meal was composed primarily of a group of sausages mixed with vegetables. The flavors were far stronger than she was accustomed to. However, the more she ate the spicy Hallandren food, the more she found herself liking it.

Hungry or not, it was strange to eat in silence. Siri was accustomed to either eating in the kitchens with the servants or at the table with her father, his generals, and whatever local people or monks he had invited to his home that evening. It was never a silent affair, yet here in Hallandren—land of colors, sounds, and ostentation—she found herself eating alone, quietly, in a room that felt dull despite its bright decorations.

Her servants watched. None of them spoke to her. Their silence was supposed to be respectful, she knew, but Siri just found it intimidating. She tried several times to draw them into conversation, but she managed to get only terse replies.

She chewed on a spiced caper. *Is this what my life is to be from now on?* she thought. *A night spent feeling half-used, half-ignored by my husband, then days spent surrounded by people, yet somehow still alone?*

She shivered, her appetite waning. She set down the fork, and her food slowly grew cold on the table before her. She stared at it, a part of her wishing she'd simply remained in the comfortable, oversized black bed.

9

VIVENNA—FIRSTBORN CHILD of Dedelin, king of Idris—gazed upon the grand city of T'Telir. It was the ugliest place she had ever seen.

People jostled their way through the streets, draped flagrantly in colors, yelling, and talking, and moving, and stinking, and coughing, and bumping. Her hair lightened to grey, she pulled her shawl close as she maintained her imitation—such that it was—of an elderly woman. She had feared that she might stand out. She needn't have worried. Who could ever stand out in this confusion?

Nevertheless, it was best to be safe. She had come—arriving in T'Telir just hours ago—to rescue her sister, not to get herself kidnapped.

It was a bold plan. Vivenna could hardly believe that she'd come up with it. Still, of the many things her tutors had taught her, one was foremost in her mind: A leader was someone who acted. Nobody else was going to help Siri, and so it was up to Vivenna.

She knew that she was inexperienced. She hoped that her awareness of that would keep her from being *too* fool-hardy, but she had the best education and political tutelage her kingdom could provide, and much of her training had focused on life in Hallandren. As a devout daughter of Austre, she'd practiced all of her life to avoid standing out. She could hide in a vast, disorganized city like T'Telir.

And vast it was. She'd memorized maps, but they hadn't prepared her for the sight, sound, scent, and *colors* of the city on market day. Even the livestock wore bright ribbons. Vivenna stood at the side of the road, stooped beside a building draped in flapping streamers. In front of her, a herdsman drove a small flock of sheep toward the market square. They had each been dyed a different color. *Won't that ruin the wool?* Vivenna thought sourly. The different colors on the animals clashed so terribly that she had to look away.

Poor Siri, she thought. *Caught up in all of this, locked in the Court of Gods, probably so overwhelmed that she can barely think.* Vivenna had been trained to deal with the terrors of Hallandren. Though the colors sickened her, she had the fortitude to withstand them. How would little Siri manage?

Vivenna tapped her foot as she stood beside the building

in the shadow of a large stone statue. *Where is that man?* she thought. Parlin had yet to return from his scouting.

There was nothing to do but wait. She glanced up at the statue beside her; it was one of the famous D'Denir Celabrin. Most of the statues depicted warriors. They stood in every imaginable pose all across the entire city, armed with weapons and often dressed in colorful clothing. According to her lessons, the people of T'Telir found dressing the statues to be an amusing pastime. Lore had it that the first ones had been commissioned by Peacegiver the Blessed, the Returned who had taken command of Hallandren at the end of the Manywar. The number of statues had increased each year as new ones were paid for by the Returned—whose money, of course, came from the people themselves.

Excess and waste, Vivenna thought, shaking her head.

Finally, she noticed Parlin coming back down the street. She frowned as she saw that he was wearing some ridiculous frippery on his head—it looked a little like a sock, though much larger. The bright green hat flopped down one side of his square face, and looked very out of place against his dull brown Idrian travel clothing. Tall but not lanky, Parlin was only a few years Vivenna's senior. She'd known him for most of her life; General Yarda's son had practically grown up in the palace. More recently, he'd been out in the forests, watching the Hallandren border or guarding one of the northern passes.

"Parlin?" she said as he approached, carefully keeping the annoyance out of her voice and her hair. "What is that on your head?"

"A hat," he said, characteristically terse. It wasn't that Parlin was rude; it just seemed he rarely felt he had much to say.

"I can see that it's a hat, Parlin. Where did you get it?"

"The man in the market said they're very popular."

Vivenna sighed. She'd hesitated to bring Parlin into the city. He was a good man—as solid and reliable as she'd ever known—but the life he knew was one of living in the wilderness and guarding isolated outposts. The city was probably overwhelming to him.

"The hat is ridiculous, Parlin," Vivenna said, hair controlled to keep the red out of it. "And makes you stand out."

Parlin removed the hat, tucking it in his pocket. He said nothing further, but did turn, watching the crowds of people pass. They seemed to make him as nervous as they did Vivenna. Perhaps more so. However, she was glad to have him. He was one of the few people she trusted not to go to her father; she knew that Parlin fancied her. During their youth, he'd often brought her gifts from the forest. Usually, those had taken the form of some animal he'd killed.

To Parlin's mind, nothing showed affection like a hunk of something dead and bleeding on the table.

"This place is strange," Parlin said. "People here move like herds." His eyes followed a pretty Hallandren girl as she walked by. The hussy was—like most of the women in T'Telir—wearing practically nothing. Blouses that were open well below the neck, skirts well above the knees— some women even wore trousers, just like men.

"What did you discover in the market?" she asked, drawing his attention back.

"There are a lot of Idrians here," he said.

"*What?*" Vivenna said, forgetting herself and showing her shock.

"Idrians," Parlin said. "In the market. Some were trading goods; many looked like common laborers. I watched them."

Vivenna frowned, folding her arms. "And the restaurant?" Vivenna asked. "Did you scout it as I asked?"

He nodded. "Looks clean. Feels strange to me that people eat food made by strangers."

"Did you see anyone suspicious there?"

"What would be 'suspicious' in this city?"

"I don't know. You're the one who insisted on scouting ahead."

"It's always a good idea when hunting. Less likely to scare away the animals."

"Unfortunately, Parlin," Vivenna said, "people aren't like animals."

"I am aware of that," Parlin said. "Animals make sense."

Vivenna sighed. However, she did notice just then that Parlin had been right on at least one count. She caught sight of a group of Idrians walking along the street nearby, one pulling a cart that had probably once held produce. They were easy to distinguish by their muted dress and the slight accent to their voices. It surprised her that they would come so far to trade. But, admittedly, commerce hadn't been particularly robust in Idris lately.

Reluctantly, she closed her eyes and—using the shawl to hide the transformation—changed her hair from grey to brown. If there were other Idrians in town, it was unlikely that she would stand out. Trying to act like an old woman would be more suspicious.

It still felt wrong to be exposed. In Bevalis, she'd have been recognized instantly. Of course, Bevalis had only a few thousand people in it. The vastly greater scale of T'Telir would require a conscious adjustment.

She gestured to Parlin and—gritting her teeth—joined the crowd and began making her way toward the market-place.

The inland sea made all the difference. T'Telir was a prime port, and the dyes it sold—made from the Tears of Edgli, a local flower—made it a center of trade. She could see the evidence all around her. Exotic silks and clothing. Brown-skinned traders from Tedradel with their long black beards bound with tight leather cords into cylindri-cal shapes. Fresh foodstuffs from cities along the coast. In Idris, the population was spread out thinly across the farms and rangelands. In Hallandren—a country that controlled a good third of the inland sea's coast—things were differ-ent. They could burgeon. Grow.

Get flamboyant.

In the distance, she could see the plateau that held the Court of Gods, the most profane place beneath Austre's colorful eyes. Inside its walls, within the God King's terrible palace, Siri was being held captive, prisoner of Susebron himself. Logically, Vivenna understood her father's decision. In raw political terms, Vivenna was more valuable to Idris. If war was certain, it made sense to send the less useful daughter as a stalling tactic.

But it was hard for Vivenna to think of Siri as "less useful." She was gregarious, but she'd also been the one who smiled when others were down. She was the one who brought gifts when nobody was expecting them. She was infuriating, but also innocent. She was Vivenna's baby sister, and someone had to look out for her.

The God King would demand an heir. That was to have been Vivenna's duty—her sacrifice for her people. She had been prepared and willing. It felt *wrong* for Siri to have to do something so terrible.

Her father had made his decision; the best one for Idris. Vivenna had made her own. If there was going to be war, then Vivenna wanted to be ready to get her sister out of the city the moment it got dangerous. In fact, Vivenna felt there *had* to be a way to rescue Siri before the war came—a way of fooling the Hallandren, making them think that Siri had died. Something that would save Vivenna's sister, yet not further provoke hostilities.

This wasn't something her father could condone. So she hadn't told him. Better for him to be able to deny involvement if things went wrong.

Vivenna moved down the street, eyes downcast, careful to not draw attention to herself. Getting away from Idris had been surprisingly easy. Who would suspect such a brash move from Vivenna—she who had always been perfect? Nobody wondered when she'd asked for food and supplies, explaining that she wanted to make emergency kits. Nobody questioned when she'd proposed an expedition to the higher reaches to gather important roots, an excuse to disguise the first few weeks of her disappearance.

Parlin had been easy enough to persuade. He trusted her, perhaps too much, and he had intimate knowledge of the paths and trails leading down to Hallandren. He'd been as far as the city walls on one scouting trip a year back. With his help, she'd been able to recruit a few of his friends—also woodsmen—to protect her and be part of her "expedition." She'd sent the rest of them back earlier that morning. They would be of little use in the city, where she had already arranged for other allies to be her protection. Parlin's friends would carry word to her father, who would already have heard of what she'd done. Before leaving, she'd arranged for her maid to deliver a letter to him. Counting off the days, she realized that her letter would be delivered that very evening.

She didn't know what her father's reaction would be. Perhaps he would covertly send soldiers to retrieve her. Perhaps he'd leave her be. She'd warned him that if she saw Idrian soldiers searching for her, she would simply go to the Court of Gods, explain that there had been a mistake, and trade herself for her sister.

She sincerely hoped she wouldn't have to do that. The God King was not to be trusted; he might take Vivenna captive and keep Siri, thereby gaining two princesses to provide pleasure instead of one.

Don't think about that, Vivenna told herself, pulling her shawl closer despite the heat.

Better to find another way. The first step was to find Lemex, her father's chief spy in Hallandren. Vivenna had corresponded with him on several occasions. Her father had wanted her to be familiar with his best intelligence agent in T'Telir, and his foresight would work against him. Lemex knew Vivenna, and had been told to take orders from her. She'd sent the spy a letter—delivered via a messenger with multiple mounts to allow quick delivery—the day she'd left Idris. Assuming the message had arrived safely, the spy would meet her in the appointed restaurant.

Her plan seemed good. She was prepared. Why, then, did she feel so utterly daunted when she entered the market?

She stood quietly, a rock in the stream of human traffic flooding down the street. It was such an enormous expanse, covered in tents, pens, buildings, and people. There were no cobblestones here, only sand and dirt with the occasional patch of grass, and there didn't appear to be much reason or direction to the arrangement of buildings. The arbitrary streets had simply been made where people felt like going. Merchants yelled out what they sold, banners waved in the wind, and entertainers vied for attention. It was an orgy of color and motion.

"Wow," Parlin said quietly.

Vivenna turned, shaking off her stupor. "Weren't you just here?"

"Yeah," Parlin said, eyes a little glazed over. "Wow again."

Vivenna shook her head. "Let's go to the restaurant."

Parlin nodded. "This way."

Vivenna followed him, annoyed. This was Hallandren—she shouldn't be awed by it. She should be disgusted. Yet she was so overwhelmed that it was hard to feel anything beyond a slight sense of sickness. She'd never realized how much she took Idris's beautiful simplicity for granted.

Parlin's familiar presence was welcome as the powerful wave of scents, sounds, and sights tried to drown her. In some places the crowds grew so thick that they had to shove their way through. On occasion, Vivenna found herself on the edge of panic, pressed in by dirty, repulsively colored bodies. Blessedly, the restaurant wasn't too far in, and they arrived just when she thought the sheer excess of the place would make her scream. On its signboard out front, the restaurant had a picture of a boat sailing merrily. If the scents coming from inside were any indication, then the ship represented the restaurant's cuisine: fish. Vivenna barely kept herself from gagging. She'd eaten fish several times in preparation for her life in Hallandren. She'd never grown to like it.

Parlin walked in, immediately stepping to the side and crouching, almost like a wolf, as he let his eyes adjust to the dimness. Vivenna gave the restaurant keeper the fake name Lemex knew to call her by. The restaurant keeper eyed Parlin, then shrugged and led the two of them to one of the tables on the far side of the room. Vivenna sat down; despite her training, she was a little uncertain what one did at a restaurant. It seemed significant to her that places like restaurants could exist in Hallandren—places meant to feed not travelers, but the locals who couldn't be bothered to prepare their own food and dine at their own homes.

Parlin didn't sit, but remained standing beside her chair, watching the room. He looked as tense as she felt. "Vivenna," he said softly, leaning down. "Your hair."

She started, realizing that her hair had lightened from the trauma of pushing her way through the crowd. It hadn't bleached completely white—she was far too well trained for that—but it had grown whiter, as if it had been powdered.

Feeling a jolt of paranoia, Vivenna replaced the shawl on her head, looking away as the restaurant owner approached to take their order. A short list of meals was scratched into the table, and Parlin finally sat down, drawing the restaurant owner's attention away from Vivenna.

You're better than this, she told herself sternly. *You've studied Hallandren for most of your life.* Her hair darkened, returning to its brown. The change was subtle enough that if someone had been watching, they would have probably thought it to be a trick of the light. She kept the shawl up, feeling ashamed. One walk through the market, and she lost control?

Think of Siri, she told herself. That gave her strength. Her mission was impromptu, even reckless, but it was important. Calm once again, she put the shawl back down and waited while Parlin chose a dish—a seafood stew—and the innkeeper walked away.

"Now what?" Parlin asked.

"We wait," Vivenna said. "In my letter, I told Lemex to check the restaurant each day at noon. We will sit here until he arrives."

Parlin nodded, fidgeting.

"What is it?" Vivenna asked calmly.

He glanced toward the door. "I don't trust this place, Vivenna. I can't smell anything but bodies and spices, can't hear anything but the chatter of people. There's no wind, no trees, no rivers, just . . . *people*."

"I know."

"I want to go back outside," he said.

"What?" she said. "Why?"

"If you aren't familiar with a place," he said awkwardly, "you need to become familiar with it." He gave no other explanation.

Vivenna felt a stab of fear at the thought of being left alone. However, it wasn't proper to demand that Parlin stay and attend her. "Do you promise to stay close?"

He nodded.

"Then go."

He did, walking from the room. He didn't move like one of the Hallandren—his motions were too fluid, too much like a prowling beast. *Perhaps I should have sent him back with the others.* But the thought of being completely alone had been too much. She needed *someone* to help her find Lemex. As it was, she felt that she was probably taking too great a risk at entering the city with only one guard, even one as skilled as Parlin.

But it was done. No use worrying now. She sat, arms folded on the table, thinking. Back in Idris, her plan to save Siri had seemed simpler. Now the true nature of it lay before her. Somehow, she had to get into the Court of Gods and sneak her sister out. How would one accomplish something so audacious? Surely the Court of Gods would be well guarded.

Lemex will have ideas, she told herself. *We don't have to do anything yet. I'm—*

A man sat down at her table. Less colorfully dressed than most Hallandren, he wore an outfit made mostly of brown leather, though he did have a token red cloth vest thrown over the top. This was not Lemex. The spy was an older man in his fifties. This stranger had a long face and styled hair, and couldn't have been older than thirty-five.

"I hate being a mercenary," the man said. "You know why?"

Shocked, Vivenna sat frozen, mouth opened slightly.

"The prejudice," the man said. "Everyone else, they work, they ask for recompense, and they are respected for it. Not mercenaries. We get a bad name just for doing our job. How many minstrels get spat on for accepting payment from the highest bidder? How many bakers feel guilty for selling pastries to one man, then selling more of those same pastries to the man's enemies?" He eyed her. "No. Only the mercenary. Unfair, wouldn't you say?"

"W . . . who are you?" Vivenna finally managed to ask. She jumped as another man sat down on her other side. Large of girth, this man had a cudgel strapped to his back. A colorful bird was sitting on the end of it.

"I'm Denth," the first man said, taking her hand and shaking it. "That's Tonk Fah."

"Pleased," Tonk Fah said, taking her hand once Denth was through with it.

"Unfortunately, Princess," Denth said, "we're here to kill you."

10

VIVENNA'S HAIR INSTANTLY bleached to a stark white. *Think!* she told herself. *You've been trained in politics! You studied hostage negotiation. But . . . what do you do when you* are *the hostage?*

Suddenly, the two men burst out laughing. The larger man thumped the table several times with his hand, causing his bird to squawk.

"Sorry, Princess," Denth—the thinner man—said, shaking his head. "Just a bit of mercenary humor."

"We kill sometimes, but we don't murder," Tonk Fah said. "That's assassin work."

"Assassins," Denth said, holding up a finger. "Now, *they* get respect. Why do you suppose that is? They're really just mercenaries with fancier names."

Vivenna blinked, struggling to get control of her nerves. "You're not here to kill me," she said, voice stiff. "So you're just going to kidnap me?"

"Gods, no," Denth said. "Bad business, that. How do you make money at it? Every time you kidnap someone worth the ransom, you upset people a whole lot more powerful than you are."

"Don't make important people angry," Tonk Fah said, yawning. "Unless you're getting paid by people who are even *more* powerful."

Denth nodded. "And that isn't even considering the feeding and care of captives, the exchanging of ransom notes, and the arranging of drop-offs. It's a headache, I tell you. Terrible way to make money."

The table fell silent. Vivenna placed her hands flat on its top to keep them from quivering. *They know who I am,* she thought, forcing herself to think logically. *Either they recognize me, or . . .*

"You work for Lemex," she said.

Denth smiled widely. "See, Tonk? He said she was a clever one."

"Guess that's why she's a princess and we're just mercenaries," Tonk Fah said.

Vivenna frowned. *Are they mocking me or not?* "Where is Lemex? Why didn't he come himself?"

Denth smiled again, nodding toward the restaurant owner as the man brought a large pot of steaming stew to the table. It smelled of hot spices, and had what appeared to be crab claws floating in it. The owner dropped a group of wooden spoons to the table, then retreated.

Denth and Tonk Fah didn't wait for permission to eat her meal. "Your friend," Denth said, grabbing a spoon, "Lemex—our employer—isn't doing so well."

"Fevers," Tonk Fah said between slurps.

"He requested that we bring you to him," Denth said. He handed her a folded piece of paper with one hand, while cracking a claw between three fingers of the other. Vivenna cringed as he slurped the contents out.

Princess, the paper read. *Please trust these men. Denth has served me well for some measure now, and he is loyal—if any mercenary can be called loyal. He and his men have been paid, and I am confident he will stay true to us for the duration of his contract. I offer proof of authenticity by virtue of this password: bluemask.*

The writing was in Lemex's hand. More than that, he had given the proper password. Not "bluemask"—that was misdirection. The true password was using the word "measure" instead of time. She glanced at Denth, who slurped out the insides of another claw.

"Ah, now," he said, tossing aside the shell. "This is the tricky part; she has to make a decision. Are we telling her the truth, or are we fooling her? Have we fabricated that letter? Or maybe we took the old spy captive and tortured him, forcing him to write the words."

"We could bring you his fingers as proof of our good faith," Tonk Fah said. "Would that help?

Vivenna raised an eyebrow. "Mercenary humor?"

"Such that it is," Denth said with a sigh. "We're not generally a clever lot. Otherwise, we'd probably have selected a profession without such a high mortality rate."

"Like your profession, Princess," Tonks said. "Good lifespans, usually. I've often wondered if I should apprentice myself to one."

Vivenna frowned as the two men chuckled. *Lemex wouldn't have broken under torture,* she thought. *He's too well trained. Even if he had broken, he wouldn't have included both the real password and the false one.*

"Let's go," she said, standing.

"Wait," Tonk Fah said, spoon to lips, "we're skipping the rest of our meal?"

Vivenna eyed the red-colored soup and its bobbing crustacean limbs. "Definitely."

⁕

LEMEX COUGHED QUIETLY. His aged face was streaked with sweat, his skin clammy and pale, and he occasionally gave a whispered mumble of delirious ramblings.

Vivenna sat on a stool beside his bed, hands in her lap. The two mercenaries waited with Parlin at the back of the room. The only other person present was a solemn nurse—the same woman who had informed Vivenna in a quiet voice that nothing more could be done.

Lemex was dying. It was unlikely that he would last the day.

This was the first Vivenna had seen Lemex's face, though she'd often corresponded with him. The face looked . . .

wrong. She knew that Lemex was growing old; that made him a better spy, for few looked for spies among the elderly. Yet he wasn't supposed to be this frail stick of a person, shaking and coughing. He was supposed to be a spry, quick-tongued old gentleman. That was what she had imagined.

She felt like she was losing one of her dearest friends, though she had never really known him. With him went her refuge in Hallandren, her secret advantage. He was the one she had supposed would make this insane plan of hers work. The skilled, crafty mentor she had counted on having at her side.

He coughed again. The nurse glanced at Vivenna. "He goes in and out of lucidity, my lady. Just this morning, he spoke of you, but now he's getting worse and worse. . . ."

"Thank you," Vivenna said quietly. "You are excused."

The woman bowed and left.

Now it is time to be a princess, Vivenna thought, rising and leaning over Lemex's bed.

"Lemex," she said. "I need you to pass on your knowledge. How do I contact your spy networks? Where are the other Idrian agents in the city? What are the passcodes that will get them to listen to me?"

He coughed, staring unseeingly, whispering something. She leaned closer.

". . . never say it," he said. "You can torture me all that you want. I won't give in."

Vivenna sat back. By design, the Idrian spy network in Hallandren was loosely organized. Her father knew all of their agents, but Vivenna had only ever communicated with Lemex, the leader and coordinator of the network. She gritted her teeth, leaning forward again. She felt like a grave robber as she shook Lemex's head slightly.

"Lemex, look at me. I'm not here to torture you. I'm the princess. You received a letter from me earlier. Now I've come to you."

"Can't fool me," the old man whispered. "Your torture is nothing. I won't give it up. Not to you."

Vivenna sighed, looking away.

Suddenly, Lemex shuddered, and a wave of color washed across the bed, over Vivenna, and pulsed along the floor before fading. Despite herself, Vivenna stepped back in shock.

Another pulse came. It wasn't color itself. It was a wave of *enhanced* color—a ripple that made the hues in the room stand out more as it passed. The floor, the sheets, her own dress—it all flared to vibrant vividness for a second, then faded back to the original hues.

"What in Austre's name was *that*?" Vivenna asked.

"BioChromatic Breath, Princess," Denth said as he stood, leaning against the doorframe. "Old Lemex has a lot of it. Couple hundred Breaths, I'd guess."

"That's impossible," Vivenna said. "He's Idrian. He'd never accept Breath."

Denth shot a look at Tonk Fah, who was scratching his parrot's neck. The bulky soldier just shrugged.

Another wave of color came from Lemex.

"He's dying, Princess," Denth said. "His Breath is going irregular."

Vivenna glared at Denth. "He doesn't have—"

Something grabbed her arm. She jumped, looking down at Lemex, who had managed to reach up and take hold of her. He was focused on her face. "Princess Vivenna," he said, eyes showing some lucidity at last.

"Lemex," she said. "Your contacts. You have to give them to me!"

"I've done something bad, Princess."

She froze.

"Breath, Princess," he said. "I inherited it from my predecessor, and I've bought more. A lot more. . . ."

God of Colors . . . Vivenna thought with a sick feeling in her stomach.

"I know it was wrong," Lemex whispered. "But . . . I felt

so powerful. I could make the very dust of the earth obey my command. It was for the good of Idris! Men with Breath are respected here in Hallandren. I could get into parties where I normally would have been excluded. I could go to the Court of Gods when I wished and hear the Court Assembly. The Breath extended my life, made me spry despite my age. I . . ."

He blinked, eyes unfocusing.

"Oh, Austre," he whispered. "I've damned myself. I've gained notoriety through abusing the souls of others. And now I'm dying."

"Lemex!" Vivenna said. "Don't think about that now. Names! I need names and passcodes. Don't leave me alone!"

"Damned," he whispered. "Someone take it. Please take it away from me!"

Vivenna tried to pull back, but he still held on to her arm. She shuddered, thinking about the Breath he held.

"You know, Princess," Denth said from behind. "Nobody really tells mercenaries anything. It's an unfortunate—but very realistic—drawback of our profession. Never trusted. Never looked to for advice."

She glanced back at him. He leaned against the door, Tonk Fah a short distance away. Parlin stood there as well, holding that ridiculous green hat in his fingers.

"Now, if someone *were* to ask my opinion," Denth continued, "I'd point out how much those Breaths are worth. Sell them, and you'd have enough money to buy your *own* spy network—or pretty much anything else you wanted."

Vivenna looked back at the dying man. He was mumbling to himself.

"If he dies," Denth said, "that Breath dies with him. All of it."

"A shame," Tonk Fah said.

Vivenna paled. "I will not traffic in the souls of men! I don't care how much they're worth."

"Suit yourself," Denth said. "Hope nobody suffers when your mission fails, though."

Siri. . . .

"No," Vivenna said, partially to herself. "I couldn't take them." It was true. Even the thought of letting someone else's Breath mingle with her own—the idea of drawing another person's soul into her own body—made her sick.

Vivenna turned back to the dying spy. His BioChroma was burning brightly now, and his sheets practically glowed. It was better to let that Breath die with him.

Yet without Lemex, she would have no help in the city, no one to guide her and provide refuge for her. She'd barely brought along enough money to cover lodging and meals, let alone bribes or supplies. She told herself that taking the Breath would be like using goods one had found in a bandit's cavern. Did you throw it away just because it had originally been acquired through crime? Her training and lessons whispered that she needed resources badly, and that the damage had already been done. . . .

No! she thought again. *It just isn't right! I can't hold it. I couldn't.*

Of course, perhaps it would be wise to let someone *else* hold the Breaths for a time. Then she could think about what to do with them at her leisure. Maybe . . . maybe even find the people they had been taken from and give them back. She turned back, glancing at Denth and Tonk Fah.

"Don't look at me like that, Princess," Denth said, chuckling. "I see the glint in your eyes. I'm not going to keep that Breath for you. Having that much BioChroma makes a man far too important."

Tonk Fah nodded. "It'd be like hiking about the city with a bag of gold on your back."

"I like my Breath the way it is," Denth said. "I only need one, and it's functioning just fine. Keeps me alive, doesn't draw attention to me, and sits there waiting to be sold if I need it."

Vivenna glanced at Parlin. But . . . no, she couldn't force the Breath on him. She turned back to Denth. "What kind of things does your agreement with Lemex provide for?"

Denth glanced at Tonk Fah, then glanced back at her. The look in his eyes was enough. He was paid to obey. He'd take the Breath if she commanded it.

"Come here," she said, nodding to a stool beside her.

Denth approached reluctantly. "You know, Princess," he said, sitting. "If you give me that Breath, then I could just run off with it. I'd be a wealthy man. You wouldn't want to put that kind of temptation into the hands of an unscrupulous mercenary, now, would you?"

She hesitated.

If he runs off with it, then what do I lose? That would solve a lot of problems for her. "Take it," she ordered.

He shook his head. "That's not the way it works. Our friend there has to give it to me."

She looked at the old man. "I . . ." She began to command Lemex to do just that, but she had second thoughts. Austre wouldn't want her to take the Breath, no matter what the circumstances—a man who took Breath from others was worse than a slaver.

"No," she said. "No, I've changed my mind. We won't take the Breath."

At that moment, Lemex stopped his mumbling. He looked up, meeting Vivenna's eyes.

His hand was still on her arm.

"My life to yours," he said in an eerily clear voice, his grip tight on her arm as she jumped back. "*My Breath become yours!*"

A vibrant cloud of shifting, iridescent air burst from his mouth, puffing toward her. Vivenna closed her mouth, eyes wide, hair white. She ripped her arm free from Lemex's grip, even as his face grew dull, his eyes losing their luster, the colors around him fading.

The Breath shot toward her. Her closed mouth had no

effect; the Breath struck, hitting her like a physical force, washing across her body. She gasped, falling to her knees, body quivering with a perverse pleasure. She could suddenly *feel* the other people in the room. She could sense them watching her. And—as if a light had been lit—everything around her became more vibrant, more real, and more alive.

She gasped, shaking in awe. She vaguely heard Parlin rushing to her side, speaking her name. But, oddly, the only thing she could think of was the melodic quality of his voice. She could pick out each tone in every word he spoke. She knew them instinctively.

Austre, God of Colors! she thought, steadying herself with one hand against the wooden floor as the shakes subsided. *What have I done?*

11

BUT SURELY WE can bend the rules a little bit," Siri said, walking quickly beside Treledees.

Treledees eyed her. The priest—high priest of the God King—would have been tall even without the elaborate miter on his head. With it, he seemed to tower over her almost like one of the Returned.

Well, a spindly, obnoxious, disdainful Returned.

"An exception?" he asked with his leisurely Hallandren accent. "No, I do not think that will be possible, Vessel."

"I don't see why not," Siri said as a servant pulled open the door in front of them, allowing them to leave a green-colored room and pass into a blue one. Treledees respectfully let her pass through the doorway first, though she sensed that he was displeased he had to do so.

Siri ground her teeth, trying to think of another avenue of attack. *Vivenna would be calm and logical,* she thought. *She'd explain why she should be allowed to leave the palace in a way that made sense so that the priest listened to her.* Siri took a deep breath, trying to ease the red from her hair and the frustration from her attitude.

"Look. Couldn't I, maybe, go on *one* trip outside? Just into the court itself?"

"Impossible," Treledees said. "If you lack for entertainment, why not have your servants send for minstrels or jugglers? I'm sure they could keep you occupied." *And out of my hair,* his tone seemed to imply.

Couldn't he understand? It wasn't lack of something to do that frustrated her. It was that she couldn't see the sky. Couldn't run away from walls and locks and rules. Barring that, she would have settled for someone to talk to. "At least let me meet with one of the gods. I mean, really— what is accomplished by keeping me locked up like this?"

"You're not 'locked up,' Vessel," Treledees said. "You are observing a period of isolation in which you can dedicate yourself to contemplating your new place in life. It is an ancient and worthy practice, one that shows respect for the God King and his divine monarchy."

"Yes, but this is Hallandren," Siri said. "It's the land of laxness and frivolity! Surely you can see your way to making an exception."

Treledees stopped short. "We do *not* make exceptions in matters of religion, Vessel. I must assume that you are testing me in some way, for I find it hard to believe that anyone worthy of touching our God King could harbor such vulgar thoughts."

Siri cringed. *Less than a week in the city,* she thought, *and I've already started letting my tongue get me into trouble.* Siri didn't dislike people—she loved to talk to them, spend time with them, laugh with them. However, she couldn't make them do what she wanted, not in the way that a politician was supposed to be able to do. That was something she should have learned from Vivenna.

She and Treledees continued walking. Siri wore a long, flowing brown skirt that covered her feet and had a train that trailed behind her. The priest was wearing golds and maroons—colors matched by the servants. It still amazed her that everyone in the palace had so many costumes, even if they were identical save for color.

She knew that she shouldn't let herself get annoyed with the priests. They already didn't seem to like her, and getting snappish wouldn't help. It was just that the last few days had been so *dull*. Trapped in the palace, unable to leave, unable to find anyone to talk to, she felt herself nearly going mad.

But there would be no exceptions. Apparently.

"Will that be all, Vessel?" Treledees asked, pausing beside a door. It almost seemed like he found it a chore to remain civil toward her.

Siri sighed, but nodded. The priest bowed, then opened the door and quickly rushed away. Siri watched him go, tapping her foot, arms folded. Her servants stood arrayed behind her, silent as always. She considered finding Bluefingers, but . . . no. He always had so much to do, and she felt bad distracting him.

Sighing again, she motioned for her servants to prepare the evening meal. Two fetched a chair from the side of the room. Siri sat, resting as food was gathered. The chair was plush, but it was still difficult to sit in a way that didn't aggravate one of her aches or cramps. Each of the last six nights, she had been forced to kneel, naked, until she finally grew so drowsy that she drifted off. Sleeping on the hard stone had left a dull, persistent pain in her back and neck.

Each morning, once the God King was gone, she moved to the bed. When she awoke the second time, she burned the sheets. After that, she chose her clothing. There was a new array each time, with no repeated outfits. She wasn't sure where the servants got such a steady supply of clothing in Siri's size, but it made her hesitant about choosing her daily costume. She knew that she'd likely never see any of the options again.

After dressing, she was free to do as she wished, assuming she didn't leave the palace. When night came, she was bathed, then given a choice of luxurious gowns to wear into the bedchamber. As a matter of comfort, she had started requesting more and more ornate gowns, with more fabric to use in sleeping. She often wondered what the dressmakers would think if they knew that their gowns were only worn for a few brief moments before being discarded to the floor, then eventually used as blankets.

She didn't own anything, yet could have whatever she wanted. Exotic foods, furniture, entertainers, books, art . . . she only needed to ask. And yet, when she was finished, it was removed. She had everything and nothing at the same time.

She yawned. The interrupted sleep schedule left her bleary-eyed and tired. The completely empty days didn't help either. *If only there were someone to talk to.* But servants, priests, and scribes were all locked into their formal roles. That accounted for everyone she interacted with.

Well, except *him.*

Could she even call that interacting? The God King appeared to enjoy looking at her body, but he'd never given her any indication that he wanted more. He simply let her kneel, those eyes of his watching and dissecting her. That was the sum total of their marriage.

The servants finished putting out her dinner, then lined up by the wall. It was getting late—almost time for her nightly bathing. *I'll have to eat quickly,* she thought, sitting at the table. *After all, I wouldn't want to be late for the evening's ogling.*

A FEW HOURS later, Siri stood bathed, perfumed, and dressed before the massive golden door that led into the God King's bedchamber. She breathed deeply, calming herself, anxiety bringing her hair to a pale brown. She still hadn't gotten used to this part.

It was silly. She knew what would happen. And yet, the anticipation—the fear—was still there. The God King's actions proved the power he had over her. One day he would take her, and it could come at any time. Part of her wished he'd just be done with it. The extended dread was even worse than that first single evening of terror.

She shivered. Bluefingers eyed her. Perhaps eventually he'd trust her to arrive at the bedchamber on time. Each night so far, he'd come to escort her.

At least he hasn't shown up while I'm bathing again. The warm water and pleasant scents should have made her relax—unfortunately, she tended to spend each bath worrying about either her impending visit to the God King or some male servant walking in on her.

She glanced at Bluefingers.

"A few more minutes, Vessel," he said.

How does he know? she thought. The man seemed to have a supernatural sense of time. She hadn't seen any form of timepiece in the palace—neither sundial, metered candle, nor water clock. In Hallandren, apparently, gods and queens didn't worry about such things. They had servants to remind them of appointments.

Bluefingers glanced at the door, then at her. When he saw that she was watching him, he immediately turned away. As he stood, he started shuffling his weight from foot to foot.

What does he *have to be nervous about?* she thought with annoyance, turning to stare at the door's intricate gold designs. *He's not the one who has to go through this every night.*

"Do . . . things go well with the God King, then?" Bluefingers asked suddenly.

Siri frowned.

"I can see that you're tired a lot of the time," Bluefingers said. "I . . . guess that means you are very . . . active at night."

"That's good, right? Everyone wants an heir as soon as possible."

"Yes, of course," Bluefingers said, wringing his hands. "It's just that . . ." He trailed off, then glanced at her, meeting her eyes. "You just might want to be careful, Vessel. Keep your wits about you. Try to stay alert."

Her hair bleached the rest of the way white. "You make it sound as if I'm in danger," she said softly.

"What? Danger?" Bluefingers said, glancing to the side. "Nonsense. What would you have to fear? I was simply suggesting that you remain alert, should the God King have needs you should fulfill. Ah, see, now it's time. Enjoy your evening, Vessel."

With that, he pushed open the door, placed a hand on her back, and guided her into the room. At the last moment, he moved his head up next to hers. "You should watch yourself, child," he whispered. "Not all here in the palace is as it seems."

Siri frowned, turning, but Bluefingers plastered on a false smile and pushed the door shut.

What in Austre's name was that? she thought, pausing for what was probably too long a time as she stared at the door. Finally, she sighed, turning away. The usual fire crackled in the hearth, but it was smaller than previously.

He was there. Siri didn't need to look to see him. As her eyes grew more accustomed to the darkness, she could notice that the fire's colors—blue, orange, even black— were far too true, far too *vibrant*. Her gown, a brilliant golden satin, seemed to burn with its own inner color. Anything that was white—some of the lace on her dress, for instance—bent slightly, giving off a rainbow of colors as if seen through a prism. Part of her wished for a well-lit room, where she could experience the full beauty of Bio-Chroma.

But, of course, that was not right. The God King's Breath was a perversion. He was fed on the souls of his people, and the colors he evoked came at their expense.

Shivering, Siri undid the side of her dress, then let the garment fall to pieces around her—the long sleeves slipping free, bodice falling forward, skirt and gown rustling as they dropped to the floor. She completed the ritual, sliding the straps of her shift off her shoulders, then dropping the garment to the floor beside the gown. She stepped free of both, then bowed herself down into her customary posture.

Her back complained, and she ruefully contemplated another uncomfortable night. *The least they could do,* she thought, *is make certain the fire is large enough.* At night in the large stone palace, it got chilly despite the Hallandren tropical climate. Particularly if one were naked.

Focus on Bluefingers, she thought, trying to distract herself. *What did he mean? Things are not what they seem in the palace?*

Was he referring to the God King and his ability to have her killed? She was well aware of the God King's power. How could she forget it, with him sitting not fifteen feet away, watching from the shadows? No, that wasn't it. He'd felt he'd needed to give this warning quietly, without others hearing. *Watch yourself. . . .*

It smelled of politics. She gritted her teeth. If she'd paid more attention to her tutors, might she have been able to pick out a more subtle meaning in Bluefingers's warning?

As if I needed something else to be confused about, she thought. If Bluefingers had something to tell her, why hadn't he just said it? As the minutes passed, his words turned over and over in her mind like a restless sleeper, but she was too uncomfortable and cold to come to any conclusions. That only left her feeling *more* annoyed.

Vivenna would have figured it out. Vivenna probably

would have known instinctively why the God King hadn't chosen to sleep with her. She would have fixed it the first night.

But Siri was incompetent. She tried so *hard* to do as Vivenna would have—to be the best wife she could, to serve Idris. To be the woman that everyone expected her to be.

But she wasn't. She *couldn't* just keep doing this. She felt trapped in the palace. She couldn't get the priests to do more than roll their eyes at her. She couldn't even tempt the God King to bed her. On top of that, she could very well be in danger, and she couldn't even understand why or how.

In simpler terms, she was just plain frustrated.

Groaning at her aching limbs, Siri sat up in the dark room and looked at the shadowy form in the corner. "Will you please just get *on* with it?" she blurted out.

Silence.

Siri felt her hair bleach a terrible bone white as she realized what she'd just done. She stiffened, casting her eyes down, weariness fleeing in the face of sudden anxiety.

What had she been *thinking*? The God King could call servants to execute her. In fact, he didn't even need that. He could bring her own dress to life, Awakening it to strangle her. He could make the rug rise up and smother her. He could probably bring the ceiling down on her, all without moving from his chair.

Siri waited, breathing with shallow anxiety, anticipating the fury and retribution. But . . . nothing happened. Minutes passed.

Finally, Siri glanced up. The God King had moved, sitting up straighter, regarding her from his darkened chair beside the bed. She could see his eyes reflecting the firelight. She couldn't make out much of his face, but he didn't *seem* angry. He just seemed cold and distant.

She almost cast her eyes down again, but hesitated. If snapping at him wouldn't provoke a reaction, then looking at him wasn't likely to either. So she turned her chin up and met his eyes, knowing full well that she was being foolish. Vivenna would never have provoked the man. She would have remained quiet and demure, either solving the problem or—if there was no solution—kneeling every night until her patience impressed even the God King of Hallandren.

But Siri was not Vivenna. She was just going to have to accept that fact.

The God King continued to look at her, and Siri found herself blushing. She'd knelt before him naked six nights in a row, but *facing* him unclothed was more embarrassing. Still, she didn't back down. She continued to kneel, watching him, forcing herself to stay awake.

It was difficult. She was tired, and the position was actually less comfortable than bowing had been. She watched anyway, waiting, the hours passing.

Eventually—at about the same time that he left the room every night—the God King stood up. Siri stiffened, shocked alert. However, he simply walked to the door. He tapped quietly, and it opened for him, servants waiting on the other side. He stepped out and the door closed.

Siri waited tensely. No soldiers came to arrest her; no priests came to chastise her. Eventually, she just walked over to the bed and burrowed into its covers, savoring the warmth.

The God King's wrath, she thought drowsily, *is decidedly less wrathful than reported.*

With that, she fell asleep.

12

EVENTUALLY, LIGHTSONG HAD to hear petitions.

It was annoying, since the Wedding Jubilation wouldn't even be over for another few days. The people, however, needed their gods. He knew he shouldn't feel annoyed. He'd gotten most of a week off for the wedding fete— conspicuously unattended by either the bride or groom— and that was enough. All he had to do was spend a few hours each day looking at art and listening to the woes of the people. It wasn't much. Even if it did wear away at his sanity.

He sighed, sitting back in his throne. He wore an embroidered cap on his head, matched by a loose robe of gold and red. The garment wrapped over both shoulders, twisted about his body, and was hung with golden tassels. Like all of his clothing, it was even *more* complicated to put on than it looked.

If my servants were to suddenly leave me, he thought with amusement, *I'd be totally incapable of getting dressed.*

He leaned his head on one fist, elbow on the throne's armrest. This room of his palace opened directly out onto the lawn—harsh weather was rare in Hallandren, and a cool breeze blew in off of the sea, smelling of brine. He closed his eyes, breathing in.

He'd dreamed of war again last night. Llarimar had found that particularly meaningful. Lightsong was just disturbed. Everyone said that if war did come, Hallandren would easily win. But if that were the case, then why did he always dream of *T'Telir* burning? Not some distant Idrian city, but his own home.

It means nothing, he told himself. *Just a manifestation of my own worries.*

"Next petition, Your Grace," Llarimar whispered from his side.

Lightsong sighed, opening his eyes. Both edges of the room were lined with priests in their coifs and robes. Where had he gotten so many? Did any god need that much attention?

He could see a line of people extending outside onto the lawn. They were a sorry, forlorn lot, several coughing from some malady or another. *So many,* he thought as a woman was led into the room. He'd been seeing petitioners for over an hour already. *I guess I should have expected this. It's been almost a week.*

"Scoot," he said, turning to his priest. "Go tell those waiting people to sit down in the grass. There's no reason for them to all stand there like that. This could take some time."

Llarimar hesitated. Standing was, of course, a sign of respect. However, he nodded, waving over a lesser priest to carry the message.

Such a crowd, waiting to see me, Lightsong thought. *What will it take to convince the people that I'm useless?* What would it take to get them to stop coming to him? After five years of petitions, he honestly wasn't certain if he could take another five.

The newest petitioner approached his throne. She carried a child in her arms.

Not a child . . . Lightsong thought, cringing mentally.

"Great One," the woman said, falling to her knees on the carpet. "Lord of Bravery."

Lightsong didn't speak.

"This is my child, Halan," the woman said, holding out the baby. As it got close enough to Lightsong's aura, the blanket burst with a sharp blue color two and half steps from pure. He could easily see that the child was suffering from a terrible sickness. It had lost so much weight that its skin was shriveled. The baby's Breath was so weak that it flickered like a candle running out of wick. It would be dead before the day was out. Perhaps before the hour was out.

"The healers, they say he has deathfever," the woman said. "I know that he's going to die." The baby made a sound—a kind of half-cough, perhaps the closest it could get to a cry.

"Please, Great One," the woman said. She sniffled, then bowed her head. "Oh, please. He was brave, like you. My Breath, it would be yours. The Breaths of my entire family. Service for a hundred years, anything. Please, just heal him."

Lightsong closed his eyes.

"Please," the woman whispered.

"I cannot," Lightsong said.

Silence.

"I *cannot*," Lightsong said.

"Thank you, my lord," the woman finally whispered.

Lightsong opened his eyes to see the woman being led away, weeping quietly, child clutched close to her breast. The line of people watched her go, looking miserable yet hopeful at the same time. One more petitioner had failed. That meant they would get a chance.

A chance to beg Lightsong to kill himself.

Lightsong stood suddenly, grabbing the cap off his head and tossing it aside. He rushed away, throwing open a door at the back of the room. It slammed against the wall as he stumbled through.

Servants and priests immediately followed after him. He turned on them. "Go!" he said, waving them away. Many of them showed looks of surprise, unaccustomed to any kind of forcefulness on their master's part.

"Leave me *be*!" he shouted, towering over them. Colors in the room flared brighter in response to his emotion, and the servants backed down, confused, stumbling back out into the petition hall and pulling the door closed.

Lightsong stood alone. He placed one hand against the wall, breathing in and out, the other hand against his forehead. Why was he sweating so? He'd been through thousands of petitions, and many had been worse than the one he'd just seen. He'd sent pregnant women to their deaths, doomed children and parents, consigned the innocent and the faithful to misery.

There was no reason to overreact. He could take it. It was a little thing, really. Just like absorbing the Breath of a new person every week. A small price to pay. . . .

The door opened and a figure stepped in.

Lightsong didn't turn. "What do they want of me, Llarimar?" he demanded. "Do they really think I'll do it? Lightsong, the selfish? Do they really think I'd give my life for one of them?"

Llarimar was quiet for a few moments. "You offer hope, Your Grace," he finally said. "A last, unlikely hope. Hope is part of faith—part of the knowledge that someday, *one* of your followers will receive a miracle."

"And if they're wrong?" Lightsong asked. "I have no desire to die. I'm an idle man, fond of luxury. People like me don't give up their lives, even if they do happen to be gods."

Llarimar didn't reply.

"The good ones are all already dead, Scoot," Lightsong said. "Calmseer, Brighthue: those were gods who would give themselves away. The rest of us are selfish. There hasn't been a petition granted in what, three years?"

"About that, Your Grace," Llarimar said quietly.

"And why should it be otherwise?" Lightsong said, laughing a bit. "I mean, we have to *die* to heal one of them. Doesn't that strike you as ridiculous? What kind of religion encourages its members to come and petition for their god's life?" Lightsong shook his head. "It's ironic. We're gods to them only until they kill us. And I think I might know why the gods give in. It's those petitions, being forced to sit day after day, knowing that you *could* save one of them— that you probably should, since your life isn't really worth anything. That's enough to drive a man mad. Enough to drive him to kill himself!"

He smiled, glancing at his high priest. "Suicide by divine manifestation. Very dramatic."

"Shall I call off the rest of the petitions, Your Grace?" Llarimar gave no sign of being annoyed by the outburst.

"Sure, why not," Lightsong said, waving a hand. "They really need a lesson in theology. They should *already* know what a useless god I am. Send them away, tell them to come back tomorrow—assuming that they are foolish enough to do so."

"Yes, Your Grace," Llarimar said, bowing.

Doesn't that man ever get mad at me? Lightsong thought. *He, more than any, should know that I'm not a person to rely upon!*

Lightsong turned, walking away as Llarimar went back into the petition room. No servants tried to follow him. Lightsong pushed his way through red-hued room after red-hued room, eventually finding his way to a stairwell and climbing up to the second story. This floor was open on all sides, really nothing more than a large covered patio. He walked to the far side—the one opposite the line of people.

The breeze was strong here. He felt it plucking at his robes, bringing with it scents that had traveled hundreds of miles, crossed the ocean, twisting around palm trees and finally entering the Court of Gods. He stood there for a long time, looking out over the city, toward the sea beyond. He had no desire, despite what he sometimes said, to leave his comfortable home in the court. He was not a man of jungles; he was a man of parties.

But sometimes he wished that he could at least *want* to be something else. Blushweaver's words still weighed upon him. *You'll have to stand for something eventually, Lightsong. You're a god to these people. . . .*

He was. Whether he wanted to be or not. That was the

frustrating part. He'd tried his best to be useless and vain. And still they came.

We could use your confidence . . . you're a better man than you give yourself credit for being.

Why did it seem that the more he demonstrated himself to be an idiot, the more convinced people became that he had some kind of hidden depths? By implication, they called him a liar in the same breath that they complimented his presumed inner virtue. Did no one understand that a man could be both likable *and* useless? Not every quick-tongued fool was a hero in disguise.

His life sense alerted him of Llarimar's return long before footsteps did. The priest walked up to join Lightsong alongside the wall. Llarimar rested his arms on the railing—which, being built for a god, was about a foot too high for the priest.

"They're gone," Llarimar said.

"Ah, very good," Lightsong said. "I do believe that we've accomplished something today. I've fled from my responsibilities, screamed at my servants, and sat about pouting. Undoubtedly, this will convince everyone that I'm even *more* noble and honorable than they previously assumed. Tomorrow, there will be twice as many petitions, and I shall continue my inexorable march toward utter madness."

"You can't go mad," Llarimar said softly. "It's impossible."

"Sure I can," Lightsong said. "I just have to concentrate long enough. You see, the great thing about madness is that it's all in your head."

Llarimar shook his head. "I see you've been restored to your normal humor."

"Scoot, you wound me. My humor is anything but normal." They stood silently for a few more minutes, Llarimar offering no chastisement or commentary on his god's actions. Just like a good little priest.

That made Lightsong think of something. "Scoot, you're my high priest."

"Yes, Your Grace."

Lightsong sighed. "You really need to pay attention to the lines I'm feeding you, Scoot. You really should have said something pithy there."

"I apologize, Your Grace."

"Just try harder next time. Anyway, you know about theology and that sort of thing, correct?"

"I've studied my share, Your Grace."

"Well then, what *is* the point—religiously—of having gods that can only heal one person, then die? It seems counterproductive to me. Easy way to depopulate your pantheon."

Llarimar leaned forward, staring out over the city. "It's complicated, Your Grace. Returned aren't just gods—they're men who died, but who decided to come back and offer blessings and knowledge. After all, only one who has died can have anything useful to say about the other side."

"True, I suppose."

"The thing is, Your Grace, Returned aren't meant to stay. We extend their lives, giving them extra time to bless us. But they're really only supposed to remain alive as long as it takes them to do what they need to."

"Need to?" Lightsong said. "That seems rather vague."

Llarimar shrugged. "Returned have . . . goals. Objectives which are their own. You knew of yours before you decided to come back, but the process of leaping across the Iridescent Wave leaves the memory fragmented. Stay long enough, and you'll remember what you came to accomplish. The petitions . . . they're a way of helping you to remember."

"So I've come back to save one person's life?" Lightsong said, frowning, but feeling embarrassed. In five years, he'd spent little time studying his own theology. But, well, that was the sort of thing priests were for.

"Not necessarily, Your Grace," Llarimar said. "You may have come back to save one person. But, more likely, there is information about the future or the afterlife that you felt you needed to share. Or perhaps some great event in which you felt you needed to participate. Remember, it was the heroic way in which you died that gave you the power to Return in the first place. What you are to do might relate to that, somehow."

Llarimar trailed off slightly, his eyes growing unfocused. "You saw something, Lightsong. On the other side, the future is visible, like a scroll that stretches into the eternal harmonics of the cosmos. Something you saw—something about the future—worried you. Rather than remaining at peace, you took the opportunity that your brave death afforded you, and you Returned to the world. Determined to fix a problem, share information, or otherwise help those who continued to live.

"Someday, once you feel that you've accomplished your task, you can use the petitions to find someone who deserves your Breath. Then you can continue your journey across the Iridescent Wave. Our job, as your followers, is to provide Breath for you and keep you alive until you can accomplish your goal, whatever it may be. In the meantime, we pray for auguries and blessings, which can be gleaned only from one who has touched the future as you have."

Lightsong didn't respond immediately. "And if I don't believe?"

"In what, Your Grace?"

"In any of it," Lightsong said. "That Returned are gods, that these visions are anything more than random inventions of my brain. What if I don't believe that I had any purpose or plan in Returning?"

"Then maybe that's what you came back to discover."

"So . . . wait. You're saying that on the other side—where I obviously *believed* in the other side—I realized that if

I Returned I wouldn't believe in the other side, so I came back with the purpose of discovering faith in the other side, which I only lost because I Returned in the first place?"

Llarimar paused. Then he smiled. "That last one breaks down a little bit in the face of logic, doesn't it?"

"Yeah, a little bit," Lightsong said, smiling back. He turned, eyes falling on the God King's palace, standing like a monument above the other court structures. "What do you think of her?"

"The new queen?" Llarimar asked. "I haven't met her, Your Grace. She won't be presented for another few days."

"Not the person. The implications."

Llarimar glanced at him. "Your Grace. That smells of an interest in politics!"

"Blah blah, yes, I know. Lightsong is a hypocrite. I'll do penance for it later. Now answer the blasted question."

Llarimar smiled. "I don't know what to think of her, Your Grace. The court of twenty years ago thought bringing a royal daughter here was a good idea."

Yes, Lightsong thought. *But that court is gone.* The gods had thought melding the royal line back into Hallandren would be a good idea. But those gods—the ones who believed they knew how to deal with the Idrian girl's arrival—were now dead. They'd left inferior replacements.

If what Llarimar said was true, then there was something important about the things Lightsong saw. Those visions of war, and the terrible sense of foreboding. For reasons he couldn't explain, it felt to him like his people were barreling headfirst down a mountain slope, completely ignorant of a bottomless chasm hidden in the cleft of the lands before them.

"The full Court Assembly meets in judgment tomorrow, doesn't it?" Lightsong said, still looking at the black palace.

"Yes, Your Grace."

"Contact Blushweaver. See if I can share a box with her during the judgments. Perhaps she will distract me. You know what a headache politics gives me."

"You can't get headaches, Your Grace."

In the distance, Lightsong could see the rejected petitioners trailing out of the gates, returning to the city, leaving their gods behind. "Could have fooled me," he said quietly.

* * *

SIRI STOOD IN the dark black bedroom, wearing her shift, looking out the window. The God King's palace was higher than the surrounding wall, and the bedroom faced east. Out over the sea. She watched the distant waves, feeling the heat of the afternoon sun. While she was wearing the thin shift, the warmth was actually pleasant, and it was tempered by a cool breeze blowing in off the ocean. The wind teased her long hair, ruffling the fabric of her shift.

She should be dead. She had spoken directly to the God King, had sat up and made a demand of him. She'd waited all morning for punishment. There had been none.

She leaned down against the windowsill, arms crossed on the stone, closing her eyes and feeling the sea breeze. A part of her was still aghast at the way she had acted. That part was growing smaller and smaller. *I've been going about things wrong here,* she thought. *I've let myself be pushed about by my fears and worries.*

She didn't usually take time to bother with fears and worries. She just did what seemed right. She was beginning to feel that she should have stood up to the God King days ago. Perhaps she wasn't being cautious enough. Perhaps punishment would still come. However, for the moment, she felt as if she'd accomplished something.

She smiled, opening her eyes, and let her hair change to a determined golden yellow.

It was time to stop being afraid.

13

"'LL GIVE IT away," Vivenna said firmly.

She sat with the mercenaries in Lemex's home. It was the day after the Breaths had been forced upon her, and she had spent a restless night, letting the mercenaries and the nurse see to the disposal of Lemex's body. She didn't remember falling asleep from the exhaustion and stress of the day, but she did remember lying down to rest for a short time in the other upstairs bedroom. When she'd awoken, she'd been surprised to find that the mercenaries were still there. Apparently, they and Parlin had slept downstairs.

A night's perspective hadn't helped her much with her problems. She still had all of that filthy Breath, and she still had no idea what she was going to do in Hallandren without Lemex. At least with the Breath, she had an idea of what to do. It could be given away.

They were in Lemex's sitting room. Like most places in Hallandren, the room was swollen with colors; the walls were made from thin strips of reedlike wood, stained in bright yellows and greens. Vivenna couldn't help but notice that she saw each color more vibrantly now. She had a strangely precise sense of color—she could divide its shades and hues, understanding instinctively how close each color was to the ideal. It was like perfect pitch for the eyes.

It was very, *very* difficult not to see beauty in the colors.

Denth leaned against the far wall. Tonk Fah lounged on a couch, yawning periodically, his colorful bird perched on his foot. Parlin had gone to stand watch outside.

"Give it away, Princess?" Denth asked.

"The Breath," Vivenna said. She sat on a kitchen stool instead of one of the overly plush chairs or couches. "We will go out and find unfortunate people who have been raped by your culture, their Breath stolen, and I will give each one a Breath."

Denth shot a glace at Tonk Fah, who simply yawned.

"Princess," Denth said, "you can't give Breath away one at a time. You have to give it all away at once."

"Including your own Breath," Tonk Fah said.

Denth nodded. "That would leave you as a Drab."

Vivenna's stomach churned at that. The thought of not only losing the new beauty and color, but her own Breath, her soul . . . well, it was almost enough to turn her hair white. "No," she said. "That's not an option, then."

The room fell silent.

"She could Awaken stuff," Tonk Fah noted, wiggling his foot, making his bird squawk. "Stick the Breath inside of a pair of pants or something."

"That's a good point," Denth said.

"What . . . does that entail?" Vivenna asked.

"You bring something to life, Princess," Denth said. "An inanimate object. That'll draw out some of your Breath and leave the object kind of alive. Most Awakeners do it temporarily, but I don't see why you couldn't just leave the Breath there."

Awakening. Taking the souls of men and using them to create unliving monstrosities. Somehow, Vivenna felt that Austre would find that an even greater sin than simply bearing the Breath. She sighed, shaking her head. The problem with the Breath was, in a way, just a distraction—one she feared she was using to keep herself from dwelling on the lack of Lemex. What was she going to do?

Denth sat down in a chair beside her, resting his feet on the sitting table. He kept himself better groomed than Tonk Fah, his dark hair pulled back into a neat tail, his face clean-shaven. "I hate being a mercenary," he said. "You know why?"

She raised an eyebrow.

"No job security," Denth said, leaning back in his chair.

"The kinds of things we do, they tend to be dangerous and unpredictable. Our employers have a habit of dying off on us."

"Though usually not from the chills," Tonk Fah noted. "Swords tend to be the method of choice."

"Take our current predicament," Denth said. "No more employer. That leaves us without any real direction."

Vivenna froze. *Does that mean their contract is over? They know I'm a princess of Idris. What will they do with that information? Is that why they stayed here last night, rather than leaving? Are they planning to blackmail me?*

Denth eyed her. "You see that?" he asked, turning to Tonk Fah.

"Yeah," Tonk Fah said. "She's thinking it."

Denth leaned back further in his chair. "This is *exactly* what I'm talking about. Why does everyone assume that when a mercenary's contract is over, he'll betray them? You think we go around stabbing people for the fun of it? Do you think a surgeon has this problem? Do people worry that the moment they're done paying him, he'll laugh maniacally and cut off their toes?"

"*I* like cutting off toes," Tonk Fah noted.

"That's different," Denth said. "You wouldn't do it simply because your contract ran out, would you?"

"Nah," Tonk Fah said. "Toes is toes."

Vivenna rolled her eyes. "Is there a point to this?"

"The point is, Princess," Denth said, "you were just thinking that we were going to betray you. Maybe rob you blind or sell you into slavery or something."

"Nonsense," Vivenna said. "I was thinking nothing of the sort."

"I'm sure," Denth replied. "Mercenary work is very respectable—it's legal in almost every kingdom I know. We're just as much a part of the community as the baker or the fishmonger."

"Not that we pay the tax collectors," Tonk Fah added. "We tend to stab them for the fun of it."

Vivenna just shook her head.

Denth leaned forward, speaking in a more serious tone. "What I'm trying to say, Princess, is that we're not criminals. We're employees. Your friend Lemex was our boss. Now he's dead. I figure that our contract transfers to you now, if you want it."

Vivenna felt a slight glimmer of hope. But could she trust them? Despite Denth's speech, she found it hard to have faith in the motives and altruism of a pair of men who fought for money. However, they hadn't taken advantage of Lemex's sickness, and they *had* stayed around even after they could have robbed the place and left while she was asleep.

"All right," she said. "How much is left on your contract?"

"No idea," Denth said. "Jewels handles that kind of thing."

"Jewels?" Vivenna asked.

"Third member of the group," Tonk Fah said. "She's off doing Jewels stuff."

Vivenna frowned. "How many of you are there?"

"Just three," Denth said.

"Unless you count pets," Tonk Fah said, balancing his bird on his foot.

"She'll be back in a while," Denth said. "She stopped in last night, but you were asleep. Anyway, I know we've got at least a few months left on our contract, and we were paid half up front. Even if you decide not to pay the rest, we probably owe you a few more weeks."

Tonk Fah nodded. "So if there's anyone you want killed, now would be the time."

Vivenna stared, and Tonk Fah chuckled.

"You're really going to have to get used to our terrible senses of humor, Princess," Denth said. "Assuming, of course, you're going to keep us around."

"I've already implied that I'll keep you," Vivenna said.

"All right," Denth replied. "But what are you going to do with us? Why did you even come to the city?"

Vivenna didn't answer immediately. *No point in holding back,* she thought. *They know the most dangerous secret—my identity—already.* "I'm here to rescue my sister," she said. "To sneak her out of the God King's palace and see her returned to Idris unharmed."

The mercenaries fell silent. Finally, Tonk Fah whistled. "Ambitious," he noted as his parrot mimicked the whistle.

"She *is* a princess," Denth said. "They tend to be ambitious sorts."

"Siri isn't ready to deal with Hallandren," Vivenna said, leaning forward. "My father sent her in my place, but I cannot stand the thought of her serving as the God King's wife. Unfortunately, if we simply grab her and go, Hallandren will likely attack my homeland. We need to make her disappear in a way that isn't traceable to my people. If necessary, we can substitute me for my sister."

Denth scratched his head.

"Well?" Vivenna asked.

"Little bit out of our realm of expertise," Denth said.

"We usually hit things," Tonk Fah said.

Denth nodded. "Or, at least, keep things from getting hit. Lemex kept us on partially just as bodyguards."

"Why wouldn't he just send for a couple of Idrian soldiers to protect him?"

Denth and Tonk Fah exchanged a look.

"How can I put this delicately?" Denth said. "Princess, your Lemex was embezzling money from the king and spending it on Breath."

"Lemex was a patriot!" Vivenna said immediately.

"That may have been the case," Denth said. "But even a good priest isn't above slipping himself a few coins out of the coffer, so to speak. I think your Lemex figured it would be better to have outside muscle, rather than inside loyalists, protecting him."

Vivenna fell silent. It was still hard to imagine the thoughtful, clever, and passionate man represented in Lemex's letters as a thief. Yet it was also hard to imagine Lemex holding as much Breath as he obviously had.

But embezzling? Stealing from Idris itself?

"You learn things as a mercenary," Denth said, resting back with hands behind his head. "You fight enough people, and you figure you start to understand them. You stay alive by anticipating them. The thing is, people aren't simple. Even Idrians."

"Boring, yes," Tonk Fah added. "But not simple."

"Your Lemex, he was involved in some big plans," Denth said. "I honestly think he *was* a patriot. There are many intrigues going on in this city, Princess—some of the projects Lemex had us working on had a grand scope, and were for the good of Idris, as near as I can tell. I guess he just thought he should be compensated a little for his patriotism."

"Quite an amiable fellow, actually," Tonk Fah said. "Didn't want to bother your father. So he just did the figures on his own, gave himself a raise, and indicated in his reports that his costs were far greater than they really were."

Vivenna fell silent, letting herself digest the words. How could anyone who stole money from Idris also be a patriot? How could a person faithful to Austre end up with several hundred BioChromatic Breaths?

She shook her head wryly. *I saw men who placed themselves above others, and I saw them cast down,* she quoted to herself. It was one of the Five Visions. She shouldn't judge Lemex, particularly now that he was dead. "Wait," she said, eyeing the mercenaries. "You said that you were just bodyguards. What, then, were you doing helping Lemex with 'projects'?"

The two men shared a look.

"Told you she was smart," Tonk Fah said. "Comes from not being a mercenary."

"We *are* bodyguards, Princess," Denth said. "However, we're not without certain . . . skills. We can make things happen."

"Things?" Vivenna asked.

Denth shrugged. "We know people. That's part of what makes us useful. Let me think about this issue with your sister. Maybe I'll be able to come up with some ideas. It's a little like kidnapping. . . ."

"Which," Tonk Fah said, "we're not too fond of. Did we mention that?"

"Yes," Vivenna said. "Bad business. No money. What were these 'projects' Lemex was working on?"

"I'm not exactly sure of the whole of them," Denth admitted. "We only saw pieces—running errands, arranging meetings, intimidating people. It had something to do with work for your father. We can find out for you, if you want."

Vivenna nodded. "I do."

Denth stood. "All right," he said. He walked past Tonk Fah's couch, smacking the larger man's leg, causing the bird to squawk. "Tonk. Come on. Time to ransack the house."

Tonk Fah yawned and sat up.

"Wait!" Vivenna said. "Ransack the house?"

"Sure," Denth said, heading up the stairs. "Break out any hidden safes. Search through papers and files. Figure out what old Lemex was up to."

"He won't care much," Tonk Fah said, standing. "Being dead and all."

Vivenna shivered. She still wished she'd been able to see that Lemex got a proper Idrian burial, rather than sending him off to the Hallandren charnel house. Having a pair of toughs search his belongings felt unseemly.

Denth must have noticed her discomfort. "We don't have to, if you don't want us to."

"Sure," Tonk Fah said. "We'll never know what Lemex was up to, though."

"Continue," Vivenna said. "But I'm going to supervise."

"Actually, I doubt that you will," Denth said.

"And why is that?"

"Because," Denth said. "Now, I know nobody ever asks mercenaries for their opinion. You see—"

"Oh, just get on with it," Vivenna said with annoyance, though she immediately chastised herself for her snappishness. What was wrong with her? The last few days must be wearing on her.

Denth just smiled, as if he found her outburst incredibly amusing. "Today's the day when the Returned hold their Court Assembly, Princess."

"So?" Vivenna asked with forced calmness.

"So," Denth replied, "it's also the day when your sister will be presented to the gods. I suspect that you'll want to go get a good look at her, see how she's holding up. If you're going to do that, you'll want to get moving. Court Assembly will begin pretty soon."

Vivenna folded her arms, not moving. "I've been tutored all about these things, Denth. Regular people can't just walk into the Court of Gods. If you want to watch the judgments at the Court Assembly, you either have to be favored by one of the gods, be extremely influential, or you have to draw and win the lottery."

"True," Denth said, leaning against the banister. "If only we knew someone with enough BioChromatic Breaths to instantly be considered important, and therefore gain entrance to the court without being questioned."

"Ah, Denth," Tonk Fah said. "Someone has to have at least fifty Breaths to be considered worthy! That's a terribly high number."

Vivenna paused. "And . . . how many Breaths do I have?"

"Oh, around five hundred or so," Denth said. "At least, that's what Lemex claimed. I'm inclined to believe him. You are, after all, making the carpet shine."

She glanced down, noticing for the first time that she was creating a pocket of enhanced color around her. It wasn't very distinct, but it *was* noticeable.

"You'd better get going, Princess," Denth said, continuing to clomp up the stairs. "You'll be late."

∼∞∼

SIRI SAT NERVOUSLY, blond with excitement, trying to contain herself as the serving women did her hair. Her Wedding Jubilation—something she found rather inappropriately named—was finally over, and it was time for her formal presentation before the Hallandren gods.

She was probably too excited. It hadn't really been that long. Yet the prospect of finally leaving—if only to attend court—made her almost giddy. She would finally get to interact with someone other than priests, scribes, and servants. She'd finally get to meet some of those gods that she'd heard so much about.

Plus, *he*'d be there at the presentation. The only times she'd been able to see the God King had been during their nightly staring matches, when he was shrouded in shadow. Today, she would at last see him in the light.

She smiled, inspecting herself in a large mirror. The servants had done her hair in an amazingly intricate style, part of it braided, the rest allowed to flow free. They'd tied several ribbons into the braids and also woven them into her free-flowing hair. The ribbons shimmered as she turned her head. Her family would have been mortified at the ostentatious colors. Siri grinned mischievously, making her hair turn a brighter shade of golden blond to better contrast with the ribbons.

The serving women smiled approvingly, a couple letting out quiet "ooo's" at the transformation. Siri sat back, hands in her lap as she inspected her clothing choices for the court appearance. The garments were ornate—not as complex as the ones she wore to the bedchambers, but far more formal than her everyday choices.

Red was the theme for the serving women and priests today. That made Siri want to choose something else. Eventually, she decided on gold, and she pointed at the two golden gowns, having the women bring them forward so she could look at them more closely. Unfortunately, as she did so, the women fetched three more golden dresses from a rolling wardrobe out in the hallway.

Siri sighed. It was as if they were determined to keep her from having a reasonably simple choice. She just hated seeing so many options disappear each day. If only . . .

She paused. "Could I try them *all* on?"

The serving women glanced at each other, a little confused. They nodded toward her, their expressions conveying a simple message. *Of course you can.* Siri felt foolish, but in Idris she'd never had a choice before. She smiled, standing and letting them take off her robe and then dress her in the first of the gowns, careful not to mess up her hair. Siri inspected herself, noting that the neckline was rather low. She was willing to splurge on color, but the amount of flesh the Hallandren showed still felt scandalous.

She nodded, letting them take off the gown. Then they dressed her in the next one—a two-piece garment with a separate corset. Once they were finished, Siri eyed this new outfit in the mirror. She liked it, but she wanted to try the others as well. So, after spinning about and inspecting the back, she nodded and moved on.

It was frivolous. But why was she so worried about being frivolous? Her father wasn't around to regard her with that stern, disapproving face of his. Vivenna was an entire kingdom away. Siri was queen of the Hallandren people. Shouldn't she try to learn their ways? She smiled at the ridiculous justification, but went on to the next gown anyway.

14

I T'S RAINING," LIGHTSONG noted.

"Very astute, Your Grace," Llarimar said, walking beside his god.

"I'm not fond of rain."

"So you have often noted, Your Grace."

"I'm a god," Lightsong said. "Shouldn't I have power over the weather? How can it rain if I don't want it to?"

"There are currently twenty-five gods in the court, Your Grace. Perhaps there are more who desire rain than those who don't."

Lightsong's robes of gold and red rustled as he walked. The grass was cool and damp beneath his sandaled toes, but a group of servants carried a wide canopy over him. Rain fell softly on the cloth. In T'Telir, rainfalls were common, but they were never very strong.

Lightsong would have liked to have seen a true rainstorm, like people said occurred out in the jungles. "I'll take a poll then," Lightsong said. "Of the other gods. See how many of them wanted it to rain today."

"If you wish, Your Grace," Llarimar said. "It won't prove much."

"It'll prove whose fault this is," Lightsong said. "And . . . if it turns out that most of us want it to stop raining, perhaps that will start a theological crisis."

Llarimar, of course, didn't seem bothered by the concept of a god trying to undermine his own religion. "Your Grace," he said, "our doctrine is *quite* sound, I assure you."

"And if the gods don't want it to rain, yet it still does?"

"Would you like it to be sunny all the time, Your Grace?"

Lightsong shrugged. "Sure."

"And the farmers?" Llarimar said. "Their crops would die without the rain."

"It can rain on the crops," Lightsong said, "just not in the city. A few selective weather patterns shouldn't be too much for a god to accomplish."

"The people need water to drink, Your Grace," Llarimar said. "The streets need to be washed clean. And what of the plants in the city? The beautiful trees—even this grass that you enjoy walking across—would die if the rain did not fall."

"Well," Lightsong said, "I could just *will* them to continue living."

"And that is what you do, Your Grace," Llarimar said. "Your soul knows that rain is best for the city, and so it rains. Despite what your consciousness thinks."

Lightsong frowned. "By that argument, you could claim that *anyone* was a god, Llarimar."

"Not just *anyone* comes back from the dead, Your Grace. Nor do they have the power to heal the sick, and they certainly don't have your ability to foresee the future."

Good points, those, Lightsong thought as they approached the arena. The large, circular structure was at the back of the Court of Gods, outside of the ring of palaces that surrounded the courtyard. Lightsong's entourage moved inside—red canopy still held above him—and entered the sand-covered arena yard. Then they moved up a ramp toward the seating area.

The arena had four rows of seats for ordinary people—stone benches, accommodating T'Telir citizens who were favored, lucky, or rich enough to get themselves into an assembly session. The upper reaches of the arena were reserved for the Returned. Here—close enough to hear what was said on the arena floor, yet far enough back to remain stately—were the boxes. Ornately carved in stone, they were large enough to hold a god's entire entourage.

Lightsong could see that several of his colleagues had

arrived, marked by the colorful canopies that sat above their boxes. Lifeblesser was there, as was Mercystar. They passed by the empty box usually reserved for Lightsong and made their way around the ring and approached a box topped by a green pavilion. Blushweaver lounged inside. Her green and silver dress was lavish and revealing, as always. Despite its rich trim and embroidery, it was little more than a long swath of cloth with a hole in the center for her head and some ties. That left it completely open on both sides from shoulder to calf, and Blushweaver's thighs curved out lusciously on either side. She sat up, smiling.

Lightsong took a deep breath. Blushweaver always treated him kindly and she certainly did have a high opinion of him, but he felt like he had to be on guard at all times when he was around her. A man could be taken in by a woman such as she.

Taken in, then never released.

"Lightsong, dear," she said, smiling more deeply as Lightsong's servants scuttled forward, setting up his chair, footrest, and snack table.

"Blushweaver," Lightsong replied. "My high priest tells me that you're to blame for this dreary weather."

Blushweaver raised an eyebrow, and to the side—standing with the other priests—Llarimar flushed. "I like the rain," Blushweaver finally said, lounging back on her couch. "It's . . . different. I like things that are different."

"Then you should be thoroughly bored by me, my dear," Lightsong said, seating himself and taking a handful of grapes—already peeled—from the bowl on his snack table.

"Bored?" Blushweaver asked.

"I strive for nothing if not mediocrity, and mediocrity is *hardly* different. In fact, I should say that it's highly in fashion in court these days."

"You shouldn't say such things," Blushweaver said. "The people might start to believe you."

"You mistake me. That's why I say them. I figure if I can't

do properly deific miracles like control the weather, then I might as well settle for the lesser miracle of being the one who tells the truth."

"Hum," she replied, stretching back, the tips of her fingers wiggling as she sighed in contentment. "Our priests say that the purpose of the gods is not to play with weather or prevent disasters, but to provide visions and service to the people. Perhaps this attitude of yours is not the best way to see to their interests."

"You're right, of course," Lightsong said. "I've just had a revelation. Mediocrity *isn't* the best way to serve our people."

"What is, then?"

"Medium rare on a bed of sweet-potato medallions," he said, popping a grape in his mouth. "With a slight garnish of garlic and a light white wine sauce."

"You're incorrigible," she said, finishing her stretch.

"I am what the universe made me to be, my dear."

"You bow before the whims of the universe, then?"

"What else would I do?"

"Fight it," Blushweaver said. She narrowed her eyes, absently reaching to take one of the grapes from Lightsong's hand. "Fight with everything, force the universe to bow to you instead."

"That's a charming concept, Blushweaver. But I believe that the universe and I are in slightly different weight categories."

"I think you're wrong."

"Are you saying I'm fat?"

She regarded him with a flat glance. "I'm saying that you needn't be so humble, Lightsong. You're a *god*."

"A god who can't even make it stop raining."

"*I* want it to storm and tempest. Maybe this drizzle is the compromise between us."

Lightsong popped another grape in his mouth, squishing it between his teeth, feeling the sweet juice leak onto his palate. He thought for a moment, chewing. "Blushweaver, dear," he finally said. "Is there some kind of subtext to our current conversation? Because, as you might know, I am absolutely *terrible* with subtext. It gives me a headache."

"You can't get headaches," Blushweaver said.

"Well I can't get subtext either. Far too subtle for me. It takes effort to understand, and effort is—unfortunately— against my religion."

Blushweaver raised an eyebrow. "A new tenet for those who worship you?"

"Oh, not that religion," Lightsong said. "I'm secretly a worshipper of Austre. His is such a delightfully blunt theology—black, white, no bothering with complications. Faith without any bothersome thinking."

Blushweaver stole another grape. "You just don't know Austrism well enough. It's complex. If you're looking for something *really* simple, you should try the Pahn Kahl faith."

Lightsong frowned. "Don't they just worship the Returned, like the rest of us?"

"No. They have their own religion."

"But everyone knows the Pahn Kahl are practically Hallandren."

Blushweaver shrugged, watching the stadium floor below.

"And how exactly did we get onto this tangent, anyway?" Lightsong said. "I swear, my dear. Sometimes our conversations remind me of a broken sword."

She raised an eyebrow.

"Sharp as hell," Lightsong said, "but lacking a point."

Blushweaver snorted quietly. "You're the one who asked to meet with me, Lightsong."

"Yes, but we both know that you wanted me to. What are you planning, Blushweaver?"

Blushweaver rolled her grape between her fingers. "Wait," she said.

Lightsong sighed, waving for a servant to bring him some nuts. One placed a bowl on the table; then another came forward and began to crack them for him. "First you imply that I should join with you, now you won't tell me what you want me to do? I swear, woman. Someday, your ridiculous sense of drama is going to cause cataclysmic problems—like, for instance, boredom in your companions."

"It's not drama," she said. "It's respect." She nodded directly across the arena, where the God King's box still stood empty, golden throne sitting on a pedestal above the box itself.

"Ah. Feeling patriotic today, are we?"

"It's more that I'm curious."

"About?"

"Her."

"The queen?"

Blushweaver gave him a flat stare. "Of course, her. Who else would I be speaking about?"

Lightsong counted off the days. It had been a week. "Huh," he said to himself. "Her period of isolation is over, then?"

"You really should pay more attention, Lightsong."

He shrugged. "Time tends to pass you by more quickly when you take no notice of it, my dear. In that, it's remarkably similar to most women I know." With that, he accepted a handful of nuts, then settled back to wait.

⟡

APPARENTLY, THE PEOPLE of T'Telir weren't fond of carriages—not even to carry gods. Siri sat, somewhat bemused, as a group of servants carried her chair across the grass toward a large, circular structure at the back of the Court of Gods. It was raining. She didn't care. She'd been cooped up for far too long.

She turned, twisting in her chair, looking back over a group of serving women who carried her dress's long golden train, keeping it off the wet grass. Around them all walked more women, who held a large canopy to shield Siri from the rain.

"Could you . . . move that aside?" Siri asked. "Let the rain fall on me?"

The serving women glanced at one another.

"Just for a little bit," Siri said. "I promise."

The women shared frowns, but slowed, allowing Siri's porters to pull ahead and expose her to the rain. She looked up, smiling as the drizzle fell on her face. *Seven days is far too long to spend indoors,* she decided. She basked for a long moment, enjoying the cool wetness on her skin and clothing. The grass looked inviting. She glanced back again. "I could walk, you know." *Feel my toes on those green blades. . . .*

The serving women looked very, very uncomfortable about that concept.

"Or not," Siri said, turning around as the women sped up, again covering the sky with their canopy. Walking was probably a bad idea, considering her dress's long train. She'd eventually chosen a gown far more daring than anything she'd ever worn before. The neckline was a touch low, and it had no sleeves. It also had a curious design that covered the front of her legs with a short skirt, yet was floor-length in back. She'd picked it partially for the novelty, though she blushed every time she thought of how much leg it showed.

They soon arrived at the arena and her porters carried her up into it. Siri was interested to see that it had no ceiling and had a sand-covered floor. Just above the floor, a colorful group of people were gathering on ranks of benches. Though some of them carried umbrellas, many ignored the light rain, chatting amiably among themselves. Siri smiled at the crowd; a hundred different colors and as many different clothing styles were represented. It was good to see some variety again, even if that variety was some-what garish.

Her porters carried her up to a large stone cleft built into the side of the building. Here, her women slid the canopy's poles into holes in the stone, allowing it to stand freely to cover the entire box. Servants scuttled about, getting things ready, and her porters lowered her chair. She stood, frowning. She was finally free of the palace. And yet it appeared she was going to have to sit above everyone else. Even the other gods—who she assumed were in the other canopied boxes—were far away and separated from her by walls.

How is it that they can make me feel alone, even when surrounded by hundreds of people? She turned to one of her serving women. "The God King. Where is he?"

The woman gestured toward the other boxes like Siri's.

"He's in one of them?" Siri asked.

"No, Vessel," the woman said, eyes downcast. "He will not arrive until the gods are all here."

Ah, Siri thought. *Makes sense, I guess.*

She sat back in her chair as several servants prepared food. To the side, a minstrel began to play a flute, as if to drown out the sounds of the people below. She would rather have heard the people. Still, she decided not to let herself get into a bad mood. At least she was outside, and she could *see* other people, even if she couldn't interact with them. She smiled to herself, leaning forward, elbows on knees, as she studied the exotic colors below.

What was she to make of T'Telir people? They were just so remarkably diverse. Some had dark skin, which meant they were from the edges of the Hallandren kingdom. Others had yellow hair, or even strange hair colors—blue and green—that came, Siri assumed, from dyes.

All wore brilliant clothing, as if there were no other option. Ornate hats were popular, both on men and women. Clothing ranged from vests and shorts to long robes and gowns. *How much time must they spend shopping!* It was difficult enough for her to choose what to wear, and she had only about a dozen choices each day—and no hats.

After she'd refused the first few, the servants had stopped offering them.

Entourage after entourage arrived bearing a different set of colors—a hue and a metallic, usually. She counted the boxes. There was room for about fifty gods, but the court had only a couple of dozen. Twenty-five, wasn't it? In each procession, she saw a figure standing taller than the others. Some—mostly the women—were carried on chairs or couches. The men generally walked, some wearing intricate robes, others wearing nothing more than sandals and skirt. Siri leaned forward, studying one god as he walked right by her box. His bare chest made her blush, but it let her see his well-muscled body and toned flesh.

He glanced at her, then nodded his head slightly in respect. His servants and priests bowed almost to the ground. The god passed on, having said nothing.

She sat back in her chair, shaking her head as one of the servants offered her food. There were still four or five gods left to arrive. Apparently, the Hallandren deities weren't as punctual as Bluefingers's schedule-keeping had led her to believe.

⊗≫

VIVENNA STEPPED THROUGH the gates, passing into the Hallandren Court of Gods, which was dominated by a group of large palaces. She hesitated, and small groups of people passed through on either side of her, though there wasn't much of a crowd.

Denth had been right; it had been easy for her to get into the court. The priests at the gate had waved Vivenna through without even asking her identity. They had even let Parlin pass, assuming him to be her attendant. She turned back, glancing at the priests in their blue robes. She could see bubbles of colorfulness around them, indications of their strong BioChroma.

She'd been tutored about this. The priests guarding the

gates had enough Breath to get them to the First Heightening, the state at which a person gained the ability to distinguish levels of Breath in other people. Vivenna had it too. It wasn't that auras or colors looked different to her. In fact, the ability to distinguish Breath was similar to the perfect pitch she had gained. Other people heard the same sounds she did, she just had the ability to pick them apart.

She saw how close a person had to get to one of the priests before the colors increased, and she saw exactly how much more colorful those hues became. This information let her know instinctively that each of the priests was of the First Heightening. Parlin had one Breath. The ordinary citizens, who had to present papers to gain entrance to the court, also each had only one Breath. She could tell how strong that Breath was, and if the person was sick or not.

The priests each had exactly fifty Breaths, as did the majority of the wealthier individuals entering through the gates. A fair number had at least two hundred Breaths, enough for the Second Heightening and the perfect pitch it granted. Only a couple had more Breaths than Vivenna, who had reached all the way to the Third Heightening and the perfect color perception it granted.

She turned away from her study of the crowd. She'd been tutored about the Heightenings, but she'd never expected to experience one firsthand. She felt dirty. Perverse. Particularly because the colors were just so *beautiful*.

Her tutors had explained how the court was composed of a wide circle of palaces, but they had not mentioned how each palace was so harmoniously balanced in color. Each was a work of art, utilizing subtle color gradients that normal people just wouldn't be able to appreciate. These sat on a perfect, uniformly green lawn. It was trimmed carefully, and it was marred by neither road nor walkway. Vivenna stepped onto it, Parlin at her side, and she felt an urge to kick off her shoes and walk barefoot in the dew-moistened grass. That wouldn't be appropriate at all, and she stifled the impulse.

The drizzle was finally starting to let up, and Parlin lowered the umbrella he'd bought to keep them both dry. "So, this is it," he said, shaking off the umbrella. "The Court of Gods."

Vivenna nodded.

"Good place to graze sheep."

"I doubt that," she said quietly.

Parlin frowned. "Goats, then?" he said finally.

Vivenna sighed, and they joined the small procession walking across the grass toward a large structure outside the circle of palaces. She'd been worried about standing out—after all, she still wore her simple Idrian dress, with its high neck, practical fabric, and muted colors. She was beginning to realize that there just *wasn't* a way to stand out in T'Telir.

The people around her wore such a stunning variety of costumes that she wondered who had the imagination to design them all. Some were as modest as Vivenna's and others even had muted colors—though these were usually accented by bright scarves or hats. Modesty in both design and color was obviously unfashionable, but not nonexistent.

It's all about drawing attention, she realized. *The whites and faded colors are a reaction against the bright colors. But because everyone tries so hard to look distinctive, nobody does!*

Feeling a little more secure, she glanced at Parlin, who seemed more at peace now that they were away from the larger crowds in the city below. "Interesting buildings," he said. "The people wear so much color, but that palace is just one color. Wonder why that is."

"It's not one color. It's many different shades of the same color."

Parlin shrugged. "Red is red."

How could she explain? Each red was different, like

notes on a musical scale. The walls were of pure red. The roof tiles, side columns, and other ornamentations were of slightly different shades, each distinct and intentional. The columns, for instance, formed stepping fifths of color, harmonizing with the base tint of the walls.

It was like a symphony of hues. The building had obviously been constructed for a person who had achieved the Third Heightening, as only such a person would be able to see the ideal resonance. To others . . . well, it was just a bunch of red.

They passed the red palace, approaching the arena. Entertainment was central to the lives of the Hallandren gods. After all, one couldn't expect gods to do anything useful with their time. Often they were diverted in their palaces or on the courtyard lawn, but for particularly large events, there was the arena—which also served as the location of Hallandren legislative debates. Today, the priests would argue for the sport of their deities.

Vivenna and Parlin waited their turn as the people crowded around the arena entrance. Vivenna glanced toward another gateway, wondering why nobody used it. The answer was made manifest as a figure approached. He was surrounded by servants, some carrying a canopy. All were dressed in blue and silver, matching their leader, who stood a good head taller than the others. He gave off a Bio-Chromatic aura such as Vivenna had never seen—though, admittedly, she'd been able to see them for only a few hours. His bubble of enhanced color was enormous; it extended nearly thirty feet. To her First Heightening senses, the god's Breath registered as infinite. Immeasurable. For the first time, Vivenna could see that there *was* something different about the Returned. They weren't just Awakeners with more power; it was like they had only a single Breath, but that Breath was so immensely powerful that it single-handedly propelled them to the upper Heightenings.

The god entered the arena through the open gateway. As

she watched him, Vivenna's sense of awe dissipated. There was an arrogance in this man's posture, a dismissiveness to the way he entered freely while others waited their turn at an overcrowded entrance.

To keep him alive, Vivenna thought, *he has to absorb a person's Breath each week.*

She'd let herself become too relaxed, and she felt her revulsion return. Color and beauty couldn't cover up such enormous conceit, nor could it hide the sin of being a parasite living on the common people.

The god disappeared into the arena. Vivenna waited, thinking for a time about her own BioChroma and what it meant. She was completely shocked when a man beside her suddenly lifted off the ground.

The man rose into the air, lifted by his unusually long cloak. The cloth had stiffened, looking a little like a hand as it held the man up high so he could see over the crowd. *How does it do that?* She'd been told that Breath could give life to objects, but what did "life" mean? It seemed as if the fibers in the cloak were taut, like muscles, but how did it lift something so much heavier than it was?

The man descended to the ground. He muttered something Vivenna couldn't hear, and his BioChromatic aura grew stronger as he recovered his Breath from the cloak. "We should be moving again soon," the man said to his friends. "The crowd is thinning up ahead."

Indeed, soon the crowd started to progress. It wasn't long before Vivenna and Parlin entered the arena itself. They moved through the stone benches, choosing a place that wasn't too crowded, and Vivenna looked urgently through the boxes set above. The building was ornate, but not really very big, and so it didn't take her long to locate Siri.

When she did, her heart sank. *My . . . sister,* Vivenna thought with a chill. *My poor sister.*

Siri was dressed in a scandalous golden dress that didn't even come down to her knees. It also had a plunging neckline. Siri's hair, which even she should have been able to keep a dark brown, was instead the golden yellow of enjoyment, and there were deep red ribbons woven through it. She was being attended by dozens of servants.

"Look what they've done to her," Vivenna said. "She must be frightened senseless, forced to wear something like that, forced to keep her hair a color that matches her clothing . . ." *Forced to be slave to the God King.*

Parlin's square-jawed face grew hard. He didn't often get angry, but Vivenna could see it in him now. She agreed. Siri was being exploited; they were carrying her around and displaying her like some kind of trophy. It seemed to Vivenna a statement. They were saying they could take a chaste, innocent Idrian woman and do whatever they wished with her.

What I'm doing is right, Vivenna thought with growing determination. *Coming to Hallandren was the best thing to do. Lemex might be dead, but I have to press onward. I have to find a way.*

I have to save my sister.

"Vivenna?" Parlin said.

"Hum?" Vivenna asked, distracted.

"Why is everyone starting to bow?"

<hr />

SIRI PLAYED IDLY with one of the tassels on her dress. The final god was seating himself in his box. *That's twenty-five,* she thought. *That should be all of them.*

Suddenly, out in the audience, people began to rise, then kneel to the ground. Siri stood, searching anxiously. What was she missing? Had the God King arrived, or was this something else? Even the gods had gone down on their knees, though they didn't prostrate themselves as the mortals did. They all seemed to be bowing toward Siri. *Some sort of ritual greeting for their new queen?*

Then she saw it. Her dress exploded with color, the

stone at her feet gained luster, and her very skin became more vibrant. In front of her, a white serving bowl began to shine; then it seemed to stretch, the white color splitting into the colors of the rainbow.

A serving woman tugged on Siri's sleeve from where she knelt below. "Vessel," the woman whispered, "behind you!"

15

B REATH CATCHING IN her chest, Siri turned. She found *him* standing behind her, though she had no idea how he had arrived. There was no entrance back there, just the stone wall.

He wore white. She hadn't expected that. Something about his BioChroma made the pure white split as she'd seen before, breaking up like light passed through a prism. Now, in daylight, she could finally see this properly. His clothing seemed to stretch, forming a robe-shaped rainbow in a colorful aura around him.

And he was young. Far younger than her shadowed meetings had suggested. He had supposedly reigned in Hallandren for decades, yet the man standing behind her appeared to be no more than twenty. She stared at him, awed, mouth opening slightly, and any words she had planned to say escaped her. This man *was* a god. The very air distorted around him. How could she have not seen it? How could she possibly have treated him as she had? She felt like a fool.

He regarded her, expression blank and unreadable, face so controlled that he reminded Siri of Vivenna. Vivenna. She wouldn't have been so belligerent. She would have deserved marriage to such a majestic creature.

The serving woman hissed quietly, tugging again at

Siri's dress. Belatedly, Siri dropped to her knees on the stone, the long train of her dress flapping slightly in the wind behind her.

———◆———

BLUSHWEAVER KNELT OBEDIENTLY on her cushion. Lightsong, however, remained standing, looking across the stadium toward a man he could barely see. The God King wore white, as he often did, for dramatic effect. As the only being to have achieved the Tenth Heightening, the God King had such a strong aura that he could draw color even from something colorless.

Blushweaver glanced up at Lightsong.

"Why do we kneel?" Lightsong asked.

"That's our king!" Blushweaver hissed. "Drop down, fool."

"What will happen if I don't?" Lightsong said. "They can't execute me. I'm a god."

"You could hurt our cause!"

"Our cause"? Lightsong thought. *One meeting and I'm already part of her plans?*

However, he wasn't so foolish that he would needlessly earn the God King's ire. Why risk his perfect life, full of people who would carry his chair through the rain and shell his nuts for him? He knelt down on his cushion. The God King's superiority was arbitrary, much like Lightsong's divinity—both part of a grand game of make-believe.

But he'd found that imaginary things were often the only items of real substance in people's lives.

———◆———

SIRI BREATHED QUICKLY, kneeling on the stone before her husband. The entire arena was hushed and still. Eyes downcast, she could still see Susebron's white-clothed feet in front of her. Even they gave off an aura of color, the white straps of his sandals bending out colorful ribbons.

Two coils of colorful rope hit the ground on either side of the God King. Siri watched as the ropes twisted with a life of their own, carefully wrapping around Susebron and pulling him into the air. His white robes fluttered as he was towed up through the space between the canopy and the back wall. Siri leaned forward, watching the ropes deliver her husband to a stone outcropping above. He sat back into a golden throne. Beside him, a pair of Awakener priests commanded their living ropes to roll up around their arms and shoulders.

The God King stretched out his hand. The people stood up—their chatter beginning again—and reseated themselves. *So . . . he's not going to sit with me,* she thought as she rose. A part of her was relieved, though another was just as frustrated. She'd been getting over her awe of being in Hallandren and being married to a god. Now he'd gone and impressed her all over again. Troubled, she sat and stared out over the crowds, barely watching as a group of priests entered the arena below.

What was she to make of Susebron? He couldn't be a god. Not really. Could he?

Austre was the true God of men, the one who *sent* the Returned. The Hallandren had worshipped him too, before the Manywar and the exile of the royal family. Only after that had they fallen, becoming pagans, worshipping the Iridescent Tones: BioChromatic Breath, the Returned, and art in general.

And yet, Siri had never seen Austre. She'd been taught about him, but what was one to make of a creature like the God King? That divine halo of color wasn't something that she could ignore. She began to understand just how the people of Hallandren—after nearly being destroyed by their enemies, then being saved by the diplomatic skills of Peacegiver the Blessed—could look to the Returned for divine guidance.

She sighed, glancing to the side as a figure walked up the steps toward her box. It was Bluefingers—hands stained with ink, characteristically scribbling away on a ledger even as he entered her pavilion. He glanced up at the God King, nodded to himself, then made another annotation on his ledger. "I see that His Immortal Majesty is positioned and that you are properly displayed, Vessel."

"Displayed?"

"Of course," Bluefingers said. "That is the main purpose of your visit here. The Returned didn't get much of a chance to see you when you first came to us."

Siri shivered, trying to maintain a better posture. "Shouldn't they be paying attention to the priests down there? Instead of studying me, I mean."

"Probably," Bluefingers said, not looking up from his ledger. "In my experience, they rarely do what they're supposed to." He didn't seem particularly reverent toward them.

Siri let the conversation lapse, thinking. Bluefingers had never explained his odd warning the other night. *Things are not what they seem.* "Bluefingers," she said. "About the thing you told me the other night. The—"

He immediately shot her a look—eyes wide and insistent—cutting her off. He turned back to his ledger. The message was obvious. Not right now.

Siri sighed, resisting the urge to slump down. Below, priests of various colors stood on short platforms, debating despite the drizzling rain. She could hear them quite well, yet little of what they said made sense to her—the current debate appeared to have something to do with the way refuse and sewage was handled in the city.

"Bluefingers," she asked. "Are they really gods?"

The scribe hesitated, then finally looked up from his ledger. "Vessel?"

"The Returned. Do you really think that they're divine? That they can see the future?"

"I . . . don't think I'm the right one to ask, Vessel. Let me fetch one of the priests. He can answer your questions. Just give me a—"

"No," Siri said, causing him to stop. "I don't want a priest's opinion—I want the opinion of a regular person, like you. A typical follower."

Bluefingers frowned. "All apologies, Vessel, but I'm *not* a follower of the Returned."

"But you work in the palace."

"And *you* live there, Vessel. Yet neither of us worship the Iridescent Tones. You are from Idris. I am from Pahn Kahl."

"Pahn Kahl is the same as Hallandren."

Bluefingers raised an eyebrow, pursing his lips. "Actually, Vessel, it's quite different."

"But you're ruled by the God King."

"We can accept him as king without worshipping him as our god," Bluefingers said. "That is one of the reasons why I'm a steward in the palace instead of a priest."

His robes, Siri thought. *Maybe that's why he always wears brown.* She turned, glancing down at the priests upon their pedestals in the sand. Each wore a different set of colors, each representing—she assumed—a different one of the Returned. "So what do you think of them?"

"Good people," Bluefingers said, "but misguided. A little like I think of you, Vessel."

She glanced at him. He, however, had already turned back to his ledgers. He wasn't the easiest man with whom to have a conversation. "But how do you explain the God King's radiance?"

"BioChroma," Bluefingers said, still scribbling, not sounding at all annoyed by her questions. He was obviously a man accustomed to dealing with interruption.

"The rest of the Returned don't bend white into colors like he does, do they?"

"No," Bluefingers said, "indeed they do not. They, however, don't hold the wealth of Breaths that he does."

"So he *is* different," Siri said. "Why was he born with more?"

"He wasn't, Vessel. The God King's power does not derive from the inherent BioChroma of being a Returned—in that, he is identical to the others. However, he holds something else. The Light of Peace, they call it. A fancy word for a treasure trove of Breath that numbers somewhere in the tens of thousands."

Tens of thousands? Siri thought. "That much?"

Bluefingers nodded distractedly. "The God Kings are said to be the only ones to ever achieve the Tenth Heightening. *That* is what makes light fracture around him, as well as gives him other abilities. The ability to break Lifeless Commands, for instance, or the ability to Awaken objects without touching them, using only the sound of his voice. These powers are less a function of divinity, and more a simple matter of holding so much Breath."

"But where did he get it?"

"The majority of it was originally gathered by Peacegiver the Blessed," Bluefingers said. "He collected thousands of Breaths during the days of the Manywar. He passed those on to the first Hallandren God King. That inheritance has been transferred from father to son for centuries—and has been enlarged, since each God King is given two Breaths a week, instead of the one that the other Returned receive."

"Oh," Siri said, sitting back, finding herself oddly disappointed by the news. Susebron was not a god, he was simply a man with far more BioChroma than normal.

But . . . what of the Returned themselves? Siri folded her arms again, still troubled. She'd never been forced to look objectively at what she believed. Austre was simply . . . well, God. You didn't question people when they talked about God. The Returned were usurpers, who had cast the followers of Austre out of Hallandren, not true deities themselves.

Yet they were so majestic. Why *had* the royal family been cast out of Hallandren? She knew the official story

taught in Idris—that the royals hadn't supported the con-
flicts that led up to the Manywar. For that, the people had
revolted against them. That revolt had been led by Kalad
the Usurper.

Kalad. Though Siri had avoided most of her tutorial sessions, even she knew the stories of that man. He was the
one who had led the people of Hallandren in the heresy of
building Lifeless. He had created a powerful army of the
creatures, one the likes of which had never been seen in
the land. The stories said Kalad's Lifeless had been more
dangerous, new and distinctive. Terrible and destructive.
He'd eventually been defeated by Peacegiver, who had
then ended the Manywar through diplomacy.

The stories said that Kalad's armies were still out there,
somewhere. Waiting to sweep down and destroy again. She
knew that story was just a legend told by hearthlight, but it
still gave her shivers to consider.

Regardless, Peacegiver had seized control and stopped
the Manywar. However, he had not restored Hallandren to
its rightful rulers. Idris's histories claimed betrayal and
treachery. The monks spoke of heresies that were too
deeply ingrained in Hallandren.

Surely the Hallandren people had their own version of
the story. Watching the Returned in their boxes made Siri
wonder. One fact was obvious: Things in Hallandren were
a whole lot less terrible than she had been taught.

VIVENNA SHIVERED, CRINGING as the people in their
colorful outfits crowded around her.

Things here are worse, even, than my tutors said, she
decided, wriggling in her seat. Parlin seemed to have lost
much of his nervousness about being in such a crowd. He
was focused on the debating priests on the floor of the arena.

She still couldn't decide if she thought the Breath she held
was horrible or wonderful. Gradually, she was coming to

appreciate that it was horrible *because* of how wonderful it felt. The more people that surged around her, the more overwhelmed she felt by her Breath-heightened perception of them. Surely if Parlin only could sense the sheer scope of all those colors, he wouldn't gawk so dumbly at the costumes. Surely if he could *feel* the people, he would feel boxed in as she did, unable to breathe.

That's it, she thought. *I've seen Siri, and I know what they've done with her. It's time to go.* Turning, she stood. And froze.

A man was standing two rows back, and he was staring directly at Vivenna. She normally wouldn't have paid him any attention. He was wearing ragged brown clothing, ripped in places, his loose trousers tied at the waist by a simple rope. His facial hair was halfway between being a beard and just scruff. His hair was unkempt and came down to his shoulders.

And he created a bubble of color around him so bright that he had to be of the Fifth Heightening. He stared at her, meeting her eyes, and she had a sudden and awful panicked sense that he knew exactly who she was.

She stumbled back. The strange man didn't take his eyes off of her. He shifted, pushing back his cloak and exposing a large, black-hilted sword at his belt. Few people in Hallandren wore weapons. This man didn't seem to care. How had he gotten that thing into the court? The people to the sides gave him a wide berth, and Vivenna swore she could sense *something* about that sword. It seemed to darken colors. Deepen them. Make tans into browns, reds into maroons, blues into navies. As if it had its own BioChroma . . .

"Parlin," she said, more sharply than she'd intended. "We're leaving."

"But—"

"Now," Vivenna said, turning and rushing away. Her newfound BioChromatic senses informed her that the man's eyes were still on her. Now that she realized it, she understood

that his eyes on her were probably what had made her so uncomfortable in the first place.

The tutors spoke of this, she thought as she and Parlin made their way to one of the stone exit passages. *Life sense, the ability to tell when there are people nearby, and to tell when they're watching you. Everyone has it to a small degree. BioChroma enhances that.*

As soon as they entered the passage, the sense of being watched vanished, and Vivenna let out a relieved breath.

"I don't see why you wanted to leave," Parlin said.

"We've seen what we needed to," Vivenna said.

"I guess," Parlin said. "I thought you might want to listen to what the priests were saying about Idris."

Vivenna froze. "What?"

Parlin frowned, looking distraught. "I think they might be declaring war. Don't we have a treaty?"

Lord God of Colors! Vivenna thought, turning and scrambling back up into the open arena.

16

". . . STILL SAY THAT we cannot *possibly* justify military action against Idris!" a priest shouted. The man wore blue and gold. It was Stillmark's high priest—Lightsong couldn't quite remember the man's name. Nanrovah?

The argument was not unexpected. Lightsong leaned forward. Nanrovah and his master, Stillmark, were both staunch traditionalists. They tended to argue against pretty much every proposal, but were well respected. Stillmark was nearly as old as Blushweaver, and was considered wise. Lightsong rubbed his chin.

Opposing Nanrovah was Blushweaver's own high priestess, Inhanna. "Oh, come now," the woman said from the sands down below. "Do we really need to have *this* argument again? Idris is nothing more than a rebel enclave set up inside the borders of our own kingdom!"

"They keep to themselves," Nanrovah said. "Holding lands we don't want anyway."

"Lands we don't want?" Blushweaver's priestess said, sputtering. "They hold every single pass to the northern kingdoms! Every workable copper mine! They have military garrisons within striking distance of T'Telir! And they *still* claim to be ruled by the rightful kings of Hallandren!"

Nanrovah fell silent, and there was a surprisingly large rumble of assent from the watching priests. Lightsong eyed them. "You've seeded the group with people sympathetic to your cause?" he asked.

"Of course," Blushweaver said. "So did the others. I just did a better job."

The debate continued, other priests stepping up to argue for and against an assault on Idris. The priests spoke the concerns of the people of the nation; part of their duty was to listen to the people and study issues of national import, then discuss them here so that the gods—who didn't have the opportunity to go out among the people—could be kept informed. If an issue came to a head, the gods would make their judgments. They were divided into subgroups, each having responsibility for a certain area. Some gods were in charge of civic issues; others governed agreements and treaties.

Idris was not a new topic for the assembly. However, Lightsong had never seen the discussion become so explicit and extreme. Sanctions had been discussed. Blockades. Even some military pressure. But war? Nobody had said the word yet, but they all knew what the priests were discussing.

He could not dispel the images from his dreams—visions of death and pain. He did not accept them as prophetic, but he did acknowledge that they must have something to do with the worries inside his subconscious. He feared what war would do to them. Perhaps he was just a coward. It did seem that suppressing Idris would solve so much.

"You're behind this debate, aren't you," he said, turning to Blushweaver.

"Behind it?" Blushweaver said sweetly. "Dear Lightsong, the priests decide the issues to be discussed. Gods don't bother with such mundanity."

"I'm sure," Lightsong said, reclining. "You want my Lifeless Commands."

"I wouldn't say that," Blushweaver said, "I just want you to be informed should you . . ."

She trailed off as Lightsong gave her a flat look.

"Aw, Colors," she swore. "Of *course* I need your Commands, Lightsong. Why else would I go to all the trouble to get you up here? You're a very difficult person to manipulate, you know."

"Nonsense," he said. "You just have to promise me that I won't have to do a thing, and then I'll do anything you want."

"Anything?"

"Anything that doesn't require doing anything."

"That's nothing, then."

"Is it?"

"Yes."

"Well, that's something!"

Blushweaver rolled her eyes.

Lightsong was more troubled than he let on. The arguments for attack had never been so strong. There was proof of a military buildup in Idris and the highlanders had been particularly stingy with the northern passes lately. Beyond that, there was a growing belief that the Returned were weaker than they'd been in previous generations. Not less powerful in BioChroma, just less . . . divine. Less benevolent, less wise. Lightsong happened to agree.

It had been three years since a Returned had given up his or her life to heal someone. The people were growing impatient with their gods. "There's more, isn't there?" he said, glancing at Blushweaver, who was still lounging back, delicately eating cherries. "What aren't they saying?"

"Lightsong, dear," she said. "You were right. Bring you to government proceedings, and it absolutely corrupts you."

"I just don't like secrets," he said. "They make my brain itch, keep me awake at nights. Engaging in politics is like pulling off a bandage—best to get the pain over with quickly."

Blushweaver pursed her lips. "Forced simile, dear."

"Best I can do at the moment, I'm afraid. Nothing dulls the wit more quickly than politics. Now, you were saying . . ."

She snorted. "I've told you already. The focus of all this is that woman."

"The queen," he said, glancing at the God King's box.

"They sent the wrong one," Blushweaver said. "The younger instead of the elder."

"I know," Lightsong said. "Clever of them."

"Clever?" Blushweaver said. "It's downright brilliant. Do you know what a fortune we paid these last twenty years to spy upon, study, and learn about the eldest daughter? Those of us who thought to be careful even studied the second daughter, the one they've made a monk. But the youngest? Nobody gave her half a thought."

And so the Idrians send a random element into court, Lightsong thought. *One that upsets plans and conniving that our politicians have been working on for decades.*

It *was* brilliant.

"Nobody knows *anything* about her," Blushweaver said, frowning deeply. She obviously did not like being taken by surprise. "My spies in Idris insist the girl is of little consequence—which makes me worry that she is even more dangerous than I'd feared."

Lightsong raised an eyebrow. "And you don't think, maybe, that you might be overreacting a tad?"

"Oh?" Blushweaver asked. "And tell me, what would

you do if you wanted to inject an agent into the court? Would you, perhaps, set up a decoy that you could display, drawing attention away from the *real* agent, whom you could train secretly with a clandestine agenda?"

Lightsong rubbed his chin. *She has a point.* Maybe. Living among so many scheming people tended to make one see plots everywhere. However, the plot that Blushweaver suggested had a very serious chance of being dangerous. What better way to get an assassin close to the God King than to send someone to marry him?

No, that wouldn't be it. Killing the God King would just cause Hallandren to go on the rampage. But if they'd sent a woman skilled in the art of manipulation—a woman who could secretly poison the mind of the God King . . .

"We need to be ready to act," Blushweaver said. "I won't sit and let my kingdom be pulled out from under me—I won't idly be cast out as the royals once were. You control a fourth of our Lifeless. That's ten thousand soldiers who don't need to eat, who can march tirelessly. If we convince the other three with Commands to join us . . ."

Lightsong thought for a moment, then nodded and stood.

"What are you doing?" Blushweaver asked, sitting up.

"I think I'll go for a stroll," Lightsong said.

"Where?"

Lightsong glanced over at the queen.

"Oh, blessed Colors," Blushweaver said with a sigh. "Lightsong, do *not* ruin this. We walk a very delicate line, here."

"I'll do my best."

"I don't suppose I can talk you out of interacting with her?"

"My dear," Lightsong said, glancing backward. "I at least have to chat with her. Nothing would be more intolerable than being overthrown by a person with whom I'd never even had a nice conversation."

—∞—

BLUEFINGERS WANDERED OFF sometime during the court proceedings. Siri didn't notice—she was too busy watching the priests debate.

She had to be misunderstanding. Surely they couldn't be thinking about attacking Idris. What would be the point? What would Hallandren gain? As the priests finished their discussion on that topic, Siri turned to one of her serving women. "What was that about?"

The woman glanced down, not answering.

"They sounded like they were discussing war," Siri said. "They wouldn't really invade, would they?"

The woman shuffled uncomfortably, then glanced at one of her companions. That woman rushed away. A few moments later, the servant returned with Treledees. Siri frowned slightly. She did *not* like speaking with the man.

"Yes, Vessel?" the tall man said, eyeing her with his usual air of disdain.

She swallowed, refusing to be intimidated. "The priests," she said. "What were they just discussing?"

"Your homeland of Idris, Vessel."

"I know that much," Siri said. "What do they want with Idris?"

"It seemed to me, Vessel, that they were arguing about whether or not to attack the rebel province and bring it back under proper royal control."

"Rebel province?"

"Yes, Vessel. Your people are in a state of rebellion against the rest of the kingdom."

"But you rebelled against us!"

Treledees raised an eyebrow.

Different viewpoints on history indeed, Siri thought. "I can see how somebody might think as you do," she said. "But . . . you wouldn't really attack us, would you? We sent you a queen, just as you demanded. Because of that, the next God King will have royal blood."

Assuming the current God King ever decides to consummate our marriage. . . .

Treledees simply shrugged. "It is likely nothing, Vessel. The gods simply needed to be apprised of the current political climate of T'Telir."

His words didn't offer Siri much comfort. She shivered. Should she be doing something? Trying to politic in Idris's defense?

"Vessel," Treledees said.

She glanced at him. His peaked hat was so tall it brushed the top of the canopy. In a city full of colors and beauty, for some reason Treledees's long face seemed even bleaker for the contrast. "Yes?" she asked.

"There is a matter of some delicacy I fear that I must discuss with you."

"What is that?"

"You are familiar with monarchies," he said. "Indeed, you are the daughter of a king. I assume that you know how important it is to a government that there be a secure, stable plan for succession."

"I guess."

"Therefore," Treledees said, "you realize that it is of no small importance that an heir be provided as *quickly* as possible."

Siri blushed. "We're working on that."

"With all due respect, Vessel," Treledees said. "There is some degree of disagreement upon whether or not you actually are."

Siri blushed further, hair reddening as she glanced away from those callous eyes.

"Such arguments, of course, are limited to those inside the palace," Treledees said. "You can trust in the discretion of our staff and priests."

"How do you know?" Siri said, looking up. "I mean,

about us. Maybe we *are* . . . working on it. Maybe you'll have your heir before you know it."

Treledees blinked once, slowly, regarding her as if she were a ledger to be added up and accounted. "Vessel," he said. "Do you honestly think that we would take an unfamiliar, foreign woman and place her in close proximity to our most holy of gods without keeping watch?"

Siri felt her breath catch, and she had a moment of horror. *Of course!* she thought. *Of course they were watching. To make sure I didn't hurt the God King, to make certain things went according to plan.*

Being naked before her husband was bad enough. To be so exposed before men like Treledees—men who saw her not as a woman, but as an annoyance—felt even worse, somehow. She found herself slouching, arms wrapping around her chest and its revealing neckline.

"Now," Treledees said, leaning in. "We understand that the God King may not be what you expected. He may even be . . . difficult to work with. You are a woman, however, and should know how to use your charms to motivate."

"How can I 'motivate' if I can't talk to him or look at him?" she snapped.

"I'm sure you'll find a way," Treledees said. "You only have one task in this palace. You want to make certain Idris is protected? Well, give the God King's priesthood what we desire, and your rebels will earn our appreciation. My colleagues and I have no small influence in the court, and we can do much to safeguard your homeland. All we ask is that you perform this single duty. Give us an heir. Give the kingdom stability. Not everything in Hallandren is as . . . cohesive as it may appear to you at first."

Siri remained slouched down, not looking at Treledees.

"I see that you understand," he said. "I feel that . . ." He trailed off, turning to the side. A procession was approaching Siri's box. Its members wore gold and red, and a tall figure at the front caused them to shine with vibrant color.

Treledees frowned, then glanced at her. "We will speak further, if it becomes necessary. Do your duty, Vessel. Or there will be consequences."

With that, the priest withdrew.

———✸———

SHE DIDN'T *LOOK* dangerous. That, more than anything else, made Lightsong inclined to believe Blushweaver's concerns. *I've been in the court for far too long,* he thought to himself as he smiled pleasantly at the queen. *All my life, actually.*

She was a small thing, much younger than he had expected. Barely a woman. She looked intimidated as he nodded to her, waiting while his priests arranged furniture for him. Then he sat, accepting some grapes from the queen's serving women, even though he wasn't hungry.

"Your Majesty," he said. "It is a pleasure to meet you, I'm sure."

The girl hesitated. "You're sure?"

"Figure of speech, my dear," Lightsong said. "A rather redundant one—which is quite appropriate, since *I* am a rather redundant person."

The girl cocked her head. *Colors,* Lightsong thought, remembering that she'd just finished with her period of isolation. *I'm probably the only Returned that she's met besides the God King. What a bad first impression.* Still, there was nothing to be done about it. Lightsong was who he was. Whoever that was.

"I'm pleased to make your acquaintance, Your Grace," the queen said slowly. She turned as a serving woman whispered his name to her. "Lightsong the Brave, Lord of Heroes," she said, smiling at him.

There was a hesitancy about her. Either she had not been trained for formal situations—which Lightsong found difficult to believe, since she'd been raised in a palace—or she was quite a good actress. He frowned inwardly.

The woman's arrival should have put an end to the discussions of war, but instead she had only exacerbated them. He kept his eyes open, for he feared the images of destruction he would see flashing inside his mind's eye if he so much as blinked. They waited like Kalad's Phantoms, hovering just beyond his vision.

He couldn't accept those dreams as foretellings. If he did, it meant that he *was* a god. And if that were the case, then he feared greatly for them all.

On the outside, he simply gave the queen his third most charming smile and popped a grape into his mouth. "No need to be so formal, Your Majesty. You will soon realize that among the Returned, I am by far the least. If cows could Return, they'd undoubtedly be ranked higher than I."

She wavered again, obviously uncertain how to deal with him. It was a common reaction. "Might I inquire as to the nature of your visitation?" she asked.

Too formal. Not at ease. Uncomfortable around those of high rank. Could it be possible that she *was* genuine? No. It was likely an act to put him at ease. To make him underestimate her. Or was he just thinking too much?

Colors take you, Blushweaver! he thought. *I really don't want to be part of this.*

He almost withdrew. But, then, that wouldn't be very pleasant of him—and contrary to some of the things he said, Lightsong *did* like being pleasant. *Best to be kind,* he thought, smiling idly to himself. *That way, if she ever does take over the kingdom, perhaps she'll behead me last.* "You ask after the nature of my visitation?" he said. "I believe it has no nature, Your Majesty, other than to appear natural—at which I have already failed by staring at you for far too long while thinking to myself about your place in this mess."

The queen frowned again.

Lightsong popped a grape in his mouth. "Wonderful things," he said, holding up another one. "Delightfully sweet, wrapped in their own little package. Deceptive, really. So hard and dry on the outside, but so delectable on the inside. Don't you think?"

"We . . . don't have many grapes in Idris, Your Grace."

"I'm rather the opposite, you know," he said. "Fluffy and pretty on the outside, without much of import on the inside. But I guess that is beside the point. You, my dear, are a very welcome sight. Much more so than a grape."

"I . . . How is that, Your Grace?"

"We haven't had a queen in such a long time," Lightsong said. "Since before my Return, in fact. And old Susebron up there really *has* been moping about the palace lately. Looking forlorn. It's good he has a woman in his life."

"Thank you for the compliment, Your Grace," the queen said.

"You're welcome. I'll make up a few more, if you like."

She fell silent.

Well, then, that's it, he thought, sighing. *Blushweaver was right. I probably shouldn't have come.*

"All right," the queen said, hair suddenly turning red as she threw her hands up in the air. "*What* is going on here?"

He hesitated. "Your Majesty?"

"Are you making fun of me?"

"Probably."

"But you're supposed to be a god!" she said, leaning back, staring up at the canopy. "Just when I thought things in this city were starting to make sense, the priests start yelling at me, then you come along! What am I supposed to do with you? You seem more like a schoolboy than a god!"

Lightsong paused, then settled back into his seat, smiling. "You have me found out," he said, opening his hands. "I killed the real god and took his place. I've come to hold you ransom for your sweets."

"There," the queen said, pointing. "Aren't you supposed to be . . . I don't know, distinguished or something?"

He spread his hands out. "My dear, this *is* what passes for being distinguished in Hallandren."

She didn't seem convinced.

"I am, of course, lying through my teeth," he said, eating another grape. "You shouldn't base your opinion of the others upon what you think of me. They're all much more deific than I am."

The queen sat back. "I thought you were the god of bravery."

"Technically."

"You seem more like the god of jesters to me."

"I've applied for the position and been turned down," he said. "You should see the person they have doing the job. Dull as a rock and twice as ugly."

Siri hesitated.

"I wasn't lying that time," Lightsong said. "Mirthgiver, god of laughter. If ever there was a god more poorly suited to his position than I, it's he."

"I don't understand you," she said. "It appears there's a *lot* I don't understand in this city."

This woman is no fake, Lightsong thought, staring into her youthful, confused eyes. *Or, if she is, then she's the best actress I've ever met.*

That meant something. Something important. It was possible there were mundane reasons why this girl had been sent instead of her sister. Sickness on the part of the elder daughter, perhaps. But Lightsong didn't buy that. She was part of something. A plot, or perhaps several. And whatever those plots were, *she* didn't know about them.

Kalad's Phantoms! Lightsong cursed mentally. *This child is going to get ripped apart and fed to the wolves!*

But what could he really do about it? He sighed, standing, causing his priests to begin packing his things. The girl watched with confusion as he nodded to her, giving her a wan smile of farewell. She stood and curtsied slightly, though she probably didn't need to. She was his queen, even if she wasn't herself Returned.

Lightsong turned to go, then stopped, recalling his own

first few months in the court, and the confusion he'd known. He reached over, laying a gentle hand on her shoulder. "Don't let them get to you, child," he whispered.

And with that, he withdrew.

17

VIVENNA WALKED BACK toward Lemex's house, dissecting the argument she'd heard at the Court of Gods. Her tutors had instructed her that discussions in the Court Assembly didn't always lead to action; just because they talked of war didn't mean it would happen.

This discussion, however, seemed to mean more. It was too passionate, with too many voices for one side. It indicated that her father was right, and that war was inevitable.

She walked with her head down on a nearly deserted street. She was beginning to learn that she could avoid the roiling masses by walking through more residential sections of the city. It appeared that people in T'Telir liked to be where everybody else was.

The street was in a wealthy neighborhood and had a slate stone sidewalk running along the side of it. It made for pleasant walking. Parlin walked beside her, occasionally pausing to study ferns or palm trees. The Hallandren liked plants; most of the homes were shaded by trees, vines, and exotic blooming shrubs. In Idris, each of the large homes along the street would have been considered a mansion, but here they were only of average size—probably the homes of merchants.

I need to stay focused, she thought. *Is Hallandren going to attack soon? Or is this just a prelude to something still months, perhaps years, away?*

Real action wouldn't occur until the gods voted, and Vivenna wasn't sure what it would take to get them to that point. She shook her head. Only one day in T'Telir, and already she knew that her training and tutorials hadn't prepared her half as well as she'd assumed.

She felt as if she knew nothing. And that left her feeling very lost. She was not the confident, competent woman she'd assumed herself to be. The frightening truth was, should she have been sent to become the God King's bride, she would have been nearly as ineffective and confused as poor Siri undoubtedly was.

They turned a corner, Vivenna trusting in Parlin's amazing sense of direction to get them back to Lemex's house, and they passed under the gaze of one of the silent D'Denir statues. The proud warrior stood with sword raised above his stone head, his armor—carved into the statue—augmented by a red scarf tied and flapping around his neck. He looked dramatic, as if he were going gloriously to war. It wasn't long before they approached the steps to Lemex's house. Vivenna froze, however, when she saw that the door was hanging from one hinge. The lower part was cracked, as if it had been kicked very hard.

Parlin pulled up beside her, then hissed, holding up a hand for her to be silent. His hand went to the long hunting knife at his belt and he glanced around. Vivenna stepped back, nerves itching to flee. And yet, where would she go? The mercenaries were her only connection in the city. Denth and Tonk Fah could have handled an attack, right?

Someone approached from the other side of the door. Her BioChromatic senses warned her of the proximity. She laid a hand on Parlin's arm, preparing to bolt.

Denth pushed the broken door open, sticking his head out. "Oh," he said. "It's you."

"What happened?" she asked. "Were you attacked?"

Denth glanced at the door and chuckled to himself. "Nah," he said, pushing the door open and waving her in.

Through the broken door she could see that furniture had been ripped apart, there were holes in the walls, and pictures were slashed and broken. Denth wandered back inside, kicking aside some stuffing from a cushion, making his way toward the stairs. Several of the steps had been broken.

He glanced back, noting her confusion. "Well, we *did* say we were going to search the house, Princess. Figured we might as well do a good job of it."

VIVENNA SAT DOWN very carefully, half-expecting the chair to collapse beneath her. Tonk Fah and Denth had been *very* thorough in their search—they had broken every bit of wood in the house, it seemed, including chair legs. Fortunately, her current chair had been propped up reasonably well, and it held her weight.

The desk in front of her—Lemex's desk—was splintered. The drawers had been removed, and a false back had been revealed, the compartment emptied. A group of papers and several bags sat on the desktop.

"That's everything," Denth said, leaning against the room's doorframe. Tonk Fah lounged on a broken couch, its stuffing sticking out awkwardly.

"Did you have to break so much?" Vivenna asked.

"Had to be certain," Denth said, shrugging. "You'd be surprised where people hide things."

"Inside the front door?" Vivenna asked flatly.

"Would *you* have thought to look there?"

"Of course not."

"Sounds like a pretty good hiding place to me, then. We knocked, and thought we found a hollow space. Just turned out to be a section of different wood, but it was important to check."

"People get really clever when it comes to hiding important stuff," Tonk Fah said with a yawn.

"You know the thing I hate most about being a mercenary?" Denth asked, holding up a hand.

Vivenna raised an eyebrow.

"Splinters," he said, wiggling several red fingers.

"No hazard pay for those," Tonk Fah added.

"Oh, now you're just being silly," Vivenna said, sorting through the items on the table. One of the bags clinked suggestively. Vivenna undid the drawstring and pulled open the top.

Gold glistened inside. A lot of it.

"Little over five thousand marks in there," Denth said lazily. "Lemex had it stashed all over the house. Found one bar of it in the leg of your chair."

"Got easier when we discovered the paper he'd used to remind himself of where he hid it all," Tonk Fah noted.

"*Five thousand marks?*" Vivenna said, feeling her hair lighten slightly in shock.

"Seems like old Lemex was storing up quite the little nest egg," Denth said, chuckling. "That, mixed with the amount of Breath he held . . . he must have extorted even more from Idris than I assumed."

Vivenna stared at the bag. Then, she looked up at Denth. "You . . . gave it to me," she said. "You could have taken it and spent it!"

"Actually, we did," Denth said. "Took about ten bits for lunch. Should be here any minute."

Vivenna met his eyes.

"Now there's what I'm talking about, eh, Tonks?" Denth said, glancing down at the larger man. "If I'd been, say, a butler, would she be looking at me like that? Just because I didn't take the money and run? Why does everyone expect a mercenary to rob them?"

Tonk Fah grunted, stretching again.

"Look through those papers, Princess," Denth said, kicking Tonk Fah's couch, then nodding toward the door. "We'll wait for you downstairs."

Vivenna watched them retreat, Tonk Fah grumbling as he had to rise, bits of stuffing sticking to the back of his clothing. They thumped their way down the stairs, and soon she heard dishes rattling. They'd likely sent one of the street boys—who passed periodically yelling that they would bring food from a local restaurant—for the meal.

Vivenna didn't move. She was increasingly uncertain of her purpose in the city. Yet she still had Denth and Tonk Fah, and—surprisingly—she was finding herself growing attached to them. How many soldiers in her father's army—good men, all of them—would have been able to resist running off with five thousand marks? There was more to these mercenaries than they let on.

She turned her attention to the books, letters, and papers on the desk.

———◦⊱⊰◦———

SEVERAL HOURS LATER, Vivenna still sat alone, a solitary candle burning and dripping wax onto the splintered desk corner. She had long since stopped reading. A plate of food sat uneaten by the door, brought by Parlin some time before.

Letters lay spread out on the desk before her. It had taken time to put them in order. Most were penned in her father's familiar hand. Not the hand of her father's scribe. Her father's *own* hand. That had been her first clue. He only wrote his most personal, or most secret, communications on his own.

Vivenna kept her hair under control. She deliberately breathed in and out. She didn't look out the darkened window at the lights of a city that should have been asleep. She simply sat.

Numb.

The final letter—the last before Lemex's death—sat on top of the pile. It was only a few weeks old.

My friend, her father's script read.

*Our conversations have worried me more than I care to
admit. I have spoken with Yarda at length. We can see no
solution.*

*War is coming. We all know that now. The continued—
and increasingly vigorous—arguments in the Court of
Gods show a disturbing trend. The money we sent to buy
you enough Breath to attend those meetings is some of the
best I have ever spent.*

*All signs point to the inevitability of Hallandren Lifeless
marching to our mountains. Therefore, I give you leave to
do as we have discussed. Any disruptions you can cause in
the city—any delays you can earn us—will be extremely
valuable. The additional funds you requested should have
arrived by now.*

*My friend, I must admit a weakness in myself. I will never
be able to send Vivenna to be a hostage in that dragon's
nest of a city. To send her would be to kill her, and I cannot
do that. Even though I know it would be best for Idris if
I did.*

*I'm not yet sure what I will do. I will not send her, for I
love her too much. However, breaking the treaty would
bring the Hallandren wrath against my people even more
quickly. I fear I may have to make a very difficult decision
in the days to come.*

But that is the essence of a king's duty.

Until we correspond again,

Dedelin, your liege and your friend.

Vivenna looked away from the letter. The room was too
perfectly silent. She wanted to scream at the letter and her
father, who was now so far away. And yet, she could not.
She had been trained for better. Tantrums were useless
displays of arrogance.

Don't draw attention to yourself. Don't set yourself above
others. He who makes himself high will be cast down
low. But what of the man who murders one of his daughters
to save the other? What of the man who claims—to your

face—that the switch was for other reasons? That it was for the good of Idris? That it wasn't about favoritism at all?

What of the king who betrayed the highest tenets of his religion by purchasing Breath for one of his spies?

Vivenna blinked at a tear in her eye, then gritted her teeth, angry at herself and the world. Her father was supposed to be a good man. The perfect king. Wise and knowing, always sure of himself and always right.

The man she saw in these letters was far more human. Why should she be so shocked to learn that?

It doesn't matter, she told herself. *None of that matters.* Factions in the Hallandren government were rallying the nation for war. Reading her father's candid words, she finally believed him completely. Hallandren troops would likely march on her homeland before the year was out. And then, the Hallandren—so colorful yet so deceptive—would hold Siri hostage and threaten to kill her unless Dedelin surrendered.

Her father would not give up his kingdom. Siri would be executed.

And that *is what I'm here to stop,* Vivenna thought. Her hands grew tighter, gripping the edges of the desktop, jaw set. She brushed away the traitorous tear. She had been trained to be strong even when surrounded by an unfamiliar city and its people. She had work to do.

She rose, leaving the letters on the table with the bag of coins and Lemex's journal. She made her way down the stairs, avoiding the broken steps, to where the mercenaries were teaching Parlin how to play a game with wooden cards. The three men looked up as Vivenna approached. She settled herself carefully on the floor, sitting with her legs beneath her in an unassuming posture.

She met their eyes as she spoke. "I know where some of Lemex's money came from," she said. "Idris and Hallandren will soon go to war. Because of this threat, my father gave much greater resources to Lemex than I'd realized.

He sent enough money for Lemex to buy fifty Breaths, allowing him to enter the court and report on its proceedings. Obviously, my father didn't know that Lemex already *had* a sizable amount of Breath."

The three men were silent. Tonk Fah shot a glance at Denth, who sat back, resting against an overturned, broken chair.

"I believe that Lemex was still loyal to Idris," she said. "His personal writings make that relatively clear. He was not a traitor; he was simply greedy. He wanted as much Breath as possible because he had heard that it extended a person's life. Lemex and my father had planned to hinder the war preparations from inside Hallandren. Lemex promised he would find a way to sabotage the Lifeless armies, damage the city's supplies, and generally undermine their ability to wage war. For him to accomplish this, my father sent him a large sum of money."

"About five thousand marks' worth?" Denth asked, rubbing his chin.

"Less than that," Vivenna said. "But a large chunk nonetheless. I believe that you are right about Lemex, Denth—he has been stealing from the Crown for some time."

She fell silent. Parlin looked confused. That wasn't uncommon. The mercenaries, however, didn't look surprised.

"I don't know if Lemex intended to do as my father asked," Vivenna said, keeping her voice even. "The way he hid the money, some of the things he wrote . . . well, maybe he was finally planning to turn traitor and run. We can't know what he would eventually have decided. We do, however, have a vague list of things he planned to accomplish. Those plans were convincing enough to persuade my father, and the urgency of his letters has convinced me. We are going to continue Lemex's work and undermine Hallandren's ability to wage war."

The room fell silent. "And . . . your sister?" Parlin finally asked.

"We will get her out," Vivenna said firmly. "Her rescue and safety is our first priority."

"That is all easier discussed than accomplished, Princess," Denth said.

"I know."

The mercenaries shared a look. "Well," Denth finally said, standing up. "Better get back to work, then." He nodded at Tonk Fah, who sighed and grumbled, standing.

"Wait," Vivenna said, frowning. "What?"

"I figured once you saw those papers that you'd want to continue," Denth said, stretching. "Now that I've seen what he was up to, I can piece together why he had us do some of the things we were involved in. One of those was to contact and support some rebellious factions here in the city, including one that was stamped out just a few weeks back. Cult of disaffection centered on a guy named Vahr."

"Always wondered why Lemex gave him support," Tonk Fah said.

"That faction's dead," Denth said, "along with Vahr himself. But a lot of his followers are still around. Waiting for trouble to come their way. We can contact them. There are a few other leads I think we can look into, things Lemex didn't explain completely, but which I might be able to figure out."

"And . . . you can handle something like this?" Vivenna asked. "You just said it wouldn't be easy."

Denth shrugged. "Won't be. But if you haven't realized it yet, this kind of thing is why Lemex hired us. A team of three high-priced, specialist mercenaries isn't exactly the type of thing you keep around to serve your tea."

"Unless you want the tea rammed up someplace uncomfortable," Tonk Fah noted.

Three mercenaries? Vivenna thought. *That's right. There's another one. A woman.* "Where's the other member of your team?"

"Jewels?" Denth asked. "You'll meet her soon enough."

worked in the past. Or had it? Her father had been perpetually angry at her, and Vivenna had always treated her like a child. The city's people had loved her, but sufferingly.

No, Siri thought suddenly. *No, I can't go back to that. The people in this palace—this court—they aren't the types you can defy just because you're annoyed.* Spurn the palace priests, and they wouldn't grumble at her like her father had. They'd show her what it really meant to be in their power.

But what to do then? She couldn't keep throwing off her clothing and kneeling on the floor, naked, could she?

Feeling confused, and a little angry at herself, she stepped into the dark room and pulled the door closed. The God King waited in his corner, shadowed as always. Siri looked at him, staring at that too-calm face. She knew that she should disrobe and kneel, but she didn't.

Not because she felt defiant. Not even because she felt angry or petulant. Because she was tired of wondering. Who was this man who could rule gods and bend light with the force of his BioChroma? Was he really just spoiled and indolent?

He stared back at her. As before, he didn't grow angry at her insolence. Watching him, Siri pulled at the strings on her dress, dropping the bulky garment to the floor. She reached for the shoulders of her shift, but hesitated.

No, she thought. *This isn't right either.*

She glanced down at the shift; the edges of the white garment fuzzed, the white bending into color. She looked up at the God King's impassive face.

Then—gritting her teeth against her nervousness—Siri took a step forward.

He tensed. She could see it in the edges of his eyes and round his lips. She took another step forward, the white her garment bending further into prismatic colors. The od King didn't do anything. He just watched as she drew oser and closer.

"Unfortunately," Tonk Fah said under his breath.

Denth elbowed his friend. "For now, let us go back out and see how things stand on our projects. Gather what you want from this house. We'll move out tomorrow."

"Move out?" Vivenna said.

"Unless you want to sleep on a mattress Tonk Fah ripped into five pieces," Denth noted. "He has a thing about mattresses."

"And chairs," Tonk Fah said cheerfully, "and tables, and doors, and walls, actually. Oh, and people."

"Either way, Princess," Denth said, "this building was well known to people who worked with Lemex. As you've discovered, he wasn't exactly the most honest fellow around. I doubt you want the baggage that comes with being associated with him."

"Best to move to another house," Tonk Fah agreed.

"We'll try not to break up the next one quite so badly," Denth said.

"No promises though," Tonk Fah said with a wink.

And then the two left.

18

SIRI STOOD BEFORE the door to her husband's bedchamber, shuffling nervously. As usual, Bluefingers stood beside her, and he was the only other one in the hallway. He scribbled on his pad, giving no indication of how he always knew when it was time for her to enter.

For once, she didn't mind the delay, nervous though she was. It gave her more time to think about what she was going to do. The day's events still buzzed about in her head: Treledees, telling her that she needed to provide an heir.

Lightsong the Bold, talking in circles, then leaving her with what had seemed like a heartfelt farewell. Her king and husband, sitting on his tower above, bending light around him. The priests below, arguing about whether or not to invade her homeland.

A lot of people wanted to push her in different directions, yet none of them were really willing to tell her how to do what they wanted—and some didn't even bother to tell her *what* they wanted. The only thing they were accomplishing was annoying her. She was not a seductress. She had no idea how to make the God King desire her—particularly since she was terrified of him doing just that.

High Priest Treledees had given her a command. Therefore, she intended to show him how she responded to commands, particularly when they had threats attached to them. Tonight, she would go into the king's bedchamber, sit down on the floor, and refuse to strip. She'd confront the God King. He didn't want her. Well, she was tired of being ogled every night.

She intended to explain all this to him in no uncertain terms. If he wanted to see her naked again, he'd have to order servants to strip her. She doubted that he'd do that. He'd made no move toward her, and when he presided over the arena debates, he'd actually done no more than sit and watch. She was getting a new impression of this God King. He was a man with so much power, he had grown lazy. He was a man who had everything, and so he bothered with nothing. He was a man who expected others to do everything for him. People like him annoyed her. She was reminded of a guard captain in Idris who had insisted on making his men work hard, while he spent his afternoons playing cards.

It was time the God King was defied. More than that, it was time that his priests learned that they couldn't bully her. She was tired of being used. Tonight, she would react. That was her decision. And it made her nervous as all Colors.

She glanced at Bluefingers. Eventually, she caught his

eye. "Do they really watch me each night?" she asked, leaning in and whispering.

He paused, paling slightly. He glanced to either side, then shook his head.

She frowned. *But Treledees knew that I hadn't been bedded by the God King.*

Bluefingers raised a finger, pointing to his eyes, then shook his head. Then he pointed to his ears and nodded. He pointed to a doorway down the hall.

They listen, Siri thought.

Bluefingers leaned in closer. "They would never watch, Vessel," he whispered. "Remember, the God King is their holiest of deities. Seeing him nude, watching him with his wife . . . no, they wouldn't dare. However, they aren't above *listening.*"

She nodded. "They are very concerned about an heir."

Bluefingers glanced about nervously.

"Am I really in danger from them?" she asked.

He met her eyes, then nodded sharply. "More danger than you know, Vessel." Then he backed away, gesturing a the doorway.

You have to help me! she mouthed at him.

He shook his head, holding up his hands. *I cannot. now.* With that, he pushed open the door, bowed, and s tled away, glancing nervously over his shoulder.

Siri glared at him. The time was swiftly approac when she'd need to corner him and find out what he knew. Until then, she had other people to annoy. She t and glanced into the dark room. Her nervousness ret

Is this wise? Being belligerent had never both before. And yet . . . her life wasn't like it had been Bluefingers's fear had left her even more on edge.

Defiance. It had always been her way to get She hadn't been obstinate out of spite. She'd sin unable to measure up to Vivenna, so she'd just opposite of what was expected of her. Her de

She stopped right in front of him. Then she turned from him and climbed up onto the bed, feeling the deep softness beneath her as she crawled to the middle of its mattress. She sat up on her knees, regarding the black marble wall with its obsidian sheen. The God King's priests waited just beyond, listening carefully to hear things that were really none of their business.

This, she thought, taking a deep breath, *is going to be exceptionally embarrassing.* But she'd been forced to lie prostrate, naked, before the God King for over a week. Was now really the time to start feeling self-conscious?

She began to bounce up and down on the bed, making its springs creak. Then, cringing slightly, she started to moan.

She hoped it was convincing. She didn't really know what it was supposed to sound like. And how long did it usually continue? She tried to make her moans get louder and louder, her bouncing more furious, for what she assumed was a proper amount of time. Then she stopped sharply, let out a final moan, and fell back onto the bed.

All was still. She glanced up, eyeing the God King. Some of his emotional mask had softened, and he displayed a very human look of confusion. She almost laughed out loud at how perplexed he seemed. She just met his eyes and shook her head. Then—her heart beating, her skin a bit sweaty—she lay back on the bed to rest.

Tired from the day's events and intrigues, it wasn't long after that she found herself rolled up in the luxurious comforter and relaxing. The God King left her alone. In fact, he'd grown tense at her approach, almost as if he were worried. Even frightened of her.

That couldn't be. He was the God and King of Hallandren, and she was just a silly girl, swimming in waters that were far over her head. No, he wasn't frightened. The concept was enough to again make her feel like laughing. She restrained herself, maintaining the illusion for the listening priests as she drifted off in the luxurious comfort of the bed.

⟨⟨⟨∞⟩⟩⟩

THE NEXT MORNING, Lightsong did not get out of bed.

His servants stood around the perimeter of his room like a flock of birds waiting for seed. As noon approached, they began to shuffle uncomfortably, shooting glances at one another.

He remained in bed, staring up at the ornate red canopy. Some servants approached tentatively, placing a tray of food atop a small table beside him. Lightsong did not reach for it.

He had dreamed of war again.

Finally, a figure walked up to the bed. Large of girth and draped in his priestly robes, Llarimar looked down at his god, betraying none of the annoyance that Lightsong was sure that he felt. "Leave us, please," Llarimar said to the servants.

They hesitated, uncertain. When was a god without his servants?

"Please," Llarimar repeated, though somehow his tone indicated that it was not a request. Slowly, the servants filed from the room. Llarimar moved the tray of food, then sat down on the edge of the low table. He studied Lightsong, expression thoughtful.

What did I ever do to earn a priest like him? Lightsong thought. He knew many of the high priests of other Returned, and most of them were various levels of insufferable. Some were quick to anger, others quick to point out fault, and still others were so fulsomely effusive toward their gods that it was downright maddening. Treledees, the God King's own high priest, was so stuck-up that he made even *gods* feel inferior.

And then there was Llarimar. Patient, understanding. He deserved a better god.

"All right, Your Grace," Llarimar said. "What is it this time?"

"I'm sick," Lightsong said.

"You can't get sick, Your Grace."

Lightsong gave a few weak coughs, to which Llarimar just rolled his eyes.

"Oh come on, Scoot," Lightsong said. "Can't you just play along a little?"

"Play along that you are sick?" Llarimar asked, showing a hint of amusement. "Your Grace, to do that would be to pretend that you're not a god. I do not believe that's a good precedent for your high priest to set."

"It's the truth," Lightsong whispered. "I'm no god."

Again, there was no sign of annoyance or anger from Llarimar. He just leaned down. "Please don't say such things, Your Grace. Even if you yourself do not believe, you should not say so."

"Why not?"

"For the sake of the many who *do* believe."

"And I should continue to deceive them?"

Llarimar shook his head. "It is no deception. It's not so uncommon for others to have more faith in someone than he has in himself."

"And that doesn't strike you as a little odd in my case?"

Llarimar smiled. "Not knowing your temperament, it doesn't. Now, what brought this on?"

Lightsong turned, looking up at the ceiling again. "Blushweaver wants my Commands for the Lifeless."

"Yes."

"She'll destroy that new queen of ours," Lightsong said. "Blushweaver worries that the Idrian royals are making a play for the Hallandren throne."

"Do you disagree?"

Lightsong shook his head. "No. They probably are. But the thing is, I don't think the girl—the queen—knows that she's part of anything. I'm worried that Blushweaver will crush the child out of fear. I'm worried that she'll be too aggressive and get us all into a war, when I don't know yet if that's the right thing to do."

"It seems that you already have a good handle on all this, Your Grace," Llarimar said.

"I don't want to be part of it, Scoot," Lightsong said. "I feel myself getting sucked in."

"It is your duty to be involved so that you can lead your kingdom. You can't avoid politics."

"I can if I don't get out of bed."

Llarimar raised an eyebrow. "You don't honestly believe that, do you, Your Grace?"

Lightsong sighed. "You're not going to give me a lecture about how even my inaction has political effects, are you?"

Llarimar hesitated. "Perhaps. Like it or not, you are a part of the workings of this kingdom—and you produce effects even if you stay in bed. If you do nothing, then the problems are as much your fault as if you had instigated them."

"No," Lightsong said. "No, I think you're wrong. If I don't do anything, then at least I can't ruin things. Sure, I can *let* them go wrong, but that's not the same thing. It really isn't, no matter what people say."

"And if, by acting, you could make things better?"

Lightsong shook his head. "Not going to happen. You know me better than that."

"I do, Your Grace," Llarimar said. "I know you better, perhaps, than you think I do. You've always been one of the best men I have known."

Lightsong rolled his eyes, but then stopped, noting the expression on Llarimar's face.

Best men I have known . . .

Lightsong sat up. "You knew me!" he accused. "*That's* why you chose to be my priest. You did know me before! Before I died!"

Llarimar said nothing.

"Who was I?" Lightsong asked. "A good man, you claim. What was it about me that made me a good man?"

"I can say nothing, Your Grace."

"You've already said something," Lightsong said, raising a finger. "You might as well go on. No turning back."

"I've said too much already."

"Come on," Lightsong said. "Just a little bit. Was I from T'Telir, then? How did I die?" *Who is she, the woman I see in my dreams?*

Llarimar said nothing further.

"I could command you to speak . . ."

"No you couldn't," Llarimar said, smiling as he stood up. "It's like the rain, Your Grace. You can *say* you want to command the weather to change, but you don't believe it, deep down. It doesn't obey, and neither would I."

Convenient bit of theology, that, Lightsong thought. *Particularly when you want to hide things from your gods.*

Llarimar turned to go. "You have paintings waiting to be judged, Your Grace. I suggest that you let your servants bathe and dress you so that you can get through the day's work."

Lightsong sighed, stretching. *How exactly did he just do that to me?* he thought. Llarimar hadn't even really revealed anything, yet Lightsong had overcome his bout of melancholy. He eyed Llarimar as the priest reached the door and waved for the servants to return. Perhaps dealing with sullen deities was part of his job description.

But . . . he knew me before, Lightsong thought. *And now he's my priest. How did that happen?* "Scoot," Lightsong said, drawing the priest's attention. Llarimar turned, guarded, obviously expecting Lightsong to pry further into his past.

"What should I do?" Lightsong asked. "About Blushweaver and the queen?"

"I cannot tell you, Your Grace," Llarimar said. "You see, it is from what *you* do that we learn. If I guide you, then we gain nothing."

"Except perhaps the life of a young girl who is being used as a pawn."

Llarimar paused. "Do your best, Your Grace," he said. "That is all I can suggest."

Great, Lightsong thought as he stood. He didn't know what his "best" was.

The truth was, he'd never bothered to find out.

19

"THIS IS NICE," Denth said, looking over the house. "Strong wood paneling. Will break very cleanly."

"Yeah," Tonk Fah added, peeking into a closet. "And it has plenty of storage. Bet we could fit a good half-dozen bodies in here alone."

Vivenna shot the two mercenaries a look, causing them to chuckle to themselves. The house wasn't as nice as Lemex's had been; she didn't want to be ostentatious. It was one of many that were built in a row along a well-maintained street. Deeper than it was wide, the building was bordered on either side with large palm trees, obscuring the view should someone try to spy from the neighboring buildings.

She was pleased. Part of her balked at living in a home that was—despite being modest by Hallandren standards— nearly as large as the king's palace back in Idris. However, she and Parlin had looked at and rejected cheaper sections of town. She didn't want to live in a place where she was afraid to go out at night, particularly since she worried that her Breath might make her a target.

She trailed down the stairs, the mercenaries following. The house had three stories—a small upper story with sleeping chambers, the main floor with a kitchen and sitting room, and a cellar for storage. The building was sparsely furnished, and Parlin had gone to the market to shop for more. She hadn't wanted to spend the money, but Denth had pointed out that they must at least *try* to keep up appearances, lest they end up drawing even more attention.

"Old Lemex's house will be taken care of soon," Denth said. "We left some hints in the underground, mentioning that the old man was dead. Whatever we didn't ransack, a gang of burglars will take care of tonight. By tomorrow, the city guard will be there, and they'll assume that the place was burgled. The nurse has been paid off, and she never knew who Lemex really was anyway. When nobody comes to pay for the funeral services, the authorities will take the house in forfeit and have the body burned with other debtors."

Vivenna stopped at the bottom of the stairs, paling. "That doesn't sound very respectful."

Denth shrugged. "What do you want to do? Go claim him at the charnel house yourself? Give him an Idrian ceremony?"

"Good way to get people asking questions, that," Tonk Fah said.

"Better to just let others deal with it," Denth said.

"I suppose," Vivenna said, turning away from the stairs and walking into the sitting room. "It just bothers me, letting his body be cared for by . . ."

"By what?" Denth said, amused. "Pagans?"

Vivenna didn't look at him.

"The old man didn't seem to care much about heathen ways," Tonk Fah noted. "Not with the number of Breaths he held. Of course, didn't your daddy give him the money to buy them?"

Vivenna closed her eyes.

You hold those same Breaths, she told herself. *You're not innocent in all of this.*

She hadn't been given a choice. She could only hope and

assume that her father had felt he was in a similar position—no choice but to do what seemed wrong.

Lacking furniture, Vivenna arranged her dress and knelt on the wooden floor, hands in her lap. Denth and Tonk Fah sat back against the wall, looking just as comfortable sitting on a hardwood floor as they were when lounging in plush chairs. "All right, Princess," Denth said, unfolding a paper from his pocket. "We've got some plans for you."

"Please continue, then."

"First," Denth said, "we can get you a meeting with some of Vahr's allies."

"Who exactly was this man?" Vivenna said, frowning. She didn't like the idea of working with revolutionaries.

"Vahr was a worker in the dye fields," Denth said. "Things can get bad out in those fields—long hours, little more than food for pay. About five years back, Vahr got the bright idea that if he could convince enough of the other workers to give him their Breath, he might be able to use the power to start a revolt against the overseers. Became enough of a hero to the people in the outer flower plantations that he actually drew the attention of the Court of Gods."

"Never truly had a chance of starting a real rebellion," Tonk Fah said.

"So what good are his men to us?" Vivenna asked. "If they never had a chance of succeeding."

"Well," Denth said, "you didn't say anything about a rebellion or anything like that. You just want to make it tough for the Hallandren when they go to war."

"Revolts in the fields would sure be a pain during war," Tonk Fah added.

Vivenna nodded. "All right," she said. "Let's meet with them."

"Just so you know, Princess," Denth said. "These aren't particularly . . . sophisticated kinds of folks."

"I am not offended by poverty or people of small means. Austre regards all people equally."

"I didn't mean that," Denth said, rubbing his chin. "It's not that they're peasants, it's that . . . well, when Vahr's little insurrection went bad, these are the people who were smart enough to get out quickly. That means they weren't all that committed to him in the first place."

"In other words," Tonk Fah said, "they were really just a bunch of thugs and crime lords who thought Vahr might be the source of some easy influence or money."

Great, Vivenna thought. "And do we want to associate with people like that?"

Denth shrugged. "We have to start somewhere."

"The other things on the list are a bit more fun," Tonk Fah said.

"And they are?" Vivenna asked.

"Raid the Lifeless storage warehouse, for one," Denth said, smiling. "We won't be able to kill the things—not without drawing the rest of them down on us. But we might be able to muck up the way the creatures work."

"That sounds dangerous," Vivenna said.

Denth glanced at Tonk Fah, who opened his eyes. They shared a smile.

"What?" Vivenna asked.

"Hazard pay," Tonk Fah said. "We may not steal your money, but we have nothing against overcharging you for extremely dangerous stunts!"

Vivenna rolled her eyes.

"Beyond that," Denth added, "from what I can tell, Lemex wanted to undermine the city's food supply. It's a good idea, I suppose. Lifeless don't need to eat, but the humans who form the support structure of the army *do*. Disrupt supply, and perhaps people here will begin to worry if they can afford a long-term war."

"That sounds more reasonable," Vivenna said. "What did you come up with?"

"We raid merchant caravans," Denth said. "Burn things up, cost them a bunch. We make it look like bandits or maybe even remnants of Vahr's supporters. That ought to confuse people in T'Telir and maybe make it more difficult for the priests to go to war."

"Priests run a lot of the trade in the city," Tonk Fah added. "They have all the money so they tend to own the supplies. Burn away the stuff they intended to use for the war, and they'll be more hesitant to attack. It'll buy your people more time."

Vivenna swallowed. "Your plans are a bit more . . . violent than I had anticipated."

The mercenaries shared a look.

"You see," Denth said. "This is where we get our bad reputation. People hire us to do difficult things—like undermine a country's ability to wage war—then complain that we're too violent."

"Very unfair," Tonk Fah agreed.

"Perhaps she'd rather we buy puppies for all of her enemies, then send them with nice apologetic notes, asking them to stop being so mean."

"And then," Tonk Fah said, "when they *don't* stop, we could kill the puppies!"

"All right," Vivenna said. "I understand that we'll have to use a firm hand, but . . . really. I don't want the Hallandren to starve because of what we do."

"Princess," Denth said, sounding more serious. "These people want to attack your homeland. They see your family as the greatest existing threat to their power—and they're going to make certain that nobody of the royal blood lives to challenge them."

"They get a child by your sister to be the next God King," Tonk Fah said, "then they kill every other person of royal blood. They never have to worry about you again."

Denth nodded. "Your father and Lemex were right. The Hallandren have *everything* to lose by not attacking you. And, from what I can see, your people are going to need every bit of help you can give them. That means doing everything we can—scaring the priests, breaking their supply reserves, weakening their armies—to help out."

"We can't stop the war," Tonk Fah added. "We can just make the fight a little more fair."

Vivenna took a deep breath, then nodded. "All right, then, we'll—"

At that moment, the door to the building flew open, slamming against the other side of the wall. Vivenna looked up. A figure stood in the doorway—a tall, bulky man with unusually large muscles and flat features. It took her a moment to register the other oddity about him.

His skin was grey. His eyes too. There was no color to him at all, and her Heightenings told her that he didn't have a single Breath. A Lifeless soldier.

Vivenna scrambled to her feet, barely keeping in a cry of distress. She backed away from the large soldier. It just stood there, immobile, not even breathing. Its eyes tracked her—they didn't just stare ahead like those of a dead man.

For some reason, she found that the most unnerving.

"Denth!" Vivenna said. "What are you doing? Attack!"

The mercenaries remained where they were, lounging on the floor. Tonk Fah barely cracked an eye open. "Ah well," Denth said. "Looks like we've been discovered by the city watch."

"Pity," Tonk Fah said. "This was looking like it would be a fun job."

"Nothing but execution for us now," Denth said.

"Attack!" Vivenna cried. "You're my bodyguards, you're . . ." She trailed off, noticing as the two men began to chuckle.

Oh, Colors, not again, she thought. "What?" she said. "Some kind of joke? Did you paint that man grey? What's going on?"

"Move it, you rock on legs," a voice said from behind the Lifeless. The creature walked into the room, carrying a couple of canvas bags over its shoulders. As it entered, it revealed a shorter woman standing behind. Thick through the thighs and through the bust, she had light brown hair that came down to her shoulders. She stood with hands on hips, looking upset.

"Denth," she snapped, "he's here. In the city."

"Good," Denth said, lounging back. "I owe that man a sword through the gut."

The woman snorted. "He killed Arsteel. What makes you think you can beat him?"

"I've always been the better swordsman," Denth said calmly.

"Arsteel was good too. Now he's dead. Who's the woman?"

"New employer."

"Hope she lives longer than the last one," the woman grumbled. "Clod, put those down and go get the other bag."

The Lifeless responded, setting down its bags and then walking back out. Vivenna watched, by now having figured out that the short woman must be Jewels, the third member of Denth's team. What was she doing with a Lifeless? And how had she found the new house? Denth must have sent her a message.

"What's wrong with you?" Jewels said, glancing at Vivenna. "Some Awakener come by and steal your colors?"

Vivenna paused. "What?"

"She means," Denth said, "why do you look so surprised?"

"That, and her hair is white," Jewels said, walking over to the canvas bags.

Vivenna flushed, realizing that her shock had gotten the better of her. She returned her hair to its proper dark color. The Lifeless was returning, carrying another bag.

"Where did that creature come from?" Vivenna asked.

"What?" Jewels asked. "Clod? Made him from a dead body, obviously. I didn't do it myself—I just paid money for someone else to."

"Too much money," Tonk Fah added.

The creature clomped back into the room. It wasn't unnaturally tall—not like a Returned. It could have been a normal, if well-muscled, man. Only the skin coloring, mixed with the emotionless face, was different.

"She bought him?" Vivenna asked. "When? Just now?"

"Nah," Tonk Fah said, "we've had Clod for months."

"It's useful to have a Lifeless around," Denth said.

"And you didn't tell me about this?" Vivenna asked, trying to keep the hysteria out of her voice. First she'd had to deal with the city and all of its colors and people. Then she was given a dose of unwanted Breath. Now she was confronted by the most unholy of abominations.

"The topic didn't come up," Denth said, shrugging. "They're pretty common in T'Telir."

"We were just talking about defeating these things," Vivenna said. "Not embracing them!"

"We talked about defeating *some* of them," Denth said. "Princess, Lifeless are like swords. They're tools. We can't destroy *all* of them in the city, nor would we want to. Just the ones being used by your enemies."

Vivenna slid down, sitting on the wooden floor. The Lifeless set down its final bag, then Jewels pointed toward the corner. It walked over and stood there, patiently waiting for further orders.

"Here," Jewels said to the other two, untying the final large bag. "You wanted these." She turned it on its side, exposing glittering metal shining within.

Denth smiled, rising. He kicked Tonk Fah back awake—the large man had an uncanny ability to fall asleep at a moment's notice—and walked over to the bag. He pulled out several swords, shiny and new-looking with long, thin blades. Denth made a few practice swings while Tonk Fah wandered over, pulling out wicked-looking daggers, some shorter swords, and then some leather jerkins.

Vivenna sat, back against the wall, using her breathing

to calm herself. She tried not to feel threatened by the Lifeless in the corner. How could they just go about, ignoring it like that? It was so unnatural that it made her itch and squirm. Eventually, Denth noticed her. He told Tonk Fah to oil the blades, then walked over and sat down in front of Vivenna, leaning back with hands against the floor behind him.

"That Lifeless is going to be a problem, Princess?" he asked.

"Yes," she said curtly.

"Then we'll need to work it out," he said, meeting her eyes. "My team can't function if you tie our hands. Jewels has invested a lot of effort into learning the proper Commands to use a Lifeless, not to mention learning to maintain the thing."

"We don't need her."

"Yes," Denth said. "Yes we *do*. Princess, you've brought a lot of biases into this city. It's not my place to tell you what to do with them. I'm just your employee. But I will tell you that you don't know half the things you think you do."

"It's not about what I 'think I know,' Denth," Vivenna said. "It's what I *believe*. A person's body shouldn't be abused by making it come back to life and serve you."

"Why not?" he asked. "Your own theology says a soul leaves when the body dies. The corpse is just recycled dirt. Why not use it?"

"It's wrong," Vivenna said.

"The family of the corpse was well paid for the body."

"Doesn't matter," Vivenna said.

Denth leaned forward. "Well, fine then. But if you order Jewels away, you order us all away. I'll give your money back, then we'll go hire you another team of bodyguards. You can use them instead."

"I thought you were my employee," Vivenna snapped.

"I am," Denth said. "But I can quit whenever I want."

She sat quietly, stomach unsettled.

"Your father was willing to use means that he didn't agree with," Denth said. "Judge him if you must, but tell me this. If using a Lifeless could save your kingdom, who are you to ignore the opportunity?"

"Why do you care?" Vivenna asked.

"I just don't like leaving things unfinished."

Vivenna glanced away.

"Look at it this way, Princess," he said. "You can work with us—which will give you chances to explain your views, maybe change our minds on things like Lifeless and BioChroma. Or you can send us away. But if you reject us because of our sins, aren't you being ostentatious? Don't the Five Visions say something about that?"

Vivenna frowned. *How does he know so much about Austrism?* "I'll think about it," she said. "Why did Jewels bring all those swords?"

"We'll need weapons," Denth said. "You know, has to do with that violence thing we mentioned earlier."

"You don't have any already?"

Denth shrugged. "Tonk usually has a cudgel or knife on him, but a full sword draws attention in T'Telir. It's best not to stand out, sometimes. Your people have some interesting wisdom in that area."

"But now . . ."

"Now we don't really have a choice," he said. "If we keep moving forward with Lemex's plans, things are going to get dangerous." He eyed her. "Which reminds me. I have something else for you to think about."

"What?"

"Those Breaths you hold," Denth said. "They're a tool. Just like the Lifeless. Now, I know you don't agree with how they were obtained. But the fact is, you have them. If a dozen slaves die to forge a sword, does it do any good to melt down the sword and refuse to use it? Or is it better to use that sword and try to stop the men who did such evil in the first place?"

"What are you saying?" Vivenna said, feeling that she probably already knew.

"You should learn to use the Breaths," Denth said. "Tonks and I could sure use an Awakener backing us up."

Vivenna closed her eyes. Did he have to hit her with that now, right after twisting around her concerns about the Lifeless? She had expected to find uncertainties and obstacles in T'Telir. She just hadn't expected so many difficult decisions. And she hadn't expected them to endanger her soul.

"I'm not going to become an Awakener, Denth," Vivenna said quietly. "I might turn a blind eye toward that Lifeless, for now. But I will *not* Awaken. I expect to take these Breaths to my death so that nobody else can benefit from harvesting them. No matter what you say, if you buy that sword forged by overworked slaves, then you'll just encourage the evil merchants."

Denth fell silent. Then he nodded, standing. "You're the boss, and it's your kingdom. If we fail, the only thing *I* lose is an employer."

"Denth," Jewels said, approaching. She barely gave Vivenna a glance. "I don't like this. I don't like the fact that *he* got here first. He has Breath—reports say he looked to have reached at least the Fourth Heightening. Maybe the Fifth. I'll bet he got it from that rebel, Vahr."

"How do you even know it's him?" Denth asked.

Jewels snorted. "Word's all over. People being found slaughtered in alleyways, the wounds corrupt and black. Sightings of a new, powerful Awakener roaming the city carrying a black-handled sword in a silver sheath. It's Tax, all right. Goes by a different name now."

Denth nodded. "Vasher. He's used it for a while. It's a joke on his part."

Vivenna frowned. *Black-handled sword. Silver sheath. The man at the arena?* "Who are we talking about?"

Jewels shot her an annoyed look, but Denth just shrugged. "Old . . . friend of ours."

"He's bad trouble," Tonk Fah said, walking up. "Tax tends to leave a lot of bodies in his wake. Has strange motivations—doesn't think like other people."

"He's interested in the war for some reason, Denth," Jewels said.

"Let him be," Denth snapped. "That will just bring him across my path all the sooner." He turned away, waving a hand indifferently. Vivenna watched him go, noting the frustration in his step, the curtness of his motions.

"What is wrong with him?" she asked Tonk Fah.

"Tax—or, I guess, Vasher—" Tonk Fah said. "He killed a good friend of ours over in Yarn Dred a couple months back. Denth used to have four people in this team."

"It shouldn't have happened," Jewels said. "Arsteel was a brilliant duelist—almost as good as Denth. Vasher's never been able to beat either of them."

"He used that . . . sword of his," Tonk Fah grumbled.

"There was no blackness around the wound," Jewels said.

"Then he cut the blackness out," Tonk Fah snapped, watching Denth belt a sword to his waist. "There's no way Vasher beat Arsteel in a fair duel. *No* way."

"This Vasher," Vivenna found herself saying. "I saw him."

Jewels and Tonk Fah turned sharply.

"He was at the court yesterday," Vivenna said. "Tall man, carrying a sword when nobody else did. It had a black hilt and a silver sheath. He looked ragged. Hair unkempt, beard scraggly, clothing ripped in places. Only a rope for a belt. He was watching me from behind. He looked . . . dangerous."

Tonk Fah cursed quietly.

"That's him," Jewels said. "Denth!"

"What?" Denth asked.

Jewels gestured at Vivenna. "He's a step ahead of us. Been tailing your princess here. She saw him watching her at the court."

"Colors!" Denth swore, snapping a dueling blade into the sheath at his waist. "Colors, Colors, *Colors*!"

"What?" Vivenna asked, paling. "Maybe it was just a coincidence. He could have just come to watch the court."

Denth shook his head. "There *are* no coincidences where that man is concerned, Princess. If he was watching you, then you can bet on the Colors that he knows exactly who you are and where you came from." He met her eyes. "And he's probably planning to kill you."

Vivenna fell silent.

Tonk Fah laid a hand on her shoulder. "Ah, don't worry, Vivenna. He wants to kill *us* too. At least you're in good company."

20

FOR THE FIRST time in her several weeks at the palace, Siri stood before the God King's door and felt neither worried nor tired.

Bluefingers, oddly, wasn't scribbling on his pad. He watched her silently, expression unreadable.

Siri almost smiled to herself. Gone were the days when she'd had to lie on the floor, awkwardly trying to kneel while her back complained. Gone were the days when she had to fall asleep on the marble, her discarded dress her only comfort. Ever since she'd grown daring enough to climb into the bed the previous week, she'd slept well each night, comfortable and warm. And not once had she been touched by the God King.

It was a nice arrangement. The priests—apparently satisfied that she was doing her wifely duty—left her alone. She didn't have to be naked in front of anyone, and she was beginning to learn the social dynamic of the palace. She'd even gone to a few more sessions of the Court Assembly, though she hadn't mingled with the Returned.

"Vessel," Bluefingers said quietly.

She turned toward him, raising an eyebrow.

He shuffled uncomfortably. "You . . . have found a way to make the king respond to your advances, then?"

"That got out, did it?" she asked, looking back at the door. Inside, her smile deepened.

"Indeed it did, Vessel," Bluefingers said, tapping his ledger from beneath. "Only those in the palace know about any of this, of course."

Good, Siri thought. She glanced to the side.

Bluefingers did not look pleased.

"What?" she asked. "I'm out of danger. The priests can stop worrying about an heir." *For a few months, at least. They'll get suspicious eventually.*

"Vessel," Bluefingers said with a harsh whisper. "Doing your duty as the Vessel *was* the danger!"

She frowned, looking at Bluefingers as the little scribe tapped his board. "Oh gods, oh gods, oh gods . . ." he whispered to himself.

"What?" she asked.

"I shouldn't say."

"Then what is the point of bringing it up in the first place! Honestly, Bluefingers, you're getting frustrating. Leave me too confused, and I might just start asking questions—"

"No!" Bluefingers said sharply, then immediately glanced behind him, cringing slightly. "Vessel, you must not speak to others of my fears. They're silly, really, nothing to bother anyone else with. Just . . ."

"What?" she asked.

"You *must* not bear him a child," Bluefingers said. "That is the danger, both to yourself and to the God King himself. This all . . . everything here in the palace . . . it is not what it appears to be."

"That's what everyone says," she snapped. "If it's not what it seems, then tell me what it *is*."

"There is no need," Bluefingers said. "And I will not speak of this again. After tonight, you will conduct yourself to the bedchamber—you obviously have the pattern down well enough. Just wait a hundred heartbeats or so after the women let you out of the dressing room."

"You have to tell me something!" Siri said.

"Vessel," Bluefingers said, leaning in. "I advise you to please keep your voice down. You don't know how many factions shift and move inside the palace. I am a member of many of them, and a stray word on your part could . . . no, *would* . . . mean my death. Do you understand that? *Can* you understand that?"

She hesitated.

"I should *not* be putting my life in danger because of you," he said. "But there are things about this arrangement with which I do not agree. And so, I give my warning. Avoid giving the God King a child. If you want to know more than that, read your histories. Honestly, I would think that you'd have come to all this a little more prepared."

And with that, the little man left.

Siri shook her head, then sighed and pushed open the door and entered the God King's chamber. She closed the door, then eyed the God King—who watched her, as always—and pulled off her dress, leaving her shift on. She went to the bed and sat down, waiting a few minutes before climbing up on her knees to do her bouncing, moaning act. She varied it sometimes, doing several different rhythms, getting creative.

Once she was done, she snuggled down in the blankets and lay back in the pillows to think. *Could Bluefingers have been any more obscure?* she thought with frustration. What little Siri knew of political intrigue told her that people preferred to be subtle—obscure, even—to protect themselves from implication.

Read your histories. . . .

It seemed an odd suggestion. If the secrets were that visible, then why would they be dangerous?

Still, as she thought, she did find herself feeling grateful for Bluefingers. She couldn't really blame him for his hesitation. He'd probably already endangered himself far more than he should have. Without him, she wouldn't have known she was in danger.

In a way, he was the only friend she had in the city—a person like herself, a person drawn in from another country. A country that was overshadowed by beautiful, bold Hallandren. A man who . . .

Her thoughts trailed off; she felt something odd. She opened her eyes.

Someone loomed over her in the darkness.

Despite herself, Siri screamed in surprise. The God King jumped back, stumbling. Heart thumping, Siri shuffled backward on the bed, pulling the covers up over her chest—though, of course, he had seen her unclothed so often that it was a ridiculous gesture.

The God King stood in his dark black clothing, looking uncertain in the hearth's wavering light. She'd never asked her servants why he wore black. One would think that he would prefer white, which he could affect so dramatically with his BioChroma.

For a few moments, Siri sat with the blankets clutched before her, then forced herself to relax. *Stop being so silly,* she told herself. *He's never so much as threatened you.*

"It's all right," she said softly. "You just startled me."

He glanced at her. And—with a jolt of surprise—she realized this was the first time she'd addressed him since her outburst the previous week. Now that he stood, she could see even better how . . . heroic he looked. Tall, broad-shouldered, like a statue. Human, but of more dramatic proportions. Carefully, showing more uncertainty than she'd ever expected from a man who had the title of

God King, he moved back to the bed. He sat down on its edge.

Then he reached to his shirt, pulling it up.

Oh, Austre, she thought with sudden shock. *Oh, God, Lord of Colors! This is it! He's finally coming for me!*

She couldn't fight off the trembles. She'd convinced herself that she was safe, comfortable. She shouldn't have to go through this. Not again!

I can't do it! I can't! I—

The God King pulled something out from underneath his shirt, then let the garment drape back down. Siri sat, breath coming in gasps, slowly realizing that he was making no further moves toward her. She calmed herself, forcing the color back into her hair. The God King laid the object on the bed, and the firelight revealed it to be . . . a book. Siri immediately thought of the histories Bluefingers had mentioned, but she quickly discarded the idea. This book, from the title on the spine, was a book of stories for children.

The God King let his fingers rest on it, then he delicately opened to the first page. The white parchment bent in the force of his BioChroma, shooting out prismatic colors. This didn't distort the text, and Siri carefully inched forward, looking at the words.

She looked up at the God King. His face seemed less stiff than usual. He nodded down at the page, then pointed at the first word.

"You want me to read this?" Siri asked in a low whisper, mindful of the priests who might be listening.

The God King nodded.

"It says 'Stories for Children,' " Siri said, confused.

He turned the book around, looking at it himself. He rubbed his chin in thought.

What's going on? she thought. It didn't seem like he was going to bed her. Did he, instead, expect her to read a story to him? She couldn't imagine him asking for something that childish. She looked up at him again. He turned the book around, pointing at the first word. He nodded toward it.

"Stories?" Siri asked.

He pointed at the word. She looked closely, trying to discern some hidden meaning or mysterious text. She sighed, looking up at him. "Why don't you just tell me?"

He paused, cocking his head. Then he opened his mouth. By the waning light of the hearth's fire, Siri saw something shocking.

The God King of Hallandren had no tongue.

There was a scar. She could just barely see it if she squinted closely. Something had happened to him, some terrible accident had ripped it free. Or . . . had it been taken purposefully? Why would anyone remove the tongue of the king himself?

The answer came to her almost immediately.

BioChromatic Breath, she realized, thinking back to a half-remembered lesson from her childhood. *To Awaken objects, a person must give a Command. Words spoken in a crisp, clear voice. No slurring or mumbling allowed, or the Breath will not function.*

The God King looked away, suddenly, seeming ashamed. He picked up the book, holding it to his chest, and moved to stand.

"No, please," Siri said, edging forward. She reached her hand forward and touched his arm.

The God King froze. She immediately pulled her hand back. "I didn't mean to look so disgusted," Siri said in her whispered voice. "That wasn't because of . . . your mouth. It was because I was realizing why it must have been done to you."

The God King studied her, then slowly seated himself again. He held himself back far enough that they were not touching, and she did not reach for him again. However, he did carefully—almost reverently—put his book back down on the bed. He opened to the first page again, then looked at her, his eyes pleading.

"You can't read, can you?" Siri asked.

He shook his head.

"That's the secret," she whispered. "The thing that scares Bluefingers so much. You're not king, you're a puppet! A *figurehead*. You're paraded around by your priests, given a BioChromatic aura so strong that it makes people fall to their knees in wonder. Yet they took your tongue so that you couldn't ever use it, and they never taught you to read, lest you learn too much or manage to communicate with others."

He sat and looked away.

"All so that they could control you." *No wonder Bluefingers is so scared. If they would do that to their own god . . . then the rest of us are nothing to them.*

It made sense, now, why they had been so adamant about her not talking to—or even kissing—the king. It made sense why they would dislike her so much. They were worried about someone spending time alone with the God King. Someone who might discover the truth.

"I'm sorry," she whispered.

He shook his head, then met her eyes. There was a strength in them she wouldn't have expected of a man who had been sheltered and isolated as he must have been. Finally, he looked down, pointing back at the words on the page. The first word. The first letter, actually.

"That is the letter 'shash,'" Siri said, smiling. "I can teach you them all, if you wish."

The priests were right to be worried.

21

VASHER STOOD ATOP the palace of the God King, watching the sun drop above the western rain forest. The sunset was vibrant amidst the clouds, colors flaring, beautiful reds and oranges painting the trees. Then the sun disappeared and the colors faded.

Some said that before a man died, his BioChromatic aura flared with sudden brightness. Like a heart giving its last beat, like the final surge of a wave before the tide retreats. Vasher had seen it happen, but not with every death. The event was rare, much like a perfect sunset.

Dramatic, Nightblood noted.

The sunset? Vasher asked.

Yes.

You can't see it, he said to the sword.

But I can feel *you seeing it. Crimson. Like blood in the air.*

Vasher didn't respond. The sword couldn't see. But with its powerful, twisted BioChroma, it could sense life and people. Both were things Nightblood had been created to protect. It was strange, how easily and quickly protection could cause destruction. Sometimes, Vasher wondered if the two weren't really the same thing. Protect a flower, destroy the pests who wanted to feed on it. Protect a building, destroy the plants that could have grown in the soil.

Protect a man. Live with the destruction he creates.

Although it was dark, Vasher's life sense was strong. He could just faintly feel the grass growing below and knew how far away it was. With more Breath, he might even have been able to sense the lichen growing on the palace stones. He knelt down, laying one hand on his trouser leg and one on the stone of the palace.

"Strengthen me," he Commanded, Breathing. His trouser legs stiffened, and a patch of color bled from the black stone beside him. Black was a color. He'd never considered that before he'd become an Awakener. Tassels hanging at his cuffs stiffened, wrapping around his ankle. With him kneeling as he was, they could also twist around the bottoms of his feet.

Vasher placed a hand on the shoulder of his shirt, touching another patch of marble as he formed an image in his mind. "Upon call, become my fingers and grip," he Commanded. The shirt quivered and a group of tassels curled up around his hand. Five of them, like fingers.

It was a difficult Command. It required far more Breath to Awaken than he would have liked—his remaining Breath barely allowed him the Second Heightening—and the visualization of the Command had taken practice to perfect. The finger tassels were worth it; they had proven very useful, and he was loath to engage in the night's activities without them.

He stood up straight, noting the scar of grey marble on the otherwise perfectly black palace surface. He smiled to think of the indignation the priests would feel when they discovered it.

He tested the strength in his legs, gripping Nightblood, then took a careful step off the side of the palace. He fell some ten feet; the palace was constructed from massive stone blocks in a steep pyramidal shape. He landed hard on the next block, but his Awakened clothing absorbed some of the shock, acting like a second, external set of bones. He stood up, nodding to himself, then jumped down the other pyramid steps.

Eventually, he landed on the soft grass north of the palace, close to the wall that surrounded the entire plateau. He crouched, watching quietly.

Sneaking, Vasher? Nightblood said. *You're terrible at sneaking.*

Vasher didn't respond.

You should attack, Nightblood said. *You're good at that.*

You just want to prove how strong you are, Vasher thought.

Well, yes, the sword replied. *But you do have to admit that you're bad at sneaking.*

Vasher ignored the sword. A lone man in ragged clothing carrying a sword across the grounds would be conspicuous. So he surveyed. He had picked a night when the gods hadn't planned any grand celebrations out in the courtyard, but there were still small groups of priests, minstrels, or servants moving between palaces.

How sure are you about this information of yours? Nightblood said. *Because, honestly, I don't trust priests.*

He isn't a priest, Vasher thought. He moved carefully, creeping through the dark starlit shadow of the wall's overhang. His contact had warned him to stay away from the palaces of influential gods like Blushweaver and Stillmark. But he had also said that the palace of a lesser god—like Giftbeacon or Peaceyearning—wouldn't work for Vasher's purpose. Instead, Vasher sought out the home of Mercystar, a Returned known for her involvement in politics, yet who wasn't all that influential.

Her palace looked relatively dark this evening, but there would still be guards. Hallandren Returned all had servants to spare. Sure enough, Vasher located two men watching the door he wanted. They wore the extravagant costumes of court servants, colored yellow and gold after the pattern of their mistress.

The men weren't armed. Who would attack the home of a Returned? They were simply there to keep anyone from wandering in and bothering their lady while she slept. They stood by their lanterns, alert and attentive, but more for the sake of appearances than anything else.

Vasher obscured Nightblood beneath his cloak, then walked out of the darkness, looking from side to side anxiously, mumbling to himself. He hunched his body to help hide the oversized hidden sword.

Oh, please, Nightblood said flatly. *The crazy disguise? You're cleverer than that.*

It'll work, Vasher thought. *This is the Court of Gods. Nothing attracts the unbalanced more than the prospect of meeting deities.*

The two guards looked up when they saw him approaching, but they didn't seem surprised. They had probably dealt with marginally insane people every day of their professional careers. Vasher had seen the types who ended up in the lines for Returned petitions.

"Here now," one of the men said as Vasher approached. "How'd you get in here?"

Vasher stepped up to them, mumbling to himself about talking to the goddess. The second man put a hand on Vasher's shoulder. "Come on, friend. Let's get you back to the gates and see if there's a shelter that's still taking people in for the night."

Vasher hesitated. Kindness. He hadn't expected that, for some reason. The emotion made him feel a tad guilty for what he had to do next.

He snapped his arm to the side, twitching his thumb twice to make the long finger tassels on his shirt sleeve begin mimicking the motions of his real fingers. He formed a fist. The tassels snapped forward, wrapping around the first guard's neck.

The man choked out a soft gasp of surprise. Before the second guard could react, Vasher brought Nightblood up, ramming the hilt into the guard's stomach. The man stumbled, and Vasher swept his feet out from beneath him. Vasher's boot followed, coming down slowly but firmly on the man's neck. He wiggled, but Vasher's legs bore Awakened strength.

Vasher stood for a long moment, both men struggling, neither managing to escape their strangulation. A short time later, Vasher stepped off the second guard's neck, then lowered the first guard to the grass, twitching his thumb twice and releasing the finger tassels.

You didn't use me much, Nightblood said, sounding hurt. *You could have used me. I'm better than a shirt. I'm a sword.*

Vasher ignored the comments, scanning the darkness to see if he had been spotted.

I really am better than a shirt. I would have killed them. Look, they're still breathing. Stupid shirt.

That was the point, Vasher thought. *Corpses cause more trouble than men who get knocked out.*

I could knock people out, Nightblood said immediately.

Vasher shook his head, ducking into the building. Returned palaces—this one included—were generally just collections of open rooms with colorful sheets on the doorways. The weather was so temperate in Hallandren that the building could be open to the air at all times.

He didn't go through the central rooms, but instead stayed in the peripheral servant hallway. If Vasher's informant had been truthful, then what he wanted could be found on the northeast side of the building. As he walked, he unraveled the rope from his waist.

Belts are stupid too, Nightblood said. *They—*

At that moment, a group of four servants rounded the corner directly ahead of Vasher. Vasher looked up, startled but not really surprised.

The servants' shock lasted a second longer than his own. Within a heartbeat, Vasher snapped the rope forward. "Hold things," he Commanded, giving up most of his remaining Breath. The rope wrapped around the arm of one of the servants, though Vasher had been aiming for the neck. Vasher cursed, yanking the person forward. The man cried out as Vasher knocked him against the angle of the corner. The others moved to run.

Vasher whipped out Nightblood with his other hand.

Yes! the sword thought.

Vasher didn't draw the sword. He simply tossed it forward. The blade skidded against the floor, then came to rest before the three men. One of the group froze, looking down at the sword, transfixed. He reached out tentatively, eyes awed.

The other two took off running, yelling about an intruder. *Blast!* Vasher thought. He yanked the rope, knocking the entangled servant off of his feet again. As the servant tried to stumble to his feet, Vasher dashed forward and wrapped the rope around the man's hands and body. To his side, the remaining servant ignored both Vasher and his friend. This man picked up Nightblood, eyes alight. He undid the snap on the hilt, moving to pull the sword.

When he had barely gotten a thin sliver of blade free, a dark, fluidlike smoke began to stream out. Some dripped to the ground; other tendrils of it snaked out and wrapped around the man's arm, drawing the color from his skin.

Vasher kicked out with an Awakened leg, knocking the man down, forcing him to drop Nightblood. Vasher left the first man squirming, tied up, then grabbed the man who had held the sword and rammed his head against the wall.

Breathing hard, Vasher grabbed Nightblood, closed the sheath, and did up the clasp. Then he reached over, touching the rope that tied the dazed servant. "Your Breath to mine," he said, recovering the Breath from the rope, leaving the man bound.

You didn't let me kill him, Nightblood said, annoyed.

No, Vasher said. *Corpses, remember?*

And . . . two ran away from me. That's not right.

You cannot tempt the hearts of men who are pure, Nightblood. No matter how much he explained that concept, it seemed beyond the sword's ability to comprehend.

Vasher moved quickly, dashing down the hallway. He had only a little farther to go, but there were already cries of alarm and calls for help. He had no desire to fight an army of servants and soldiers. He stopped, uncertain, in the unadorned hallway. He noticed, idly, that Awakening the rope had inadvertently stolen the color from his boots and cloak—the only pieces of clothing he wore that weren't themselves Awakened.

The grey clothing would instantly brand him for what he was. But the thought of backing down made him cringe. He gritted his teeth in frustration, punching the wall. This was supposed to have gone a lot more smoothly.

I told you, you aren't sneaky, Nightblood said.

Shut up, Vasher thought, determined not to run. He reached into a pouch at his belt, pulling out the object within: a dead squirrel.

Yuck, Nightblood said with a sniff.

Vasher knelt, putting a hand on the creature.

"Awaken to my Breath," he Commanded, "serve my needs, live at my Command and my word. Fallen Rope."

Those last words, "fallen rope," formed the security phrase. Vasher could have chosen anything, but he picked the first thing that came to mind.

One Breath was leached from his body, going down into the small rodent's corpse. The thing began to twitch. That was a Breath Vasher would never be able to recover, for creating a Lifeless was a permanent act. The squirrel lost all color, bleeding to grey, the Awakening feeding off the body's own colors to help fuel the transformation. The squirrel had been grey in the first place, so the difference was tough to see. That's why Vasher liked to use them.

"Fallen Rope," he said to the creature, its grey eyes looking up at him. The security phrase pronounced, Vasher could now imprint the creature with an order, much as he did when performing a standard Awakening. "Make noise. Run around. Bite people who are not me. Fallen Rope." The second use of the words closed its impressionability, so it could no longer be Commanded.

The squirrel hopped up to its feet, then scampered down the hallway, heading for the open doorway the fleeing servants had disappeared into. Vasher stood and began to run again, hoping that this distraction would earn him time. Indeed, a few moments later he heard cries coming from the doorway. Clangs and screams followed. Lifeless could be difficult to stop, particularly a fresh one with orders to bite.

Vasher smiled.

We could have taken them, Nightblood said.

Vasher rushed to the place his information had indicated. The location was marked by a splintered board in the wall, ostensibly just normal wear of the building. Vasher crouched, hoping that his informant had not lied. He searched around on the floor, then froze as he found the hidden latch.

He pulled it open, revealing a trapdoor. Returned palaces were only supposed to be one story. He smiled.

What if this tunnel doesn't have another way out? Nightblood asked as Vasher dropped into the hole, trusting his Awakened clothing to absorb the fall.

Then you'll probably get to kill a lot of people, Vasher thought. However, his information had been good so far. He suspected that the rest was good as well.

The priests of the Iridescent Tones, it appeared, were hiding things from the rest of the kingdom. And from their gods.

22

WEATHERLOVE, GOD OF storms, selected one of the wooden spheres from the rack, then hefted it in his hand. It had been built to fill the palm of a god, and was weighted in the middle with lead. Carved with rings across the surface, it was painted a deep blue.

"A doubling sphere?" asked Lifeblesser. "A bold move."

Weatherlove eyed the small group of gods behind him. Lightsong was among them, sipping on a sweet orange fruited drink with some kind of alcohol enhancement. It had been several days since he'd allowed Llarimar to talk him out of bed, but he still had come to no conclusion on how to proceed.

"A bold move indeed," Weatherlove said, tossing the sphere up into the air, then catching it. "Tell me, Lightsong the Bold. Do you favor this throw?"

The other gods chuckled. There were four of them playing. As usual, Weatherlove wore a green and gold robe that hung from only one shoulder with a wrap around his waist that came down to mid-thigh. The outfit—patterned after the ancient dress of the Returned from paintings centuries past—revealed his sculpted muscles and divine figure. He stood at the edge of the balcony, as it was his turn to throw.

Seated behind him were the three others. Lightsong on the left and Lifeblesser—god of healing—in the middle. Truthcall, god of nature, sat on the far right, wearing his ornate cloak and uniform of maroon and white.

The three gods were variations on a theme. If Lightsong hadn't known them well, he would have had trouble telling them apart. Each stood almost exactly seven feet tall, with bulging muscles that any mortal would have envied. True, Lifeblesser had brown hair, while Weatherlove had blond and Truthcall had black. But all three had that same set of square-jawed features, perfect coiffure, and innate seamless grace that marked them as Returned divinities. Only their costumes really offered any variety.

Lightsong sipped his drink. "Do I bless your throw, Weatherlove?" he asked. "Are we not in competition against one another?"

"I suppose," the god said, tossing the wooden ball up and down.

"Then why would I bless you when you throw against me?"

Weatherlove just smirked, then pulled back his arm and launched the ball out across the pitch. It bounced, then rolled over the grass, eventually coming to rest. This section of the courtyard had been divided into an expansive game board with ropes and stakes. Priests and servants scurried about on the sides, making notations and keeping track of the score so that the gods wouldn't have to. Tarachin was a complex game, played only by the wealthy. Lightsong had never bothered to learn the rules.

He found it more amusing to play when he had no idea what he was doing.

It was his throw next. He stood up, selecting one of the wooden spheres from the rack because it matched the color of his drink. He tossed the orange sphere up and down; then—not paying attention to where he was throwing—he tossed it out onto the field. The sphere flew much farther than it probably should have; he had the strength of a perfect body. That was part of the reason the field was so vast; it had to be built to the scale of gods, and so when they played, they required the elevated perspective of a balcony to view their game.

Tarachin was supposed to be one of the most difficult games in the world; it required strength to throw the spheres correctly, keen wit to understand where to place them, coordination to do so with the necessary precision, and a great understanding of strategy to pick the proper sphere and dominate the game field.

"Four hundred and thirteen points," a servant announced after being fed the number by scribes working below.

"Another magnificent throw," Truthcall said, perking up in his wooden lounging chair. "How do you do it? I'd *never* have thought to use a reversal sphere for that throw."

Is that what the orange ones are called? Lightsong thought, returning to his seat. "You just have to understand the playing field," he said, "and learn to get inside the mind of the sphere. Think like it does, reason as it might."

"Reason like a sphere?" Lifeblesser said, standing up. He wore flowing robes of his colors, blue and silver. He selected a green sphere off the rack, then stared at it. "What type of reasoning does a wooden sphere do?"

"The circular type, I should think," Lightsong said lightly. "And, by coincidence, it is my favorite type as well. Perhaps that's why I'm so good at the game."

Lifeblesser frowned, opening his mouth to reply. He finally shut it, looking confused by Lightsong's comment. Becoming a god did not, unfortunately, increase one's mental capacity along with one's physical attributes. Lightsong didn't mind. For him, the real sport of a game of Tarachin never involved where the spheres landed.

Lifeblesser made his throw, then sat down. "I do say, Lightsong," he said, smiling. "I mean this as a compliment, but having you around can be draining!"

"Yes," Lightsong said, sipping his drink, "I'm remarkably like a mosquito in that regard. Truthcall, isn't it your throw?"

"Actually, it's yours again," Weatherlove said. "You achieved the crown pairing during your last toss, remember?"

"Ah yes, how could I forget," Lightsong said, rising. He took another sphere, tossed it over his shoulder out onto the green, then sat down.

"Five hundred and seven points," the priest announced.

"Now you're just showing off," Truthcall said.

Lightsong said nothing. In his opinion, it revealed an inherent flaw in the game that the one who knew least about it tended to do the best. He doubted, however, that the others would take it that way. All three were very dedicated to their sport, and they played every week. There was blessed little else for them to do with their time.

Lightsong suspected that they kept inviting him only

because they wanted to prove, at last, that they could defeat him. If he'd fathomed the rules, he'd have tried to lose on purpose to keep them from insisting that he come play with them. Still, he liked the way his victories annoyed them—though, of course, they never showed him anything other than perfect decorum. Either way, under the circumstances, he suspected that he couldn't lose if he wanted to. It was rather difficult to throw a game when you had no idea what you were doing to win it in the first place.

Truthcall finally stepped up to throw. He always wore clothing of a martial style, and the colors maroon and white were very handsome on him. Lightsong suspected that he'd always been jealous that instead of being given Lifeless Commands as his duty to the court, he'd been given a vote over issues of trade with other kingdoms.

"I hear that you spoke with the queen a few days back, Lightsong," Truthcall said as he threw.

"Yes, indeed," Lightsong said, sipping his drink. "She was extraordinarily pleasant, I must say."

Weatherlove gave a quiet laugh, obviously thinking that last comment to be sarcasm—which was a little annoying, since Lightsong had meant it sincerely.

"The entire court is abuzz," Truthcall said, turning and flipping back his cape, then leaning against the balcony railing as he waited for the points from his throw to be tabulated. "The Idrians betrayed the treaty, one could say."

"The wrong princess," Weatherlove agreed. "It gives us an opening."

"Yes," Truthcall said musingly, "but an opening for what?"

"To attack!" Lifeblesser said in his usual, dense way. The other two regarded him wincingly.

"There is so much more to be gained than that, Lifeblesser."

"Yes," Weatherlove said, idly spinning the last bit of wine in his cup. "My plans are already in motion, of course."

"And what plans would those be, divine brother?" Truthcall said.

Weatherlove smiled. "I wouldn't want to spoil the surprise, now, would I?"

"That depends," Truthcall said evenly. "Will it keep me from demanding the Idrians give us more access to the passes? I'm willing to bet that some . . . pressures could be placed on the new queen to gain her favor for such a proposal. She's said to be rather naive."

Lightsong felt a slight nausea as they spoke. He knew how they plotted, always scheming. They played their game with spheres, but just as much of their reason for seeing one another at these events was to posture and make deals.

"Her ignorance must be an act," Lifeblesser said in a rare moment of thoughtfulness. "They wouldn't have sent her if she was really that inexperienced."

"She's Idrian," Truthcall said dismissively. "Their most important city has fewer people than a small T'Telir neighborhood. They barely understand the concept of politics, I'll warrant. They are more used to talking to sheep than humans."

Weatherlove nodded. "Even if she's 'well trained' by their standards, she'll be easy to manipulate here. The real trick is going to be to make certain others don't get to her first. Lightsong, what was your impression? Will she be quick to do as the gods tell her?"

"I really wouldn't know," he said, waving for more juice. "As you know, I'm not much interested in political games."

Weatherlove and Truthcall shared a smirking look; like most in the court, they considered Lightsong hopeless when it came to practical matters. And by their definition, "practical" meant "taking advantage of others."

"Lightsong," Lifeblesser said with his tactlessly honest voice. "You really need to take more of an interest in politics. It can be very diverting. Why, if you only knew the secrets to which I'm privy!"

"My dear Lifeblesser," Lightsong replied, "please trust me when I say that I have *no* desire to know any secrets which involve you and a privy."

Lifeblesser frowned, obviously trying to work through that one.

The other two began to discuss the queen again as the priests reported the score from the last throw. Oddly, Lightsong found himself increasingly troubled. As Lifeblesser stood up to take his next toss, Lightsong found himself rising as well.

"My divine brothers," he said, "I suddenly feel quite weary. Perhaps it was something I ingested."

"Not something I served, I hope?" Truthcall said. It was his palace.

"Food, no," Lightsong said. "The other things you're serving today, perhaps. I really must be on my way."

"But you're in the lead!" Truthcall said. "If you leave now, we'll have to play again next week!"

"Your threats roll off of me like water, my divine brother," Lightsong said, nodding respectfully to each in turn. "I bid you farewell until such time as you drag me up here again to play this tragic game of yours."

They laughed. He wasn't sure whether to be amused or insulted that they so often confused his jokes for serious statements and the other way around.

He collected his priests—Llarimar included—from the room just inside the balcony, but didn't feel like speaking with any of them. He just made his way through the palace of deep reds and whites, still troubled. The men on the balcony were rank amateurs compared to the *real* political masters, like Blushweaver. They were so blunt and obvious with their plans.

But even men who were blunt and obvious could be dangerous, particularly to a woman like the queen, who obviously had little experience with such things.

I've already determined that I can't help her, Lightsong

thought, leaving the palace and entering the green outside. To the right, a complex network of rope squares and patterns marked the Tarachin pitch. A sphere bounced with a distant thud in the grass. Lightsong walked the other direction on the springy lawn, not even waiting for his priests to erect a canopy to shade him from the afternoon sun.

He still worried that if he tried to help, he'd just make things worse. But then there were the dreams. War and violence. Over and over again, he saw the fall of T'Telir itself, the destruction of his homeland. He couldn't continue to ignore the dreams, even if he didn't accept them as prophetic.

Blushweaver thought that war was important. Or, at least, that it was important to prepare for. He trusted her more than any other god or goddess, but he also worried about how aggressive she was. She had come to him, asking him to be a part of her plans. Had she done it, perhaps, because she knew he would be more temperate than she? Was she intentionally balancing herself?

He heard petitions, even though he didn't intend to ever give up his Breath and die. He interpreted paintings, even though he didn't think he was seeing anything prophetic in them. Couldn't he help secure power in the court in order to be prepared when he didn't believe that his visions meant anything? Particularly if those preparations helped protect a young woman who, undoubtedly, would have no other allies?

Llarimar had told him to do his best. That sounded like an awful lot of work. Unfortunately, doing nothing was beginning to seem like even *more* work. Sometimes, when you stepped in something foul, the only thing to do was to stop walking and make the effort to clean it off.

He sighed, shaking his head. "I'm probably going to regret this," he muttered to himself.

Then he went looking for Blushweaver.

—◆◆◆—

THE MAN WAS slight, almost skeletal, and each shellfish he slurped made Vivenna cringe for two reasons. Not only did she have trouble believing that anyone would enjoy such slimy, sluglike food, but the mussels were also of a very rare and expensive variety.

And she was paying.

The afternoon restaurant crowd was large—people usually ate out at midday, when it made more sense to buy food than return home for a meal. The entire concept of restaurants still seemed strange to her. Didn't these men have wives or servants to make them meals? Didn't they feel uncomfortable eating in such a public place? It was so . . . impersonal.

Denth and Tonk Fah sat on either side of her. And, of course, they helped themselves to the plate of mussels as well. Vivenna wasn't certain—she'd pointedly not asked—but she thought that the shellfish were raw.

The thin man across from her slurped down another one. He didn't seem to be enjoying himself much despite the expensive surroundings and free food. He had a sneer on his lips and while he didn't appear nervous, she did notice that he kept an eye on the restaurant entrance.

"So," Denth said, setting another empty shell on the table, then wiping his fingers on the tablecloth—a common practice in T'Telir. "Can you help us or not?"

The little man—he called himself Fob—shrugged. "You tell a wild tale, mercenary."

"You know me, Fob. When have I lied to you?"

"Whenever you've been paid to do it," Fob said with a snort. "I've just never been able to catch you."

Tonk Fah chuckled, reaching for another mussel. It slipped free of the shell as he brought it to his lips; Vivenna had to steel herself to keep from gagging at the slimy plop it made when it hit the table.

"You don't disagree that war is coming, though," Denth said.

"Of course not," Fob said. "But it's been coming for decades now. What makes you think that it will finally happen this year?"

"Can you afford to ignore the chance that it might?" Denth asked.

Fob squirmed a bit, then began eating mussels again. Tonk Fah began stacking the shells, seeing how many he could get balanced on top of one another. Vivenna said nothing for the moment. Her minor part in the meetings didn't bother her. She watched, she learned, and she thought.

Fob was a landowner. He cleared forests, then rented the land to growers. He often relied on Lifeless to help with his clearing—workers loaned to him through the government. There was only one stipulation upon the lending. Should war come, all of the food produced on his holdings during wartime immediately became the property of the Returned.

It was a good deal. The government would probably seize his lands during a war anyway, so he didn't really lose anything save for his right to complain.

He ate another mussel. *How does he keep packing them down?* she thought. Fob had managed to slurp away nearly twice as many of the disgusting little creatures as Tonk Fah.

"That harvest won't come in, Fob," Denth said. "You will lose quite a bit this year, should we prove right."

"But," Tonk Fah said, adding another shell to his stack, "harvest early, sell your stockpiles, and you stand to get ahead of your competitors."

"And what do you gain?" Fob asked. "How do I know those same competitors haven't hired you to *convince* me a war is coming?"

The table fell silent, making noticeable the other diners clattering at their own meals. Denth finally turned, eyeing Vivenna, and nodded.

She pulled up her shawl—not the matronly one she'd brought from Idris, but a silken, gossamer one that Denth had found for her. She met Fob's eyes, then changed her hair to a deep red. With the shawl up, only those at the table and watching closely would be able to see the change.

He froze. "Do that again," he said.

She changed it to blond.

Fob sat back, letting his mussel fall free of its shell. It splatted against the table near the one Tonk Fah had dropped. "The *queen*?" he asked with shock.

"No," Vivenna said. "Her sister."

"What's going on here?" Fob asked.

Denth smiled. "She's here to organize a resistance against the Returned gods and to prepare Idrian interests here in T'Telir for the coming war."

"You don't think that old royal up in the highlands would send his daughter for nothing?" Tonk Fah said. "War. It's the only thing that would call for such desperation."

"Your sister," Fob said, eyeing Vivenna. "They sent the younger one into the court. Why?"

"The king's plans are his own, Fob," Denth said.

Fob looked thoughtful. Finally, he flipped the fallen mussel onto the plate of shells and reached for a fresh one. "I *knew* there was more behind that girl's arrival than simple chance."

"So you'll harvest?" Denth asked.

"I'll think about it," Fob said.

Denth nodded. "Good enough, I guess."

He nodded to Vivenna and Tonk Fah, and the three of them left Fob eating his shellfish. Vivenna settled the tab—which was even higher than she'd feared—and then they joined Parlin, Jewels, and Clod the Lifeless waiting outside. The group moved away from the restaurant, pushing through the crowd easily, if only because of the massive Lifeless that walked before them.

"Where now?" Vivenna asked.

Denth eyed her. "Not tired even a little?"

Vivenna didn't acknowledge her sore feet or her drowsiness. "We're working for the good of my people, Denth. A little weariness is a small price."

Denth shot a glance toward Tonk Fah, but the overweight mercenary had split off into the crowd toward a merchant's stand, Parlin tagging along behind. Parlin, Vivenna noticed, had gone back to wearing his ridiculous green hat despite her disapproval. What was wrong with that man? He wasn't terribly bright, true, but he had always been levelheaded.

"Jewels," Denth called up ahead. "Take us to the Raymar place."

Jewels nodded, giving instructions to Clod that Vivenna couldn't hear. The group turned in another direction through the crowd.

"It only responds to her?" Vivenna said.

Denth shrugged. "It has basic instructions to do what Tonks and I say and I've got a security phrase I can use if I need more control."

Vivenna frowned. "Security phrase?"

Denth eyed her. "This is a rather heretical discussion we're getting into. You sure you want to continue?"

Vivenna ignored the amusement in his tone. "I still do *not* like the idea of that thing being with us, particularly if I don't have any way to control it."

"All Awakening works by way of the Command, Princess," Denth said. "You infuse something with life, then give it an order. Lifeless are valuable because you can give them Commands *after* you create them, unlike regular Awakened objects, which you can only Command once in advance. Plus, Lifeless can remember a long list of complicated orders and are generally good about not misunderstanding them. They retain a bit of their humanity, I guess."

Vivenna shivered. That made them seem far too sentient for her liking.

"However, that means pretty much anyone can control a Lifeless," Denth said. "Not just the person who created them. So we give them security phrases. A couple words you can say that will let you imprint the creature with new Commands."

"So what's the security phrase for Clod?"

"I'll have to ask Jewels if you can have it."

Vivenna opened her mouth to complain, but thought better of it. Denth obviously didn't like interfering with Jewels or her work. Vivenna would simply have to make a point of it later, once they were in a more private location. Instead, she just eyed Clod. He was dressed in simple clothing. Grey trousers and grey shirt, with a leather jerkin that had been drained of color. He carried a large blade at his waist. Not a dueling sword—a more brutal, broad-bladed weapon.

All in grey, Vivenna thought. *Is that because they want everyone to recognize Clod for a Lifeless?* Despite what Denth said about Lifeless being common, many people gave the thing a wide berth. *Snakes might be common in the jungle,* she thought, *but that doesn't mean that people are pleased to see them.*

Jewels chatted quietly at the Lifeless, though it never responded. It simply walked, face forward, inhuman in the steady rhythm of its steps.

"Does she always . . . talk to it like that?" Vivenna asked, shivering.

"Yeah," Denth said.

"That doesn't seem very healthy."

Denth looked troubled, though he said nothing. A few moments later, Tonk Fah and Parlin returned. Tonk Fah, Vivenna was displeased to see, had a small monkey on his shoulder. It chittered a bit, then ran behind Tonk Fah's neck, moving to the other shoulder.

"A new pet?" Vivenna asked. "What happened to that parrot of yours, anyway?"

Tonk Fah looked ashamed, and Denth just shook his head. "Tonks isn't very good with pets."

"That parrot was boring anyway," Tonk Fah said. "Monkeys are *much* more interesting."

Vivenna shook her head. It wasn't long before they arrived at the next restaurant, one far less lavish than the previous one. Jewels, Parlin, and the Lifeless took up places outside, as usual, and Vivenna and the two male mercenaries walked in.

The meetings were becoming routine. During the last couple of weeks, they'd met with at least a dozen people of varying usefulness. Some were underground leaders Denth thought might be capable of making a ruckus. Others were merchants, like Fob. All in all, Vivenna was impressed with the variety of covert ways Denth had come up with to disrupt things in T'Telir.

Most of the schemes did, however, require a display of Vivenna's Royal Locks as a clincher. Most people instantly grasped the importance of a royal daughter being in the city, and she was left wondering just how Lemex had intended to achieve results without such convincing proof.

Denth led them to a table in the corner, and Vivenna frowned at how dirty the restaurant was. The only light came in the form of slim slatlike windows shining beams of sunlight through the ceiling, but even that was enough to show the grime. Despite her hunger, she quickly determined that she would not be eating anything at *this* establishment. "Why do we keep switching restaurants, anyway?" she said, sitting down—but only after wiping off the stool with her handkerchief.

"Harder to spy on us that way," Denth said. "I keep warning you, Princess. This is more dangerous than it seems. Don't let the simple meetings over food throw you off. In any other city, we'd be meeting in lairs, gambling parlors, or alleyways. Best to keep moving."

They settled down, and as if they hadn't just come from their second lunch of the day, Denth and Tonk Fah ordered food. Vivenna sat quietly in her chair, preparing for the meeting. Gods Feast was something of a holy day in Hallandren—though, from what she'd seen, the people of the pagan city had no real concept of what a "holy day" should be. Instead of helping the monks in their fields or caring for the needy, the people took the evening off and splurged on meals—as if the gods wanted them to be extravagant.

And perhaps they did. From what she'd heard, the Returned were profligate beings. It made sense for their followers to spend their "holy day" being idle and gluttonous.

Their contact arrived before the food did. He walked in with two bodyguards of his own. He wore nice clothing—which meant bright clothing, in T'Telir—but his beard was long and greasy, and he appeared to be short several teeth. He pointed, and his bodyguards pulled a second table over next to Vivenna's, then arranged three chairs by it. The man took a seat, careful to keep his distance from Denth and Tonk Fah.

"A little paranoid, aren't we?" Denth said.

The man raised his hands. "Caution never hurt a man."

"More food for us, then," Tonk Fah said as the plate arrived. It was covered with bits of . . . something that had been battered and fried. The monkey immediately scrambled down Tonk Fah's arm and snatched a few pieces.

"So," the man said, "you're the infamous Denth."

"I am. I assume you're Grable?"

The man nodded.

One of the city's less reputable thieving lords, Vivenna thought. *A strong ally of Vahr's rebellion.* They had been waiting weeks to set up this meeting.

"Good," Denth said. "We have some interest in making certain supply carts disappear on the way to the city." He said it so openly. Vivenna glanced about, making certain no other tables were close.

"Grable owns this restaurant, Princess," Tonk Fah whispered. "Every second man in this room is probably a bodyguard."

Great, she thought, annoyed they hadn't told her before they entered. She glanced around again, feeling far more jumpy this time.

"Is that so?" Grable asked, bringing Vivenna's attention back to the conversation. "You want to make things disappear? Caravans of food?"

"It's a difficult job we're asking for," Denth said grimly. "These aren't long-distance caravans. Most of them will simply be coming into the city from the outlying farms." He nodded to Vivenna, and she pulled out a small pouch of coins. She handed them to him, and he tossed them to a nearby table.

One of the bodyguards investigated.

"For your trouble in coming today," Denth said.

Vivenna watched the money go with a crimp in her stomach. It felt downright *wrong* to be using royal funds to bribe men like Grable. What she had just given away wasn't even a real bribe—it was simply "grease money," as Denth put it.

"Now," Denth said, "the carts we're talking about—"

"Wait," Grable said. "Let's see the hair first."

Vivenna sighed, moving to put up the shawl.

"No shawl," Grable said. "No tricks. The men in this room are loyal."

Vivenna shot a glance at Denth, and he nodded. So she shifted colors a couple of times. Grable watched intently, scratching at his beard.

"Nice," he finally said. "Nice indeed. Where'd you find her?"

Denth frowned. "What?"

"A person with enough royal blood to imitate one of the princesses."

"She's no impostor," Denth said as Tonk Fah continued to work on the plate of fried somethings.

"Come now," Grable said, smiling with a wide, uneven smile. "You can tell me."

"It's true," Vivenna said. "Being royal is about more than just blood. It's about lineage and the holy calling of Austre. My children will not have the Royal Locks unless I become queen of Idris. Only potential heirs have the ability to change their hair color."

"Superstitious nonsense," Grable said. He leaned forward, ignoring her and focusing on Denth. "I don't care about your caravans, Denth. I want to buy the girl from you. How much?"

Denth was silent.

"Word of her is spreading about town," Grable said. "I see what you're doing. You could move a lot of people, make a lot of noise, with a person who seemed to be of the royal family. I don't know where you found her, or how you trained her so well, but I want her."

Denth stood up slowly. "We're leaving," he said. Grable's bodyguards stood up too.

Denth moved.

There were flashes—reflections of sunlight, and bodies moving too fast for Vivenna's shocked mind to follow. Then the motion stopped. Grable remained in his chair. Denth stood poised, his dueling blade sticking through the neck of one of the bodyguards.

The bodyguard looked surprised, his hand still on his sword. Vivenna hadn't even seen Denth draw his weapon. The other bodyguard stumbled, blood staining the front of his jerkin from where—shockingly—Denth seemed to have managed to stab him as well.

He slipped to the ground, bumping Grable's table in his death throes.

Lord of Colors . . . Vivenna thought. *So fast!*

"So, you *are* as good as they say," Grable said, still looking unconcerned. Around the room, other men had stood. Some twenty of them. Tonk Fah grabbed another handful of fried things, then nudged Vivenna. "We might want to get up," he whispered.

Denth pulled his sword free of the bodyguard's neck, and the man joined his friend, bleeding and dying on the floor. Denth slammed his sword into its sheath without wiping it, never breaking Grable's gaze.

"People speak of you," Grable said. "Say you appeared out of nowhere a decade or so back. Gathered yourself a team of the best—stole them from important men. Or important prisons. Nobody knows much about you, other than the fact that you're fast. Some say inhumanly so."

Denth nodded toward the doorway. Vivenna stood nervously, then let Tonk Fah pull her through the room. The guards stood with their hands on their swords, but nobody attacked.

"It's a pity we couldn't do business," Grable said, sighing. "I hope you'll think of me for future dealings."

Denth finally turned away, joining Vivenna and Tonk Fah as they left the restaurant and moved out onto the sunny street. Parlin and Jewels hurried to catch up.

"He's letting us go?" Vivenna asked, heart thumping.

"He just wanted to see my blade," Denth said. He still seemed tense. "It happens sometimes."

"Barring that, he wanted to steal himself a princess," Tonk Fah added. "He either got to verify Denth's skill or he got you."

"But . . . you could have killed him!" Vivenna said.

Tonk Fah snorted. "And bring down the wrath of half the thieves, assassins, and burglars in the city? No, Grable knew he wasn't ever in any danger from us."

Denth looked back at her. "I'm sorry for wasting your time—I thought he'd be more useful."

She frowned, noting for the first time the careful mask that Denth kept on his emotions. She'd always thought of him as carefree, like Tonk Fah, but now she saw hints of something else. Control. Control that was, for the first time since they'd met, in danger of cracking.

"Well, no harm done," she said.

"Except for those slobs that Denth poked," Tonk Fah added, happily feeding another morsel to his monkey.

"We need to—"

"Princess?" a voice asked from the crowd.

Denth and Tonk Fah both spun. Once again, Denth's sword was out before Vivenna could track. This time, however, he didn't strike. The man behind them didn't seem much of a threat. He wore ragged brown clothing, and had a leathery suntanned face. He had the look of a farmer.

"Oh, Princess," the man said, hurrying forward, ignoring the blades. "It is you. I heard rumors, but . . . oh, you're here!"

Denth shot a look at Tonk Fah, and the larger mercenary reached out, putting a hand in front of the newcomer before he got too close to Vivenna. She would have thought the caution unnecessary had she just not seen Denth kill two men in an eyeblink. The danger Denth always talked about was slowly seeping into her mind. If this man had a hidden weapon and a little skill, he could kill her before she knew what was happening.

It was a chilling realization.

"Princess," the man said, falling to his knees. "I am your servant."

"Please," she said. "Do not put me above others."

"Oh," the man said, looking up. "I'm sorry. It's been so long since I left Idris! But, it *is* you!"

"How did you know I was here?"

"The Idrians in T'Telir," the man said. "They say you've come to take the throne back. We've been oppressed here for so long that I thought people were just making up stories. But it's true! You're here!"

Denth glanced at her, then at Grable's restaurant, which was still close behind them. He nodded to Tonk Fah. "Grab him, search him, and we'll talk somewhere else."

THE "SOMEWHERE ELSE" turned out to be a ragged dump of a building in a poor section of town about fifteen minutes from the restaurant.

Vivenna found the slums of T'Telir to be very interesting, on an intellectual level at least. Even here, there was color. People wore faded clothing. Bright strips of cloth hung from windows, stretched across overhangs, and even sat in puddles on the street. Colors, muted or dirty. Like a carnival that had been hit by a mudslide.

Vivenna stood outside the shack with Jewels, Parlin, and the Idrian, waiting as Denth and Tonk Fah made sure the building wasn't hiding any unseen threats. She wrapped her arms around herself, feeling an odd sense of despair. The faded colors in the alley felt wrong. They were dead things. Like a beautiful bird that had fallen motionless to the ground, its shape intact, but the magic gone.

Ruined reds, stained yellows, broken greens. In T'Telir, even simple things—like chair legs and storage sacks— were dyed bright colors. How much must the people of the city spend on dyes and inks? If it hadn't been for the Tears of Edgli, the vibrant flowers that grew only in the T'Telir climate, it would have been impossible. Hallandren had made an entire economy out of growing, harvesting, and producing dyes from the special flowers.

Vivenna wrinkled her nose at the smell of refuse. Scents were more vibrant to her now, too, much like colors. It wasn't that her ability to smell was any better, the things that she smelled just seemed rich. She shivered. Even now, weeks after the infusion of Breath, she didn't feel normal. She could *sense* the teeming people of the city, could sense Parlin beside her, watching the nearby alleys with suspicion. She could sense Denth and Tonk Fah inside—one of them appeared to be inspecting the basement.

She could . . .

She froze. She *couldn't* feel Jewels. She glanced to the side, but the shorter woman was there, hands on hips, muttering to herself about being left with the "kids." Her Lifeless abomination was beside her; Vivenna hadn't expected to be able to feel it. Why couldn't she feel Jewels? Vivenna had a sharp moment of panic, thinking that Jewels might be some twisted Lifeless creation. Then, however, she realized that there was a simple explanation.

Jewels had no Breath. She was a Drab.

Now that Vivenna knew what to look for, it was obvious. Even without her wealth of Breath, Vivenna thought she might have been able to tell. There was less of a sparkle of life in Jewels's eyes. She seemed more grumpy, less pleasant. She seemed to put others on edge.

Plus Jewels never noticed when Vivenna was watching her. Whatever sense made others glance about if they were watched for too long, Jewels didn't have it. Vivenna turned away, and found herself blushing. Seeing a person without Breath . . . it felt like spying on someone when they were changing. Seeing them exposed.

Poor woman, she thought. *I wonder how it happened.* Had she sold it herself? Or had it been taken from her? Suddenly, Vivenna felt awkward. *Why should I have so much, when she has nothing?* It was the worst kind of ostentation.

She felt Denth approach before he actually pushed the door open. It looked ready to fall off its hinges. "Safe," he said. Then he eyed Vivenna. "You don't have to be involved with this, if you don't want to waste your time, Princess. Jewels can take you back to the house. We'll question the man and bring you word."

She shook her head. "No. I want to hear what he has to say."

"I figured as much," Denth said. "We'll want to cancel our next appointment, though. Jewels, you—"

"I'll do it," Parlin said.

Denth paused, glancing at Vivenna.

"Look, I may not understand everything going on in this

city," Parlin said, "but I can deliver a simple message. I'm not an idiot."

"Let him go," Vivenna said. "I trust him."

Denth shrugged. "All right. Head straight down this alley until you find the square with the broken statue of a horseman, then turn east and follow that road through its curves. That'll take you out of the slum. The next appointment was to happen at a restaurant called the Armsman's Way; you'll find it in the market on the west side."

Parlin nodded and took off. Denth waved for Vivenna and the others to enter the building. The nervous Idrian man— Thame—went first. Vivenna followed him in, and was surprised to find that the inside of the building looked quite a bit sturdier than the outside had indicated. Tonk Fah found a stool, and he put it down in the center of the room.

"Have a seat, friend," Denth said, gesturing.

Thame nervously settled on the stool.

"Now," Denth said, "why don't you tell us how you found out that the princess was going to be in that particular restaurant today?"

Thame glanced from side to side. "I just happened to be walking in the area and I—"

Tonk Fah cracked his knuckles. Vivenna glanced at him, suddenly noticing that Tonk Fah seemed more . . . dangerous. The idle, overweight man who liked to nap had vanished. In his place was a thug with sleeves rolled up, showing off muscles that bulged impressively.

Thame was sweating. To the side, Clod the Lifeless stepped into the room, his inhuman eyes falling into shadow, his face looking like something molded in wax. A simulacrum of a human.

"I . . . run jobs for one of the bosses in the city," Thame said. "Little things. Nothing big. When you're one of us, you take the jobs you can get."

"One of us?" Denth asked, resting his hand on the pommel of his sword.

"Idrian."

"I've seen Idrians in good positions in the city, friend," Denth said. "Merchants. Moneylenders."

"The lucky ones, sir," Thame said, gulping. "They have their own money. People will work with anyone who has money. If you're just an ordinary man, things are different. People look at your clothing, listen to your accent, and they find others to do their work. They say we're not trustworthy. Or that we're boring. Or that we steal."

"And do you?" Vivenna found herself asking.

Thame looked at her, then glanced down at the building's dirt floor. "Sometimes," he said. "But not at first. I only do it now, when my boss asks me to."

"That still doesn't answer how you knew where to find us, friend," Denth said quietly. His pointed use of the word "friend," when contrasted with Tonk Fah on one side and the Lifeless on the other, made Vivenna shiver.

"My boss talks too much," Thame said. "He knew what was happening at that restaurant—he sold the information to a couple of people. I heard for free."

Denth glanced at Tonk Fah.

"Everyone knows she's in the city," Thame said quickly. "We've all heard the rumors. It's no coincidence. Things are bad for us. Worse than they've ever been. The princess came to help, right?"

"Friend," Denth said. "I think it's best that you forget this entire meeting. I realize that there will be the temptation to sell information. But I promise you, we can find out if you do that. And we can—"

"Denth, that's enough," Vivenna said. "Stop scaring the man."

The mercenary glanced at her, causing Thame to jump.

"Oh, for the Colors' sake," she said walking forward, crouching beside Thame's stool. "No harm will come to you, Thame. You have done well in seeking me out, and I trust you to keep news of our meeting quiet. But, tell me, if things are so bad in T'Telir, why not return to Idris?"

"Travel costs money, Your Highness," he said. "I can't afford it—most of us can't."

"Are there many of you here?" Vivenna asked.

"Yes, Your Highness."

Vivenna nodded. "I want to meet with the others."

"Princess—" Denth said, but she silenced him with a glance.

"I can gather some together," Thame said, nodding eagerly. "I promise. I'm known to a lot of the Idrians."

"Good," Vivenna said. "Because I *have* come to help. How shall we contact you?"

"Ask around for Rira," he said. "That's my boss."

Vivenna rose and then gestured toward the doorway. Thame fled without further prompting. Jewels, who stood guarding the doorway, reluctantly stepped aside and let the man scuttle away.

The room was silent for a moment.

"Jewels," Denth said. "Follow him."

She nodded and was gone.

Vivenna glanced back at the two mercenaries, expecting to find them angry at her.

"Aw, did you have to let him go so fast?" Tonk Fah said, sitting down on the floor, looking morose. Whatever he'd done to look dangerous was gone, evaporating faster than water on metal in the sun.

"Now you've done it," Denth said. "He'll be sullen for the rest of the day."

"I *never* get to be the bad guy anymore," Tonk Fah said, falling back and staring up at the ceiling. His monkey wandered over and sat atop his ample stomach.

"You'll get over it," Vivenna said, rolling her eyes. "Why were you so hard on him, anyway?"

Denth shrugged. "You know what I like least about being a mercenary?"

"I suspect that you're going to tell me," Vivenna said, folding her arms.

"People are always trying to fool you," he said, sitting down on the floor beside Tonk Fah. "They all think that because you're hired muscle, you're an idiot."

He paused, as if expecting Tonk Fah to give his usual counterpoint. Instead, however, the bulky mercenary just continued to stare at the ceiling. "Arsteel *always* got to be the mean one," he said.

Denth sighed, giving Vivenna a "This is your fault" look. "Anyway," he continued. "I couldn't be sure that our friend there wasn't a plant arranged by Grable. He could have pretended to be a loyal subject, gotten inside our defenses, then knifed you in the back. Best to be safe."

She sat down on the stool, and was tempted to say that he was overreacting, but . . . well, she had just seen him kill two men in her defense. *I'm paying them,* she thought. *I should probably just let them do their job.* "Tonk Fah," she said. "You can be the mean one next time."

He looked up. "You promise?"

"Yes," she said.

"Can I yell at the person we are interrogating?"

"Sure," she said.

"Can I growl at him?" he asked.

"I guess," she said.

"Can I break his fingers?"

She frowned. "No!"

"Not even the unimportant ones?" Tonk Fah asked. "I mean, people have *five* after all. The little ones don't even do that much."

Vivenna paused, then Tonk Fah and Denth started laughing.

"Oh, honestly," she said, turning away. "I can never tell when you shift from being serious to being ridiculous."

"That's what makes it so funny," Tonk Fah said, still chuckling.

"Are we leaving, then?" Vivenna said, rising.

"Nah," Denth said. "Let's wait a bit. I'm still not sure that Grable isn't looking for us. Best to lay low for a few hours."

She frowned, glancing at Denth. Tonk Fah, amazingly, was already snoring softly.

"I thought you said that Grable would let us go," she said. "That he was just testing us—that he wanted to see how good you were."

"It's likely," Denth said. "But I've been known to be wrong. He might have let us go because he was worried about my sword being so close to him. He could be having second thoughts. We'll give it a few hours, then head back and ask my watchers if anyone has been poking around the house."

"Watchers?" Vivenna asked. "You have people watching our house?"

"Of course," Denth said. "Kids work cheap in the city. Worth the coin, even when you're not protecting a princess from a rival kingdom."

She folded her arms, standing. She didn't feel like sitting, so she began to pace.

"I wouldn't worry too much about Grable," Denth said, eyes closed as he sat back, leaning against the wall. "This is just a precaution."

She shook her head. "It makes sense that he'd want revenge, Denth," she said. "You killed two of his men."

"Men can be cheap in this city too, Princess."

"You say he was testing you," Vivenna said. "But what would be the point of that? Provoking you to action just to let you go?"

"To see how much of a threat I was," Denth said, shrugging, eyes still closed. "Or, more likely, to see if I was worth the pay I usually demand. Again, I wouldn't worry so much."

She sighed, then wandered over to the window so she could watch the street.

"You should probably stay away from the window," Denth said. "Just to be safe."

First he tells me not to worry, then he tells me not to let myself be seen, she thought with frustration, walking toward the back of the room, moving toward the door down to the cellar.

"I wouldn't do that, either," Denth noted. "Stairs are broken in a few places. Not much to see, anyway. Dirt floor. Dirt walls. Dirt ceiling."

She sighed again, turning away from the door.

"What is with you, anyway?" he asked, still not opening his eyes. "You're not usually this nervous."

"I don't know," she said. "Being locked in like this makes me anxious."

"I thought princesses were taught to be patient," Denth noted.

He's right, she realized. *That sounded like something Siri would say. What* is *wrong with me lately?* She forced herself to sit down on the stool, folding her hands in her lap, reasserting control of her hair, which had rebelliously started to lighten to a brown. "Please," she said, forcing herself to sound patient, "tell me of this place. Why did you select this building?"

Denth cracked an eyelid. "We rent it," he finally said. "It's nice to have safe houses around the city. Since we don't use them very often, we find the cheapest ones we can."

I noticed, Vivenna thought, but fell silent, recognizing how stilted her attempt at conversation had sounded. She sat quietly, looking down at her hands, trying to figure out just what had set her on edge.

It was more than the fight. The truth was, she was worried about how long things in T'Telir were taking. Her father would have received her letter two weeks before and would know that *two* of his daughters were in Hallandren. She could only hope that the logic of her letter, mixed with her threats, would keep him from doing anything foolish.

She was glad Denth had made her abandon Lemex's house. If her father did send agents to retrieve her, they would naturally try to find Lemex first—just as she had. However, a cowardly part of her wished that Denth hadn't shown such foresight. If they were still living in Lemex's home, she might have been discovered already. And be on her way back to Idris.

She acted so determined. Indeed, sometimes she *felt* quite determined. Those were the times when she thought about Siri or her kingdom's needs. However, those times— the royal times—were actually rather rare. The rest of the time, she wondered.

What was she doing? She didn't know about subterfuge or warfare. Denth was really behind everything she was "doing" to help Idris. What she had suspected on that first day had proved true. Her preparation and study amounted to little. She didn't know how to go about saving Siri. She didn't know what to do about the Breath she held within her. She didn't even know, really, if she wanted to stay in this insane, overcrowded, over*colored* city.

In short, she was useless. And that was the one thing, above all else, that her training had never prepared her to deal with.

"You really want to meet with the Idrians?" Denth asked. Vivenna looked up. Outside, it was growing darker as evening approached.

Do I? she thought. *If my father has agents in the city, they might be there. But, if there's something I can do for those people . . .*

"I'd like to," she said.

He fell silent.

"You don't like it," she said.

He shook his head. "It will be hard to arrange, hard to keep quiet, and will make you hard to protect. These meetings we've been having—they've all been in controlled areas. If you meet with the common folk, that won't be possible."

She nodded quietly. "I want to do it anyway. I have to do something, Denth. Something useful. Being paraded before these contacts of yours is helping. But I need to do more. If war is coming, we need to prepare these people. Help them, somehow."

She looked up, staring out toward the windows. Clod the Lifeless stood in the corner where Jewels had left him. Vivenna shivered, looking away. "I want to help my sister," she said. "And I want to be useful to my people. But I can't help feeling that I'm not doing much for Idris by staying in the city."

"Better than leaving," Denth said.

"Why?"

"Because if you left, there wouldn't be anyone to pay me."

She rolled her eyes.

"I wasn't joking," Denth noted. "I really do like getting paid. However, there are better reasons to stay."

"Like what?" she asked.

He shrugged. "Depends, I guess. Look, Princess, I'm not the type to give brilliant advice or deep counsel. I'm a mercenary. You pay me, you point me, and I go stab things. But I figure that if you think about it, you'll find that running back to Idris is about the *least* useful thing you could do. You won't be able to do anything there other than sit about and knit doilies. Your father has other heirs. Here, you might be largely ineffective—but there you're completely redundant."

He fell silent, stretching, leaning back a little more. *Tough man to have a conversation with, sometimes,* Vivenna thought to herself, shaking her head. Still, she found his words comforting. She smiled, turning.

And found Clod standing right beside her stool.

She yelped, half-scrambling, half-falling backward.

Denth was on his feet in a heartbeat, sword drawn, and Tonk Fah wasn't far behind.

Vivenna stumbled to her feet, her skirts getting in the way, and placed a hand against her chest, as if to still her heartbeat. The Lifeless stood, watching her.

"He does that sometimes," Denth said, chuckling, though it sounded false to Vivenna. "Just walks up to people."

"Like he was curious about them," Tonk Fah said.

"They *can't* be curious," Denth said. "No emotion at all. Clod. Go back to your corner."

The Lifeless turned and began to walk.

"No," Vivenna said, shivering. "Put it in the basement."

"But, the stairs—" Denth said.

"*Now!*" Vivenna snapped, hair tingeing red at the tips.

Denth sighed. "Clod, to the cellar."

The Lifeless turned and walked to the door at the back. As he went down the steps, Vivenna heard one crack slightly, but the creature made it safely, judging by the sound of his footsteps. She sat back down, trying to calm her breathing.

"Sorry about that," Denth said.

"I can't feel him," Vivenna said. "It's unnerving. I forget that he's there, and don't notice when he approaches."

Denth nodded. "I know."

"Jewels, too," she said, glancing at him. "She is a Drab."

"Yeah," Denth said, settling back down. "Has been since she was a child. Her parents sold her Breath to one of the gods."

"They each need a Breath a week to survive," Tonk Fah added.

"How horrible," Vivenna said. *I really need to show her more kindness.*

"It's really not so bad," Denth said. "I've been without Breath myself."

"You have?"

He nodded. "Everyone goes through times when they're

short of coin. The nice thing about Breath is that you can always buy one off someone else."

"Somebody is always selling," Tonk Fah said.

Vivenna shook her head, shivering. "But you have to live without it for a time. Have no soul."

Denth laughed—and this time it was definitely genuine. "Oh, that's just superstition, Princess. Lacking Breath doesn't change you that much."

"It makes you less kind," Vivenna said. "More irritable. Like . . ."

"Jewels?" Denth asked, amused. "Nah, she'd be like that anyway. I'm sure of it. Either way, when I've sold my Breath, I didn't feel much different. You really have to pay attention to even notice it's missing."

Vivenna turned away. She didn't expect him to understand. It was easy to call her beliefs superstition, but she could just as easily turn the words back on Denth. People saw what they wanted to see. If he believed he felt the same without Breath, that was just an easy way to rationalize the selling of it—and then the purchase of another Breath from an innocent person. Besides, why even bother buying one back if it didn't matter?

The conversation died off until Jewels returned. She walked in and, once again, Vivenna barely noticed her. *I'm starting to rely on that life sense far too much,* she thought with annoyance, standing as Jewels nodded to Denth.

"He is who he says he is," Jewels said. "I asked around, got three confirmations from people I kind of trust."

"All right, then," Denth said, stretching and climbing to his feet. He kicked Tonk Fah awake. "Let's *carefully* head back to the house."

23

LIGHTSONG FOUND BLUSHWEAVER in the grassy portion of the courtyard behind her palace. She was enjoying the art of one of the city's master gardeners.

Lightsong strolled through the grass, his entourage hovering around him, holding up a large parasol to shield him from the sun, and generally seeing that he was suitably pampered. He passed hundreds of planters, pots, and vases filled with various kinds of growing things, all arranged into elaborate formal patterns and rows.

Temporary flower beds. The gods were too godly to leave the court and visit the city gardens, so the gardens had to be brought to them. Such an enormous undertaking required dozens of workers and carts full of plants. Nothing was too good for the gods.

Except, of course, freedom.

Blushweaver stood admiring one of the patterns of vases. She noticed Lightsong as he approached, his moving BioChroma successively making the flowers shine more vibrantly in the afternoon sunlight. She was wearing a surprisingly modest dress. It had no sleeves and appeared to be made entirely of a single wrapping of green silk, but it covered up the essential bits and then some.

"Lightsong, dear," she said, smiling. "Visiting a lady in her home? How charmingly forward. Well, enough of this small talk. Let us retire to the bedroom."

He smiled, holding up a sheet of paper as he approached her.

She paused, then accepted it. The front was covered with colored dots—the artisans' script. "What is this?" she asked.

"I figured I knew how our conversation would begin,"

he said. "And so I saved us the trouble of having to go through it. I had it written out beforehand."

Blushweaver raised an eyebrow, then read. " 'To start, Blushweaver says something that is mildly suggestive.' " She glanced at him. "Mildly? I invited you to the bedroom. I'd call that blatant."

"I underestimated you," Lightsong said. "Please continue."

" 'Then Lightsong says something to deflect her,' " Blushweaver read. " 'It is so incredibly charming and clever that she is left stunned by his brilliance and cannot speak for several minutes . . .' Oh, honestly, Lightsong. Do I have to read this?"

"It's a masterpiece," he said. "Best work I've ever done. Please, the next part is important."

She sighed. " 'Blushweaver says something about politics which is dreadfully boring but she offsets it by wiggling her chest. After that, Lightsong apologizes for being so distant lately. He explains that he had some things to work out.' " She paused, eyeing him. "Does this mean that you're finally ready to be part of my plans?"

He nodded. To the side, a group of gardeners removed the flowers. They returned in waves, building a pattern of small blossoming trees in large pots around Blushweaver and Lightsong, a living kaleidoscope with the two Returned gods at its center.

"I don't think that the queen is involved in a plot to take the throne," Lightsong said. "Although I've spoken with her only briefly, I am convinced."

"Then why agree to join with me?"

He stood quietly for a moment, enjoying the blossoms. "Because," he said. "I intend to see that you don't crush her. Or the rest of us."

"My dear Lightsong," Blushweaver said, pursing bright red lips. "I assure you that I'm harmless."

He raised an eyebrow. "I doubt that."

"Now, now," she said, "you should never point out a lady's departure from strict truth. Anyway, I'm glad you came. We have work to do."

"Work?" he said. "That sounds like . . . work."

"Of course, dear," she said, walking away. Gardeners immediately ran forward, pulling aside the small trees to clear a path for them. The master gardener himself stood by directing the evolving composition like the conductor of a botanical orchestra.

Lightsong hurried and caught up. "Work," he said. "Do you know what my philosophy on that word is?"

"I have somehow gotten the subtle impression that you do not approve of it," Blushweaver said.

"Oh, I wouldn't say that. Work, my dear Blushweaver, is like fertilizer."

"It smells?"

He smiled. "No, I was thinking that work is like fertilizer in that I'm glad it exists; I just don't ever want to get stuck in it."

"That's unfortunate," Blushweaver said. "Because you just agreed to do so."

He sighed. "I thought I smelled something."

"Don't be tedious," she said, smiling to some workers as they lined her path with vases of flowers. "This is going to be fun." She turned back to him, eyes twinkling. "Mercystar got attacked last night."

⚬⚬⚬

"OH, MY DEAR Blushweaver. It was positively *tragic*."

Lightsong raised an eyebrow. Mercystar was a gorgeously voluptuous woman who offered a striking contrast with Blushweaver. Both were, of course, perfect examples of feminine beauty. Blushweaver was simply the slim— yet busty—type while Mercystar was the curvaceous—yet busty—type. Mercystar lounged back on a plush couch, being fanned with large palm leaves by several of her serving men.

She didn't have Blushweaver's subtle sense of style. There was a skill to choosing bright clothing that didn't edge into garishness. Lightsong himself didn't have it—but he had servants who did. Mercystar, apparently, didn't even know such a skill existed.

Though admittedly, he thought, *orange and gold aren't exactly the easiest colors to wear with dignity.*

"Mercystar, dear," Blushweaver said warmly. One of the servants provided a cushioned stool, sliding it beneath Blushweaver just as she sat at Mercystar's elbow. "I can understand how you must feel."

"Can you?" Mercystar asked. "Can you possibly? This is terrible. Some . . . some *miscreant* snuck into my palace, accosting my servants! The very home of a goddess! Who would do such a thing?"

"Indeed, he must have been deranged," Blushweaver said soothingly. Lightsong stood beside her, smiling sympathetically, hands clasped behind his back. A cool afternoon breeze blew across the courtyard and through the pavilion. Some of Blushweaver's gardeners had brought over flowers and trees, surrounding the pavilion's canopy, filling the air with their mingled perfumes.

"I can't understand it," Mercystar said. "The guards at the gates are supposed to prevent these kinds of things! Why do we have walls if people can just walk in and violate our homes? I just don't feel safe anymore."

"I'm certain the guards will be more diligent in the future," Blushweaver said.

Lightsong frowned, glancing toward Mercystar's palace, where servants buzzed about like bees around a disturbed hive. "What was the intruder after, do you suppose?" he said, almost to himself. "Works of art, perhaps? Surely there are merchants who would be much easier to rob."

"We may not know what they want," Blushweaver said smoothly, "but we at least know *something* about them."

"We do?" Mercystar said, perking up.

"Yes, dear," Blushweaver said. "Only someone with no respect for tradition, propriety, or religion would dare trespass in the home of a god. Someone base. Disrespectful. Unbelieving . . ."

"An Idrian?" Mercystar asked.

"Did you ever wonder, dear," Blushweaver said, "why they sent their *youngest* daughter to the God King instead of their eldest?"

Mercystar frowned. "They did?"

"Yes, dear," Blushweaver said.

"That is rather suspicious, now, isn't it?"

"Something is going on in the Court of Gods, Mercystar," Blushweaver said, leaning over. "These could be dangerous times for the Crown."

"Blushweaver," Lightsong said. "A word, if you please?"

She eyed him in annoyance. He met her gaze steadily, which eventually caused her to sigh. She patted Mercystar's hand and then retreated from the pavilion with Lightsong, their servants and priests trailing behind.

"What are you doing?" Lightsong said as soon as they were out of Mercystar's hearing.

"Recruiting," Blushweaver said, a glint in her eye. "We're going to need her Lifeless Commands."

"I'm still not myself persuaded that we will need them," Lightsong said. "War may not be necessary."

"As I said," Blushweaver replied, "we need to be careful. I'm just making preparations."

"All right," he said. There was a wisdom to that. "But we don't know that it was an Idrian who broke into Mercystar's palace. Why are you implying that it was?"

"And you think it's just coincidence? Someone sneaks into one of our palaces *now,* with the war approaching?"

"Coincidence."

"And the intruder just *happened* to pick one of the four Returned who hold Lifeless access Commands? If I were going to go to war with Hallandren, the first thing I'd do would be to try to search out those commands. Maybe see if they were written down anywhere, or perhaps try to kill the gods who held them."

Lightsong glanced back at the palace. Blushweaver's arguments held some merit, but they weren't enough. He had an odd impulse to look into this more deeply. However, that sounded like work. He really couldn't afford to make an exception to his usual habits, particularly without a lot of complaining first. It set a poor precedent. So he just nodded his head, and Blushweaver led them back to the pavilion.

"Dear," Blushweaver said, quickly sitting back beside Mercystar and looking a little bit more anxious. She leaned in. "We've talked it over and decided to trust you."

Mercystar sat up. "Trust me? With what?"

"Knowledge," Blushweaver whispered. "There are those of us who fear that the Idrians aren't content with their mountains and are determined to control the lowlands as well."

"But we'll be joined by blood," Mercystar said. "There will be a Hallandren God King with royal blood on our throne."

"Oh?" Blushweaver said. "And could that not also be interpreted as an *Idrian* king with Hallandren blood on the throne?"

Mercystar wavered. Then, oddly, she glanced at Lightsong. "Do you believe this?"

Why did people look toward him? He did everything to discourage such behavior, but they still tended to act like he was some kind of moral authority. "I think that some . . . preparation would be wise," he said. "Though, of course, the same can be said for dinner."

Blushweaver gave him an annoyed look, though by the

time she looked back at Mercystar, she had her consoling face on again. "We understand that you've had a difficult day," she said. "But please, consider our offer. We would like you to join with us in our precautions."

"What kind of precautions are you talking about?" Mercystar asked.

"Simple ones," Blushweaver said quickly. "Thinking, talking, planning. Eventually, if we think we have enough evidence, we will bring what we know to the God King."

This seemed to ease Mercystar's mind. She nodded. "Yes, I can see. Preparation. It *would* be wise."

"Rest now, dear," Blushweaver said, rising and leading Lightsong away from the pavilion. They walked leisurely across the perfect lawn back toward Blushweaver's own palace. He felt a reluctance to go, however. Something about the meeting bothered him.

"She's a dear," Blushweaver said, smiling.

"You just say that because she's so easy to manipulate."

"Of course," Blushweaver said. "I positively *love* people who do as they should. 'Should' being defined as whatever I think is best."

"At least you're open about it," Lightsong said.

"To you, my dear, I'm as easy to read as a book."

He snorted. "Maybe one that hasn't been translated to Hallandren yet."

"You just say that because you've never *really* tried reading me," she said, smiling at him. "Though, I must say that there is one thing about dear Mercystar that positively annoys me."

"And that is?"

"Her armies," Blushweaver said, folding her arms. "Why did *she,* goddess of kindness, get command of ten thousand Lifeless? It's obviously a dire error in judgment. Particularly since I don't have command of *any* troops."

"Blushweaver," he said with amusement, "you're the

goddess of honesty, communication, and interpersonal relationships. Why in the world would you be given stewardship of armies?"

"There are many interpersonal relationships related to armies," she said. "After all, what do you call one man hitting another with a sword? That's interpersonal."

"Quite so," Lightsong said, glancing back at Mercystar's pavilion.

"Now," Blushweaver said, "I should think that you'd appreciate my arguments, since relationships are, in fact, war. As is clear in *our* relationship, dear Lightsong. We . . ." She trailed off, then poked him in the shoulder. "Lightsong? Pay attention to me!"

"Yes?"

She folded her arms petulantly. "I must say, your banter has been decidedly off today. I may just have to find someone else to play with."

"Hum, yes," he said, studying Mercystar's palace. "Tragic. Now, the break-in at Mercystar's. It was just one person?"

"Supposedly," Blushweaver said. "It's not important."

"Was anyone injured?"

"A couple of servants," Blushweaver said with a wave of the hand. "One was found dead, I believe. You should be paying attention to *me,* not that—"

Lightsong froze. "Someone was *killed*?"

She shrugged. "So they say."

He turned around. "I'm going to go back and talk to her some more."

"Fine," Blushweaver snapped. "But you'll do it without me. I have gardens to enjoy."

"All right," Lightsong said, already turning away. "I'll talk to you later."

Blushweaver let out a huff of indignation, her hands on her hips, watching him go. Lightsong ignored her irritation, however, more focused on . . .

What? So some servants had been hurt. It wasn't his

place to be involved in criminal disturbances. And yet, he walked straight to Mercystar's pavilion again, his servants and priests trailing behind, as ever.

She was still reclining on her couch. "Lightsong?" she asked with a frown.

"I returned because I just heard that one of your servants was killed in the attack."

"Ah, yes," she said. "The poor man. What a terrible occurrence. I'm sure he's found his blessings in heaven."

"Funny, how they're always in the last place you consider looking," Lightsong said. "Tell me, how did the murder happen?"

"It's very odd, actually," she said. "The two guards at the door were knocked unconscious. The intruder was discovered by four of my servants who were walking through the service hallway. He fought them, knocked out one, killed another, and two escaped."

"How was the man killed?"

Mercystar sighed. "I really don't know," she said with a wave of the hand. "My priests can tell you. I fear I was too traumatized to take in the details."

"It would be all right if I talked to them?"

"If you must," Mercystar said. "Have I mentioned exactly how thoroughly out of sorts I am? One would think that you'd prefer to stay and comfort me."

"My dear Mercystar," he said. "If you know anything of me, then you will realize that leaving you alone is by far the best comfort I can offer."

She frowned, looking up.

"It was a joke, my dear," he said. "I am, unfortunately, quite bad at them. Scoot, you coming?"

Llarimar, who stood—as always—with the rest of the priests, looked toward him. "Your Grace?"

"No need to upset the others any further," Lightsong said. "I think that you and I alone will be sufficient for this exercise."

"As you command, Your Grace," Llarimar said. Once again, Lightsong's servants found themselves separated from their god. They clustered uncertainly on the grass—like a group of children abandoned by their parents.

"What is this about, Your Grace?" Llarimar asked quietly as they walked up to the palace.

"I honestly have no idea," Lightsong said. "I just feel that there's something odd going on here. The break-in. The death of that man. Something is wrong."

Llarimar looked at him, a strange expression on his face.

"What?" Lightsong asked.

"It is nothing, Your Grace," Llarimar finally said. "This is just very uncharacteristic of you."

"I know," Lightsong said, feeling confident about the decision nonetheless. "I honestly can't say what prompted it. Curiosity, I guess."

"Curiosity that outweighs your desire to avoid doing . . . well, anything at all?"

Lightsong shrugged. He felt energized as he walked into the palace. His normal lethargy retreated, and instead he felt excitement. It was almost familiar. He found a group of priests chatting inside the servants' corridor. Lightsong walked right up to them, and they turned to regard him with shock.

"Ah, good," Lightsong said. "I assume you can tell me more of this break-in?"

"Your Grace," one said as all three bowed their heads. "I assure you, we have everything under control. There is no danger to you or your people."

"Yes, yes," Lightsong said, looking over the corridor. "Is this where the man was killed, then?"

They glanced at one another. "Over there," one of them said reluctantly, pointing to a turn in the hallway.

"Wonderful. Accompany me, if you please." Lightsong walked up to the indicated section. A group of workers were removing the boards from the floor, probably to be replaced. Bloodstained wood, no matter how well cleaned, would not do for a goddess's home.

"Hum," Lightsong said. "Looks messy. How did it happen?"

"We aren't sure, Your Grace," said one of the priests. "The intruder knocked the men at the doorway unconscious, but did not otherwise harm them."

"Yes, Mercystar mentioned that," Lightsong said. "But then he fought with four of the servants?"

"Well, 'fought' isn't quite the right word," the priest said, sighing. Though Lightsong wasn't their god, he was *a* god. They were bound by oath to answer his questions.

"He immobilized one of them with an Awakened rope," the priest continued. "Then, while one remained behind to delay the intruder, the other two ran for aid. The intruder quickly knocked the remaining man unconscious. At that time, the one who had been tied up was still alive." The priest glanced at his colleagues. "When help finally came— delayed by a Lifeless animal that was causing confusion— they found the second man still unconscious. The first, still tied up, was dead. Stabbed through the heart with a dueling blade."

Lightsong nodded, kneeling beside the broken boards. The servants who had been working there bowed their heads and retreated. He wasn't certain what he expected to find. The floor had been scrubbed clean, then torn apart. However, there was a strange patch a short distance away. He walked over and knelt, inspecting it more closely. *Completely devoid of color,* he thought. He looked up, focusing on the priests. "An Awakener, you say?"

"Undoubtedly, Your Grace."

He looked back down at the grey patch. *There's no chance an Idrian did this,* he realized. *Not if he used Awakening.* "What was this Lifeless creature you mentioned?"

"A Lifeless squirrel, Your Grace," one of the men said. "The intruder used it as a diversion."

"Well made?" he asked.

They nodded. "Using modern Command words, if its actions were any judge," one said. "It even had ichor-alcohol instead of blood. Took us the better part of the night to catch the thing!"

"I see," Lightsong said, standing. "But the intruder escaped?"

"Yes, Your Grace," one of them said.

"What do you suppose he was after?"

The priests wavered. "We don't know for sure, Your Grace," one of them said. "We scared him away before he could reach his goal—one of our men saw him fleeing back out the way he had come. Perhaps the resistance was too much for him."

"We think that he may have been a common burglar, Your Grace," one said. "Here to sneak into the gallery and steal the art."

"Sounds likely enough to me," Lightsong said, standing. "Good work with this, and all that." He turned, walking back down the hallway toward the entrance. He felt strangely surreal.

The priests were lying to him.

He didn't know how he could tell. Yet he did—he knew it deep inside, with some instincts he hadn't realized he possessed. Instead of disturbing him, for some reason the lies excited him.

"Your Grace," Llarimar said, hurrying up. "Did you find what you wanted?"

"That was no Idrian who broke in," Lightsong said quietly as they walked into the sunlight.

Llarimar raised an eyebrow. "There have been cases of Idrians coming to Hallandren and buying themselves Breath, Your Grace."

"And have you ever heard of one using a Lifeless?"

Llarimar fell quiet. "No, Your Grace," he finally admitted.

"Idrians hate Lifeless. Consider them abominations, or some such nonsense. Either way, it wouldn't make sense for an Idrian to try and get in like that. What would be the point? Assassinating a single one of the Returned? He or she would only be replaced, and the protocols in place would be certain that even the Lifeless armies weren't without someone to direct them for long. The possibility for retaliation would far outweigh the benefit."

"So you believe that it was a thief?"

"Of course not," Lightsong said. "A 'common burglar' with enough money or Breath that he can *waste* a Lifeless, just for a diversion? Whoever broke in, he was already rich. Besides, why sneak through the servants' hallway? There are no valuables there. The *interior* of the palace holds far more wealth."

Llarimar fell quiet again. He looked over at Lightsong, the same curious expression as before on his face. "That's some very solid reasoning, Your Grace."

"I know," Lightsong said. "I feel positively unlike myself. Perhaps I need to go get drunk."

"You can't get drunk."

"Ah, but I certainly enjoy trying."

They walked back toward his palace, picking up his servants on the way. Llarimar seemed unsettled. Lightsong, however, simply felt excited. *Murder in the Court of Gods,* he thought. *True, it was only a servant—but I'm supposed to be a god for all people, not just important ones. I wonder how long it's been since someone was killed in the court? Hasn't happened in my lifetime, certainly.*

Mercystar's priests were hiding something. Why had the intruder released a diversion—particularly such an expensive one—if he were simply going to run away? The servants of the Returned were not formidable soldiers or warriors. So why had he given up so easily?

All good questions. Good questions that he, of all people, shouldn't have bothered to wonder about. And yet, he did.

All the way back to the palace, through a nice meal, and even into the night.

24

SIRI'S SERVANTS CLUSTERED around her uncertainly as she walked into the chaotic room. She wore a blue and white gown with a ten-foot train. As she entered, scribes and priests looked up in shock; some immediately scrambled to their feet, bowing. Others just stared as she passed, her serving women doing their best to hold her train with dignity.

Determined, Siri continued through the chamber—which was more like a hallway than a proper room. Long tables lined the walls, stacks of paper cluttered those tables, and scribes—Pahn Kahl men in brown, Hallandren men in the day's colors—worked on the papers. The walls were, of course, black. Colored rooms were only found in the center of the palace, where the God King and Siri spent most of their time. Separately, of course.

Though, things are a little different at night, she thought, smiling. It felt very conspiratorial of her to be teaching him letters. She had a secret that she was keeping from the rest of the kingdom, a secret that involved one of the most powerful men in the entire world. That gave her a thrill. She supposed she should have been more worried. Indeed, in her more thoughtful moments, the reality behind Bluefingers's warnings did worry her. That's why she had come to the scribes' quarters.

I wonder why the bedchamber is out here, she thought. *Outside the main body of the palace, in the black part.*

Either way, the servants' section of the palace—God King's bedchamber excluded—was the last place the scribes expected to be disturbed by their queen. Siri noticed that some of her serving women looked apologetically at the men in the room as Siri arrived at the doors on the far side. A servant opened the door for her, and she entered the room beyond.

A relaxed group of priests stood leafing through books in the medium-sized chamber. They looked over at her. One dropped his book to the floor in shock.

"I," Siri proclaimed, "want some books!"

The priests stared at her. "Books?" one finally asked.

"Yes," Siri said, hands on hips. "This is the palace library, is it not?"

"Well, yes, Vessel," the priest said, glancing at his companions. All wore the robes of their office, and this day's colors were violet and silver.

"Well, then," Siri said. "I'd like to borrow some of the books. I am tired of common entertainment and shall be reading to myself in my spare time."

"Surely you don't want *these* books, Vessel," another priest said. "They are about boring topics like religion or city finances. Surely a book of stories would be more appropriate."

Siri raised an eyebrow. "And where might I find such a 'more appropriate' volume?"

"We could have a reader bring the book from the city collection," the priest said, stepping forward smoothly. "He'd be here shortly."

Siri hesitated. "No. I do not like that option. I shall take some of these books here."

"No, you shall not," a new voice said from behind.

Siri turned. Treledees, high priest of the God King,

stood behind her, fingers laced, miter on his head, frown on his face.

"You cannot refuse me," Siri said. "I am your queen."

"I can and *will* refuse you, Vessel," Treledees said. "You see, these books are quite valuable, and should something happen to them, the kingdom would suffer grave consequences. Even our priests are not allowed to bear them out of the room."

"What could happen to them in the *palace,* of all places?" she demanded.

"It is the principle, Vessel. These are the property of a god. Susebron has made it clear that he wishes the books to stay here."

Oh he has, has he? For Treledees and the priests, having a tongueless god was very convenient. The priests could claim that he'd told them whatever served the purposes of the moment, and he could never correct them.

"If you absolutely must read these volumes," Treledees said, "you can stay here to do it."

She glanced at the room and thought of the stuffy priests standing in a flock around her, listening to her sound out words, making a fool of herself. If anything in these volumes was sensitive, they'd probably find a way to distract her and keep her from finding it.

"No," Siri said, retreating from the crowded room. "Perhaps another time."

❧

I TOLD YOU that they would not let you have the books, the God King wrote.

Siri rolled her eyes and flopped back onto the bed. She still wore her heavy evening dress. For some reason, being able to communicate with the God King made her even shyer. She only took off the dresses right before she went to sleep—which, lately, was getting later and later. Susebron sat in his usual place—not on the mattress, as he had that first night. Instead, he had pulled his chair up beside the bed. He still seemed so large and imposing. At least, he did until he looked at her, his face open, honest. He waved her back toward him where he sat with a board, writing with a bit of charcoal that she'd smuggled in.

You shud not anger the prests so, he wrote. His spelling, as one might expect, was awful.

Priests. She had pilfered a cup, then had hidden it in the room. If she held it to the wall and listened, she could sometimes faintly hear talking on the other side. After her nightly moaning and bouncing, she could usually hear chairs moving and a door closing. After that, there was silence in the other room.

Either the priests left each night once they were sure the deed was done or they were suspicious and trying to fool her into thinking they were gone. Her instinct said the former, though she made certain to whisper when she spoke to the God King, just in case.

Siri? he wrote. *What are you thinking about?*

"Your priests," she whispered. "They frustrate me! They intentionally do things to spite me."

They are good men, he wrote. *They work very hard to mayntayn my kingdom.*

"They cut out your tongue," she said.

The God King sat quietly for a few moments. *It was nesisary,* he wrote. *I have too much power.*

She moved over. As usual, he shied back when she approached, moving his arm out of the way. There was no arrogance in this reaction. She had begun to think that he just had very little experience with touching.

"Susebron," she whispered. "These men are *not* looking after your best interests. They did more than cut out your tongue. They speak in your name, doing whatever they please."

They are not my enemies, he wrote stubbornly. *They are good men.*

"Oh?" she said. "Then why do you hide from them the fact that you're learning to read?"

He paused again, glancing downward.

So much humility for one who has ruled Hallandren for fifty years, she thought. *In many ways, he's like a child.*

I do not want them to know, he finally wrote. *I do not want to upset them.*

"I'm sure," Siri said flatly.

He paused. *You are shur?* he wrote. *Does that mean you beleve me?*

"No," Siri said. "That was sarcasm, Susebron."

He frowned. *I do not know this thing. Sarkazm.*

"Sarcasm," she said, spelling it. "It's . . ." She trailed off. "It's when you say one thing, but you really mean the opposite."

He frowned at her, then furiously erased his board and began writing again. *This thing makes no sense. Why not say what you mean?*

"Because," Siri said. "It's just like . . . oh, I don't know. It's a way to be clever when you make fun of people."

Make fun of people? he wrote.

God of Colors! Siri thought, trying to think of how to explain. It seemed ridiculous to her that he would know nothing of mockery. And yet, he had lived his entire life as a revered deity and monarch. "Mockery is when you say things to tease," Siri said. "Things that might be hurtful to someone if said in anger, but you say them in an affectionate or playful way. Sometimes you *do* just say them to be mean. Sarcasm is one of the ways we mock—we say the opposite, but in an exaggerated way."

How do you know if the person is affekshonate, playful, or mean?

"I don't know," Siri said. "It's the way they say it, I guess."

The God King sat, looking confused but thoughtful. *You are very normal,* he finally wrote.

Siri frowned. "Um. Thank you?"

Was that good sarcasm? he wrote. *Because in reality, you are quite strange.*

She smiled. "I try my best."

He looked up.

"That was sarcasm again," she said. "I don't 'try' to be strange. It just happens."

He looked at her. How had she ever been frightened of this man? How had she misunderstood? The look in his eyes, it wasn't arrogance or emotionlessness. It was the look of a man who was trying very hard to understand the world around him. It was innocence. Earnestness.

However, he was not simple. The speed at which he'd learned to write proved that. True, he'd already understood the spoken version of the language—and he'd memorized all of the letters in the book years before meeting her. She'd only needed to explain the rules of spelling and sound for him to make the final jump.

She still found it amazing how quickly he picked things up. She smiled at him, and he hesitantly smiled back.

"Why do you say that I'm strange?" she asked.

You do not do things like other people, he wrote. *Everyone else bows before me all of the time. Nobody talks to me. Even the prests, they only okashonally give me instrukshons—and they haven't done that in years.*

"Does it offend you that I don't bow, and that I talk to you like a friend?"

He erased his board. *Offend me? Why would it offend me? Do you do it in sarcasm?*

"No," she said quickly. "I really like talking to you."

Then I do not understand.

"Everyone else is afraid of you," Siri said. "Because of how powerful you are."

But they took away my tongue to make me safe.

"It's not your Breath that scares them," Siri said. "It's your power over armies and people. You're the God King. You could order anyone in the kingdom killed."

But why would I do that? he wrote. *I would not kill a good person. They must know that.*

Siri sat back, resting on the plush bed, the fire crackling in the hearth behind them. "I know that, now," she said. "But nobody else does. They don't know you—they know only how powerful you are. So they fear you. And so they show their respect for you."

He paused. *And so, you do not respect me?*

"Of course I do," she said, sighing. "I've just never been very good at following rules. In fact, if someone tells me what to do, I usually want to do the opposite."

That is very strange, he wrote. *I thought all people did what they were told.*

"I think you'll find that most do not," she said, smiling.

That will get you into trouble.

"Is that what the priests taught you?"

He shook his head; then he reached over and took out his book. The book of stories for children. He brought it with him always, and she could see from his reverent touch that he valued it greatly.

It's probably his only real possession, she thought. *Everything else is taken from him every day, then replaced the next morning.*

This book, he wrote. *My mother read the stories to me when I was a child. I memorized them all, before she was taken away. It speaks of many children who do not do as they are told. They are often eaten by monsters.*

"Oh are they?" Siri said, smiling.

Do not be afraid, he wrote. *My mother taught me that the monsters are not real. But I remember the lessons the stories taught. Obediance is good. You shud treat people well. Do not go into the jungle by yourself. Do not lie. Do not hurt others.*

Siri's smile deepened. Everything he'd learned in his life, he'd either gotten from moralistic folktales or from priests who were teaching him to be a figurehead. Once she realized that, the simple, honest man that he had become was not so difficult to understand.

Yet what had prompted him to defy that learning and ask her to teach him? Why was he willing to keep his learning secret from the men he had been taught all his life to obey and trust? He was not quite so innocent as he appeared.

"These stories," she said. "Your desire to treat people well. Is that what kept you from . . . taking me on any of those nights when I first came into the room?"

From taking you? I do not understand.

Siri blushed, hair turning red to match. "I mean, why did you just sit there?"

Because I did not know what else to do, he said. *I knew that we need to have a child. So I sat and waited for it to happen. We must be doing something wrong, for no child has come.*

Siri paused, then blinked. He couldn't possibly . . . "You don't know how to have children?"

In the stories, he wrote, *a man and a woman spend the night together. Then they have a child. We spent many nights together, and there were no children.*

"And nobody—none of your priests—explained the process to you?"

No. What process do you mean?

She sat for a moment. *No,* she thought, feeling her blush deepen. *I am* not *going to have that conversation with him.* "I think we'll talk about it another time."

It was a very strange experiance when you came into the room that first night, he wrote. *I must admit, I was very scared of you.*

Siri smiled as she remembered her own terror. It hadn't even occurred to her that he would be frightened. Why would it have? He was the God King.

"So," she said, tapping the bedspread with one finger, "you were never taken to other women?"

No, he wrote. *I did find it very interesting to see you naked.*

She flushed again, though her hair had apparently decided to just stay red. "That's not what we're talking about right now," she said. "I want to know about other women. No mistresses? No concubines?"

No.

"They really are scared of you having a child."

Why say that? he wrote. *They sent you to me.*

"Only after fifty years of rule," she said. "And only under very controlled circumstances, with the proper lineage to produce a child with the right bloodline. Bluefingers thinks that child might be a danger to us."

I do not understand why, he wrote. *This is what everyone wants. There must be an heir.*

"Why?" Siri said. "You still look like you're barely two decades old. Your aging is slowed by your BioChroma."

Without an heir, the kingdom is in danger. Should I be killed, there will be nobody to rule.

"And that wasn't a danger for the last fifty years?"

He paused, frowning, then slowly erased his board.

"They must think that you're in danger now," she said slowly. "But not from sickness—even I know that Returned don't suffer from diseases. In fact, do they even age at all?"

I don't think so, the God King wrote.

"How did the previous God Kings die?"

There have been only four, he wrote. *I do not know how they died for certain.*

"Only four kings in several hundred years, all dead of mysterious circumstances. . . ."

My father died before I was old enough to remember him, Susebron wrote. *I was told he gave his life for the kingdom—that he released his BioChromatic Breath, as all Returned can, to cure a terrible disease. The other Returned can only cure one person. A God King, however, can cure many. That is what I was told.*

"There must be a record of that then," she said. "Somewhere in those books the priests have guarded so tightly."

I am sorry that they would not let you read them, he wrote.

She waved an indifferent hand. "There wasn't much chance of it working. I'll need to find another way to get at those histories." *Having a child* is *the danger,* she thought. *That's what Bluefingers said. So whatever threat there is to my life, it will only come after there is an heir. Bluefingers mentioned a threat to the God King too. That almost makes it sound like the danger comes from the priests themselves. Why would they want to harm their own god?*

She glanced at Susebron, who was flipping intently through his book of stories. She smiled at the look of concentration on his face as he deciphered the text.

Well, she thought, *considering what he knows of sex, I'd say that we don't have to worry much about having a child in the near future.*

Of course, she was also worried that the lack of a child would prove just as dangerous as the presence of one.

25

VIVENNA WENT AMONG the people of T'Telir and couldn't help feeling that every one of them recognized her.

She fought the feeling down. It was actually a miracle that Thame—who came from her own home city—had been able to pick her out. The people around her would have no way of connecting Vivenna to the rumors they might have heard, especially considering her clothing.

Immodest reds and yellows layered one atop the other

on her dress. The garment had been the only one that Parlin and Tonk Fah had been able to find that met her stringent requirements for modesty. The tubelike dress was made after a foreign cut, from Tedradel, across the Inner Sea. It came down almost to her ankles, and though its snugness emphasized her bust, at least the garment covered her almost up to the neck, and had full-length sleeves.

Rebelliously, she did find herself stealing glances at the other women in their loose, short skirts and sleeveless tops. That much exposed skin was scandalous, but with the blazing sun and the cursed coastal humidity, she could see why they did it.

After a month in the city, she was also beginning to get the hang of moving with the flow of traffic. She still wasn't sure she wanted to be out, but Denth had been persuasive.

You know the worst thing that can happen to a bodyguard? he had asked. *Letting your charge get killed when you aren't even there. We have a small team, Princess. We can either divide and leave you behind with one guard or you can come with us. Personally, I'd like to have you along where I can keep an eye on you.*

And so she'd come. Dressed in one of her new gowns, her hair turned an uncomfortable—yet un-Idrian—yellow and left loose, blowing behind her. She walked around the garden square, as if out on a stroll, moving so that she wouldn't look nervous. The people of T'Telir liked gardens—they had all kinds all over the city. In fact, from what Vivenna had seen, most of the city practically *was* a garden. Palms and ferns grew on every street, and exotic flowers bloomed everywhere year-round.

Four streets crossed in the square, with four plots of cultivated ground forming a checkerboard pattern. Each sprouted a dozen different palms. The buildings surrounding the gardens were more rich than the ones in the market up the way. And while there was plenty of foot traffic, people made certain to stick to the slate sidewalks, for carriages were common. This was a wealthy shopping district. No tents. Fewer performers. Higher quality—and more expensive—shops.

Vivenna strolled along the perimeter of the northwestern garden block. There were ferns and grass to her right. Shops of a quaint, rich, and—of course—colorful variety lay across the street to her left. Tonk Fah and Parlin lounged between two of these. Parlin had the monkey on his shoulder, and had taken to wearing a colorful red vest with his green hat. She couldn't help thinking that the woodsman was even more out of place in T'Telir than she was, but he didn't seem to attract any attention.

Vivenna kept walking. Jewels trailed her somewhere in the crowd. The woman was good—Vivenna only rarely caught a glimpse of her, and that was because she'd been told where to look. She never saw Denth. He was there somewhere, far too stealthy for her to spot. As she reached the end of the street and turned around to walk back, she did catch sight of Clod. The Lifeless stood as still as one of the D'Denir statues that lined the gardens, impassively watching the crowds pass. Most of the people ignored him.

Denth was right. Lifeless weren't plentiful, but they also weren't uncommon. Several walked through the market carrying packages for their owners. None of these were as muscular or as tall as Clod—Lifeless came in as many shapes and sizes as people. They were put to work guarding shops. Acting as packmen. Sweeping the walkway. All around her.

She continued to walk, and she caught a brief glimpse of Jewels in the crowd as she passed. *How does she manage to look so relaxed?* Vivenna thought. Each of the mercenaries looked as calm as if they were at a leisurely picnic.

Don't think about the danger, Vivenna thought, clenching her fists. She focused on the gardens. The truth was, she was a little jealous of the T'Telirites. People lounged, sitting on the grass, lying in the shade of trees, their children playing and laughing. D'Denir statues stood in a solemn line, arms upraised, weapons at the ready, as if in defense of the people. Trees climbed high into the sky, spreading branches that grew strange flowerlike bundles.

Wide-petaled flowers bloomed in planters; some of them were actually Tears of Edgli. Austre had placed the flowers where he wanted them. To cut and bring them back, to use them to adorn a room or house, was ostentation. Yet was it ostentatious to plant them in the middle of the city, where all were free to enjoy them?

She turned away. Her BioChroma continued to sense the beauty. The density of life in one area made a sort of buzz inside her chest.

No wonder they like to live so close together, she thought, noticing how a group of flowers scaled in color, fanning toward the inside of their planter. *And if you're going to live this compactly, the only way to see nature would be to bring it in.*

"Help! Fire!"

Vivenna spun, as did most of the other people on the street. The building Tonk Fah and Parlin had been standing next to was burning. Vivenna didn't continue to gawk, but turned and looked toward the center of the gardens. Most of the people in the garden itself were stunned, looking toward the smoke billowing into the air.

Distraction one.

People ran to help, crossing the street, causing carriages to pull up abruptly. At that moment, Clod stepped forward—surging with the crowd—and swung a club at the leg of a horse. Vivenna couldn't hear the leg break, but she did see the beast scream and fall, upsetting the carriage it had been pulling. A trunk fell from the top of the vehicle, plunging to the street.

The carriage belonged to one Nanrovah, high priest of the god Stillmark. Denth's intelligence said the carriage would be carrying valuables. Even if it weren't, a high priest in danger would draw a lot of attention. The trunk hit the street. And, in a twist of good fortune, it shattered, spraying out gold coins.

Distraction two.

Vivenna caught a glimpse of Jewels standing on the other side of the carriage. She looked at Vivenna and nodded. Time to go. As people ran toward either gold or fire, Vivenna walked away. Nearby, Denth would be raiding one of the shops with a gang of thieves. The thieves got to keep the goods. Vivenna just wanted to make certain those goods disappeared.

Vivenna was joined by Jewels and Parlin on the way out. She was surprised to feel how quickly her heart was thumping. Almost nothing had happened. No real danger. No threat to herself. Just a couple of "accidents."

But, then, that was the idea.

———✿———

HOURS LATER, DENTH and Tonk Fah still hadn't returned to the house. Vivenna sat quietly on their new furniture, hands in her lap. The furniture was green. Apparently, brown was not an option in T'Telir.

"What time is it?" Vivenna asked quietly.

"I don't know," Jewels snapped, standing beside the window, looking out at the street.

Patience, Vivenna told herself. *It's not her fault she's so abrasive. She had her Breath stolen.*

"Should they be back yet?" Vivenna asked calmly.

Jewels shrugged. "Maybe. Depends on if they decided to go to a safe house to let things cool down first or not."

"I see. How long do you think we should wait?"

"As long as we have to," Jewels said. "Look, do you think you could just not talk to me? I'd really appreciate it." She turned back to look out the window.

Vivenna stiffened at the insult. *Patience!* she told herself. *Understand her place. That's what the Five Visions teach.*

Vivenna stood up, then walked quietly over to Jewels.

Tentatively, she laid an arm on the other woman's shoulder. Jewels jumped immediately—obviously, without Breath, it was harder for her to notice when people approached her.

"It's all right," Vivenna said. "I understand."

"Understand?" Jewels asked. "Understand what?"

"They took your Breath," Vivenna said. "They had no right to do something so terrible."

Vivenna smiled, then withdrew, walking to the stairs.

Jewels started laughing. Vivenna stopped, glancing back.

"You think you *understand* me?" Jewels asked. "What? You feel sorry for me because I'm a Drab?"

"Your parents shouldn't have done what they did."

"My parents served our God King," Jewels said. "My Breath was given to him directly. It's a greater honor than you could possibly understand."

Vivenna stood still for a moment, absorbing that comment. "You *believe* in the Iridescent Tones?"

"Of course I do," Jewels said. "I'm a Hallandren, aren't I?"

"But the others—"

"Tonk Fah is from Pahn Kahl," Jewels said. "And I don't know where in the Colors *Denth* is from. But I'm from T'Telir itself."

"But surely you can't still worship those so-called gods," Vivenna said. "Not after what was done to you."

"What was done to me? I'll have you know that I gave away my Breath willingly."

"You were a child!"

"I was eleven and my parents gave me the choice. I made the right one. My father had been in the dye industry, but had slipped and fallen. The damage to his back wouldn't allow him to work, and I had five brothers and sisters. Do you know what it's like to watch your brothers and sisters starve? Years before, my parents had already sold their Breath to get enough money to start the business. By selling mine, we got enough money to live for nearly a year!"

"No price is worth a soul," Vivenna said. "You—"

"Stop judging me!" Jewels snapped. "Kalad's Phantoms take you, woman. I was *proud* to sell my Breath! I still am. A part of me lives inside the God King. Because of me, he continues to live. I'm *part* of this kingdom in a way that few others are."

Jewels shook her head, turning away. "That's why we get annoyed by you Idrians. So high, so certain that what you do is *right*. If your god asked you to give up your Breath—or even the Breath of your child—wouldn't you do it? You give up your children to become monks, forcing them into a life of servitude, don't you? That's seen as a sign of faith. Yet when we do something to serve *our* gods, you twist your lips at us and call us blasphemers."

Vivenna opened her mouth, but could come up with no response. Sending children away to become monks was different.

"We sacrifice for our gods," Jewels said, still staring out the window. "But that doesn't mean we're being exploited. My family was blessed because of what we did. Not only was there enough money to buy food, but my father recovered, and a few years later, he was able to open up the dye business again. My brothers still run it.

"You don't have to believe in my miracles. You can call them accidents or coincidences, if you must. But don't pity me for my faith. And don't presume that you're better, just because you believe something different."

Vivenna closed her mouth. Obviously, there was no point in arguing. Jewels was in no mood for her sympathy. Vivenna retreated back up the stairs.

⁂

A FEW HOURS later, it began to grow dark. Vivenna stood on the house's second-story balcony, looking out over the city. Most of the buildings on their street had such balconies on the front. Ostentatious or not, from their hillside location they did provide a good view of T'Telir.

The city glowed with light. On the larger streets, pole-mounted lamps lined the sidewalks, lit each night by city workers. Many of the buildings were illuminated as well. Such expenditure of oil and candles still amazed her. Yet with the Inner Sea to hand, oil was far cheaper than it was in the highlands.

She didn't know what to make of Jewels's outburst. How could someone be *proud* that their Breath had been stolen and then fed to a greedy Returned? The woman's tone seemed to indicate she was being sincere. She'd clearly thought about these things before. Obviously, she had to rationalize her experiences to live with them.

Vivenna was trapped. The Five Visions taught that she must try to understand others. They told her not to place herself above them. And yet, Austrism taught that what Jewels had done was an abomination.

The two seemed contradictory. To believe that Jewels was wrong was to place herself above the woman. Yet to accept what Jewels said was to deny Austrism. Some might have laughed at her turmoil, but Vivenna had always tried very hard to be devout. She'd understood that she'd need strict devotion to survive in heathen Hallandren.

Heathen. Didn't she place herself above Hallandren by calling it that word? But they *were* heathen. She couldn't accept the Returned as true gods. It seemed that to believe in any faith was to become arrogant.

Perhaps she deserved the things Jewels had said to her.

Someone approached. Vivenna turned as Denth pushed open the wooden door and stepped out onto the balcony. "We're back," he announced.

"I know," she said, looking out over the city and its specks of light. "I felt you enter the building a little while ago."

He chuckled, joining her. "I forget that you have so much Breath, Princess. You never use it."

Except to feel when people are nearby, she thought. *But I can't help that, can I?*

"I recognize that look of frustration," Denth noted. "Still worried that the plan isn't working fast enough?"

She shook her head. "Other things entirely, Denth."

"Probably shouldn't have left you alone so long with Jewels. I hope she didn't take *too* many bites out of you."

Vivenna didn't respond. Finally, she sighed, then turned toward him. "How did the job go?"

"Perfectly," Denth said. "By the time we hit the shop, *nobody* was looking. Considering the guards they put there every night, they must be feeling pretty stupid to have been robbed in broad daylight."

"I still don't understand what good it will do," she said. "A spice merchant's shop?"

"Not his shop," Denth said. "His stores. We ruined or carted off every barrel of salt in that cellar. He's one of only three men who store salt in any great amount; most of the other spice merchants buy from him."

"Yes, but salt," Vivenna said. "What's the point?"

"How hot was it today?" Denth asked.

Vivenna shrugged. "Too hot."

"What happens to meat when it's hot?"

"It rots," Vivenna said. "But they don't have to use salt to preserve meat. They can use . . ."

"Ice?" Denth asked, chuckling. "No, not down here, Princess. You want to preserve meat, you salt it. And if you want an army to carry fish with them from the Inner Sea to attack a place as far away as Idris . . ."

Vivenna smiled.

"The thieves we worked with will ship the salt away," Denth said. "Smuggle it to the distant kingdoms where it can be sold openly. By the time this war comes, the Crown will have some real trouble keeping its men supplied with meat. Just another small strike, but those should add up."

"Thank you," Vivenna said.

"Don't thank us," Denth said. "Just pay us."

Vivenna nodded. They fell silent for a time, looking out over the city.

"Does Jewels really believe in the Iridescent Tones?" Vivenna finally asked.

"As passionately as Tonk Fah likes to nap," Denth said. He eyed her. "You didn't challenge her, did you?"

"Kind of."

Denth whistled. "And you're still standing? I'll have to thank her for her restraint."

"How can she believe?" Vivenna said.

Denth shrugged. "Seems like a good enough religion to me. I mean, you can go and *see* her gods. Talk to them, watch them shine. It isn't all that tough to understand."

"But she's working for an Idrian," Vivenna said. "Working to undermine her own gods' ability to wage war. That was a *priest's* carriage we knocked over today."

"And a fairly important one, actually," Denth said with a chuckle. "Ah, Princess. It's a little difficult to understand. Mind-set of a mercenary. We're paid to do things—but *we're* not the ones doing them. It's *you* who do these things. We're just your tools."

"Tools that work against the Hallandren gods."

"That isn't a reason to stop believing," Denth said. "We get pretty good at separating ourselves from the things we have to do. Maybe that's what makes people hate us so much. They can't see that if we kill a friend on a battlefield, it doesn't mean that we're callous or untrustworthy. We do what we're paid to do. Just like anyone else."

"It's different," Vivenna said.

Denth shrugged. "Do you think the refiner ever considers that the iron he purifies could end up in a sword that kills a friend of his?"

Vivenna stared out over the lights of the city and all of the people they represented, with all their different beliefs, different ways of thinking, different contradictions. Perhaps she wasn't the only one who struggled to believe two seemingly opposing things at the same time.

"What about you, Denth?" she asked. "Are you Hallandren?"

"Gods, no," he said.

"Then what do you believe?"

"Haven't believed much," he said. "Not in a long time."

"What about your family?" Vivenna asked. "What did they believe?"

"Family's all dead. They believed faiths that most everybody has forgotten by now. I never joined them."

Vivenna frowned. "You have to believe in something. If not a religion, then somebody. A way of living."

"I did once."

"Do you always have to answer so vaguely?"

He glanced at her. "Yes," he said. "Except, perhaps, for that question."

She rolled her eyes.

He leaned against the banister. "The things I believed," he said, "I don't know that they'd make sense, or that you'd even hear me out if I told you about them."

"You claim to seek money," she said. "But you don't. I've seen Lemex's ledgers. He wasn't paying you that much. Not as much as I'd assumed by far. And, if you'd wanted, you could have hit that priest's carriage and taken the money. You could have stolen it twice as easily as you did the salt."

He didn't respond.

"You don't serve any kingdom or king that I can figure out," she continued. "You're a better swordsman than any simple bodyguard—I suspect better than almost anyone, if you can impress a crime boss with your skill so easily. You could have fame, students, and prizes if you decided to become a sport duelist. You claim to obey your employer, but you give the orders more often than take them—and besides, since you don't care about money, that whole employee thing is probably just a front."

She paused. "In fact," she said, "the only thing I've ever seen you express even a spark of emotion about is that man, Vasher. The one with the sword."

Even as she said the name, Denth grew more tense.

"Who *are* you?" she asked.

He turned toward her, eyes hard, showing her—once again—that the jovial man he showed the world was a mask. A charade. A softness to cover the stone within.

"I'm a mercenary," he said.

"All right," she said, "then who *were* you?"

"You don't want to know the answer to that," he said. And then he left, stomping away through the door and leaving her alone on the dark wooden balcony.

26

LIGHTSONG AWOKE AND immediately climbed from bed. He stood up, stretched, and smiled. "Beautiful day," he said.

His servants stood at the edges of the room, watching uncertainly.

"What?" Lightsong asked, holding out his arms. "Come on, let's get dressed."

They rushed forward. Llarimar entered shortly after. Lightsong often wondered how early he got up, since each morning when Lightsong rose, Llarimar was always there.

Llarimar watched him with a raised eyebrow. "You're chipper this morning, Your Grace."

Lightsong shrugged. "It just felt like it was time to get up."

"A full hour earlier than usual."

Lightsong cocked his head as the servants tied off his robes. "Really?"

"Yes, Your Grace."

"Fancy that," Lightsong said, nodding to his servants as they stepped back, leaving him dressed.

"Shall we go over your dreams, then?" Llarimar asked.

Lightsong paused, an image flashing in his head. Rain. Tempest. Storms. And a brilliant red panther.

"Nope," Lightsong said, walking toward the doorway.

"Your Grace . . ."

"We'll talk about the dreams another time, Scoot," Lightsong said. "We have more important work."

"More important work?"

Lightsong smiled, reaching the doorway and turning back. "I want to go back to Mercystar's palace."

"What ever for?"

"I don't know," Lightsong said happily.

Llarimar sighed. "Very well, Your Grace. But can we at least look over some art, first? There are people who paid good money to get your opinion, and some are waiting quite eagerly to hear what you think of their pieces."

"All right," Lightsong said. "But let's be quick about it."

⸎

LIGHTSONG STARED AT the painting.

Red upon red, shades so subtle that the painter must have been of the Third Heightening at least. Violent, terrible reds, clashing against one another like waves—waves that only vaguely resembled men, yet that somehow managed to convey the idea of armies fighting much better than any detailed realistic depiction could have.

Chaos. Bloody wounds upon bloody uniforms upon bloody skin. There was so much violence in red. His own color. He almost felt as if he were *in* the painting—felt its turmoil shaking him, disorienting him, *pulling* on him.

The waves of men pointed toward one figure at the center. A woman, vaguely depicted by a couple of curved brushstrokes. And yet it was obvious. She stood high, as if atop a cresting wave of crashing soldiers, caught in mid-motion, head flung back, her arm upraised.

Holding a deep black sword that darkened the red sky around it.

"The Battle of Twilight Falls," Llarimar said quietly, standing beside him in the white hallway. "Last conflict of the Manywar."

Lightsong nodded. He'd known that, somehow. The faces of many of the soldiers were tinged with grey. They were Lifeless. The Manywar had been the first time they had been used in large numbers on the battlefield.

"I know you don't prefer war scenes," Llarimar said. "But—"

"I like it," Lightsong said, cutting off the priest. "I like it a lot."

Llarimar fell silent.

Lightsong stared into the painting with its flowing reds, painted so subtly that they gave a *feeling* of war, rather than just an image. "It might be the best painting that has ever passed through my hall."

The priests on the other side of the room began writing furiously. Llarimar just stared at him, troubled.

"What?" Lightsong asked.

"It's nothing," Llarimar said.

"Scoot . . ." Lightsong said, eyeing him.

The priest sighed. "I can't speak, Your Grace. I cannot taint your impression of the paintings."

"A lot of gods have been giving favorable reviews of war paintings lately, eh?" Lightsong said, looking back at the artwork.

Llarimar didn't answer.

"It's probably nothing," Lightsong said. "Just our response to those arguments in the court, I'd guess."

"Likely," Llarimar said.

Lightsong fell silent. He knew it wasn't "nothing" to Llarimar. To him, Lightsong wasn't just giving his impression of art—he was foretelling the future. What did it augur that he liked a depiction of war with such vibrant, brutal colorings? Was it a reaction to his dreams? But last night, he hadn't dreamed of a war. Finally. He'd dreamed of a storm, true, but that wasn't the same thing.

I shouldn't have spoken, he thought. And yet, reacting to the art seemed like the only truly important thing he did.

He stared at the sharp smears of paint, each figure just a couple of triangular strokes. It was beautiful. Could war be beautiful? How could he find beauty in those grey faces confronting flesh, the Lifeless killing men? This battle hadn't even meant anything. It hadn't decided the outcome of the war, even though the leader of the Pahn Unity—the kingdoms united against Hallandren—had been killed in the battle. Diplomacy had finally ended the Manywar, not bloodshed.

Are we thinking of starting this up again? Lightsong thought, still transfixed by the beauty. *Is what I do going to lead to war?*

No, he thought to himself. *No, I'm just being careful. Helping Blushweaver secure a political faction. Better that than letting things just pass me by. The Manywar started because the royal family wasn't careful.*

The painting continued to call to him. "What's that sword?" Lightsong asked.

"Sword?"

"The black one," Lightsong said. "In the woman's hand."

"I . . . I don't see a sword, Your Grace," Llarimar said. "To tell you the truth, I don't see a woman, either. It's all just wild strokes of paint, to me."

"You called it the Battle of Twilight Falls."

"The title of the piece, Your Grace," Llarimar said. "I assumed that you were as confused by it as I was, so I told you what the artist had named it."

The two fell silent. Finally, Lightsong turned, walking away from the painting. "I'm done reviewing art for the day." He hesitated. "Don't burn that painting. Keep it for my collection."

Llarimar acknowledged the command with a nod. As Lightsong made his way out of the palace, he tried to regain some of his eagerness, and he succeeded—though memory of the terrible, beautiful scene stayed with him. Mixing with his memories of last night's dream, with its clashing tempest of winds.

Not even that could dampen his mood. Something was different. Something excited him. There had been a murder in the Court of Gods.

He didn't know why he should find that so intriguing. If anything, he should find it tragic or upsetting. And yet for as long as he had lived, everything had been provided for him. Answers to his questions, entertainment to sate his whims. Almost by accident, he had become a glutton. Only two things had been withheld from him: knowledge of his past and freedom to leave the court.

Neither of those restrictions was going to change soon. But here, inside the court—the place of too much safety and comfort—something had gone wrong. A little thing. A thing most Returned would ignore. Nobody cared. Nobody wanted to care. Who, therefore, would object to Lightsong's questions?

"You're acting very oddly, Your Grace," Llarimar said, catching up to him as they crossed the grass, servants following behind in a chaotic cluster as they worked to get a large red parasol open.

"I know," Lightsong said. "However, I believe we can agree that I have *always* been rather odd, for a god."

"I must admit that is true."

"Then I'm actually being very like myself," Lightsong said. "And all is right in the universe."

"Are we really going back to Mercystar's palace?"

"Indeed we are. Do you suppose she'll be annoyed at us? That might prove interesting."

Llarimar just sighed. "Are you ready to talk about your dreams yet?"

Lightsong did not immediately reply. The servants finally got the parasol up and held it over him. "I dreamed of a storm," Lightsong finally said. "I was standing in it, without anything to brace myself. It was raining and blowing against me, forcing me backward. In fact, it was so strong that even the ground beneath me seemed to undulate."

Llarimar looked disturbed.

More signs of war, Lightsong thought. *Or, at least, that's how he'll see it.*

"Anything else?"

"Yes," Lightsong said. "A red panther. It seemed to shine, reflective, like it was made of glass or something like that. It was waiting in the storm."

Llarimar eyed him. "Are you making things up, Your Grace?"

"What? No! That's really what I dreamed."

Llarimar sighed, but nodded to a lesser priest, who rushed up to take his dictation. It wasn't long before they reached Mercystar's palace of yellow and gold. Lightsong paused before the building, realizing that he'd never before visited another god's palace without first sending a messenger.

"Do you want me to send in someone to announce you, Your Grace?" Llarimar asked.

Lightsong hesitated. "No," he finally said, noticing a pair of guards standing at the main doorway. The two men looked far more muscular than the average servant and they wore swords. Dueling blades, Lightsong assumed—though he'd never actually seen one.

He walked up to the men. "Is your mistress here?"

"I am afraid not, Your Grace," one of them said. "She went to visit Allmother for the afternoon."

Allmother, Lightsong thought. *Another with Lifeless Commands. Blushweaver's doing?* Perhaps he would drop by later—he missed chatting with Allmother. She, unfortunately, hated him violently. "Ah," Lightsong said to the guard. "Well, regardless, I need to inspect the corridor just inside here, where the attack happened the other night."

The guards glanced at each other. "I . . . don't know if we can let you do that, Your Grace."

"Scoot!" Lightsong said. "Can they forbid me?"

"Only if they have a direct command to do so from Mercystar."

Lightsong looked back at the men. Reluctantly, they stepped aside. "It's perfectly all right," he told them. "She asked me to take care of things. Kind of. Coming, Scoot?"

Llarimar followed him into the corridors. Once again, Lightsong felt an odd satisfaction. Instincts he hadn't known he had drove him to seek out the place where the servant had died.

The wood had been replaced—his Heightened eyes could easily tell the difference between the new wood and the old. He walked a little farther. The patch where the wood had turned grey was gone as well, seamlessly replaced with new material.

Interesting, he thought. *But not unexpected. I wonder . . . are there any other patches?* He walked a little further and was rewarded by another patch of new wood. It formed an exact square.

"Your Grace?" a new voice asked.

Lightsong looked up to see the curt young priest he had spoken with the day before. Lightsong smiled. "Ah, good. I was hoping that you would come."

"This is most irregular, Your Grace," the man said.

"I hear that eating a lot of figs can cure you of that," Lightsong said. "Now, I need to speak with the guards who saw the intruder the other night."

"But why, Your Grace?" the priest said.

"Because I'm eccentric," Lightsong said. "Send for them.

I need to speak to *all* of the servants or guards who saw the man who committed the murder."

"Your Grace," the priest said uncomfortably. "The city authorities have already dealt with this. They have determined that the intruder was a thief after Mercystar's art, and they have committed to—"

"Scoot," Lightsong said, turning. "Can this man ignore my demand?"

"Only at great peril to his soul, Your Grace," Llarimar said.

The priest eyed them both angrily, then turned and sent a servant to do as Lightsong asked. Lightsong knelt down, causing several servants to whisper in alarm. They obviously thought it improper for a god to stoop.

Lightsong ignored them, looking at the square of new wood. It was larger than the other two that had been ripped up, and the colors matched far better. It was just a square patch of wood that was just a *slightly* different color than its neighbors. Without Breath—and a lot of it—he wouldn't even have noticed the distinction.

A trapdoor, he thought with sudden shock. The priest was watching him closely. *This patch isn't as new as the other ones back there. It's only new in relation to the other boards.*

Lightsong crawled along the floor, deliberately ignoring the door in the floor. Once again, unexpected instincts warned him not to reveal what he'd discovered. Why was he so wary all of a sudden? Was it the influence of his violent dreams and imagery from the painting earlier? Or was it something more? He felt as if he were dredging deep within himself, pulling forth an awareness he had never before needed.

Either way, he moved on from the patch, pretending that he hadn't noticed the trapdoor, and was instead searching for threads that might have been caught on the wood. He picked up one that had obviously come from a servant's robe and held it up.

The priest seemed to relax slightly.

So he knows about the trapdoor, Lightsong thought. *And . . . perhaps the intruder did as well?*

Lightsong crawled some more, discomforting the servants until the men he had requested were assembled. He stood—letting a couple of his servants dust off his robes—then walked over to the newcomers. The hallway was growing quite crowded, so he shooed them back out into the sunlight.

Outside, he regarded the group of six men. "Identify yourselves. You on the left, who are you?"

"My name is Gagaril," the man said.

"I'm sorry," Lightsong said.

The man flushed. "I was named after my father, Your Grace."

"After he what? Spent an unusual amount of time at the local tavern? Anyway, how are you involved in this mess?"

"I was one of the guards at the door when the intruder broke in."

"Were you alone?" Lightsong asked.

"No," said another of the men. "I was with him."

"Good," Lightsong said. "You two, go over there somewhere." He waved his hand at the lawn. The men looked at each other, then walked away as indicated.

"Far enough that you can't hear us!" Lightsong called at them.

The men nodded and continued.

"All right," Lightsong said, looking back at the others. "Who are you four?"

"We were attacked by the man in the hallway," one of the servants said. He pointed at two of the others. "All three of us. And . . . one other. The man who was killed."

"Terribly unfortunate, that," Lightsong said, pointing at

another section of the lawn. "Off you go. Walk until you can't hear me anymore, then wait."

The three men trudged off.

"And now you," Lightsong said, hands on hips, regarding the last man—a shorter priest.

"I saw the intruder flee, Your Grace," the priest said. "I was watching out a window."

"Very timely of you," Lightsong said, pointing at a third spot on the lawn, far enough from the others to be sequestered. The man walked away. Lightsong turned back to the priest who was obviously in charge.

"You said that the intruder released a Lifeless animal?" Lightsong asked.

"A squirrel, Your Grace," the priest said. "We captured it."

"Go and fetch it for me."

"Your Grace, it's quite wild and—" He stopped, recognizing the look in Lightsong's eyes, then waved for a servant.

"No," Lightsong said. "Not a servant. You go and get it personally."

The priest looked incredulous.

"Yes, yes," Lightsong said, waving him away. "I know. It's an offense to your dignity. Perhaps you should think about converting to Austrism. For now, get going."

The priest left, grumbling.

"The rest of you," Lightsong said, addressing his own servants and priests. "You wait here."

They looked resigned. Perhaps they were growing accustomed to him dismissing them.

"Come on, Scoot," Lightsong said, walking toward the first group he had sent off onto the lawn—the two guards. Llarimar scurried forward to keep up as Lightsong took long strides over to the two men. "Now," Lightsong said to the two, out of earshot of the others, "tell me what you saw."

"He came to us pretending to be a madman, Your Grace,"

one of the guards said. "He sauntered out of the shadows, mumbling to himself. It was just an act, though, and when he got close enough, he knocked us both out."

"How?" Lightsong asked.

"He grabbed me around the neck with tassels from his Awakened coat," the guard said. He nodded to his companion. "Knocked him in the stomach with the hilt of a sword."

The second guard raised his shirt to show a large bruise on his stomach, then cocked his head to the side, showing another one on his neck.

"Choked us both," the first guard said. "Me with those tassels, Fran with a boot on his neck. That's the last thing we knew. By the time we awoke, he was gone."

"He choked you," Lightsong said, "but didn't kill you. Just enough to knock you out?"

"That's right, Your Grace," the guard said.

"Please describe this man," Lightsong said.

"He was big," the guard said. "Had a scraggly beard. Not too long, but not trimmed either."

"He wasn't smelly or dirty," the other said. "He just didn't seem to take much care for how he looked. His hair was long—came down to his neck—and hadn't seen a brush in a long while."

"Wore ragged clothing," the first said. "Patched in places, nothing bright, but not really dark either. Just kind of . . . bland. Rather un-Hallandren, now that I think on it."

"And he was armed?" Lightsong said.

"With the sword that hit me," the second guard said. "Big thing. Not a dueling blade, more like an Easterner sword. Straight and really long. Had it hidden under his cloak, and we would have seen it, if he hadn't covered it up by walking so oddly."

Lightsong nodded. "Thank you. Stay here."

With that, he turned and walked toward the second group.

"This is very interesting, Your Grace," Llarimar said. "But I really don't see the point."

"I'm just curious," Lightsong said.

"Excuse me, Your Grace," Llarimar said. "But you're not really the curious type."

Lightsong continued walking. The things he was doing, he did mostly without thinking. They just felt natural. He approached the next group. "You were the ones who saw the intruder in the hallway, right?" Lightsong said to them.

The men nodded. One shot a glance back at Mercystar's palace. The lawn in front of it was now crowded with a colorful assortment of priests and servants, both Mercystar's and Lightsong's own.

"Tell me what happened," Lightsong said.

"We were walking through the servants' hallway," one said. "We'd been released for the evening, and were going to go out into the city to a nearby tavern."

"Then we saw someone in the hallway," another said. "He didn't belong there."

"Describe him," Lightsong said.

"Big man," one said. The others nodded. "Had ragged clothing and a beard. Kind of dirty-looking."

"No," another said. "The clothing was old, but the man wasn't dirty. Just slovenly."

Lightsong nodded. "Continue."

"Well, there isn't much to say," one of the men said. "He attacked us. Threw an Awakened rope at poor Taff, who got tied up immediately. Rariv and I ran for help. Lolan stayed behind."

Lightsong looked at the third man. "You stayed back? Why?"

"To help Taff, of course," the man said.

Lying, Lightsong thought. *Looks too nervous.* "Really?" he said, stepping closer.

The man looked down. "Well, mostly. I mean, there was the sword, too . . ."

"Oh, right," another said. "He threw a sword at us. Strangest thing."

"He didn't draw it?" Lightsong asked. "He *threw* it?"

The men shook their heads. "He threw it at us, sheath and all. Lolan picked it up."

"I thought I'd fight him," Lolan said.

"Interesting," Lightsong said. "So you two left?"

"Yeah," one of the men said. "When we came back with the others—after getting around that blasted squirrel—we found Lolan on the ground, unconscious, and poor Taff . . . well, he was still tied up, though the rope wasn't Awakened anymore. He'd been stabbed straight through."

"You saw him die?"

"No," Lolan said, bringing his hands up in denial. He had—Lightsong noticed—a bandage on one hand. "The intruder knocked me out with a fist to the head."

"But you had the sword," Lightsong said.

"It was too big to use," the man said, looking down.

"So he threw the sword at you, then ran up and *punched* you?" Lightsong said.

The man nodded.

"And your hand?" Lightsong asked.

The man paused, unconsciously retracting his hand. "It got twisted. Nothing important."

"And you need a bandage for a twisted wrist?" Lightsong said, raising an eyebrow. "Show me."

The man hesitated.

"Show me, or lose your soul, my son," Lightsong said in what he hoped was a suitably divine voice.

The man slowly extended his hand. Llarimar stepped forward and removed the bandage.

The hand was completely grey, drained of color.

Impossible, Lightsong thought with shock. *Awakening doesn't do that to living flesh. It can't draw color from someone alive, only objects. Floorboards, clothing, furniture.*

The man withdrew his hand.

"What is that?" Lightsong asked.

"I don't know," the man said. "I woke up, and it was like that."

"Is that so?" Lightsong said flatly. "And I'm to believe that you had nothing else to do with this? That you weren't working with the intruder?"

The man fell to his knees suddenly, beginning to cry. "Please, my lord! Don't take my soul. I'm not the best of men. I go to the brothels. I cheat when we gamble."

The other two looked startled at this.

"But I didn't know anything about this intruder," Lolan continued. "Please, you have to believe me. I just wanted that sword. That beautiful, black sword! I wanted to draw it, swing it, attack the man with it. I reached for it and while I was distracted, he attacked me. But I didn't see him kill Taff! I promise, I hadn't ever seen this intruder before! You have to believe me!"

Lightsong paused. "I do," he finally said. "Let this be a warning. Be good. Stop cheating."

"Yes, my lord."

Lightsong nodded to the men, then he and Llarimar left them behind.

"I actually kind of feel like a god," Lightsong said. "Did you see me make that man repent?"

"Amazing, Your Grace," Llarimar said.

"So what do you think about their testimonies?" Lightsong said. "Something strange *is* going on, isn't it?"

"I'm still wondering why you think you should be the one to investigate it, Your Grace."

"It's not like I have anything else to do."

"Besides be a god."

"Overrated," Lightsong said, walking up to the final man. "It has nice perks, but the hours are awful."

Llarimar snorted quietly as Lightsong turned to address the final witness, the short priest who stood in his robes of yellow and gold. He was distinctly younger than the other priest.

Was he chosen to tell me lies with the hopes that he'd seem innocent? Lightsong wondered idly. *Or am I just making assumptions?* "What is your story?" Lightsong asked.

The young priest bowed. "I was going about my duties, carrying to the records sanctuary several prophecies we had inscribed from the Lady's mouth. I heard a distant disturbance in the building. I looked out the window toward the sound, but I saw nothing."

"Where were you?" Lightsong asked.

The young man pointed toward a window. "There, Your Grace."

Lightsong frowned. The priest had been on the opposite side of the palace from where the killing had occurred. However, that *was* the side of the building where the intruder had first entered. "You could see the doorway where the intruder disabled the two guards?"

"Yes, Your Grace," the man said. "Though I didn't see them at first. I almost left the window to search for the source of the noise. However, at that point I *did* see something odd in the lantern light of the entryway: a figure moving. It was then that I noticed the guards on the ground. I thought they were dead bodies, and I was frightened by the shadowy figure moving between them. I yelled, and ran for help. By the time anyone paid attention to me, the figure was gone."

"You went down to look for him?" Lightsong asked.

The man nodded.

"And how long did it take you?"

"Several minutes, Your Grace."

Lightsong nodded slowly. "Very well, then. Thank you."

The young priest began to walk over to the main group of his colleagues.

"Oh, wait," Lightsong said. "Did you, by any chance, get a clear look at the intruder?"

"Not really, Your Grace," the priest said. "He was in dark clothing, kind of nondescript. It was too far away to see well."

Lightsong waved the man away. He rubbed his chin thoughtfully for a moment, then eyed Llarimar. "Well?"

The priest raised an eyebrow. "Well what, Your Grace?"

"What do you think?"

Llarimar shook his head. "I . . . honestly don't know, Your Grace. This is obviously important, however."

Lightsong paused. "It is?"

Llarimar nodded. "Yes, Your Grace. Because of what that man said—the one who was wounded in the hand. He mentioned a black sword. You predicted it, remember? In the painting this morning?"

"That wasn't a prediction," Lightsong said. "That was really there, in the painting."

"That's the way prophecy works, Your Grace," Llarimar said. "Don't you see? You look at a painting and an entire image appears to your eyes. All I see is random strokes of red. The scene you describe—the things you see—are prophetic. You are a god."

"But I saw exactly what the painting was said to depict!" Lightsong said. "Before you even told me what the title was!"

Llarimar nodded knowingly, as if that proved his point.

"Oh, never mind. Priests! Insufferable fanatics, every one of you. Either way, you agree with me that there is something strange here."

"Definitely, Your Grace."

"Good," Lightsong said. "Then you'll kindly stop complaining when I investigate it."

"Actually, Your Grace," Llarimar said, "it's even *more* imperative that you *not* get involved. You predicted this would occur, but you are an oracle. You must not interact with the subject of your predictions. If you get involved, you could unbalance a great many things."

"I like being unbalanced," Lightsong said. "Besides, this is *far* too much fun."

As usual, Llarimar didn't react to having his advice ignored. As they began to walk back toward the main group, however, the priest did ask a question. "Your Grace. Just to sate my own curiosity, what do *you* think about the murder?"

"It's obvious," Lightsong said idly. "There were two intruders. The first is the large man with the sword—he knocked out the guards, attacked those servants, released the Lifeless, then disappeared. The second man—the one the young priest saw—came in after the first intruder. That second man is the murderer."

Llarimar frowned. "Why do you suppose that?"

"The first man took care not to kill," Lightsong said. "He left the guards alive at risk to himself, since they could have regained consciousness at any moment to raise the alarm. He didn't draw his sword against the servants but simply tried to subdue them. There was no reason for him to kill a bound captive—particularly since he'd already left witnesses. If there were a second man, however . . . well, that would make sense. The servant who was killed, he was the one who was conscious when this second intruder came through. That servant was the only one who *saw* the second intruder."

"So, you think someone else followed the man with the sword, killed the only witness, and then . . ."

"Both of them vanished," Lightsong said. "I found a trapdoor. I'm thinking there must be passages beneath the palace. It all seems fairly obvious to me. One thing, however, is *not* obvious." He glanced at Llarimar, slowing before they reached the main group of priests and servants.

"And what is that, Your Grace?" Llarimar asked.

"How in the name of the Colors I figured all of this out!"

"I'm trying to grasp that myself, Your Grace."

Lightsong shook his head. "This comes from before, Scoot. Everything I'm doing, it feels *natural*. Who was I before I died?"

"I don't know what you mean, Your Grace," Llarimar said, turning away.

"Oh, come now, Scoot. I've spent most of my Returned life just lounging about, but then the *moment* someone is killed, I leap out of bed and can't resist poking around. Doesn't that sound suspicious to you?"

Llarimar didn't look at him.

"Colors!" Lightsong swore. "I was someone *useful*? I was just beginning to convince myself that I'd died in a reasonable way—such as falling off a stump when I was drunk."

"You know you died in a brave way, Your Grace."

"It could have been a really high stump."

Llarimar just shook his head. "Either way, Your Grace, you know I can't say anything about who you were before."

"Well, these instincts came from somewhere," Lightsong said as they walked over to the main group of watching priests and servants. The head priest had returned with a small wooden box. Wild scratching came from inside. "Thank you," Lightsong snapped, grabbing the box and passing by without even breaking stride. "I'm telling you, Scoot, I am *not* pleased."

"You seemed rather happy this morning, Your Grace," Llarimar noted as they walked away from Mercystar's palace. Her priest was left behind, a complaint dying on his lips, Lightsong's entourage trailing after their god.

"I was happy," Lightsong said, "because I didn't know what was going on. How am I going to be properly indolent if I keep itching to investigate things? Honestly, this murder will completely destroy my hard-won reputation."

"My sympathies, Your Grace, that you have been inconvenienced by a semblance of motivation."

"Quite right," Lightsong said, sighing. He handed over the box with its furious Lifeless rodent. "Here. You think my Awakeners can break its security phrase?"

"Eventually," Llarimar said. "Though it's an animal, Your Grace. It won't be able to tell us anything directly."

"Have them do it anyway," Lightsong said. "Meanwhile, I need to think about this case some more."

They walked back to his palace. However, the thing that now struck Lightsong was the fact that he'd used the word "case" in reference to the murder. It was a word he'd never heard used in that particular context. Yet he knew that it fit. Instinctively, automatically.

I didn't have to learn to speak again when I Returned, he thought. *I didn't have to learn to walk again, or read again, or anything like that. Only my personal memory was lost.*

But not all of it, apparently.

And that left him wondering what else he could do, if he tried.

27

SOMETHING HAPPENED TO *those previous God Kings,* Siri thought, striding through the endless rooms of the God King's palace, her servants scurrying behind. *Something that Bluefingers fears will happen to Susebron. It will be dangerous to both the God King and myself.*

She continued to walk, trailing a train made from countless tassels of translucent green silk behind her. The day's gown was nearly gossamer thin—she'd chosen it, then had asked her servants to fetch an opaque slip for her. It was funny how quickly she'd stopped worrying about what was "ostentatious" and what was not.

There were many much more important problems to worry about.

The priests do *fear that something will happen to Susebron,* she thought firmly. *They are so eager for me to produce an heir. They claim it's about the succession, but they went fifty years without bothering. They were willing to wait twenty years to get their bride from Idris. Whatever the danger is, it's not urgent.*

And yet the priests act like it is.

Perhaps they'd wanted a bride of the royal line so badly that they'd been willing to risk the danger. Surely they needn't have waited twenty years, though. Vivenna could have borne children years ago.

Though perhaps the treaty specified a time and not an age. Maybe it just said that the king of Idris had twenty years to provide a bride for the God King. That would explain why her father had been able to send Siri instead. Siri cursed herself for ignoring her lessons about the treaty. She didn't really know *what* it said. For all she knew, the danger could be spelled out in the document itself.

She needed more information. Unfortunately, the priests were obstructive, the servants silent, and Bluefingers, well . . .

She finally caught sight of him moving through one of the rooms, writing on his ledger. Siri hurried up, train rustling. He turned, glimpsing her. His eyes opened wide, and he increased his speed, ducking through the open doorway into another room. Siri called after him, moving as quickly as the dress would allow, but when she arrived, the room was empty.

"Colors!" she swore, feeling her hair grow a deep red in annoyance. "You still think he isn't avoiding me?" she demanded, turning to the most senior of her servants.

The woman lowered her gaze. "It would be improper for a servant of the palace to avoid his queen, Vessel. He must not have seen you."

Right, Siri thought, *just like every other time.* When she sent for him, he always arrived after she'd given up and left. When she had a letter scribed to him, he responded so vaguely that it only frustrated her even further.

She couldn't take books from the palace library, and the priests were disruptively distracting if she tried to read inside the library chamber itself. She'd requested books from the city, but the priests had insisted that they be brought by a priest, then read to her, so as to not "strain her eyes." She was pretty sure that if there was anything in the book that the priests didn't want her to know, the reader would simply skip it.

She depended so much upon the priests and scribes for everything, including information.

Except . . . she thought, still standing in the bright red room. There *was* another source of information. She turned to her head servant. "What activities are going on today in the courtyard?"

"Many, Vessel," the woman said. "Some artists have come and are doing paintings and sketches. There are some animal handlers showing exotic creatures from the South— I believe they have both elephants and zebras on display. There are also several dye merchants showing off their newest color combinations. And—of course—there are minstrels."

"What about at that building we went to before?"

"The arena, Vessel? I believe there will be games there later in the evening. Contests of physical prowess."

Siri nodded. "Prepare a box. I want to attend."

⌘

BACK IN HER homeland, Siri had occasionally watched running contests. They were usually spontaneous, as the monks did not approve of men showing off. Austre gave all men talents. Flaunting them was seen as arrogance.

Boys cannot be so easily contained. She had seen them run, had even encouraged them. Those contests, however, had been *nothing* like what the Hallandren men now put on.

There were a half-dozen different events going on at once. Some men threw large stones, competing for distance. Others raced in a wide circle around the interior of the arena floor, kicking up sand, sweating heavily in the muggy Hallandren heat. Others tossed javelins, shot arrows, or engaged in leaping contests.

Siri watched with a deepening blush—one that ran all the way to the ends of her hair. The men wore only loincloths. During her weeks in the grand city, she had never seen anything quite so . . . interesting.

A lady shouldn't stare at young men, her mother had taught. *It's unseemly.*

Yet what was the point, if not to stare? Siri couldn't help herself, and it wasn't just because of the naked skin. These were men who had trained extensively—who had mastered their physical abilities to wondrous effect. As Siri watched, she saw that relatively little regard was given to the winners of each particular event. The contests weren't really about victory, but about the skill required to compete.

In that respect, these contests were almost in line with Idrian sensibilities—yet, at the same time, they were ironically opposite.

The beauty of the games kept her distracted for much longer than she'd intended, her hair permanently locked into a deep maroon blush, even after she got used to the idea of men competing in so little clothing. Eventually, she forced herself to stand and turn away from the performance. She had work to do.

Her servants perked up. They had brought all kinds of luxuries. Full couches and cushions, fruits and wines, even a few men with fans to keep her cool. After only a few weeks in the palace, such comfort was beginning to seem commonplace to her.

"There was a god who came and spoke to me before,"

Siri said, scanning the amphitheater, where many of the stone boxes were decorated with colorful canopies. "Which one was it?"

"Lightsong the Bold, Vessel," one of the serving women said. "God of bravery."

Siri nodded. "And his colors are?"

"Gold and red, Vessel."

Siri smiled. His canopy showed that he was there. He wasn't the only god to have introduced himself to her during her weeks in the palace, but he *was* the only one who had spent any amount of time chatting with her. He'd been confusing, but at least he'd been willing to talk. She left her box, beautiful dress trailing on the stone. She'd had to force herself to stop feeling guilty for ruining them, since apparently each dress was burned the day after she wore it.

Her servants burst into frantic motion, gathering up furniture and foods, following behind Siri. As before, there were people on the benches below—merchants rich enough to buy entrance to the court or peasants who had won a special lottery. Many turned and looked up as she passed, whispering among themselves.

It's the only way they get to see me, she realized. *Their queen.*

That was one thing that Idris certainly handled better than Hallandren. The Idrians had easy access to their king and their government, while in Hallandren the leaders were kept aloof—and therefore made remote, even mysterious.

She approached the red and gold pavilion. The god she had seen before lounged inside, relaxing on a couch, sipping from a large, beautifully engraved glass cup filled with an icy red liquid. He looked much as he had before— the chiseled masculine features that she was already coming to associate with godhood, perfectly styled black hair, golden tan skin, and a distinctly blasé attitude.

That's something else Idris was right about, she thought.

My people may be too stern, but it also isn't good to be-come as self-indulgent as some of these Returned.

The god, Lightsong, eyed her and nodded in deference. "My queen."

"Lightsong the Bold," she said as one of her servants brought her chair. "I trust your day has been pleasant?"

"So far this day I have discovered several disturbing and redefining elements of my soul which are slowly restructuring the very nature of my existence." He took a sip from his drink. "Other than that, it was uneventful. You?"

"Fewer revelations," Siri said, sitting. "More confusion. I'm still inexperienced in the way things work here. I was hoping you could answer some of my questions, give me some information, perhaps . . ."

"Afraid not," Lightsong said.

Siri paused, then flushed, embarrassed. "I'm sorry. Did I do something wrong. I—"

"No, nothing wrong, child," Lightsong said, his smile deepening. "The reason I cannot help you is because I, unfortunately, know nothing. I'm useless. Haven't you heard?"

"Um . . . I'm afraid I haven't."

"You should pay better attention," he said, raising his cup toward her. "Shame on you," he said, smilingly.

Siri frowned, growing more embarrassed. Lightsong's high priest—distinguished by his oversized headgear—looked on disapprovingly, and that only caused her to be more self-conscious. *Why should I be the ashamed one?* she thought, growing annoyed. *Lightsong is the one who is making veiled insults against me—and making overt ones against himself! It's like he* enjoys *self-deprecation.*

"Actually," Siri said, looking over at him, lifting her chin, "I *have* heard of your reputation, Lightsong the Bold. 'Useless' wasn't the word I heard used, however."

"Oh?" he said.

"No. I was told you were harmless, though I can see that

is not true—for in speaking to you, my sense of reason has certainly been harmed. Not to mention my head, which is beginning to ache."

"Both common symptoms of dealing with me, I'm afraid," he said with an exaggerated sigh.

"That could be solved," Siri said. "Perhaps it would help if you refrained from speaking when others are present. I think I should find you quite amiable in those circumstances."

Lightsong laughed. Not a belly laugh, like her father or some of the men back in Idris, but a more refined laugh. Still, it seemed genuine.

"I *knew* I liked you, girl," he said.

"I'm not sure if I should feel complimented or not."

"Depends upon how seriously you take yourself," Lightsong said. "Come, abandon that silly chair and recline on one of these couches. Enjoy the evening."

"I'm not sure that would be proper," Siri said.

"I'm a god," Lightsong said with a wave of his hand. "I define propriety."

"I think I'll sit anyway," Siri said, smiling, though she did stand and have her servants bring the chair farther under the canopy so that she didn't have to speak so loudly. She also tried not to pay too much attention to the contests, lest she be drawn in by them again.

Lightsong smiled. He seemed to enjoy making others uncomfortable. But, then, he also seemed to have no concern for how he himself appeared.

"I meant what I said before, Lightsong," she said. "I need information."

"And I, my dear, was quite honest as well. I *am* useless, mostly. However, I'll try my best to answer your questions— assuming, of course, you will provide answers to mine."

"And if I don't know the answers to your questions?"

"Then make something up," he said. "I'll never know

the difference. Unknowing ignorance is preferable to informed stupidity."

"I'll try to remember that."

"Do so and you defeat the point. Now, your questions?"

"What happened to the previous God Kings?"

"Died," Lightsong said. "Oh, don't look so surprised. It happens to people sometimes, even gods. We make, if you haven't noticed, laughable immortals. We keep forgetting about that 'live forever' part and instead find ourselves unexpectedly dead. And for the *second time* at that. You might say that we're twice as bad at staying alive as regular folk."

"How do the God Kings die?"

"Gave away their Breath," Lightsong said. "Isn't that right, Scoot?"

Lightsong's high priest nodded. "It is, Your Grace. His Divine Majesty Susebron the Fourth died to cure the plague of distrentia that struck T'Telir fifty years ago."

"Wait," Lightsong said. "Isn't distrentia a disease of the bowels?"

"Indeed," the high priest said.

Lightsong frowned. "You mean to tell me that our God King—the most holy and divine personage in our pantheon—died to cure a few tummy aches?"

"I wouldn't exactly put it that way, Your Grace."

Lightsong leaned over to Siri. "I'm expected to do that someday, you know. Kill myself so that some old lady will be able to stop messing herself in public. No wonder I'm such an embarrassing god. Must have to do with subconscious self-worth issues."

The high priest looked apologetically at Siri. For the first time, she realized that the overweight priest's disapproval wasn't directed at her, but at his god. To her, he smiled.

Maybe they're not all like Treledees, she thought, smiling back.

"The God King's sacrifice was not an empty gesture, Vessel," the priest said. "True, diarrhea may not be a great danger to most, but to the elderly and the young it can be quite deadly. Plus, the epidemic conditions were spreading other diseases, and the city's commerce—and therefore the kingdom's—had slowed to a crawl. People in outlying villages went months without necessary supplies."

"I wonder how those who were cured felt," Lightsong said musingly, "waking to find their God King dead."

"One would think they'd be honored, Your Grace."

"I think they'd be annoyed. The king came all that way, and they were too sick to notice. Anyway, my queen, there you go. That was actually helpful information. You now have me worried that I've broken my promise to you about being useless."

"If it's any consolation," she said, "you weren't all that helpful yourself. It's your priest who actually seems useful."

"Yes, I know. I've tried for years to corrupt him. Never seems to work. I can't even get him to acknowledge the theological paradox it causes when I try to tempt him to do evil."

Siri paused, then found herself smiling even more broadly.

"What?" Lightsong asked, then finished off the last of his drink. It was immediately replaced by another, this one blue.

"Talking to you is like swimming in a river," she said. "I keep getting pulled along with the current and I'm never sure when I'll be able to take another breath."

"Watch out for the rocks, Vessel," the high priest noted. "They look rather insignificant, but have sharp edges under the surface."

"Bah," Lightsong said. "It's the *crocodiles* you have to watch for. They can bite. And . . . what exactly were we talking about, anyway?"

"The God Kings," Siri said. "When the last one died, an heir had already been produced?"

"Indeed," the high priest said. "In fact, he had just been married the year before. The child was born only weeks before he died."

Siri sat back in her chair, thoughtful. "And the God King before him?"

"Died to heal the children of a village which had been attacked by bandits," Lightsong said. "The commoners love the story. The king was so moved by their suffering that he gave himself up for the simple people."

"And had he been married the year before?"

"No, Vessel," the high priest said. "It was several years after his marriage. Though, he *did* die only a month after his second child was born."

Siri looked up. "Was the first child a daughter?"

"Yes," the priest said. "A woman of no divine powers. How did you know?"

Colors! Siri thought. *Both times, right after the heir was born.* Did having a child somehow make the God Kings wish to give their lives away? Or was it something more sinister? A cured plague or healed village were both things that, with a little creative propaganda, could be invented to cover up some other cause of death.

"I'm not truly an expert on these things, I'm afraid, Vessel," the high priest continued. "And I'm afraid that Lord Lightsong is not either. If you press him, he *could* very well just start making things up."

"Scoot!" Lightsong said indignantly. "That's slanderous. Oh, and by the way, your hat is on fire."

"Thank you," Siri said. "Both of you. This has actually been rather helpful."

"If I might suggest . . ." the high priest said.

"Please," she replied.

"Try a professional storyteller, Vessel," the priest said. "You can order one in from the city, and he can recite both histories and tales of imagination to you. They will provide much better information than we can."

Siri nodded. *Why can't the priests in our palace be this helpful?* Of course, if they really *were* covering up the true reason their God Kings died, they had good reason to avoid helping her. In fact, it was likely that if she asked for a storyteller, they would just provide one who would tell her what *they* wanted her to hear.

She frowned. "Could . . . you do that for me, Lightsong?"

"What?"

"Order in a storyteller," she said. "I should like you to be there, in case I have any questions."

Lightsong shrugged. "I guess I could. Haven't heard a storyteller in some time. Just let me know when."

It wasn't a perfect plan. Her servants were listening and they might report to the priests. However, if the storyteller came to Lightsong's palace, there was at least some chance of Siri hearing the truth.

"Thank you," she said, rising.

"Ah, ah, ah! Not so fast," Lightsong said, raising a finger.

She stopped.

He drank from his cup.

"Well?" she finally asked.

He held up the finger again as he continued to drink, tipping his head back, getting the last bits of slushy ice from the bottom of the cup. He set it aside, mouth blue. "How refreshing. Idris. Wonderful place. Lots of ice. Costs quite a bit to bring it here, so I've heard. Good thing I don't ever have to pay for anything, eh?"

Siri raised an eyebrow. "And I'm standing here waiting because . . ."

"You promised to answer some of *my* questions."

"Oh," she said, sitting back down. "Of course."

"Now, then," he said. "Did you know any city guards back in your home?"

She cocked her head. "City guards?"

"You know, fellows who enforce the law. Police. Sheriffs. The men who catch crooks and guard dungeons. That sort."

"I knew a couple, I guess," she said. "My home city wasn't large but it was the capital. It did attract people who could be difficult sometimes."

"Ah, good," Lightsong said. "Kindly describe them for me. Not the difficult fellows. The city watch."

Siri shrugged. "I don't know. They tended to be careful. They'd interview newcomers to the village, walk the streets looking for wrongdoing, that sort of thing."

"Would you call them inquisitive types?"

"Yes," Siri said. "I guess. I mean, as much as anybody. Maybe more."

"Were there ever any murders in your village?"

"A couple," Siri said, glancing down. "There shouldn't have been—my father always said things like that shouldn't happen in Idris. Said murder was a thing of . . . well, Hallandren."

Lightsong chuckled. "Yes, we do it all the time. Quite the party trick. Now, did these policemen investigate the murders?"

"Of course."

"Without having to be asked to do so?"

Siri nodded.

"How'd they go about it?"

"I don't know," Siri said. "They asked questions, talked to witnesses, looked for clues. I wasn't involved."

"No, no," Lightsong said. "Of course you weren't. Why, if you'd been a murderer, they would have done something terrible to you, yes? Like exile you to another country?"

Siri felt herself pale, hair growing lighter.

Lightsong just laughed. "Don't go taking me so seriously, Your Majesty. Honestly, I gave up wondering if you were an assassin *days* ago. Now, if your servants and mine will stay behind for a second, I think I may have something important to tell you."

Siri started as Lightsong stood up. He began to walk from the pavilion, and his servants remained where they were. Confused but excited, Siri rose from her own seat and hurried after him. She caught up with him a short distance away, on the stone walkway that ran between the various boxes in the arena. Down below, the athletes continued their display.

Lightsong looked down at her, smiling.

They really are tall, she thought, craning a bit. A single foot of extra height made such a difference. Standing next to a man like Lightsong—and not really being that tall herself—she felt dwarfed. *Maybe he'll tell me the thing I've been looking for,* Siri thought. *The secret!*

"You are playing a dangerous game, my queen," Lightsong said, leaning against the stone railing. It was built for Returned proportions, so it was too high for her to rest against comfortably.

"Game?" she asked.

"Politics," he said, watching the athletes.

"I don't want to play politics."

"If you don't, it will play you, I'm afraid. I always get sucked in, regardless of what I do. Complaining doesn't stop that—though it does annoy people, which is satisfying in its own right."

Siri frowned. "So you pulled me aside to give me a warning?"

"Colors, no," Lightsong said, chuckling. "If you haven't already figured out that this is dangerous, then you're far too dense to appreciate a warning. I just wanted to give some advice. The first is about your persona."

"My persona?"

"Yes," he said. "It needs work. Choosing the persona of an innocent newcomer was a good instinct. It suits you. But you need to refine it. Work on it."

"It's not a persona," she said sincerely. "I *am* confused and new to all this."

Lightsong raised a finger. "That's the trick to politics, child. Sometimes, although you can't disguise who you are and how you really feel, you *can* make use of who you are. People distrust that which they can't understand and predict. As long as you feel like an unpredictable element in court, you will appear to be a threat. If you can skillfully—and honestly—portray yourself as someone they understand, then you'll begin to fit in."

Siri frowned.

"Take me as an example," Lightsong said. "I'm a useless fool. I always have been, as long as I can remember—which actually isn't all that long. Anyway, I know how people regard me. I enhance it. Play with it."

"So it's a lie?"

"Of course not. This is who I am. However, I make certain that people never forget it. You can't control everything. But if you can control how people regard you, then you can find a place in this mess. And once you have that, you can begin to influence factions. Should you want to. I rarely do because it's such a bother."

Siri cocked her head. Then she smiled. "You're a good man, Lightsong," she said. "I knew it, even when you were insulting me. You mean no harm. Is that part of your persona?"

"Of course," he said, smiling. "But I'm not sure *what* it is that convinces people to trust me. I'd get rid of it if I could. It only serves to make people expect too much. Just give what I said some practice. The best thing about being locked in this beautiful prison is that you *can* do some good, you *can* change things. I've seen others do it. People I respected. Even if there haven't been many of those around the court lately."

"All right," she said. "I will."

"You're digging for something—I can sense it. And it has

to do with the priests. Don't make too many waves until you're ready to strike. Sudden and surprising, that's how you want to be. You don't want to appear *too* nonthreatening—people are always suspicious of the innocent. The trick is to appear *average*. Just as crafty as everyone else. That way, everyone else will assume that they can beat you with just a little advantage."

Siri nodded. "Kind of an Idrian philosophy."

"You came from us," Lightsong said. "Or, perhaps, we came from you. Either way, we're more similar than our outward trappings make us seem. What is that Idrian philosophy of extreme plainness except a means of contrasting with Hallandren? All those whites you people use? That makes you stand out on a national scale. You act like us, we act like you, we just do the same things in opposite ways."

She nodded slowly.

He smiled. "Oh, and one thing. Please, *please* don't depend on me too much. I mean that. I'm not going to be of much help. If your plots come to a head—if things go wrong at the last moment and you're in danger or distress—don't think of me. I will fail you. *That* I promise from my heart with absolute sincerity."

"You're a very strange man."

"Product of my society," he said. "And since most of the time, my society consists pretty much only of myself, I blame God. Good day, my queen."

With that, he sauntered off back to his box and waved for her servants—who had been watching with concern—to finally rejoin her.

28

"THE MEETING IS set, my lady," Thame said. "The men are eager. Your work in T'Telir is gaining more and more notoriety."

Vivenna wasn't sure what she thought of that. She sipped her juice. The lukewarm liquid was addictively flavorful, although she wished for some Idrian ice.

Thame looked at her eagerly. The short Idrian was, according to Denth's investigations, trustworthy enough. His story of being "forced" into a life of crime was a tad overstated. He filled a niche in Hallandren society—he acted as a liaison between the Idrian workers and the various criminal elements.

He was also, apparently, a staunch patriot. Despite the fact that he tended to exploit his own people, particularly newcomers to the city.

"How many will be at the meeting?" Vivenna asked, watching traffic pass on the street out beyond the restaurant's patio gate.

"Over a hundred, my lady," Thame said. "Loyal to our king, I promise. And they're influential men, all of them—for Idrians in T'Telir, that is."

Which, according to Denth, meant that they were men who wielded power in the city because they could provide cheap Idrian workers and could sway the opinion of the underprivileged Idrian masses. They were men who, like Thame, thrived because of the Idrian expatriates. A strange duality. These men had stature among an oppressed minority, and without the oppression, they would be powerless.

Like Lemex, she thought, *who served my father—even seemed to respect and love him—all the while stealing every bit of gold he could lay his hands on.*

She leaned back, wearing a white dress with a long pleated skirt that rippled and blew in the wind. She tapped the side of her cup, which caused a serving man to refill her juice. Thame smiled, taking more juice as well, though he looked out of place in the fine restaurant.

"How many are there, you suppose?" she asked. "Idrians in the city, I mean."

"Perhaps as many as ten thousand."

"That many?"

"Trouble on the lower farms," Thame said, shrugging. "It's hard, sometimes, living up in those mountains. Crops fail, and what do you have? The king owns your land, so you can't sell. You need to pay your levies . . ."

"Yes, but one can petition in the case of disaster," Vivenna said.

"Ah, my lady, but most of these men are several weeks' travel from the king. Should they leave their families to make a petition, when they fear their loved ones will starve during the weeks it will take to bring food from the king's storehouse if they are successful? Or do they travel the much shorter distance down to T'Telir? Take work there, loading on the docks or harvesting flowers in the jungle plantations? It's hard work, but steady."

And, in doing so, they betray their people.

But who was she to judge? The Fifth Vision would define it as haughtiness. Here she sat in the cool shade of a canopy, enjoying a nice breeze and expensive juice while other men slaved to provide for their families. She had no right to sneer at their motivations.

Idrians shouldn't have to seek for work in Hallandren. She didn't like to admit fault in her father, yet his was not a bureaucratically efficient kingdom. It consisted of dozens of scattered villages with poor highways that were often blocked by snows or rockslides. In addition, he was forced to expend a lot of resources keeping his army strong in case of a Hallandren assault.

He had a difficult job. Was that a good enough excuse for the poverty of her people who had been forced to flee their homeland? The more she listened and learned, the more she realized that many Idrians had never known anything like the idyllic life she'd lived in her lovely mountain valley.

"The meeting is three days hence, my lady," Thame said. "Some of these men are hesitant after Vahr and his failure, but they will listen to you."

"I will be there."

"Thank you." Thame rose—bowed, despite the fact that she'd asked him not to draw attention to her—and withdrew.

Vivenna sat and sipped her juice. She felt Denth before he arrived. "You know what interests me?" he said, taking the seat Thame had been using.

"What?"

"People," he said, tapping an empty cup, drawing the serving man back over. "People interest me. Particularly people who don't act like they're supposed to. People who surprise me."

"I hope you aren't talking about Thame," Vivenna asked, raising an eyebrow.

Denth shook his head. "I'm talking about you, Princess. Wasn't too long ago that—no matter what or who you looked at—you had a look of quiet displeasure in your eyes. You've lost it. You're starting to fit in."

"Then that's a problem, Denth," Vivenna said. "I don't want to fit in. I hate Hallandren."

"You seem to like that juice all right."

Vivenna set it aside. "You're right, of course. I shouldn't be drinking it."

"If you say so," Denth said, shrugging. "Now, if you were to ask the mercenary—which, of course, nobody ever does—he might mention that it's *good* for you to start acting like a Hallandren. The less you stand out, the less likely people are to connect you to that Idrian princess hiding in the city. Take your friend Parlin."

"He looks like a fool in those bright colors," she said, glancing across the street toward where he and Jewels were chatting as they watched the escape route.

"Does he?" Denth said. "Or does he just look like a Hallandren? Would you hesitate at all if you were in the jungle and saw him put on the fur of a beast, or perhaps shroud himself in a cloak colored like fallen leaves?"

She looked again. Parlin lounged against the side of a building much like street toughs his age she'd seen elsewhere in the city.

"You both fit better here than you once did," Denth said. "You're learning."

Vivenna looked down. Some things in her new life were actually starting to feel natural. The raids, for instance, were becoming surprisingly easy. She was also growing used to moving with the crowds and being part of an underground element. Two months earlier, she would have been indignantly opposed to dealing with a man like Denth, simply because of his profession.

She found it very difficult to reconcile herself to some of these changes. It was growing harder and harder to understand herself, and to decide what she believed.

"Though," Denth said, eyeing Vivenna's dress, "you might want to think about switching to trousers."

Vivenna frowned, looking up.

"Just a suggestion," Denth said, then gulped down some juice. "You don't like the short Hallandren skirts, but the only decent clothing we can buy you that are 'modest' are of foreign make—and that makes them expensive. That means we have to use expensive restaurants, lest we stand out. That means you have to deal with all of this terrible lavishness. Trousers, however, are modest *and* cheap."

"Trousers are *not* modest."

"Don't show knees," he said.

"Doesn't matter."

Denth shrugged. "Just giving my opinion."

Vivenna looked away, then sighed quietly. "I appreciate the advice, Denth. Really. I just . . . I'm confused by a lot of my life lately."

"World's a confusing place," Denth said. "That's what makes it fun."

"The men we're working with," Vivenna said. "They lead the Idrians in the city but exploit them at the same time. Lemex stole from my father but still worked for the interests of my country. And here I am, wearing an overpriced dress and sipping expensive juice while my sister is being abused by an awful dictator and while this wonderful, terrible city prepares to launch a war on my homeland."

Denth leaned back in his chair, looking out over the short railing toward the street, watching the crowds with their colors both beautiful and terrible. "The motivations of men. They never make sense. And they always make sense."

"Right now, *you* don't make sense."

Denth smiled. "What I'm trying to say is that you don't understand a man until you understand what makes him do what he does. Every man is a hero in his own story, Princess. Murderers don't believe that they're to blame for what they do. Thieves, they think they deserve the money they take. Dictators, they believe they have the right—for the safety of their people and the good of the nation—to do whatever they wish."

He stared off, shaking his head. "I think even Vasher sees himself as a hero. The truth is, most people who do what you'd call 'wrong' do it for what they call 'right' reasons. Only mercenaries make any sense. We do what we're paid to do. That's it. Perhaps that's why people look down on us so. We're the only ones who don't pretend to have higher motives."

He paused, then met her eyes. "In a way, we're the most honest men you'll ever meet."

The two of them fell silent, the crowd passing by just a short distance away, a river of flashing colors. Another figure approached the table. "That's right," Tonk Fah said, "but, you forgot to mention that in addition to being honest, we're also clever. And handsome."

"Those both go without saying," Denth said.

Vivenna turned. Tonk Fah had been watching from nearby, ready to provide backup. They were letting her start to take the lead in some of the meetings. "Honest, perhaps," Vivenna said. "But I certainly *hope* that you're not the most handsome men I'll ever meet. Are we ready to go?"

"Assuming you're finished with your juice," Denth said, smirking at her.

Vivenna glanced at her cup. It was *very* good. Feeling guilty, she drained the juice. *It would be a sin to waste it,* she thought. Then she rose and swished her way from the building, leaving Denth—who now handled most of the coins—to settle the bill. Outside on the street, they were joined by Clod, who'd been given orders to come if she screamed for help.

She turned, looking back at Tonk Fah and Denth. "Tonks," she said. "Where's your monkey?"

He sighed. "Monkeys are boring anyway."

She rolled her eyes. "You lost *another* one?"

Denth chuckled. "Get used to it, Princess. Of all the happy miracles in the universe, one of the greatest is that Tonks has never fathered a child. He'd probably lose it before the week was out."

She shook her head. "You may be right," she said. "Next appointment. D'Denir garden, right?"

Denth nodded.

"Let's go," she said, walking down the street. The others trailed behind, picking up Parlin and Jewels on the way.

Vivenna didn't wait for Clod to force a way through the crowd. The less she depended on that Lifeless, the better. Moving through the streets really wasn't that difficult. There was an art to it—one moved with a crowd, rather than trying to swim against its flow. It wasn't long before, Vivenna at the front, the group turned off into the wide grassy field that was the D'Denir garden. Like the crossroads square, this place was an open space of green life set among the buildings and colors. Yet, here no flowers or trees broke the landscape, nor did people bustle about. This was a more reverent place.

And it was filled with statues. Hundreds of them. They looked much like the other D'Denir in the city—with their oversized bodies and heroic poses, many tied with colorful cloths or garments. These were some of the oldest statues she had seen, their stone weathered from years spent enduring the frequent T'Telir rainfalls. This group was the final gift from Peacegiver the Blessed. The statues had been made as a memorial to those who had died in the Manywar. A monument and a warning. So the legends said. Vivenna couldn't help thinking that if the people really did honor those who had fallen, they wouldn't dress the statues up in such ridiculous costumes.

Still, the place was far more serene than most in T'Telir, and she could appreciate that. She walked down the steps onto the lawn, wandering between the silent stone figures.

Denth moved up beside her. "Remember who we're meeting?"

She nodded. "Forgers."

Denth eyed her. "You all right with this?"

"Denth, during our months together I've met with thief lords, murderers, and—most frighteningly—mercenaries. I think I can deal with a couple of spindly scribes."

Denth shook his head. "These are the men who *sell* the documents, not the scribes who do the work. You won't meet more dangerous men than forgers. Within the Hallandren bureaucracy, they can make anything seem legal by putting the right documents in the right places."

Vivenna nodded slowly.

"You remember what to have them make?" Denth asked.

"Of course I do," she said. "This particular plan was *my* idea, remember?"

"Just checking," he said.

"You're worried that I'll mess things up, aren't you?"

He shrugged. "You're the leader in this little dance, Princess. I'm just the guy who mops the floor afterward." He eyed her. "I hate mopping up blood."

"Oh, please," she said, rolling her eyes, walking faster and leaving him behind. As he fell back, she could hear him talking to Tonk Fah. "Bad metaphor?" Denth asked.

"Nah," Tonk Fah said. "It had blood in it. That makes it a good metaphor."

"I think it lacked poetic style."

"Find something that rhymes with 'blood' then," Tonk Fah suggested. He paused. "Mud? Thud? Uh . . . taste-bud?"

They sure are literate, for a bunch of thugs, she thought.

She didn't have to go far before she spotted the men. They waited beside the agreed meeting place—a large D'Denir with a weathered axe. The group of people were having a picnic and chatting among themselves, a picture of harmless innocence.

Vivenna slowed.

"That's them," Denth whispered. "Let's go sit beside the D'Denir across from them."

Jewels, Clod, and Parlin hung back while Tonk Fah strolled away to watch the perimeter. Vivenna and Denth approached the statue near the forgers. Denth spread out a blanket for her, then stood to the side, as if he were a man-servant.

One of the men beside the other statue looked across as

Vivenna sat down; then he nodded. The others continued to eat. The Hallandren underground's penchant for working in broad daylight still unnerved Vivenna, but she supposed it had advantages over skulking about at night.

"You want some work commissioned?" the forger closest to her asked, just loudly enough that Vivenna could hear. It almost seemed part of his conversation with his friends.

"Yes," she said.

"It costs."

"I can pay."

"You're the princess everyone is talking about?"

She paused, noticing Denth's hand leisurely going to his sword hilt.

"Yes," she said.

"Good," the forger said. "Royalty always seems to know how to handle itself. What is it you desire?"

"Letters," Vivenna said. "I want them to appear as if they were between certain members of the Hallandren priesthood and the king of Idris. They need to have official seals and convincing signatures."

"Difficult," the man said.

Vivenna pulled something from her dress pocket. "I have a letter written in King Dedelin's hand. It has his seal on the wax, his signature at the bottom."

The man seemed intrigued, though she could only see the side of his face. "That makes it possible. Still hard. What do you want these documents to prove?"

"That these particular priests are corrupt," Vivenna said. "I have a list on this sheet. I want you to make it look like they've been extorting Idris for years, forcing our king to pay outrageous sums and make extreme promises in order to prevent war. I want you to show that Idris doesn't want war and that the priests are hypocrites."

The man nodded. "Is that everything?"

"Yes."

"It can be done. We'll be in touch. Instructions and explanations are on the back of the paper?"

"As requested," Vivenna said.

The group of men stood, a servant moving forward to pack up their lunch. As he did so, he let a napkin blow in the wind, then rushed over and picked it up, grabbing Vivenna's paper too. Soon, all of them were gone.

"Well?" Vivenna asked, looking up.

"Good," Denth said, nodding to himself. "You're becoming an expert."

Vivenna smiled, settling back on her blanket to wait. The next appointment consisted of a group of thieves who had stolen—at Vivenna and Denth's request—various goods from the war offices in the Hallandren bureaucratic building. The documents were of relatively little import themselves, but their absence would cause confusion and frustration.

That appointment wasn't for a few hours, which meant she could enjoy some time relaxing on the lawn, away from the unnatural colors of the city. Denth seemed to sense her inclination, and he sat down, leaning back against the side of the statue's bare pedestal. As Vivenna waited, she saw that Parlin was over talking to Jewels again. Denth was right; though his clothing looked ridiculous to her, that was because she *knew* him as an Idrian. Looking at him more objectively, she saw that he fit in remarkably well with other young men in the city.

That's well and good for him, Vivenna thought with annoyance, looking away. *He can dress as he wishes—he doesn't have to worry about his neckline or hemline.*

Jewels laughed. It was almost a snort of derision, but there was *some* mirth in it. Vivenna looked back immediately, watching Jewels roll her eyes at Parlin, who had a self-effacing smirk on his face. He knew he'd said something wrong. He didn't know what. Vivenna knew him well enough to read the expression and to know that he'd just smile and go along with it.

Jewels saw his face, then laughed again.

Vivenna gritted her teeth. "I should send him back to Idris," she said.

Denth turned, looking down at her. "Hum?"

"Parlin," she said. "I sent my other guides back. I should have sent him too. He serves no function."

"He's quick at adapting to situations," Denth said. "And he's trustworthy. That's good enough reason to keep him."

"He's a fool," Vivenna said. "Has trouble understanding half of what goes on around him."

"He's not got the wit of a scholar, true, but he seems to instinctively know how to blend in. Besides, we can't all be geniuses like you."

She glanced at Denth. "What does that mean?"

"It means," Denth said, "that you shouldn't let your hair change colors in public, Princess."

Vivenna started, noticing that her hair had shifted from a still, calm black to the red of frustration. *Lord of Colors!* she thought. *I used to be so good at controlling that. What is happening to me?*

"Don't worry," Denth said, settling back. "Jewels has *no* interest in your friend. I promise you."

Vivenna snorted. "Parlin? Why should I care?"

"Oh, I don't know," Denth said. "Maybe because you and he have been practically engaged since you were children?"

"That's completely untrue," Vivenna said. "I've been engaged to the God King since before my birth!"

"And your father always wished you could marry the son of his best friend instead," Denth said. "At least, that's what Parlin says." He eyed her with a smirk.

"That boy talks too much."

"Actually, he's usually rather quiet," Denth said. "You have to pry to get him to talk about himself. Either way, Jewels has other ties. So stop your worrying."

"I'm not worried," Vivenna said. "And I'm *not* interested in Parlin.

"Of course not."

Vivenna opened her mouth to object, but she noticed Tonk Fah wandering over, and didn't want *him* to join this discussion as well. She snapped her jaw shut as the hefty mercenary arrived.

"Flood," Tonk Fah said.

"Hum?" Denth asked.

"Rhymes with blood," Tonk Fah said. "Now you can be poetic. Flood of Blood. It is a nice visual image. Far better than tastebud." ·

"Ah, I see," Denth said flatly. "Tonk Fah?"

"Yes?"

"You're an idiot."

"Thanks."

Vivenna stood up and began to walk through the statues, studying them—if only to escape having to watch Parlin and Jewels. Tonk Fah and Denth trailed along behind at a comfortable distance, keeping a watchful eye.

There was a beauty to the statues. They weren't like the other kinds of art in T'Telir—flashy paintings, colorful buildings, exaggerated clothing. The D'Denir were solid blocks that had aged with dignity. The Hallandren, of course, did their best to destroy this with the scarves, hats, or other colorful bits they tied on the stone memorials. Fortunately, there were too many in this garden for all to be decorated.

They stood, as if on guard, somehow more solid than much of the city. Most stared up into the sky or looked straight ahead. Each one was different, each pose distinct, each face unique. *It must have taken decades to create all of these,* she thought. *Perhaps that's where the Hallandren got their penchant for art.*

Hallandren was such a place of contradictions. Warriors to represent peace. Idrians who exploited and protected each other at the same time. Mercenaries who seemed to be among the best men she had ever known. Bright colors that created a kind of uniformity.

And, over it all, BioChromatic Breath. It was exploitive, yet people like Jewels saw giving up their Breath as a privilege. Contradictions. The question was, could Vivenna afford to become another contradiction? A person who bent her beliefs in order to see that they were preserved?

The Breaths *were* wonderful. It was more than just the beauty or the ability to hear changes in sound and sense intrinsically the distinct hues of color. It was more even than the ability to sense life around her. More than the sounds of the wind and the tones of people talking, or her ability to feel her way through a group of people and move easily with the motions of a crowd.

It was a connection. The world around her felt *close*. Even inanimate things like her clothing or fallen twigs felt near to her. They were dead, yet seemed to yearn for life again.

She could give it to them. They remembered life and she could Awaken those memories. But what good would it do to save her people if she lost herself?

Denth doesn't seem lost, she thought. *He and the other mercenaries can separate what they believe from what they are forced to do.*

In her opinion, that was why people regarded mercenaries as they did. If you divorced belief from action, then you were on dangerous ground.

No, she thought. *No Awakening for me.*

The Breath would remain untapped. If it tempted her too much further, she would give the lot away to somebody who had none.

And become a Drab herself.

29

*T*ELL ME ABOUT *the mountains,* Susebron wrote.

Siri smiled. "Mountains?"

Please, he wrote, sitting in his chair beside the bed. Siri lay on one side; her bulky dress had been too hot for this evening, so she sat in her shift with a sheet over her, resting on one elbow so she could see what he wrote. The fire crackled.

"I don't know what to tell you," she said. "I mean, the mountains aren't amazing like the wonders you have in T'Telir. You have so many colors, so much variety."

I think that rocks sticking from the ground and rising thousands of feet into the air count as a wonder, he wrote.

"I guess," she said. "I liked it in Idris—I didn't want to know anything else. For someone like you, though, it would probably be boring."

More boring than sitting in the same palace every day, not allowed to leave, not allowed to speak, being dressed and pampered?

"Okay, you win."

Tell me of them, please. His handwriting was getting very good. Plus, the more he wrote, the more he seemed to understand. She wished so much that she could find him books to read—she suspected that he'd absorb them quickly, becoming as learned as any of the scholars who had tried to tutor her.

And yet, all he had was Siri. He seemed to appreciate what he gave him—but that was probably only because he didn't know just how ignorant she was. *I suspect,* she thought, *that my tutors would laugh themselves silly if they knew how much I'd come to regret ignoring them.*

"The mountains are vast," she said. "You can't really get

a sense of it here, in the lowlands. It's by seeing them that you know just how insignificant people really are. I mean, no matter how long we worked and built, we could never pile up *anything* as high as one of the mountains.

"They're rocks, like you said, but they're not lifeless. They're green—as green as your jungles. But it's a different green. I heard some of the traveling merchants complain that the mountains cut off their view, but I think you can see *more*. They let you see the surface of the land as it extends upward, toward Austre's domain in the sky."

He paused. *Austre?*

Siri flushed, hair blushing as well. "I'm sorry. I probably shouldn't talk about other gods in front of you."

Other gods? he wrote. *Like those in the court?*

"No," Siri said. "Austre is the Idrian god."

I understand, Susebron wrote. *Is he very handsome?*

Siri laughed. "No, you don't understand. He's not a Returned, like you or Lightsong. He's . . . well, I don't know. Didn't the priests mention other religions to you?"

Other religions? he wrote.

"Sure," she said. "I mean, not everybody worships the Returned. The Idrians like me worship Austre, and the Pahn Kahl people—like Bluefingers . . . well, I don't actually know what they worship, but it's not you."

That is very strange to consider, he wrote. *If your gods are not Returned, then what are they?*

"Not they," Siri said. "Just one. We call him Austre. The Hallandren used to worship him too before . . ." She almost said before they became heretics. "Before Peacegiver arrived, and they decided to worship the Returned instead."

But who is this Austre? he wrote.

"He's not a person," Siri said. "He's more of a force. You know, the thing that watches over all people, who punishes those who don't do what is right and who blesses those who are worthy."

Have you met this creature?

Siri laughed. "Of course not. You can't see Austre."

Susebron frowned, looking at her.

"I know," she said. "It must seem silly to you. But, well, we know he's there. When I see something beautiful in nature—when I look at the mountains, with their wild-flowers growing in patterns that are somehow more *right* than a man could have planted—I know. Beauty is real. That's what reminds me of Austre. Plus, we've got the Returned—including the First Returned, Vo. He had the Five Visions before he died, and they *must* have come from somewhere."

But you don't believe in worshiping the Returned?

Siri shrugged. "I haven't decided yet. My people teach strongly against it. They're not fond of the way that the Hallandren understand religion."

He sat quietly for a long moment.

So . . . you do not like those such as me?

"What? Of course I like you! You're sweet!"

He frowned, writing. *I don't think God Kings are supposed to be "sweet."*

"Fine, then," she said, rolling her eyes. "You're terrible and mighty. Awesome and deific. And sweet."

Much better, he wrote, smiling. *I should very much like to meet this Austre.*

"I'll introduce you to some monks sometime," Siri said. "They should be able to help you with that."

Now you are mocking me.

Siri smiled as he looked up at her. There was no hurt in his eyes. He didn't appear to mind being mocked; indeed, he seemed to find it very interesting. He particularly liked trying to pick out when she was being serious and when she wasn't.

He looked down again. *More than meeting with this god, however, I should like to see the mountains. You seem to love them very much.*

"I do," Siri said. It had been a long time since she'd

thought of Idris. But as he mentioned it, she remembered the cool, open feeling of the meadows she had run through not so long ago. The crispness of the chilly air—something that she suspected one could never find in Hallandren.

Plants in the Court of Gods were kept perfectly clipped, cultivated, and arranged. They were beautiful, but the wild fields of her homeland had their own special feel.

Susebron was writing again. *I suspect that the mountains are beautiful, as you have said. However, I believe the most beautiful thing in them has already come down to me.*

Siri started, then flushed. He seemed so open, not even a little embarrassed or shy about the bold compliment. "Susebron!" she said. "You have the heart of a charmer."

Charmer? he wrote. *I must only speak what I see. There is nothing so wonderful as you, even in my entire court. The mountains must be special indeed, to produce such beauty.*

"See, now you've gone too far," she said. "I've *seen* the goddesses of your court. They're far more beautiful than I am."

Beauty is not about how a person looks, Susebron wrote. *My mother taught me this. The travelers in my storybook must not judge the old woman ugly, for she might be a beautiful goddess inside.*

"This isn't a story, Susebron."

Yes it is, he wrote. *All of those stories are just tales told by people who lived lives before ours. What they say about humankind is true. I have watched and seen how people act.* He erased, then continued. *It is strange, for me, to interpret these things, for I do not see as normal men do. I am the God King. Everything, to my eyes, has the same beauty.*

Siri frowned. "I don't understand."

I have thousands of Breaths, he wrote. *It is hard to see as other people do—only through the stories of my mother can I understand their ways. All colors are beauty in my eyes. When others look at something—a person—one may sometimes seem more beautiful than another.*

This is not so for me. I see only the color. The rich, wondrous colors that make up all things and give them life. I cannot focus only on the face, as so many do. I see the sparkle of the eyes, the blush of the cheeks, the tones of skin—even each blemish is a distinct pattern. All people are wonderful.

He erased. *And so, when I speak of beauty, I must speak of things other than these colors. And you are different. I do not know how to describe it.*

He looked up, and suddenly Siri was aware of just how close they were to each other. She, only in her shift, with the thin sheet covering her. He, tall and broad, shining with a soul that made the colors of the sheets bend out like light through a prism. He smiled in the firelight.

Oh, dear . . . she thought. *This is dangerous.*

She cleared her throat, sitting up, flushing yet again. "Well. Um, yes. Very nice. Thank you."

He looked back down. *I wish I could let you go home, to see your mountains again. Perhaps I could explain this to the priests.*

She paled. "I don't think it would be good to let them know that you can read."

I could use the artisans' script. It is very difficult to write, but they taught it to me so I could communicate with them, if I needed to.

"Still," she said. "Telling them you want to send me home could hint that you've been talking to me."

He stopped writing for a few moments.

Maybe that would be a good thing, he wrote.

"Susebron, they're planning to *kill* you."

You have no proof of that.

"Well, it's suspicious, at least," she said. "The last two God Kings died within months of producing an heir."

You're too untrusting, Susebron wrote. *I keep telling you. My priests are good people.*

She regarded him flatly, catching his eyes.

Except for removing my tongue, he admitted.

"And keeping you locked up, and not telling you anything. Look, even if they aren't planning to kill you, they know things they're not telling you. Perhaps it's something to do with BioChroma—something that makes you die once your heir arrives."

She frowned, leaning back. *Could that be it?* she wondered suddenly. "Susebron, how do you pass on your Breaths?"

He paused. *I don't know,* he wrote. *I . . . don't know a lot about it.*

"I don't either," she said. "Can they take them from you? Give them to your son? What if that kills you?"

They wouldn't do that, he wrote.

"But maybe it's possible," she said. "And maybe that's what happens. That's why having a child is so dangerous! They have to make a new God King and it kills you to do so."

He sat with his board in his lap, then shook his head, writing. *I am a god. I am not given Breaths, I am born with them.*

"No," Siri said. "Bluefingers told me you'd been collecting them for centuries. That each God King gets two Breaths a week, instead of one, building up his reserves."

Actually, he admitted, *some weeks I get three or four.*

"But you only need one a week to survive."

Yes.

"And they can't let that wealth die with you! They're too afraid of it to let you use it, but they also can't let themselves lose it. So, when a new child is born, they take the Breath from the old king—killing him—and give it to the new one."

But Returned cannot use their Breath for Awakening, he wrote. *So my treasure of Breaths is useless.*

This gave her pause. She *had* heard that. "Does that mean only the Breath you're born with, or does it include the extra Breaths that have been added on top?"

I do not know, he wrote.

"I'll bet you could use those extra Breaths if you wanted," she said. "Otherwise, why remove your tongue? You may not be able to access and use that Breath that makes you Returned in the first place, but you have thousands and thousands of Breaths above that."

Susebron sat for a few moments, and then finally he rose, walking across to the window. He stared out at the darkness beyond. Siri frowned, then picked up his board and crossed the room. She got off the bed and approached hesitantly, wearing only her shift.

"Susebron?" she asked.

He continued to stare out the window. She joined him, careful not to touch him, looking out. Colorful lights sparkled amidst the city beyond the wall of the Court of Gods. Beyond that was darkness. The still sea.

"Please," she said, pushing the board into his hands. "What is it?"

He paused, then took it. *I am sorry,* he wrote. *I do not wish to appear petulant.*

"Is it because I keep challenging your priests?"

No, he wrote. *You have interesting theories, but I think they are just guesses. You do not know that the priests plan what you claim. That doesn't bother me.*

"What is it, then?"

He hesitated, then erased with the sleeve of his robe. *You do not believe that the Returned are divine.*

"I thought we already talked about this."

We did. However, I realized now that this *is the reason why you treat me as you do. You are different because you*

*do not believe in my godhood. Is that the only reason I find
you interesting?*

*And, if you do not believe, it makes me sad. Because a
god is who I am, it is what I am, and if you do not believe
in it, it makes me think you do not understand me.*

He paused.

Yes. It does sound petulant. I am sorry.

She smiled, then tentatively touched his arm. He froze,
looking down, but didn't pull back as he had times before.
So she moved up beside him, resting against his arm.

"I don't have to believe in you to understand you," she
said. "I'd say that those people who worship you are the ones
who don't understand. They can't get close to you, see who
you really are. They're too focused on the aura and the
divinity."

He didn't respond.

"And," she said, "I'm not different *just* because I don't
believe in you. There are a lot of people in the palace who
don't believe. Bluefingers, some of the serving girls who
wear brown, other scribes. They serve you just as reverently
as the priests. I'm just . . . well, I'm an irreverent type. I
didn't really listen to my father or the monks back home,
either. Maybe that's what you need. Someone who would be
willing to look beyond your godhood and just get to know
you."

He nodded slowly. *That is comforting,* he wrote. *Though,
it is very strange to be a god whose wife does not believe
in him.*

Wife, she thought. Sometimes that was tough to remember. "Well," she said, "I should think it would do every man
good to have a wife who isn't as in awe of him as everyone
else is. Somebody has to keep you humble."

Humility is, I believe, somewhat opposite to godhood.

"Like sweetness?" she asked.

He chuckled. *Yes, just like that.* He put the board down.

Then, hesitantly—a little frightened—he put his arm around her shoulders, pulling her closer as they looked out the window at the lights of a city that remained colorful, even at night.

———∽∞∾———

BODIES. FOUR OF them. They all lay dead on the ground, blood an oddly dark color against the grass.

It was the day after Vivenna's visit to the D'Denir garden to meet with the forgers. She was back again. Sunlight streamed down, hot upon her head and neck as she stood with the rest of the gawking crowd. The silent D'Denir waited in rows behind her, soldiers of stone who would never march. Only they had seen the four men die.

People chattered with hushed voices, waiting for the city guard to finish their inspection. Denth had brought Vivenna quickly, before the bodies could be cleared. He had done so at her request. Now she wished she'd never asked.

To her enhanced eyes, the colors of the blood on grass were powerfully distinct. Red and green. It made almost a violet in combination. She stared at the corpses, feeling an odd sense of disconnection. Color. So strange to see the colors of skin paled. She could tell the difference—the intrinsic difference—between skin that was alive and skin that was dead.

Dead skin was ten shades whiter than live skin. It was caused by blood seeping down and out of the veins. Almost like . . . like the blood *was* the color, drained out of its casks. The paint of a human life which had been carelessly spilled, leaving the canvas blank.

She looked away.

"You see it?" Denth said, at her side.

She nodded silently.

"You asked about him. Well, here's what he does. *This* is why we're so worried. Look at those wounds."

She turned back. In the growing morning light, she

could see something she'd missed before. The skin directly around the sword wounds had been completely drained of color. The wounds themselves had a dark black tinge to them. As if they had been infected with some terrible disease.

She turned back to Denth.

"Let's go," Denth said, leading her away from the crowd as the city Guards finally began to order people back, annoyed by the number of gawkers.

"Who were they?" she asked quietly.

Denth stared straight ahead. "A gang of thieves. Ones we'd worked with."

"You think he might come for us?"

"I'm not sure," Denth said. "He could probably find us if he wanted. I don't know."

Tonk Fah approached across the green as they passed through the D'Denir statues. "Jewels and Clod are on alert," Tonk Fah said. "None of us see him anywhere."

"What happened to the skin of those men?" Vivenna asked.

"It's that sword of his," Denth growled. "We *have* to find a way to deal with it, Tonks. We're going to end up crossing him, eventually. I can feel it."

"But what is the sword?" Vivenna asked. "And how did it drain the color from their skin?"

"We'll have to steal the thing, Denth," Tonk Fah said, rubbing his chin as Jewels and Clod filled in around them, making a protective pattern as they moved out into the human river of the street.

"Steal the sword?" Denth asked. "I'm not touching the thing! No, we have to make him use it. Draw it. He won't be able to keep it out for long. After that, we'll be able to take him easily. I'll kill him myself."

"He beat Arsteel," Jewels said quietly.

Denth froze. "He did *not* beat Arsteel! Not in a duel, at least."

"Vasher didn't use the sword," Jewels said. "There was no blackness to Arsteel's wounds."

"Then Vasher used a trick!" Denth said. "Ambush. Accomplices. Something. Vasher is no duelist."

Vivenna let herself get pulled along, thinking of those bodies. Denth and the others had spoken of the deaths this Vasher was causing. She'd wanted to see them. Well, now she had. And it left her feeling disturbed. Unsettled. And . . .

She frowned, itching slightly.

Someone with a lot of Breath was watching her.

⸺⊗⸺

HEY! NIGHTBLOOD SAID. *It's VaraTreledees! We should go talk to him. He'll be happy to see me.*

Vasher stood openly atop the building. He didn't really care who saw him. He rarely did. An endless flow of people passed on the colorful street. VaraTreledees—Denth, as he called himself now—walked among them with his team. The woman, Jewels. Tonk Fah, as always. The clueless princess. And the abomination.

Is Shashara here? Nightblood asked, excitement in his nebulous voice. *We need to go see her! She'll be worried about what happened to me.*

"We killed Shashara long ago, Nightblood," Vasher said. "Just like we killed Arsteel." *Just like we'll eventually kill Denth.*

As usual, Nightblood refused to acknowledge Shashara's death. *She made me, you know,* Nightblood said. *Made me to destroy things that were evil. I'm rather good at it. I think she'd be proud of me. We should go talk to her. Show her how well I do my job.*

"You are good at it," Vasher whispered. "Too good."

Nightblood began to hum quietly, pleased at the perceived praise. Vasher, however, focused on the princess, walking in her obviously exotic dress, standing out like a flake of snow in the tropical heat. He would need to do something about her. Because of her, so many things were falling apart. Plans toppling like badly stacked boxes, creating a racket with their collapse. He didn't know where Denth had found her or how he kept control of her. However, Vasher was sorely tempted to jump down and let Nightblood take her.

The deaths the night before had already drawn too much attention. Nightblood was right. Vasher wasn't good at sneaking about. Rumors regarding him were widespread in the city. That was both good and bad.

Later, he thought, turning from the silly girl and her mercenary entourage. *Later.*

30

LIGHTSONG!" BLUSHWEAVER SAID, hands on hips. "What in the name of the Iridescent Tones are you doing?"

Lightsong ignored her, instead applying his hands to the clump of muddy clay in front of him. His servants and priests stood in a large ring, looking nearly as confused as Blushweaver—who had arrived at his pavilion just a few moments before.

The pottery wheel spun. He held the clay, trying to get it to stay in place. Sunlight shone in through the sides of the pavilion, and the neatly manicured grass under his table was flecked with clay. As the wheel sped up, the clay twirled round, flipping out clods and clumps. Lightsong's hands became soaked with grimy, slick clay, and it didn't take long for the entire mess to flip off the wheel and squish to the ground.

"Hum," he said, regarding it.

"Have you taken leave of your senses?" Blushweaver

asked. She wore one of her customary dresses—which meant nothing on the sides, very little at the top, and only slightly more through the front and back. She had her hair up in an intricately twisting woven pattern of braids and ribbon. Likely the work of a master stylist, who had been invited into the court to perform for one of the gods.

Lightsong hopped to his feet, holding his hands out to either side as servants rushed to wash them off. Others came and wiped the bits of clay from his fine robes. He stood thoughtfully as other servants removed the pottery wheel.

"Well?" Blushweaver asked. "What *was* that?"

"I just discovered that I am no good at pottery," Lightsong said. "Actually, I am worse than 'no good.' I am pathetic. Ridiculously bad. Can't even get the blasted clay to stay on the wheel."

"Well what did you expect?"

"I'm not sure," Lightsong said, walking across the pavilion toward a long table. Blushweaver—obviously annoyed at being led along—followed. Lightsong suddenly grabbed five lemons off of the table and threw them into the air. He proceeded to juggle them.

Blushweaver watched. And, for just a moment, she looked honestly concerned. "Lightsong?" she asked. "Dear. Is . . . everything all right?"

"I have never practiced juggling," he said, watching the lemons. "Now, please grab that guava fruit."

She hesitated, then carefully picked up the guava.

"Throw it," Lightsong said.

She tossed it at him. He deftly plucked it from the air, then threw it into the pattern with the lemons. "I didn't know I could do this," he said. "Not before today. What do you make of it?"

"I . . ." she cocked her head.

He laughed. "I don't think I've ever seen you at a loss for words, my dear."

"I don't know that I've ever seen another god throwing fruit into the air."

"It's more than this," Lightsong said, dipping down as he nearly lost one of the lemons. "Today I have discovered that I know a surprising number of sailing terms, that I am fantastic at mathematics, and that I have a fairly good eye for sketching. On the other hand, I know nothing about the dyeing industry, horses, or gardening. I have no talent for sculpting, I can't speak any foreign languages, and—as you've seen—I'm terrible at pottery."

Blushweaver watched him for a second.

He looked at her, letting the lemons drop but snatching the guava out of the air. He tossed it to a servant, who began peeling it for him. "My previous life, Blushweaver. These are skills that I—Lightsong—have no right to know. Whoever I was before I died, *he* could juggle. He knew about sailing. And he could sketch."

"We're not supposed to worry about the people we were before," Blushweaver said.

"I'm a god," Lightsong said, taking back a plate containing the peeled and sliced guava, then offering a piece to Blushweaver. "And, by Kalad's Phantoms, I'll worry about whatever I please."

She paused, then smiled and took a slice. "Just when I thought I had you figured out . . ."

"You didn't have me figured out," he said lightly. "And neither did I. That's the point. Shall we go?"

She nodded, joining him as they began to cross the lawn, their servants bringing parasols to shade them. "You can't tell me that you've never wondered," Lightsong said.

"My dear," she replied, sucking on a guava piece, "I was *boring* before."

"How do you know?"

"Because I was an ordinary person! I would have been . . . Well, have you *seen* regular women?"

"Their proportions aren't quite up to your standards, I know," he said. "But many are quite attractive."

Blushweaver shivered. "Please. Why would you want to know about your normal life? What if you were a murderer or a rapist? Worse, what if you had bad fashion sense?"

He snorted at the twinkle in her eye. "You act so shallow. But I see the curiosity. You should try some of these things, let them tell you a little of who you were. There must have been something special about you for you to have Returned."

"Hum," she said, smiling and sidling up to him. He stopped as she ran her finger down the front of his chest. "Well, if you're trying new things today, maybe there's something else you ought to think about. . . ."

"Don't try to change the subject."

"I'm not," she said. "But, how will you know who you were if you don't try? It would be an . . . experiment."

Lightsong laughed, pushing her hand away. "My dear, I fear you would find me less than satisfactory."

"I think you overestimate me."

"That's impossible."

She paused, flushing slightly.

"Uh . . ." Lightsong said. "Hum. I didn't exactly mean . . ."

"Oh, bother," she said. "Now you've spoiled the moment. I was about to say something very clever, I just know it."

He smiled. "Both of us, at a loss for words in one afternoon. I do believe we're losing our touch."

"*My* touch is perfectly fine, which you'd discover if you'd just let me show you."

He rolled his eyes and continued to walk. "You're hopeless."

"When all else fails, use sexual innuendo," she said lightly, joining him. "It always brings the focus back to where it belongs. On me."

"Hopeless," he said again. "But, I doubt we have time for me to chastise you again. We've arrived."

Indeed, Hopefinder's palace was before them. Lavender and silver, it had a pavilion out front prepared with three tables and food. Naturally, Blushweaver and Lightsong had arranged for the meeting ahead of time.

Hopefinder the Just, god of innocence and beauty, stood up as they approached. He appeared to be about thirteen years old. By apparent physical age, he was the youngest of the gods in the court. But they weren't supposed to acknowledge such discrepancies. After all, he'd Returned when his body had been two, which made him—in god years—Lightsong's senior by six years. In a place where most gods didn't last twenty years, and the average age was probably closer to ten, six years' difference was very significant.

"Lightsong, Blushweaver," Hopefinder said, stiff and formal. "Welcome."

"Thank you, dear," Blushweaver said, smiling at him.

Hopefinder nodded, then gestured toward the tables. The three small tables were separate, but set close enough together for the meal to remain intimate while giving each god his or her own space.

"How have you been, Hopefinder?" Lightsong asked, sitting.

"Very well," Hopefinder said. His voice always seemed a little too mature for his body. Like a boy trying to imitate his father. "There was a particularly difficult case during petitions this morning. A mother with a child who was dying of the fevers. She'd already lost her other three, as well as her husband. All in the space of a year. Tragic."

"My dear," Blushweaver said with concern. "You're not actually considering . . . passing your Breath, are you?"

Hopefinder sat. "I don't know, Blushweaver. I am old. I feel old. Perhaps it is time for me to go. I'm fifth most aged, you know."

"Yes, but with the times growing so exciting!"

"Exciting?" he asked. "Why, they're calming down. The

new queen is here, and my sources in the palace say that she's pursuing her duties to produce an heir with great vigor. Stability will soon arrive."

"Stability?" Blushweaver asked as the servants brought them each a chilled soup. "Hopefinder, I find it hard to believe that you're *so* uninformed."

"You think the Idrians plan to use the new queen in a play for the throne," Hopefinder said. "I know what you've been doing, Blushweaver. I disagree."

"And the rumors out in the city?" Blushweaver said. "The Idrian agents who are causing such a ruckus? This so-called second princess somewhere in the city?"

Lightsong paused, spoon halfway to his lips. *What was that?*

"The city's Idrians are *always* creating one crisis or another," Hopefinder said, waving his fingers dismissively. "What was that disturbance six months ago, the rebel on the outer dye plantations? He died in prison, I recall. Foreign workers rarely provide a stable societal underclass, but I don't fear them."

"They've never claimed to have a royal agent working with them," Blushweaver said. "Things could get out of hand *very* quickly."

"My interests in the city are quite secure," Hopefinder said, lacing his fingers in front of him. The servants took away his soup. He'd taken only three sips. "How about yours?"

"That's what this meeting is for," Blushweaver said.

"Excuse me," Lightsong said, raising a finger. "But what in the *Colors* are we talking about?"

"Unrest in the city, Lightsong," Hopefinder said. "Some of the locals are unsettled by the prospect of war."

"They could turn dangerous very easily," Blushweaver said, stirring her soup with a lazy motion. "I think that we should be prepared."

"I am," Hopefinder said, watching Blushweaver with his

too-young face. Like all younger Returned—the God King included—Hopefinder would continue to age until his body reached maturity. Then, he would stop aging—just over the brink into the prime adulthood—until he gave up his Breath.

He acted so much like an adult. Lightsong hadn't interacted much with children, but some of his attendants—when training—were youths. Hopefinder was not like those. All accounts said that Hopefinder, like other young Returned, had matured very quickly during his first year of life, coming to think and speak as an adult while his body was still that of a young child.

Hopefinder and Blushweaver continued to talk about the stability of the city, mentioning various acts of vandalism that had occurred. War plans stolen, city supply stations poisoned. Lightsong let them talk. *He doesn't seem to find Blushweaver's beauty distracting,* he thought as he watched. She turned to the fruit course, acting characteristically lascivious as she sucked on pieces of pineapple. Hopefinder either didn't care, or didn't notice, as she leaned forward, showing an impressive amount of cleavage.

Something is *different about him,* Lightsong thought. *He Returned when he was a child and acted like one for a very short time. Now, he's an adult in some ways, but a child in others.*

The transformation had made Hopefinder more mature. He was also taller and more physically impressive than ordinary boys his age, even if he didn't have the chiseled, majestic features of a fully grown god.

And yet, Lightsong thought, eating a piece of pineapple, *different gods have different body styles. Blushweaver is inhumanly well endowed, particularly for how thin she is. Yet Mercystar is plump and curvaceous all around. Others, like Allmother, look physically old.*

Lightsong knew he didn't deserve his powerful physique. Like the knowledge of how to juggle, he somehow understood that a person usually had to work hard at manual labor to have such a muscular body. Lounging about, eating and drinking, should have made him plump and flabby.

But there have been gods who were fat, he thought, remembering some of the pictures he had seen of Returned who had come before him. *There was a time in our culture's history when that was seen as the ideal. . . .* Did Returned looks have something to do with the way society saw them? Perhaps their opinion of ideal beauty? That would certainly explain Blushweaver.

Some things survived the transformation. Language. Skills. And, as he thought about it, social competence. Considering the fact that the gods spent their lives locked up atop a plateau, they probably should have been far less well adjusted than they were. At the very least, they should have been ignorant and naive. Yet most of them were consummate schemers, sophisticates with a surprisingly good grasp of what happened in the outside world.

Memory itself didn't survive. Why? Why could Lightsong juggle and understand the meaning of the word "bowsprit," yet at the same time be unable to remember who his parents had been? And who was that face he saw in his dreams? Why had storms and tempests dominated his dreams lately? What was the red panther that had appeared, yet again, in his nightmares the night before?

"Blushweaver," Hopefinder said, holding up a hand. "Enough. Before we go any further, I must point out that your obvious attempts to seduce me will gain you nothing."

Blushweaver glanced away, looking embarrassed.

Lightsong shook himself out of his contemplations. "My dear Hopefinder," he said. "She was *not* trying to seduce you. You must understand; Blushweaver's aura of allure is simply a part of who she is; it's part of what makes her so charming."

"Regardless," he said. "I will not be swayed by it or by her paranoid arguments and fears."

"My contacts do not think that these things are simple

'paranoia,'" Blushweaver said as the fruit dishes were removed. A small chilled fish fillet arrived next.

"Contacts?" Hopefinder asked. "And just who are these 'contacts' you keep mentioning?"

"People within the God King's palace itself."

"We all have people in the God King's palace," Hopefinder said.

"I don't," Lightsong said. "Can I have one of yours?"

Blushweaver rolled her eyes. "My contact is *quite* important. He hears things, knows things. War *is* coming."

"I don't believe you," he said, picking at his food, "but that doesn't really matter now, does it? You're not here to get me to believe you. You just want my army."

"Your codes," Blushweaver said. "Lifeless security phrases. What will it cost us to get them?"

Hopefinder picked at his fish some more. "Do you know, Blushweaver, why I find my existence so boring?"

She shook her head. "Honestly, I *still* think you're bluffing on that count."

"I'm not," he said. "Eleven years. Eleven years of peace. Eleven years to grow to sincerely loathe this system of government we have. We all attend the assembly court of judgment. We listen to the arguments. But most of us don't matter. In any given vote, only those with sway in that field have any real say over anything. During war times, those of us with Lifeless Commands are important. The rest of the time, our opinion rarely matters.

"You want my Lifeless? Be welcome to them! I have had no opportunity to use them in eleven years, and I venture that another eleven will pass without incident. I will give you those Commands, Blushweaver—but only in exchange for *your* vote. You sit on the council of social ills. You have an important vote practically every week. In exchange for my security phrases, you must promise to vote in social matters as I say, from now until one of us dies."

The pavilion fell silent.

"Ah, so now you reconsider," Hopefinder said, smiling. "I've heard you complain about your duties in court—that you find your votes trivial. Well, it's not so easy to let go of them, is it? Your vote is all the influence you have. It isn't flashy, but it is potent. It—"

"Done," Blushweaver said sharply.

Hopefinder cut off.

"My vote is yours," Blushweaver said, meeting his eyes. "The terms are acceptable. I swear it in front of your priests and mine, before another god even."

By the Colors, Lightsong thought. *She really* is *serious.* Part of him had presumed, all along, that her posturing about the war was just another game. Yet the woman who stared Hopefinder in the eyes was not playing. She sincerely believed that Hallandren was in danger, and she wanted to make certain that the armies were unified and prepared. She cared.

And that left him worried. What had he gotten himself into? What if there really was a war? As he watched the interaction of the two gods, he was left chilled by how easily and quickly they dealt with the fate of the Hallandren people. To Hopefinder, his control of a quarter of the Hallandren armies should have been a sacred obligation. He was ready to toss that aside simply because he had grown bored.

Who am I to chastise another's lack of piety? Lightsong thought. *I, who don't even believe in my own divinity.*

And yet . . . at that moment, as Hopefinder prepared to release his Commands to Blushweaver, Lightsong thought he saw something. Like a remembered fragment of a memory. A dream that he might never have dreamed.

A shining room, glowing, reflecting light. A room of steel.

A prison.

"Servants and priests, withdraw," Hopefinder commanded.

They retreated, leaving the three gods alone beside their half-eaten meals, pavilion silk flapping slightly in the wind.

"The security phrase," Hopefinder said, looking at Blushweaver, "is 'A candle by which to see.'"

It was the title of a famous poem; even Lightsong knew it. Blushweaver smiled. Speaking those words to any of Hopefinder's ten thousand Lifeless in the barracks would allow her to override their current orders and take complete control of them. Lightsong suspected that by the end of the day, she'd make the trip down to the barracks—which lay at the base of the court, and were considered part of it—and begin imprinting Hopefinder's soldiers with a new security phrase, known only to her and perhaps a few of her most trusted priests.

"And now, I withdraw," Hopefinder said, standing. "There is a vote this evening at the court. You will attend, Blushweaver, and you will cast your vote in favor of the reformist arguments."

With that, he left.

"Why do I feel like we've just been manipulated?" Lightsong asked.

"We only got manipulated, my dear, if there *isn't* war. If there is, then we may have just set ourselves up to save the entire court—perhaps the kingdom itself."

"How very altruistic of us," Lightsong said.

"We're like that," Blushweaver said as the servants returned. "So selfless at times it's painful. Either way, that means we control two gods' worth of Lifeless."

"Mine and Hopefinder's?"

"Actually," she said, "I was speaking of Hopefinder's and Mercystar's. She confided hers to me yesterday, all the while talking about how comforting she found it that you'd taken a personal interest in the incident at her palace. That was very well done, by the way."

She seemed to be fishing for something. Lightsong smiled. "No, I didn't know that would encourage her to release her Commands to you. I was just curious."

"Curious about a murdered servant?"

"Actually, yes," Lightsong said. "The death of a servant of the Returned is quite disconcerting to me, particularly in its proximity to our own palaces."

Blushweaver raised an eyebrow.

"Would I lie to you?" Lightsong asked.

"Only every time you claim you don't want to sleep with me. Lies, brazen lies."

"Innuendo again, my dear?"

"Of course not," she said. "That was quite blatant. Regardless, I know that you are lying about that investigation. What was the *real* purpose of it?"

Lightsong paused, then sighed, shaking his head, waving for a servant to bring back the fruit—he liked that better. "I don't know, Blushweaver. In all honesty, I'm beginning to wonder if I might have been a kind of officer of the law in my previous life."

She frowned.

"You know, like city watch. I was *extremely* good at interrogating those servants. At least, that's my own humble opinion."

"Which we've already established is quite altruistic."

"Quite," he agreed. "I think this might explain how I ended up dying in a 'bold' way, giving me my name."

Blushweaver raised an eyebrow. "I just always assumed you were found in bed with a much younger woman and her father killed you. Seems far more bold than dying from stab wounds while trying to catch some petty thief."

"Your mockery slides right off of my altruistic humility."

"Ah, indeed."

"Either way," Lightsong said, eating another chunk of pineapple. "I was a sheriff or investigator of some kind. I'll bet that if I ever got my hands on a sword, I'd prove one of the best duelists this city has ever seen."

She regarded him for a moment. "You're serious."

"Dead serious. Dead as a squirrel serious."

She paused, looking puzzled.

"Personal joke," he said, sighing. "But yes, I believe it. Though, there's one thing I can't figure out."

"And that is?"

"How juggling lemons fits into it all."

31

I FEEL I HAVE to ask one more time," Denth said. "Do we *have* to go through with this?" Denth walked with Vivenna, Tonk Fah, Jewels, and Clod. Parlin had stayed behind at Denth's suggestion. He was worried about the dangers of the meeting, and didn't want another body to keep track of.

"Yes, we have to go through with this," Vivenna said. "They're my people, Denth."

"So?" he asked. "Princess, mercenaries are *my* people, and you don't see me spending that much time with them. They're a smelly, annoying lot."

"Not to mention rude," Tonk Fah added.

Vivenna rolled her eyes. "Denth, I'm their *princess*. Besides, you yourself said that they were influential."

"Their leaders are," Denth said. "And they'd be perfectly happy to meet with you on neutral ground. Going into the slums isn't necessary—the common people, they really aren't all that important."

She eyed him. "That is the difference between Hallandren and Idrians. We pay attention to our people."

Behind, Jewels snorted in derision.

"I'm not Hallandren," Denth noted. However, he let the statement drop as they approached the slums. Vivenna had to admit that as they grew closer, she did feel a little more apprehensive.

This slum felt different from the others. Darker, somehow. Something more than just the run-down shops and unrepaired streets. Small groups of men stood on street corners, watching her with suspicious eyes. Every once in a while, Vivenna would catch a glimpse of a building with women in very revealing clothing—even for Hallandren— hanging about the front. Some even whistled toward Denth and Tonk Fah.

This was a foreign place. Everywhere else in T'Telir, she felt like she didn't fit in. Here, she felt unwelcome. Distrusted. Even hated.

She steeled herself. Somewhere in this place was a group of tired, overworked, frightened Idrians. The threatening atmosphere made her feel even sorrier for her people. She didn't know if they would be much help in trying to sabotage the Hallandren war effort, but she did know one thing: She intended to help them. If her people had slipped through the monarchy's fingers, then it was her duty to try and pick them back up.

"That look on your face," Denth said. "What's it for?"

"I'm worried about my people," she said, shivering as they passed a large group of street toughs dressed in black with red armbands, their faces stained and dirtied. "I came by this slum when Parlin and I were searching for a new home. I didn't want to get close, even though I'd heard that rents were cheap. I can't believe that my people are so oppressed that they would have to live somewhere in here, surrounded by all of *this*."

Denth frowned. "Surrounded by it?"

Vivenna nodded. "Living among prostitutes and gangs, having to walk past such things every day . . ."

Denth started laughing, startling her. "Princess," he said, "your people don't live *among* prostitutes and gangs. Your people *are* the prostitutes and gangs."

Vivenna stopped in the middle of the street. "What?"

Denth glanced back at her. "This is the Idrian quarter of

the city. These slums are called the Highlands, for Color's sake."

"Impossible," she snapped.

"Very possible," Denth replied. "I've seen it in cities across the world. Immigrants gather, make a little enclave. That enclave gets conveniently ignored by the rest of the city. When roads are repaired, other places come first. When guards are sent to patrol, they avoid the foreign sections."

"The slum becomes its own little world," Tonk Fah said, walking up beside her.

"Everyone you pass in here is an Idrian," Denth said, waving for her to keep walking. "There's a reason your kind have a bad reputation in the rest of the city."

Vivenna felt a numb chillness. *No,* she thought. *No, it's not possible.*

Unfortunately, she soon began to see signs. Symbols of Austre placed—unobtrusive by intention—in the corners of windowsills or on doorsteps. People in greys and whites. Mementos of the highlands in the form of shepherd's caps or wool cloaks. And yet, if these people were of Idris, then they'd been completely corrupted. Colors marred their costumes, not to mention the air of danger and hostility they exuded. And how could any Idrian even *think* of becoming a prostitute?

"I don't understand, Denth. We are a peaceful people. A people of mountain villages. We are open. Friendly."

"That kind doesn't last long in a slum," he said, walking beside her. "They change or they get beaten down."

Vivenna shivered, feeling a stab of anger at Hallandren. *I could have forgiven the Hallandren for making my people poor. But this? They've made thugs and thieves out of caring shepherds and farmers. They've turned our women into prostitutes and our children to urchins.*

She knew she shouldn't let herself get angry. And yet, she had to grit her teeth and work very, *very* hard to keep her hair from bleeding to a smoldering red. The images awoke something within her. Something she had consistently avoided thinking about.

Hallandren has ruined these people. Just as it ruined me by dominating my childhood, by forcing me to honor the obligation to be taken and raped in the name of protecting my country.

I hate this city.

They were unseemly thoughts. She couldn't afford to hate Hallandren. She had been told that on many occasions. She had trouble lately remembering why.

But she succeeded in keeping her hatred, and hair, under control. A few moments later, Thame joined them and led them the rest of the distance. She had been told they would be meeting in a large park, but Vivenna soon saw that the term "park" had been used loosely. The plot of land was barren, strewn with garbage, and hemmed in by buildings on all sides.

Her group stopped at the edge of this dreary garden and waited as Thame went ahead. People had gathered as Thame had promised. Most were of the same type she had seen earlier. Men wearing dark, ominous colors and cynical expressions. Cocky street toughs. Women in the garb of prostitutes. Some worn-down older people.

Vivenna forced a smile, but it felt insincere, even to her. For their benefit, she changed her hair color to yellow. The color of happiness and excitement. The people muttered among themselves.

Thame soon returned and waved her forward.

"Wait," Vivenna said. "I wanted to talk to the common people before we meet with the leaders."

Thame shrugged. "If you wish . . ."

Vivenna stepped forward. "People of Idris," she said. "I've come to offer you comfort and hope."

The people continued to talk among themselves. Very few seemed to pay any attention to her at all. Vivenna swallowed. "I know that you've had hard lives. But I want to promise you that the king *does* care for you and wants to support you. I will find a way to bring you home."

"Home?" one of the men said. "Back to the highlands?"

Vivenna nodded.

Several people snorted at that comment, and a few trailed away. Vivenna watched them go with concern. "Wait," she said. "Don't you want to hear me? I bring news from your king."

The people ignored her.

"Most of them just wanted confirmation that you were who you were rumored to be, Your Highness," Thame said quietly.

Vivenna turned back toward the groups still talking quietly in the garden. "Your lives can get better," she promised. "I will see you cared for."

"Our lives are already better," one of the men said. "There is nothing for us in the highlands. I carn twice as much here as I did back there." Others nodded in agreement.

"Then why even come to see me?" she whispered.

"I told you, Princess," Thame said. "They're patriots— they cling to being Idrian. City Idrians. We stick together, we do. You being here, it means something to them, don't worry. They may seem indifferent, but they'll do *anything* to get back at the Hallandren."

Austre, Lord of Colors, she thought, growing even more deeply upset. *These people aren't even Idrians anymore.* Thame called them "patriots," but all she saw was a group held together by the eternal pressures of Hallandren disdain.

She turned, giving up on her speech. These people were not interested in hope or comfort. They only wanted revenge. She could use that, perhaps, but it made her feel dirty even to consider it. Thame led her and the others down a pathway beaten into the ugly field of weeds and trash. Near the far side of the "park," they found a wide structure that was partially a storage shed, partially an open wooden pavilion. She could see the leaders waiting inside.

There were three of them, each with his own complement of bodyguards. She had been told of them ahead of time. The leaders wore rich, vibrant T'Telir colors. Slumlords. Vivenna felt her stomach twist. All three of the men had at least the First Heightening. One of them had attained the Third.

Jewels and Clod took their places outside the building, guarding Vivenna's escape route. Vivenna walked in and sat in the last open chair. Denth and Tonk Fah took up protective places behind her.

Vivenna regarded the slumlords. All three were variations on the same theme. The one on the left looked most comfortable in his rich clothing. That would be Paxen—the "gentleman Idrian," he was called. He'd gotten his money from running brothels. The one on the right looked like he needed a haircut to match his fine garments. That would be Ashu, who was known for running and funding underground fighting leagues where men could watch Idrians box each other to unconsciousness. The one in the center seemed the self-indulgent type. He was sloppy—but in a purposefully relaxed way, perhaps because it was a nice accent to his handsome, youthful face. Rira, Thame's employer.

She reminded herself not to put too much stock in any facile interpretation of their appearances. These were dangerous men.

The room was silent.

"I'm not sure what to say to you," Vivenna said finally. "I came to find something that doesn't exist. I was hoping that the people still cared about their heritage."

Rira leaned forward, sloppy clothing out of place compared with the clothing of the others in the room. "You're our princess," he said. "Daughter of our king. We care about that."

"Kind of," said Paxen.

"Really, Princess," Rira said. "We're honored to meet with you. And curious at your intentions in our city. You've been making quite a stir."

Vivenna regarded them with a serious expression. Finally, she sighed. "You all know that war is coming."

Rira nodded. Ashu, however, shook his head. "I'm not convinced there will be war. Not yet."

"It *is* coming," Vivenna said sharply. "I promise you that. My intentions in this city, therefore, are to make certain that the war goes as well for Idris as possible."

"And what would that entail?" Ashu asked. "A royal on the throne of Hallandren?"

Was that what she wanted? "I just want our people to survive."

"A weak middle ground," said Paxen, polishing the top of his fine cane. "Wars are fought to be won, Your Highness. The Hallandren have Lifeless. Beat them, and they'll just make more. I think that an Idrian military presence in the city would be an absolute *necessity* if you wanted to bring our homeland freedom."

Vivenna frowned.

"You think to overthrow the city?" asked Ashu. "If you do, what do we get out of it?"

"Wait," said Paxen. "Overthrow the city? Are we sure we want to get involved in *that* sort of thing again? What of Vahr's failure? We all lost a lot of money in that venture."

"Vahr was from Pahn Kahl," said Ashu. "Not one of us at all. I'm willing to take another risk if there are real royals involved this time."

"I didn't say anything about overthrowing the kingdom," Vivenna said. "I just want to bring the people some hope." *Or, at least, I did . . .*

"Hope?" asked Paxen. "Who cares about hope? I want commitments. Will titles be handed out? Who gets the trade contracts if Idris wins?"

"You have a sister," Rira said. "A third one, unmarried.

Is her hand bargainable? Royal blood could gain *my* support for your war."

Vivenna's stomach twisted. "Gentlemen," she said in her diplomat's voice, "this is not about seeking personal gain. This is about patriotism."

"Of course, of course," Rira said. "But even patriots should earn rewards. Right?"

All three looked at her expectantly.

Vivenna stood up. "I will be going, now."

Denth, looking surprised, laid a hand on her shoulder. "Are you sure?" he asked. "It took quite a bit of effort to set up this meeting."

"I have been willing to work with thugs and thieves, Denth," she said quietly. "But seeing these and knowing they're my own people is too hard."

"You judge us quickly, Princess," Rira said from behind, chuckling. "Don't tell me that you didn't expect this?"

"Expecting something is different from seeing it firsthand, Rira. I expected you three. I didn't expect to see what had happened to our people."

"And the Five Visions?" Rira asked. "You sweep in here, judge us beneath you, then sweep away? That's not very Idrian of you."

She turned back toward the men. The long-haired Ashu had already stood and was gathering his bodyguards to go, grumbling about the "waste of time."

"What do you know of being Idrian?" she snapped. "Where is your obedience to Austre?"

Rira reached beneath his shirt, pulling out a small white disk, inscribed with his parents' names. An Austrin charm of obedience. "My father *carried* me down here from the highlands, Princess. He died working the Edgli fields. I've pulled myself up by the pain of my scraped, bleeding hands. I worked very hard to make things better for your people. When Vahr spoke of revolution, I gave him coin to feed his supporters."

"You buy Breath," she said. "And you make prostitutes of housewives."

"I live," he said. "And I make sure that everyone else has enough food. Will *you* do better for them?"

Vivenna frowned. "I . . ."

She fell silent as she heard the screams.

Her life sense jolted her, warning of large groups of people approaching. She spun as the slumlords cursed, standing. Outside, through the garden, she saw something terrible. Purple-and-yellow uniforms on hulking men with grey faces.

Lifeless soldiers. The city watch.

Peasants scattered, screaming as the Lifeless tromped into the garden, led by a number of uniformed living city guards. Denth cursed, shoving Vivenna to the side. "Run!" he said, whipping his sword free.

"But—"

Tonk Fah grabbed her arm, towing her out of the building as Denth charged the guards. The slumlords and their people were in disarray as they fled, though the city guards were quickly moving to cut off the exits.

Tonk Fah cursed, pulling Vivenna into a small alleyway across from the garden.

"What's going on?" she asked, heart thumping.

"Raid," Tonk Fah said. "Shouldn't be too dangerous, unless . . ."

Blades sounded, metal clashing against metal, and the screams grew more desperate. Vivenna glanced backward. The men from the slumlords' groups, feeling trapped, had engaged the Lifeless. Vivenna felt a sense of horror, watching the terrible, grey-faced men wade among the swords and daggers, ignoring wounds. The creatures pulled out their weapons and began to attack. Men yelled and screamed, falling, bloody.

Denth moved to defend the mouth of Vivenna's alleyway. She didn't know where Jewels had gone.

"Kalad's Phantoms!" Tonk Fah cursed, pushing her ahead of him as they retreated. "Those fools decided to resist. Now we're in trouble."

"But how did they find us!"

"Don't know," he said. "Don't care. They might be after you. They might just be after those slumlords. I hope we never find out. *Keep moving!*"

Vivenna obeyed, rushing down the dark alleyway, trying to keep from tripping on her long dress. It proved very impractical to run in, and Tonk Fah kept shooing her forward, looking back anxiously. She heard grunts and echoing yells as Denth fought something at the mouth of the alleyway.

Vivenna and Tonk Fah burst out of the alleyway. There, standing in the street waiting, was a group of five Lifeless. Vivenna lurched to a halt. Tonk Fah cursed.

The Lifeless looked as if they were stone, their expressions eerily grim in the waning light. Tonk Fah glanced backward, obviously decided that Denth wasn't going to be arriving anytime soon, then resignedly held his hands up and dropped his sword. "I can't take five on my own, Princess," he whispered. "Not Lifeless. We'll have to let them arrest us."

Vivenna slowly held her hands up as well.

The Lifeless pulled out their weapons.

"Uh . . ." Tonk Fah said. "We surrender?"

The creatures charged.

"Run!" he shouted, reaching down and snatching his sword off the ground.

Vivenna stumbled to the side as several of the lifeless charged Tonk Fah. She scrambled away as quickly as she could. Tonk Fah tried to follow, but had to stop to defend himself. She slowed, glancing back in time to see him ram his dueling blade through the neck of a Lifeless.

The creature gushed something that was not blood. Three others got around Tonk Fah, though he did manage to whip his blade to the side, taking one in the back of the leg. It fell to the cobbles.

Two ran toward her.

Vivenna watched them come, mind numb. Should she stay? Try to help . . .

Help how? something screamed within her. That something was visceral and primal. *Run!*

And she did. She dashed away, overwhelmed with terror, taking the first corner she saw, ducking into an alleyway. She raced for the other end, but in her haste she tripped on her skirt.

She hit the cobblestones roughly, crying out. She heard footsteps behind her, and she yelled for help, ignoring her bruised elbow as she quickly tore her skirt off, leaving only her underbreeches. She scrambled to her feet, screaming again.

Something darkened the other end of the alleyway. A hulking figure with grey skin. Vivenna stopped, then spun. The other two entered the alleyway behind her. She backed against the wall, feeling suddenly cold. Shocked.

Austre, God of Colors, she thought, trembling. *Please . . .*

The three Lifeless advanced on her, weapons drawn. She looked down. A bit of rope, frayed but still useful, sat in the refuse beside her discarded green skirt.

Like everything else, the rope called to her. As if it *knew* that it could live again. She couldn't sense the Lifeless bearing down on her, but ironically she felt as if she could sense the rope. Could imagine it, twisting around legs, tying the creatures up.

Those Breaths you hold, Denth had said. *They're a tool. Almost priceless. Certainly powerful . . .*

She glanced back at the Lifeless, with their inhumanly human eyes. She felt her heart thumping so hard it felt like someone was pounding on her chest. She watched them approach.

And saw her death reflected in their unfeeling eyes.

Tears on her face, she fell to her knees, trembling as she grabbed the rope. She knew the mechanics. Her tutors had trained her. She'd need to touch the fallen skirt to drain color out of it.

"Come to life," she begged the rope.

Nothing happened.

She knew the mechanics, but that obviously wasn't enough. She wept, eyes blurry. "Please," she begged. "Please. Save me."

The first Lifeless reached her—the one who had cut her off at the far end of the alleyway. She cringed, cowering to the dirty street.

The creature leaped over her.

She looked up in shock as the creature slammed its weapon into one of the others as they arrived. Vivenna blinked her eyes clear, and only then did she recognize the newcomer.

Not Denth. Not Tonk Fah. A creature with skin as grey as that of the men attacking her, which was why she hadn't recognized him at first.

Clod.

He expertly took off the head of his first opponent, wielding his thick-bladed sword. Something clear sprayed from the neck of the beheaded creature as it fell backward, tumbling to the ground. Dead—apparently—as any man would have been.

Clod blocked an attack from the remaining Lifeless guard. Behind, in the mouth of the alleyway, two more appeared. They charged as Clod backed up, firmly planting one foot on either side of Vivenna, his sword held before him. It dripped clear liquid.

The remaining lifeless guard waited for the other two to approach. Vivenna trembled, too tired—too numb—to flee. She glanced upward, and saw something almost human in Clod's eyes as he raised his sword against the three. It was the first emotion she'd seen in any Lifeless, though she might have imagined it.

Determination.

The three attacked. She had assumed—in her ignorance back in Idris—that Lifeless were like decaying skeletons or corpses. She'd imagined them attacking in waves, lacking skill, but having relentless, dark power.

She'd been wrong. These creatures moved with proficiency and coordination, just as a human might. Except there was no speaking. No yelling or grunting. Just silence as Clod fended off one attack, then rammed his elbow into the face of a second Lifeless. He moved with a fluidity she had rarely seen, his skill matching the brief moment of dazzling speed that Denth had displayed in the restaurant.

Clod whipped his sword around and took the third Lifeless in the leg. One of the others, however, rammed his blade through Clod's stomach. Something clear squirted out both sides, spraying Vivenna. Clod didn't even grunt as he brought his weapon around and took off a second head.

The Lifeless guard died, falling to the ground and leaving his weapon sticking from Clod's stomach. One of the other guards stumbled away, leg bleeding clear blood, and then it fell backward to the ground too. Clod efficiently turned his attention to the last standing Lifeless, which did not retreat, but took an obviously defensive stance.

The stance didn't work; Clod took this last one down in a matter of seconds, slamming his sword repeatedly against that of his opponent before spinning it around in an unexpected motion and taking off his enemy's sword hand. That was followed by a blow to the stomach, dropping the creature. In a final motion, he efficiently rammed his blade through the neck of a fallen creature, stopping it from trying to crawl toward Vivenna, a knife in its hand.

The alleyway fell still. Clod turned toward her, eyes lacking emotion, square jaw and rectangular face set above a thick, muscled neck. He began to twitch. He shook his head, as if trying to clear his vision. An awful lot of clear liquid was pouring from his torso. He placed one hand against the wall, then slumped to his knees.

Vivenna hesitated, then reached out a hand toward him. Her hand fell on his arm. The skin was cold.

A shadow moved on the other side of the alleyway. She looked up, apprehensive, still in shock.

"Aw, Colors," Tonk Fah said, running forward, outfit wet with clear liquid. "Denth! She's here!" He knelt down beside Vivenna. "You okay?"

She nodded dully, only barely aware that she was still holding her skirt in one hand. That meant her legs—to just above her knees—were exposed. She couldn't find it in herself to care. Nor did she care that her hair was bleached white. She just stared at Clod, who knelt before her, head bowed, as if worshiping at some strange altar. His weapon slipped from his twitching fingers and clanged to the cobbles. His eyes stared forward, glassy.

Tonk Fah followed her gaze, looking at Clod. "Yeah," he said. "Jewels is *not* going to be pleased. Come on, we need to get out of here."

32

H E WAS ALWAYS gone when Siri awoke.

She lay in the deep, well-stuffed bed, morning light streaming through the window. Already, the day was growing warm, and even her single sheet was too hot. She threw it off but remained on the bed, looking up at the ceiling.

She could tell from the sunlight that it was nearly noon. She and Susebron tended to stay up late talking. That was probably a good thing. Some might see that she was getting up later and later each morning, and think that it was due to other activities.

She stretched. At first, it had been strange to communicate with the God King. As the days progressed, however, it was feeling more and more natural to her. She found his writing—uncertain, unpracticed letters that explained such interesting thoughts—to be endearing. If he spoke, she suspected that his voice would be kindly. He was so tender. She'd never have expected that.

She smiled, sinking back into her pillow, idly wishing for him to still be there when she awoke. She was happy. That, also, was something she'd never expected from Hallandren. She did miss the highlands, and her inability to leave the Court of Gods frustrated her, particularly considering the politics.

And yet there were other things. Marvelous things. The brilliant colors, the performers, the sheer *overwhelming* experience of T'Telir. And there was the opportunity to speak with Susebron each night. Her brashness had been such a shame and an embarrassment to her family, but Susebron found it fascinating, even alluring.

She smiled again, letting herself dream. However, real life began to intrude. Susebron was in danger. Real, serious danger. He refused to believe that his priests could bear him any sort of malice or be a threat. That same innocence which made him so appealing was also a terrible liability.

But what to do? Nobody else knew of his predicament. There was only one person who could help him. That person, unfortunately, wasn't up to the task. She had ignored her lessons, and had come to her fate wholly unprepared.

So what? a part of her mind whispered.

Siri stared at the ceiling. She found it hard to summon her customary shame at having ignored her lessons. She'd made a mistake. How much time was she going to spend moping, annoyed at herself for something done and gone?

All right, she told herself. *Enough excuses. I might not have prepared as well as I should, but I'm here, now, and I need to do something.*

Because nobody else will.

She climbed out of bed, running her fingers through her long hair. Susebron liked it long—he found it as fascinating as her serving women did. With them to help her care for it, the length was worth the trouble. She folded her arms, wearing only her shift, pacing. She needed to play their game. She hated thinking of it that way. "Game" implied small stakes. This was no game. It was the God King's life.

She searched through her memory, dredging up what scraps she could from her lessons. Politics was about exchanges. It was about giving what you had—or what you implied that you had—in order to gain more. It was like being a merchant. You started with a certain stock, and by the end of the year, you hoped to have increased that stock. Or maybe even have changed it into a completely different and better stock.

Don't make too many waves until you're ready to strike, Lightsong had told her. *Don't appear too innocent, but don't appear too smart either. Be average.*

She stopped beside the bed, then gathered up the bedsheets and towed them over to the smoldering fire to burn, as was her daily chore.

Exchanges, she thought, watching the sheets catch fire in the large hearth. *What do I have to trade or exchange? Not much.*

It would have to do.

She walked over and pulled open the door. As usual, a group of serving women waited outside. Siri's standard ladies moved around her, bringing clothing. Another group of servants, however, moved to tidy the room. Several of these wore brown.

As her servants dressed her, she watched one of the girls

in brown. At a convenient moment, Siri stepped over, putting a hand on the girl's shoulder.

"You're from Pahn Kahl," Siri said quietly.

The girl nodded, surprised.

"I have a message I want you to give to Bluefingers," Siri whispered. "Tell him I have vital information he needs to know. I'd like to trade. Tell him it could change his plans drastically."

The girl paled, but nodded, and Siri stepped back to continue dressing. Several of the other serving women had heard the exchange, but it was a sacred tenet of the Hallandren religion that the servants of a god weren't to repeat what they heard in confidence. Hopefully that would hold true. If it didn't, then she hadn't really given that much away.

Now she just had to decide just what "vital information" she had, and why exactly Bluefingers should care about it.

━━━◦◦◦◦━━━

"MY DEAR QUEEN!" Lightsong said, actually going so far as to embrace Siri as she stepped into his box at the arena.

Siri smiled as Lightsong waved for her to seat herself in one of his chaise longues. Siri sat with care—she was coming to favor the elaborate Hallandren gowns, but moving gracefully in them took quite a bit of skill. As she settled, Lightsong called for fruit.

"You treat me too kindly," Siri said.

"Nonsense," Lightsong said. "You're my queen! Besides, you remind me of someone of whom I was very fond."

"And who is that?"

"I honestly have no idea," Lightsong said, accepting a plate of sliced grapes, then handing them to Siri. "I can barely remember her. Grapes?"

Siri raised an eyebrow, but she knew by now not to

encourage him *too* much. "Tell me," she asked, using a little wooden spear to eat her grape slices. "Why do they call you Lightsong the Bold?"

"There is an easy answer to that," he said, leaning back. "It is because of all the gods, only I am bold enough to act like a complete idiot."

Siri raised an eyebrow.

"My station requires true courage," he continued. "You see, I am *normally* quite a solemn and boring person. At nights my fondest desire is to sit and compose interminably periphrastic lectures on morality for my priests to read to my followers. Alas, I cannot. Instead, I go out each evening, abandoning didactic theology in favor of something which requires true courage: spending time with the other gods."

"Why does *that* take courage?"

He looked at her. "My lady. Have you *seen* how positively tedious they all can be?"

Siri laughed. "No, really," she said. "Where did the name come from?"

"It's a complete misnomer," Lightsong said. "Obviously you're intelligent enough to see that. Our names and titles are assigned randomly by a small monkey who has been fed an exceedingly large amount of gin."

"Now you're just being silly."

"Now?" Lightsong asked. "*Now?*" He raised a cup of wine toward her. "My dear, I am *always* silly. Please be good enough to retract that statement at once!"

Siri just shook her head. Lightsong, it appeared, was in rare form this afternoon. *Great,* she thought. *My husband is in danger of being murdered by unknown forces and my only allies are a scribe who's afraid of me and a god who makes no sense.*

"It has to do with death," Lightsong finally said as the priests began to file into the arena floor below for this day's round of arguments.

Siri looked toward him.

"All men die," Lightsong said. "Some, however, die in ways that exemplify a particular attribute or emotion. They show a spark of something greater than the rest of mankind. That is what is said to bring us back."

He fell silent.

"You died showing great bravery, then?" Siri asked.

"Apparently," he said. "I don't know for sure. Something in my dreams suggests that I may have insulted a very large panther. That sounds rather brave, don't you think?"

"You don't know how you died?"

He shook his head. "We forget," he said. "We awake without memories. I don't even know what work I did."

Siri smiled. "I suspect that you were a diplomat or a salesman of some sort. Something that required you to talk a lot, but say very little!"

"Yes," he said quietly, seeming unlike himself as he stared down at the priests below. "Yes, no doubt that was it exactly . . ." He shook his head, then smiled at her. "Regardless, my dear queen, I have provided a surprise for you this day!"

Do I want to be surprised by Lightsong? She glanced about nervously.

He laughed. "No need to fear," he said. "My surprises rarely cause bodily harm, and never to beautiful queens." He waved his hand, and an elderly man with an extraordinarily long white beard approached.

Siri frowned.

"This is Hoid," Lightsong said. "Master storyteller. I believe you had some questions you wished to ask . . ."

Siri laughed in relief, remembering only now her request to Lightsong. She glanced at the priests below. "Um, shouldn't we be paying attention to the speeches?"

Lightsong waved indifferently. "Pay attention? Ridiculous! That would be far too responsible of us. We're gods,

for the Colors' sake. Or, well, I am. You're close enough.
A god-in-law, one might say. Anyway, do *you* really want
to listen to a bunch of stuffy priests talk about sewage
treatment?"

Siri grimaced.

"I thought not. Besides, neither of us has votes pertaining to this issue. So let us spend our time wisely. We never
know when we will run out!"

"Of time?" Siri asked. "But you're immortal!"

"Not run out of time," Lightsong said, holding up his
plate. "Of grapes. I *hate* listening to storytellers without
grapes."

Siri rolled her eyes, but continued to eat the grape slices.
The storyteller waited patiently. As she looked more closely,
she could tell that he wasn't quite as old as he seemed at first
glance. The beard must be a badge of his profession, and
while it didn't appear to be fake, she suspected that it
had been bleached. He was really much younger than he
wanted to appear.

Still, she doubted Lightsong would have settled for anyone other than the very best. She settled back in her chair—
which, she noticed, had been crafted for someone of her
size. *I should be careful with my questions,* she thought. *I
can't ask directly about the deaths of the old God Kings;
that would be too obvious.*

"Storyteller," she said. "What do you know of Hallandren history?"

"Much, my queen," he said, bowing his head.

"Tell me of the days before the division between Idris
and Hallandren."

"Ah," the man said, reaching into a pocket. He pulled
out a handful of sand and began to rub it between his fingers, letting it drop in a soft stream toward the ground, its
grains blown slightly in the wind. "Her Majesty wishes one
of the *deep* stories, from long before. A story before time
began?"

"I wish to know the origins of the Hallandren God Kings."

"Then we begin in the distant haze," the storyteller said, bringing up another hand, letting powdery black sand drop from it, mixing with the sand that fell from the first hand. As Siri watched, the black sand turned white, and she cocked her head, smiling at the display.

"The first God King of Hallandren is ancient," Hoid said. "Ancient, yes. Older than kingdoms and cities, older than monarchs and religions. Not older than the mountains, for *they* were already here. Like the knuckles of the sleeping giants below, they formed this valley, where panthers and flowers both make their home.

"We speak of just 'the valley' then, a place before it had a name. The people of Chedesh still dominated the world. They sailed the Inner Sea, coming from the east, and it was they who first discovered this strange land. Their writings are sparse, their empire has long since been taken by the dust, but memory remains. Perhaps you can imagine their surprise upon arriving here? A place with beaches of fine, soft sand, with fruits aplenty, and with strange, alien forests?"

Hoid reached into his robes and pulled out a handful of something else. He began to drop it before him—small green leaves from the fronds of a fern.

"Paradise, they called it," Hoid whispered. "A paradise hidden between the mountains, a land with pleasant rains that never grew cold, a land where succulent food grew spontaneously." He threw the handful of leaves into the air, and in the center of them puffed a burst of colorful dust, like a tiny flameless firework. Deep reds and blues mixed in the air, blowing around him.

"A land of color," he said. "Because of the Tears of Edgli, the striking flowers of such brilliance that could yield dyes that would hold fast in any cloth."

Siri had never really thought about how Hallandren

would look to people who came across the Inner Sea. She'd heard stories from the ramblemen who came into Idris, and they spoke of distant places. In other lands, one found prairies and steppes, mountains and deserts. But not jungles. Hallandren was unique.

"The First Returned was born during this time," Hoid said, sprinkling a handful of silver glitter into the air before him. "Aboard a ship that was sailing the coast. Returned can now be found in all parts of the world, but the first one—the man whom you call Vo, but we name only by his title—was born here, in the waters of this very bay. He declared the Five Visions. He died a week later.

"The men of his ship founded a kingdom upon these beaches, then called Hanald. Before their arrival, all that had existed in these jungles was the people of Pahn Kahl, more a mere collection of fishing villages than a true kingdom."

The glitter ran out, and Hoid began to drop a powdery brown dirt from his other hand as he reached into another pocket. "Now, you may wonder why I must travel back so far. Should I not speak of the Manywar, of the shattering of kingdoms, of the Five Scholars, of Kalad the Usurper and his phantom army, which some say still hides in these jungles, waiting?

"Those are the events we focus upon, the ones men know the best. To speak only of them, however, is to ignore the history of three hundred years that led up to them. Would there have been a Manywar without knowledge of the Returned? It was a Returned, after all, who predicted the war and prompted Strifelover to attack the kingdoms across the mountains."

"Strifelover?" Siri interrupted.

"Yes, Your Majesty," Hoid said, switching to a black dust. "Strifelover. Another name for Kalad the Usurper."

"That sounds like the name of a Returned."

Hoid nodded. "Indeed," he said. "Kalad *was* Returned, as

was Peacegiver, the man who overthrew him and founded Hallandren. We haven't arrived at *that* part yet. We are still back in Hanald, the outpost-become-kingdom founded by the men of the First Returned's crew. They were the ones who chose the First Returned's wife as their queen, then used the Tears of Edgli to create fantastic dyes which sold for untold riches across the world. This soon became a bustling center of trade."

He removed a handful of flower petals and began to let them fall before him. "The Tears of Edgli. The source of Hallandren wealth. Such small things, so easy to grow here. And yet, this is the only soil where they will live. In other parts of the world, dyes are very difficult to produce. Expensive. Some scholars say that the Manywar was fought over these flower petals, that the kingdoms of Kuth and Huth were destroyed by little drips of color."

The petals fell to the floor.

"But only *some* of the scholars say that, storyteller?" Lightsong said. Siri turned, having almost forgotten that he was with her. "What do the rest say? Why was the Manywar fought in *their* opinions?"

The storyteller fell silent for a moment. And then he pulled out two handfuls and began to release dust of a half-dozen different colors. "Breath, Your Grace. Most agree that the Manywar was not *only* about petals squeezed dry, but a much greater prize. *People* squeezed dry.

"You know, perhaps, that the royal family was growing increasingly interested in the process by which Breath could be used to bring objects to life. Awakening, it was then first being called. It was a fresh and poorly understood art, then. It still is, in many ways. The workings of the souls of men— their power to animate ordinary objects and the dead to life—is something discovered barely four centuries ago. A short time, by the accounting of gods."

"Unlike a court proceeding," Lightsong mumbled, glancing over at the priests who were still talking about sanitation. "Those seem to last an eternity, according to the accounting of this god."

The storyteller didn't break stride at the interruption. "Breath," he said. "The years leading up to the Manywar, those were the days of the Five Scholars and the discovery of new Commands. To some, this was a time of great enlightenment and learning. Others call them the darkest days of men, for it was then we learned to best exploit one another."

He began to drop two handfuls of dust, one bright yellow, the other black. Siri watched, amused. He seemed to be slanting what he said toward her, careful not to offend her Idrian sensibilities. What did she really know of Breath? She'd rarely even seen any Awakeners in the court. Even when she did, she didn't really care. The monks had spoken against such things, but, well, she had paid about as much attention to them as she had to her tutors.

"One of the Five Scholars made a discovery," Hoid continued, dropping a handful of white scraps, small torn pieces of paper with writing on them. "Commands. Methods. The means by which a Lifeless could be created from a *single Breath*.

"This, perhaps, seems a small thing to you. But you must look at the past of this kingdom and its founding. Hallandren began with the servants of a Returned and was developed by an expansive mercantile effort. It controlled a uniquely lucrative region which, through the discovery and maintenance of the northern passes—combined with increasingly skillful navigation—was becoming a jewel coveted by the rest of the world."

He paused and his second hand came up, dropping little bits of metal, which fell to the stonework with a sound not unlike falling rain. "And so the war came," he said. "The Five Scholars split, joining different sides. Some kingdoms gained the use of Lifeless while others did not. Some kingdoms had weapons others could only envy.

"To answer the god's question, my story claims one other reason for the Manywar: the ability to create Lifeless so cheaply. Before the discovery of the single-Breath Command, Lifeless took fifty Breaths to make. Extra soldiers—even a Lifeless one—are of limited use if you can gain only one for every fifty men you already have. However, being able to create a Lifeless with a single Breath . . . one for one . . . that will double your troops. And half of them won't need to eat."

The metal stopped falling.

"Lifeless are no stronger than living men," Hoid said. "They are the same. They are not more skilled than living men. They are the same. However, not having to *eat* like regular men? That advantage was enormous. Mix that with their ability to ignore pain and never feel fear . . . and suddenly you had an army that others could not stand against. It was taken even further by Kalad, who was said to have created a new and more powerful type of Lifeless, gaining an advantage even more frightening."

"What kind of new Lifeless?" Siri asked, curious.

"Nobody remembers, Your Majesty," Hoid explained. "The records of that time have been lost. Some say they were burned intentionally. Whatever the true nature of Kalad's Phantoms, they were frightening and terrible—so much so that even though the details have been lost in time, the phantoms themselves live on in our lore. And our curses."

"Do they really still exist out there?" Siri asked, shivering slightly, glancing toward the unseen jungles. "Like the stories say? An unseen army, waiting for Kalad to return and command them again?"

"Alas," Hoid said, "I can tell only stories. As I said, so much from that time is lost to us now."

"But we know of the royal family," Siri said. "They broke away because they didn't agree with what Kalad was doing, right? They saw moral problems with using Lifeless?"

The storyteller hesitated. "Why, yes," he finally said, smiling through his beard. "Yes, they did, Your Majesty."

She raised an eyebrow.

"Psst," Lightsong said, leaning in. "He's lying to you."

"Your Grace," the storyteller said, bowing deeply. "I beg your pardon. There are diverging explanations! Why, I am a teller of stories—all stories."

"And what do other stories say?" Siri asked.

"None of them agree, Your Majesty," Hoid said. "Your people speak of religious indignation and of treachery by Kalad the Usurper. The Pahn Kahl people tell of the royal family working hard to gain powerful Lifeless and Awakeners, then being surprised when their tools turned against them. In Hallandren, they tell of the royal family aligning themselves with Kalad, making him their general and ignoring the will of the people by seeking war with bloodlust."

He looked up, and then began to trail two handfuls of black, burned charcoal. "But time burns away behind us, leaving only ash and memory. That memory passes from mind to mind, then finally to my lips. When all is truth, and all are lies, does it matter if some say the royal family sought to create Lifeless? Your belief is your own."

"Either way, the Returned took control of Hallandren," she said.

"Yes," Hoid said. "And they gave it a new name, a variation on the old one. And yet, some still speak regretfully of the royals who left, bearing the blood of the First Returned to their highlands."

Siri frowned. "Blood of the First Returned?"

"Yes, of course," Hoid said. "It was his wife, pregnant with his child, who became the first queen of this land. You are his descendant."

She sat back.

Lightsong turned, curious. "You didn't know this?" he asked, in a tone lacking his normal flippancy.

She shook her head. "If this fact is known to my people, we do not speak of it."

Lightsong seemed to find that interesting. Down below, the priests were moving on to a different topic—something about security in the city and increasing patrols in the slums.

She smiled, sensing a subtle way to get to the questions she *really* wanted to ask. "That means that the God Kings of Hallandren carried on *without* the blood of the First Returned."

"Yes, Your Majesty," Hoid said, crumbling clay out into the air before him.

"And how many God Kings have there been?"

"Five, Your Majesty," the man said. "Including His Immortal Majesty, Lord Susebron, but not including Peacegiver."

"Five kings," she said. "In three hundred years?"

"Yes, Your Majesty," Hoid said, bringing out a handful of golden dust, letting it fall before him. "The dynasty of Hallandren was founded at the conclusion of the Manywar, the first one gaining his Breath and life from Peacegiver himself, who was revered for dispelling Kalad's Phantoms and bringing a peaceful end to the Manywar. Since that day, each God King has fathered a stillborn son who then Returned and took his place."

Siri leaned forward. "Wait. How did Peacegiver create a new God King?"

"Ah," Hoid said, switching back to sand with his left hand. "Now *there* is a story lost in time. How indeed? Breath can be passed from one man to another, but Breath—no matter how much—does not make one a god. Legends say that Peacegiver died by granting his Breath to his successor. After all, can a god not give his life away to bless another?"

"Not exactly a sign of mental stability, in my opinion," Lightsong said, waving for some more grapes. "You don't encourage confidence in our predecessors, storyteller.

Besides, even if a god gives away his Breath, it doesn't make the recipient divine."

"I only tell stories, Your Grace," Hoid repeated. "They may be truths, they may be fictions. All I know is that the stories themselves exist and that I must tell them."

With as much flair as possible, Siri thought, watching him reach into yet another pocket and pull free a handful of small bits of grass and earth. He let bits fall slowly between his fingers.

"I speak of foundations, Your Grace," Hoid said. "Peacegiver was no ordinary Returned, for he managed to stop the Lifeless from rampaging. Indeed, he sent away Kalad's Phantoms, which formed the main bulk of the Hallandren army. By doing so, he left his own people powerless. He did so in an effort to bring peace. By then, of course, it was too late for Kuth and Huth. However, the other kingdoms— Pahn Kahl, Tedradel, Gys, and Hallandren itself—were brought out of the conflict.

"Can we not assume more from this god of gods who was able to accomplish so much? Perhaps he *did* do something unique, as the priests claim. Leave some seed within the God Kings of Hallandren, allowing them to pass their power and divinity from father to son?"

Heritage which would give them a claim to rule, Siri thought, idly slipping a sliced grape into her mouth. *With such an amazing god as their progenitor, they could become God Kings. And the only one who could threaten them would be . . .*

The royal family of Idris, who can apparently trace their line back to the First Returned. Another heritage of divinity, a challenger for rightful rule in Hallandren.

That didn't tell her how the God Kings had died. Nor did it tell her why some gods—such as the First Returned— could bear children, while others could not.

"They're immortal, correct?" Siri asked.

Hoid nodded, smoothly dropping the rest of his grass and dirt, moving into a different discussion by bringing forth a handful of white powder. "Indeed, Your Majesty. Like all Returned, the God Kings do not age. Agelessness is a gift for all who reach the Fifth Heightening."

"But why have there been five God Kings?" she asked. "Why did the first one die?"

"Why do any Returned pass on, Your Majesty?" Hoid asked.

"Because they are loony," Lightsong said.

The storyteller smiled. "Because they tire. Gods are not like ordinary men. They come back for *us,* not for themselves, and when they can no longer endure life, they pass on. God Kings live only as long as it takes them to produce an heir."

Siri started. "That's commonly known?" she asked, then cringed slightly at the potentially suspicious comment.

"Of course it is, Your Majesty," the storyteller said. "At least, to storytellers and scholars. Each God King has passed from this world shortly after his son and heir was born. It is natural. Once the heir has arrived, the God King grows restless. Each one has sought out an opportunity to use up his Breath to benefit the realm. And then . . ."

He threw up a hand, snapping his fingers, throwing up a little spray of water, which puffed to mist.

"And then they pass on," he said. "Leaving their people blessed and their heir to rule."

The group fell silent, the mist evaporating in front of Hoid.

"Not exactly the most pleasant thing to inform a newly-wed wife, storyteller," Lightsong noted. "That her husband is going to grow bored with life as soon as she bears him a son?"

"I seek not to be charming, Your Grace," Hoid said, bowing. At his feet, the various dusts, sands, and glitters mixed together in the faint breeze. "I only tell stories. This one is known to most. I should think that Her Majesty would like to be aware of it as well."

"Thank you," Siri said quietly. "It was good of you to speak of it. Tell me, where did you learn such an . . . unusual method of storytelling?"

Hoid looked up, smiling. "I learned it many, many years ago from a man who didn't know who he was, Your Majesty. It was a distant place where two lands meet and gods have died. But that is unimportant."

Siri ascribed the vague explanation to Hoid's desire to create a suitably romantic and mysterious past for himself. Of far more interest to her was what he'd said about the God Kings' deaths.

So there is an official explanation, she thought, stomach twisting. *And it's actually a pretty good one. Theologically, it makes sense that the God Kings would depart once they had arranged for a suitable successor.*

But that doesn't explain how Peacegiver's Treasure— that wealth of Breath—passes from God King to God King when they have no tongues. And it doesn't explain why a man like Susebron would get tired of life when he seems so excited by it.

The official story would work fine for those who didn't know the God King. It fell flat for Siri. Susebron would never do such a thing. Not now.

Yet . . . Would things change if she bore him a son? Would Susebron grow tired of her that easily?

"Maybe we should be *hoping* for old Susebron to pass, my queen," Lightsong said idly, picking at the grapes. "You were forced into all this, I suspect. If Susebron died, you might even be able to go home. No harm done, people healed, new heir on the throne. Everyone is either happy or dead."

The priests continued to argue below. Hoid bowed, waiting for dismissal.

Happy . . . or dead. Her stomach twisted. "Excuse me," she said, rising. "I would like to walk about a bit. Thank you for your storytelling, Hoid."

With that—entourage in tow—she quickly left the pavilion, preferring that Lightsong not see her tears.

33

JEWELS WORKED QUIETLY, ignoring Vivenna and pulling another stitch tight. Clod's guts—intestines, stomach, and some other things Vivenna didn't want to identify—lay on the floor beside him, carefully pulled out and arranged so that they could be repaired. Jewels was working on the intestines at the moment, sewing with a special thick thread and curved needle.

It was gruesome. And yet it didn't really affect Vivenna, not after the shock she'd had earlier. They were in the safe house. Tonk Fah had gone to scout the regular house to see if Parlin was all right. Denth was downstairs, fetching something.

Vivenna sat on the floor. She'd changed to a long dress, purchased on the way—her skirt was filthy from its time in the mud—and she sat with legs pulled up against her chest. Jewels continued to ignore Vivenna, working atop a sheet on the floor. She was muttering to herself, still angry. "Stupid thing," Jewels said under her breath. "Can't believe we let you get hurt like this just to protect *her*."

Hurt. Did that even mean anything to a creature like Clod? He was awake; she could see that his eyes were open. What was the point of sewing up his insides? Would they heal? He didn't need to eat. Why bother with intestines? Vivenna shivered, looking away. She felt, in a way, as if her own insides had been ripped out. Exposed. For the world to see.

Vivenna closed her eyes. Hours later, and she was *still* shaking from the terror of huddling in that alleyway, thinking that she'd be dead in a moment. What had she learned about herself when finally threatened? Modesty had meant nothing—she'd pulled off her skirt rather than let it trip her again. Her hair had meant nothing; she'd ignored it as soon as the danger arrived. Her religion, apparently, meant nothing. Not that she'd been able to use the Breath—she hadn't even managed to commit blasphemy successfully.

"I'm half-tempted to just leave," Jewels muttered. "You and I. Go away."

Clod began to shuffle, and Vivenna opened her eyes to see him trying to stand up, even though his insides were hanging out.

Jewels swore. "Lie back down," she hissed, barely audible. "Colors-cursed thing. Howl of the sun. Go inactive. Howl of the sun."

Vivenna watched as Clod lay down and then stopped moving. *They might obey commands,* she thought. *But they aren't very smart. It tried to walk out, obeying Jewels's apparent Command to "go away."* And what was that nonsense Jewels had said about the sun? Was that one of the security phrases Denth had mentioned?

Vivenna heard footsteps on the stairs leading down to the cellar, and then the door opened and Denth appeared. He closed the door, then came over and handed Jewels something that looked like a large wineskin. The woman took it and immediately turned back to her work.

Denth walked over and sat down beside Vivenna.

"They say a man doesn't know himself until he faces death for the first time," he said in a conversational tone. "I don't know about that. It seems to me that the person you are when you're about to die isn't as important as the person you are during the rest of your life. Why should a few moments matter more than an entire lifetime?"

Vivenna didn't respond.

"Everyone gets scared, Princess. Even brave men sometimes run the first time they see battle. In armies, that's why there's so much training. The ones who hold aren't the courageous ones, they're the well-trained ones. We have instincts like any other animal. They take over sometimes. That's all right."

Vivenna continued to watch as Jewels carefully placed the intestines back into Clod's belly. She took out a small package and removed something that looked like a strip of meat.

"You did well, actually," Denth said. "Kept your wits about you. Didn't freeze. Found the quickest way out. I've protected some people who will just stand there and die unless you shake them and force them to run."

"I want you to teach me Awakening," Vivenna whispered.

He started, glancing at her. "Do you . . . want to think about that a bit first?"

"I have," she whispered, arms around knees, chin resting against them. "I thought I was stronger than I am. I thought I'd rather die than use it. That was a lie. In that moment, I would have done *anything* to survive."

Denth smiled. "You'd make a good mercenary."

"It's wrong," she said, still staring forward. "But I can't claim to be pure anymore. I might as well understand what I have. Use it. If that damns me, then so be it. At least it will have helped me survive long enough to destroy the Hallandren."

Denth raised an eyebrow. "You want to *destroy* them now, eh? No more simple sabotage and undermining?"

She shook her head. "I want this kingdom overthrown," she whispered. "Just like the slumlords said. It can corrupt those poor people. It can corrupt even me. I hate it."

"I—"

"No, Denth," Vivenna said. Her hair bled to a deep red, and for once she didn't care. "I *really* hate it. I've always hated this people. They took my childhood. I had to prepare. Become their queen. Get ready to marry their God King. Everyone said he was unholy and a heretic. Yet *I* was supposed to have sex with him!

"I hate this entire city, with its colors and its gods! I hate the fact that it stole away my life, then demanded that I leave behind all that I love! I hate the busy streets, the placating gardens, the commerce, and the suffocating weather.

"I hate their arrogance most of all. Thinking they could push my father around, force him into that treaty twenty years ago. They've controlled my life. Dominated it. *Ruined* it. And now they have my sister."

She drew in a deep breath through gritted teeth.

"You'll have your vengeance, Princess," Denth whispered.

She looked at him. "I want them to hurt, Denth. The attack today wasn't about subduing a rebellious element. The Hallandren sent those soldiers in to kill. Kill the poor that *they* created. We're going to stop them from doing things like that. I don't care what it takes. I'm tired of being pretty and nice and ignoring ostentation. I want to *do* something."

Denth nodded slowly. "All right. We'll change course, start making our attacks a little more painful."

"Good," she said. She squeezed her eyes shut, feeling frustrated, wishing that she was strong enough to keep all of these emotions away. But she wasn't. She'd kept them in too long. That was the problem.

"This was never about your sister, was it?" Denth asked. "Coming here?"

She shook her head, eyes still shut.

"Why, then?"

"I had trained all of my life," she whispered. "I was the

one who would sacrifice herself. When Siri left in my place, I became nothing. I had to come and get it back."

"But you just said that you've always hated Hallandren," he said, sounding confused.

"I have. And I do. That's why I had to come."

He was silent for a few moments. "Too complicated for a mercenary, I guess."

She opened her eyes. She wasn't sure if she understood, either. She'd always kept a firm grip on her hatred, only letting it manifest in disdain for Hallandren and its ways. She confronted the hatred now. Acknowledged it. Somehow, Hallandren could be loathsome yet enticing at the same time. It was as if . . . she knew that until she came and saw the place for herself, she wouldn't have a real focus—a real understanding, a real image—of what it was that had destroyed her life.

Now she understood. If her Breaths would help, then she would use them. Just like Lemex. Just like those slumlords. She wasn't above that. She never had been.

She doubted Denth would understand. Instead, Vivenna nodded toward Jewels. "What is she doing?"

Denth turned. "Attaching a new muscle," he said. "One of the ones in his side got cut, sheared right through. Muscles won't work right if you just sew them together. She has to replace the whole thing."

"With screws?"

Denth nodded. "Right into the bone. It works all right. Not perfectly, but all right. No wound can ever be *perfectly* fixed on a Lifeless, though he will heal some. You just sew them up and pump them full of fresh ichor-alcohol. If you fix them enough times, the body will stop working right and you'll have to spend another Breath to keep them going. By then, it's usually just best to buy another body."

Saved by a monster. Perhaps that was what made her so determined to use her Breath. She should be dead, but Clod had saved her. A Lifeless. She owed her life to something that should not exist. Even worse, if she looked deep within herself, she found herself feeling a traitorous pity for the thing. Even an affection. Considering that, she figured that she was already damned to the point where using her Breaths wouldn't matter.

"He fought well," she whispered. "Better than the Lifeless that the city guard was using."

Denth glanced at Clod. "They're not all equal. Most Lifeless, they're just made out of whatever body happens to be around. If you pay good money, you can get one who was very skillful in life."

She felt a chill, remembering then that moment of humanity she'd seen on Clod's face as he defended her. If an undead monstrosity could be a hero, then a pious princess could blaspheme. Or was she still just trying to justify her actions?

"Skill," she whispered. "They keep it?"

Denth nodded. "Some semblance of it, at least. Considering what we paid for this guy, he must have been quite the soldier. And that's why it's worth the money, time, and trouble to repair him, rather than buy a new Lifeless."

They treat him just like a thing, Vivenna thought. Just as she should. And yet, more and more, she thought of Clod as a "he." He had saved her life. Not Denth, not Tonk Fah. Clod. It seemed to her that they should show more respect for him.

Jewels finished with the muscles, then sewed the skin closed with a thick string.

"Though he'll kind of heal," Denth said, "it's best to use something strong in the repair, so the wound doesn't rip apart again."

Vivenna nodded. "And the . . . juice."

"Ichor-alcohol," Denth said. "Discovered by the Five Scholars. Wonderful stuff. Keeps a Lifeless going really well."

"That's what let the Manywar occur?" she whispered. "Getting the mixture right?"

"That's part of it. That and the discovery—again by one of the Five Scholars, I forget which one—of some new Commands. If you really want to be an Awakener, Princess, that's what you have to learn. The Commands."

She nodded. "Teach me."

To the side Jewels got out a small pump and attached a small hose to a little valve at the base of Clod's neck. She began to pump the ichor-alcohol, moving the pump very slowly, probably in order to keep from bursting the blood vessels.

"Well," Denth said, "there are a *lot* of Commands. If you want to bring a rope to life—like that one you tried to use back in the alleyway—a good Command is 'hold things.' Speak it with a clear voice, willing your Breath to act. If you do it right, the rope will grab whatever is closest. 'Protect me' is another good one, though it can be interpreted in fairly strange ways if you don't imagine exactly what you want."

"Imagine?" Vivenna asked.

He nodded. "You have to form the Command in your head, not just speak it. The Breath you give up, it's part of your life. Your soul, you Idrians would say. When you Awaken something, it becomes part of you. If you're good— and practiced—the things you Awaken will do what you expect of them. They're part of you. They understand, just like your hands understand what you want them to do."

"I'll start practicing, then," she said.

He nodded. "You should pick it up fairly quickly. You're a clever woman, and you have a lot of Breaths."

"That makes a difference?"

He nodded, looking somewhat distant. As if distracted by his own thoughts. "The more Breaths you hold when you start, the easier it is for you to learn how to Awaken.

It's like . . . I don't know, the Breath is more part of you. Or you're more part of it."

She sat back, contemplating that. "Thank you," she finally said.

"What? For explaining Awakening? Half the children on the streets could have told you that much."

"No," she said. "Though I appreciate the instruction, the thanks is for other things. For not condemning me as a hypocrite. For being willing to change plans and take risks. For protecting me today."

"Last I checked, those were all the things a good employee should do. At least if that employee is a mercenary."

She shook her head. "It's more than that. You're a good man, Denth."

He met her eyes, and she could see something in them. An emotion she couldn't describe. Again, she thought of the mask he wore—the persona of the laughing, joking mercenary. That man seemed just a front, when she looked into those eyes, and saw so much more.

"A good man," he said, turning away. "Sometimes, I wish that were still true, Princess. I haven't been a good man for some years now."

She opened her mouth to reply, but something made her hesitate. Outside, a shadow passed the window. Tonk Fah entered a few moments later. Denth stood up without glancing at her. "Well?" he asked Tonk Fah.

"Looks safe," Tonk Fah said, eyeing Clod. "How's the stiff?"

"Just finished," Jewels said. She leaned down, saying something very soft to the Lifeless. Clod started moving again, sitting up, looking about. Vivenna waited as his eyes passed over her, but there didn't seem to be recognition in them. He wore the same dull expression.

Of course, Vivenna thought, standing. *He's Lifeless, after all.* Jewels had said something to make him start working

again. It was probably the same thing Jewels had used to
make him stop moving in the first place. That odd phrase . . .

Howl of the sun. Vivenna filed it away, then followed as
they left the building.

───❦───

A SHORT TIME later, they were home. Parlin rushed out,
expressing his fears for their safety. He went to Jewels first,
though she brushed him off. As Vivenna entered the building, he moved up to her. "Vivenna? What happened?"

She just shook her head.

"There was fighting," he said, following her up the
stairs. "I heard about it."

"There was an attack on the camp we visited," Vivenna
said wearily, reaching the top of the stairs. "A squad of Lifeless. They started killing people."

"Lord of Colors!" Parlin said. "Is Jewels all right?"

Vivenna flushed, turning on the landing, looking down
the stairs toward him. "Why do you ask about *her*?"

Parlin shrugged. "I think she's nice."

"Should you be saying things like that?" Vivenna asked,
noticing halfheartedly that her hair was turning red again.
"Aren't you engaged to *me*?"

He frowned. "You were engaged to the God King,
Vivenna."

"But you know what our fathers wanted," she said, hands
on hips.

"I did," Parlin said. "But, well, when we left Idris, I figured we were both going to get disinherited. There's really
no reason to keep up the charade."

Charade?

"I mean, let's be honest, Vivenna," he said, smiling. "You
really haven't ever been that nice to me. I know you think
I'm stupid; I guess you're probably right. But if you really
cared, I figured that you wouldn't make me *feel* stupid, too.

Jewels grumbles at me, but she laughs at my jokes some-times. You've never done that."

"But . . ." Vivenna said, finding herself at a slight loss for words. "But why did you follow me down to Hallan-dren?"

He blinked. "Well, for Siri, of course. Isn't that why we came? To rescue her?" He smiled fondly, then shrugged. "Good night, Vivenna." He trailed down the steps, calling to Jewels to see if she was hurt.

Vivenna watched him go.

He's twice the person I am, she thought with shame, turning toward her room. *But I'm just finding it hard to care anymore.* Everything had been taken from her. Why not Parlin, too? Her hatred for Hallandren grew a little more firm as she stepped into her room.

I just need to sleep, she thought. *Maybe after that, I can figure out just what in the name of the Colors I'm doing in this city.*

One thing remained firm. She was going to learn how to Awaken. The Vivenna from before—the one who had a right to stand tall and denounce Breath as unholy—no lon-ger had a place in T'Telir. The real Vivenna hadn't come to Hallandren to save her sister. She'd come because she couldn't stand being unimportant.

She'd learn. That was her punishment.

Inside her room, she pushed the door closed, locking the bolt. Then she walked over to pull the drapes closed.

A figure stood on her balcony, resting easily against the railing. He wore several days' worth of stubble on his face and his dark clothing was worn, almost tattered. He carried a deep black sword.

Vivenna jumped, eyes wide.

"You," he said in an angry voice, "are causing a lot of trouble."

She opened her mouth to scream, but the drapes snapped

forward, muffling her neck and mouth. They squeezed tightly, choking her. They wrapped around her entire body, pinning her arms to her sides.

No! she thought. *I survive the attack and the Lifeless, and then fall in my own room?*

She struggled, hoping someone would hear her thrashing and come for her. But nobody did. At least, not before she fell unconscious.

34

LIGHTSONG WATCHED THE young queen dart away from his pavilion and felt an odd sense of guilt. *How very uncharacteristic of me,* he thought, taking a sip of wine. After the grapes, it tasted a little sour.

Maybe the sourness was from something else. He'd spoken to Siri about the God King's death in his usual flippant way. In his opinion, it was usually best for people to hear the truth bluntly—and, if possible, amusingly.

He hadn't expected such a reaction from the queen. What was the God King to her? She'd been sent to be his bride, probably against her will. Yet she seemed to take the prospect of his death with grief. He eyed her appraisingly as she fled.

Such a small, young thing she was, all dressed up in gold and blue. *Young?* he thought. *Yet she's been alive longer than I have.*

He retained some things from his former life—such as his perception of his own age. He didn't feel like he was five. He felt far older. That age should have taught him to hold his tongue when speaking of making widows out of young women. Could the girl actually have feelings for the God King?

She'd been in the city for only a couple of months, and he knew—through rumors—what her life must be like. Forced to perform her duty as a wife for a man to whom she could not speak and whom she could not know. A man who represented all the things that her culture taught were profane. The only thing Lightsong could suppose, then, was that she was worried about what might happen to her if her husband killed himself. A legitimate worry. The queen would lose most of her stature if she lost her husband.

Lightsong nodded to himself, turning to look down at the arguing priests. They were done with sewage and guard patrols and had moved on to other topics. "We *must* prepare ourselves for war," one of them was saying. "Recent events make it clear that we cannot coexist with the Idrians with any assurance of peace or security. This conflict will come, whether we wish it or not."

Lightsong sat listening, tapping one finger against the arm rest of his chair.

For five years, I've been irrelevant, he thought. *I didn't have a vote on any of the important court councils, I simply held the codes to a division of the Lifeless. I've crafted a divine reputation of being useless.*

The tone below was even more hostile than it had been during previous meetings. That wasn't what worried him. The problem was the priest spearheading the movement for war. Nanrovah, high priest of Stillmark the Noble. Normally, Lightsong wouldn't have bothered paying attention. Yet Nanrovah had always been the most outspoken *against* war.

What had made him change his mind?

It wasn't long before Blushweaver made her way to his box. By the time she arrived, Lightsong's taste for the wine had returned, and he was sipping thoughtfully. The voices against war from below were soft and infrequent.

Blushweaver sat beside him, a rustle of cloth and a waft of perfume. Lightsong didn't look toward her.

"How did you get to Nanrovah?" he finally asked.

"I didn't," Blushweaver said. "I don't know why he changed his mind. I wish he hadn't done it so quickly—it seems suspicious and makes people think I manipulated him. Either way, I'll take the support."

"You wish for war so much?"

"I wish for our people to be aware of the threat," Blushweaver said. "You think I *want* this to happen? You think I want to send our people to die and to kill?"

Lightsong looked at her, judging her sincerity. She had such beautiful eyes. One rarely noticed that, considering how she proffered the rest of her assets so blatantly. "No," he said. "I don't think you want a war."

She nodded sharply. Her dress was sleek and trim this day, as always, but it was particularly revealing up top, where her breasts were pressed up and forward, demanding attention. Lightsong looked away.

"You're boring today," Blushweaver said.

"I'm distracted."

"We should be happy," Blushweaver said. "The priests have almost all come around. Soon there will be a call for attack made to the main assembly of gods."

Lightsong nodded. The main assembly of gods was called to deliberate only in the most important of situations. In that case, they all had a vote. If the vote was for war, the gods with Lifeless Commands—gods like Lightsong—would be called upon to administer and lead the battle.

"You've changed the Commands on Hopefinder's ten thousand?" Lightsong asked.

She nodded. "They're mine now, as are Mercystar's."

Colors, he thought. *Between the two of us, we now control three-quarters of the kingdom's armies.*

What in the name of the Iridescent Tones am I getting myself into?

Blushweaver settled back in her chair, eyeing the smaller one that Siri had vacated. "I am annoyed, however, at All-mother."

"Because she's prettier than you, or because she's smarter?"

Blushweaver didn't dignify that with a verbal response; she just shot him a look of annoyance.

"Just trying to act less boring, my dear," he said.

"Allmother controls the last group of Lifeless," Blushweaver said.

"An odd choice, don't you think?" Lightsong said. "I mean, *I* am a logical choice—assuming you don't know me, of course—since I'm supposedly bold. Hopefinder represents justice, a nice mix with soldiers. Even Mercy-star, who represents benevolence, makes a kind of sense for one who controls soldiers. But Allmother? Goddess of matrons and families? Giving her ten thousand Lifeless is enough to make even me consider my drunk-monkey theory."

"The one who chooses names and titles of the Re-turned?"

"Exactly," Lightsong said. "I've actually considered expanding the theory. I am now proposing to believe that God—or the universe, or time, or whatever you think controls all of this—is *all* really just a drunk monkey."

She leaned over, squeezing her arms together, seriously threatening to pop her bosom out the front of her dress. "And, you think *my* title was chosen by happenstance? Goddess of honesty and interpersonal relations. Seems to fit, wouldn't you say?"

He hesitated. Then he smiled. "My dear, did you just try to prove the existence of God with your cleavage?"

She smiled. "You'd be surprised what a good wriggle of the chest can accomplish."

"Hum. I'd never considered the theological power of your breasts, my dear. If there were a Church devoted to them, perhaps you'd make a theist out of me after all. Regardless, are you going to tell me what specifically Allmother did to annoy you?"

"She won't give me her Lifeless Commands."

"Not surprising," Lightsong said. "*I* hardly trust you, and I'm your friend."

"We need those security phrases, Lightsong."

"Why?" he asked. "We've got three of the four—we dominate the armies already."

"We can't afford infighting or divisiveness," Blushweaver said. "If her ten were to turn against our thirty, we'd win, but we'd be left badly weakened."

He frowned. "Surely she wouldn't do that."

"Surely we'd rather be certain."

Lightsong sighed. "Very well, then. I'll talk to her."

"That might not be a good idea."

He raised an eyebrow.

"She doesn't like you very much."

"Yes, I know," he said. "She has remarkably good taste. Unlike some other people I know."

She glared at him. "Do I need to wriggle my breasts at you again?"

"No, please. I don't know if I'd be able to stand the theological debate that would follow."

"All right, then," she said, sitting back, looking down at the priests who were still arguing.

They sure are taking a long time on this one, he thought. He glanced toward the other side, where Siri had paused to look out over the arena, her arms resting on the stonework; it was too high for her to do so comfortably.

Perhaps it wasn't thinking of her husband's death that bothered her, he thought. *Maybe it was because the discussion turned to war.*

A war her people couldn't win. That was another good reason why the conflict was becoming inevitable. As Hoid had implied, when one side had an unbeatable advantage, war was the result. Hallandren had been building its Lifeless armies for centuries, and the size was becoming daunting. Hallandren had less and less to lose from an attack. He should have realized that earlier, rather than assuming this would all blow over once the new queen arrived.

Blushweaver huffed beside him, and he noticed that *she* had noticed his study of Siri. She was watching the queen with obvious dislike.

Lightsong immediately changed the topic. "Do you know anything about a tunnel complex beneath the Court of Gods?"

Blushweaver turned back toward him, shrugging. "Sure. Some of the palaces have tunnels beneath them, places for storage and the like."

"Have you ever been down in any of them?"

"Please. Why would I go crawling about in storage tunnels? I only know about them because of my high priestess. When she joined my service, she asked me if I wanted mine connected to the main complex of tunnels. I said I didn't."

"Because you didn't want others to have access to your palace?"

"No," she said, turning back to watching the priests below. "Because I didn't want to put up with the racket of all that digging. Can I have some more wine, please?"

SIRI WATCHED THE proceedings for quite a long time. She felt a little like Lightsong said he did. Because she didn't have a say about what the court did, it was frustrating to pay attention. Yet she wanted to know. The arguments of the priests were, in a way, her only connection to the outside world.

She was not encouraged by what she heard. As the time passed, the sun falling close to the horizon and servants lighting massive torches along the walkway, Siri found her-

self feeling more and more daunted. Her husband was probably either going to be killed or persuaded to kill himself in
the upcoming year. Her homeland, in turn, was about to be
invaded by the very kingdom her husband ruled—yet
he could do nothing to stop it because he had no way to
communicate.

Then there was the guilt she felt for actually *enjoying* all
the challenges and problems. Back home, she'd had to be
contrary and disobedient to find any kind of excitement.
Here she only had to stand and watch, and things would
begin to topple against each other and cause a clatter. There
was far *too* much clatter at present, but that didn't stop her
from thrilling at her part in it.

Silly fool, she told herself. *Everything you love is in
danger and you're thinking about how exciting it is?*

She needed to find a way to help Susebron. In doing so,
perhaps she could bring him out from beneath the oppres-
sive control of the priests. Then he might be able to do
something to help her homeland. As she followed that line
of thought, she almost missed a comment from below. It
was spoken by one of the priests most strongly in favor of
attacking.

"Have you not heard of the Idrian agent who has been
causing havoc in the city?" the priest asked. "The Idrians
are preparing for the war! *They* know that a conflict is inevitable and so they've begun to work against us!"

Siri perked up. *Idrian agents in the city?*

"Bah," said another of the priests. "The 'infiltrator' you
speak of is said to be a princess of the royal family. That's
obviously a story for the common people. Why would a
princess come in secret to T'Telir? These stories are ridiculous and unfounded."

Siri grimaced. That, at least, was obviously true. Her
sisters were not the types to come and work as "Idrian
agents." She smiled, imagining her soft-spoken monk of a

sister—or even Vivenna in her prim outfits and stony attitude—coming to T'Telir in secret. Part of her had a little trouble believing that Vivenna had really been intended to become Susebron's bride. Starchy Vivenna? Having to deal with the exotic court and the wild costumes?

Vivenna's stoic coldness would never have coaxed Susebron out of his imperial mask. Vivenna's obvious disapproval would have alienated her from gods like Lightsong. Vivenna would have hated wearing the beautiful dresses and would never have appreciated the colors and variety in the city. Siri might not have been ideal for the position, but she was slowly coming to realize that Vivenna hadn't been a good choice either.

A group of people was approaching along the walkway. Siri remained where she was; she was too distracted by her thoughts to pay much attention.

"Are they talking about a relative of yours?" a voice asked.

Siri started, spinning. Behind her stood a dark-haired goddess wearing a lavish—and revealing—gown of green and silver. Like most of the gods, she stood a good head taller than a mortal person, and she looked down at Siri with a raised eyebrow.

"Your . . . Grace?" Siri responded, confused.

"They're discussing the famous hidden princess," the goddess said with a wave of her hand. "She'd be a relative of yours, if she really does have the Royal Locks."

Siri glanced back at the priests. "They must be mistaken. I'm the only princess here."

"The stories of her are quite pervasive."

Siri fell silent.

"My Lightsong has taken a liking to you, Princess," the goddess said, folding her arms.

"He has been very kind to me," Siri said carefully, trying to present the right image—that of the person she was, only less threatening. A little more confused. "Might I ask which goddess you are, Your Grace?"

"I am Blushweaver," the goddess said.

"I am pleased to meet you."

"No you aren't," Blushweaver said. She leaned in, eyes narrowing. "I don't like what you're doing here."

"Excuse me?"

Blushweaver raised a finger. "He's a better man than any of us, *Princess.* Don't you go spoiling him and pulling him into your schemes."

"I don't know what you mean."

"You don't fool me with your false naïveté," Blushweaver said. "Lightsong is a good person—one of the last ones we have left in this court. If you taint him, I will destroy you. Do you understand?"

Siri nodded dumbly; then Blushweaver turned and moved away, muttering, "Find someone else's bed to climb into, you little slut."

Siri watched her go, shocked. When she finally regained her composure, she blushed furiously, then fled.

⊶∞⊷

BY THE TIME she got back to the palace, Siri was quite ready for her bath. She entered the bathing chamber, letting her serving women undress her. They retreated with the clothing, then exited to prepare the evening's gown. That left Siri in the hands of a group of lesser attendants, the ones whose job it was to follow her into the massive tub and scrub her clean.

Siri relaxed and leaned back, sighing as the women went to work. Another group—standing fully clothed in the deep water—pulled her hair straight and then cut most of it free, something she'd ordered them to do every night.

For a few moments, Siri floated and let herself forget the threats to her people and her husband. She even let herself forget Blushweaver and her snappish misunderstanding. She just enjoyed the heat and the scents of the perfumed water.

"You wanted to speak with me, My Queen?" a voice asked.

Siri started, splashing as she dunked her body beneath the water. "Bluefingers," she snapped. "I thought we'd cleared this up on the first day!"

He stood at the rim of the tub, fingers blue, typically anxious as he began to pace. "Oh, please," he said. "I have daughters twice your age. You sent word that you wanted to talk to me. Well, this is where I will talk. Away from random ears."

He nodded to several of the serving girls, and they began to splash just a bit more, speaking quietly, creating a low noise. Siri flushed, her short hair a deep red—though a few cut-off strands that floated in the water remained blond.

"Haven't you gotten over your shyness yet?" Bluefingers asked. "You've been in Hallandren for months."

Siri eyed him, but didn't relax her concealing posture, even if she did let the serving women continue to work on her hair and scrub her back. "Won't it seem suspicious to have the serving women making so much noise?" she asked.

Bluefingers waved a hand. "They're already considered second-class servants by most in the palace." She understood what he meant. These women, as opposed to her regular servants, wore brown. They were from Pahn Kahl.

"You sent me a message earlier," Bluefingers said. "What did you mean by claiming to have information relating to my plans?"

Siri bit her lip, sorting through the dozens of ideas she had considered, discarding them all. What did she know? How could she make Bluefingers willing to trade?

He gave me clues, she thought. *He tried to scare me into not sleeping with the king. But he had no reason to help me. He barely knew me. He must have other motives for not wanting an heir to be born.*

"What happens when a new God King takes the throne?" she asked carefully.

He eyed her. "So you've figured that out, then?"

Figured out what? "Of course I have," she said out loud.

He wrung his hands nervously. "Of course, of course. Then you can see why I'm so nervous? We worked hard to get me where I am. It isn't easy for a Pahn Kahl man to rise high in the theocracy of Hallandren. Once I got into place, I worked so hard to provide work for my people. The serving girls who wash you, they have far better lives than the Pahn Kahl who work the dye fields. That will all be lost. We don't believe in their gods. Why would we be treated as well as people of their own faith?"

"I still don't see why it has to happen," Siri said carefully.

He waved a nervous hand. "Of course it doesn't *have* to, but tradition is tradition. The Hallandren are very lax in every area but religion. When a new God King is chosen, his servants are replaced. They won't kill us to send us into the afterlife along with our lord—that horrid custom hasn't been in effect since the days before the Manywar—but we *will* be dismissed. A new God King represents a fresh start."

He stopped pacing, looking at her. She was still naked in the water, awkwardly covering herself as best she could. "But," he said, "I guess my job security is the lesser of our problems."

Siri snorted. "Don't tell me you're worried about *my* safety above your own place in the palace."

"Of course not," he said, kneeling down beside the tub, speaking quietly. "But the God King's life . . . well, that worries me."

"So," Siri said, "I haven't been able to decide yet. Do the God Kings give up their lives willingly once they have an heir, or are they coerced into it?"

"I'm not sure," Bluefingers admitted. "There are stories, spoken of by my people regarding the last God King's death. They say that the plague he cured—well, he wasn't even in the city when the 'curing' happened. My suspicion is that they somehow coerced him to give up his Breaths to his son and that killed him."

He doesn't know, Siri thought. *He doesn't realize that Susebron is a mute.* "How closely have you served the God King?"

He shrugged. "As close as any servant considered unholy. I'm not allowed to touch him or speak to him. But, Princess, I've *served* him all my life. He's not my god, but he's something better. I think these priests look upon their gods as placeholders. It doesn't really matter to them who is holding the station. Me, I've served His Majesty for my entire life. I was hired by the palace as a lad and I remember Susebron's childhood. I cleaned his quarters. He's not my god, but he *is* my liege. And now these priests are planning to kill him."

He turned back to his pacing, wringing his hands. "But there's nothing to be done."

"Yes, there is," she said.

He waved a hand. "I gave you a warning and you ignored it. I know that you've been performing your duties as a wife. Perhaps we could find some way of making certain that no pregnancy of yours comes to term."

Siri flushed. "I would never do such a thing! Austre forbids it."

"Even to save the life of the God King? But . . . of course. What is he to you? Your captor and imprisoner. Yes. Perhaps my warnings were useless."

"I *do* care, Bluefingers," she said. "And I think we can stop this before it gets to the point of worrying about an heir. I've been talking to the God King."

Bluefingers froze, looking directly at her. "What?" ·

"I've been talking to him," Siri admitted. "He's not as heartless as you might think. I don't think this has to end with him dying or your people losing their places in the palace."

Bluefingers studied her, staring at her to the point that she flushed again, ducking further down into the water.

"I see that you've found yourself a position of power," he noted.

Or, at least, one that looks powerful, she thought ruefully. "If things turn out as I want them to, I'll make certain your people are cared for."

"And my side of the bargain?" he asked.

"If things don't turn out as I want them to," she said, taking a deep breath, heart fluttering, "I want you to get Susebron and me out of the palace."

Silence.

"Deal," he said. "But let us make certain it does not come to that. Is the God King aware of the danger from his own priests?"

"He is," Siri lied. "In fact, he knew about it before I did. He's the one who told me I needed to contact you."

"He did?" Bluefingers asked, frowning slightly.

"Yes," Siri said. "I will be in touch on how to make this turn out well for all of us. And, until then, I would appreciate it if you'd let me get back to my bath."

Bluefingers nodded slowly, then retreated from the bathing chamber. Siri, however, found it hard to still her nerves. She wasn't certain if she'd handled the exchange well or not. She seemed to have gained something. Now she just had to figure out how to use it.

35

VIVENNA AWOKE SORE, tired, and terrified. She tried struggling, but her hands and legs were tied. She succeeded only in rolling herself into an even less comfortable position.

She was in a dark room, gagged, her face pressing awkwardly against a splintering wood floor. She still wore her skirt, an expensive foreign one like those that Denth complained about. Her hands were tied behind her.

Someone was in the room with her. Someone with a lot of Breath. She could feel it without even trying. She twisted, rolling onto her back in an awkward motion. She could see a figure silhouetted against a starlit sky, standing on a balcony a short distance away.

It was him.

He turned toward her, face shadowed in the unlit room, and she began to squirm with panic. What was this man planning to do with her? Horrible possibilities leaped to mind.

The man walked toward her, feet thumping roughly on the floor, the wood shaking. He knelt down, pulling her head up by the hair. "I'm still deciding whether or not to kill you, Princess," he said. "If I were you, I'd avoid doing anything more to antagonize me."

His voice was deep, thick, and had an accent she couldn't place. She froze in his grip, trembling, hair bleached white. He appeared to be studying her, eyes reflecting starlight. He dropped her back to the wooden floor.

She groaned through the gag as he lit a lantern, then pushed the balcony doors closed. He reached to his belt and removed a large hunting dagger. Vivenna felt a stab of fear, but he simply walked over and cut the bonds on her hands.

He tossed the dagger aside, and it made a *thock* as it stuck into the wood of the far wall. He reached for something on the bed. His large, black-hilted sword.

Vivenna scrambled back, hands free, and pulled at her gag, intending to scream. He whipped the scabbarded sword toward her, making her freeze.

"You will remain quiet," he said sharply.

She huddled back into the corner. *How is this happening to me?* she thought. Why hadn't she fled back to Idris long ago? She'd been deeply unsettled when Denth had killed the ruffians in the restaurant. She'd known then that she was dealing with people and situations that were truly dangerous.

She'd been an arrogant fool to think that she could do anything in this city. This monstrous, overwhelming, terrible city. She was nothing. Barely a peasant from the countryside. Why had she been determined to get herself involved in this people's politics and schemes?

The man, Vasher, stepped forward. He undid the clasp on that deep, black sword, and Vivenna felt a strange nausea strike her. A thin wisp of black smoke began to curl up from the blade.

Vasher approached, backlit by the lantern, the sheathed tip of the sword dragging along the floor behind him. Then he dropped the sword to the floor in front of Vivenna.

"Pick it up," he said.

She untensed slightly, looking up, though she still huddled in the corner. She felt tears on her cheeks.

"Pick up the sword, Princess."

She had no training with weapons, but maybe . . . She reached for the sword, but felt her nausea grow far stronger. She groaned, her hand twitching as it approached the strange black blade.

She shied away.

"*Pick it up!*" Vasher bellowed.

She complied with a gagged cry of desperation, grabbing

the weapon, feeling a terrible sickness travel like a wave up her arm and into her stomach. She found herself ripping away her gag with desperate fingers.

Hello, a voice said in her head. *Would you like to kill someone today?*

She dropped the horrid weapon and fell to her knees, retching onto the floor. There wasn't much in her stomach, but she couldn't stop herself. When she was done, she crawled away and huddled down against the wall again, mouth dripping with bile, feeling too sick to yell for help or even wipe her face.

She was crying again. That seemed the least of her humiliations. Through teary eyes, she watched as Vasher stood quietly. Then he grunted—as if in surprise—and picked up the sword. He clicked the clasp on its sheath, locking the weapon back inside, then threw a towel onto what she'd retched up.

"We are in one of the slums," he said. "You may scream if you wish, but nobody will think anything of it. Except me. I'll be annoyed." He glanced back at her. "I warn you. I'm not known for my ability to keep my temper."

Vivenna shivered, still feeling hints of nausea. This man held even more Breath than she did. Yet, when he'd kidnapped her, she hadn't felt anyone standing in her room. How had he hidden it?

And what was that voice?

They seemed silly things to distract her, considering her current situation. However, she used them to keep from thinking about what this man might do to her. What—

He was walking toward her again. He picked up the gag, his expression dark. She finally screamed, trying to scramble away, and he cursed, putting a foot on her back and forcing her down against the floor. He tied her hands again before forcing on the gag. She cried, her voice muffled as he jerked her backward. He stood, then slung her over his shoulder and carried her out of the room.

"Colors-cursed slums," he muttered. "Everyone's too poor to afford cellars." He pushed her into a sitting position in the doorway of a second, much smaller room and retied her hands to the doorknob. He stepped back, looking her over, obviously unsatisfied. Then he knelt beside her, unshaven face close to hers, breath vile. "I have work to do," he said. "Work that *you* have forced me to do. You will not run. If you do, I'll find you and kill you. Understand?"

She nodded weakly.

She caught sight of him retrieving his sword from the other room, then he ran down the stairs. The door below slammed and locked, leaving her alone and helpless.

⁂

AN HOUR OR so later, Vivenna had finished crying herself dry. She sat slumped, hands tied awkwardly above her. Part of her kept waiting for the others to find her. Denth, Tonk Fah, Jewels. They were experts. They'd be able to save her.

No rescue came. Dazed, drowsy, and sick though she was, she realized something. This man—this Vasher—was someone that even Denth had feared. Vasher had killed one of their friends some months before. He was at least as skilled as they were.

How did they all end up here, then? she thought, her wrists rubbed raw. *It seems an unlikely coincidence.* Perhaps Vasher had followed Denth to the city and was acting out some kind of twisted rivalry by working against them.

They'll find me and save me.

But she knew that they wouldn't, not if Vasher was as dangerous as they said. He'd know how to hide from Denth. If she was going to escape, she'd have to do it herself. The concept terrified her. Strangely, however, memories from her tutors returned to her.

There are things to do if you are kidnapped, one had taught. *Things that every princess should know.* During her time in T'Telir, she'd begun to feel that her lessons were use-less. Now she was surprised to find herself remembering sessions that related directly to her situation.

If a person kidnaps you, the tutor had taught, *your best time to escape is near the beginning, when you are still strong. They will starve you and beat you so that soon you will be too weak to flee. Do not expect to be rescued, though friends will undoubtedly be working to help you. Never expect to be redeemed for a ransom. Most kidnappings end in death.*

The best thing you can do for your country is try to escape. If you don't succeed, then perhaps the captor will kill you. That is preferable to what you might have to endure as a captive. Plus, if you die, the kidnappers will no longer have a hostage.

It was a harsh, blunt lesson—but many of her lessons had been like that. Better to die than to be held captive and used against Idris. That was the same lesson that warned her that the Hallandren might try to use her against Idris once she was there as queen. In such a case, she was told that her father might be forced to order her assassination.

That was a problem she didn't have to worry about anymore. The kidnapping advice, however, seemed useful. It frightened her, made her want to cower in place and simply wait, hoping that Vasher would find a reason to let her go. But the more she thought, the more she knew that she had to be strong.

He'd been extremely harsh with her—exaggeratedly so. He'd wanted to frighten her so that she wouldn't try to escape. He'd cursed not having a cellar, for that would have been a good place to secret her. When he returned, he would probably move her to a more secure location. The tutors were right. The only chance she had to escape was now.

Her hands were bound tightly. She'd tried pulling them free several times already. Vasher knew his knots. She wiggled, rubbing more skin off, and she cringed in pain. Blood began to drip down her wrist, but even that slickness wasn't enough to get her hands free. She began to cry again, not in fear, but in pain and frustration.

She couldn't wiggle her way out. But . . . could she perhaps make the ropes untie themselves?

Why didn't I let Denth train me with Breath sooner?

Her stubborn self-righteousness seemed even more flagrant to her now. Of course it was better to use the Breath than it was to be killed—or worse—by Vasher. She thought she understood Lemex and his desire to gather enough Bio-Chroma to extend his life. She tried to speak some Commands through her gag.

That was useless. Even she knew that the Commands had to be spoken clearly. She began to wiggle her chin, pushing on the gag with her tongue. It didn't appear to be as tight as her wrist bonds. Plus, it was wet from her tears and saliva. She worked at it, moving her lips and her teeth. She was actually surprised when it finally dropped loose below her chin.

She licked her lips, working her sore jaw. *Now what?* she thought. Her apprehension was rising. Now she *really* needed to get free. If Vasher returned and saw that she'd managed to work her gag off, he'd never leave her with such an opportunity again. He might punish her for disobeying him.

"Ropes," she said. "Untie yourself."

Nothing happened.

She gritted her teeth, trying to remember the Commands that Denth had told her. *Hold things* and *Protect me*. Neither seemed all that useful in her situation. She certainly didn't want the ropes to hold her wrists more tightly. However, he had said something else. Something about imagining what you wanted in your mind. She tried that, picturing the ropes untying themselves.

"Untie yourselves," she said clearly.

Again, nothing happened.

Vivenna leaned her head back in frustration. Awakening seemed such a vague art, which was odd, considering the number of rules and restrictions it appeared to have. Or maybe it just seemed vague to her because it was so complicated.

She closed her eyes. *I have to get this,* she thought. *I must figure it out. If I don't, I will be killed.*

She opened her eyes, focusing on her bonds. She pictured them untying again, but somehow that felt wrong. She was like a child, sitting and staring at a leaf, trying to make it move just by concentrating on it.

That wasn't the way her newfound senses worked. They were part of her. So, instead of concentrating, she relaxed, letting her unconscious mind do the work. A little like she did when she changed the color of her hair.

"Untie," she Commanded.

The Breath flowed from her. It was like blowing bubbles beneath the water, exhaling a piece of herself but feeling it flow into something else. That something else became part of her—a limb she could only slightly control. It was more of a *sense* of the rope than an ability to move it. As the Breath left her, she could feel the world dull, colors becoming slightly less bold, the wind a little more difficult to hear, the life of the city a little more distant. The ropes around her hands jerked, causing her wrists to burn.

Then the ropes unraveled and dropped to the ground. Her arms came free, and she sat, staring at her wrists, shocked.

Austre, Lord of Colors, she thought. *I did it.* She wasn't certain whether to be impressed or ashamed.

Either way, she knew she needed to run. She untied her ankles, then scrambled to her feet, noticing that a section of the wooden door had been completely drained of color in a circular pattern around her hands. She paused only briefly, then grabbed the rope and ran down the stairs. She unlocked the door and peeked out the doorway onto the street, but it was dark, and she could see little.

Taking a deep breath, she rushed out into the night.

～∞～

SHE WALKED AIMLESSLY for a time, trying to put space between herself and Vasher's lair. She knew that she should probably find a place to hide, but she was afraid. She was distinctive in her fine dress and would be remembered by all who passed. Her only real hope was to get out of the slums and into the city proper, where she could find her way back to Denth and the others.

She carried the rope tucked into the dress's pocket pouch, hidden behind a fold of cloth on the side. She'd grown so accustomed to having a certain amount of Breath that missing a fraction, even the small bit contained in the rope, felt wrong. Awakeners could recover Breath they invested into objects; she'd been tutored on that. She just didn't know the Commands to do it. So she brought the rope, hoping that Denth would be able to help her recover its Breath.

She maintained a quick pace, head down, trying to watch for a discarded cloak or piece of cloth she could wrap around herself to hide the dress. Fortunately, it seemed as if the hour was too late, even, for most ruffians. She did occasionally see shadowed figures on the sides of the road, and she had trouble keeping her heart stilled as she passed them.

If only the sun were up! she thought. It was just beginning to grow light with morning's arrival, but it was still dark enough that she had trouble telling which direction she was going. The slums were convoluted enough that she felt she was going in circles. The tall buildings loomed around her, blocking off the sky. This area had once been much more rich; the shadowed fronts of the buildings held worn engravings and faded colors. The square down the street to her left held an old, broken statue of a man atop a horse, perhaps part of a fountain or—

Vivenna stopped. A broken statue of a horseman. Why did that seem familiar?

Denth's directions, she thought. *When he explained to Parlin how to get from the safe house to the restaurant.* That day, weeks back, seemed so vague to her now. But she did remember the exchange. She'd been worried that Parlin would get lost.

For the first time in hours, she felt a sense of hope. The directions had been simple. Could she remember them? She worked, walking hesitantly, partially just on instinct. After just a few minutes, she realized that the dark street around her looked familiar. There were no lamps in the slums, but the light of false dawn was enough.

She turned around, and sure enough, the safe house lay huddled between two larger buildings across from her. *Blessed Austre!* she thought with relief, quickly crossing the street and pushing her way into the building. The main room was empty, and she hurriedly opened the door down to the cellar, seeking a place to hide.

She searched around with her fingers, and sure enough, she found a lantern with flint and steel beside the stairway. She pulled the door closed and found it more sturdy than she would have assumed. That felt good, though she couldn't lock it from this side. She left it unlatched and bent down to light the lantern.

A set of worn, broken stairs led down into the cellar. Vivenna paused, remembering that Denth had warned her about the steps. She walked down carefully, feeling them creak beneath her, and could see why he'd been worried. Still, she made it down all right. At the bottom, she wrinkled her nose at the musty scent. The carcasses of several small game hung on the wall; someone had been here recently, which was a good sign.

She rounded the stairs. The main space of the cellar was

built beneath the floor of the upper room. She would rest there for a few hours, and if Denth didn't arrive, she'd venture out. Then she—

She froze, jerking to a halt, lantern swinging in her hand. Its unsteady light shone on a figure sitting before her, head bowed, face shadowed. His arms were tied behind his back and his ankles were bound to the legs of the chair.

"Parlin?" Vivenna asked with shock, rushing to his side. She quickly set down the lantern, then froze. There was blood on the floor.

"Parlin!" she said louder, urgently lifting his head. His eyes stared forward, sightless, his face scratched and bloody. Her life sense couldn't feel him. His eyes were dead.

Vivenna's hands began to shake. She stumbled back, horrified. "Oh, Colors," she found herself mumbling. "Colors, Colors, Colors . . ."

A hand fell on her shoulder. She screamed, spinning. A large figure stood in the darkness behind her, half-hidden beneath the stairs.

"Hello, Princess," Tonk Fah said. He smiled.

Vivenna stumbled back, nearly colliding with Parlin's body. She began to gasp, hand at her chest. Only then did she notice the bodies on the walls.

Not game animals. What she had mistaken for a pheasant in the dim light of her lantern now reflected back green. A dead parrot. A monkey hung beside, body sliced and cut. The freshest corpse was that of a large lizard. All had been tortured.

"Oh, Austre," she whispered.

Tonk Fah stepped forward, grabbing for her, and Vivenna finally shocked herself into motion. She ducked to the side, escaping his reach. She ran around the large man, scrambling toward the stairs. She came up short as she collided with someone's chest.

She looked up, blinking.

"Do you know what I hate most about being a mercenary, Princess?" Denth asked quietly, grabbing her arm. "Fulfilling the stereotypes. Everyone assumes that they can't trust you. The thing is, they really can't."

"We do what we're paid to," Tonk Fah said, stepping up behind her.

"It's not exactly the most desirable work," Denth said, holding her tightly. "But the money is good. I was hoping we wouldn't have to do this. Everything was going so nicely. Why did you run away? What tipped you off?"

He pushed her forward with a careful hand, still holding her arm, as Jewels and Clod moved down the steps behind him. The stairs groaned beneath the weight.

"You've been lying to me the entire time," she whispered, tears almost unnoticed on her cheeks, heart thumping as she tried to make sense of the world. "Why?"

"Kidnapping is hard work," Denth said.

"Terrible business," Tonk Fah added.

"It's better if your subject never even knows they've been kidnapped."

They always kept an eye on me. Staying near. "Lemex . . ."

"Didn't do what we needed him to," Denth said. "Poison was too good a death for that one. You should have known, Princess. With as much Breath as he held . . ."

He couldn't have died from sickness, she realized. *Austre!* Her mind was numb. She glanced at Parlin. *He's dead. Parlin is dead. They killed him.*

"Don't look at him," Denth said, delicately turning her head away from the corpse. "That was an accident. Listen to me, Princess. You'll be all right. We won't hurt you. Just tell me why you ran away. Parlin insisted he didn't know where you had gone, though we knew he spoke to you on the stairs right before you vanished. Did you really leave without telling him? Why? What made you suspect us? Did one of your father's agents contact you? I thought we found all of those when they entered the city."

She shook her head dumbly.

"This is important, Princess," Denth said calmly. "I need to know. Whom did you contact? What did you tell the slumlords about me?" He began to squeeze her arm tightly.

"We wouldn't want to have to break anything," Tonk Fah said. "You Idrians. You break too easily."

What had once seemed lighthearted banter to her now seemed terrible and callous. Tonk Fah loomed in the shadowy lantern light to her right, Denth was a slimmer form in front of her. She remembered his speed, the way he'd slain those bodyguards at the restaurant.

Remembered the way they'd destroyed Lemex's house. Remembered their flippancy toward death. They'd hidden it all behind a veil of humor. Now that Denth had brought another lantern, she could see a couple of large sacks stuffed underneath the stairs; a foot was hanging out of one of them. The boot bore the crest of the Idrian army on its side.

Her father *had* sent people to recover her. Denth had just found them before they found her. How many had he killed? Bodies wouldn't keep for long in this basement. Those two corpses must be relatively new, awaiting disposal somewhere else.

"Why?" she asked again, nearly too stunned to speak. "You seemed like my friends."

"We are," Denth said. "I like you, Princess." He smiled—a genuine smile, not a dangerous leer, like Tonk Fah. "If it means anything, I really am sorry. Parlin wasn't supposed to die—that *was* an accident. But, well, a job is a job. We do what we're paid to do. I explained this all to you several times, I'm sure you recall."

"I never really believed . . ." she whispered.

"They never do," Tonk Fah said.

Vivenna blinked. *Get away quickly. While you still have strength.*

She'd escaped once. Wasn't that enough? Didn't she deserve some peace?

Quickly!

She twisted her arm, slapping it against the back of Tonk Fah's cloak. "Grab—"

Denth, however, was too fast. He yanked her back, covered her mouth, then snatched her other hand, holding it tightly. Tonk Fah stood surprised as Vivenna's dress bled free of color, turning grey, and some of her Breath passed through Denth's fingers and into Tonk Fah's cloak. Yet without a Command, that Breath couldn't do anything. It had been wasted, and Vivenna felt the world around her grow more dull.

Denth released her mouth and slapped Tonk Fah on the back of the head.

"Hey," Tonk Fah said, rubbing his head.

"Pay attention," Denth said. Then he glanced at Vivenna, holding her arm tightly.

Blood seeped between his fingers from her wounded wrist. Denth froze, obviously seeing her bloodied wrists for the first time; the dark cellar had obscured them. He looked up, meeting her eyes. "Aw, hell," he cursed. "You didn't run from us, did you?"

"Huh?" Tonk Fah asked.

Vivenna was numb.

"What happened?" Denth asked. "Was it *him*?"

She didn't respond.

Denth grimaced, then twisted her arm, causing her to yelp. "All right. It looks like my hand has been forced. Let's deal with that Breath of yours first, and then we can have a chat—nicely, like friends—about what has happened to you."

Clod stepped up beside Denth, grey eyes staring forward, empty as always. Except . . . could she see something in them? Was she imagining it? Her emotions were so strained lately that she really couldn't trust her perceptions. Clod seemed to meet her eyes.

"Now," Denth said, face growing harder. "Repeat after me. My Life to yours. My Breath become yours."

Vivenna looked up at him, meeting his eyes. "Howl of the sun," she whispered.

Denth frowned. "What?"

"Attack Denth. Howl of the sun."

"I—" Denth began. At that moment, Clod's fist hit his face.

The blow threw Denth to the side and into Tonk Fah, who cursed and stumbled. Vivenna wrenched free, ducking past Clod—nearly tripping on her dress—and threw her shoulder into the surprised Jewels.

Jewels fell. Vivenna scrambled up the stairs.

"You let her hear the security phrase?" Denth bellowed, sounds of struggle coming from where he was wrestling with Clod.

Jewels gained her feet and followed Vivenna. The woman's foot broke through a step, however. Vivenna stumbled into the room above, then threw the door shut. She reached over, turning the latch.

Won't hold them for long, she thought, feeling helpless. *They'll keep coming. Chasing me. Just like Vasher. God of Colors. What am I going to do?*

She rushed out onto the street, now lit by the dawn light filling the city, and ducked down an alleyway. Then she just kept running—this time trying to pick the smallest, dirtiest, darkest alleyways she could.

36

I WILL NOT leave you, Susebron wrote, sitting on the floor beside the bed, his back propped up by pillows. *I promise.*

"How can you be sure?" Siri asked from her place on the bed. "Maybe once you have an heir, you'll grow tired of life, then give away your Breath."

First of all, he wrote, *I'm still not even sure how I would get an heir. You refuse to explain it to me, nor will you answer my questions.*

"They're embarrassing!" Siri said, feeling her short hair grow red. She turned it back to yellow in an instant.

Secondly, he wrote, *I cannot give away my Breath, not if what I understand about BioChroma is true. Do you think I've been lied to about how Breath works?*

He's getting much more articulate in his writing, Siri thought as she watched him erase. *It's such a shame that he's been locked up his entire life.*

"I really don't know that much about it," she said. "Bio-Chroma isn't exactly something we focus on in Idris. I suspect that half of the things I know are rumors and exaggerations. For instance, back in Idris, they think you sacrifice people on altars in the court here—I heard that a dozen times from different people."

He paused, then continued writing. *Regardless, we argue something that is absurd. I will not change. I am not going to suddenly decide to kill myself. You do not need to worry.*

She sighed.

Siri, he wrote, *I lived for fifty years with no information, no knowledge, barely able to communicate. Can you re-*

ally think that I would kill myself now? Now, when I've discovered how to write? When I've discovered someone to talk to? When I've discovered you?

She smiled. "All right. I believe you. But I still think we have to worry about your priests."

He didn't respond, looking away.

Why is he so cursedly loyal to them? she thought.

Finally, he looked back at her. *Would you grow your hair?*

She raised an eyebrow. "And what color am I to make it?"

Red, he wrote.

"You Hallandren and your bright colors," she said, shaking her head. "Do you realize that my people considered red the most flagrant of all colors?"

He paused. *I'm sorry,* he wrote. *I did not mean to offend you. I—*

He broke off as she reached down and touched his arm. "No," she said. "Look, I wasn't arguing. I was just being flirtatious. I'm sorry."

Flirtatious? he wrote. *My storybook doesn't use this term.*

"I know," Siri said. "That book is too full of stories about children getting eaten by trees and things."

The stories are metaphors meant to teach—

"Yes, I know," she said, interrupting him again.

So, what is flirtatious?

"It's . . ." *Colors! How do I get myself into these situations?* "It's when a girl acts hesitant—or sometimes silly—in order to make a man pay more attention to her."

Why would that make a man pay attention to her?

"Well, like this." She looked at him, leaning forward a bit. "Do you want me to grow my hair?"

Yes.

"Do you *really* want me to?"

Of course.

"Well then, if I must," she said, tossing her head and commanding her hair become a deep auburn red. It flushed midtoss, flaring from yellow to red like ink bleeding into a pool of clear water. Then she made it grow. The ability was more instinctive than conscious—like flexing a muscle. In this case, it was a "muscle" she'd been using a lot lately, since she tended to cut her hair off in the evenings rather than spending the time combing it.

Even as the hair whipped past her face, it grew in length. She tossed her head, one final time—the hair making it feel more heavy, her neck warm from the locks that now tumbled down around her shoulders and down her back, twisting in loose curls.

Susebron looked at her with wide eyes. She met them, then tried a seductive glance. The result seemed so ridiculous to her, however, that she just found herself laughing. She fell back on the bed, newly grown hair flaring around her.

Susebron tapped her leg. She looked over at him, and he stood up, sitting on the side of the bed so that she could see his tablet as he wrote.

You are very strange, he said.

She smiled. "I know. I'm not meant to be a seductress. I can't keep a straight face."

Seductress, he wrote. *I know that word. It is used in a story when the evil queen tries to tempt the young prince with something, though I don't know what.*

She smiled.

I think she must have been planning to offer him food.

"Yeah," Siri said. "Good interpretation, there, Seb. Completely right."

He hesitated. *She wasn't offering food, was she?*

Siri smiled again.

He flushed. *I feel like such an idiot. There is so much that everyone else understands intrinsically. Yet I have only the stories of a children's book to guide me. I've read them so often that it's hard to separate myself—and the way I view them—from the child I was when I first read them.*

He began to erase furiously. She sat up, then laid a hand on his arm.

I know that there are things I'm missing, he wrote. *Things that embarrass you, and I have guesses. I am not a fool. And yet, I get frustrated. With your flirtation and sarcasm—both behaviors where you apparently act opposite to what you want—I fear that I will never understand you.*

He stared with frustration at his board, wiping cloth held in one hand, charcoal in the other. The fire cracked quietly in the fireplace, throwing waves of overbright yellow against his clean-shaven face.

"I'm sorry," she said, scooting closer to him. She wrapped her arms around his elbow, laying her head against his upper arm. He actually didn't seem that much bigger than she, now that she was used to it. There had been men back in Idris who had stood as much as six and a half feet tall, and Susebron was only a few inches taller than that. Plus, because his body was so perfectly proportioned, he didn't seem spindly or unnatural. He was normal, just bigger.

He glanced at her as she rested her head on his arm and closed her eyes. "I think you are doing better than you think. Most people back in my homeland didn't understand me half as well as you do."

He began to write, and she opened her eyes.

I find that hard to believe.

"It's true," she said. "They kept telling me to become someone else."

Who?

"My sister," she said with a sigh. "The woman you were supposed to marry. She was everything the daughter of a king should be. Controlled, soft spoken, obedient, learned."

She sounds boring, he wrote, smiling.

"Vivenna is a wonderful person," Siri said. "She was always very kind to me. It's just that . . . well, I think even she felt that I should have been more reserved."

I can't understand that, he wrote. *You're wonderful. So full of life and excitement. The priests and servants of the palace, they wear colors, but there's no color inside of them. They just go about their duties, eyes down, solemn. You've got color on the inside, so much of it that it bursts out and colors everything around you.*

She smiled. "That sounds like BioChroma."

You are more honest than BioChroma, he wrote. *My Breath, it makes things more bright, but it isn't mine. It was given to me. Yours is your own.*

She felt her hair shift from the deep red into a golden tone, and she sighed softly with contentment, pulling herself a little closer to him.

How do you do that? he wrote.

"Do what?"

Change your hair.

"That one was unconscious," she said. "It goes blond if I feel happy or content."

You're happy, then? he wrote. *With me?*

"Of course."

But when you speak of the mountains, there is such longing in your voice.

"I miss them," she said. "But if I left here, I'd miss you too. Sometimes, you can't have everything you want, since the wants contradict each other."

They fell silent for a time, and he set aside his board, hesitantly wrapping his arm around her and leaning back against the headboard. A blushful tinge of red crept into her hair as she realized that they were still sitting on the bed, and she was snuggling up beside him wearing only her shift.

But, well, she thought, *we are married, after all.*

The only thing that spoiled the moment was the occasional rumbling of her stomach. After a few minutes, Susebron reached for his board.

You are hungry? he wrote.

"No," she said. "My stomach is an anarchist; it likes to growl when it's full."

He paused. *Sarcasm?*

"A poor attempt," she said. "It's all right—I'll survive."

Didn't you eat before you came to my chambers?

"I did," she said. "But growing that much hair is draining. It always leaves me hungry."

It makes you hungry every night? he asked, writing quickly. *And you didn't say anything?*

She shrugged.

I will get you food.

"No, we can't afford to expose ourselves."

Expose what? he wrote. *I am God King—I have food whenever I wish it. I have sent for it at night before. This will not be odd.* He stood, walking toward the doorway.

"Wait!" she said.

He turned, glancing back at her.

"You can't go to the door like that, Susebron," she said, keeping her voice quiet, in case someone was listening. "You're still fully dressed."

He looked down, then frowned.

"Make your clothing look disheveled at least," she said, quickly hiding his writing board.

He undid his neck buttons, then threw off his deep black overrobe, revealing an undergown. Like everything white near him, it gave off a halo of rainbow colors. He reached up, mussing his dark hair. He turned back to her, eyes questioning.

"Good enough," she said, pulling the bedsheets up to her neck, covering herself. She watched curiously as Susebron rapped on the door with his knuckles.

It immediately opened. *He's too important to open his own door,* Siri thought.

He commanded food by putting a hand to his stomach, then pointing away. The servants—barely visible to Siri through the doorway—scuttled away at his order. He turned as the door closed, walking back to sit beside her on the bed.

A few minutes later, servants arrived at the room with a dining table and a chair. They set the table with large amounts of food—everything from roasted fish to pickled vegetables and simmering shellfish.

Siri watched with amazement. *There's no way they fixed it that quickly. They simply had it waiting in the kitchens, should their god happen to grow hungry.*

It was wasteful to the point of extravagance, but it was also wondrous. It bespoke a lifestyle that her people back in Idris couldn't even imagine, one representative of an uncomfortable imbalance in the world. Some people starved; others were so wealthy that they never even *saw* most meals that were made for them.

The servants set only one chair at the table. Siri watched as they brought in plate after plate. They couldn't know what the God King wanted, so they apparently brought him some of everything. They filled the table, then retreated as Susebron pointed for them to go.

The scents were almost too much for Siri in her hungered state. She waited, tense, until the door closed. Then she threw off the sheets and rushed over. She had thought the meals prepared for her were extravagant, but they were nothing compared with this feast. Susebron gestured toward the chair.

"Aren't you going to eat?" she asked.

He shrugged.

She walked over and took one of the blankets from the bed, then spread it on the stone floor. "What looks good to you?" she said, approaching the table.

He pointed at the plate of simmering mussels and several of the breads. She moved these, along with a dish that didn't appear to have any fish in it—a bowl of exotic fruits tossed in some kind of creamy sauce—to the cloth. She then sat down and began eating.

Susebron carefully situated himself on the floor. He managed to look dignified even when wearing only his undergown. Siri reached over and handed him his board.

This is very odd, he said.

"What?" she asked. "Eating on the floor?"

He nodded. *Dining is such a production for me. I eat some of what is on a plate, then servants pull it away, wipe my face, and bring me another one. I never finish an entire dish, even if I like it.*

Siri snorted. "I'm surprised they don't hold the spoon for you."

They did when I was younger, Susebron wrote, flushing. *I eventually got them to let me do it myself. It's hard, when you can't speak with anyone.*

"I can imagine," Siri said between mouthfuls. She eyed Susebron, who ate with small, reserved bites. She felt a slight stab of shame at how fast she was eating, then decided she didn't care. She put aside the fruit dish and fetched several pastries from the table.

Susebron eyed her as she began to eat one after another. *Those are Pahn Kahl tinkfans,* he wrote. *One takes only small bites, making sure to eat a piece of bread between to clear away the taste. They are a delicacy and—*

He broke off as Siri picked up an entire pastry and shoved it into her mouth. She smiled at him, then continued chewing.

After a moment of looking stunned, he wrote on his board again. *You realize that children in the stories who gorged themselves usually ended up being thrown off of cliffs?*

Siri stuffed another crispbread into her mouth beside the first, dusting her fingers and face with powdered sugar in the process, her cheeks bulging.

Susebron watched her, then reached over and took a

whole one himself. He inspected it, then shoved it into his mouth.

Siri laughed, nearly spitting out bits of pastry onto the blanket. "And so my corruption of the God King continues," she said once she could speak.

He smiled. *This is very curious,* he wrote, eating another crispbread. Then another. Then another.

Siri watched him, raising an eyebrow. "One would think that as God King, you would *at least* be able to eat sweets whenever you want."

I have many rules that others need not follow, he wrote as he chewed. *The stories explained this. Much is required of a prince or a king. I would rather have been born a peasant.*

Siri raised an eyebrow. She had a feeling that he'd be surprised if he actually had to experience things like hunger, poverty, or even discomfort. However, she left him his illusions. Who was she to chastise?

You are the one who was hungry, he wrote. *But I am the one doing all the eating!*

"They obviously don't feed you enough," Siri said, trying a slice of bread.

He shrugged, continuing to eat. She watched him, wondering if eating was different for him, with no tongue. Did that affect his ability to taste? He certainly still seemed to like the sweets. Thinking of her tongue made her mind turn to darker topics. *We can't just keep going on like this,* she thought. *Playing around at night, pretending like the world isn't going on without us. We're going to get crushed.*

"Susebron," she said. "I think we need to find a way to expose what your priests have been doing to you."

He looked up, then wrote, *What do you mean?*

"I mean that we should have you try to talk to the common people," she said. "Or maybe some of the other gods. The priests gain all of their power by associating with you. If you choose to communicate through someone else, it would overthrow them."

Do we need to do that?

"Pretend with me for a moment that we do," she said.

Very well, he wrote. *But how, exactly, would I communicate with someone else? I can't exactly stand up and begin shouting.*

"I don't know. Notes, perhaps?"

He smiled. *There is a story about that in my book. A princess trapped in a tower who throws notes out into the ocean waters. The king of the fishes finds them.*

"I doubt the king of fishes cares about our predicament," Siri said flatly.

Such a creature is only slightly less fantastic than the possibility of my notes being found and interpreted correctly. If I threw them out the window, nobody would believe that the God King had written them.

"And if you passed them to servants?"

He frowned. *Assuming that you are right, and that my priests are working against me, then wouldn't it be foolhardy to trust the servants they employ?*

"Perhaps. We could try a Pahn Kahl servant."

None of them attend me, for I am the God King, he wrote. *Besides, what if we did get a servant or two on our side? How would that expose the priests? Nobody would believe a Pahn Kahl servant who contradicted the priests.*

She shook her head. "I suppose you could try making a scene, running away or causing a distraction."

When outside of the palace, I am constantly attended by a troop of hundreds. Awakeners, soldiers, guards, priests, and Lifeless warriors. Do you honestly think I could make any kind of a scene without being rushed away before I could communicate with anyone?

"No," she admitted. "But we have to do something! There has to be a way out of this."

I do not see one. We need to work with the priests, not against them. Perhaps they know more about why the God

Kings die. They could tell us—I can speak to them, using the artisans' script.

"No," Siri said. "Not yet. Let me think first."

Very well, he wrote, then tried another pastry.

"Susebron . . ." she finally said. "Would you consider running away with me? Back to Idris?"

He frowned. *Perhaps,* he finally wrote. *That seems extreme.*

"What if I could prove that the priests are trying to kill you? And what if I could provide a way out—someone to smuggle us from the palace and out of the city?"

The concept obviously bothered him. *If it is the only way,* he wrote, *then I will go with you. But I do not believe that we will get to that point.*

"I hope you're right," she said. *But if you're not,* she thought, *then we're escaping. We'll take our chances back with my family, war or no war.*

37

IN THE SLUMS it could seem like night, even during the full light of day.

Vivenna wandered, aimless, stepping over soiled bits of colorful trash. She knew that she should find a place to hide and stay there. Yet she wasn't really thinking straight anymore.

Parlin was dead. He'd been her friend since childhood. She'd convinced him to come with her on what now seemed the most idiotic of quests. His death was her fault.

Denth and his team had betrayed her. No. They had *never* worked for her. Now that she looked back, she could see the signs. How conveniently they'd found her in the restaurant. How they'd used her to get at Lemex's Breath. How they'd manipulated her, letting her feel that she was in control. They'd just been playing along.

She'd been a prisoner and never known it.

The betrayal felt so much the worse for how she'd come to trust, even befriend, them. She should have seen the warnings. Tonk Fah's joking brutality. Denth's explanations that mercenaries had no allegiances. He'd pointed out that Jewels would work against her own gods. Compared with that, what was betraying a friend?

She stumbled down yet another alleyway, hand on the wall of a brick building beside her. Dirt and soot stained her fingers. Her hair was a bleached white. It still hadn't recovered.

The attack in the slum had been frightening. Getting captured by Vasher had been terrifying. But seeing Parlin, tied to that chair, blood coming from his nose, his cheeks sliced open to reveal the inside of his mouth . . .

She would never forget. Something inside of her seemed broken. Her ability to care. She was just . . . numb.

She reached the end of the alleyway, then looked up dully. There was a wall in front of her. A dead end. She turned to go back.

"You," a voice said.

Vivenna turned, surprised at the speed of her own reaction. Her mind remained shocked, but a carnal part of her was still awake. Capable of defensive instinct.

She stood in a narrow alley like those she had walked down all day. She'd kept to the slums, figuring that Denth would expect her to run for the open city. He knew it better than she did. In her addled mind, staying in the cluttered, quiet slum seemed a much better idea.

A man sat on a small stack of boxes behind her, legs swinging over the sides. He was short, dark-haired, and wore typical slum clothing—a mixture of garments going through various stages of wear.

"You've been causing quite a stir," the man said.

She stood quietly.

"Woman wandering the slums in a beautiful white dress, eyes dark, hair white and ragged. If everyone hadn't been so paranoid following the raid the other day, you'd have been seen to hours ago."

The man seemed faintly familiar. "You're Idrian," she whispered. "You were there, in the crowd, when I visited the slumlords."

He shrugged.

"That means you know who I am," she said.

"I don't know anything," he said. "Particularly not things that could get me into trouble."

"Please," she said. "You have to help me." She took a step forward.

He hopped off his boxes, a knife flashing in his hand. "Help you?" he asked. "I saw that look in your eyes when you came to the meeting. You look down on us. Just like the Hallandren."

She shied back.

"A lot of people have seen you wandering about like a wraith," he said. "But nobody seems to know exactly where to find you. There's quite a search going in some parts."

Denth, she thought. *It's a miracle I've stayed free so long. I need to do something. Stop wandering. Find a place to hide.*

"I figure that someone will find you eventually," the man said. "So I'm going to act first."

"Please," she whispered.

He raised the knife. "I won't turn you in. You deserve at least that much. Besides, I don't want to draw attention to myself. That dress, though. That will sell for a lot, even damaged like it is. I could feed my family for weeks on that cloth."

She hesitated.

"Scream and I'll cut you," he said quietly. "It's not a threat. It's just an inevitability. The dress, Princess. You'll be better without it. It's what is making everyone take notice of you."

She considered using her Breath. But what if it didn't work? She couldn't concentrate, and had a feeling that she wouldn't be able to get the Commands to work. She wavered, but the looming knife convinced her. So, staring straight ahead and feeling like she was someone else, she reached up and began undoing the buttons.

"Don't drop it to the ground," the man said. "It's dirty enough already."

She pulled it off, then shivered, standing only in her underleggings and her shift. He took the dress, then opened her pocket pouch. He frowned as he tossed aside the rope inside of it. "No money?"

She shook her head dully.

"The leggings. They're silk, right?"

Her shift came down to her midthighs. She stooped down, pulling off the leggings, then handed them over. He took them, and she saw a glint of greed—or perhaps something else—in his eyes.

"The shift," he said, waving his knife.

"No," she said quietly.

He took a step forward.

Something snapped inside of her.

"No!" she yelled. "No, no, NO! You take your city, your colors and clothing, and go! Leave me!" She fell to her knees, crying, and grabbed handfuls of refuse and mud, rubbing it on the shift. "There!" she screamed. "You want it! Take it from me! Sell it like this!"

Contrary to his threat, the man wavered. He looked around, then clutched the valuable cloth to his chest and dashed away.

Vivenna knelt. Where had she found more tears? She curled up, heedless of the trash and mud, and wept.

IT STARTED RAINING sometime while she was curled in the mud. It was one of the soft, hazy Hallandren rainfalls. The wet drops kissed her cheek; little streams ran down the sides of the alleyway walls.

She was hungry and exhausted. But with the falling rain came a shred of lucidity.

She needed to move. The thief had been right—the dress had been a hindrance. She felt naked in the shift, particularly now that it was wet, but she had seen women in the slums wearing just as little. She needed to go on, become just another waif in the dirt and grime.

She crawled over to a refuse pile, noticing a bit of cloth sticking from it. She pulled free a muddy, stinking shawl. Or maybe it had been a rug. Either way, she wrapped it around her shoulders, pulling it tight across her chest to offer some measure of modesty. She tried to make her hair black, but it refused.

She sat down, too apathetic to be frustrated. Instead, she simply rubbed mud and dirt into her hair, changing the pale white into a sickly brown.

It's still too long, she thought. *I'll need to do something about that. It stands out. No beggar would keep hair that long—it would be difficult to care for.*

She began to make her way out of the alleyway, then paused. The shawl had become brighter, now that she was wearing it. *Breath. I'll be immediately visible to anyone with the First Heightening. I can't hide in the slums!*

She still felt the loss of the Breath she'd sent into the rope and then the larger amount she'd wasted on Tonk's cloak. Yet she had the greater portion left. She huddled down by the side of the wall, nearly losing control again as she considered the situation.

And then she realized something.

Tonk Fah snuck up on me down in that cellar. I couldn't

feel his Breath. Just like I couldn't feel Vasher's when he ambushed me in my rooms.

The answer felt so easy it was ridiculous. She couldn't feel the Breath in the rope she'd made. She picked it up, tying it around her ankle. Then she took the shawl, holding it in front of her. It was such a pathetic thing, frayed at the edges, its original red color barely peeking through the grime.

"My life to yours," she said, speaking the words Denth had tried to get her to say. "My Breath become yours." They were the same words Lemex had spoken when he'd given her his Breath.

It worked on the shawl too. Her Breath drained from her body, all of it, invested into the shawl. It was no Command—the shawl wouldn't be able do anything—but her Breath, hopefully, would be safe. She wouldn't give off an aura.

None at all. She almost fell to the ground with the shock of losing it all. Where she had once been able to sense the city around her, now everything became still. It was as if it had been silenced. The entire city becoming dead.

Or maybe it was Vivenna who had become dead. A Drab. She stood slowly, shivering in the drizzling rain, and wiped the water from her eyes. Then she pulled the shawl—Breaths and all—close and shuffled away.

38

LIGHTSONG SAT ON the edge of his bed, sweat thick on his brow as he stared down at the floor in front of him. He was breathing heavily.

Llarimar eyed a lesser scribe, who lowered his pen. Servants clustered around the edges of the bedchamber. They had, at his request, woken him up unusually early in the morning.

"Your Grace?" Llarimar asked.

It's nothing, Lightsong thought. *I dream of war because I'm thinking about it. Not because of prophecy. Not because I'm a god.*

It felt so real. In the dream he had been a man, on the battlefield, with no weapon. Soldiers had died around him. Friend after friend. He had known them, each one close to him.

A war against Idris wouldn't be like that, he thought. *It would be fought by our Lifeless.*

He didn't want to acknowledge that his friends during the dream hadn't been wearing bright colors. He hadn't been seeing through the eyes of a Hallandren soldier, but an Idrian. Perhaps that was why it had been such a slaughter.

The Idrians are the ones threatening us. They're the rebels who broke off, maintaining a second throne inside of Hallandren borders. They need to be quelled.

They deserve it.

"What did you see, Your Grace?" Llarimar asked again.

Lightsong closed his eyes. There were other images. The recurring ones. The glowing red panther. The tempest. A young woman's face, being absorbed by darkness. Eaten alive.

"I saw Blushweaver," he said, speaking only of the very last part of the dreams. "Her face red and flushed. I saw you, and you were sleeping. And I saw the God King."

"The God King?" Llarimar asked, sounding excited.

Lightsong nodded. "He was crying."

The scribe wrote the images down. Llarimar, for once, didn't prompt further. Lightsong stood, forcing the images out of his mind. Yet he couldn't ignore that his body felt weak. It was his feast day, and he would have to take in a Breath or he would die.

"I'm going to need some urns," Lightsong said. "Two

dozen of them, one for each of the gods, painted after their colors."

Llarimar gave the order without even asking why.

"I'll also need some pebbles," Lightsong said as the servants dressed him. "Lots of them."

Llarimar nodded. Once Lightsong was dressed, he turned to leave the room. Off once again to feed on the soul of a child.

<hr />

LIGHTSONG THREW A pebble into one of the urns in front of him. It made a slight ringing sound.

"Well done, Your Grace," Llarimar complimented him, standing beside Lightsong's chair.

"Nothing to it," Lightsong said, tossing another pebble. It fell short of the intended urn, and a servant rushed forward, plucking it off the ground and depositing it in the proper container.

"I appear to be a natural," Lightsong noted. "I get it in every time." He felt much better, having been given fresh Breath.

"Indeed, Your Grace," Llarimar said. "I believe that Her Grace the goddess Blushweaver is approaching."

"Good," Lightsong said, throwing another pebble. He hit the target this time. Of course, the urns were only a few feet from his seat. "I can show off my pebble-throwing skills."

He sat on the green of the courtyard, a cool breeze blowing, his pavilion set up just inside the court's gates. He could see the blocking wall, the one that kept him from looking out at the city proper. With the wall in the way, it was a rather depressing sight.

If they're going to lock us in here, he thought, *they could at least give us the courtesy of a decent view out.*

"What in the name of the Iridescent Tones are you doing!*

Lightsong didn't need to look to know that Blushweaver was standing with hands on hips beside him. He threw another pebble.

"You know," he said, "it's always struck me as strange. When we say oaths like that, we use the colors. Why not use our own names? We are, allegedly, gods."

"Most gods don't like their names being used as an oath," Blushweaver said, sitting beside him.

"Then they are far too pompous for my taste," Lightsong said, tossing a pebble. It missed, and a servant deposited it. "I, personally, should find it very flattering to have my name used as an oath. Lightsong the Brave! Or, by Lightsong the Bold! I suppose that's a bit of a mouthful. Perhaps we could shorten it to a simple Lightsong!"

"I swear," she said. "You are getting stranger by the day."

"No, actually," he said. "You *didn't* swear in that particular statement. Unless you're proposing we should swear using the personal pronoun. *You!* So, your line at this point is 'What in the name of You are you doing?' "

She grumbled at him under her breath.

He eyed her. "I certainly don't deserve that yet. I've barely gotten started. Something else must be bothering you."

"Allmother," she said.

"Still won't give you the Commands?"

"Refuses to even speak with me now."

Lightsong threw a pebble into one of the urns. "Ah, if only she knew the refreshing sense of frustration she was missing out on knowing by refusing your acquaintance."

"I'm not that frustrating!" Blushweaver said. "I've actually been rather charming with her."

"Then that is your problem, I surmise," Lightsong said. "We're gods, my dear, and we quickly grow tired of our immortal existences. Surely we seek for extreme ranges in emotion—good or bad, it doesn't matter. In a way, it's the *absolute value* of emotion that is important, rather than the positive or negative nature of that emotion."

Blushweaver paused. So did Lightsong.

"Lightsong, dear," she said. "What in the name of You did that mean?"

"I'm not exactly sure," he said. "It just kind of came out. I can visualize what it means in my head, though. With numbers."

"Are you all right?" she asked, sounding genuinely concerned.

Images of warfare flashed in his mind. His best friend, a man he didn't know, dying with a sword through the chest. "I'm not sure," he said. "Things have been rather strange for me lately."

She sat quietly for a moment. "You want to go back to my palace and frolic? That always makes me feel better."

He tossed a pebble, smiling. "You, my dear, are incorrigible."

"I'm the goddess of lust, for Your sake," she said. "I've got to fill the role."

"Last I checked," he said, "you were goddess of honesty."

"Honesty and honest emotions, my dear," she said sweetly. "And let me tell you, lust is one of the most honest of all emotions. Now, what *are* you doing with those silly pebbles?"

"Counting," he said.

"Counting your inanities?"

"That," Lightsong said, tossing another pebble, "and counting the number of priests who come through the gates wearing the colors of each god or goddess."

Blushweaver frowned. It was midday, and the gates were fairly busy with the comings and goings of servants and performers. There were only occasionally priests or priestesses, however, since they would have been required to come in early to attend their gods.

"Each time a priest of a particular god enters," Lightsong said, "I toss a pebble into the urn representing that god."

Blushweaver watched him toss—and miss—with another pebble. As he'd instructed, the servants picked the pebble up and put it in the proper urn. Violet and silver. To the side, one of Hopefinder's priestesses rushed across the green toward her god's palace.

"I'm baffled," Blushweaver finally said.

"It's easy," Lightsong said. "You see someone wearing purple, you throw a pebble in the urn of the same color."

"Yes, dear," she said. "But *why*?"

"To keep track of how many priests of each god enter the court, of course," Lightsong said. "They've slowed to nearly a trickle. Scoot, would you mind counting?"

Llarimar bowed and then gathered several servants and scribes, ordering them to empty the urns and count the contents of each one.

"My dear Lightsong," Blushweaver said. "I *do* apologize if I've been ignoring you lately. Allmother has been rudely unresponsive to my suggestions. If my lack of attention has caused your fragile mind to snap . . ."

"My mind is quite unsnapped, thank you," Lightsong said, sitting up, watching the servants count.

"Then, you must be so very bored," Blushweaver continued. "Perhaps we can come up with something to entertain you."

"I'm well entertained." He smiled even before the counting results were in. Mercystar had one of the smallest piles.

"Lightsong?" Blushweaver asked. Nearly all of her playful attitude was gone.

"I ordered my priests in early today," Lightsong said, glancing at her. "And to set up position here, in front of the gates, before the sun even rose. We've been counting priests for some six hours now."

Llarimar walked over, handing Lightsong a list of the

gods and the number of priests who had entered wearing their colors. Lightsong scanned it, nodding to himself.

"Some of the gods have had over a hundred priests report for service, yet a couple of them have had barely a dozen. Mercystar is one of those."

"So?" Blushweaver asked.

"So," Lightsong said. "I'm going to send my servants to watch and count at Mercystar's palace, keeping track of the number of priests who are there. I already suspect that I know what they'll find. Mercystar doesn't have fewer priests than the rest of us. They're just getting into the court by a different route."

Blushweaver looked at him blankly, but then cocked her head. "The tunnels?"

Lightsong nodded.

Blushweaver leaned back, sighing. "Well at least you're not insane or bored. You're just obsessed."

"Something's going on with those tunnels, Blushweaver. And it relates to the servant who was murdered."

"Lightsong, we have *much* bigger problems to worry about!" Blushweaver shook her head, holding her forehead as if she could have a headache. "I can't believe that you're still bothering with this. Honestly! The kingdom is about to go to war—for the first time, your position in the assembly is important—and you're worrying about how priests are getting into the court?"

Lightsong didn't respond immediately. "Here," he finally said, "let me prove my point to you."

He reached over to the side of his couch and picked a small box up off the ground. He held it up, showing it to Blushweaver.

"A box," she said flatly. "What a convincing argument you make."

He pulled the top off of the box, leaving a small grey squirrel sitting in his hand. It stood perfectly still, staring forward, fur blowing in the breeze.

"A Lifeless rodent," Blushweaver said. "That's *much* better. I feel myself being swayed already."

"The person who broke into Mercystar's palace used this as a distraction," Lightsong said. "Do you know anything about breaking Lifeless, my dear?"

She shrugged.

"I didn't either," Lightsong said. "Not until I required my priests to break this one. Apparently, it requires *weeks* to take control of a Lifeless for which you do not have the right security phrases. I'm not even sure how the process goes—has something to do with Breath and torture, apparently."

"Torture?" she said. "Lifeless can't feel."

Lightsong shrugged. "Anyway, my servants broke this one for me. The stronger and more skilled the Awakener who created the Lifeless, the more difficult it is to break it."

"That's why we need to get the Commands from Allmother," Blushweaver said. "If something were to happen to her, her ten thousand would become useless to us. It would take years to break that many Lifeless!"

"The God King and some of Allmother's priestesses have the codes as well," Lightsong said.

"Oh," Blushweaver said, "and you think *he* is going to just give them over to us? Assuming we're even allowed to talk to him?"

"I'm just pointing out that a single assassination couldn't ruin our entire army," Lightsong said, holding up the squirrel. "That's not the point. The point is that whoever made this squirrel held quite a bit of Breath and knew what he was doing. The creature's blood has been replaced with ichoralcohol. The sutures are perfect. The Commands controlling the rodent were extremely strong. It's a marvelous piece of BioChromatic art."

"And?" she asked.

"And he released it in Mercystar's palace," Lightsong said. "Creating a distraction so that he could sneak into those tunnels. Someone else followed the intruder, and this second person killed a man to keep him from revealing what he'd seen. Whatever is in those tunnels—wherever they lead—it's important enough to waste Breath on. Important enough to kill for."

Blushweaver shook her head. "I still can't believe you are even worrying about this."

"You said you knew about the tunnels," Lightsong said. "I had Llarimar ask around, and others know of them too. They're used for storage beneath the palaces, as said. Different gods have ordered them constructed at various times during the history of the court.

"But," he continued, excited, "they would also be the perfect place to set up a clandestine operation! The court is outside the jurisdiction of the regular city guards. Each palace is like a little autonomous country! Expand a few of those cellars so that their tunnels connect with others, dig them out past the walls so that you can come and go secretly . . ."

"Lightsong," Blushweaver said. "If something *that* secret were going on, then why would the priests use those tunnels to come into the court? Wouldn't that be a little suspicious? I mean, if you noticed it, how hard could it be to discover?"

Lightsong paused, then flushed slightly. "Of course," he said. "I got so wrapped up in pretending to be useful that I forgot myself! Thank you so much for reminding me that I am an idiot."

"Lightsong, I didn't mean—"

"No, it's quite all right," he said, standing. "Why bother? I need to remember who I am. Lightsong, self-hating god. The most useless person ever granted immortality. Just answer one question for me."

Blushweaver paused. "What question?"

"Why?" he asked, looking at her. "*Why* do I hate being a god? Why do I act so frivolous? Why do I undermine my own authority. Why?"

"I always assumed it was because you were amused by the contrast."

"No," he said. "Blushweaver, I was *like this from the first day*. When I awoke, I refused to believe I was a god. Refused to accept my place in this pantheon and this court. I've acted accordingly ever since. And, if I might say, I've gotten quite a bit more clever about it as the years have passed. Which is beside the point. The thing I must focus on—the important point here—is *why*."

"I don't know," she confessed.

"I don't either," he said. "But whoever I was before, he's trying to get out. He keeps whispering for me to dig at this mystery. Keeps warning me that I'm no god. Keeps prompting me to deal with all this in a frivolous way." He shook his head. "I don't know who I was—nobody will tell me. But I'm beginning to have suspicions. I was a person who couldn't simply sit and let something unexplained slide away into the fog of memory. I was a man who hated secrets. And I'm only just beginning to understand how many secrets there are in this court."

Blushweaver looked taken aback.

"Now," he said, walking away from the pavilion, his servants hurrying to catch up, "if you will excuse me, I have some business to attend to."

"What business?" Blushweaver demanded, rising.

He glanced back. "To see Allmother. There are some Lifeless Commands that need to be dealt with."

39

A WEEK LIVING in the gutters served to drastically change Vivenna's perspective on life.

She sold her hair on the second day for a depressingly small amount of money. The food that she'd bought hadn't even filled her stomach, and she didn't have the strength to regrow the locks. The haircut didn't even have the dignity of being cleanly shorn—it was a ragged job of hackwork, and the remaining hair would have still been a pale white, save for the fact that it was matted and blackened with dirt and soot.

She'd thought about selling her Breath, but wouldn't even know where to go or how to go about it. Besides, she had a strong feeling that Denth would be watching places where she might sell the Breath. Beyond that, she had no idea how to get the Breaths back from her shawl, now that she'd put them into it.

No. She had to remain secret, unseen. Couldn't draw attention to herself.

She sat on the side of the street, holding out her hand to the passing crowds, keeping her eyes down. No offerings came. She wasn't certain how the other beggars did it; their meager earnings seemed an amazing treasure. They knew so much she didn't—where to sit, how to plead. Passers learned to avoid beggars, even with their eyes. The successful beggars, then, were those who managed to draw attention.

Vivenna wasn't certain if she wanted the attention or not. Though the gnawing pain of hunger had eventually driven her out onto busy streets, she was still frightened that Denth or Vasher might find her.

The more hungry she got, the less other worries bothered

her. Eating was a problem for *now*. Being killed by Denth or Vasher was a problem for *later*.

The flood of people in their colors continued to pass. Vivenna watched them without focusing on faces or bodies. Just colors. Like a spinning wheel, each spoke a different hue. *Denth won't find me here,* she thought. *He won't see the princess in the beggar on the side of the street.*

Her stomach growled. She was learning to ignore it. Just as the people ignored her. She didn't feel like she was a true beggar or child of the street, not after just one week. But she *was* learning to imitate them, and her mind felt so fuzzy lately. Ever since she'd gotten rid of her Breath.

She pulled the shawl close. She kept it with her always.

She still hardly believed what Denth and the others had done. She had such fond memories of their joking. She couldn't connect that to what she'd seen in the cellar. In fact, sometimes she found herself rising to seek them out. Surely the things she'd seen had been hallucinations. Surely they couldn't be such terrible men.

That's foolish, she thought. *I need to focus. Why isn't my mind working right anymore?*

Focus on what? There wasn't much to think about. She couldn't go to Denth. Parlin was dead. The city authorities would be no help—she had now heard the rumors of the Idrian princess who had been causing such troubles. She'd be arrested in a heartbeat. If there were any more of her father's agents in the city, she had no idea how to locate them without exposing herself to Denth. Besides, there was a good chance that Denth had found those agents and killed them. He'd been so clever at keeping her captive, quietly eliminating those who could have taken her to safety. What did her father think? Vivenna lost to him, every man he sent to retrieve her vanishing mysteriously, Hallandren inching closer and closer to declaring war.

Those were distant worries. Her stomach growled. There were soup kitchens in the city, but at the first one she'd gone to, she'd spotted Tonk Fah lounging in a doorway across the street. She'd turned and scurried away, hoping he hadn't seen her. For the same reason, she didn't dare leave the city. Denth was sure to have agents watching the gates. Besides, where would she go? She didn't have the supplies for a trip back to Idris.

Perhaps she could leave if she managed to save up enough money. That was hard, almost impossible. Every time she got a coin, she spent it on food. She couldn't help herself. Nothing else seemed to matter.

She'd already lost weight. Her stomach growled again.

So she sat, sweaty and filthy in the meager shade. She still wore only her shift and the shawl, though she was dirty enough that it was difficult to tell where clothing ended and skin began. Her former arrogant refusal to wear anything but the elegant dresses now seemed ridiculous.

She shook her head, trying to clear the fog from it. One week on the street felt like an eternity—yet she knew that she'd only just begun to experience the life of the poor. How did they survive, sleeping in alleyways, getting rained on every day, jumping at every sound, feeling so hungry they were tempted to pick at and eat the rotting garbage they found in gutters? She'd tried that. She'd even managed to keep some down.

It was the only thing she'd had to eat in two days.

Someone stopped beside her. She looked up, eager, hand stretching out further until she saw the colors he wore. Yellow and blue. City guard. She grabbed at her shawl, pulling it closer. It was foolish, she knew—nobody knew about the Breaths it contained. The move was reflexive. The shawl was the only thing she owned, and—meager though it was—several urchins had already tried to steal it from her while she slept.

The guard didn't reach for her shawl. He just nudged her with his truncheon. "Hey," he said. "Move. No begging on this corner."

He didn't explain. They never did. There were apparently rules about where beggars could sit and where they couldn't, but nobody bothered to provide the specifics to the beggars. Laws were things of lords and gods, not the lowly.

I'm already starting to think about lords as if they were some other species.

Vivenna rose and felt a moment of nausea and dizziness. She rested against the side of the building, and the guard nudged her again, prompting her to shuffle away.

She bowed her head and moved along with the crowd, though most of them kept their distance from her. Ironic that they would leave her space now that she didn't care. She didn't want to think about how she smelled—though more than the scent, it was the fear of being robbed that probably kept the others away. They needn't have worried. She wasn't skilled enough to cut purses or pick pockets, and she couldn't afford to get caught trying.

She'd stopped worrying about the morality of stealing days ago. Even before leaving the slum alleys for the streets, she hadn't been so naive as to believe that she wouldn't steal if she were denied food, though she had assumed that it would take her far longer to reach that state.

She didn't head to another corner, but instead shuffled out of the crowds, making her way back into the Idrian slums. Here she'd gained some small measure of acceptance. At least she was considered one of them. None knew that she was the princess—after that first man, nobody had recognized her. However, her accent had earned her a place.

She began to seek out a location to spend the night. That was one of the reasons she'd decided not to continue begging for the evening. It was a profitable time, true, but she was just so tired. She wanted a good place to sleep. She wouldn't have thought that it would make much difference which alleyway one huddled in, but some were warmer than others and some had better cover from the rain. Some were safer. She was beginning to learn these things, as well as who to avoid angering.

In her case, that last group included pretty much everyone—including the urchins. They were all above her in the pecking order. She'd learned that the second day. She'd tried to bring back a coin from selling her hair, intending to save it for a chance at leaving the city. She wasn't certain how the urchins had known that she had coin, but she'd gotten her first beating that day.

Her favorite alleyway turned out to be occupied by a group of men with dark expressions, doing something that was obviously illegal. She left quickly, going to her second-favorite. It was crowded with a gang of urchins. The ones who had beaten her before. She left that one quickly as well.

The third alley was empty. This one was beside a building with a bakery. The ovens hadn't yet been stoked for the night's baking, but they would provide some warmth through the walls in the early morning.

She lay down, curling up with her back against the bricks, clutching her shawl close. Despite the lack of pillow or blanket, she was asleep in moments.

40

SIRI WAS ENJOYING a meal on the court green when Treledees found her. She ignored him, content to pick at the dishes in front of her.

The sea, she had decided, was quite strange. What else could be said of a place that could spawn creatures with such wiggly tentacles and boneless bodies, and yet others

452   BRANDON SANDERSON

with such needly skins? She poked at something the locals called a cucumber, but which—in actuality—tasted nothing like one.

She tried each dish, testing them with her eyes closed, focusing on the flavor. Some hadn't been as bad as the others. She hadn't really liked any of them. Seafood just wasn't appetizing to her.

I would have trouble becoming a true Hallandren, she decided, sipping her fruit juice.

Fortunately, the juice was delicious. The variety, and flavor, of the numerous Hallandren fruits were almost as remarkable as the oddity of its sea life.

Treledees cleared his throat. The God King's high priest was not one accustomed to waiting.

Siri nodded to her serving women, motioning for them to prepare another series of plates. Susebron had been coaching Siri on how to eat with etiquette, and she wanted to practice. Coincidentally, his way of eating—taking small bites, never really finishing anything—was a good one for testing out new dishes. She wanted to become familiar with Hallandren, its ways, its people, its tastes. She'd forced her servants to begin talking to her more, and she planned to meet with more of the gods. In the distance, she saw Lightsong wandering by, and she waved to him fondly. He seemed uncharacteristically preoccupied; he waved back, but didn't come over to visit her.

Pity, she thought. *I would have liked a good excuse to keep Treledees waiting even longer.*

The high priest cleared his throat again, this time more demandingly. Finally, Siri stood, gesturing for her servants to stay behind.

"Would you mind walking with me for a bit, Your Excellency?" she asked lightly. She passed him, moving languidly in a gorgeous violet dress with a gossamer train that trailed through the grass behind her.

He hurried to catch up. "I need to speak to you about something."

"Yes," she said. "I deduced that by the way that you summoned me several times today."

"You didn't come," he said.

"It seems to me that the consort of the God King should not make a habit of responding to demands and hopping to attend upon others whenever she is requested."

Treledees frowned.

"However," she continued, "I will of course make time for the high priest himself, should he come to speak to me."

He eyed her, standing tall and straight-backed, wearing the God King's colors of the day—blue and copper. "You should not antagonize me, Your Highness."

Siri felt a brief flush of anxiety, but caught her hair before it bleached white. "I am not antagonizing you," she said. "I am simply establishing some rules that should have been understood from the beginning."

Treledees got a hint of a smile on his face.

What? Siri thought with surprise. *Why that reaction?*

As they walked, he drew himself up. "Is that so?" he said, his voice turning condescending. "You know very little of what you presume, Your Highness."

Blast! she thought. *How did this conversation get away from me so quickly?*

"I might say the same to you, Your Excellency." The massive black temple of a palace loomed above them, sheer ebony blocks stacked like the playthings of a gigantic child.

"Oh?" he said, glancing at her. "Somehow I doubt that."

She had to force back another spear of anxiety. Treledees smiled again.

Wait, she thought. *It's like he can read my emotions. Like he can see . . .*

Her hair hadn't changed colors, at least not discernibly.

She glanced at Treledees, trying to figure out what was wrong. She noticed something interesting. In a circle around Treledees, the grass seemed just a shade more colorful.

Breath, she thought. *Of course he'd have it! He's one of the most powerful men in the kingdom.*

People with lots of Breath were supposed to be able to see very minute changes in color. Could he really be reading her from such faint reactions in her hair? Was that why he had always been so dismissive? Could he see her fear?

She gritted her teeth. In her youth, Siri had ignored the exercises that Vivenna had done to make sure she had complete control over her hair. Siri was an emotional person, and people had been able to read her regardless of her hair, so she'd figured that there was no point in learning to manipulate the Royal Locks.

She hadn't imagined a Court of Gods and men with the power of BioChroma. Those tutors had been a *whole* lot more intelligent than Siri had credited. As were the priests. Now that she thought about it, it was obvious that Treledees and the others would have studied the meanings of all the shades of hair changes.

She needed to get the conversation back on course. "Do not forget, Treledees," she said. "You are the one who came to see me. Obviously, I have *some* power here, if I could force even the high priest to do as I wish."

He glanced at her, eyes cold. Focusing, she kept her hair the deepest black. Black, for confidence. She met his eyes, and let not even a slight tinge color her locks.

He finally turned away. "I have heard disturbing rumors."

"Oh?"

"Yes. It appears that you are no longer fulfilling your wifely duties. Are you pregnant?"

"No," she said. "I had my women's issue just a couple of days ago. You can ask my servants."

"Then why have you stopped trying?"

"What?" she asked lightly. "Are your spies disappointed to be missing their nightly show?"

Treledees flushed just slightly. He glanced at her, and she still managed to keep her hair perfectly black. Not even a glimmer of white or red. He seemed more uncertain.

"You Idrians," the priest spat. "Living up in your lofty mountains, dirty and uncultured, but still assuming that you're better than us. Don't judge me. Don't judge us. You know nothing."

"I know that you've been listening in on the God King's chamber."

"Not just listening," Treledees said. "The first few nights, there was a spy in the chamber itself."

Siri couldn't mask this blush. Her hair remained mostly black, but if Treledees really did have enough BioChroma to distinguish subtle changes, he would have seen a hint of red.

"I am well aware of the poisonous things your monks teach," Treledees said, turning away. "The hatred into which you're indoctrinated. Do you really think that we'd let a woman from Idris confront the God King himself, alone, unwatched? We had to make certain you weren't intending to kill him. We're still not convinced."

"You speak with remarkable frankness," she noted.

"Merely saying some things that *I* should have established from the beginning." They stopped in the shadow of the massive palace. "You are not important here. Not compared to our God King. He is everything, and you are *nothing*. Just like the rest of us."

If Susebron is so important, Siri thought, meeting Treledees's eyes, *then why are you planning to kill him?* She held his eyes. The woman she'd been a few months ago would have looked away. But when she felt weak, she remembered Susebron. Treledees was orchestrating the plot to subdue, control, and eventually kill his own God King.

And Siri wanted to know why.

"I stopped having sex with the God King on purpose," she said, keeping her hair dark with some effort. "I knew it would get your attention."

In truth, she had simply stopped her little performances each night. Treledees's reaction, fortunately, proved that the priests believed her acting. For that she blessed her luck. They might still be unaware that she could communicate with Susebron. She was extra careful to whisper at night, and had even taken to writing things herself, to keep up the charade.

"You must produce an heir," Treledees said.

"Or what? Why are you so eager, Treledees?"

"It is none of your concern," he said. "Suffice it to say that I have obligations that you cannot comprehend. I am subject to the gods, and I do their will, *not* yours."

"Well you're going to have to bend on that last part if you want your heir," Siri said.

Treledees obviously did not like how the conversation was going. He glanced at her hair. And, somehow, she kept it from showing even a slight bit of uncertainty. He looked back at her eyes.

"You can't kill me, Treledees," she said. "Not if you want a royal heir. You can't bully me or force me. Only the God King could do that. And, we know how *he* is."

"I don't know what you mean," Treledees said flatly.

"Oh, come now," Siri said. "Did you honestly expect me to sleep with the man and not find out he has no tongue? That he's virtually a child? I doubt he can even go to the privy without help from some servants."

Treledees flushed with anger.

He really does care, Siri noted abstractedly. *Or, at least, insulting his God King insults him. He's more devoted than I would have expected.*

So it probably wasn't about money. She couldn't be sure, but she suspected that this was not the type of man to sell out his religion. Whatever the reasons for what was happening inside the palace, it probably had to do with true conviction.

Revealing what she knew about Susebron was a gamble. She figured that Treledees would guess anyway, and so it would be better to indicate that she thought Susebron a fool with the mind of a child. Give away one bit of information, but also mislead with another. If they assumed that she thought Susebron a fool, they wouldn't suspect a conspiracy between her and her husband.

Siri wasn't certain if she was doing the right thing. But she needed to learn, or Susebron would die. And the only way to learn was to do. She didn't have much, but she *did* have one thing that the priests wanted: her womb.

It seemed that she could hold it for ransom effectively, for Treledees suppressed his anger and maintained a semblance of calm. Turning from her, he glanced up at the palace. "Do you know much about the history of this kingdom? After your family departed, of course."

Siri frowned, surprised at the question. *More than you probably think,* she thought. "Not really," she said out loud.

"Lord Peacegiver left us with a challenge," Treledees said. "He gave us the treasure our God King now holds, a wealth of BioChromatic Breath such as nobody had ever seen. Over fifty thousand Breaths. He told us to keep them safe." Treledees turned back to her. "And he warned us not to use it."

Siri felt a slight shiver.

"I do not expect you to understand what we have done," Treledees said. "But it was necessary."

"Necessary to keep a man in bondage?" Siri said. "To deprive him of the ability to speak, to make a permanent child out of a grown man? He didn't even understand what he was supposed to do with a woman!"

"It was necessary," Treledees said, jaw set. "You Idrians. You don't even try to understand. I've had dealings with your father for years, and I sense the same ignorant prejudice in him."

He's baiting me, Siri thought, keeping her emotions in check. It was harder than she'd expected. "Believing in Austre instead of your living gods is not ignorance. After all, you're the ones who abandoned our faith and took an easier path."

"We follow the god who came to protect us when your Austre—an unseen, unknown thing—abandoned us to the destroyer Kalad. Peacegiver returned to life with a specific purpose—to stop the conflict between men, to bring peace again to Hallandren."

He glanced at her. "His name is holy. *He* is the one who gave us life, Vessel. And he only asked one thing of us: to care for his power. He died to give it to us, but demanded that it be held in case he should Return again and need it. We couldn't let it be used. We couldn't let it be profaned. Not even by our God King."

He fell silent.

So how do you get that treasure away from him to pass on? she thought. She was tempted to ask. Would that be giving away too much?

Finally, Treledees continued. "I see now why your father sent you instead of the other one. We should have studied all of the daughters, not just the first. You are far more capable than we had been led to believe." The statement surprised her, but she kept her hair in check. Treledees sighed, looking away. "What are your demands? What will it take to make you return to your . . . duties each night?"

"My servants," she said. "I want to replace my main serving women with the women from Pahn Kahl."

"You are displeased with your serving women?"

"Not particularly," Siri said. "I simply feel that I have more in common with the women of Pahn Kahl. They, like me, are living in exile from their own people. Besides, I like the browns they wear."

"Of course," Treledees said, obviously thinking her Idrian prejudices were behind the request.

"The Hallandren girls can continue to serve in the roles that the Pahn Kahl women did," Siri said. "They don't have to leave me completely—in fact, I still want to talk to some of them. However, the main women who are with me always, they are to be from Pahn Kahl."

"As I said," Treledees said. "It shall be done. You'll return to your efforts, then?"

"For now," Siri said. "That will earn you a few more weeks."

Treledees frowned, but what could he really do? Siri smiled at him, then turned and walked away. However, she found herself dissatisfied with the way the conversation had gone. She'd achieved a victory—but at the cost of antagonizing Treledees even further.

I doubt he would have taken a liking to me, no matter how hard I tried, she decided, sitting down in her pavilion. *This is probably the better way.*

She still didn't know what was going to happen to Susebron; at least she had confirmed that manipulating the priests was possible. That meant something, though she knew she was treading dangerous ground. She turned back to her meal, ready to try another round of seafood. She did her best to learn about Hallandren, but if it came down to Susebron's life, she was going to get him out. She hoped that giving Bluefingers's Pahn Kahl a more prominent role in her service would facilitate that escape. She hoped.

With a sigh, she raised the first bit of food to her lips and continued with her tasting.

41

VIVENNA PRESENTED HER coin.

"One bit?" Cads asked. "That's all? One *single* bit?" He was among the dirtiest men she'd met, even in the streets. He liked fancy clothing, though. It was his style— worn and dirty clothing in the latest designs. He seemed to think it was funny. A mockery of the highborn.

He turned her coin over in his grime-covered fingers. "One bit," he repeated.

"Please," Vivenna whispered. They stood at the mouth of an alley at the back of two restaurants. Just inside the alley, she could see urchins rooting in the garbage. Fresh garbage from *two* restaurants. She salivated.

"I find it hard to believe, lady girly," he said, "that *this* is all you made today."

"Please, Cads," she said again. "You know . . . you know I don't beg well." It was starting to rain. Again.

"You should do better," he said. "Even the children can bring me at least two."

Behind him, the fortunates who had pleased him continued to feast. It smelled so good. Or maybe that was the restaurants.

"I haven't eaten in days," she whispered, blinking away the rain.

"Then do better tomorrow," he said, shooing her away.

"My coin—"

Cads immediately waved for his toughs as she reached toward him. Vivenna shied away reflexively, stumbling.

"Two tomorrow," Cads said, walking into his alleyway. "I have to pay the restaurant owners, you know. Can't let you eat for free."

Vivenna stood, staring at him. Not because she thought she could get him to change his mind. But because she just had trouble making her mind understand. It was her last chance for food this day. One bit wouldn't buy anything more than a mouthful elsewhere, but here—last time—it had allowed her to eat until she was full.

That had been a week ago. How long had she been on the streets now? She didn't know. She turned, dully, and pulled her shawl tight. It was dusk. She should go beg some more.

She couldn't. Not after losing that bit. She felt shaken, as if her most valuable possession had been stolen.

No. *No.* She still had that. She pulled the shawl close.

Why was it important? She had trouble remembering.

She shuffled back toward the Highlands. Her home. A part of her realized that she shouldn't feel so distant from the person she had been. She was a princess, wasn't she? But she felt so sick lately, sick enough that she didn't even think she could feel the hunger anymore. It was all so wrong. So very, very wrong.

She entered the slums and crept along, careful to keep her head bowed, her back cowed, lest someone take offense at her. She hesitated as she walked, however, passing a street to her right. It was where the whores waited, protected from the drizzle by an awning.

Vivenna stared at them, standing in their revealing clothing. It was only two streets into the slum, a place that wasn't too threatening for outsiders. Everyone knew not to rob a man on his way to visit the whores. The slumlords didn't like it when their customers got scared away. Bad for business, as Denth might say.

Vivenna stood for a long moment. The whores looked fed. They weren't dirty. Several of them laughed. She could join them. An urchin had spoken of it the other day, mentioned that she was still young. He'd wanted her to come to the slumlord with him, hoping to get some coin for recruiting a willing girl.

It was so tempting. Food. Warmth. A dry bed.

Blessed Austre, she thought, shaking herself. *What am I thinking? What is wrong with my mind?* It was so hard to focus. As if she were in a trance all the time.

She forced herself to keep moving, stumbling away from the women. She wouldn't do that. Not yet.

Not yet.

Oh, Lord of Colors, she thought with horror. *I need to get out of this city. Better for me to die, starving on the road back to Idris—better to get taken by Denth and tortured—than to end up in the brothel.*

However, much like the morality of stealing, the morality of using her body seemed much vaguer to her now, when her hunger was such a constant need. She made her way to her latest alleyway. She'd been kicked out of the others. But this one was good. It was secluded, yet often filled with younger urchins. Their company made her feel better, though she knew they searched her at night for coins.

I can't believe how tired I am . . . she thought, head spinning, putting her hand against the wall. She took a few deep breaths. The dizzy spells struck often these days.

She started forward again. The alleyway was empty, everyone else staying out in the evening to try for a few extra coins. She took the best of the spots—an earthen mound which had managed to grow a small tuft of grass. There weren't even that many lumps in the dirt, though it would be wet with mud from the light rain. She didn't care about that.

Shadows darkened the alleyway behind her.

Her reaction was immediate. She started to run. Living on the streets taught quick lessons. Weak as she was, in her panic she managed a burst of speed. Then another shadow stepped across the other end of the alley ahead of her. She froze, then turned to see a group of thugs moving up the alleyway behind her.

At their back was the man who had robbed her a few weeks ago, the one who had taken her dress. He looked chagrined. "Sorry, Princess," he said. "Bounty just got too high. Took me blasted long enough to find you, though. You did a great job of hiding."

Vivenna blinked. And then she simply let herself slide down to the ground.

I just can't take any more, she thought, wrapping her arms around herself. She was exhausted. Mentally, emotionally, completely. In a way, she was glad it was over. She didn't know what the men would do to her, but she did know it was over. Whomever they sold her to wouldn't be careless enough to let her escape again.

The thugs clustered around her. She heard one mention taking her to Denth. Rough hands grabbed her arm, towing her to her feet. She followed with head bowed. They led her out onto the main street. It was growing dim, but no urchins or beggars made their way toward the alley.

I should have realized, she thought. *It was too deserted.*

Everything, finally, overwhelmed her. She couldn't summon the energy to care about escaping, not again. A part of her, deep inside, realized that her tutors had been right. When you were weak and hungry, it was hard to summon the energy to care about anything, even escape.

She had trouble remembering her tutors now. She had trouble even remembering what it was like to not be hungry.

The thugs stopped walking. Vivenna looked up, blinking away her dizziness. There was something in the dark, wet street in front of them. A black sword. The weapon, silver sheath and all, had been rammed into the dirt.

The street grew still. One of the thugs stepped forward, pulling the sword from the ground. He undid the sheath clasp. Vivenna felt a sudden nausea, more of a memory than a real sensation. She stumbled back, horrified.

The other thugs, transfixed, gathered up around their friend. One of them reached for the hilt.

The man carrying the sword struck. He swung the weapon, sheath and all, into the face of his friend. A black smoke began to twist off the sword, rising from the tiny sliver of blade that was visible.

Men cried out, each one scrambling for the sword. The man holding it continued to swing, the weapon hitting with far more force and damage than it should have. Bones broke, blood began to run on the cobblestones. The man continued to attack, moving with terrible speed. Vivenna, still stumbling backward, could see his eyes.

They were terrified.

He killed his last friend—the one who had robbed her on that day that now seemed so long ago—by slamming the sheathed sword down against the man's back. Bones cracked. By now, the clothing on the sword wielder's arm had disintegrated, and a blackness—like vines growing on a wall—had twisted up around his shoulder. Black, pulsing veins that bulged out of the skin. The man screamed a piercing, desperate cry.

Then he twisted the sword around and rammed it, sheath and all, through his chest. It cut skin and flesh, though the sheath itself didn't look sharpened. The man stumbled to his knees, then slumped backward, twitching, staring up into the air as the black veins on his arm began to evaporate. He died like that, kneeling, held upright by the sword that came out through his back, propping him up from behind.

Vivenna stood alone on a street littered with corpses. A figure descended from a rooftop, lowered by two twisting lengths of animated rope. He landed softly, ropes falling dead. He passed Vivenna, ignoring her, and grabbed the sword. He paused for a moment, then did up the clasp and pulled the weapon—sheath and all—free from the corpse.

The dead man finally fell to the ground.

Vivenna stared dully ahead. Then, numb, she sat down in the street. She didn't even flinch as Vasher picked her up and slung her over his shoulder.

42

HER GRACE IS not interested in seeing you," the priestess said, maintaining a reverent posture.

"Well I'm not interested in her uninterest," Lightsong said. "Perhaps you should ask her again, just to be sure."

The priestess bowed her head. "My pardons, Your Grace, but I have already asked fourteen times. Goddess Allmother is growing impatient with your requests, and she instructed me not to respond to them anymore."

"Did she give the same command to the other priestesses?"

The priestess paused. "Well, no, Your Grace."

"Wonderful," Lightsong said. "Send for one of them. Then send *her* to ask Allmother if she will see me."

The priestess sighed audibly; Lightsong considered that something of a victory. Allmother's priests were among the most pious—and most humble—in the court. If he could annoy them, he could annoy anyone.

He waited, hands on hips, as the priestess went to do his bidding. Allmother could give them orders and commands, but she couldn't tell them to completely ignore Lightsong. After all, he was a god too. As long as he asked them to do something other than what Allmother had explicitly forbidden, they had to obey.

Even if it annoyed their goddess.

"I'm developing a new skill," Lightsong said. "Irritation by proxy!"

Llarimar sighed. "What about your speech to Goddess Blushweaver a few days ago, Your Grace? It seemed to imply that you were *not* going to annoy people as much."

"I said nothing of the sort," Lightsong said. "I simply said that I was coming to recognize within myself a little more of the person I used to be. That doesn't mean I'm going to discard all the progress I've made over the last few years."

"Your sense of self-awareness is remarkable, Your Grace."

"I know! Now, hush. The priestess is coming back."

Indeed, the woman approached and bowed before Lightsong on the grass. "My apologies, Your Grace. Our goddess, however, has now requested that *no* priestess be allowed to ask her if you can come in to see her."

"Did she tell them that they couldn't ask if she would come out here?"

"Yes, Your Grace," the priestess said. "And every other phrasing that would imply asking her to come within Your Grace's proximity, or communicate with him by letter, or relay messages from him in any form."

"Hum," he said, tapping his chin. "She's getting better. Well, I guess there's nothing to be done."

The priestess relaxed visibly.

"Scoot, set up my pavilion here in front of her palace," Lightsong said. "I'm going to be sleeping here tonight."

The priestess looked up.

"You're going to do *what*?" Llarimar asked.

Lightsong shrugged. "I'm not moving until I meet with her. That means staying until she acknowledges me. It's been over a week! If she wants to be stubborn, then I'll prove that I can be *equally* stubborn." He eyed the priestess. "I'm quite practiced at it, you know. Comes from being an insufferable buffoon, and all. I don't suppose she forbade you from allowing squirrels into the building?"

"Squirrels, Your Grace?" the woman asked.

"Excellent," Lightsong said, sitting down as his servants erected the pavilion. He pulled the Lifeless squirrel from its box and held it forward.

"Almond grass," he said quietly, giving the new Command he'd had his people imprint on the Lifeless. Then he spoke louder, so that the priestess could hear. "Go into the building, search out the Returned who lives in it, and run around in circles squeaking as loudly as you can. Don't let anyone catch you. Oh, and destroy as much furniture as you can." Then, more quietly, he repeated, "Almond grass."

The squirrel immediately jumped off his hand and shot toward the palace. The priestess twisted her head to follow it, horrified. The squirrel began to screech with a sound that seemed amazingly un-squirrel-like. It disappeared into the building, slipping between the legs of a startled guard.

"What a delightful afternoon it's becoming," Lightsong said, reaching for a handful of grapes as the priestess rushed after the squirrel.

"It won't be able to follow all of those orders, Your Grace," Llarimar said. "It has the mind of a squirrel, despite the power that Breath gives it to obey Commands."

Lightsong shrugged. "We shall see."

He began to hear shouts of annoyance from inside the palace. He smiled.

It took longer than he had expected. Allmother was stubborn, as proved by Blushweaver's complete inability to manipulate her. As he sat—idly listening to a group of musicians—a priestess occasionally checked on him. Several hours passed. He didn't eat or drink very much so he didn't need to visit the privy.

He ordered his musicians to play louder. He had picked a group with a lot of percussion.

Finally, a frazzled-looking priestess came out of the palace. "Her Grace will see you," the woman said, bowing before Lightsong

"Hum?" Lightsong said. "Oh, that. Do I have to go now? Can't I finish listening to this song?"

The priestess glanced up. "I—"

"Oh, very well then," Lightsong said, rising.

⸺⸺⸺

ALLMOTHER WAS STILL in her audience chamber. Lightsong hesitated in the doorway—which, like those in every palace, was designed at the godly scale. He frowned to himself.

People still waited in a line and Allmother sat on a throne at the front of the room. She was stocky for a goddess, and he had always considered her white hair and wrinkled face an oddity within the pantheon. In bodily age, she was the oldest of the gods.

It had been a while since he'd come to visit her. In fact . . . *The last time I was here was the night before Calmseer gave up her Breath,* he realized. *That evening, years ago, when we shared what would be her last meal.*

He'd never come back. What would have been the point? They'd only gotten together in the first place because of Calmseer. On most of those occasions, Allmother had been quite vocal about what she thought of Lightsong. At least she was honest.

That was more than he could say for himself.

She didn't acknowledge him as he entered. She continued to sit, a little stooped over, listening to the man presenting his petition. He was middle-aged and stood awkwardly, leaning on a walking staff.

". . . my children are starving now," he said. "I cannot afford the food. I figured if my leg worked, I could go back to the docks." He looked down.

"Your faith is commendable," Allmother said. "Tell me, how did you lose the use of your leg?"

"A fishing accident, Your Grace," the man said. "I came down from the highlands a few years back, when early frosts took my crops. I took a job on one of the stormrunners—the ships that go out during the spring tempests, catching fish when others remain in the harbor. The accident crushed a barrel against me leg. Nobody will take me on to work the boats, not with a lame leg."

Allmother nodded.

"I wouldn't have come to you," he said. "But with my wife sick and my daughter crying with such hunger . . ."

Allmother reached a hand out, laying it on the man's shoulder. "I understand your difficulties, but your problems are not as severe as you may think. Go and speak with my high priest. I have a man on the docks who owes me allegiance. You have two good hands; you will be put to work sewing nets."

The man looked up, hope glimmering in his eyes.

"We will send you back with enough food to care for your family until you learn your new trade," Allmother said. "Go with my blessing."

The man rose, then fell back to his knees and began to cry. "Thank you," he whispered. "Thank you."

Priests walked forward and led the man away. The room fell still, and Allmother looked over, meeting Lightsong's eyes. She nodded to the side, where a priest stepped up, holding a small bundle of fur tied tightly with ropes.

"That is yours, I am told?" Allmother asked.

"Ah, yes," Lightsong said, flushing slightly. "Terribly sorry. It kind of got away from me."

"With an accidental Command to find me?" Allmother asked. "Then run around in circles screaming?"

"That actually worked?" Lightsong said. "Interesting. My high priest didn't think the squirrel's brain would be capable of following such complicated Commands."

Allmother regarded him with a stern look.

"Oh," Lightsong said. "I mean, 'Whoops. It completely misunderstood me. Stupid squirrel.' My deepest apologies, honored sister."

Allmother sighed, then waved toward a doorway on the side of the room. Lightsong walked that way and she followed, a few servants trailing. Allmother moved with the stiffness of age. *Is it me, or does she look older than she did before?* That was, of course, impossible. Returned did not age. At least, not the ones who had reached maturity.

Once they were out of earshot and view of the petitioners, Allmother grabbed his arm. "What in the name of the Colors do you think you are doing?" she snapped.

Lightsong turned, raising an eyebrow. "Well, you wouldn't see me, and—"

"Do you intend to destroy what little authority we have left, you idiot?" Allmother asked. "Already, people in the city are saying that the Returned are growing weak, that the best of us died years ago."

"Maybe they're right."

Allmother scowled. "If too many of them believe that, then we lose our access to Breaths. Have you considered that? Have you considered what your lack of decorum, your flippancy, could cost all of us?"

"Is that the reason for the show then?" he asked, glancing back through the doorway.

"Once, the Returned didn't just listen to petitions and say yes or no," Allmother said. "They would take the time to hear each person who came to them, then seek to help them as best they could."

"Seems like an awful lot of trouble."

"We're their *gods*. Should a bit of trouble deter us?" She eyed him. "Oh, of course. We wouldn't want to let something as simple as the pains of our people interfere with our leisure time. Why am I even talking to you?" She turned to leave the room.

"I came to give you my Lifeless Commands," Lightsong said.

Allmother froze.

"Blushweaver has control of two sets of the Commands,"

Lightsong said, "which gives her control of half of our armies. That worries me. I mean, I trust her as much as I trust any other Returned. But if war does come, then she'll quickly become the second-most-powerful person in the kingdom. Only the God King would have more authority."

Allmother regarded him with an unreadable expression.

"I figure that the best way to counter her is to have someone else who has two sets of Commands," Lightsong said. "Perhaps it will give her pause. Keep her from doing anything rash."

There was silence in the room.

"Calmseer trusted you," Allmother finally said.

"Her one flaw, I must profess," Lightsong said. "Even goddesses have them, or so it seems. I've found it gentlemanly to never point out such things."

"She was the best of us," Allmother said, glancing out in the direction of her supplicants. "She would meet with people all day. They loved her."

"Bottom line blue," Lightsong said. "That's my core security phrase. Please, take it. I'll tell Blushweaver that you bullied me into giving it to you. She'll be angry at me, of course, but it won't be the first time."

"No," Allmother finally said. "No, I'm not letting you out of this so easily, Lightsong."

"What?" he asked, startled.

"Can't you feel it?" she asked. "Something is happening in the city. This mess with the Idrians and their slums, the increasingly fierce arguments among our priests." She shook her head. "I'm not letting you wiggle out of your part. You were chosen for that place of yours. You're a god, like the rest of us, even if you do your best to pretend otherwise."

"You already have my Command, Allmother," he said with a shrug, walking toward a doorway to leave. "Do what you will with it."

"Verdant bells," Allmother said. "That's mine."

Lightsong froze in midstep.

"Now two of us know both of them," Allmother said. "If what you said earlier was true, then it's better that our Commands be distributed."

He spun. "You were just calling me a fool! Now you entrust me with command of your soldiers? I must ask, Allmother, and please think me not rude. But what in the name of the *Colors* is wrong with you?"

"I dreamed that you would come," she said, meeting his gaze. "I saw it in the pictures a week ago. All week, I've seen patterns of circles in the paintings, all red and gold. Your colors."

"Coincidence," he said.

She snorted quietly. "Someday, you'll have to get over your foolish selfishness, Lightsong. This isn't just about us. I've decided to start doing a better job of things. Perhaps you should take a look at who you are and what you are doing."

"Ah, my dear Allmother," Lightsong said. "You see, the problem in that challenge is the presumption that I haven't *tried* to be something other than what I am. Every time I do, disaster is the result."

"Well, you now have my Commands. For better, or for worse." The aged goddess turned away, walking back toward her room of supplicants. "I, for one, am curious to see how you handle them."

43

VIVENNA AWOKE, SICK, tired, thirsty, starving.

But alive.

She opened her eyes, feeling a strange sensation. Comfort. She was in a comfortable soft bed. She sat up immediately; her head spun.

"I'd be careful," a voice said. "Your body is weak."

She blinked fuzzy eyes, focusing on a figure sitting at a table a short distance away, his back to her. He appeared to be eating.

A black sword in a silver sheath rested against the table.

"You," she whispered.

"Me," he said between bites.

She looked down at herself. She wasn't wearing her shift anymore, but instead had on a set of soft cotton sleeping garments. Her body was clean. She raised a hand to her hair, feeling that the tangles and mats were gone. It was still white.

She felt so strange to be clean.

"Did you rape me?" she asked quietly.

He snorted. "A woman who's been to Denth's bed holds no temptation for me."

"I never slept with him," she said, though she didn't know why she cared to tell him.

Vasher turned, face still framed by the patchy, ragged beard. His clothing was far less fine than her own. He studied her eyes. "He had you fooled, didn't he?"

She nodded.

"Idiot."

She nodded again.

He turned back to his meal. "The woman who runs this building," he said. "I paid her to bathe you, dress you, and change your bedpan. I never touched you."

She frowned. "What . . . happened?"

"Do you remember the fight on the street?"

"With your sword?"

He nodded.

"Vaguely. You saved me."

"I kept a tool out of Denth's hands," he said. "That's all that really matters."

"Thank you anyway."

He was silent for a few moments. "You're welcome," he finally said.

"Why do I feel so ill?"

"Tramaria," the man said. "It's a disease you don't have in the highlands. Insect bites spread it. You probably got it a few weeks before I found you. It stays with you, if you're weak."

She put a hand to her head.

"You probably had a pretty bad time lately," Vasher noted. "What with the dizziness, the dementia, and the hunger."

"Yes," she said.

"You deserved it." He continued to eat.

She didn't move for a long moment. His food smelled so good, but she'd apparently been fed during the fevers, for she wasn't as famished as she might have expected. Just mildly hungry. "How long was I unconscious?" she asked.

"A week," he said. "You should sleep some more."

"What are you going to do with me?"

He didn't reply. "The BioChromatic Breaths you had," he said. "You gave them to Denth?"

She paused, thinking. "Yes."

He glanced at her, raising an eyebrow.

"No," she admitted, looking away. "I put them in the shawl I was wearing."

He stood, leaving the room. She considered running. Instead, she got out of the bed and began to eat his food—a fish, whole and fried. Seafood didn't bother her anymore.

He returned, then stopped in the doorway, watching her ravage the fish bones. He didn't force her out of the seat; he simply took the other chair at the table. Finally, he held up the shawl, washed and clean.

"This?" he asked.

She froze, a bit of fish on her cheek.

He set the shawl on the table beside her.

"You're giving it back to me?" she asked.

He shrugged. "If there really is Breath stored in it, I can't get to it. Only you can."

She picked it up. "I don't know the Command."

He raised an eyebrow. "You escaped those ropes of mine without Awakening them?"

She shook her head. "I guessed that one."

"I should have gagged you better. What do you mean you 'guessed' it?"

"It was the first time I'd ever used Breath."

"That's right, you're of the royal line."

"What does that mean?"

He just shook his head, pointing toward the shawl. "Your Breath to mine," he said. "That's the Command you want."

She laid her hand on the shawl and said the words. Immediately, everything changed.

Her dizziness went away. Her deadness to the world vanished. She gasped, shaking with the pleasure of Breath restored. It was so strong that she actually fell from the chair, quivering like a person having a fit with the wonder of it. It was amazing. She could sense life. Could sense Vasher making a pocket of color around him that was bright and beautiful. She was *alive* again.

She basked in that for a long moment.

"It's shocking, when you first get it," Vasher said. "It's usually not too bad if you take the Breath back after only an hour or so. Wait weeks, or even a few days, and it's like taking it in for the first time."

Smiling, feeling amazing, she climbed back into the seat and wiped the fish from her face. "My sickness is gone!"

"Of course," he said. "You've got enough Breath for at least the Third Heightening, if I'm reading you right. You'll never know sickness. You'll barely even age. Assuming you manage to hang on to the Breath, of course."

She looked up at him in a panic.

"No," he said. "I'm not going to force you to give it to me. Though I probably should. You're far more trouble than you're worth, Princess."

She turned back to the food, feeling more confident. It seemed now as if the last few weeks had been a nightmare. A bubble, surreal, disconnected from her life. Had it really been she who had sat on the street, begging? Had she really slept in the rain, lived in the mud? Had she really considered turning to prostitution?

She had. She couldn't forget that just because she now had Breath again. But had becoming a Drab had a hand in her actions? Had the sickness had a part in it too? Either way, the greatest part had been simple desperation.

- "All right," he said, standing, picking up the black sword. "Time to go."

"Go where?" she asked, suspicious. The last time she had met this man, he'd bound her, forced her to touch that sword of his, and left her gagged.

He ignored her concern, tossing a pile of clothing onto the table. "Put this on."

She picked through it. Thick trousers, a tunic that tucked into them, a vest to go over the tunic. All of various shades of blue. There were undergarments of a less bright color.

"That's a man's clothing," she said.

"It's utilitarian," Vasher said, walking toward the doorway. "I'm not going to waste money buying you fancy dresses, Princess. You'll just have to get used to those."

She opened her mouth, but then shut it, discarding her complaint. She'd just spent . . . she didn't know how long running around in a thin, nearly translucent shift that had only covered her to midthigh. She took the trousers and shirts gratefully.

"Please," she said, turning toward him. "I appreciate this clothing. But can I at least know what you intend to do with me?"

Vasher hesitated in the doorway. "I have work for you to do."

She shivered, thinking of the bodies Denth had shown

her, and of the men Vasher had killed. "You're going to kill again, aren't you?"

He turned back toward her, frowning. "Denth is working toward something. I'm going to block him."

"Denth was working for me," she said. "Or, at least, he was pretending to. All of those things he did, they were at my command. He was just playing along to keep me complacent."

Vasher gave a barking laugh, and Vivenna flushed. Her hair—responding to her mood for the first time since her shock at seeing Parlin dead—turned red.

It felt so surreal. Two weeks on the street? It felt so much longer. But now, suddenly, she was cleaned and fed, and somehow she felt like her old self again. Part of it was the Breath. The beautiful, wonderful Breath. She never wanted to be parted from it again.

Not her old self at all. Who was she, then? Did it matter?

"You laugh at me," she said, turning to Vasher. "But I was just doing the best I could. I wanted to help my people in the upcoming war. Fight against Hallandren."

"Hallandren isn't your enemy."

"It is," she said sharply. "And it is planning to march on my people."

"The priests have good reasons for acting as they do."

Vivenna snorted. "Denth said that every man thinks he's doing the right thing."

"Denth is too smart for his own good. He was playing with you, Princess."

"What do you mean?"

"Didn't it ever occur to you?" Vasher asked. "Attacking supply caravans? Rousing the Idrian poor to rebel? Reminding them of Vahr and his promises of freedom, which were so fresh in their minds? Showing yourself to thug lords, making them think that Idris was working to undermine the Hallandren government? Princess, you say every man thinks he's on the right side, that every man who opposed you was deluding himself." He met her eyes. "Didn't you ever once stop to think that maybe *you* were the one on the wrong side?"

Vivenna froze.

"Denth wasn't working for you," Vasher said. "He wasn't even pretending to. Someone in this city hired him to start a war between Idris and Hallandren, and he's spent these last few months using you to make it happen. I'm trying to figure out why. Who's behind it, and why would a war serve them?"

Vivenna sat back, eyes wide. It couldn't be. He had to be wrong.

"You were the perfect pawn," Vasher said. "You reminded the people in the slums of their true heritage, giving Denth someone to rally them behind. The Court of Gods is a hair's breadth away from marching on your homeland. Not because they hate Idrians, but because they feel like Idrian insurgents have *already* been attacking them."

He shook his head. "I couldn't believe that you didn't realize what you were doing. I assumed you had to be working with him intentionally to start the war." He eyed her. "I underestimated your stupidity. Get dressed. I don't know if we have enough time to undo what you've done, but I intend to try."

⸺⸺⸺

THE CLOTHING FELT strange. The trousers pulled at her thighs, making her feel like she was exposed. It was odd not to have the swishing of skirts at her ankles.

She walked beside Vasher without comment, head bowed, hair too short to even put into a braid. She didn't try to regrow it yet. That would draw needed nourishment from her body.

They passed through the Idrian slum, and Vivenna had

to fight to keep herself from jumping at every sound, looking over her shoulder to see if someone was following her. Was that an urchin wanting to steal the money she'd begged? Was that a group of thugs, wishing to sell her to Denth? Were those shadows grey-eyed Lifeless, come to attack and slaughter? They passed a waif beside the road, a young woman of indeterminable age but with a soot-covered face and bright eyes that watched them. Vivenna could read the hunger in those eyes. The woman was trying to decide whether or not to try stealing from them.

The sword in Vasher's hand was obviously enough to ward the girl away. Vivenna watched her scurry down an alleyway, feeling an odd sense of connection.

Colors, she thought. *Was that really me?*

No. She hadn't even been as capable as that girl. Vivenna had been so naive that she'd been kidnapped without knowing it, then worked to start a war without realizing what she was doing.

Didn't you ever stop to think that maybe you were on the wrong side?

She wasn't sure what to believe. She'd been taken in so quickly by Denth that she was hesitant to accept anything this Vasher said. However, she *could* see signs that some of what he had told her was true.

Denth had always taken her to meet with the less reputable elements in the city. Not only were they the ones a mercenary like him would know, but they would be more likely to prefer the chaos of war. Attacking the Hallandren supplies wouldn't only make it more difficult to administer the war, it would make the priests more likely to attack while they were still strong. The losses would also serve to make them angrier.

It made chilling sense—sense it was hard for her to ignore. "Denth made me think that the war was inevitable," Vivenna whispered as they walked through the slums. "My father thinks it's inevitable. Everyone says it's going to happen."

"They're wrong," Vasher said. "War between Hallandren and Idris has been close for decades, but never inevitable. Getting this kingdom to attack requires convincing the Returned—and they're generally too focused on themselves to want something as disruptive as a war. Only an extended effort—first convincing the priests, then getting them to argue until the gods believed them—would be successful."

Vivenna stared ahead down the dirty streets with their colorful refuse. "I really am useless, aren't I?" she whispered.

Vasher glanced over at her.

"First, my father sent my sister to marry the God King instead of me. I followed, but I didn't even know what I was doing—Denth took me on the very first day I was here. When I finally escaped him, I couldn't make it a month on the street without getting robbed, beaten, and then captured. Now you claim that I've single-handedly brought my people to the edge of war."

Vasher snorted. "Don't give yourself *too* much credit. Denth has been working on this war for a long time. From what I hear, he corrupted the Idrian ambassador himself. Plus there are elements in the Hallandren government—the ones who hired Denth in the first place—who want this conflict to happen."

It was all so confusing. What he said made sense, but Denth had made sense too. She needed to know more. "Do you have any guesses who they might be? The ones who hired Denth?"

Vasher shook his head. "One of the gods, I think—or perhaps a cabal of them. Maybe a group of priests, working on their own."

They fell silent again.

"Why?" Vivenna finally asked.

"How should I know?" Vasher asked. "I can't even figure out *who's* behind it."

"No," Vivenna said. "Not that. I mean, why are you involved? Why do you care?"

"Because," Vasher said.

"Because why?"

Vasher sighed. "Look, Princess. I'm not like Denth; I don't have his ability with words, and I don't really like people in the first place. Don't expect me to chat with you. All right?"

Vivenna shut her mouth in surprise. *If he's trying to manipulate me,* she thought, *he has a very strange way of doing it.*

Their destination turned out to be a run-down building on the corner of a run-down intersection. As they approached, Vivenna paused to wonder exactly how slums like this one came to exist. Did people build them cramped and shoddy on purpose? Had these streets, like others she'd seen, once been part of a better section of town that had fallen into disrepair?

Vasher grabbed her arm as she stood there, then pulled her up to the door and pounded on it with the hilt of his sword. The door creaked open a second later, and a pair of nervous eyes glanced out.

"Get out of the way," Vasher said, testily shoving the door open the rest of the way and pulling Vivenna inside. A young man stumbled back, pressing up against the wall of the hallway and letting Vasher and Vivenna pass. He closed the door behind them.

Vivenna felt as if she should be frightened, or at least angry, at the treatment. However, after what she had been through, it just didn't seem like much. Vasher let go of her and thumped his way down a set of stairs. Vivenna followed more carefully, the dark stairwell reminding her of the cellar in Denth's hideout. She shivered. At the bottom, fortunately, the similarities between cellars ended. This one had a wooden floor and walls. A rug sat in the middle of the room with a group of men sitting on it. A couple of them rose as Vasher rounded the stairs.

"Vasher!" one said. "Welcome. Do you want something to drink?"

"No."

The men glanced uncomfortably at each other as Vasher tossed his sword toward the side of the room. It hit with a clank, skidding on the wood. Then he reached back and pulled Vivenna forward.

"Hair," he said.

She hesitated. He was using her just as Denth had. But rather than make him angry, she obliged, changing the color of her hair. The men watched with awe; then several of them bowed their heads. "Princess," one whispered.

"Tell them you don't want them to go to war," Vasher said.

"I don't," she said honestly. "I have never wanted my people to fight Hallandren. They would lose, almost certainly."

The men turned to Vasher. "But she was working with the slumlords. Why did she change her mind?"

Vasher looked at her. "Well?"

Why did she change her mind? *Had* she changed her mind? It was all too quick.

"I . . ." she said. "I'm sorry. I . . . didn't realize. I've *never* wanted war. I thought it was inevitable, and so I tried to plan for it. I might have been manipulated, though."

Vasher nodded, then pushed her aside. He left her and joined the men as they sat back on the rug. Vivenna remained where she was. She wrapped her hands around herself, feeling the unfamiliar cloth of the tunic and coat.

These men are Idrians, she realized, listening to their accents. *And now they've seen me, their princess, wearing a man's clothing. How is it that I can still care about such things, considering everything else that is happening?*

"All right," Vasher said, squatting. "What are you doing to stop this?"

"Wait," one of the men said. "You expect that to change our minds? A few words from the princess, and we're supposed to believe everything you've been telling us?"

"If Hallandren goes to war, you're dead," Vasher snapped. "Can't you see that? What do you think will happen to the Idrians in these slums? You think things are bad now, wait until you're seen as enemy sympathizers."

"We know that, Vasher," another said. "But what do you expect us to do? Submit to Hallandren treatment of us? Cave in and worship their indolent gods?"

"I don't really care what you do," Vasher said, "as long as it doesn't involve threatening the security of the Hallandren government."

"Maybe we *should* just admit that war is coming and fight," another said. "Maybe the slumlords are right. Maybe the best thing to do is hope that Idris wins."

"They hate us," another of them said, a man in his twenties with anger in his eyes. "They treat us worse than they do the statues in their streets! We're less than Lifeless, to them."

I know that anger, Vivenna realized. *I felt it. Feel it still. Anger at Hallandren.*

The man's words rang hollow to her now. The truth was, she hadn't really felt any ire from the Hallandren people. If anything, she'd felt indifference. She was just another body on the street to them.

Perhaps that's why she hated them. She'd worked all of her life to become something important for them—in her mind, she'd been dominated by the monster that was Hallandren and its God King. And then, in the end, the city and its people had simply ignored her. She didn't matter to them. And that was infuriating.

One of the Idrian men, an older man wearing a dark tan cap, shook his head in thought. "The people are restless,

Vasher. Half the men talk of storming the Court of Gods in anger. The women store up food, waiting for the inevitable. Our youths go out in secret groups, searching the jungles for Kalad's legendary army."

"They believe that old myth?" Vasher asked.

The man shrugged. "It offers hope. A hidden army, powerful enough that it nearly ended the Manywar itself."

"Believing myths isn't what frightens me," another man said. "It's that our youths would even *think* of using Lifeless as soldiers. Kalad's Phantoms. Bah!" He spat to the side.

"What it means is that we're desperate," one of the older men said. "The people are angry. We can't stop the riots, Vasher. Not after that slaughter a few weeks back."

Vasher pounded the floor with a fist. "That's what they want! Can't you fools see that you're giving your enemies perfect scapegoats? Those Lifeless that attacked the slum weren't given their orders by the government. Someone slipped a few broken Lifeless into the group with orders to kill so that things would turn ugly!"

What? Vivenna thought.

"The Hallandren theocracy is a top-heavy structure laden with bureaucratic foolishness and inertia," Vasher said. "It never moves unless someone pushes it! If we have riots in the street, that will be just what the war faction needs."

I could help him, Vivenna thought, watching the reactions of the Idrians. She knew them instinctively in a way Vasher obviously didn't. He made good arguments, but he approached them in the wrong way. He needed credibility.

She could help. But should she?

Vivenna didn't know what to think anymore. If Vasher was right, she'd been played like a puppet by Denth. She believed that was true, but how could she know that Vasher wasn't doing the same thing?

Did she want war? No, of course she didn't. Particularly

The Idrians here in the slums—I've seen their strength. If you tell them that they've been used, maybe they can avoid being manipulated further."

The men fell silent.

"I don't know if everything this man says is true," she said, nodding to Vasher. "But I do know that Idris will not win this war. We should be doing everything we can to prevent a conflict, not to encourage one." She felt a tear on her cheek, and her hair had grown a pale white. "You can see. I . . . no longer have the control a princess and follower of Austre should show. I am a disgrace to you, but please don't let my failure doom you. The Hallandren don't hate us. They barely even notice us. I know this is frustrating, but if you *make* them notice you by rioting and destroying, they will only be shaken into anger against our homeland."

"So we should just roll over?" the younger man asked. "Let them step on us? What does it matter if they do it unintentionally? We still get crushed."

"No," Vivenna said. "There must be a better way. An Idrian is their queen, now. Perhaps, if we give them time, they will get over their prejudice. We *must* focus our energies now on keeping them from attacking!"

"Your words make sense, Princess," said the older man wearing the cap. "But—and forgive me for my ostentation— those of us here in Hallandren find it difficult to care about Idris much anymore. It failed us before we even left, and now we can't really go back."

"We *are* Idrians," one of the others said. "But . . . well, our families here are more important."

A month ago, Vivenna would have been offended. Her sojourn on the streets, though, had taught her a little of what desperation could do to a person. What was Idris to them if their families starved? She could not blame them for their attitude.

"You think you will fare better if Idris is conquered?"

not a war Idris would have a very hard time surviving alone winning. Vivenna had worked so hard to undermine Hallandren's ability to wage war. Why hadn't she ever considered trying to head it off?

I did, she realized. *That was my original plan when I was back in Idris. I'd intended to talk the God King out of war when I became his bride.*

She'd given up on that plan. No, she'd been manipulated into giving up on it. Either by her father's sense of inevitability or by Denth's subtlety—or by both—it didn't really matter. Her initial instinct had been to prevent the conflict. That was the best way to protect Idris; and it was—she now realized—also the best way to protect Siri. She'd practically given up on saving her sister, focusing on her own hate and arrogance instead.

Stopping the war wouldn't protect Siri from being abused by the God King. But it would probably keep her from being used as a pawn or a hostage. It could save her life.

That was enough for Vivenna.

"It's too late," one of the men said.

"No," Vivenna said. "Please."

The men in the circle paused, looking over at her. She walked back to the circle and then knelt before them. "Please do not say such things."

"But Princess," one of the men said, "what can we do? The slumlords rile the people to anger. We have no power compared to them."

"You must have some influence," she said. "You seem like men of wisdom."

"We're family men and workers," another said. "We have no riches."

"But people listen to you?" she asked.

"Some do."

"Then tell them that there *are* more options," Vivenna said, bowing her head. "Tell them to be stronger than I was.

Vasher asked. "If there's war, you'll be treated even worse than you are now."

"There *are* other options," Vivenna said. "I know of your plight. If I return to my father and explain it, perhaps we can find a way to return you to Idris."

"Return us to Idris?" one of the men said. "My family has been here in Hallandren for fifty years now!"

"Yes, but as long as the king of Idris lives," Vivenna said, "you have an ally. We can work with diplomacy to make things better for you."

"The king doesn't care about us," another said sadly.

"I care," Vivenna said.

And she did. She found it strange, but a part of her felt more of a kinship with the Idrians in the city than with those she had left behind. She understood.

"We must find a way to bring attention to your suffering without bringing hatred as well," she said. "We will find a way. As I said, my sister is married to the God King himself. Perhaps through her, he can be persuaded to improve the slums. Not because he's afraid of the violence our people might cause, but because of the pity he feels for their situation."

She continued to kneel, ashamed before these men. Ashamed to be crying, to be seen in the immodest clothing and with ragged, short hair. Ashamed to have failed them so completely.

How could I fail so easily? she thought. *I, who was supposed to be so prepared, so in control. How could I be so angry that I ignored my people's needs just because I wanted to see Hallandren pay?*

"She is sincere," one of the men finally said. "I will give her that."

"I don't know," said another. "I still feel it's too late."

"If that's the case," Vivenna said, still looking at the floor, "what do you have to lose? Think of the lives you could save. I promise, Idris will not forget you any longer.

If you make peace with Hallandren, I will ensure that you are seen as heroes back in our homeland."

"Heroes, eh?" one of them said. "It would be nice to be known as a hero, rather than the ones who left the highlands to live in brazen Hallandren."

"Please," Vivenna whispered.

"I'll see what I can do," one of the men said, standing.

Several of the others voiced agreement. They stood as well, shaking hands with Vasher. Vivenna remained kneeling as they left.

Eventually, the room was empty save for her and Vasher. He sat down across from her.

"Thanks," he said.

"I didn't do it for you," she whispered.

"Get up," he said. "Let's go. I want to meet with someone else."

"I . . ." She sat up on the rug, trying to make sense of her feelings. "Why should I do as you tell me? How do I know that you're not just using me? Lying to me. Like Denth did."

"You don't know," Vasher said, recovering his sword from the corner. "You'll just have to do what I say."

"Am I a prisoner then?"

He glanced at her. Then he walked over and squatted. "Look," he said. "We both agree that war is bad for Idris. I'm not going to take you on raids or make you meet with slumlords. All you have to do is tell people you don't want a war."

"And if I'm not willing to do that?" she said. "Will you force me?"

He watched her for a moment, then swore under his breath, standing. He pulled out a bag of something and tossed it at her. It clinked as it hit her chest and then fell to the floor.

"Go," he said. "Get back to Idris. I'll do it without you."

She just continued to sit, staring. He began to walk away.

"Denth used me," she found herself whispering. "And the worst part is, I still feel like this must all be just a misunderstanding. I feel that he's really my friend, and that I should go to him and find out why he did what he did. Maybe we are all just confused."

She closed her eyes, resting her head on her knees. "But then I remember the things I saw him do. My friend Parlin is dead. Other soldiers sent by my father, stuffed in sacks. I'm so confused."

The room fell silent. "You're not the first one he's taken in, Princess," Vasher finally said. "Denth . . . he's a subtle one. A man like him can be evil to the core, but if he is charismatic and amusing, people will listen to him. They'll even like him."

She looked up, blinking teary eyes.

Vasher turned away. "Me," he said. "I'm not like that. I have trouble talking. I get frustrated. I snap at people. Doesn't make me very popular. But I promise you that I won't lie to you." He met her eyes. "I want to stop this war. That's all that really matters to me right now. I promise you."

She wasn't sure if she believed him. Yet she found herself wanting to. *Idiot,* she thought. *You're just going to get taken in again.*

She hadn't proven herself a very good judge of character. Still, she didn't pick up the bag of coins. "I am willing to help. Assuming it doesn't involve anything more than telling others that I wish to keep Idris from harm."

"Good enough."

She hesitated. "Do you really think we can do it. Stop the war?"

He shrugged. "Maybe. Assuming I can keep myself from beating the Colors out of all these Idrians for acting like idiots."

A pacifist with temper-control issues, she thought ruefully. *What a combination. A little like a devout Idrian*

*princess who holds enough BioChromatic Breath to popu-
late a small village.*

"There are more places like this," Vasher said. "I would
show you to the people there."

"All right," she said, trying not to look at the blade as
she stood. Even now, it had a strange ability to make her
feel sick.

Vasher nodded. "There won't be many people at each
meeting. I don't have Denth's connections, and I'm not
friendly with important people. The ones I know are workers. We'll have to go visit the dye vats, perhaps even some of
the fields."

"I understand," she said.

Without further comment, Vasher picked up his bag of
coins, then led her out onto the street. *And so,* she thought,
I begin again.

I can only hope that this time, I'm on the right side.

44

SIRI WATCHED SUSEBRON with affection as he ate a
third dessert. Their night's meal lay spread out on the
table and floor, some dishes completely devoured, others
barely tasted. That first night when Susebron had ordered
a meal had started a tradition. Now they ordered food every night—though only after Siri did her act for the listening priests. Susebron claimed to find it very amusing,
though she noticed the curiosity in his eyes as he watched
her.

Susebron had proven to have quite a sweet tooth now
that disapproving priests and their sense of etiquette were
absent. "You should probably watch out," she noted as he

finished another pastry. "If you eat too many of those, you will get fat."

He reached for his writing board. *No I won't.*

"Yes you will," she said, smiling. "That's the way it works."

Not for gods, he wrote. *My mother explained it. Some men become more bulky if they exercise a lot and become fat if they eat a lot. That doesn't happen to Returned. We always look the same.*

Siri couldn't offer argument. What did she know of Returned?

Is food in Idris like this? Susebron wrote.

Siri smiled. He was always so curious about her homeland. She could sense a longing in him, the wish to be free of his palace and see the outside. And yet, he didn't want to be disobedient, even when the rules were harsh.

"I really need to work on corrupting you some more," she noted.

He paused. *What does that have to do with food?*

"Nothing," she said. "But it's true nonetheless. You're far too good a person, Susebron."

Sarcasm? he wrote. *I certainly hope that it is.*

"Only half," she said, lying down on her stomach and watching him across their impromptu picnic setting.

Half-sarcasm? he wrote. *Is this something new?*

"No," she said, sighing. "There is truth sometimes even in sarcasm. I don't *really* want to corrupt you, but I do think that you're just too perfectly obedient. You need to be a little more reckless. Impulsive and independent."

It's hard to be impulsive when you are locked in a palace surrounded by hundreds of servants, he wrote.

"Good point."

However, I have been thinking about the things you've said. Please don't be mad at me.

Siri perked up, noting the embarrassment in his expression. "All right. What did you do?"

I talked to my priests, he said. *With the artisans' script.*

Siri felt a moment of panic. "You told them about us?"

No, no, he wrote quickly. *I did tell them I was worried about having a child. I asked why my father died right after he had a child.*

Siri frowned. Part of her wished that he'd let her handle such negotiations. However, she said nothing. She didn't want to keep him pinned down as his priests did. It was his life that was being threatened—he deserved the chance to work on the problem too.

"Good," she said.

You're not mad?

She shrugged. "I was just encouraging you to be more impulsive! I can't complain now. What did they say?"

He erased, then continued. *They told me not to worry. They said everything would be all right. So I asked them again, and again they gave me a vague answer.*

Siri nodded slowly.

It hurts me to write this, but I'm beginning to think that you are right. I've noticed that my guards and Awakeners are staying particularly close lately. We even skipped going to the Court Assembly yesterday.

"That's a bad sign," she agreed. "I haven't had much luck finding out what is going to happen. I've ordered in three other storytellers but none of them had any better information than what Hoid gave me."

You still think it's about the Breath I hold?

She nodded. "Remember what I said about my conversation with Treledees? He talked about that Breath of yours with reverence. To him, it's something to be passed from generation to generation, like a family tapestry."

In one of the children's stories in my book, he wrote, *there is a magic sword. A young boy is given it by his grandfather, and it turns out the sword was an heirloom— the symbol of kingship in the land.*

"What are you saying?" she asked.

Perhaps the entire monarchy of Hallandren is nothing more than a way to guard the Breath. The only way to safely pass Breath between individuals and generations is to use people as hosts. So they created a dynasty of God Kings who could hold the treasure and pass it from father to son.

Siri nodded slowly. "That would mean that the God King is more of a vessel than I am. A sheath for a magic weapon."

Exactly, Susebron wrote, hand moving quickly. *They had to make my family kings because of how much Breath was in that treasure. And they had to give it to a Returned—otherwise their king and their gods might have competed for power.*

"Perhaps. It seems awfully convenient that the God King always bears a stillborn son who becomes Returned . . ."

She trailed off. Susebron saw it too.

Unless the next God King isn't really the son of the current one, he wrote, hand shaking slightly.

"Austre!" Siri said. "God of Colors! That's it. Somewhere in the kingdom, a baby died and Returned. That's why it's so urgent that I get pregnant! They already have the next God King, now they just need to keep up the farce. They marry me to you, hope for a child as quickly as possible, then switch the baby for the Returned one."

Then they kill me and somehow take my Breaths away, he wrote. *And give it to this child, who can become the next God King.*

"Wait. Do infants even Return?" she asked.

Yes, he wrote.

"But, how does an *infant* Return in a way that is heroic, or virtuous, or anything like that?"

Susebron hesitated, and she could tell he didn't have an answer for her. Infant Returned. Among her own people, they didn't believe that a person was chosen to Return because of some virtue they exemplified. That was a Hallandren belief. To her, it seemed a hole in their theology, but she didn't want to challenge Susebron on it further. He already worried about how she didn't believe in his divinity.

Siri sat back. "That doesn't really matter. The real question is more important. If the God Kings are just vessels to hold Breath, then why bother changing them? Why not just leave one man holding the Breath?"

I don't know, Susebron wrote. *It doesn't seem to make sense, does it? Maybe they are worried about keeping a single God King captive that long. Children are easier to control, perhaps?*

"If that's the case, they would want to change *more* often," Siri said. "Some of those God Kings lasted centuries. Of course, it could just have to do with how rebellious they think their king is."

I do everything I'm supposed to! You just complained that I am too obedient.

"Compared to me, you are," she said. "Maybe from their viewpoint, you're a wild man. After all, you did hide that book your mother gave you, and then you learned to write. Perhaps they know you well enough to realize that you weren't going to stay docile. So now that they have an opportunity to replace you, they're intending to take it."

Maybe, he wrote.

Siri thought through their conclusions again. Looked at critically, she could see that they were just speculations. Yet everyone said that the other Returned couldn't have children, and so why would the God King be different? That might just be a means of obfuscating the fact that they were bringing in a new person to be God King when they found one.

That still didn't answer the most important question. What were they going to do to Susebron to get his Breaths away from him?

Susebron leaned back, staring up at the dark ceiling. Siri watched him, noting the look of sadness in his eyes. "What?" she asked.

He just shook his head.

"Please? What is it?"

He sat for a moment, then looked down, writing. *If what you say is true, then the woman who raised me was not my mother. I would have been born to someone random out in the countryside. The priests would have taken me once I Returned, then raised me in the palace as the "son" of the God King they'd just killed.*

Seeing him in pain made her insides twist. She moved around the blanket, sitting beside him, putting her arms around him and resting her head on his arm.

She's the only person to have shown me real kindness in my life, he wrote. *The priests, they revere me and care for me—or, at least, I assumed that they did. However, they never really loved me. Only my mother did that. And now I'm not sure I even know who she is.*

"If she raised you, she's your mother," Siri said. "It doesn't matter who gave birth to you."

He didn't respond to that.

"Maybe she was your real mother," Siri said. "If they were going to bring you to the palace in secret, they might as well bring your mother too. Who better to care for you?"

He nodded, then scribbled on the board with one hand— the other was around Siri's waist. *Perhaps you are right. Though it now seems suspicious to me that she would die as she did. She was one of the few who could have told me the truth.*

This seemed to make him even more sad, and Siri pulled him closer, laying her head on his chest.

Please, he wrote. *Tell me of your family.*

"My father was often frustrated with me," Siri said. "But he did love me. *Does* love me. He just wanted me to do what they thought was right. And . . . well, the more time I spend in Hallandren, the more I wish I had listened to him, at least a little bit.

"Ridger is my older brother. I was always getting him into trouble. He was the heir, and I had him *thoroughly* corrupted, at least until he got old enough to appreciate his duties. He's a little like you. Very kindhearted, always trying to do what is right. He didn't eat as many sweets, though."

Susebron smiled faintly, squeezing her shoulder.

"Between us is Fafen. I didn't really know her that well. She joined a monastery when I was still quite young—and I was glad. It's seen as a duty in Idris to provide at least one child for the monasteries. They're the ones who grow the food for the needy and take care of things that need to be done around the city. Pruning, washing, painting. Anything to be of service."

He reached over. *A little like a king,* he wrote. *Living a life to serve others.*

"Sure," Siri said. "Only they don't get locked up and they can stop doing it, if they want. Either way, I'm glad it was Fafen and not me. I would have gone *crazy* living as a monk. They have to be pious all the time, and are supposed to be the least ostentatious in the city."

Not a good match for your hair, he wrote.

"Definitely," she said.

Though, he wrote, frowning slightly. *It's stopped changing colors so often lately.*

"I've had to learn to control it better," Siri said with a grimace. "People can read me too easily by it. Here." She changed it from black to yellow, and he smiled, running his fingers through its lengthy locks.

"After Fafen and Ridger," Siri said, "there's just the eldest, Vivenna. She's the one you were supposed to marry. She spent her entire life preparing to move to Hallandren."

She must hate me, Susebron wrote. *Growing up knowing she would have to leave her family and live with a man she didn't know.*

"Nonsense," Siri said. "Vivenna looked forward to it. I don't think she *can* feel hatred. She was always just calm and careful and perfect."

Susebron frowned.

"I sound bitter, don't I?" Siri said, sighing. "I don't mean to. I really do love Vivenna. She was always there, watching out for me. But it seemed to me that she made too many efforts to cover up for me. My big sister, pulling me out of trouble, scolding me calmly, then seeing that I wasn't punished as much as I should have been." She hesitated. "They're all probably at home right now, worried sick about me."

You sound like you're worried about them, he wrote.

"I am," she said. "I've been listening to the priests argue in the court. It doesn't sound good, Seb. There are a lot of Idrians in the city and they're being very reckless. The city guard was forced to send troops into one of the slums a few weeks back. That isn't helping reduce tensions between our countries."

Susebron didn't write a response, but instead wrapped his arm around her again, pulling her close. It felt good to be held against him. Very good.

After a few minutes, he pulled his arm away and wrote again, awkwardly erasing first. *I was wrong, you know.*

"About what?"

About one of the things I said earlier. I wrote that my mother was the only person to ever show me love and kindness. That's not true. There's been another.

He stopped writing and looked at her. Then he glanced at the board again. *You didn't have to show me kindness,* he wrote. *You could have hated me for taking you from your family and your homeland. Instead, you taught me to read, befriended me. Loved me.*

He stared at her. She stared at him. Then, hesitant, he leaned down and kissed her.

Oh, dear . . . Siri thought, a dozen objections popping into her head. She found it difficult to move, to resist, or to do anything.

Anything other than kiss him back.

She felt hot. She knew that they needed to stop, lest the priesthood get exactly what they were waiting for. She *understood* all of these things. Yet those objections began to seem less and less rational as she kissed him, as her breathing grew more hurried.

He paused, obviously uncertain what to do next. Siri looked up at him, breathing heavily, then pulled him down to kiss him again, feeling her hair bleed to a deep, passionate red.

At that point, she stopped caring about anything else. Susebron didn't know what to do. But she did. *I really am too hasty,* she thought as she pulled off her shift. *I need to get better at controlling my impulses.*

Some other time.

45

THAT NIGHT, LIGHTSONG dreamed of T'Telir burning. Of the God King dead and of soldiers in the streets. Of Lifeless killing people in colorful clothing.

And of a black sword.

46

V IVENNA CHOKED DOWN her meal. The dried meat tasted strongly of fish, but she had learned that by breathing through her mouth, she could ignore much of the flavor. She ate every bite, then washed the taste away with a few mouthfuls of warm boiled water.

She was alone in the room. It was a small chamber built onto the side of a building near the slums. Vasher had paid a few coins for a day in it, though he wasn't there at the moment. He'd rushed off to deal with something.

She leaned back, food consumed, closing her eyes. She'd reached the point where she was so exhausted that she actually found it difficult to sleep. The fact that the room was so small didn't help. She couldn't even stretch out all the way.

Vasher hadn't been exaggerating when he'd said that their work would be rigorous. Stop after stop, she spoke with the Idrians, consoling them, begging them not to push Hallandren to war. There were no restaurants as there had been with Denth. No dinners with men in fine clothing and guards. Just group after group of tired, working-class men and women. Many of them weren't rebellious and a large number of them didn't even live in the slums. But they were part of the Idrian community in T'Telir, and they could influence how their friends and family felt.

She liked them. Empathized with them. She felt far better about her new efforts than she had about her work with Denth, and so far as she could tell, Vasher was being honest with her. She had decided to trust those instincts. That was her decision, and that decision meant helping Vasher, for now.

Vasher didn't ask her if she wanted to continue. He simply

led her from location to location, expecting her to keep up. And so she did, meeting with the people and begging their forgiveness, despite how emotionally draining it was. She wasn't certain if she could repair what she had done, but she was willing to try. This determination seemed to gain her some respect from Vasher. It was much more reluctantly given than Denth's respect had been.

Denth was fooling me the entire time. It was still hard to remember that fact. Part of her didn't want to. She leaned forward, staring at the bland wall in front of her in the box-like room. She shivered. It was a good thing that she'd been working herself so hard lately. It kept her from thinking about things.

Discomforting things.

Who was she? How did she define herself now that everything she'd been, and everything she'd tried, had collapsed around her? She couldn't be Vivenna the confident princess anymore. That person was dead, left behind in that cellar with Parlin's bloody corpse. Her confidence had come from naïveté.

Now she knew how easily she had been played. She knew the cost of ignorance, and she had glimpsed the grim truths of real poverty.

Yet, she also couldn't be *that* woman—the waif of the streets, the thief, the beaten-down wretch. That wasn't her. She felt as if those weeks had been a dream, brought on by the stress of isolation and trauma of her betrayal, fueled by becoming a Drab and being suffocated by disease. To pretend that was the real her would be to parody those who truly lived on the streets. The people she'd hidden among and tried to imitate.

Where did that leave her? Was she the penitent, quiet princess who knelt with bowed head, pleading with the peasants? This, too, was partially an act. She really did feel sorry. However, she was using her stripped pride as a tool. That wasn't her.

Who was she?

She stood up, feeling cramped in the tiny room, and pushed open the door. The neighborhood outside wasn't quite a slum, but it wasn't rich either. It was simply a place where people lived. There were enough colors along the street to be welcoming, but the buildings were small and held a number of families each.

She walked along the street, careful not to stray too far from the room Vasher had rented. She passed trees, admiring their blooms.

Who was she really? What was left, when one stripped away the princess and the hatred of Hallandren? She was determined. That part of her, she liked. She'd forced herself to become the woman she needed to be in order to marry the God King. She'd worked hard, sacrificing, to reach her goal.

She was also a hypocrite. Now she knew what it was to be truly humble. Compared to that, her former life seemed more brash and arrogant than any colorful skirt or shirt.

She did believe in Austre. She loved the teachings of the Five Visions. Humility. Sacrifice. Seeing another's problems before your own. Yet she was beginning to think that she—along with many others—had taken this belief too far, letting her desire to seem humble become a form of pride itself. She now saw that when her faith had become about clothing instead of people, it had taken a wrong turn.

She wanted to learn to Awaken. Why? What did that say about her? That she was willing to accept a tool her religion rejected, just because it would make her powerful?

No, that wasn't it. At least, she hoped it wasn't.

Looking back on her recent life, she felt frustrated at her frequent helplessness. And *that* felt like part of who she really was. The woman who would do anything to be sure she wasn't helpless. That was why she'd studied so hard with the tutors in Idris. That was also why she wanted to learn how to Awaken. She wanted as much information as she could get and wanted to be prepared for the problems that might come at her.

She wanted to be capable. That might be arrogant, but it was the truth. She wanted to learn everything she could about how to survive in the world. The most humiliating aspect of her time in T'Telir was her ignorance. She wouldn't make that mistake again.

She nodded to herself.

Time to practice, then, she thought, returning to the room. Inside, she pulled out a piece of rope—the one that Vasher had used to tie her up, the first thing that she had Awakened. She'd since retrieved the Breath from it.

She went back outside, holding the rope between her fingers, twisting it, thinking. *The Commands that Denth taught me were simple phrases. Hold things. Protect me.* He'd implied that the intent was important. When she'd Awakened her bonds, she'd made them move as if part of her body. It was more than just the Command. The Command brought the life, but the intent—the instructions from her mind—brought focus and action.

She stopped beside a large tree with thin, blossom-laden branches that drooped toward the ground. She stood beside a branch, touched the bark of the tree's trunk itself to use its color. She held out the rope to the branch. "Hold things," she Commanded, reflexively letting out some of her Breath. She felt an instant of panic as her sense of the world dimmed.

The rope twitched. However, instead of drawing color from the tree, the Awakening pulled color from her tunic. The garment bled grey, and the rope moved, wrapping like a snake around the branch. Wood cracked slightly as the rope pulled tight. However, the other end of the rope twisted in an odd pattern, writhing.

Vivenna watched, frowning, until she figured out what was happening. The rope was twisting around her hand, trying to hold it as well.

"Stop," Vivenna said.

Nothing happened. It continued to pull tight.

"Your Breath to mine," she Commanded.

The rope stopped twisting and her Breath returned. She shook the rope free. *All right,* she thought. *"Hold things" works, but it's not very specific. It will wrap around my fingers as well as the thing I want it to tie up. What if I tried something else?*

"Hold that branch," she Commanded. Again, Breath left her. More of it this time. Her trousers drained of color, and the rope end twisted, wrapping around the branch. The rest of it remained still.

She smiled in satisfaction. *So the more complicated the Command, the more Breath it requires.*

She took back her Breath. As Vasher had explained, doing so didn't shock her senses, for it was a mere restoration to a normal state for her. If she'd gone several days without that Breath, she'd have been overwhelmed by recovering its power. It was a little like taking a first bite of something very flavorful.

She eyed her clothes, which were now completely grey. Out of curiosity, she tried Awakening the rope again. Nothing happened. She picked up a stick, then Awakened the rope. It worked this time, the stick losing its color, though it took a *lot* more breath. Perhaps this was because the stick wasn't very colorful. The tree trunk didn't work for color, though. Presumably, one couldn't draw color from something that was itself alive.

She discarded the branch and fetched a few of Vasher's colored handkerchiefs from the room. She walked back to the tree. *Now what?* she thought. Could she put the Breath into the rope now, then command it to hold something later? How would she even phrase that?

"Hold things that I tell you to hold," she Commanded.

Nothing happened.

"Hold that branch when I tell you."

Again, nothing.

"Hold whatever I say."

Nothing.

A voice came from behind. "Tell it to 'Hold when thrown.'"

Vivenna jumped, spinning. Vasher stood behind her, Nightblood held before him, point down. He had his pack over his shoulder.

Vivenna flushed, glancing back at the rope. "Hold when thrown," she said, using a handkerchief for color. Her Breath left her, but the rope remained limp. So she tossed it to the side, hitting one of the hanging tree branches.

The rope immediately twisted about, locking the branches together and holding them tightly.

"That's useful," Vivenna said.

Vasher raised an eyebrow. "Perhaps. Dangerous though."

"Why?"

"Get the rope back."

Vivenna paused, realizing that the rope had twisted around branches that were too high for her to reach. She hopped up, trying to grab it.

"I prefer to use a longer rope," Vasher said, raising Nightblood by the blade and using its hooked crossguard to pull the branches down. "If you always keep hold of one end, then you don't have to worry about it getting taken from you. Plus, you can Awaken when you need to, rather than leaving a bunch of Breath locked into a rope that you may or may not need."

Vivenna nodded, recovering her Breath from the rope.

"Come on," he said, walking back toward the room. "You've made enough of a spectacle for one day."

Vivenna followed, noticing that several people on the street had stopped to watch her. "How did they notice?" she asked. "I wasn't *that* obvious about what I was doing."

Vasher snorted. "And how many people in T'Telir walk around in grey clothing?"

Vivenna blushed as she followed Vasher into the cramped room. He set down his pack and then leaned Nightblood against one wall. Vivenna eyed the sword. She still wasn't certain what to make of the weapon. She felt a little nauseated every time she looked at it, and the memory of how violently sick she'd felt when touching it was still fresh.

Plus there had been that voice in her head. Had she really heard it? Vasher had been characteristically tight-lipped when she'd asked about it, rebuffing her questions.

"Aren't you an Idrian?" Vasher asked, drawing her attention as he settled down.

"Last I checked," she replied.

"You seem oddly fascinated with Awakening for a follower of Austre." He spoke with eyes closed as he rested his head against the door.

"I'm not a very good Idrian," she said, sitting down. "Not anymore. I might as well learn to use what I have."

Vasher nodded. "Good enough. I've never really understood why Austrism suddenly turned its back on Awakening."

"Suddenly?"

He nodded, eyes still closed. "Wasn't like that before the Manywar."

"Really?"

"Of course," he said.

He often spoke that way, mentioning things that seemed farfetched to her, yet saying them as if he knew exactly what he was talking about. No conjecture. No wavering. As if he knew everything. She could see why it was sometimes hard for him to get along with people.

"Anyway," Vasher said, opening his eyes. "Did you eat all of that squid?"

She nodded. "Is that what that was?"

"Yes," he said, opening his pack, getting out another dried chunk of meat. He held it up. "Want more?"

She felt sick. "No, thank you."

He paused, noticing the look in her eyes. "What? Did I give you a bad piece?"

She shook her head.

"What?" he asked.

"It's nothing."

He raised an eyebrow.

"I said it's nothing." She glanced away. "I just don't care for fish very much."

"You don't?" he asked. "I've been feeding it to you for five days now."

She nodded silently.

"You ate it every time."

"I'm dependent upon you for food," she said. "I don't intend to complain about what you give me."

He frowned, then took a bite of squid and began chewing. He still wore his torn, almost-ragged clothing, but Vivenna had now been around him enough to know that he kept it clean. He obviously had the resources to get new clothing, yet he chose to wear the worn and tattered things instead. He also wore the same half-scrub, half-beard on his face. It never seemed to get longer, yet she never saw him trim it or shave it. How did he manage to keep it just the right length? Was that intentional, or was she reading too much into it?

"You aren't what I expected," he said.

"I would have been," she said. "A few weeks ago."

"I doubt it," he said, gnawing on his chunk of squid. "That tenacious spirit you've got doesn't come from a few weeks on the streets. Neither does that sense of martyrdom."

She met his eyes. "I want you to teach me more about Awakening."

He shrugged. "What do you want to know?"

"I don't even know how to answer that," she said. "Denth taught me a few Commands, but that was the same day that you took me captive."

Vasher nodded. They sat silent for a few minutes.

"Well?" she finally asked. "Are you going to say anything?"

"I'm thinking," he said.

She raised an eyebrow.

He scowled. "Awakening is something I've done for a very, very long time. I always have trouble trying to explain it. Don't rush me."

"It's okay," she said. "Take your time."

He shot her a glance. "Don't patronize me either."

"I'm not patronizing; I'm being polite."

"Well next time, be polite with less condescension in your voice," he said.

Condescension? she thought. *I wasn't condescending!* She eyed him as he sat, chewing on his dried squid. The more time she spent with him, the less frightening she found him, but the more frustrating. *He is a dangerous man,* she reminded herself. *He has left corpses strewn all over the city, using that sword of his to make people slaughter each other.*

She'd considered running from him on several occasions, but had eventually decided that she'd be a fool to do so. She could find no fault in his efforts to stop the war, and his solemn promise in the basement that first day still stuck with her. She believed him. Hesitantly.

She just intended to keep her eyes open a little wider from now on.

"All right," he said. "I guess this is for the best. I'm getting tired of you walking around with that bright aura of yours that you can't even use."

"Well?"

"Well, I think we should start with theory," he said. "There are four kinds of BioChromatic entities. The first, and most spectacular, are the Returned. They're called gods here in Hallandren, but I'd rather call them Spontaneous Sentient BioChromatic Manifestations in a Deceased Host.

What is odd about them is that they're the only naturally oc-
curring BioChromatic entity, which is theoretically the explanation for why they can't use or bestow their BioChromatic
Investiture. Of course, the fact is that *every* living being is
born with a certain BioChromatic Investiture. This could
also explain why Type Ones retain sentience."

Vivenna blinked. That wasn't what she had been expecting.

"You're more interested in Type Two and Type Three entities," Vasher continued. "Type Two being Mindless Manifestations in a Deceased Host. They are cheap to make, even
with awkward Commands. This is per the Law of BioChromatic Parallelism: the closer a host is to a living shape and
form, the easier it is to Awaken. BioChroma is the power of
life, and so it seeks patterns of life. That, however, leads us
to another law—the Law of Comparability. It states that the
amount of Breath required to Awaken something isn't necessarily indicative of its power once Awakened. A piece of
cloth cut into a square and a piece of cloth cut into the shape
of a person will take very different amounts of Breath to
Awaken, but will be essentially the same once they have
been Invested.

"The explanation for this is simple. Some people think
of Awakening as pouring water into a cup. You pour until
the cup is filled, and then the object comes to life. This is a
false analogy. Instead, think of Awakening as beating down
a door. You pound and pound, and some doors are easier to
open than others, but once they're open, they do about the
same thing."

He glanced at her. "Understand?"

"Uh . . ." she said. She'd spent her youth training with
the tutors, but this was beyond even their methods of teaching. "It's a little dense."

"Well, do you want to learn or not?"

You asked me if I understood, she thought. *And I an-*

swered. However, she didn't voice her objections. Better for him to keep talking.

"Type Two BioChromatic entities," he said, "are what people in Hallandren call Lifeless. They are different from Type One entities in several ways. Lifeless can be created at will, and require only a few Breaths to Awaken—anywhere between one and hundreds, depending on the Commands used—and they feed off of their own color when being Invested. They don't present an aura when Awakened, but the Breath sustains them, keeping them from needing to eat. They can die, and need a special alcohol solution to remain functional past a few years of Awakened status. Because of their organic host, their Breath clings to the body, and cannot be withdrawn once Invested."

"I know a little about them," Vivenna said, "Denth and his team have a Lifeless."

Vasher fell silent. "Yes," he finally said. "I know."

Vivenna frowned, noticing a strange look in his eyes. They sat silently for a few moments. "You were talking about Lifeless and their Commands?" she prompted.

Vasher nodded. "They need a Command to Awaken them, just like anything else. Even your religion teaches about Commands—it says that Austre is the one who Commands the Returned to come back."

She nodded.

"Understanding the theory of Commands is tough. Look at Lifeless, for instance. It's taken us centuries to discover the most efficient ways to bring a body to a Lifeless state. Even now, we're not sure if we understand how it works. I guess *this* is the first thing I'd like to get across to you—that BioChroma is complicated, and we really don't understand most of it."

"What do you mean?" she asked.

"Just what I said," Vasher replied, shrugging. "We don't really know what we're doing."

"But you sound so technical and precise in your descriptions."

"We've figured out some things," he said. "But Awakeners really haven't been around that long. The more you learn about BioChroma, the more you'll realize that there are more things that we *don't* know than there are things we do. Why are the specific Commands so important, and why do they have to be spoken in your native language? What brings Type One entities—Returned—back to life in the first place? Why are Lifeless so dull-minded, while Returned fully sentient?"

Vivenna nodded.

"Creating Type Three BioChromatic entities is what we traditionally call 'Awakening,'" Vasher continued. "That's when you create a BioChromatic manifestation in an organic host that is far removed from having been alive. Cloth works the best, though sticks, reeds, and other plant matter can be used."

"What about bones?" Vivenna asked.

"They're strange," Vasher said. "They take far more Breath to awaken than a body held together with flesh and aren't as flexible as something like cloth. Still, Breath will stick to them fairly easily, since they were once alive and maintain the form of a living thing."

"So Idrian stories that talk about skeletal armies *aren't* just fabrications?"

He chuckled. "Oh, they are. If you wanted to Awaken a skeleton, you'd have to arrange all the bones together in their correct places. That's a lot of work for something that will take upwards of fifty or a hundred Breaths to Awaken. Intact corpses make far more sense economically, even if the Breath sticks to them so well that it becomes impossible to recover. Still, I've seen some very interesting things done with skeletons which have been Awakened.

"Anyway, Type Three entities—regular Awakened objects—are different. BioChroma doesn't stick to them very well at all. The result is that they require quite a bit of Investiture—often well over a hundred Breaths—to Awaken them. The benefit of this, of course, is that the Breath can be drawn back out again. This has allowed for quite a bit more experimentation, and that has resulted in a more comprehensive understanding of Awakening techniques."

"You mean the Commands?" Vivenna asked.

"Right," Vasher said. "As you've seen, most basic Commands work easily. If the Command is something the object could do, and you state it in a simple way, the Command will usually work."

"I tried some simple Commands," she said. "On the rope. They didn't work."

"Those may have sounded simple, but they weren't. Simple Commands are only two words long. Grab something. Hold something. Move up. Move down. Twist around. Even some two-word Commands can be more complicated, and it takes practice visualizing—or, well, imagining. Well, using your mind to—"

"I understand that part," she said. "Like flexing a muscle."

He nodded. "The Command 'Protect me,' though only two words, is extremely complicated. So are others, like Fetch something. You have to give the right impulse to the object. This area is where you really begin to understand how little we know. There are probably thousands of Commands we don't know. The more words you add, the more complicated the mental component becomes, which is why discovering a new Command can take years of study."

"Like the discovery of a new Command to make Lifeless," she said thoughtfully. "Three hundred years ago, those who had the one-Breath Command could make their Lifeless much more cheaply than those who didn't. That disparity started the Manywar."

"Yes," Vasher said. "Or, at least, that was part of what caused the war. It's not really important. The thing to understand is that we're still children when it comes to

Awakening. It doesn't help that a lot of people who learn new, valuable Commands never share them, and probably die with the knowledge."

Vivenna nodded, noticing how his lesson grew more relaxed and conversational as he got into the topic. His expertise surprised her.

He sits on the floor, she thought, *eating a dry piece of squid, not having shaven in weeks and wearing clothing that looks like it's about to fall off. Yet he talks like a scholar giving a lecture. He carries a sword that leaks black smoke and causes people to kill each other, yet he works so hard to stop a war. Who is this man?*

She glanced to the side, to where Nightblood sat leaning against the wall. Perhaps it was the discussion of the technical aspects of BioChroma, or perhaps it was simply her growing suspicion. She was beginning to understand what wasn't right about the sword.

"What is a Type Four BioChromatic entity?" Vivenna asked, glancing back at Vasher.

He fell silent.

"Type One is a human body with sentience," Vivenna said. "Type Two is a human body without sentience. Type three is an Awakened object like a rope—an object with no sentience. Is there a way to create an Awakened object *with* sentience? Like a Returned, but inside of something other than a human body?"

Vasher stood. "We've covered enough for one day."

"You didn't answer my question."

"And I'm not going to," he said. "And I advise you never to ask it again. Understand?" He glanced at her, and she felt a chill at the harshness in his voice.

"All right," she said, though she didn't glance away.

He snorted to himself, then reached into his large pack, yanking something out. "Here," he said. "I brought you something."

He tossed a long, cloth-wrapped object to the floor. Vivenna stood, walking over to pull the cloth off. Inside was a thin, well-polished dueling blade.

"I don't know how to use one of these," she said.

"Then learn," he replied. "If you know how to fight, you'll be far less annoying to have around. I won't have to keep pulling you out of trouble all the time."

She flushed. "One time."

"It'll happen again," he said.

She hesitantly picked up the sheathed sword, surprised at how light it was.

"Let's go," Vasher said. "I've got another group for us to visit."

47

LIGHTSONG TRIED NOT to think about his dreams. He tried not to think about T'Telir in flames. Of people dying. Of the world, essentially, ending.

He stood on the second story of his palace, looking over the Court of Gods. The second story was essentially a covered roof, open on all sides. Wind blew through his hair. The sun was close to setting. Already, torches were arrayed on the lawn. It was so perfect. The palaces set in a circle, lit by torches and lanterns matching the colors of the nearest building.

Some of the palaces were dark; the buildings that currently held no gods.

What would happen if too many others Returned before we killed ourselves? he thought idly. *Would they build more palaces?* As far as he knew, there had always been enough space.

At the head of the court sat the God King's palace, tall

and black. It had obviously been built so that it would dominate even the extravagant mansions of the others, and it threw a wide, warped shadow across the back wall.

Perfect. So perfect. The torches were arranged in patterns he could only see by standing atop a building. The grass was kept manicured, and the massive wall tapestries were replaced often so that they showed no wear, stains, or fading.

The people put forth such effort for their gods. Why? Sometimes it baffled him. But what to think of other faiths, ones with no visible gods, only incorporeal imaginings or wishes? Surely those 'gods' did even less for their people than the Hallandren court, yet they still were worshipped.

Lightsong shook his head. Meeting with Allmother had reminded him of days he hadn't thought of in a long time. Calmseer. She had been his mentor when he'd first Returned. Blushweaver was jealous of his memories of her, but she didn't understand the truth. Nor could he, really, explain it. Calmseer had come closer to being a divinity than any Returned Lightsong had known. She'd cared for her followers much as Allmother now tried to do, but there had been genuine concern in Calmseer's regard. She hadn't helped the people because she feared that they would stop worshiping, and she had no arrogance of presumed superiority.

Real kindness. Real love. Real mercy.

Yet even Calmseer had felt inadequate. She had often said she felt guilty because she couldn't live up to what people expected. How could she? How could anyone? In the end, he suspected this was what drove her to answer a petition. There had only been one way, in her estimation, to be the goddess everyone demanded she be. And that was to give up her life.

They push us into it, Lightsong thought. *They craft all of this splendor and luxury, they give us whatever we de-*

*sire, then they subtly poke at us. Be a god. Prophesy.
Maintain our illusion for us.*

Die. Die so that we can keep believing.

He usually stayed off his roof. He preferred to be down
below, where the limited perspective made it so much easier to ignore the larger view. So much easier to focus on
simple things, like his life in the moment.

"Your Grace?" Llarimar asked quietly, approaching.

Lightsong didn't reply.

"Are you all right, Your Grace?"

"No man should be this important," Lightsong said.

"Your Grace?" Llarimar asked, walking up beside
him.

"It does strange things to you. We weren't built for it."

"You're a god, Your Grace. You *were* built for it."

"No," he said. "I'm no god."

"Excuse me, but you don't really get to choose. We worship you, and that makes you our god." Llarimar spoke the
words in his usual calm fashion. Didn't the man *ever* get
upset?

"You're not helping."

"I apologize, Your Grace. But perhaps you should stop
arguing about the same old things."

Lightsong shook his head. "This is something different
today. I'm not sure what to do."

"You mean about Allmother's Commands?"

Lightsong nodded. "I thought I had it figured out, Scoot.
I can't keep up with all of the things Blushweaver is
plotting—I've never been good at details."

Llarimar didn't respond.

"I was going to give it up," Lightsong said. "Allmother
was doing a fantastic job of standing up for herself. I figured that if I gave her my Commands, then *she'd* know
what to do. She'd understand if it's better to support Blushweaver or oppose her."

"You could still just let her," Llarimar said. "You gave her your Commands too."

"I know," Lightsong said.

They fell silent.

So it comes down to this, he thought. *The first of us who changes those Commands takes control of all twenty thousand. The other will be locked out.*

What did he choose? Did he sit back and let history happen, or did he jump in and make a mess of it?

Whoever you are, he thought, *whatever is out there that sent me back, why couldn't you just let me be? I'd already lived one life. I'd already made my choices. Why did you have to send me back?*

He'd tried everything, and yet people still looked to him. He knew for a fact that he was one of the most popular Returned, visited by more petitioners and given more art than almost anyone else. *Honestly,* he thought. *What is wrong with these people?* Were they so in need of something to worship that they chose him rather than worry that their religion might be false?

Allmother claimed that some *did* think that. She worried about the perceived lack of faith among the common people. Lightsong wasn't certain he agreed with her. He knew of the theories—that the gods who lived the longest were the weak ones because the system encouraged the best to sacrifice themselves quickly. However, the same number of petitioners came to him now as when he first started. Plus, too few gods were chosen on the whole for that to be statistically valid.

Or was he just distracting himself with irrelevant details? He leaned on the railing, looking out over the green and its glowing pavilions.

This could be the crowning moment for him. He could finally prove himself to be an indolent wastrel. It was perfect. If he did nothing, then Allmother would be forced to take up the armies and resist Blushweaver.

Was that what he wanted? Allmother kept herself isolated from the other gods. She didn't attend many Court assemblies and didn't listen to the debates. Blushweaver was intimately involved. She knew every god and goddess well. She understood the issues, and she was very clever. Of all of the gods, only she had begun taking steps to secure their armies.

Siri is no threat, he thought. But if someone else were manipulating her? Would Allmother have the political savvy to understand the danger? Without his concerned guidance, would Blushweaver see that Siri wasn't crushed?

If he did walk away, there would be a cost. He would be to blame, for he'd given up.

"Who was she, Llarimar?" Lightsong asked quietly. "The young woman in my dreams. Was she my wife?"

The high priest didn't answer.

"I need to know," Lightsong said, turning. "This time, I *really* need to know."

"I . . ." Llarimar frowned, then looked away. "No," he said quietly. "She was not your wife."

"My lover?"

He shook his head.

"But she was important to me?"

"Very," Llarimar said.

"And is she still alive?"

Llarimar wavered, then finally nodded his head.

Still alive, Lightsong thought.

If this city fell, then she would be in danger. Everyone who worshiped Lightsong—everyone who counted on him despite his best efforts—would be in danger.

T'Telir couldn't fall. Even if there were war, the fighting wouldn't come here. Hallandren was not in danger. It was the most powerful kingdom in the world.

And what of his dreams?

He had been given only one real duty in the government. That of taking command of ten thousand Lifeless. Of deciding when they should be used. And when they should not be.

Still alive . . .

He turned and walked toward the steps.

———∞∞∞———

THE LIFELESS ENCLAVE was technically part of the Court of Gods. The huge building was built at the base of the court plateau, and a long, covered walkway ran down to it.

Lightsong moved down the steps with his entourage. They passed several guard posts, though he wasn't sure why they needed guards in a hallway leading from the court. He had only visited the enclave a couple of times—primarily during his first few weeks as a Returned, when he had been required to give the security phrase to his ten thousand soldiers.

Perhaps I should have come more often, he thought. What would have been the point? Servants cared for the Lifeless, making certain their ichor-alcohol was fresh, that they exercised, and . . . did whatever else it was that Lifeless did.

Llarimar and several of the other priests were puffing from the long, brisk walk by the time they reached the bottom of the steps. Lightsong, of course, had no trouble, as he was in perfect physical condition. There were some things about godhood that never made him complain. A couple of guards opened the doors into the compound. It was gigantic, of course—it contained space for forty thousand Lifeless. There were four large warehouse-like storage areas for the different groups of Lifeless, a track for them to run around, a room filled with various stones and blocks of metal for them to lift to keep their muscles strong, and a medical area where their ichor-alcohol was tested and refreshed.

They passed through several twisting passages, designed to confuse invaders who might try to strike at the Lifeless, then approached a guard post set beside a large open doorway. Lightsong passed the living human guards and looked in at the Lifeless.

He'd forgotten that they kept them in the dark.

Llarimar waved for a couple of priests to hold up lamps. The door opened onto a viewing platform. The floor of the warehouse extended below, filled with line upon line of silent, waiting soldiers. They wore their armor and carried their weapons in sheaths.

"There are holes in the ranks," Lightsong said.

"Some of them will be exercising," Llarimar replied. "I have sent a servant to fetch them."

Lightsong nodded. The Lifeless stood with eyes open. They didn't shuffle or cough. Staring out over them, Lightsong suddenly remembered why he never felt any desire to return and inspect his troops. They were simply too unnerving.

"Everyone out," Lightsong said.

"Your Grace?" Llarimar asked. "Don't you want a few priests to stay?"

Lightsong shook his head. "No. I will bear this phrase myself."

Llarimar hesitated, but then nodded, doing as ordered.

In Lightsong's opinion, there was no good way of keeping Command phrases. Leaving them in the hands of a single god was to risk losing the phrase through assassination. However, the more people who knew the Command phrases, the more likely it was that the secret would be bribed or tortured out of someone.

The only mitigating factor was the God King. Apparently, with his powerful BioChroma, he could break Lifeless more quickly. Still, taking control of ten thousand would require weeks, even for the God King.

The choice was left to the individual Returned. They could let some of their priests hear the Command phrase so that if something happened to the god, the priests could pass the phrase on to the next Returned. If the god chose not to give the phrase to his priests, then he placed an even larger burden on himself. Lightsong had found that option silly, years before, and had included Llarimar and several others in the secret.

This time he saw wisdom in keeping the phrase to himself. Should he get the chance, he would whisper it to the God King. But only him. "Bottom line blue," he said. "I give you a new Command phrase." He paused. "Red panther. Red panther. Step to the right side of the room."

A group of the Lifeless near the front—those who could hear his voice—moved over to the side. Lightsong sighed, closing his eyes. A part of him had hoped that Allmother had come here first, that she had already changed the Command phrase.

But she hadn't. He opened his eyes then took the steps down to the warehouse floor. He spoke again, changing the phrase for another group. He could do about twenty or thirty at a time—he remembered the process taking hours the last time.

He continued. He would leave the Lifeless with their basic instructions to obey the servants when they asked the creatures to exercise or go to the infirmary. He'd give them a lesser Command that could be used to move them about and make them march to specific locations, as when they had been placed in ranks outside the city to greet Siri, and another to make them go with members of the city guard to provide extra muscle.

Yet there would only be one person with ultimate command of them. One person who could make them go to war. When he was done in this room, he would move on, taking utter command of Allmother's ten thousand as well.

He would draw both armies to him. And in doing so, he would take his place at the very heart of the fate of two kingdoms.

48

SUSEBRON DIDN'T LEAVE in the mornings anymore.

Siri lay in the bed beside him, curled slightly, her skin against his. He slept peacefully, chest going up and down, the white bed sheets throwing out prismatic colors around him as they inevitably reacted to his presence. A few months back, who could have understood where she'd find herself? Not only married to the God King of Hallandren, but in love with him as well.

She still thought it amazing. He was the most important religious and secular figure in the whole of the Inner Sea area. He was the basis for worship of the Hallandren Iridescent Tones. He was a creature feared and hated by most people in Idris.

And he was dozing quietly at her side. A god of color and beauty, his body as perfectly sculpted as a statue. And what was Siri? Not perfect, of that she was sure. And yet, somehow, she'd brought to him something that he needed. A hint of spontaneity. A breath from the outside, untamed by his priests or his reputation.

She sighed, head resting on his chest. There would be a price to be paid for their enjoyment these last few nights. *We really are fools,* she thought idly. *We only have to avoid one thing: giving the priests a child. We're aiming ourselves straight toward disaster.*

She found it hard to berate herself too firmly. She suspected that her act wouldn't have fooled the priests for much longer. They would grow suspicious, or at least frustrated, if she continued it without producing an heir. She could imagine them interfering if faced with more stalling.

Whatever she and Susebron did to change events, they would have to do it quickly.

He stirred beside her, and she twisted, looking at his face as he opened his eyes. He regarded her for a few minutes, stroking her hair. It was amazing how quickly they had become comfortable in their intimacy.

He reached for his writing board. *I love you.*

She smiled. It was always the first thing he wrote in the mornings. "And I love you," she said.

However, he continued, *we are probably in trouble, aren't we?*

"Yes."

How long? he asked. *Until it's obvious that you will bear a child, I mean?*

"I'm not sure," she said, frowning. "I don't have much experience with this, obviously. I know that some of the women back in Idris complained of not being able to have children as quickly as they wanted, so maybe it doesn't always happen immediately. I know other women who bore children almost exactly nine months after their wedding night."

Susebron looked thoughtful.

A year from now, I could be a mother, Siri thought. She found the concept daunting. Up until a short time ago, she hadn't really thought of herself as an adult. *Of course,* she thought, feeling a bit sick, *according to what we've been told, any children I bear the God King would be stillborn anyway.* Even if that was a lie, her child would be in danger. She still suspected that the priests would spirit it away, then replace it with a Returned. In all likelihood, Siri would then be made to disappear as well.

Bluefingers tried to warn me, she thought. *He spoke of danger, not only to Susebron, but to me.*

Susebron was writing. *I've made a decision,* he wrote.

Siri raised an eyebrow.

I want to try making myself known to the people, he wrote, *and the other gods. I want to take control of my kingdom for myself.*

"I thought we decided that would be too dangerous."

It will be, he wrote. *But I'm beginning to think that it is a risk we must take.*

"And your objections from before?" she asked. "You can't shout out the truth, and your guards are likely to rush you away if you try something like escaping."

Yes, Susebron wrote, *but you have far fewer guards, and you* can *yell.*

Siri paused. "Yes," she said. "But would anyone believe me? What would they think if I just started screaming about how the God King is being held prisoner by his own priests?"

Susebron cocked his head.

"Trust me," she said. "They'd think that I was crazy."

What if you gained the confidence of the Returned you often speak about? he wrote. *Lightsong the Bold.*

Siri gave that some thought.

You could go to him, Susebron wrote. *Tell him the truth. Perhaps he will lead you to other Returned he thinks might listen. The priests will not be able to silence us all.*

Siri lay beside him for a moment, head still resting on his chest. "It sounds possible, Seb, but why not just run? My serving women are from Pahn Kahl now. Bluefingers has said that he will try to get us out, if I ask. We can flee to Idris."

If we flee, Hallandren troops will follow, Siri. We would not be safe in Idris.

"We could go somewhere else, then."

He shook his head. *Siri, I have been listening to the arguments in the court of judgment. There will soon be war between our kingdoms. If we run, we will be abandoning Idris to invasion.*

"The invasion will happen if we stay, too."

Not if I take control of my throne, Susebron wrote. *The people of Hallandren, even the gods, are obligated to obey me. There will be no war if they know I disapprove.* He erased, then continued, writing faster. *I have told the priests that I don't wish to go to war, and they appeared sympathetic. However, they have done nothing.*

"They are probably worried," Siri said. "If they let you start making policy, then you may begin to think that you don't need them."

They'd be right, he wrote, smiling. *I need to become the leader of my people, Siri. That is the only way to protect your beautiful hills and the family you love so much.*

Siri fell silent, offering no further objections. To do as he was saying would be to play their hand. Make a gamble for everything. If they failed, the priests would undoubtedly figure out that Siri and Susebron were in communication. That would spell the end of their time alone together.

Susebron obviously noticed her concern. *It is dangerous, but it is the best option. Fleeing would be just as risky, and it would leave us in far worse circumstances. In Idris, we would be seen as the reason the Hallandren armies had come. Other countries would be even more dangerous.*

Siri slowly nodded. In another country, they'd have no money and would make perfect subjects for ransom. They'd escape the priests only to find themselves being held captive to be used against Hallandren. The Kingdom of Iridescence was still widely disliked because of the Manywar.

"We'd be taken captive, as you say," she acknowledged. "Plus, if we were in another country, I doubt we'd be able to get you a Breath every week. Without them, you'd die."

He looked hesitant.

"What?" she asked.

I would not die without Breath, he wrote. *But that is not an argument in favor of flight.*

"You mean the stories of Returned needing Breath to live are lies?" Siri asked incredulously.

Not at all, he wrote quickly. *We do need Breath—but you forget that I hold the wealth of Breath passed down for generations in my family. I heard my priests speak of this once. If it were necessary to move me, I could survive on the extra Breaths I hold. Those over and above the Breath that makes me Returned. My body would simply feed off those extra Breaths, absorbing one a week.*

Siri sat back thoughtfully. That seemed to imply something about Breath that she couldn't quite figure out. Unfortunately, she just didn't have the experience to sort through it.

"All right," she said. "So we *could* go into hiding if we needed to."

I said this was not an argument for fleeing, Susebron wrote. *My treasure of Breaths might keep me alive, but it would also make me a very valuable target. Everyone will want those Breaths—even if I weren't the God King, I would be in danger.*

That was very true. Siri nodded. "All right," she said. "If we're really going to try exposing what the priests have done, I think we make our move soon. If I display any signs of being pregnant, I bet it will take the priests all of two heartbeats to sequester me."

Susebron nodded. *There will be a general assembly of the court in a couple of days. I have heard my priests say that this will be an important meeting—it is rare that the gods are all called together to vote. That meeting will decide whether or not we march on Idris.*

Siri nodded nervously. "I could sit with Lightsong," she said, "and plead for his help. If we go to several of the other gods, perhaps they—in front of the crowds—can demand to know whether or not I am lying."

And I will open my mouth and reveal that I have no tongue, he wrote. *Then let us see what the priests do. They will be forced to bow to the will of their own pantheon.*

Siri nodded. "All right," she said. "Let's try it."

49

V ASHER FOUND HER practicing again.

He hovered outside the window, lowered down from the roof via an Awakened rope which gripped him about the waist. Inside, Vivenna repeatedly Awakened a strip of cloth, unaware of Vasher. She Commanded the cloth to wiggle across the room, wrap around a cup, then bring that cup back without spilling.

She's learning so quickly, he thought. The Commands themselves were simple to say, but providing the right mental impulse was difficult. It was like learning to control a second body. Vivenna was quick. Yes, she had a lot of Breath. That made it easier, but true Instinctive Awakening—the ability to Awaken objects without training or practice—was a gift granted only by the Sixth Heightening. That was one step beyond even what Returned had, with their single deific Breath. Vivenna was far from that stage. She learned faster than she should have, even if he knew she was frustrated by how often she got things wrong.

Even as he watched, she made a mistake. The cloth wiggled across the room, but climbed into the cup instead of wrapping around it. It shook, making the cup fall over, then the cloth finally returned, leaving a soggy trail. Vivenna cursed and walked over to refill the cup. She never noticed Vasher hanging just outside. He wasn't surprised—he was currently a Drab, his excess Breath stored in his shirt.

She replaced the cup, and he pulled himself up as she walked back. Of course, the mechanics of how he moved about with the ropes were far more complicated than they seemed. His Command incorporated making the rope respond to taps of his finger along its length. Awakening was different from creating a Lifeless—Lifeless had brains and could interpret Commands and requests. The rope had none of that; it could only act on its original instructions.

With a few taps, he lowered himself again, Vivenna faced away from him as she picked up another colored swatch to use as fuel when she Awakened her cup-fetching ribbon.

I like her, Nightblood said. *I'm glad we didn't kill her.*

Vasher didn't respond.

She's very pretty, don't you think? Nightblood asked.

You can't tell, Vasher replied.

I can tell, Nightblood said. *I've decided that I can.*

Vasher shook his head. Pretty or not, the woman should never have come to Hallandren. She'd given Denth a perfect tool. *Of course,* he admitted wryly, *Denth probably didn't need that tool.* Hallandren and Idris were close to snapping. Vasher had stayed away too long. He knew that. He also knew that there was no way he would have come back earlier.

Inside the room, Vivenna successfully managed to get the cloth to bring her cup, and she drank from it with a satisfied look that Vasher could just barely see from the side. He had the rope lower him to the ground. He ordered it to let go up above, then—once it had twisted down around his arm—he recovered his Breath and climbed the external steps to the room.

<hr />

VIVENNA TURNED AS Vasher entered. She set down the cup, hurriedly stuffing the cloth in her pocket. *What does it matter if he sees me practicing?* she thought, flushing. *It's not like I have anything to hide.* But practicing before him was embarrassing. He was so stern, so unforgiving of faults. She didn't like him to see her fail.

"Well?" she asked.

He shook his head. "Both the house you were using and the safe house in the slums are empty," he said. "Denth is too clever to get caught like that. He must have figured that you would reveal his location."

Vivenna ground her teeth in frustration, settling back against the wall. Like the other rooms they had stayed in, this one was utterly simple. Their only possessions were a pair of bedrolls and their changes of clothing, all of which Vasher carried about in his duffel.

Denth lived far more luxuriously. He could afford to—he now held all of Lemex's money. *Clever bit, that,* she thought. *Giving me the money, making me feel like I was in charge. He knew all along that the gold was never out of his hands, just as I never was.*

"I was hoping we'd be able to watch him," she said. "Maybe get a jump on what he's planning next."

Vasher shrugged. "Didn't work. No use crying about it. Come on. I think I can get us in to meet with some of the Idrian workers at one of the orchards, assuming we arrive during the lunch break."

Vivenna frowned as he turned to go. "Vasher," she said. "We can't keep doing this."

"This?"

"When I was with Denth, we met with crime lords and politicians. You and I are meeting with peasants on corners and in fields."

"They're good people!"

"I know they are," Vivenna said quickly. "But, do you really think we're making a difference? Compared to what Denth is probably doing, I mean?"

He frowned, but instead of arguing with her, he just pounded his fist against the side of the wall. "I know," he said. "I've tried other leads, but most everything I do seems a step behind Denth. I can kill his gangs of thieves, but he has more of them than I can find. I've tried to figure out who is behind the war—even followed leads in the Court of Gods itself—but everyone is growing more and more tight-lipped. They assume the war to be inevitable, now, and don't want to be seen as being on the losing side of the argument."

"What about priests?" Vivenna said. "Aren't they the ones who bring things to the attention of the gods? If we can get more of them to argue against the war, then maybe we can stop it."

"Priests are fickle," Vasher said with a shake of his head. "Most of those who argued against the war have caved in. Even Nanrovah switched sides on me."

"Nanrovah?"

"High priest of Stillmark," Vasher said. "I thought he was solid—he even met with me a few times to talk about his opposition to the war. Now he refuses to see me anymore and has switched sides. Colorless liar."

Vivenna frowned. *Nanrovah . . .* "Vasher," she said. "We did something to him."

"What?"

"Denth and his team," Vivenna said. "We helped a gang of thieves rob from a salt peddler. We used a couple of distractions to cover the burglary. We set a fire in a nearby building and overturned a carriage that was passing through the garden. The carriage belonged to a high priest. I think his name was Nanrovah."

Vasher cursed quietly.

"You think it might be connected?" she asked.

"Maybe. You know which thieves were actually doing the robbery?"

She shook her head.

"I'll be back," he said. "Wait here."

———✦———

SO SHE DID. She waited for hours. She tried practicing her Awakening, but she'd already spent most of the day working on that. She was mentally exhausted and found it difficult to concentrate. Eventually, she found herself staring out the window in annoyance. Denth had always let her go along on his information gathering forays.

That was just because he wanted to keep me close, she thought. Now that she looked back, there were obviously lots of things Denth had been hiding from her. Vasher just didn't care to placate her.

He wasn't stingy with information, though, when she asked. His answers were grumpy, but he did usually answer. She still mulled over their conversation about Awakening. Less because of what he'd said. More because of the way he'd said it.

She'd been wrong about him. She was almost certain of that now. She had to stop judging people. But was that possible? Wasn't interaction based, in part, on judgments? A person's background and attitudes influenced how she responded to them.

The answer, then, wasn't to stop judging. It was to hold those judgments as mutable. She'd judged Denth to be a friend, but she shouldn't have ignored the way he talked about mercenaries having no friends.

The door slammed open. Vivenna jumped, putting a hand to her chest.

Vasher walked in. "Start reaching for that sword when you're startled," he said. "There's little reason to grab your shirt, unless you're planning to rip it off."

Vivenna flushed, hair twinging red. The sword he had bought her lay at the side of the room; they hadn't had much opportunity to practice, and she still barely even knew how to hold the thing properly. "Well?" she asked as he closed the door. It was already dark outside, and the city was beginning to sparkle with lights.

"The robbery was a cover," Vasher said. "The real hit was that carriage. Denth promised the thieves something valuable if they committed a robbery and started a fire, both as distractions to get at the carriage."

"Why?" Vivenna asked.

"I'm not sure."

"Coins?" Vivenna asked. "When Clod hit the horse, it knocked a chest off the top. It was filled with gold."

"What happened then?" Vasher asked.

"I left with some others. I thought the carriage itself was the distraction, and once it went down, I was supposed to pull out."

"Denth?"

"He wasn't there, come to think of it," Vivenna said. "The others told me he was working with the thieves."

Vasher nodded, walking over to his pack. He threw aside the bedrolls, then took out several articles of clothing. He pulled off his shirt, exposing a well-muscled—and rather hairy—torso. Vivenna blinked in surprise, then blushed. She probably should have turned aside, but the curious part of her was too strong. What was he doing?

He didn't remove his trousers, thankfully, but instead threw on a different shirt. The sleeves of this one were cut into long ribbons near the wrists.

"Upon call," he said, "become my fingers and grip that which I must."

The cuff tassels wiggled.

"Wait," Vivenna said. "What was that? A Command?"

"Too complicated for you," he said, kneeling and undoing the cuff of his trousers. She could see that here, too, there were extra lengths of cloth. "Become as my legs and give them strength," he Commanded.

The leg-tassels crossed under his feet, growing tight. Vivenna didn't argue with his insistence that the Commands were "too complicated." She just memorized them anyway.

Finally, Vasher threw on his tattered cloak, which was ripped in places. "Protect me," he Commanded, and she could see a lot of his remaining Breath drain into the cloak. He wrapped his rope belt around his waist—it was thin, for a rope, but strong, and she knew its purpose was not to keep his trousers up.

Finally, he picked up Nightblood. "You coming?"

"Where?"

"We're going to go capture a few of those thieves. Ask them exactly what Denth wanted with that carriage."

Vivenna felt a stab of fear. "Why invite me? Won't I just make it harder for you?"

"Depends," he said. "If we get into a fight, and you get in the way, then it will be more difficult. If we get into a fight and half of them attack you instead of me, it will make things easier."

"Assuming you don't defend me."

"That's a good assumption," he said, looking into her eyes. "If you want to come, come. But don't expect me to protect you, and—whatever you do—don't try and follow on your own."

"I wouldn't do such a thing," she said.

He shrugged. "I thought I'd make the offer. You're no prisoner here, Princess. You can do whatever you want. Just don't get in my way when you do it, understand?"

"I understand," she said, feeling a chill as she made her decision. "And I'm coming."

He didn't try to dissuade her. He simply pointed at her sword. "Keep that on."

She nodded, tying it on.

"Draw it," he said.

She did so, and he corrected her grip.

"What good will holding it properly do?" she asked. "I still don't know how to use it."

"Look threatening and it might make someone attacking you pause. Make them hesitate for a couple seconds in a fight, and that could mean a lot."

She nodded nervously, sliding the weapon back in its sheath. Then she grabbed several lengths of rope. "Hold when thrown," she said to the smaller one, then stuffed it into her pocket.

Vasher eyed her.

"Better to lose the Breath than get killed," she said.

"Few Awakeners agree with you," he noted. "To most of them, the thought of losing Breath is far more frightening than the prospect of death."

"Well, I'm not like most Awakeners," she said. "Half of me still finds the process blasphemous."

He nodded. "Put the rest of your Breath somewhere else," he said, opening the door. "We can't afford to draw attention."

She grimaced, then did as told, putting her Breath into her shirt with a basic, and non-active, Command. It was actually the same as giving a half-spoken Command, or one that was mumbled. Those would draw out the Breath, but leave the item unable to act.

As soon as she placed the Breath, the dullness returned. Everything seemed dead around her.

"Let's go," Vasher said, moving out into the darkness.

Night in T'Telir was very different from her homeland. There, it had been possible to see so many stars overhead that it looked like a bucket of white sand had been dashed into the air. Here, there were street lamps, taverns, restaurants, and houses of entertainment. The result was a city full of lights—a little like the stars themselves had come down to inspect grand T'Telir. And yet, Vivenna was still saddened by how few real stars she saw in the sky.

None of that meant that the places they were going were by any means bright. Vasher led her through the streets, and he quickly became little more than a hulking shadow. They left behind places with street lights, and even lit windows, moving into an unfamiliar slum. This was one of those she'd been afraid to enter, even when she lived on the streets. The night seemed to grow even darker as they entered and walked down one of the twisting, dark alleys that passed for streets in such places. They remained silent. Vivenna knew not to speak and draw attention.

Eventually, Vasher pulled to a stop. He pointed toward a building: single-story, flat-topped, and wide. It sat alone, in a depression, shanties built from refuse covering the low hill behind it. Vasher waved for her to stay back, then quietly put the rest of his Breath into his rope and crept forward up the hill.

Vivenna waited, nervous, kneeling beside a decaying shanty that appeared to have been built from half-crumbling bricks. *Why did I come?* she thought. *He didn't tell me to—he simply said that I could. I could just as easily have stayed behind.*

But she was tired of things happening *to* her. She had been the one to point out that maybe there was a connection between the priest and Denth's plan. She wanted to see this to the end. Do something.

That had been easy to think back in the lit room. It didn't help her nerves that, looming to the left side of the shanty was one of the D'Denir statues. There had been some of them in the Highland slums as well, though most of those had been defaced or broken.

She couldn't feel anything with her life sense. She felt almost as if she'd been blinded. The Breath's absence brought memories of nights sleeping in the mud of a cold alleyway. Beatings administered by urchins half her size but with twice her competence. Hunger. Terrible, omnipresent, depressing, and draining hunger.

A footstep cracked and a shadow loomed. She nearly gasped in shock, but managed to keep it in as she recognized Nightblood in the figure's hand.

"Two guards," Vasher said. "Both silenced."

"Will they do for answering our questions?"

Vasher shook a silhouetted head. "Practically kids. We need someone more important. We'll have to go in. Either that, or sit and watch for a few days to determine who is in charge, then grab him when he's alone."

"That would take too long," Vivenna whispered.

"I agree," he said. "I can't use the sword, though. When Nightblood is done with a group, there's never anyone to question."

Vivenna shivered.

"Come on," he whispered. She followed as quietly as she could, moving for the front door. Vasher grabbed her arm and shook his head. She followed him around to the side, barely noticing the two lumps of unconscious bodies rolled into a ditch. At the back of the building, Vasher began to feel around on the ground. After a few moments without success, he cursed quietly and pulled something from his pocket. A handful of straw.

In just a few seconds, he had constructed three little men from the straw and some thread, then used Breath reclaimed from his cloak to animate them. He gave each one the same command: "Find tunnels."

Vivenna watched with fascination. *That's far more abstract a Command than he led me to believe was possible,* she thought as the little men scuttled around on the ground. Vasher himself returned to his searching. *Apparently experience—and ability to use mental images—is the most important aspect of Awakening.*

He's been doing this a long time, and the way he spoke before—like a scholar—indicates he's studied Awakening very seriously.

One of the straw men began to jump up and down. The other two rushed over to it and then they began to bounce as well. Vasher joined them, as did Vivenna, and she watched as he uncovered a trapdoor hidden beneath a thick layer of dirt. He raised it a tad, then reached underneath. His hand came back out with several small bells, which had apparently been rigged there to ring if the door were opened all the way.

"No group like this has a hideout without bolt-holes," Vasher said. "Usually a couple of them. Always trapped."

Vivenna watched as he recovered the Breath from the straw men, quietly thanking each one. She frowned at the curious words. They were just piles of straw. Why thank them?

He put the Breath back into his cloak with a protection Command, then led the way down through the trapdoor. Vivenna followed, stepping softly, skipping a particular step when Vasher indicated. The bottom was a roughly cut tunnel—or, so she got from feeling along the sides of the lightless earthen chamber.

Vasher moved forward; she could only tell because of the quiet rustling of his clothing. She followed and was curious to see light ahead. She could also hear voices. Men talking, and laughing.

Soon she could see Vasher's silhouette; she moved up next to him, peeking out of their tunnel and into an earthen room. There was a fire burning at the center, the smoke twisting up through a hole in the ceiling. The upper chamber—the building itself—was probably just a front, for the chamber down here looked very lived-in. There were piles of cloth, bed rolls, pots and pans. All of it as dirty as the men who sat around the fire, laughing.

Vasher gestured to the side. There was another tunnel a few feet to the side of the one they were hiding in. Vivenna's heart jumped in shock as Vasher crept into the room and toward the second tunnel. She glanced at the fire. The men were very focused on their drinking, and were blinded by the light. They didn't seem to notice Vasher.

She took a deep breath, then followed into the shadows of the large room, feeling exposed with the firelight to her back. Vasher didn't go far, however, before stopping. Vivenna nearly collided with him. He stood there for a few moments; finally, Vivenna poked him in the back, trying to get him to move so that she could see what he was doing. He shuffled aside, letting her see what was before him.

This tunnel ended abruptly—apparently, it wasn't so much a tunnel as a nook. Nestled against the back of the nook was a cage, about as high as Vivenna's waist. Inside the cage was a child.

Vivenna gasped softly, pushing past Vasher and kneeling down beside the cage. *The valuable thing in the carriage,* she thought, making the connection. *It wasn't the coins. It was the priest's daughter. The perfect bargaining chip if you wanted to blackmail someone into changing their position at court.*

As Vivenna knelt, the girl pulled back in the cage, sniffling quietly and quivering. The cage stank of human waste, and the child was covered in grime—all except for lines on her cheeks, which had been streaked clean by tears.

Vivenna looked up at Vasher. His eyes were shadowed, his back to the fire, but she could see him gritting his teeth. She could see tension in his muscles. He turned his head to the side, half-illuminating his face with the light of the red fire.

In that single lit eye, Vivenna saw fury.

"Hey!" one of the thieves called.

"Get the child out," Vasher said in a harsh whisper.

"How did you get here!" another man yelled.

Vasher met her eyes with his single illuminated one, and she felt herself shrink before him. She nodded, and Vasher turned away from her, one hand clenching into a fist, the other grabbing Nightblood in a hard-knuckled grip. He stepped slowly, deliberately, as he approached the men, his cloak rustling. Vivenna intended to do as asked, but she found it hard to look away from him.

The men drew blades. Vasher moved suddenly.

Nightblood, still sheathed, took one man in the chest, and Vivenna heard bones snap. Another man attacked, and Vasher spun, whipping out a hand. The tassels on his sleeve moved on their own, wrapping around the blade of the thief's sword, catching it. Vasher's momentum ripped the blade free, and he tossed it aside, the tassels releasing it.

The sword hit the dirt of the cellar floor; Vasher's hand snapped up, grabbing the thief's face. The tassels wrapped around the man's head like a squid's tentacles. Vasher slammed the man backward and down into the ground—kneeling as he did to add momentum—even as he rammed the sheathed Nightblood into another man's legs, dropping him. A third tried to cut Vasher from behind, and Vivenna cried a warning. Vasher's cloak, however, suddenly whipped out—moving on its own—and grabbed the surprised man by the arms.

Vasher turned, anger in his face, and swung Nightblood toward the entangled man. Vivenna cringed at the sound of the cracking bones, and she turned away from the fight as the screaming continued. With shaking fingers, she tried to open the cage.

It was locked, of course. She drew out some Breath from a rope, then tried to Awaken the lock, but nothing happened.

Metal, she thought. *Of course. It hasn't been alive, so it can't be Awakened.*

Instead she pulled a thread free from her shirt, trying to ignore the cries of pain from behind. Vasher began to bellow as he fought, losing any semblance of being a cold, professional killer. This was a man enraged.

She raised the thread.

"Unlock things," she Commanded.

The thread wiggled a bit, but when she stuck it into the lock, nothing happened.

She withdrew the Breath, took a few calming breaths of her own, then closed her eyes.

Have to get the intention right. Need it to go inside, twist the tumbler free.

"Twist things," she said, feeling the Breath leave her. She

stuck the thread into the lock. It spun about, and she heard a click. The door opened. The sounds of fighting from behind stopped, though men continued to moan.

Vivenna recovered her Breath, then reached into the cage. The girl cringed, crying out and hiding her face.

"I'm a friend," Vivenna said soothingly. "Please, I'm here to help you." But the girl wiggled, screaming when touched. Frustrated, Vivenna turned back toward Vasher.

He stood beside the fire, head bowed, bodies strewn around him. He held Nightblood in one hand, sheathed tip resting back against the dirty floor. And, for some reason, he seemed *larger* than he had a few moments ago. Taller. Broader of shoulder. More threatening.

Vasher's other hand was on Nightblood's hilt. The sheath clasp was undone, and black smoke crept out, off of the blade, some pouring toward the ground, some floating up toward the ceiling. As if it couldn't decide.

Vasher's arm was quivering.

Draw . . . me . . . a distant voice seemed to say in Vivenna's head. *Kill them . . .*

Many of the men still twitched on the ground. Vasher began to slide the blade free. It was dark black, and it seemed to suck in the firelight.

This isn't good, she thought. "Vasher!" she yelled. "Vasher, the girl won't come to me!"

He froze, then glanced at her, eyes glazed over.

"You defeated them, Vasher. No need to draw the sword."

Yes . . . yes there is . . .

He blinked, then saw her. He snapped Nightblood back into place, shaking his head and rushing toward her. He kicked a body as he passed, earning a grunt.

"Colorless monsters," he whispered, looking into the cage. He no longer seemed larger, and she decided that what she'd seen must have just been a trick of the light. He reached into the cage, holding out his hands. And, oddly, the child immediately went to him, grabbing his chest and weeping.

Vivenna watched with shock. Vasher picked the child up, tears in his own eyes.

"You know her?" Vivenna asked.

He shook his head. "I've met Nanrovah, and knew he had young children, but I never met any of them."

"Then how? Why did she come to *you*?"

He didn't answer. "Come on," he said. "I attacked the ones who came running down when they heard screams. But more might return."

He looked like he almost wished that would happen. He turned toward the exit tunnel, and Vivenna followed.

<hr/>

THEY IMMEDIATELY MOVED toward one of the rich neighborhoods of T'Telir. Vasher didn't say much as they walked, and the girl was even more unresponsive. Vivenna worried for the child's mind. She had obviously had a rough couple of months.

They passed from shanties, to tenements, to decent homes on tree-lined streets with burning lanterns. As they reached the mansions, Vasher paused on the street, setting the girl down. "Child," he said. "I'm going to say some words to you. I want you to repeat them. Repeat them, and *mean* them."

The girl regarded him absently, nodding slightly.

He glanced at Vivenna. "Back away."

She opened her mouth to object, but thought better of it. She stepped back out of earshot. Fortunately, Vasher was near a lit streetlamp, so she could see him well. He spoke to the little girl, and she spoke back to him.

After opening the cage, Vivenna had taken the Breath back from the thread. She hadn't stowed it somewhere else. And, with the extra awareness she had, she thought she saw something. The girl's BioChromatic aura—the normal one that all people had—flickered just slightly.

It was faint. Yet with the First Heightening, Vivenna could have sworn she saw it.

But Denth told me it was all or nothing, she thought. *You have to give away all the Breath you hold. And you certainly can't give away* part *of a breath.*

Denth, it had been proven in other instances, was also a liar.

Vasher stood, the girl climbing back into his arms. Vivenna walked up and was surprised to hear the girl talking. "Where's Daddy?" she asked.

Vasher didn't reply.

"I'm dirty," the girl said, looking down. "Mommy doesn't like it when I get dirty. The dress is dirty too."

Vasher began walking. Vivenna hurriedly caught up.

"Are we going home?" the girl asked. "Where have we been? It's late, and I shouldn't be out. Who's that woman?"

She doesn't remember, Vivenna realized. *Doesn't remember where she's been . . . probably doesn't remember anything of the entire experience.*

Vivenna looked again at Vasher, walking with his ragged beard, eyes forward, child in one arm, Nightblood in the other. He walked right up to a mansion's gates, then kicked them open. He moved onto the mansion grounds, Vivenna following more nervously.

A pair of guard dogs began barking. They howled and growled, getting closer. Vivenna cringed. Yet, as soon as they saw Vasher, they grew quiet, then trailed along happily, one hopping up and trying to lick his hands.

What in the name of the Colors is going on?

Some people were gathering at the front of the mansion, holding lanterns, trying to see what had caused the barking. One saw Vasher, said something to the others, then disappeared back inside. By the time Vivenna and Vasher had reached the front patio, a man had appeared at the front doors. He wore a white nightgown and was guarded by a couple of soldiers. They stepped forward to block Vasher, but the man in the nightgown rushed between them, crying out. He wept as he took the child from Vasher's arms.

"Thank you," he whispered. "Thank you."

Vivenna stood quietly, staying back. The dogs continued to lick Vasher's hands, though they noticeably avoided Nightblood.

The man clutched his child before finally surrendering her to a woman who had just arrived—the child's mother, Vivenna assumed. The woman exclaimed in joy, taking the girl.

"Why have you returned her?" the man said, looking at Vasher.

"Those who took her have been punished," Vasher said in his quiet, gruff voice. "That's all that should matter to you right now."

The man squinted. "Do I know you, stranger?"

"We've met," Vasher said. "I asked you to argue against the war."

"That's right!" the man said. "You didn't need to encourage me. But when they took Misel away from me . . . I had to stay quiet about what had happened, had to change my arguments, or they said they'd kill her."

Vasher turned away, moving to walk back down the path. "Take your child, keep her safe." He paused, turning back. "And make certain this kingdom doesn't use its Lifeless for a slaughter."

The man nodded, still weeping. "Yes, yes. Of course. Thank you. Thank you so much."

Vasher continued walking. Vivenna rushed after him, eyeing the dogs. "How did you make them stop barking?"

He didn't respond.

She glanced back at the mansion.

"You have redeemed yourself," he said quietly, passing the dark gates.

"What?"

"Kidnapping that girl is something Denth would have done, even if you hadn't come to T'Telir," Vasher said. "I would never have found her. Denth worked with too many different groups of thieves, and I thought that burglary was simply intended to disrupt supplies. Like everyone else, I ignored the carriage."

He stopped, then looked at Vivenna in the darkness. "You saved that girl's life."

"By happenstance," she said. She couldn't see her hair in the dark, but she could feel it going red.

"Regardless."

Vivenna smiled, the compliment affecting her—for some reason—far more than it should have. "Thank you."

"I'm sorry I lost my temper," he said. "Back in that lair. A warrior is supposed to be calm. When you duel or fight, you can't let anger control you. That's why I've never been that good a duelist."

"You did the job," she said, "and Denth has lost another pawn." They moved out onto the street. "Though," she added, "I wish I hadn't seen that lavish mansion. Doesn't raise my opinion of the Hallandren priests."

Vasher shook his head. "Nanrovah's father was one of the wealthiest merchants in the city. The son dedicated himself to serving the gods out of gratitude for their blessings. He takes no pay for his service."

Vivenna paused. "Oh."

Vasher shrugged in the darkness. "Priests are always easy to blame. They make convenient scapegoats—after all, anyone with a strong faith different from your own must either be a crazy zealot or a lying manipulator."

Vivenna flushed yet again.

Vasher stopped in the street, then turned to her. "I'm sorry," he said. "I didn't mean to say it that way." He cursed, turning and walking again. "I told you I'm no good at this."

"It's all right," she said. "I'm getting used to it."

He nodded in the darkness, seeming distracted.

He is a good man, she thought. *Or, at least, an earnest man trying to be good.* A part of her felt foolish for making yet another judgment.

Yet she knew she couldn't live—couldn't interact—without making some judgments. So she judged Vasher. Not as she'd judged Denth, who had said amusing things and given her what she'd expected to see. She judged Vasher by what she had seen him do. Cry when he saw a child being held captive. Return that child to her father, his only reward an opportunity to make a rough plea for peace. Living with barely any money, dedicating himself to preventing a war.

He was rough. He was brutal. He had a terrible temper. But he was a good man. And, walking beside him, she felt safe for the first time in weeks.

50

"AND SO WE each have twenty thousand," Blushweaver said, walking beside Lightsong on the stone pathway that led in a circle around the arena.

"Yes," Lightsong said.

Their priests, attendants, and servants followed in a holy herd, though the two gods had refused palanquin or parasol. They walked alone, side by side. Lightsong in gold and red. Blushweaver, for once, wearing a gown that actually covered her.

Amazing, how good she looks in something like that, he found himself thinking, *when she takes the time to respect herself.* He wasn't certain what made him dislike her revealing outfits. Maybe he'd been a prude in his former life.

Or maybe he simply was one now. He smiled ruefully to himself. *How much can I really blame on my "old" self? That man is dead. He wasn't the one who got himself involved in the kingdom's politics.*

The arena was filling, and—in a rare show—all of the

gods would be in attendance. Only Weatherlove was late, but he was often unpredictable.

Important events are imminent, Lightsong thought. *They have been building for years now. Why should I be at the center of them?*

His dreams the night before had been so odd. Finally, no visions of war. Just the moon. And some odd twisting passages. Like . . . tunnels.

Many of the gods nodded in respect as he passed their pavilions—though, admittedly, some scowled at him, and a few just ignored him. *What a strange system of rule,* he thought. *Immortals who only last a decade or two—and who have never seen the outside world. And yet the people trust us.*

The people trust us.

"I think we should share the Command phrases with each other, Lightsong," Blushweaver said. "So that we each have all four, just in case."

He didn't say anything.

She turned away from him, looking at the people in their colorful clothing, clogging the benches and seats. "My, my," Blushweaver said, "quite the crowd. And so few of them paying attention to me. Quite rude of them, wouldn't you say?"

Lightsong shrugged.

"Oh, that's right," she said. "Perhaps they're just . . . what was it? Stunned, dazzled, and dumbfounded?"

Lightsong smiled faintly, remembering their conversation a few months back. The day this all had started. Blushweaver looked at him, a longing in her eyes.

"Indeed," Lightsong said. "Or, perhaps, they're really just ignoring you. In order to compliment you."

Blushweaver smiled. "And how, exactly, does ignoring me make a compliment?

"It provokes you to be indignant," Lightsong said. "And we all know that is when you are in best form."

"You like my form, then?"

"It has its uses. Unfortunately, I cannot compliment you by ignoring you as the others do. You see, only truly, *sincerely* ignoring you would provide the intended compliment. I am, actually, helpless and unable to ignore you. I do apologize."

"I see," Blushweaver said. "I'm flattered. I think. Yet you seem very good at ignoring *some* things. Your own divinity. General good manners. My feminine wiles."

"You're hardly wily, my dear," Lightsong said. "A wily man is one who fights with a small, carefully hidden dagger in reserve. You are more like a man who crushes his opponent with a stone block. Regardless, I do have another method of dealing with you, one that you shall likely find quite flattering."

"Somehow I find myself doubting."

"You should have more faith in me," he said with a suave wave of the hand. "I am, after all, a god. In my divine wisdom, I have realized that the only way to truly compliment one such as you—Blushweaver—is to be far more attractive, intelligent, and interesting than you."

She snorted. "Well, then, I feel rather insulted by *your* presence."

"Touché," Lightsong said.

"And are you going to explain *why* you consider competing with me to be the most sincere form of compliment?"

"Of course I am," Lightsong said. "My dear, have you ever known me to make an inflammatorily ridiculous statement without providing an equally ridiculous explanation to substantiate it?"

"Of course not," she agreed. "You are nothing if not exhaustive in your self-congratulatory made-up logic."

"I am rather exceptional in that regard."

"Undoubtedly."

"Anyway," Lightsong said, holding up a finger, "by being far more stunning than you are, I invite people to ignore you and pay attention to me. That, in turn, invites *you* to be your usual charming self—throwing little tantrums and being overly seductive—to draw their attention back to you. And that, as I explained, is when you are most majestic. Therefore, the only way to make certain you receive the attention you deserve is to draw it all away from you. It's really *quite* difficult. I hope you appreciate all the work I do to be so wonderful."

"Let me assure you," she said, "I do appreciate it. In fact, I appreciate it so very much that I would like to give you a break. You can back off. I will bear the awful burden of being the most wonderful of the gods."

"I couldn't possibly let you."

"But if you are *too* wonderful, my dear, you will completely destroy your image."

"That image is getting tiresome anyway," Lightsong said. "I've long sought to be the most notoriously lazy of the gods, but I'm realizing more and more that the task is beyond me. The others are all naturally so much more delightfully useless than I am. They just pretend not to be aware of it."

"Lightsong!" she said. "One could say you begin to sound jealous!"

"One could also say that my feet smell like guava fruit," he said. "Just because one *could* say it doesn't mean it's relevant."

She laughed. "You're incorrigible."

"Really? I thought I was in T'Telir. When did we move?"

She held up a finger. "That pun was a stretch."

"Perhaps it was just a feint."

"A feint?"

"Yes, an intentionally weak joke to distract from the *real* one."

"Which is?"

Lightsong hesitated, glancing at the arena. "The joke that has been played on all of us," he said, voice growing softer. "The joke the others in the pantheon have played by giving me so much influence over what our kingdom will do."

Blushweaver frowned at him, obviously sensing the growing bitterness in his voice. They stopped on the walkway, Blushweaver facing him, her back to the arena floor. Lightsong feigned a smile, but the moment was dying. They couldn't go on as they had. Not amidst the weighty matters in motion all around them.

"Our brothers and sisters aren't as bad as you imply," she said quietly.

"Only a matchless group of idiots would give *me* control of their armies."

"They trust you."

"They're *lazy*," Lightsong said. "They want others to make the difficult decisions. That's what this system encourages, Blushweaver. We're all locked in here, expected to spend our time in idleness and pleasure. And then we're supposed to know what is best for our country?" He shook his head. "We're more afraid of the outside than we're willing to admit. All we have are artworks and dreams. That's why you and I ended up with these armies. Nobody else wants to be the one who actually sends our troops out to kill and die. They all want to be involved, but nobody wants to be *responsible*."

He fell silent. She looked up at him, a goddess of perfect form. So much stronger than the others, but she hid it behind her own veil of triviality. "I know one thing that you said is true," she said quietly.

"And that is?"

"You *are* wonderful, Lightsong."

He stood there, looking into her eyes for a time. Widely set, beautiful green eyes.

"You're not going to give me your Command Phrases, are you?" she asked.

He shook his head.

"I brought you into this," she said. "You always talk about being useless, but we all know that you're one of the few who always goes through every picture, sculpture, and tapestry in his gallery. The one who hears every poem and song. The one who listens most deeply to the pleas of his petitioners."

"You are all fools," he said. "There is nothing in me to respect."

"No," she said. "You're the one who makes us laugh, even while you insult us. Can't you see what *that* does? Can't you see how you've inadvertently set yourself above everyone else? You didn't do it intentionally, Lightsong, and that's what makes it work so well. In a city of frivolity, you're the only one who's shown any measure of wisdom. In my opinion, that's why you hold the armies."

He didn't reply.

"I knew you might resist me," she said. "But I thought that I'd be able to influence you anyway."

"You can," he said. "As you've said, it's your doing that I'm involved in all of this."

She shook her head, still staring into his eyes. "I can't decide which feeling for you is stronger, Lightsong. My love or my frustration."

He took her hand and kissed it. "I accept them both, Blushweaver. With honor." And with that, he turned from her and went to his box. Weatherlove had arrived; that left only the God King and his bride. Lightsong sat down, wondering where Siri was. She usually got to the arena long before it was time to begin.

He found it difficult to focus his attention on the young queen. Blushweaver still stood on the walkway where he had left her, watching him.

Finally, she turned, and made her way to her own pavilion.

SIRI WALKED THROUGH the palace corridors, surrounded by her brown-uniformed serving women, a dozen worries circling through her brain.

First, go to Lightsong, she told herself, going over the plan. *It won't look odd for me to sit with him—we often spend time together at these things.*

I wait for Susebron to arrive. Then I ask Lightsong if we can talk in private, without our servants or his priests. I explain what I have discovered about the God King. I tell him about the way Susebron is being held captive. Then we see what he does.

Her biggest fear was that Lightsong would already know. Could he be part of the entire conspiracy? She trusted him as much as she trusted anyone except Susebron, but her nerves had a way of making her question everything and everyone.

She passed through room after room, each one decorated in its own color theme. She didn't notice how bright those were anymore.

Assuming Lightsong agrees to help, she thought, *I wait for the break. Once the priests leave the sand, Lightsong goes and speaks with several other gods. They each go to their priests and instruct them to begin a discussion in the arena about why the God King never speaks to them. They force the God King's priests to let him offer his own defense.*

She didn't like depending on the priests, even those who weren't members of Susebron's priesthood, but this did seem like the best way. Besides, if the priests of the various gods didn't do as instructed, Lightsong and the others would realize that they were being undermined by their own servants. Either way, Siri realized she was getting into very dangerous territory.

I started in dangerous territory, she thought, leaving the formal rooms of the palace and entering the dark outer hallway. *The man I love is threatened with death, and any children I bear will be taken from me.* She either had to act or let the priests continue to push her around. Susebron and she were in agreement. The best plan was—

Siri slowed. At the end of the hallway, in front of the doors out to the court, a small group of priests stood with several Lifeless soldiers. They were silhouetted by the evening light. The priests turned toward her, and one pointed.

Colors! Siri thought, spinning. Another group of priests was approaching up the back hallway. *No! Not now!*

The two groups of priests closed on her. Siri considered running, but where? Dashing in her long dress—pushing through servants and Lifeless—was hopeless. She raised her chin—eyeing the priests with a haughty stare—and kept her hair completely under control. "What is the meaning of this?" she demanded.

"We're terribly sorry, Vessel," the lead priest said. "But it has been decided that you shouldn't be exerting yourself while in your condition."

"My condition?" Siri asked icily. "What foolishness is this?"

"The child, Vessel," the priest said. "We can't risk danger to it. There are many who would try to harm you, should they know that you are carrying."

Siri froze. *Child?* she thought with shock. *How could they know that Susebron and I have actually started . . .*

But no. She would know if she were with child. However, she'd supposedly been sleeping with the God King for months now. That was just enough time for a pregnancy to have begun to show. It would sound plausible to the people of the city.

Fool! She thought to herself in a sudden panic. *Assuming they've already found their replacement God King, I don't actually need to bear them a child. They just have to make everyone* think *I was pregnant!*

"There is no child," she said. "You were just waiting— you just had to stall until you had an excuse to lock me away."

"Please, Vessel," one of the priests said, gesturing for a Lifeless to take her arm. She didn't struggle; she forced herself to remain calm, looking the priest in the eyes.

He looked away. "This will be for the best," he said. "It's for your own good."

"I'm sure it is," she snapped, but allowed herself to be led back to her rooms.

———⟨∞⟩———

VIVENNA SAT AMONG the crowds, watching and waiting. Part of her found it foolish to come out into the open so flagrantly. However, that part of her—the cautious Idrian princess—was growing more and more quiet.

Denth's people had found her when she'd been hiding in the slums. She'd probably be safer in the crowds with Vasher than she ever had been in the alleyways, particularly considering how well she now blended in. She hadn't realized how natural it could feel to sit in trousers and a tunic, brightly colored and completely ignored.

Vasher appeared at the railing above the benches. She carefully slipped out of her seat—someone else took it immediately—and walked toward him. The priests had already begun their arguments down below. Nanrovah, his daughter restored to him, had started by announcing the retraction of his previous position. He currently was leading the discussion against war.

He had very little support.

Vivenna joined Vasher along the railing, and he quite unapologetically elbowed open a space for her. He didn't carry Nightblood—at her insistence, he had left the sword behind with her own dueling blade. She wasn't certain how he'd managed to sneak the blade in the last time he'd come to the court, but the last thing they wanted was to draw attention.

"Well?" she asked quietly.

He shook his head. "If Denth is here, I couldn't find him."

"No surprise, considering the size of this crowd," Vivenna said quietly. There were bodies all around them—hundreds lining the railing alone. "Where did they all come from? This is far more jammed than the other assembly sessions."

He shrugged. "People who are granted a one-time visit to the court can hold their token of entry until they want to use it. A lot of them use those at a general Court Assembly, rather than one of the smaller meetings. It's their one chance to see all of the gods together."

Vivenna turned back to look over the throng. She suspected it also had to do with the rumors she'd heard. People thought that this session would be the one where the Pantheon of Returned finally declared war on Idris.

"Nanrovah argues well," she said, although she was having trouble hearing him because of the crowds—the Returned apparently had messengers relaying transcripts. She wondered why someone just didn't order all the people to be quiet. That didn't seem to be the Hallandren way. They liked chaos. Or, at least, they liked the opportunity to sit and chat while important events were in progress.

"Nanrovah is being ignored," Vasher said. "He's changed his mind twice now on the same issue. He lacks credibility."

"He should explain why he changed his mind, then."

"He might, but I don't know. If the people knew his child had been kidnapped, it would make some more afraid and they would decide that Idrian instigators had been behind it, no matter what he said. Plus there's that stubborn Hallandren pride. Priests are particularly bad. Mentioning that his daughter had been taken, and that he had been pressured into changing his politics . . ."

"I thought you liked the priests," she said.

"Some of them," he said. "Not others." When he said that, he eyed the God King's pedestal. Susebron had yet to arrive, and they had started without him.

Siri wasn't there either. That annoyed Vivenna, since

she'd been anticipating checking in on the girl, if only from a distance.

I'll help you, Siri. For real this time. The first step has to be stopping this war.

Vasher looked back at the floor of the arena, leaning on the railing, looking anxious.

"What?" she asked.

He shrugged.

She rolled her eyes. "Tell me."

"I just don't like leaving Nightblood alone for too long," he said.

"What's it going to do?" Vivenna asked. "We locked it in the closet."

He shrugged again.

"Honestly," she said. "You would think that you'd admit that bringing a five-foot-long black sword out in public would be rather conspicuous. It doesn't help, mind you, that said sword bleeds smoke and can talk in people's minds."

"I don't mind being conspicuous."

"I do," she replied.

Vasher grimaced, and she thought he'd argue some more, but he finally just nodded. "You're right, of course," he said. "I've just never been good at being unobtrusive. Denth used to make fun of me for that too."

Vivenna frowned. "You were friends?"

Vasher turned away and fell silent.

Kalad's Phantoms! she thought in frustration. *One of these days, someone in this Colors-cursed city is going to tell me the whole truth. I'll probably die of shock.*

"I'm going to go see if I can find out why the God King is taking so long," Vasher said, leaving the railing. "I'll be back."

She nodded, and he was gone. She leaned down, wishing she hadn't relinquished her seat. Once, she would have felt stifled by the large mass of people, but she'd grown used to the busy market streets, and so being surrounded by people wasn't as intimidating as it had been. Besides, there was her Breath. She'd put some of it into her shirt, but she'd held onto a portion—she needed to be of at least the First Heightening to pass through the gates into the court without being questioned.

Her Breath let her feel life as an ordinary person felt the air: always there, cool against the skin. Having so many people in such close proximity left her feeling a little intoxicated. So much life, so many hopes and desires. So much Breath. She closed her eyes, drinking it in, listening to the voices of the priests down below rise over the crowd.

She felt Vasher approach before he arrived. Not only did he have a lot of Breath, but he was watching her, and she could feel the slight familiarity of that gaze. She turned, picking him out of the crowd. He stood out far more than she did, in his darker, ragged clothing.

"Congratulations," he said as he approached, taking her arm.

"Why?"

"You'll soon be an aunt."

"What are you . . ." She trailed off. "*Siri?*"

"Your sister is pregnant," he said. "The priests are going to make an announcement later this evening. The God King is apparently remaining in his palace to celebrate."

Vivenna stood, stunned. *Siri. Pregnant.* Siri, who was still a little girl in Vivenna's mind, bearing the child of that *thing* in the palace. And yet wasn't Vivenna now fighting to keep that thing on his throne?

No, she thought. *I haven't forgiven Hallandren, even if I am learning not to hate it. I can't let Idris be attacked and destroyed.*

She felt a panic. Suddenly, all of her plans seemed meaningless. What would the Hallandren do to her once they had their heir? "We have to get her out," Vivenna found herself saying. "Vasher, we have to rescue her."

He remained quiet.

"*Please,* Vasher," she whispered. "She's my *sister.* I thought to protect her by ending this war, but if your hunch is right, then the God King himself is one of those who wants to invade Idris. Siri won't be safe with him."

"All right," Vasher said. "I will do what I can."

Vivenna nodded, turning back to the arena. The priests were withdrawing. "Where are they going?"

"To their gods," Vasher said. "To seek the Will of the Pantheon in formal vote."

"About the war?" Vivenna asked, feeling a chill.

Vasher nodded. "It is time."

———◦∞◦———

LIGHTSONG WAITED BENEATH his canopy, a couple of serving men fanning him, a cup of chilled juice in his hand, lavish snacks spread out to his side.

Blushweaver brought me into this, he thought. *Because she was worried that Hallandren would be taken by surprise.*

The priests were consulting with their gods. He could see several of them kneeling before their Returned, heads bowed. It was the way that government worked in Hallandren. The priests debated their options and then they sought the will of the gods. That would become the Will of the Pantheon. That would become the Will of Hallandren itself. Only the God King could veto a decision of the full Pantheon.

And he had chosen not to attend this meeting.

So self-congratulatory on spawning a child that he couldn't even bother with the future of his people? Lightsong thought with annoyance. *I had hoped he was better than that.*

Llarimar approached. Though he had been down below with the other high priests, he had offered no arguments to the court. Llarimar tended to keep his thoughts to himself.

The high priest knelt before him. "Please, favor us with your will, Lightsong my god."

Lightsong didn't respond. He looked up, across the open arena to where Blushweaver's canopy stood, verdant in the dimming evening light.

"Oh, God," Llarimar said. "Please. Give me the knowledge I seek. Should we go to war with our kinsmen, the Idrians? Are they rebels who need to be quelled?"

Priests were already returning from their supplications. Each held aloft a flag indicating the will of their god or goddess. Green for a favorable response. Red for dissatisfaction with the petition. In this case green meant war. So far, five of the returning seven flew green.

"Your Grace?" Llarimar asked, looking up.

Lightsong stood. *They vote, but what good are their votes?* he thought, walking out from beneath his canopy. *They hold no authority. Only two votes really matter.*

More green. Flags flapped as priests ran down the walkways. The arena was abuzz with people. They could see the inevitable. To the side, Lightsong could see Llarimar following him. The man must be frustrated. Why didn't he ever show it?

Lightsong approached Blushweaver's pavilion. Almost all of the priests had gotten their answers, and the vast majority of them carried flags of green. Blushweaver's high priestess still knelt before her. Blushweaver, of course, waited upon the drama of the moment.

Lightsong stopped outside of her canopy. Blushweaver reclined inside, watching him calmly, though he could sense her true anxiety. He knew her too well.

"Are you going to make your will known?" she asked.

He looked down at the center of the arena. "If I resist," he said, "this declaration will be for naught. The gods can shout 'war' until they are blue, but *I* control the armies. If I don't allow them my Lifeless, then Hallandren will not win any wars."

"You would defy the Will of the Pantheon?"

"It is my right to do so," he said. "Just as any of them have the same right."

"But you have the Lifeless."

"That doesn't mean I have to do what I'm told."

There was a moment of silence before Blushweaver waved to her priestess. The woman stood, then raised a flag of green and ran down to join the others. This brought forth a roar. The people must know that Blushweaver's political wranglings had left her in a position of power. Not bad, for a person who had started without command of a single soldier.

With her control of that many troops, she'll be an integral part of the planning, diplomacy, and execution of the war. Blushweaver could emerge from this as one of the most powerful Returned in the history of the kingdom.

And so could I.

He stared for a long moment. He hadn't spoken of his dreams the last night to Llarimar. He'd kept them to himself. Those dreams of twisting tunnels and of the rising moon, just barely cresting the horizon. Could it be possible that they actually meant something?

He couldn't decide. About anything.

"I need to think about this some more," Lightsong said, turning to go.

"What?" Blushweaver demanded. "What about the vote?"

Lightsong shook his head.

"Lightsong!" she said as he left. "Lightsong, you can't leave us hanging like this!"

He shrugged, glancing back. "Actually, I can." He smiled. "I'm frustrating like that."

And with that, he left the arena, heading back to his palace without giving his vote.

51

I'M GLAD YOU came back for me, Nightblood said. *It was very lonely in that closet.*

Vasher didn't reply as he walked across the top of the wall surrounding the Court of Gods. It was late, dark, and quiet, though a few of the palaces still shone with light. One of those belonged to Lightsong the Bold.

I don't like the darkness, Nightblood said.

"You mean darkness like now?" Vasher asked.

No. In the closet.

"You can't even see."

A person knows when they're in darkness, Nightblood said. *Even when they can't see.*

Vasher didn't know how to respond to that. He paused atop the wall, overlooking Lightsong's palace. Red and gold. Bold colors indeed.

You shouldn't ignore me, Nightblood said. *I don't like it.*

Vasher knelt down, studying the palace. He'd never met the one called Lightsong, but he had heard rumors. The most scurrilous of the gods, the most condescending and mocking. And this was the person who held the fate of two kingdoms in his hands.

There was an easy way to influence that fate.

We're going to kill him, aren't we? Nightblood said, eagerness sharp in his voice.

Vasher just stared at the palace.

We should kill him, Nightblood continued. *Come on. We should do it. We* really *should do it.*

"Why do you care?" Vasher whispered. "You don't know him."

He's evil, Nightblood said.

Vasher snorted. "You don't even know what that is."

For once, Nightblood was silent.

That was the great crux of the problem, the issue that had dominated most of Vasher's life. A thousand Breaths. That was what it took to Awaken an object of steel and give it sentience. Even Shashara hadn't fully understood the process, though she had first devised it.

It took a person who had reached the Ninth Heightening to Awaken stone or steel. Even then, this process shouldn't have worked. It should have created an Awakened object with no more of a mind than the tassels on his cloak.

Nightblood should not be alive. And yet he was. Shashara had always been the most talented of them, far more capable than Vasher himself, who had used tricks—like encasing bones in steel or stone—to make his creations. Shashara had been spurred on by the knowledge that she'd been shown up by Yesteel and the development of ichoralcohol. She had studied, experimented, practiced. And she'd done it. She'd learned to forge the Breath of a thousand people into a piece of steel, Awaken it to sentience, and give it a Command. That single Command took on immense power, providing a foundation for the personality of the object Awakened.

With Nightblood, she and Vasher had spent much time in thought, then finally chosen a simple, yet elegant, Command. "Destroy evil." It had seemed like such a perfect, logical choice. There was only one problem, something neither of them had foreseen.

How was an object of steel—an object that was so removed from life that it would find the experience of living strange and alien—supposed to understand what "evil" was?

I'm figuring it out, Nightblood said. *I've had a lot of practice.*

The sword wasn't really to blame. It was a terrible, destructive thing—but it had been created to destroy. It still didn't understand life or what that life meant. It only knew its Command, and it tried so very hard to fulfill it.

That man down there, Nightblood said. *The god in the palace. He holds the power to start this war. You don't want this war to start. That's why he's evil.*

"Why does that make him evil?"

Because he will do what you don't want him to.

"We don't know that for certain," Vasher said. "Plus, who is to say that my judgment is best?"

It is, Nightblood said. *Let's go. Let's kill him. You told me war is bad. He will start a war. He's evil. Let's kill him. Let's kill him.*

The sword was getting excited; Vasher could feel it— feel the danger in its blade, the twisted power of Breaths that had been pulled from living hosts and shoved into something unnatural. He could picture them breathing out, black and corrupted, twisting in the wind. Drawing him toward Lightsong. Pushing him to kill.

"No," Vasher said.

Nightblood sighed. *You locked me in a closet,* he reminded. *You should apologize.*

"I'm not going to apologize by killing someone."

Just throw me in there, Nightblood said. *If he's evil, he'll kill himself.*

This gave Vasher pause. *Colors,* he thought. The sword seemed to be getting more subtle each year, though Vasher knew he was just imagining things, projecting. Awakened objects didn't change or grow, they simply were what they were.

It was still a good idea.

"Maybe later," Vasher said, turning away from the building.

You are afraid, Nightblood said.

"You don't know what fear is," Vasher replied.

I do. You don't like killing Returned. You're afraid of them.

The sword was wrong, of course. But, on the outside, Vasher supposed that his hesitation did look like fear. It had been a long time since he'd dealt with the Returned. Too many memories. Too much pain.

He made his way to the God King's palace. The structure was old, far older than the palaces that surrounded it. Once, this place had been a seaside outpost, overlooking the bay. No city. No colors. Just the stark, black tower. It amused Vasher that it had become the home of the God King of the Iridescent Tones.

Vasher slid Nightblood into a strap on his back, then jumped from the wall toward the palace. Awakened tassels around his legs gave him extra strength, letting him leap some twenty feet. He slammed against the side of the building, smooth onyx blocks rubbing his skin. He twitched his fingers, and the tassels on his sleeves grabbed on to the ledge above him, holding him tight.

He Breathed. The belt at his waist—touching his skin, as always—Awakened. Color drained from the kerchief tied to his leg beneath his trousers.

"Climb things, then grab things, then pull me up," he Commanded. Three Commands in one Awakening, a difficult task for some. For him, however, it had become as simple as blinking.

The belt untied itself, revealing it to be far longer than it looked when wrapped around him. The twenty-five feet of rope snaked up the side of the building, curling inside of a window. Seconds later, the rope hauled Vasher up and into the air. Awakened objects could, if created well, have much more strength than regular muscles. He'd once seen a small group of ropes not much thicker than his own lift and toss boulders at an enemy fortification.

He released his tassel grips, then pulled Nightblood free as the rope deposited him inside the building. He knelt silently, eyes searching the darkness. The room was unoccupied. Carefully, he drew back his Breath, then wrapped the rope around his arm and held it in a loose coil. He stalked forward.

Who are we going to kill? Nightblood asked.

It's not always about killing, Vasher said.

Vivenna. Is she in here?

The sword was trying to interpret his thoughts again. It had trouble with things that weren't fully formed in Vasher's head. Most thoughts passing through a man's mind were fleeting and momentary. Flashes of image, sound, or scent. Connections made, then lost, then recovered again. That sort of thing was difficult for Nightblood to interpret.

Vivenna. The source of a lot of his troubles. His work in the city had been easier when he'd been able to assume that she was working willingly with Denth. Then, at least, he'd been able to blame her.

Where is she? Is she here? She doesn't like me, but I like her.

Vasher hesitated in the dark hallway. *You do?*

Yes. She's nice. And she's pretty.

Nice and pretty—words that Nightblood didn't really understand. He had simply learned when to use them. Still, the sword did have opinions, and it rarely lied. It must like Vivenna, even if it couldn't explain why.

She reminds me of a Returned, the sword said.

Ah, Vasher thought. *Of course. That makes sense.* He moved on.

What? Nightblood said.

She's descended from one, he thought. *You can tell by the hair. There's a bit of Returned in her.*

Nightblood didn't respond to that, but Vasher could feel it thinking.

He paused at an intersection. He was pretty sure he knew where the God King's chambers would be. However, a lot of the interior seemed different now. The fortress had been stark, built with odd twists and turns to confuse an invading foe. Those remained—all the stonework was the same—but the open dining halls or garrison rooms had been split into many, smaller rooms, colorfully decorated in the mode of the Hallandren upper class.

Where would the God King's wife be? If she was pregnant, she'd be under the care of servants. One of the larger complex of chambers, he assumed, on a higher level. He made his way to a stairwell. Fortunately, it seemed late enough that there were very few people awake.

The sister, Nightblood said. *That's who you're after. You're rescuing Vivenna's sister!*

Vasher nodded quietly in the darkness, feeling his way up the stairs, counting on his BioChroma to let him know if he approached anyone. Though most of his Breath was stored in his clothing, he had just enough to awaken the rope and to keep him aware.

You like Vivenna too! Nightblood said.

Nonsense, Vasher thought.

Then why?

Her sister, he thought. *She's a key to all of this, somehow. I realized it today. As soon as the queen arrived, the real move to start the war surged.*

Nightblood fell silent. That kind of logical leap was a bit too complex for it. *I see,* he said, though Vasher smiled at the confusion he sensed in the voice.

At the very least, Vasher thought, *she's a very handy hostage for the Hallandren. The God King's priests—or whoever's behind this—can threaten the girl's life, should the war go poorly for them. She makes an excellent tool.*

One you intend to remove, Nightblood said.

Vasher nodded, reaching the top of the stairwell and slinking through one of the corridors. He walked until he sensed someone nearby—a maid servant approaching.

Vasher Awakened his rope, stood in the shadows of an alcove, and waited. As she passed, the rope shot from the shadows, wrapped around her waist, and yanked her into the darkness. Vasher had one of his tassel hands wrapped around her mouth before she could scream.

She squirmed, but the rope tied her tightly. He felt a little stab of guilt as he loomed over her, her terrified eyes tearing up. He reached for Nightblood and pulled the sword slightly out of its sheath. The girl immediately looked sick. A good sign.

"I need to know where the queen is," Vasher said, forcing Nightblood up so that his hilt touched her cheek. "You're going to tell me."

He held her like that for a time, watching her squirm, feeling unhappy with himself. Finally, he relaxed the tassels, keeping the sword against her cheek. She began to vomit, and he turned her to the side.

"Tell me," he whispered.

"Southern corner," the girl whispered, trembling, spittle on her cheek. "This floor."

Vasher nodded, then tied her up with the rope, gagged her, and took his Breath back. He pushed Nightblood back into the sheath and then rushed down the hallway.

You won't kill a god who plans to march his armies to war? Nightblood asked. *But you'll nearly choke a young woman to death?*

It was a complicated statement for the sword. However, it lacked the accusation that a human would have put into the words. To Nightblood it really was just a question.

I don't understand my morality either, Vasher thought. *I'd suggest you avoid confusing yourself.*

He found the place easily. It was guarded by a large group of brutish men who seemed rather out of place in the fine palace hallways.

Vasher paused. *Something strange is going on here.*

What do you mean? Nightblood asked.

He hadn't meant to address the sword, but that was the trouble with an object that could read minds. Any thoughts Vasher formed in his head, Nightblood thought were directed at it. After all, in the sword's opinion, *everything really should have been directed toward it.*

Guards at the door. Soldiers, not servants. So they had already taken her captive. Was she really even pregnant? Were the priests just securing their power?

That many men would be impossible to kill without making noise. The best he could hope for was to take them fast. Maybe they were far enough from anyone else that a brief fight wouldn't be heard.

He sat for a few minutes, jaw clenched. Then, finally, he stepped closer and tossed Nightblood in amongst the men. He'd let them fight each other and then be ready to deal with any who weren't taken into the sword's influence.

Nightblood clanged to the stones. All of the men's eyes turned toward it. And, at that moment, something grabbed Vasher by the shoulder and yanked him backward.

He cursed, spinning, throwing his hands up to wrestle with whatever had him. An Awakened rope. Men started to fight behind him. Vasher grunted, pulling out the knife in his boot, then slicing the Awakened rope. Someone tackled him as he got free, and he was thrown back against the wall.

He grabbed his attacker by the face with one of his arm tassels, then twisted the man back and threw him into the wall. Another figure charged him from behind, but Vasher's Awakened cloak caught that one, tripping him.

"Grab things other than me," Vasher said quickly, snatching the cloak of one of the fallen men and Awakening it. That cloak whipped about, taking down another man, whom Vasher then killed with a swipe of his dagger. He kicked another man, throwing him backward, opening a pathway.

Vasher lunged, making for Nightblood, but three more figures burst out of the rooms around him, cutting him off. They were the same kind of brutish men that were now fighting over the sword. Men were all around. Dozens of them. Vasher kicked out, breaking a leg, but one man pulled Vasher's cloak off with a lucky twist. Others piled on top of him. And then, another Awakened rope snapped out, tying his legs together.

Vasher reached for his vest. "Your Breath to—" he began, trying to draw in some Breath to use for an attack, but three men grabbed his hand and pulled it away. Within seconds, he was wrapped·up in the Awakened rope. His cloak still fought against three men who were struggling to cut it up, but Vasher himself was pinned.

Someone emerged from the room to his left.

"Denth," Vasher spat, struggling.

"My good friend," Denth said, nodding for one of his lackeys—the one known as Tonk Fah—to move down the hallway toward the queen's room. Denth knelt beside Vasher. "Very good to see you."

Vasher spat again.

"Still as eloquent as ever, I see," Denth said with a sigh. "You know the best thing about you, Vasher? You're solid. Predictable. I guess I am too, in a way. Hard to live as long as we have without falling into patterns, eh?"

Vasher didn't reply, though he did try to yell as some men gagged him. He noticed with satisfaction that he'd taken down a good dozen opponents before they'd managed to stop him.

Denth eyed the fallen soldiers. "Mercenaries," he said. "No risk is too great, assuming the pay is right." He said it with a twinkle in his eye. Then he leaned down, his joviality gone as he met Vasher's eyes. "And you were always to be *my* payment, Vasher. I owe you. For Shashara, even still. We've been waiting, hidden in the palace here for a good two weeks, knowing that eventually the good Princess Vivenna would send you to save her sister."

Tonk Fah returned with a bundle held in a blanket. Nightblood.

Denth eyed it. "Throw that out somewhere far away," he said, grimacing.

"I don't know, Denth," Tonk Fah said. "I kind of think we should keep it. It could be very useful. . . ." The beginnings of the lust began to show in his eyes, the desire to draw Nightblood, to use the sword. To destroy evil. Or, really, just to destroy.

Denth stood and snatched the bundle away. Then he smacked Tonk Fah on the back of the head.

"Ow!" Tonk Fah said.

Denth rolled his eyes. "Stop whining; I just saved your life. Go check on the queen and then clean up that mess. I'll take care of the sword myself."

"You always get so nasty when Vasher's around," Tonk Fah grumbled, waddling away. Denth wrapped up Nightblood securely; Vasher watched, hoping to see the lust appear in Denth's eyes. Unfortunately, Denth was far too strong-willed to be taken by the sword. He had nearly as much history with it as Vasher did.

"Take away all his Awakened clothing," Denth said to his men, walking away. "Then hang him up in that room over there. He and I are going to have a long talk about what he did to my sister."

52

LIGHTSONG SAT IN one of the rooms of his palace, surrounded by finery, a cup of wine in his hand. Despite the very late hour, servants moved in and out, piling up furniture, paintings, vases, and small sculptures. Anything that could be moved.

The riches sat in heaps. Lightsong lounged back on his couch, ignoring empty plates of food and broken cups, which he refused to let his servants take away.

A pair of servants entered, carrying a red and gold couch. They propped it up by the far wall, nearly toppling a pile of rugs. Lightsong watched them leave, then downed the rest of his wine. He dropped the empty cup to the floor beside the others and held out his hand for another full one. A servant provided, as always.

He wasn't drunk. He couldn't get drunk.

"Do you ever feel," Lightsong said, "like something is going on? Something far greater than you are? Like a painting you can only see the corner of, no matter how you squint and search?"

"Every day, Your Grace," Llarimar said. He sat on a stool beside Lightsong's couch. As always, he watched events calmly, though Lightsong could sense the man's disapproval as another group of servants piled several marble figurines in the corner.

"How do you deal with it?" Lightsong asked.

"I have faith, Your Grace, that someone understands."

"Not me, I hope," Lightsong noted.

"You are part of it. But it is much larger than you."

Lightsong frowned to himself, watching more servants enter. Soon the room would be so piled with his wealth that his servants wouldn't be able to move in and out. "It's odd, isn't it," Lightsong said, gesturing toward a pile of paintings. "Arranged like this, none of it looks beautiful anymore. When you put it together in piles, it just seems like junk."

Llarimar raised an eyebrow. "The value in something relates to how it is treated, Your Grace. If you see these items as junk, then they are, regardless of what someone else would pay for them."

"There's a lesson in there somewhere, isn't there?"

Llarimar shrugged. "I *am* a priest, after all. We have a tendency to preach."

Lightsong snorted, then waved toward the servants. "That's enough," he said. "You can go now."

The servants, having grown resigned to being banished,

left the room promptly. Soon Lightsong and Llarimar were alone with piles and piles of riches, all stolen from other parts of his palace and brought into this one room.

Llarimar surveyed the mounds. "So what *is* the point of all this, Your Grace?"

"This is what I mean to them," Lightsong said, gulping down some more wine. "The people. They'll give up their riches for me. They sacrifice the Breath of their souls to keep me alive. I suspect that many would even die for me."

Llarimar nodded quietly.

"And," Lightsong said, "all I'm expected to do at the moment is choose their fates for them. Do we go to war or do we remain at peace? What do you think?"

"I could argue for either side, Your Grace," Llarimar said. "It would be easy to sit here and condemn the war on mere principle. War is a terrible, terrible thing. And yet, it seems that few great accomplishments in history ever occur without the unfortunate fact of military action. Even the Manywar, which caused so much destruction, can be regarded as the foundation of modern Hallandren power in the Inner Sea region."

Lightsong nodded.

"But," Llarimar continued. "To attack our brethren? Despite provocation, I cannot help but think that invading is too extreme. How much death, how much suffering, are we willing to cause simply to prove that we won't be pushed around?"

"And what would you decide?"

"Fortunately, I don't have to."

"And if you were forced to?" Lightsong asked.

Llarimar sat for a moment. Then, carefully, he removed the large miter from his head, revealing his thinning black hair plastered to the skull with sweat. He set aside the ceremonial headgear.

"I speak to you as a friend, Lightsong, not your priest,"

Llarimar said quietly. "The priest cannot influence his god for fear of disrupting the future."

Lightsong nodded.

"And as a friend," Llarimar said, "I honestly have trouble deciding what I would do. I didn't argue on the floor of the court."

"You rarely do," Lightsong said.

"I'm worried," Llarimar said, wiping his brow with a kerchief, shaking his head. "I don't think we can ignore the threat to our kingdom. The fact of the matter is, Idris *is* a rebel faction living within our borders. We've ignored them for years, enduring their almost tyrannical control of the northern passes."

"So you're for attacking?"

Llarimar paused, then shook his head. "No. No, I don't think that even Idris's rebellion can justify the slaughter it would take to get those passes back."

"Great," Lightsong said flatly. "So, you think we should go to war, but not attack."

"Actually, yes," Llarimar said. "We declare war, we make a show of force, and we frighten them into realizing just how precarious their position is. If we then hold peace talks, I'll bet we could forge more favorable treaties for use of the passes. They formally renounce their claim to our throne; we recognize their independent sovereignty. Wouldn't we both get what we want?"

Lightsong sat thoughtfully. "I don't know," he said. "That's a very reasonable solution, but I don't think those who are calling for war would accept it. It seems that we're missing something, Scoot. Why now? Why are tensions so high after the wedding, which *should* have unified us?"

"I don't know, Your Grace," Llarimar said.

Lightsong smiled, standing. "Well then," he said, eyeing his high priest. "Let's find out."

∞

SIRI WOULD HAVE been annoyed if she hadn't been so terrified. She sat alone in the black bedchamber. It felt wrong for Susebron to not be there with her.

She'd hoped that maybe he would still be allowed to come to her when night fell. But, of course, he didn't arrive. Whatever the priests were planning, it didn't require her to actually be pregnant. Not now that they'd played their hand and locked her up.

The door creaked, and she sat up on the bed, hope reviving. But it was only the guard checking on her again. One of the crass, soldierlike men who had been guarding her in recent hours. *Why did they change to these men?* she wondered as the guard closed the door. *What happened to the Lifeless and the priests who were watching me before?*

She lay back down on the bed, staring up at the canopy, still dressed in her fine gown. Her mind kept flashing to her first week in the palace, when she'd been locked inside for her "Wedding Jubilation." It had been difficult enough then, and she'd known when it would be over. Now she didn't even have an assurance that she'd live through the next few days.

No, she thought. *They'll keep me around long enough for my "baby" to be born. I'm insurance. If something goes wrong, they'll still need me to show off.*

That was little comfort. The thought of six months cooped up inside the palace—not allowed to see anyone lest they see that she wasn't really pregnant—was frightening enough to make her want to scream.

But what could she do?

Hope in Susebron, she thought. *I taught him to read, and I gave him the determination that he needed to break free from his priests.*

That will have to be enough.

⟐

"YOUR GRACE," LLARIMAR said, his voice hesitant, "are you certain you want to do this?"

Lightsong crouched down, peeking through the bushes toward Mercystar's palace. Most of the windows were dark. That was good. However, she still had a number of guards patrolling the palace. She was afraid of another break-in.

And rightly so.

In the distance, he saw the moon just barely rising into the night sky. It almost matched the position he had seen in his dream the night before, the same dream where he'd seen the tunnels. Were these things really symbols? Signs from the future?

He still resisted. The truth was, he didn't want to believe he was a god. It implied too many things. But he couldn't ignore the images, even if they were just spoken from his subconscious. He had to get into those passages beneath the Court of Gods. Had to see if, at last, there *was* something prophetic about what he had seen.

The timing seemed important. The rising moon . . . just another degree or so.

There, he thought, looking down from the sky. A guard patrol was approaching.

"Your Grace?" Llarimar asked, sounding more nervous. The portly high priest knelt on the grass beside Lightsong.

"I should have brought a sword," Lightsong said thoughtfully.

"You don't know how to use one, Your Grace."

"We don't know that," Lightsong said.

"Your Grace, this is foolishness. Let's go back to your palace. If we *must* see what is in those tunnels, we can hire someone from the city to sneak in."

"That would take too long," Lightsong said. A guard patrol passed their side of the palace. "You ready?" he asked once the patrol had passed.

"No."

"Then wait here," Lightsong said, taking off in a dash toward the palace.

After a moment, he heard a hissed "Kalad's Phantoms!" from Llarimar, followed by bushes rustling as the priest followed.

Why, I don't believe I've ever heard him curse before, Lightsong thought with amused energy. He didn't look back; he just kept running toward the open window. As in most Returned palaces, the doorways and windows were open. The tropical climate encouraged such designs. Lightsong reached the side of the building, feeling exhilarated. He climbed up through the window, then reached a hand out to help Llarimar when he arrived. The hefty priest puffed and sweated, but Lightsong managed to pull him up and into the room.

They took a few moments, Llarimar resting with his back to the outer wall, gasping for breath.

"You really need to exercise more regularly, Scoot," Lightsong said, creeping toward the doorway and peeking out into the hall beyond.

Llarimar didn't answer. He just sat, puffing, shaking his head as if he couldn't believe what was happening.

"I wonder why the man who attacked the building didn't come in through the window," Lightsong said. Then he noticed that the guards standing at the inner doorway had an easy view of this particular room. *Ah,* he thought. *Well, then. Time for the backup plan.* Lightsong stood up, walking out into the hallway. Llarimar followed, then jumped when he saw the guards. They had similar expressions of amazement on their faces.

"Hello," Lightsong said to the guards, then turned from them and walked down the hallway.

"Wait!" one said. "Stop!"

Lightsong turned toward them, frowning. "You dare command a god?"

They froze. Then they glanced at each other. One took off running in the opposite direction.

"They're going to alert others!" Llarimar said, rushing up. "We'll be caught."

"Then we should move quickly!" Lightsong said, taking off in another run. He smiled, hearing Llarimar grudgingly break into a jog behind him. They quickly reached the trapdoor.

Lightsong knelt, feeling around for a few moments before finding the hidden clasp. He triumphantly pulled the trapdoor open, then pointed down. Llarimar shook his head in resignation, then climbed down the ladder into darkness. Lightsong grabbed a lamp off the wall and followed. The remaining guard—unable to interfere with a god—simply watched with concern.

The bottom wasn't very far down. Lightsong found a tired Llarimar sitting on some boxes in what was obviously a small storage cellar.

"Congratulations, Your Grace," Llarimar said. "We've found the secret hiding place of their flour."

Lightsong snorted, moving through the chamber, poking at the walls. "Something living," he said, pointing at one wall. "That direction. I can feel it with my life sense."

Llarimar raised an eyebrow, standing. They pulled back a few boxes, and behind them was a small tunnel entrance cut into the wall. Lightsong smiled, then crawled down through it, pushing the lamp ahead of him.

"I'm not sure I'll fit," Llarimar said.

"If I fit, you will," Lightsong said, voice muffled by the close confines. He heard another sigh from Llarimar, followed by shuffling as the portly man entered the hole. Eventually, Lightsong passed out of another hole into a much larger tunnel, lit by several lanterns hanging from one of the walls. He stood up, feeling self-satisfied as Llarimar squeezed through. "There," Lightsong said, throwing a lever

and letting a grate drop down over the opening. "They'll
have trouble following now!"

"And we'll have trouble escaping," Llarimar said.

"Escape?" Lightsong said, raising his lamp, inspecting
the tunnel. "Why would we want to do that?"

"Pardon me, Your Grace," Llarimar said. "But it seems
to me that you are getting far too much enjoyment from
this experience."

. "Well, I'm called Lightsong the *Bold*," Lightsong said.
"It feels good to finally be living up to the title. Now, hush.
I can still feel life nearby."

The tunnel was obviously man-made, and resembled
Lightsong's idea of a mine shaft. Just like the image from
his dreams. The tunnels had several branches, and the life
he sensed was straight ahead. Lightsong didn't go that way,
but instead turned left, toward a tunnel that sloped steeply
downward. He followed it for a few minutes to judge its
likely trajectory.

"Figured it out yet?" Lightsong asked, turning to Llarimar, who had taken one of the lanterns, as this tunnel
didn't have any light of its own.

"The Lifeless barracks," Llarimar said. "If this tunnel
continues this way, it will lead directly to them."

Lightsong nodded. "Why would they need a secret tunnel to the barracks? Any god can go there whenever he
wants."

Llarimar shook his head, and they continued down the
tunnel. Sure enough, after a short time, they arrived at a
trapdoor in the ceiling that—when pushed up—led into
one of the dark Lifeless warehouses. Lightsong shivered,
looking out at the endless rows of legs, barely illuminated
by his lamp. He pulled his head back down, closed the
trapdoor, and they followed the tunnel further.

"It goes in a square," he said quietly.

"With doors up into each of the Lifeless barracks I'll
bet," Llarimar said. He reached out, taking a piece of dirt

from the wall and crumbling it between his fingers. "This tunnel is newer than the one we were in up above."

Lightsong nodded. "We should keep moving," he said. "Those guards in Mercystar's palace know we're down here. I don't know who they'll tell, but I'd rather finish exploring before we get chased out."

Llarimar shivered visibly at that. They walked back up the steep tunnel to the main one just below the palace. Lightsong still felt life down a side tunnel, but he chose the other branch to explore. It soon became apparent that this one split and turned numerous times.

"Tunnels to some of the other palaces," he guessed, poking at a wooden beam used to support the shaft. "Old— much older than the tunnel to the barracks."

Llarimar nodded.

"All right, then," Lightsong said. "Time to find out where the main tunnel goes."

Llarimar followed as Lightsong approached the main tunnel. Lightsong closed his eyes, trying to determine how close the life was. It was faint. Almost beyond his ability to sense. If everything else in this catacomb hadn't been merely rocks and dirt, he wouldn't even have noticed the life in the first place. He nodded to Llarimar, and they continued down the tunnel as quietly as possible.

Did it seem that he was able to move with surprising stealth? Did he have unremembered experience with sneaking about? He was certainly better at it than Llarimar. Of course, a tumbling boulder was probably better at moving quietly than Llarimar, considering his bulky clothing and his puffing exhalations.

The tunnel went on straight for a time without branches. Lightsong looked up, trying to estimate what was above them. *The God King's palace?* he guessed. He couldn't be certain; it was difficult to judge direction and distance under the ground.

He felt excited. Thrilled. This was something no god was

supposed to do. Sneaking at night, moving through secret tunnels, looking for secrets and clues. *Odd,* he thought. *They give us everything they think that we might want; they glut us with sensation and experience. And yet real feelings—fear, anxiety, excitement—are completely lost to us.*

He smiled. In the distance, he could hear voices. He turned down the lamp and crept forward extra quietly, waving for Llarimar to stay behind.

". . . have him up above," a masculine voice was saying. "He came for the princess's sister, as I said he would."

"You have what you want, then," said another voice. "Really, you pay far too much attention to that one."

"Do not underestimate Vasher," the first voice said. "He has accomplished more in his life than a hundred men, and has done more for the good of all people than you will ever be able to appreciate."

Silence.

"Aren't you planning to kill him?" said the second voice.

"Yes."

Silence.

"You're a strange one, Denth," the second voice said. "However, our goal is accomplished."

"You people don't have your war yet."

"We will."

Lightsong crouched beside a small pile of rubble. He could see light up ahead, but couldn't distinguish much beyond some moving shadows. His luck seemed remarkably good in arriving to hear this conversation. Was that proof that his dreams were, indeed, foretellings? Or was it just coincidence? It was very late at night, and anyone still up was likely to be engaged in clandestine activities.

"I have a job for you," the second voice said. "We've got someone I need you to interrogate."

"Too bad," the first voice said, growing distant. "I've got an old friend to torture. I just had to pause to dispose of his monstrosity of a sword."

"Denth! Come back here!"

"You didn't hire me, little man," the first voice said, growing fainter. "If you want to make me do something, go get your boss. Until then, you know where to find me."

Silence. And then, something moved behind Lightsong. He spun, and could just barely make out Llarimar creeping forward. Lightsong waved him back, then joined him.

"What?" Llarimar whispered.

"Voices, ahead," Lightsong whispered back, the tunnel dark around them. "Talking about the war."

"Who were they?" Llarimar asked.

"I don't know," Lightsong whispered. "But I'm going to find out. Wait here while I—"

He was interrupted by a loud scream. Lightsong jumped. The sound came from the same place he had heard the voices, and it sounded like . . .

"Let go of me!" Blushweaver yelled. "What do you think you're doing! I'm a goddess!"

Lightsong stood up abruptly. A voice said something back to Blushweaver, but Lightsong was too far down the tunnel to make out the words.

"You will let me go!" Blushweaver yelled. "I—" she cut off sharply, crying out in pain.

Lightsong's heart was pounding. He took a step.

"Your Grace!" Llarimar said, standing. "We should go for help!"

"We *are* help," Lightsong said. He took a deep breath. Then—surprising himself—he charged down the tunnel. He quickly approached the light, rounding a corner and coming into a section of tunnel that had been worked with rock. In seconds, he was running on a smooth stone floor and burst into what appeared to be a dungeon.

Blushweaver was tied into a chair. A group of men wearing the robes of the God King's priests stood around her with several uniformed soldiers. Blushweaver's lip was bleeding, and she was crying through a gag that had been placed over her mouth. She wore a beautiful nightgown, but it was dirty and disheveled.

The men in the room looked up in surprise, obviously shocked to see someone come up behind them. Lightsong took advantage of this shock and threw his shoulder against the soldier nearest to him. He sent the man flying back into the wall, Lightsong's superior size and weight knocking him aside with ease. Lightsong knelt down and quickly pulled the fallen soldier's sword from its sheath.

"Aha!" Lightsong said, pointing the weapon at the men in front of him. "Who's first?"

The soldiers regarded him dumbly.

"I say, you!" Lightsong said, lunging at the next-closest guard.

He missed the man by a good three inches, fumbling and off-balance from the lunge. The guard finally realized what was going on and pulled out his own sword. The priests backed against the wall. Blushweaver blinked through her tears, looking shocked.

The soldier nearest Lightsong attacked, and Lightsong raised his blade awkwardly, trying to block, doing a horrible job of it. The guard at his feet suddenly threw himself at Lightsong's legs, toppling him to the ground. Then one of the standing guards thrust his sword into Lightsong's thigh.

The leg bled blood as red as that of any mortal. Suddenly, Lightsong knew pain. Pain literally greater than any he'd known in his short life.

He screamed.

He saw, through tears, Llarimar heroically trying to tackle a guard from behind, but the attack was almost as poorly executed as Lightsong's own. The soldiers stepped away, several guarding the tunnel, another holding his bloodied blade toward Lightsong's throat.

Funny, Lightsong thought, gritting his teeth against the pain. *That was not at all how I imagined this going.*

53

VIVENNA WAITED UP for Vasher. He did not return.

She paced in the small, one-room hideout—the sixth in a series. They never spent more than a few days in each location. Unadorned, it held only their bedrolls, Vasher's pack, and a single flickering candle.

Vasher would have chastised her for wasting the candle. For a man who held a king's fortune in Breaths, he was surprisingly frugal.

She continued pacing. She knew that she should probably just go to sleep. Vasher could take care of himself. It seemed that the only one in the city who couldn't do *that* was Vivenna.

And yet he'd told her he was only going on a quick scouting mission. Though he was a solitary person himself, he apparently understood her desire to be a part of things, so he usually let her know where he was going and when to expect him back.

She'd never waited up for Denth to come back from a night mission, and she'd been working with Vasher for a fraction of the time she'd spent with the mercenaries. Why did she worry so much now?

Though she had felt like she was Denth's friend, she hadn't really cared about him. He'd been amusing and charming, but distant. Vasher was . . . well, who he was. There was no guile in him. He wore no false mask. She'd only met one other person like that: her sister, the one who would bear the God King's child.

Lord of Colors! Vivenna thought, still pacing. *How did things turn into such a mess?*

SIRI AWOKE WITH a start. There was shouting coming from outside her room. She roused herself quickly, moving over to the door and putting her ear to it. She could hear fighting. If she were going to run, perhaps now would be the time. She rattled the door, hoping for some reason that it was unlocked. It wasn't.

She cursed. She'd heard fighting earlier—screaming, and men dying. And now again. *Someone trying to rescue me, perhaps?* she thought hopefully. *But who?*

The door shook suddenly, and she jumped back as it opened. Treledees, high priest of the God King, stood in the doorway. "Quickly, child," he said, waving to her. "You must come with me."

Siri looked desperately for a way to run. She backed away from the priest, and he cursed quietly, waving for a couple of soldiers in city guard uniforms to rush in and grab her. She screamed for help.

"Quiet, you fool!" Treledees said. "We're trying to help you."

His lies rang hollow in her ears, and she struggled as the soldiers pulled her from the room. Outside, bodies were lying on the ground, some in guard uniforms, others in nondescript armor, still others with grey skin.

She heard fighting down the hallway, and she screamed toward it as the soldiers roughly pulled her away.

———◈———

OLD CHAPPS, THEY called him. Those who called him anything, that is.

He sat in his little boat, moving slowly across the dark water of the bay. Night fishing. During the day, one had to pay a fee to fish in T'Telir waters. Well, technically, during the night you were supposed to pay too.

But the thing about night was, nobody could see you. Old Chapps chuckled to himself, lowering his net over the side of the boat. The waters made their characteristic lap,

lap, lap against the side of the boat. Dark. He liked it dark. Lap, lap, lap.

Occasionally, he was given better work. Taking bodies from one of the city's slumlords, weighting them down with rocks tied in a sack to the foot, then tossing them into the bay. There were probably hundreds of them down there, floating in the current with their feet weighted to the floor. A party of skeletons, having a dance. Dance, dance, dance.

No bodies tonight, though. Too bad. That meant fish. Free fish he didn't have to pay tariffs on. And free fish were good fish.

No . . . a voice said to him. *A little bit more to your right.*

The sea talked to him sometimes. Coaxed him this way or that. He happily made his way in the direction indicated. He was out on the waters almost every night. They should know him pretty well by now.

Good. Drop the net.

He did so. It wasn't too deep in this part of the bay. He could drag the net behind his boat, pulling the weighted edges along the bottom, catching the smaller fish that came up into the shallows to feed. Not the best fish, but the sky was looking too dangerous to be out far from the shore. A storm brewing?

His net struck something. He grumbled, yanking it. Sometimes it got caught on debris or coral. It was heavy. Too heavy. He pulled the net back up over the side, then opened the shield on his lantern, risking a bit of light.

Tangled in the net, a sword lay in the bottom of his boat. Silvery, with a black handle.

Lap, lap, lap.

Ah, very nice, the voice said, much clearer now. *I hate the water. So wet and icky down there.*

Transfixed, Old Chapps reached out, picking up the weapon. It felt heavy in his hand.

I don't suppose you'd want to go destroy some evil,

would you? the voice said. *I'm not really sure what that means, to be honest. I'll just trust you to decide.*

Old Chapps smiled.

Oh, all right, the sword said. *You can admire me a little bit longer, if you must. After that, though, we really need to get back to shore.*

———⊸⊷⊷⊶———

VASHER AWOKE GROGGILY.

He was tied by his wrists to a hook in the ceiling of a stone room. The rope that had been used to tie him, he noticed, was the same one he'd used to tie up the maid. It had been completely drained of color.

In fact, everything around him was a uniform grey. He had been stripped save for his short, white underbreeches. He groaned, his arms feeling numb from the awkward angle of being hung by his wrists.

He wasn't gagged, but he had no Breath left—he'd used the last of it in the fight, to Awaken the cloak of the fallen man. He groaned.

A lantern burned in the corner. A figure stood next to it. "And so we both return," Denth said quietly.

Vasher didn't reply.

"I still owe you for Arsteel's death, too," Denth said quietly. "I want to know how you killed him."

"In a duel," Vasher said in a croaking voice.

"You didn't beat him in a duel, Vasher," Denth said, stepping forward. "I know it."

"Then maybe I snuck up and stabbed him from behind," Vasher said. "It's what he deserved."

Denth backhanded him across the face, causing him to swing from the hook. "Arsteel was a good man!"

"Once," Vasher said, tasting blood. "Once, we were all good men, Denth. Once."

Denth was quiet. "You think your little quest here will undo what you've done?"

"Better than becoming a mercenary," Vasher said. "Working for whomever will pay."

"I am what you made me," Denth said quietly.

"That girl trusted you. Vivenna."

Denth turned, eyes darkened, the lantern light not quite reaching his face. "She was supposed to."

"She liked you. Then you killed her friend."

"Things got a little out of hand."

"They always do, with you," Vasher said.

Denth raised an eyebrow, his face growing amused in the wan light. "*I* get out of hand, Vasher? Me? When's the last time *I* started a war? Slaughtered tens of thousands? You're the one who betrayed his closest friend and killed the woman who loved him."

Vasher didn't respond. What argument could he offer? That Shashara had needed to die? It had been bad enough when she'd revealed the Commands to make Lifeless from a single breath. What if the way of making Awakened steel, like Nightblood, had entered the Manywar? Undead monsters slaughtering people with Awakened swords thirsting for blood?

None of that mattered to a man who'd seen his sister murdered by Vasher's hand. Besides, Vasher knew he had little credibility to stand on. He'd created his own monsters to fight in that war. Not Awakened steel like Nightblood, but deadly enough in their own right.

"I was going to let Tonk Fah have you," Denth said, turning away again. "He likes hurting things. It's a weakness he has. We all have weaknesses. With my direction, he's been able to restrict it to animals."

Denth turned to him, holding up a knife. "I've always wondered what he finds so enjoyable about causing pain."

⸺◦⸺

DAWN WAS APPROACHING. Vivenna threw off her blanket, unable to sleep. She dressed, frustrated, but not sure why. Vasher was probably just fine. He was likely out carousing somewhere.

Of course, she thought wryly, *carousing. That sounds just like him.*

He'd never stayed out an entire night before. Something had gone wrong. She slowed as she pulled on her belt, glancing over at Vasher's pack and the change of clothing he had inside of it. *Every single thing I've tried since I left Idris has failed miserably,* she thought, continuing to dress. *I failed as a revolutionary, I failed as a beggar, and I failed as a sister. What am I supposed to do? Find him? I don't even know where to start.*

She looked away from the pack. Failure. It wasn't something she'd been accustomed to, back in Idris. Everything she'd done there had turned out well.

Maybe that's what this is all about, she thought, sitting. *My hatred of Hallandren. My insistence on saving Siri, on taking her place.* When their father had chosen Siri over her, it had been the first time in her life she'd felt that she wasn't good enough. So she'd come to T'Telir, determined to prove the problem wasn't with her. It'd been with someone else. Anyone else. As long as Vivenna wasn't flawed.

But Hallandren had repeatedly proved that she *was* flawed. And now that she'd tried and failed so often, she found it hard to act. By choosing to act, she might fail—and that was so daunting that doing nothing seemed preferable.

It was the crowning arrogance in Vivenna's life. She bowed her head. One last bit of feathered hypocrisy to adorn her royal hair.

You want to be competent? she thought. *You want to learn to be in control of what goes on around you, rather than just being pushed around? Then you'll have to learn to deal with failure.*

It was frightening, but she knew it was true. She stood up and walked over to Vasher's pack. She pulled out a wrinkled overshirt and a pair of leggings. Both had tassels hanging from the cuffs.

Vivenna put them on. Vasher's spare cloak followed. It smelled like him, and was cut—like his other one—into the vague shape of a man. She understood, at least, one of the reasons his clothing looked so tattered.

She pulled out a couple of colorful handkerchiefs. "Protect me," she Commanded the cloak, imagining it grabbing people who tried to attack her. She placed a hand on the sleeve of the shirt.

"Upon call," she Commanded, "become my fingers and grip that which I must." She'd only heard Vasher give the Command a couple of times, and she still wasn't quite sure how to visualize what she wanted the shirt to do. She imagined the tassels closing around her hands as she had seen them do for Vasher.

She Awakened the leggings, commanding them to strengthen her legs. The leg tassels began to twist, and she raised each foot in turn, letting the tassels wrap around the bottoms. Her stance felt firmer, the leggings pulled tight against her skin.

Finally, she tied on the sword Vasher had given her. She still didn't know how to use it, though she could hold it properly. It felt right to bring it.

Then she left.

———⋘⋙———

LIGHTSONG HAD RARELY seen a goddess cry.

"It wasn't supposed to go this way," Blushweaver said, heedless of the tears streaming down her cheeks. "I had things under control."

The dungeon beneath the God King's palace was a cramped room. Cages—like the kind that might be used for animals—lined both walls. They were large enough to hold a god. Lightsong couldn't decide if that was just a coincidence.

Blushweaver sniffled. "I thought I had the God King's priesthood on my side. We were working together."

Something's wrong about this, Lightsong thought, glancing at the group of priests chatting anxiously at the side of the room. Llarimar sat in his own cage—the one next to Lightsong's—head bowed.

Lightsong looked back at Blushweaver. "How long?" he asked. "How long were you working with them?"

"From the beginning," Blushweaver said. "I was supposed to get the Command phrases. We came up with the plan together!"

"Why did they turn on you?"

She shook her head, glancing down. "They claimed I didn't do my part. That I was withholding things from them."

"Were you?"

She looked away, eyes tearstained. She looked very odd, sitting in her cell. A beautiful woman of deific proportions, wearing a delicate silk gown, sitting on the ground, surrounded by bars. Crying.

We have to get out of here, Lightsong thought. He crawled over to the bars separating his cage from Llarimar's, ignoring the pain of his thigh. "Scoot," he hissed. "Scoot!"

Llarimar glanced up. He looked haggard.

"What does one use to pick a lock?" Lightsong asked.

Llarimar blinked. "What?"

"Pick a lock," Lightsong said, pointing. "Maybe I'll discover that I know how to do it, if I get my hands into the right position. I still haven't figured out why my swordsmanship skills were so poor. But surely I can do this. If I can only remember what to use."

Llarimar stared at him.

"Maybe I—" Lightsong began.

"What is wrong with you?" Llarimar whispered.

Lightsong paused.

"What is wrong with you!" Llarimar bellowed, standing.

"You were a *scribe,* Lightsong. A Colors-cursed *scribe.* Not a soldier. Not a detective. Not a thief. You were an accountant for a local moneylender!"

What? Lightsong thought.

"You were as much an idiot then as you are now!" Llarimar shouted. "Don't you ever *think* about what you're going to do before you just saunter off and do it! Why can't you just stop, occasionally, and ask yourself if you're being a complete fool or not? I'll give you a hint! The answer is *usually* yes!"

Lightsong stumbled back from the bars, shocked. Llarimar. *Llarimar* was yelling.

"And every time," Llarimar said, turning away, "*I* get in trouble with you. Nothing has changed. You become a god, and I *still* end up in prison!"

The heavy priest slumped down, breathing in deep gasps, shaking his head in obvious frustration. Blushweaver was staring at them. And so were the priests.

What is it I find odd about them? Lightsong thought, trying to sort out his thoughts and emotions as the group of priests approached.

"Lightsong," one of them said, stooping down beside his cage. "We need your Command phrases."

He snorted. "I'm sorry to say that I've forgotten them. You probably know my reputation for being weak-minded. I mean, what kind of fool would come charging in here and get himself captured so easily?"

He smiled at them.

The priest by his cage sighed, then waved a hand at the others. They unlocked Blushweaver's cage and pulled her out. She yelled and fought, and Lightsong smiled at the trouble she gave them. Yet there were six priests, and they finally managed to get her out.

Then one got out a knife and slit her throat.

The shock of the moment hit Lightsong like a physical

force. He froze, eyes wide, watching in horror as the red blood spilled out the front of Blushweaver's throat, staining her beautiful nightgown.

Far more disturbing was the look of panicked terror in her eyes. Such beautiful eyes.

"*No!*" Lightsong screamed, slamming against the bars, reaching helplessly toward her. He strained his godly muscles, pressing himself against the steel as he felt his body begin to shake. It was useless. Even a perfect body couldn't push its way through steel.

"You bastards!" he yelled. "You Colors-cursed bastards!" He struggled, pounding the bars with one hand as Blushweaver's eyes began to dim.

And then her BioChroma faded. Like a blazing bonfire dimming down to a single candle. It puffed out.

"No . . ." Lightsong said, sliding down to his knees, numb.

The priest regarded him. "So you *did* care for her," he said. "I'm sorry that we had to do that." He knelt down, solemn. "However, Lightsong, we decided that we had to kill her so that you would understand that we're serious. I do know your reputation, and I know that you usually take things lightheartedly. That is a fine attribute to have in many situations. Right now, you must realize how dangerous things are. We have shown you that we will kill. If you don't do as we ask, others will die."

"Bastard . . ." Lightsong whispered.

"I need your Command phrases," the priest said. "This is important. More important than you can understand."

"You can beat them out of me," Lightsong growled, feeling rage slowly overwhelm his shock.

"No," the priest said, shaking his head. "We're actually new to all of this. We don't know how to torture very well, and it would take too much time to force you to talk that way. Those who *are* skilled at torture aren't being very cooperative right now. Never pay a mercenary before the job is done."

The priest waved, and the others left Blushweaver's corpse on the ground. Then they moved to Llarimar's cage.

"No!" Lightsong screamed.

"We are serious, Lightsong," the man said. "Very, very, serious. We know how much you care for your high priest. You now know that we will kill him if you don't do as we say."

"Why?" Lightsong said. "What is this even about? The God King you serve could order us to move the armies if he wanted to! We'd listen to him. Why do you care so much about those Command phrases?"

The priests forced Llarimar from his cage, then pushed him to his knees. One put a knife to his throat.

"Red panther!" Lightsong yelled, weeping. "That's the Command phrase. Please. Leave him be."

The priest nodded to the others, and they put Llarimar back in his cell. They left Blushweaver's corpse on the ground, facedown in the blood.

"I hope that you haven't lied to us, Lightsong," the main priest said. "We're not playing games. It would be unfortunate if we discovered that you still are." He shook his head. "We are not cruel men. But we are working for something very important. Do not test us."

With that, he left. Lightsong barely noticed. He was still staring at Blushweaver, trying to convince himself that he was hallucinating, or that she was faking, or that *something* would change to make him realize that it was all just an elaborate scam.

"Please," he whispered. "Please, no. . . ."

54

"WHAT'S THE WORD on the street, Tuft?" Vivenna asked, sidling up to a beggar.

He snorted, holding out his cup to those few who passed in the early light. Tuft was always one of the first to arrive in the mornings. "What do I care?" he said.

"Come on," Vivenna said. "You kicked me out of this spot on three different occasions. I figure you owe me something."

"I don't owe nobody nothing," he said, squinting at the passersby with his one eye. The other eye was simply an empty hole. He didn't wear a patch. "Particularly don't owe you nothing," he said. "You were a plant all the time. Not a real beggar."

"I . . ." Vivenna paused. "I wasn't a plant, Tuft. I just thought I should know what it was like."

"Huh?"

"Living among you," she said. "I figured your life couldn't be easy. But I couldn't know—not really *know*—until I tried it for myself. So I came to the streets. Determined to live here for a time."

"Foolish thing to do."

"No," she said. "The fools are those who pass, without even thinking about what it must be like to live like you. Maybe if they knew, they'd give you something."

She reached into her pocket, pulling out one of the bright handkerchiefs. She placed one in the cup. "I don't have any coins, but I know you can sell that."

He grunted, eyeing it. "What do you mean by word on the street?"

"Disturbances," Vivenna said. "Ones that are out of the ordinary. Perhaps involving Awakeners."

"Go to the Third Dock slums," Tuft said. "Look around the buildings near the wharf. Maybe you'll find what you're looking for there."

LIGHT PEEKED THROUGH the window.

Morning already? Vasher thought, head down, still hanging by his wrists.

He knew what to expect from torture. He was not new to it. He knew how to scream, how to give the torturer what he wanted. He knew how to not expend his strength in resisting too much.

He also knew that none of that was likely to do any good. How would he be after a week of torture? Blood dripped down his chest, staining his undershorts. A dozen small pains nagged at his skin, cuts that had been drenched in lemon juice.

Denth stood with his back facing Vasher, bloodied knives on the ground around him.

Vasher looked up, forcing a smile. "Not as much fun as you thought it would be, is it, Denth?"

Denth didn't turn.

There's still a good man in there, Vasher thought. *Even after all these years.*

He's just been beaten down. Bloodied. Cut up worse than I have been.

"Torturing me won't bring her back," Vasher said.

Denth turned, eyes dark. "No. It won't." He picked up another knife.

THE PRIESTS PUSHED Siri through the passageways of the palace. They occasionally passed corpses in the dark black hallways, and she could still hear fighting in places.

What is going on? Someone was attacking the palace. But who? For a moment, she hoped it was her people—her father's soldiers, coming to save her. She discarded that immediately. The men opposing the priests were using Lifeless soldiers; that ruled out Idris.

It was someone else. A third force. And they wanted to free her from the grip of the priests. Hopefully, her calls for help would not go unheeded. Treledees and his men led her quickly through the palace, passing through the colorful inner rooms in their rush to get to wherever they were going.

The white cuffs of Siri's dress suddenly began to bend with color. She looked up with hope as they entered a last room. The God King stood inside the room, surrounded by a group of priests and soldiers.

"Susebron!" she said, straining against her captives.

He took a step toward her, but a guard held his arm, pulling him back. *They're touching him,* Siri thought. *All semblance of respect is gone. No need to pretend now.*

The God King looked down at his arm, frowning. He tried to tug it free, but another soldier stepped up to help hold him. Susebron glanced at this man, then at Siri, confused.

"I don't understand either," she said.

Treledees entered the room. "Bless the Colors," he said. "You've arrived. Quickly, we must go. This place is not safe."

"Treledees," Siri said, turning to glare at him. "What is going on?"

He ignored her.

"I am your *queen*," Siri said. "You will answer my question!"

He actually stopped, surprising her. He turned with an annoyed look. "A group of Lifeless has attacked the palace, Vessel. They are trying to get to the God King."

"I figured out that much, priest," Siri snapped. "Who are they?"

"We don't know," Treledees said, turning from her. As

he did, a distant scream came from outside the room. It was followed by the sound of fighting.

Treledees glanced toward the sounds. "We have to move," he said to one of the other priests. There were, perhaps, a dozen of them in the room, as well as a half-dozen soldiers. "The palace has too many doorways and passages. It would be too easy to surround us."

"The back exit?" the other priest said.

"If we can get to it," Treledees responded. "Where is that squadron of reinforcements I demanded?"

"They're not coming, Your Grace," a new voice said. Siri turned to see Bluefingers, looking haggard, enter through the far door with a couple of wounded soldiers. "The enemy has taken the east wing and is pushing this way."

Treledees cursed.

"We have to get His Majesty to safety!" Bluefingers said.

"I'm well aware of that," Treledees snapped.

"If the east wing has fallen," the other priest said, "we won't be able to get out that way."

Siri watched, helpless, trying to get Bluefingers's attention. He met her eyes, then nodded covertly, smiling. "Your Grace," Bluefingers said. "We can escape through the tunnels."

The sounds of fighting were growing closer. It seemed to Siri that their room was virtually surrounded by combat.

"Perhaps," Treledees said as one of his priests rushed to the door to peek out. The soldiers who had come with Bluefingers were resting by the wall, bleeding. One of them seemed to have stopped breathing.

"We should go," Bluefingers said urgently.

Treledees was quiet. Then he walked over to one of the fallen soldiers and picked up the man's sword. "Very well," he said. "Gendren, take half of the soldiers and go with Bluefingers. Take His Majesty to safety." He looked at Bluefingers. "Seek the docks, if you can."

"Yes, Your Grace," Bluefingers said, looking relieved. The priests released the God King, and he rushed to Siri, taking her in his arms. She held him, tense, trying to sort through her emotions.

Bluefingers. Going with him made sense—the look in his eyes indicated that he had a plan to save her and the God King, get them away from the priests. And yet . . . something felt wrong to her.

One of the priests gathered three of the soldiers and then moved to the far side of the room, peeking out. They waved to Siri and the God King. The other priests joined Treledees, taking weapons from the dead guards, their expressions grim.

Bluefingers pulled on Siri's arm. "Come, my queen," he whispered. "I made you a promise before. Let's get you out of this mess."

"What about the priests?" she asked.

Treledees glanced at her. "Foolish girl. Go! The attackers are moving in this direction. We will let them see us, then we will lead them in another direction. They will assume we know where the God King is." The priests with him did not look hopeful. If—when—they were caught, they would be slaughtered.

"Come on!" Bluefingers hissed.

Susebron looked at her, frightened. She slowly let Bluefingers tug her and the God King to the side, to where the solitary priest and three soldiers had been joined by a group of servants in brown. Something whispered in her mind. Something . . . Lightsong had told her.

Don't make too many waves until you're ready to strike, he had said. *Sudden and surprising, that's how you want to do things. You don't want to appear nonthreatening— people are always suspicious of the innocent. The trick is to appear average.*

Average.

It was good advice. Advice that, likely, others knew.

And understood. She glanced at Bluefingers, walking beside her, urging her forward. Nervous, as always.

The fighting, she thought. *Several groups have been contending back and forth, seizing control of my room. One force belongs to the priests. The second force—the one with the Lifeless—belongs to someone else. This mysterious third party.*

Someone in T'Telir had been pushing the kingdom toward war. But who would have anything at all to gain from such a disaster? Hallandren, which would expend huge resources to quell rebels, fighting a battle that they would win—but likely at great cost? It didn't make sense.

Who would gain the most if Hallandren and Idris went to war?

"Wait!" Siri said, stopping. Things were suddenly falling into place.

"Vessel?" Bluefingers asked. Susebron laid a hand on her shoulder, looking at her with confusion. *Why would the priests sacrifice themselves if they were planning to kill Susebron? Why would they simply let us go, allow us to flee, if the God King's safety were not their prime concern?*

She looked into Bluefingers's eyes, and saw him grow more nervous. His face paled, and she knew. "How does it feel, Bluefingers?" she asked. "You're from Pahn Kahl, yet everyone always just assumes that your people are Hallandren. The Pahn Kahl people were here first, in this land, but it was taken from you. Now you're just another province, part of the kingdom of your conquerors.

"You want to be free, but your people have no military of their own. And so here you are. Unable to fight. Unable to free yourselves. Considered second-class. And yet, if your oppressors were to get into a war, it might give you an opening. A chance to break away . . ."

He met her eyes, then took off in a dash, fleeing from the room.

"What in the name of the Colors?" Treledees said.

Siri ignored him, looking up into the God King's face. "You were right all along," she said. "We *should* have trusted your priests."

"Vessel?" Treledees said, stalking over.

"We can't go that way," Siri said. "Bluefingers was leading us into a trap."

The high priest opened his mouth to respond, but she met his eyes sternly and turned her hair the deep red of anger. Bluefingers had betrayed her. The *one* person she'd thought she could trust to help them.

"We go for the front gates, then," Treledees said, looking over their motley collection of priests and wounded soldiers. "And try to fight our way out."

———

IT WAS EASY for Vivenna to find the location the beggar had mentioned. The building—a slum tenement—was surrounded by gawkers, despite the morning hour. People whispered, talking about spirits and death and ghosts from the sea. Vivenna stopped at the perimeter, trying to see what had drawn their attention.

The docks were to her left, the sea brine pungent. The dock slums, where many of the dockhands lived and drank, were a small section of buildings clustered between warehouses and shipyards. Why would Vasher have come here? He had been planning to visit the Court of Gods. From what she could gather, there had been a murder in the building where the crowd had formed. People whispered of ghosts and of Kalad's Phantoms, but Vivenna simply shook her head. This wasn't what she was looking for. She'd have to—

Vivenna? The voice was faint, but she could just barely make it out. And recognize it.

"Nightblood?" she whispered.

Vivenna. Come get me.

She shivered. She wanted to turn and run—even thinking about the sword was nauseating. Yet Vasher had taken Nightblood with him. She was in the right place after all.

The gawkers spoke of a murder. Was Vasher the person who had been killed?

Suddenly concerned, she shoved her way through the crowd, ignoring yells that she should stay back. She climbed up the stairs, passing door after door. In her haste, she almost missed the one with black smoke creeping out under it.

She froze. Then, taking a deep breath, she pushed the door open and stepped inside.

The room was poorly kept, the floor littered with trash, the furniture rickety and worn. Four dead bodies lay on the floor. Nightblood was stuck in the chest of the fourth, an old man with a leathery face who lay on his side, dead eyes wide.

Vivenna! Nightblood said happily. *You found me. I'm so excited. I tried to get them to take me to the Court of Gods, but it didn't turn out well. He did draw me a little bit. That's good, right?*

She fell to her knees, feeling sick.

Vivenna? Nightblood asked. *I did well, right? Vara-Treledees threw me into the ocean, but I got back out. I'm quite satisfied. You should tell me that I did well.*

She didn't respond.

Oh, Nightblood said. *And Vasher is hurt, I think. We should go find him.*

She looked up. "Where?" she asked, uncertain if the sword would even be able to hear her.

The God King's palace, Nightblood said. *He went to get your sister out. I think he likes you, even though he says he doesn't. He says you're annoying.*

Vivenna blinked. "Siri? You went after Siri?"

Yes, but VaraTreledees stopped us.

"Who is that?" she asked, frowning.

You call him Denth. He's Shashara's brother. I wonder

if she's here too. I'm not sure why he threw me in the water. I thought he liked me.

"Vasher . . ." she said, climbing back to her feet, feeling woozy from the sword's influence. Vasher had been taken by Denth. She shivered, remembering the anger in Denth's voice when he'd spoken of Vasher. She gritted her teeth and grabbed a dirty blanket off the crude bed and wrapped it around Nightblood so that she wouldn't have to touch him.

Ah, Nightblood said. *You don't really need to do that. I had the old man clean me off after he got me out of the water.*

She ignored the sword, managing to lift the bundle with only slight nausea. Then she left, heading for the Court of Gods.

⸺∞⸺

LIGHTSONG SAT, STARING at the stones in front of him. A trickle of Blushweaver's blood was making its way down a crack in the rock.

"Your Grace?" Llarimar asked quietly. He stood up against the bars between their cages.

Lightsong didn't respond.

"Your Grace, I'm sorry. I shouldn't have yelled at you."

"What good is godhood?" Lightsong whispered.

Silence. Lanterns flickered on either side of the small chamber. Nobody had cleaned up Blushweaver's body, though they had left a couple of priests and Lifeless behind to watch Lightsong. They still needed him, should it turn out that he'd lied about the Command phrases.

He hadn't.

"What?" Llarimar finally asked.

"What good is it?" Lightsong said. "We aren't gods. Gods don't die like that. A little cut. Not even as wide as my palm."

"I'm sorry," Llarimar said. "She was a good woman, even among gods."

"She wasn't a god," Lightsong said. "None of us are. Those dreams are lies, if they led me to this. I've always known the truth, but nobody pays attention to what I say. Shouldn't they listen to the one they worship? Particularly if he's telling you *not* to worship him?"

"I . . ." Llarimar seemed at a loss for words.

"They should have seen," Lightsong hissed. "They should have seen the truth about me! An idiot. Not a god, but a scribe. A silly little scribe who was allowed to play god for a few years! A coward."

"You're no coward," Llarimar said.

"I couldn't save her," Lightsong said. "I couldn't do anything. I just sat there and screamed. Maybe if I'd been more brave, I'd have joined with her and taken control of the armies. But I hesitated. And now she's dead."

Silence.

"You were a scribe," Llarimar said quietly to the damp air. "And you were one of the best men I'd ever known. You were my brother."

Lightsong looked up.

Llarimar stared out through the bars, at one of the flickering lanterns hanging from the stark stone wall. "I was a priest, even then. I worked in the palace of Kindwinds the Honest. I saw how he lied to play political games. The longer I stayed in that palace, the more my faith waned."

He fell silent for a moment, then he looked up. "And then you died. Died rescuing my daughter. That's the girl you see in your visions, Lightsong. The description is perfect. She was your favorite niece. Still would be, I assume. If you hadn't . . ." He shook his head. "When we found you dead, I lost hope. I was going to resign my position. I knelt above your body, weeping. And then, the Colors started to glow.

You lifted your head, body changing, getting larger, muscles growing stronger.

"I knew it at that moment. I knew that if a man like *you* were chosen to Return—a man who had died to save another—then the Iridescent Tones were real. The visions were real. And the gods were real. You gave me back my faith, Stennimar."

He met Lightsong's eyes. "You *are* a god. To me, at least. It doesn't matter how easily you can be killed, how much Breath you have, or how you look. It has to do with who you are and what you mean."

55

THERE IS FIGHTING at the front gates, Your Excellency," the bloodied soldier said. "The insurgents are fighting each other there. We . . . we might be able to get out."

Siri felt a stab of relief. Finally, something going right.

Treledees turned toward her. "If we can get into the city, the people will rally around their God King. We should be safe there."

"Where did they get so many Lifeless?" Siri asked.

Treledees shook his head. They had paused in a room near the front of the palace, desperate, yet unsure. Breaking through the Pahn Kahl fortification of the Court of Gods was bound to be difficult.

She looked up at Susebron. His priests treated him like a child—they gave him respect, but they obviously gave no thought to ask his opinion. For his part, he stood, hand on her shoulder. She saw thoughts and ideas working behind those eyes of his, but there was nothing for him to write on to tell her.

"Vessel," Treledees said, drawing her attention. "You need to know something."

She looked at him.

"I hesitate to mention this," Treledees said, "as you are not a priest. But . . . if you survive and we do not . . ."

"Speak it," she commanded.

"You cannot bear the God King a child," he said. "Like all Returned, he is unable to sire children. We have not yet learned how the First Returned managed to have a child all those years ago. In fact . . ."

"You don't even think he did," she said. "You think the royal line is a fabrication." *Of course the priests dispute the record of the royal line coming from the First Returned,* she thought. *They wouldn't want to give credibility to Idris's claim to the throne.*

He flushed. "It's what people believe that matters. Regardless, we . . . have a child . . ."

"Yes," Siri said. "A Returned child you are going to make the next God King."

He looked at her, shocked. "You *know*?"

"You're planning to kill him, aren't you?" she hissed. "Take Susebron's Breath and leave him dead!"

"Colors, no!" Treledees said, shocked. "How—how could you think? No, we'd never do such a thing! Vessel, the God King needs only give away the treasure of Breaths he holds, investing them into the next God King, and then he can live the rest of his life—so long as he should desire—in peace. We change God Kings whenever an infant Returns. It is our sign that the previous God King has done his duty, and should be allowed to live the rest of his life without bearing his terrible burdens."

Siri looked at him skeptically. "That's foolish, Treledees. If the God King gives away his Breath, he will die."

"No, there is a way," the priest said.

"That is supposed to be impossible."

"Not at all. Think about it. The God King has *two*

sources of Breath. One is his innate, divine Breath—that which makes him Returned. The other is the Breath given to him as the Treasure of Peacegiver, fifty thousand Breaths strong. *That* he could use as any Awakener could, as long as he is careful about the Commands he uses. He could also survive quite easily as a Returned without it. Any of the other gods could do the same, should they gain Breath beyond the one a week which sustains them. They'd consume them at a rate of one a week, of course, but they could stockpile them and use the extras in the meantime."

"You keep them from realizing that, though," Siri said.

"Not *keep* specifically," the priest said, looking away. "It does not arise. Why would the Returned care about Awakening? They have everything they need."

"Except knowledge," Siri said. "You keep them in ignorance. I'm surprised you didn't cut out all their tongues to hide your precious secrets."

Treledees looked back at her, expression hardening. "You judge us still. We do what we do because it is what we *must,* Vessel. The power he holds in that Treasure— fifty thousand Breaths—could destroy kingdoms. It is too great a weapon; we were charged as our sole, divine mission to keep it safe and *not* let it be used. If Kalad's army ever returns from where it was exiled, we—"

A sound came from a nearby room. Treledees looked up, concerned, and Susebron's grip on Siri's shoulder tightened.

Her glance hardened. "Treledees," she said. "I need to know. How? How can Susebron give away his Breath? He can speak no Command!"

"I—"

Treledees was interrupted by a group of Lifeless bursting through the doorway to their left. Treledees yelled for her to flee, but another group of the creatures came through the other way. Siri cursed, grabbing Susebron's hand, pulling him toward yet another doorway. She pulled it open.

Bluefingers stood on the other side. He looked into her eyes, face grim. Lifeless stood behind him.

Siri felt a stab of terror, backing away. Sounds of fighting came from behind her, but she was too focused on the Lifeless stepping around Bluefingers toward her and Susebron. The God King cried out, a tongueless, wordless groan of anger.

And then the priests were there. They threw themselves in front of the Lifeless, trying to beat them back, trying desperately to protect their God King. Siri clung to her husband in the ruddy room, watching as the priests were slaughtered by emotionless warriors with grey faces. Priest after priest jumped in the way, some with weapons, others simply waving their arms in a hopeless attack.

She saw Treledees grit his teeth, terror showing in his eyes as he ran forward, trying to attack a Lifeless. He died like the others. His secrets died with him.

The Lifeless stepped over the corpses. Susebron pushed Siri behind him, arms shaking as he backed them toward a wall, facing down the bloodied monsters. The Lifeless finally stopped, and Bluefingers walked around them, looking past Susebron toward her.

"And now, Vessel, I believe we were going somewhere."

<hr />

"I'M SORRY, MISS," the guard said, holding up a hand. "All access to the Court of Gods is forbidden."

Vivenna ground her teeth. "This is unacceptable," she said. "I'm to report to the goddess Allmother at once! Can't you see how many Breaths I hold? I'm not someone you can just turn away!"

The guards remained firm. There were a good two dozen of them at the gates, stopping anyone who tried to enter. Vivenna turned away. Whatever Vasher had done inside the night before, he'd apparently caused quite a stir. People clustered around the gateway to the court, demanding answers, asking if something was wrong. Vivenna made her way back through them, leaving the gates behind.

Go to the side, Nightblood said. *Vasher never asks if he can enter. He just goes in.*

Vivenna glanced at the side of the plateau. There was a short rocky ledge running around the outside of the wall. With the guards so distracted by the people wanting in . . .

She slipped to the side. It was early in the morning yet, the sun not having crested the eastern mountains. There were guards on the wall above—she could feel them with her life sense—but she was below their angle of view as long as they looked outward. She might be able to sneak by them.

She waited until one patrol had passed, then Awakened one of the tapestries. "Lift me," she said, dropping a drained handkerchief. The tapestry twisted into the air, wrapping around her, the top end still attached to the wall. Like a muscular arm, it lifted her up, twisting and depositing her atop the wall. She glanced around, recovering her breath. To the side, some distance away, a group of guards was pointing at her.

You're not any better at this than Vasher is, Nightblood noted. *You people can't sneak at all! Yesteel would be so disappointed in you.*

She cursed, Awakened the tapestry again and had it lower her into the court. She recovered her breath, then took off running across the grassy lawn. Few people were about, but that only made her stand out even more.

The palace, Nightblood said. *Go there.*

That was where she *was* going. However, the longer she held the sword, the more she understood that it said whatever came to its steely mind, whether or not its comments were relevant. It was like a child, speaking or asking questions without inhibition.

The front of the palace was very well guarded by a group of men who weren't wearing uniforms. *He's in there,* Nightblood said. *I can feel him. Third floor. Where he and I were before.*

Vivenna got an image of the room shoved into her head. She frowned. *Remarkably useful,* she thought, *for an evil weapon of destruction.*

I'm not evil, Nightblood said, voice not defensive, simply informative. As if reminding her of something she'd forgotten. *I destroy evil. I think maybe we should destroy those men up ahead. They look evil. You should pull me out.*

For some reason, she doubted that would be a good idea.

Come on, Nightblood said.

The soldiers were pointing at her. She glanced behind, and saw others rushing across the lawn. *Austre, forgive me,* she thought. Then, gritting her teeth, she threw Nightblood—blanket and all—toward the guards in front of the building.

They halted. To a man, they looked down at the sword as it rolled free of the blanket, silver sheath glistening on the lawn. *Well, I guess this works too,* Nightblood noted, voice feeling distant now.

One of the soldiers picked up the sword. Vivenna dashed past them, ignored by the soldiers. They started to fight.

Can't go that way, she thought, eyeing the front entrance, not wanting to risk pushing her way through fighting men. So instead she ran to the side of the massive palace. The lower levels were made of the steplike black blocks that gave the palace its pyramidlike quality. Above these, it grew into a more traditional fortress, with steep walls. There were windows, if she could reach them.

She twitched her fingers, making the tassels on her sleeves clench and unclench. Then she jumped, her Awakened leggings tossing her up a few extra feet. She reached up and made the tassels grab the edge of the large, black block. The tassels just barely held, gripping the stone like footlong fingers. With difficulty, Vivenna pulled herself up onto the block.

Men yelled and screamed below, and she spared them a

glance. The guard who had grabbed Nightblood was fighting off the others, a small trail of black smoke swirling around him. As she watched, he backed into the palace itself, the other men following him.

So much evil, Nightblood said, like a woman tisking as she cleaned cobwebs from her ceiling.

Vivenna turned away, feeling slightly guilty for giving the sword to the men. She jumped up and pulled herself onto the next block, continuing as the soldiers who had seen her from the walls arrived. They wore the colors of the city guard, and while a couple of them got caught up in the Nightblood fight, most of them ignored it.

Vivenna continued up.

To the right, Nightblood said distantly. *That window on the third floor. Two over. He's in there . . .*

As his voice faded, Vivenna looked up at the window indicated. She still had to climb up a number of blocks, then somehow reach a window that was an entire story up a sheer wall. There did appear to be some decorative stonework that could serve as handholds, but she grew dizzy even thinking about climbing them.

An arrow snapped against the stone beside her, making her jump. Several guards below had bows.

Colors! she thought, pulling herself up to the next block. She heard a whoosh behind her, and cringed, feeling as if she should have been struck, but nothing happened. She pulled herself up onto the block, then twisted around.

She could just barely see a corner of her cloak holding an arrow. She started, grateful that she had Awakened it. It dropped the arrow, then returned to normal.

Handy, that, she thought, climbing up the last block. By the time she got on top of it, her arms were sore. Fortunately, her Awakened fingers were still gripping as well as ever. She took a deep breath, then began to climb straight up the upper wall of the black fortress, using the carvings as handholds.

And decided, for her own sanity, that she'd better avoid looking down.

∽∽∽∽

LIGHTSONG STARED AHEAD. Too much information. Too much was happening. Blushweaver's murder, then Llarimar's revelation, the betrayal of the God King's priests all in such quick succession.

He sat in his cell, arms wrapped around himself, gold and red robes dirtied from crawling through the tunnel, then sitting in his cage. His thigh ached from where it had been struck with the sword, though the wound had not been bad, and it was barely bleeding anymore. He ignored the pain. It was insignificant compared to the pain inside.

The priests talked quietly on the far side of the room. Oddly, as he glanced at them, something caught his eye. He let his mind be diverted by the realization—he finally grasped what was bothering him about them. He should have seen it earlier. It had to do with color—not the color of their clothing, but the color of their faces. It was just slightly off. The deviation in one man would have been easy to ignore. But all of them together was a pattern.

No regular person could have noticed it. To a man with his Heightenings, it was obvious, once he knew what to look for.

These men were not from Hallandren.

Anyone can wear a set of robes, he realized. *That doesn't mean that they're priests.* In fact, judging by the faces, he realized the men must be from Pahn Kahl.

And then it all made sense to him, that quickly. They'd all been played for fools.

∽∽∽∽

"BLUEFINGERS," SIRI DEMANDED. "Talk to me. What are you going to do with us?"

The labyrinth of the God King's palace was complex,

and it was sometimes difficult even now for her to find her way around. They'd traveled down a stairwell but now were going up another one.

Bluefingers didn't answer. He walked with his customary nervousness, wringing his hands. The fighting in the hallways seemed to be decreasing. In fact, once they left the stairwell, this newest hallway was dreadfully quiet.

Siri walked with Susebron's nervous arm around her waist. She didn't know what he was thinking—they hadn't been able to pause long enough for him to write anything. He gave her a comforting smile, but she knew that this all must be just as terrifying for him as it was for her. Probably more so.

"You can't do this, Bluefingers," Siri said, snapping at the little balding man.

"It is the only way we'd ever be able to break free," Bluefingers said, not turning, but finally responding to her.

"But you can't!" Siri said. "The Idrians are innocent!"

Bluefingers shook his head. "How many of my people would you sacrifice, if it would mean freedom for yours?"

"None!" she said.

"I should like to see you say that if our positions were reversed," he said, still not meeting her eyes. "I'm . . . sorry for your pain. But your people are *not* innocent. They're just like the Hallandren. In the Manywar, you rolled over us, made us your workers and slaves. Only at the end, when the royal family fled, did Idris and Hallandren split."

"Please," Siri said.

Susebron suddenly punched a Lifeless.

The God King growled, struggling as he kicked at another. There were dozens of them. He looked at her, waving a hand, motioning for her to flee. She didn't intend to leave him. Instead, she tried to grab Bluefingers, but a Lifeless was too quick. It took her arm, holding her firm, even when she batted at it. A couple of men wearing the robes of Susebron's priesthood came out of a stairwell ahead of them, carrying lanterns. Siri, looking closely, immediately recognized them as being from Pahn Kahl. They were too short and their skin color was just slightly off.

I've been a fool, she thought.

Bluefingers had played the game so well. He'd driven a wedge between her and the priests from the start. Most of her fears and worries, she'd gotten from him—and it had been reinforced by the priests' arrogance. All part of the scribe's plan to someday use her to gain freedom for his people.

"We have Lightsong's security phrase," one of the new men said to Bluefingers. "We have checked it, and it works. We changed it to the new one. The rest of the Lifeless are ours."

Siri glanced to the side. The Lifeless had pulled Susebron to the ground. He yelled—though it came out more as a moan. Siri yanked, trying to escape her Lifeless and help him. She began to cry.

To the side, Bluefingers nodded to his accomplices, looking fatigued. "Very well. Give the Command. Order the Lifeless to march on Idris."

"It will be done," the man said, laying a hand on Bluefingers's shoulder.

Bluefingers nodded, looking morose as the others withdrew.

"What do you have to be sad about?" she spat.

Bluefingers turned toward her. "My friends now are the only ones who know the Command phrases for Hallandren's Lifeless army. Once those Lifeless leave for Idris—with orders to destroy everything they find there—my friends will kill themselves with poison. There won't be anyone who can stop the creatures."

Austre . . . Siri thought, feeling numb. *Lord of Colors . . .*

"Take the God King below," Bluefingers said, waving to several Lifeless. "Hold him until it is time." They were joined by a Pahn Kahl scribe wearing fake priest's robes as they towed Susebron toward the stairwell. Siri reached for him. He continued to struggle, reaching back, but the Lifeless were too strong. She listened to his inarticulate yells echoing down the stairwell.

"What will you do with him?" Siri asked, tears cold on her cheeks.

Bluefingers glanced at her, but once again, would not meet her eyes. "There will be many in the Hallandren government who see the Lifeless attack as a political mistake, and they may seek to stop the war. Unless Hallandren actually commits itself to this fight, our sacrifice will be useless."

"I don't understand."

"We will take the bodies of Lightsong and Blushweaver—the two gods with the Command phrases—and leave them in the Lifeless barracks, surrounded by dead Idrians we took from the city. Then we will leave the corpse of the God King to be discovered in the palace dungeons. Those who investigate will assume that Idrian assassins attacked and killed him—we've hired enough mercenaries from the Idrian slums that it shouldn't be too difficult to believe. Those of my scribes who survive the night will confirm the story."

Siri blinked out tears. *Everyone will assume that Blushweaver and Lightsong sent the armies as retribution for the death of the God King.*

And with the king dead, the people will be furious.

"I wish you hadn't gotten involved in all of this," Bluefingers said, motioning for her Lifeless captors to pull her along. "It would have been easier for me if you'd been able to keep yourself from getting pregnant."

"I'm not!" she said.

"The people think you are," he said with a sigh as they walked toward the stairwell. "And that's enough. We have to break this government *and* we have to make the Idrians angry enough to want to destroy the Hallandren. I think your people will do better in this war than everyone says, especially if the Lifeless march without leadership. Your people will ambush them, making sure this is not an easy war for either side."

He glanced at her. "But for this war to work right, the Idrians have to *want* to fight. Otherwise, they'll flee and vanish into those highlands. No, both sides have to hate each other, pull as many allies into the battle as possible so that everyone is too distracted . . ."

And what better way to make Idris willing to fight, she thought with horror, *than to kill me? Both sides will see the death of my supposed child as an act of war. This won't simply be a fight for domination. It will be a drawn-out war of hatred. The fighting could last for decades.*

And nobody will ever realize that our real enemy—the one who started it all—is the peaceful, quiet province to the south of Hallandren.

56

VIVENNA HUNG OUTSIDE the window, breathing deeply, sweating heavily. She'd peeked inside. Denth was in there, as was Tonk Fah. Vasher was hanging from a hook on the ceiling. He was bloodied, and he held no Breath, but he seemed to be alive.

Can I stop both Denth and Tonk Fah? she thought. Her arms were tired. She had a couple of lengths of rope in her pocket she could Awaken. What if she threw and missed? She had seen Denth fight. He was faster than she'd thought possible. She would have to surprise him. And if she missed, she would die.

What am I doing? she thought. *Hanging from a wall, about to challenge two professional soldiers?*

Her recent past gave her the strength to push down her fear. They might kill her, but that would be a quick end. She'd survived betrayals, the death of a dear friend, and a time going mad from the illness, hunger, and terror of living on the streets. She'd been pushed down, forced to admit that she'd betrayed her people. There wasn't really any more they could do to her.

For some reason, those thoughts gave her power. Surprised at her own determination, she quietly recovered the Breath from her cloak and her leggings. She Awakened a pair of rope pieces, telling them to grab when thrown. She said a quiet prayer to Austre, then pulled herself up through the window and into the room.

Vasher was groaning. Tonk Fah was dozing in the corner. Denth, holding a bloody knife, looked up immediately as she landed. The look of utter shock on his face was, in itself, almost worth everything she'd been through. She tossed the rope at him, threw the other at Tonk Fah, then dashed into the room.

Denth reacted immediately, cutting the rope out of the air with his dagger. The pieces of it twisted and wriggled, but weren't long enough to grab anything. The one she threw at Tonk Fah, however, hit. He cried out, waking as it wrapped around his face and neck.

Vivenna pulled to a halt beside Vasher's swinging body. Denth had his sword out; he'd pulled it free more quickly than she could track. She gulped, then pulled out her own sword, holding it forward as Vasher had taught her. Denth paused just briefly in surprise.

That was enough. She swung—not for Denth, but for the rope holding Vasher to the ceiling. He fell with a grunt, and Denth struck, slamming the point of his dueling blade through her shoulder.

She fell, gasping in pain.

Denth stepped back. "Well, Princess," he said, warily holding his blade. "I didn't expect to see you here."

Tonk Fah made a gagging sound as the rope twisted around his neck, choking him. He struggled to pull it free with little success.

Once, the pain in her shoulder might have been debilitating. But after the beatings she'd taken on the street, it seemed somewhat familiar to her. She looked up, and met Denth's eyes.

"Was this supposed to be a rescue?" Denth asked. "Because honestly, I'm not very impressed."

Tonk Fah knocked over his stool in his thrashing. Denth glanced at him, then back at Vivenna. There was a moment of silence, save for Tonk Fah's weakening struggles. Finally, Denth cursed and jumped over to cut at the rope on his friend's neck.

"You all right?" Vasher asked from beside her. She was shocked by how solid his voice sounded, despite his bloodied body.

She nodded.

"They're going to send Lifeless marching on your homeland," he said. "We've been wrong about this all along. I don't know who's behind it, but I think they're winning the fight for the palace."

Denth finally got the rope cut free.

"You need to run," Vasher said, wiggling his hands free from their rope bonds. "Get back to your people, tell them not to fight the Lifeless. They need to flee through the northern passes, hide in the highlands. *Do not fight* or bring other kingdoms into the war."

Vivenna glanced back at Denth, who was smacking Tonk Fah back to consciousness. Then she closed her eyes. "Your Breath to mine," she said, drawing back the Breath from her hand tassels, adding it to the large amount she still held from before. She reached out, placing her hand on Vasher.

"Vivenna . . ." he said.

"My life to yours," she said. "My Breath become yours."

Her world became a thing of dullness. Beside her, Vasher gasped, then began to convulse at the bestowal of Breath. Denth stood up, spinning.

"You do it, Vasher," Vivenna whispered. "You'll be far better at it than I will be."

"Stubborn woman," Vasher said as he overcame the convulsions. He reached out, as if to restore her Breath to her, but noticed Denth.

Denth smiled, raising his blade. Vivenna put a hand to her shoulder, stopping the blood flow, and she began to push herself back toward the window—though, without Breath, she wasn't certain what she intended to do there.

Vasher stood up, taking her sword in his hand. He wore only the bloody, knee-length underbreeches, but his stance was firm. He slowly wrapped the rope he'd been hanging from around his waist, forming his characteristic belt.

How does he do it? she thought. *Where does his strength come from?*

"I should have hurt you more," Denth said. "I took my time. Savoring it too much."

Vasher snorted, tying off the belt. Denth seemed to be waiting, anticipating something.

"I've always found it funny that we bleed, just like ordinary men," Denth said. "We might be stronger, might live much longer, but we die just the same."

"Not the same," Vasher said, raising Vivenna's blade. "Other men die with far more honor than we, Denth."

Denth smiled. Vivenna could see excitement in his eyes. *He always claimed that there was no way Vasher could have beaten his friend, Arsteel, in a duel,* she thought. *He wants to fight Vasher. He wants to prove to himself that Vasher isn't as good as he is.*

Blades whipped into motion. And after just a quick exchange, Vivenna could see that there was no contest. Denth was clearly the better. Perhaps it was Vasher's wounds.

Perhaps it was the growing anger she saw in Vasher's eyes as he fought, marring his ability to be calm and collected during the fight. Maybe he just really wasn't as good as Denth. However, as Vivenna watched, she realized that Vasher was going to lose.

I didn't do all this so you could just die! she thought, rising to try to help.

A hand fell on her shoulder, pushing her back down. "I don't think so," Tonk Fah said, looming over her. "Nice trick with the rope, by the way. Very clever. I know a few tricks with ropes myself. Did you know, for instance, that a rope can be used to burn a person's flesh?" He smiled, then leaned down. "Mercenary humor, you see."

His cloak slid slightly off his shoulder, falling against her cheek.

It can't be, she thought. *I escaped from him. I tried to Awaken his cloak, but used a bad Command. Could he have been stupid enough to keep wearing it?*

She smiled, glancing over her shoulder. Vasher had backed against the far wall, to the window, and he was sweating profusely, bloody drops falling to the ground. Denth forced him back again, and Vasher stepped up on the table by the far wall, seeking high ground.

She looked back at Tonk Fah, his cloak still touching her cheek. "Your Breath to mine," she said.

She felt a sudden, welcoming burst of Breath.

"Huh?" Tonk Fah said.

"Nothing," she said. "Just . . . Attack and grab Denth!" Command made, visualization made, the cloak began to quiver. Tonk Fah's shirt drained of color, and his eyes widened with surprise. The cloak suddenly whipped into the air, yanking Tonk Fah to the side and causing him to stumble away from her.

That's why I'm the princess, and you're just a mercenary, she thought with satisfaction, rolling over.

Tonk Fah cried out. Denth spun at the sound, yelling as the very large, very uncoordinated Pahn Kahl man crashed into him, cloak whipping about.

Denth slammed backward, catching Vasher by surprise as they rammed together. Tonk Fah grunted. Denth cursed.

And Vasher was shoved backward out the window.

Vivenna blinked in surprise. That wasn't what she'd been intending. Denth cut away the cloak, pushing Tonk Fah back.

All was silent in the room for a moment.

"Go grab our squad of Lifeless!" Denth said. "Now!"

"You think he'll live?" Tonk Fah asked.

"He just fell out the third-story window, plummeting toward certain doom," Denth said. "Of course he'll live! Send the squad to the front doors to slow him!" Denth glanced at Vivenna. "You, Princess, are far more trouble than you're worth."

"So people are fond of telling me," she said with a sigh, raising her bloodied hand to her shoulder again, too exhausted to be as scared as she probably should have been.

VASHER FELL TOWARD the hard stone blocks below. He watched the window retreat above him. *Almost,* he thought with frustration. *I just about had him!*

Wind whistled. He screamed in frustration, pulling free the rope at his waist, Vivenna's Breath a lively strength within him.

"Grab things," he Commanded, whipping the rope out, drawing color from his bloodstained shorts. They bled to grey, and the rope wrapped around an outcropping of stone on the palace wall. It pulled taut, and he ran sideways along the ebony blocks, slowing his fall.

"Your Breath to mine," he yelled as his momentum slowed. The rope dropped free and he landed on the first block. "Become as my leg and give it strength!" he Commanded, drawing color from the blood on his chest. The rope twisted down, wrapping around his leg and foot as he leaped off. He landed on the next block, one foot down, the coiled rope—and its strange, inhuman muscles—bearing the brunt of the shock.

Four hops and he hit the ground. A group of soldiers stood amidst some bodies at the front gates, looking confused. Vasher barreled toward them, colorless translucent blood dropping from his skin as he drew his Breath back from the rope.

He scooped a sword from a fallen soldier. The men before the gates turned and readied their weapons. He didn't have the time, or the patience, for pleasantries. He struck, cutting men down with quick efficiency. He wasn't as good as Denth, but he had practiced for a very, very long time.

Unfortunately, there were a lot of men. Maybe too many to fight. Vasher cursed, spinning between them, dropping another one. He bent down, slapping his hand against the waist of a fallen soldier, touching both shirt and· pants, looping his finger around the colored inner undershirt.

"Fight for me, as if you were me," he Commanded, draining the man's undershirt completely grey. Vasher spun, blocking a sword strike. Another came from the side, and another. He couldn't block them all.

A sword flashed in the air, blocking a weapon that would have hit Vasher. The dead man's shirt and trousers, having pulled themselves free, stood holding a blade. They struck, as if controlled by an invisible person inside, blocking and attacking with skill. Vasher put his back to the Awakened construct. When he had a chance, he made another one, draining away his remaining Breath.

They fought in a trio, Vasher and his two sets of Awakened clothing. The guards cursed, much more wary now. Vasher eyed them, planning an attack. At that moment, a troop of some fifty Lifeless barreled around the corner, charging toward him.

Colors! Vasher thought. He growled in rage, striking and taking down another soldier.

Colors, Colors, Colors!

You shouldn't swear, a voice said in his head. *Shashara told me that was evil.*

Vasher spun toward the sound. A little line of black smoke was trailing out from beneath the closed front doors of the palace.

Aren't you going to thank me? Nightblood said. *I came to save you.*

One of his sets of clothing fell, the leg cut off by a soldier's clever strike. Vasher reached back, drawing the Breath back from the second set of clothing, then stepped with an unclothed toe on the fallen set, recovering the Breath from it as well. The soldiers backed away, wary, more than happy to let the Lifeless take him.

And in that moment of peace, Vasher charged for the gates to the palace. He threw his shoulder against them, slamming them open, skidding into the entryway.

A large group of men lay dead on the ground. Nightblood sprouted from one man's chest, as usual, hilt pointing toward the sky. Vasher hesitated only briefly. He could hear Lifeless charging up behind him.

He ran forward and grabbed Nightblood's hilt and pulled the sword free, leaving the sheath behind in the body.

The blade sprayed a wave of black liquid as he swung it. The liquid dissolved into smoke before touching walls or floor, like water in an oven. Smoke twisted, some rising from the blade, some falling in a stream to the floor, dripping like black blood.

Destroy! Nightblood's voice boomed in his head. *The evil must be destroyed!* Pain shot up Vasher's arm, and he felt his Breath being leached away, sucked into the blade, fueling its hunger. Drawing the weapon had a terrible cost. At that moment, he didn't really care. He spun toward the charging Lifeless and—enraged—attacked.

Each creature he struck with the blade immediately flashed and became smoke. A single scratch and the bodies dissolved like paper being consumed by an invisible fire, leaving behind only a large stain of blackness in the air. Vasher spun among them, striking with wrath, killing Lifeless after Lifeless. Black smoke churned around him, and his arm twisted with pain as veinlike tendrils climbed up the hilt and around his forearm—like black blood vessels that latched on to his skin, feeding off his Breath.

In a matter of minutes, the Breath Vivenna had given him had been reduced by half. Yet in those moments, he destroyed all fifty Lifeless. The soldiers outside pulled to a halt, watching the display. Vasher stood amidst a churning mass of deep ebony smoke. It slowly rose into the air, the only remnants of the fifty creatures he had destroyed.

The soldiers ran away.

Vasher screamed, charging toward the side of the room. He slammed Nightblood through a wall. The stone dissolved just as easily as flesh had, evaporating away before him. He burst through the dissipating black smoke, entering the next room. He didn't bother with a stairwell. He simply jumped onto a table and rammed Nightblood into the ceiling.

A circle ten feet wide vanished. Dark, mistlike smoke fell around him like streaks of paint. He Awakened his rope again and then tossed it up, using it to pull himself up onto the next floor. A moment later, he did it again, climbing onto the third floor.

He spun, slashing through walls, bellowing as he ran back toward Denth. The pain in his arm was incredible, and his Breath was draining away at an alarming rate. Once it was gone, Nightblood would kill him.

Everything was growing fuzzy. He slashed through a final wall, finding the room where he had been tortured.

It was empty.

He cried out, arm shaking. *Destroy . . . evil . . .* Nightblood said in his mind, all lightness gone from the tone, all familiarity. It boomed like a command. An awful, inhuman thing. The longer Vasher held the sword, the faster it drained his Breath.

Gasping, he threw the sword aside and fell to his knees. It skidded, tearing a rip in the floor that puffed away into smoke, but hit a wall with a *pling* and fell still. Smoke rose from the blade.

Vasher knelt, arm twitching. The black veins on his skin slowly evaporated. He was left with just barely enough Breath to reach the First Heightening. Another few seconds, and Nightblood would have sucked the rest away. He shook his head, trying to clear his vision.

Something fell to the tiled floor in front of him. A dueling blade. Vasher looked up.

"Stand up," Denth said, eyes hard. "We're going to finish what we started."

57

BLUEFINGERS LED SIRI—held by several Lifeless—up to the fourth floor of the palace. The top floor. They entered a room lavishly decorated with rich colors, even for Hallandren. Lifeless guards there let them pass, bowing their heads to Bluefingers.

All the Lifeless in the city are controlled by Bluefingers and his scribes, she thought. *But even before that, the scribes had great power over the bureaucracy and work-*

ings of the kingdom. Did the Hallandren realize that they were dooming themselves by relegating the Pahn Kahl people to such lowly—yet important—positions?

"My people will not fall for this," Siri found herself saying as she was pulled to the front of the room. "They won't fight Hallandren. They'll retreat through the passes. Take refuge in the highland valleys or one of the outer kingdoms."

The front of the room held a black block of stone, shaped like an altar. Siri frowned. From behind, a group of Lifeless entered the room, carrying the corpses of several priests. She saw Treledees's body among them.

What? Siri thought.

Bluefingers turned toward her. "We'll make certain they're angry," he said. "Trust me. When this is through, Princess, Idris will fight until either it or Hallandren is destroyed."

THEY TOSSED SOMEONE into the cell next to Lightsong. He looked up with weary eyes, uncaring. It was another Returned. Which of the gods had they taken captive now?

The God King, he thought. *Interesting.*

He looked down again. What did it matter? He'd failed Blushweaver. He'd failed everyone. The Lifeless armies were probably already marching on Idris. Hallandren and Idris would fight and the Pahn Kahl would have their revenge. It had been three hundred years coming.

VASHER STOOD UP with difficulty. He held the dueling sword in a weak hand, looking at Denth, still shaken by his use of Nightblood. The empty black hallway was now open around them. Vasher had destroyed several of the walls. It was amazing the roof hadn't fallen in.

Corpses littered the floor, the result of the fights when Denth's men had taken over the palace.

"I'll let you die easily," Denth said, raising his blade. "Just tell me the truth. You never beat Arsteel in a duel, did you?"

Vasher raised his own blade. The cuts, the pain in his arm, the exhaustion of being awake so long . . . it was all wearing on him. Adrenaline could only get him so far, and even *his* body could only take so much. He didn't reply.

"Have it your way," Denth said, attacking.

Vasher backed away, forced to the defensive. Denth had always been better at swordplay. Vasher had been better at research, but what had that earned him? Discoveries that had caused the Manywar, an army of monsters that had killed so many.

He fought. He fought well, he knew, considering how tired he was. But it did little good. Denth drove his blade through Vasher's left shoulder—Denth's favorite place for a first strike. It allowed his opponent to keep fighting, wounded, and drew out the fight for Denth's enjoyment.

"You *never* beat Arsteel," Denth whispered.

※

"YOU'RE GOING TO kill me on an altar," Siri said, standing in the strange room, held by Lifeless. Around her, other Lifeless placed bodies on the floor. Priests. "It doesn't make sense, Bluefingers. You don't follow their religion. Why do this?"

Bluefingers stood to the side, holding a knife. She could see the shame in his eyes. "Bluefingers," she said, forcing her voice to remain even, her hair to stay black. "Bluefingers, you don't have to do this."

Bluefingers finally looked at her. "After all I've already done, do you think one more death means anything to me?"

"After all you've done," she said, "do you really think one more death will matter for your cause?"

He glanced at the altar. "Yes," he said. "You know how

the Idrians whisper of the things that go on in the Court of Gods. Your people hate and distrust the Hallandren priests; they speak of murders done on dark altars in the backs of the palaces. Well, we are going to let a group of those Idrian mercenaries see this, once you are dead. We'll show them that we were too late to save you, that the twisted priests had already killed you on one of their profane altars. We'll show them the dead priests we killed trying to save you.

"The Idrians will riot in the city. They're strained to snapping anyway—we have you to thank for that. The city will be in chaos, and there will be a slaughter the like of which hasn't been seen since the Manywar as the Hallandren kill Idrian peasants to maintain order. Those Idrians who live will return to their homeland to tell the tale. They'll let everyone know that the Hallandren only wanted a princess of the royal blood so that they could sacrifice her to their God King. It is exaggerated and foolish to think that the Hallandren would really do such a thing, but sometimes the wildest tales are the ones best believed, and the Idrians will accept this one. You know they will."

And she did. She'd heard similar stories since her childhood. Hallandren was remote to her people: frightening, bizarre. Siri struggled, feeling even more worried.

Bluefingers glanced back at her. "I truly am sorry."

⚬⚬⚬⚬⚬

I AM NOTHING, Lightsong thought. *Why couldn't I save her? Why couldn't I protect her?*

He was crying again. Oddly, someone else was too. The man in the cell next to him. The God King. Susebron moaned with frustration, pounding against the bars of his cage. He didn't speak, though, or denounce his captors.

I wonder why that is, Lightsong thought.

Men approached the God King's cell. Pahn Kahl men, with weapons. Their expressions were grim.

Lightsong found it hard to care.

You are a god. Llarimar's words still challenged him. The high priest lay in his own cell, to Lightsong's left, eyes closed against the terrors around them.

You are a god. To me at least.

Lightsong shook his head. *No. I'm nothing! No god. Not even a good man.*

You are . . . to me . . .

Water splashed against him. Lightsong shook his head, shocked. Thunder sounded, distant, in his head. Nobody else seemed to notice.

It was growing dark.

What?

He was on a ship. Tossing, pitching, on a dark sea. Lightsong stood on the deck, trying to stay upright on the slick boards. Part of him knew it was simply a hallucination, that he was still back in the prison cell, but it felt real. Very real.

The waves churned, black sky ripped by lightning ahead, and the ship's motion slammed his face against the wall of the ship's cabin. Light from a pole-mounted lantern flickered uncertainly. It seemed weak compared with the lightning, which was so violent and angry.

Lightsong blinked. His face was pressed up against something painted on the wood. A red panther, glistening in the lanternlight and the rain.

The name of the ship, he remembered, *the* Red Panther.

He wasn't Lightsong. Or he was, but he was a much smaller, pudgier version of himself. A man accustomed to being a scribe. To working long hours counting coins. Checking ledgers.

Seeking for lost money. That's what he'd done. People hired him to discover where they'd been cheated or if a contract hadn't been paid properly. His job was to look through the books, searching out hidden or confusing twists of arithmetic. A detective. Just not the sort he had imagined.

Waves crashed against the boat. Llarimar, looking a few years younger, yelled for help from the prow. Deckhands rushed to his aid. It wasn't Llarimar's ship, or even Lightsong's. They had borrowed it for a simple pleasure trip. Sailing was a hobby of Llarimar's.

The storm had come on suddenly. Lightsong lurched back to his feet, barely managing to stay up as he made his way forward, clutching the railing. Waves surged across the deck, and sailors struggled to keep the boat from capsizing. The sails were gone, only tattered shreds remaining. Wood creaked and cracked around him. Dark, black water churned in the ocean just to his right.

Llarimar yelled to Lightsong, asking him to lash down the barrels. Lightsong nodded, grabbing a rope and tying one end to a davit. A wave hit, and he skidded, almost falling over the rail into the water.

He froze, gripping the rope, looking into the sea's mad, terrifying depths. He shook himself free, then tied the rope in a wide slipknot. It came naturally to him. Llarimar had taken him on enough sailing trips now.

Llarimar called for help again. And, suddenly, a young woman left the cabin and ran across the deck, grabbing ropes as if to lend assistance. "Tatara!" a woman called from the cabin. There was terror in her voice.

Lightsong looked up. He recognized the girl. He reached out, rope looped in his hands. He shouted for her to go back below, but his voice was lost in the thunder.

She turned to look at him.

The next wave tossed her into the ocean.

Llarimar cried out in despair. Lightsong watched, shocked. The deep blackness claimed his niece. Engulfed her. Swallowed her.

Such great, horrible chaos. The sea in a storm at night. He felt useless, his heart thumping with fright as he watched the young woman get swept into the churning current. He saw flashes of her golden hair twisting in the water. A weak splash of color passing his side of the ship. It would soon be gone.

Men cursed. Llarimar screamed. A woman wept. Lightsong just stared into the bubbling deep, with its alternating froth and blackness. The terrible, terrible blackness.

He still held the rope in his hand.

Without thinking, he leaped up onto the railing and threw himself into the darkness. Icy water took him, but he reached out, thrashing and churning in the tempest. He barely knew how to swim. Something passed him.

He grabbed it. Her foot. He threw the loop around her ankle, somehow managing to get the knot tight despite the water and the waves. As soon as he did, a surge in the undulating water yanked him away. Sucking him down. He reached upward, toward where lightning lit the surface. That light grew distant as he sank.

Down. Into the black deep.

Claimed by the void.

He blinked, waves and thunder fading. He sat on the cool stones of his cell. The void had taken him, but something had sent him back. He'd Returned.

Because he'd seen war and destruction.

The God King was yelling in fear. Lightsong looked over as the fake priests grabbed Susebron, and Lightsong could see into the God King's mouth. *No tongue*, Lightsong thought. *Of course. To keep him from using all that BioChroma. It makes sense.*

He turned to the side. Blushweaver's body lay red and bloodied. He'd seen that in a vision. In the vague shadows of morning memory, he'd thought that the image had been of her blushing, but now he remembered. He looked to the side. Llarimar, eyes closed as if asleep—that image had been in his dream as well. Lightsong realized the man had them shut as he wept.

The God King in prison. Lightsong had seen that too. But above it all, he remembered standing on the other side of a brilliant, colorful wave of light, looking down at the world from the other side. And seeing everything he loved dissolve into the destruction of war. A war greater than any the world had known, a war more deadly—even—than the Manywar.

He remembered the other side. And he remembered a voice, calm and comforting, offering him an opportunity.

To Return.

By the Colors . . . Lightsong thought, standing up as the priests forced the God King to his knees. *I am a god.*

Lightsong stepped forward, moving up to the bars of his cage. He saw pain and tears in the God King's face and somehow understood them. The man *did* love Siri. Lightsong had seen the same thing in the queen's eyes. She had somehow come to care for the man who was to oppress her.

"You are my king," Lightsong whispered. "And lord of the gods."

The Pahn Kahl men forced the God King facedown on the stones. One of the priests raised a sword. The God King's arm jutted out, his hand toward Lightsong.

I have seen the void, he thought. *And I came back.*

And then Lightsong reached through the bars and grasped the God King's hand. A fake priest looked up with alarm.

Lightsong met the man's eyes, then smiled broadly, looking down at the God King. "My life to yours," Lightsong said. "My Breath become yours."

<hr />

DENTH SLASHED, WOUNDING Vasher in the leg.

Vasher stumbled, going down on one knee. Denth struck again, and Vasher barely managed to keep the sword away.

Denth backed off, shaking his head. "You are pathetic, Vasher. There you kneel, about to die. And you still think you're better than the rest of us. You judge me for becoming a mercenary? What else was I to do? Take over kingdoms? Rule them and start wars, as you did?"

Vasher bowed his head. Denth growled and ran forward, lashing out with his sword. Vasher tried to defend himself, but he was just too weak. Denth knocked Vasher's weapon aside, then kicked him in the stomach, sending Vasher backward against the wall.

Vasher slumped down, sword lost. He reached for a knife on the belt of a fallen soldier, but Denth stepped up and put his booted foot on Vasher's hand.

"You think I should just go back to the way I was before?" Denth spat. "The happy, friendly man everyone loved?"

"You were a good person," Vasher whispered.

"That man saw and did terrible things," Denth said. "I've tried, Vasher. I've *tried* going back. But the darkness . . . it's inside. I can't escape it. My laughter has an edge to it. I can't forget."

"I can make you," Vasher said. "I know the Commands."

Denth froze.

"I promise," Vasher said. "I will take it all from you, if you wish."

Denth stood for a long moment, foot on Vasher's arm, sword lowered. Then, finally, he shook his head. "No. I don't deserve that. Neither of us do. Goodbye, Vasher."

He raised his blade to strike. And Vasher moved his arm up, touching Denth's leg.

"My life to yours, my Breath become yours."

Denth froze, then stumbled. Fifty Breaths fled from Vasher's chest and surged into Denth's body. They would be unwelcome, but he couldn't turn them away. Fifty Breaths. Not many.

But enough. Enough to make Denth shake with pleasure. Enough to make him lose control for just a second, falling to his knees. And, in that second, Vasher stood—

ripping the dagger free from the corpse beside him—then slashed it through Denth's throat.

The mercenary fell back, eyes wide, neck bleeding. He shook amidst the pleasure of gaining new Breaths even as his life flowed from him.

"Nobody ever expects it," Vasher whispered, stepping forward. "Breath is worth a fortune. To put it into someone, then kill them, is to lose more wealth than most men will ever know. They never expect it."

Denth shook, bleeding, and lost control. His hair suddenly bled to deep black, then blond, then an angry red.

Finally, the hair turned white with terror and stayed there. He stopped moving, life fading away, new Breaths and old both vanishing.

"You wanted to know how I killed Arsteel," Vasher said, spitting blood to the side. "Well, now you do."

———⚬———

BLUEFINGERS PICKED UP a knife. "The least I can do," he decided, "is to kill you myself, rather than letting the Lifeless do it. I promise it will be quick. We will make it look like a pagan ritual afterward, sparing you the need to die in a painful way." He turned to her Lifeless captors. "Tie her to the altar."

Siri struggled against the Lifeless holding her by the shoulders, but it was useless. They were terribly strong, and her hands were tied together. "Bluefingers!" she snapped, holding his eyes. "I will *not* die tied to some rock like a useless maid from one of the stories. You want me dead, then have the decency to let me die standing up."

Bluefingers hesitated, but the authority in her voice actually seemed to make him cringe. He raised a hand, stopping the Lifeless as they pulled her to the altar.

"Very well," he said. "Hold her tightly."

"You realize the wonderful opportunity you waste by

killing me," she said as he approached. "The wife of the God King would make a wonderful hostage. You are a fool to kill me, and . . ."

He ignored her this time, taking the knife, placing it against her chest, picking his spot. She started to feel numb. She was going to die. She was actually going to *die*.

And the war would start.

"Please," she whispered.

He looked at her, hesitated, then grew grim and drew back the dagger.

The building began to shake.

Bluefingers looked to the side in alarm, glancing toward several of his scribes. They shook their heads in confusion.

"Earthquake?" one asked.

The floor began to turn white. The color moved like a wave of sunlight crossing the land as the sun rose above the mountains. The walls, the ceiling, the floor—all of the black stone faded. The priests stepped away from it, looking frightened, one hopping onto a rug to keep from touching the strange white stones.

Bluefingers looked at her, confused. The ground continued to tremble, but he raised his blade anyway, held in fingers that had been stained repeatedly by ink. And, strangely, Siri saw the whites of his eyes bend and release a rainbow of colors.

The entire room burst with color, the white stones fuzzing and splitting, like light through a prism. The doors to the room exploded. A twisting mass of colorful cloths shot through it, like the countless tentacles of an enraged sea leviathan. They churned and curled, and Siri recognized tapestries, carpets, and long lengths of silk from the palace decorations.

Awakened cloth slapped aside Lifeless, curling around them, tossing them into the air. Priests cried out as they were snatched up, and a long, thin length of violet cloth snapped forward and wrapped around Bluefingers's arm.

The surging mass undulated, churning, and Siri could finally see a figure walking in the middle of it. A man of epic proportions. Black of hair, pale of face, youthful in appearance, but of great age. Bluefingers struggled to ram his knife into Siri's chest, but the God King raised a hand.

"You will *stop!*" Susebron said in a clear voice.

Bluefingers froze, looking toward the God King in amazement. The dagger slipped from his stunned fingers as an Awakened carpet twisted around him, pulling him away from Siri.

Siri stood, dumbfounded. Susebron's cloths lifted him up and over beside her, and a pair of small silken handkerchiefs reached forward, sliding around the ropes binding her hands, untying them with ease.

Freed, she grabbed him and let him lift her into his arms, weeping.

58

THE CLOSET DOOR opened, letting in lantern light. Vivenna looked up, gagged and bound, at Vasher's silhouette. He dragged Nightblood behind him, covered—as usual—by his silver sheath.

Looking very tired, Vasher knelt and undid her gag.

"About time," she noted.

He smiled wanly. "I don't have any Breath remaining," he said quietly. "It was very hard to locate you."

"Where did it all go?" she asked as he undid the ropes on her hands.

"Nightblood devoured most of it."

I don't believe him, Nightblood said happily. *I . . . can't really remember what happened. But we did slay a lot of evil!*

"You drew him?" Vivenna asked as Vasher untied her feet.

Vasher nodded.

Vivenna rubbed her hands. "Denth?"

"Dead," Vasher said. "No sign of Tonk Fah or the woman, Jewels. I think they took their money and fled."

"So it's over."

Vasher nodded, sliding down to seat himself, resting his head against the wall. "And we lost."

She frowned, grimacing at the pain of her wounded shoulder. "What do you mean?"

"Denth was being employed by some of the Pahn Kahl scribes in the palace," Vasher said. "They wanted to start a war between Idris and Hallandren in the hope that it would weaken both kingdoms and let Pahn Kahl gain independence."

"So? Denth is dead now."

"So are the scribes who had the Command phrases for the Lifeless armies," Vasher said. "And they already dispatched the troops. The Lifeless left the city over an hour ago, charging for Idris."

Vivenna fell silent.

"All of this fighting, everything with Denth, that was secondary," Vasher said, knocking his head back against the wall. "It distracted us. I couldn't get to the Lifeless in time. The war has begun. There's no way to stop it."

❦

SUSEBRON LED SIRI down into the depths of the palace. Siri walked beside him, carefully cradled in his arm, a hundred twisting lengths of cloth spinning around them.

Even with that many things Awakened, he still had

enough Breath to make every color they passed glow brightly. Of course, that didn't work for many of the stones they passed. Though large chunks of the building were still black, at least half of it had been turned white.

Not just the grey of normal Awakening. They had been made bone white. And, becoming that white, they now reacted to his incredible BioChroma, splitting back into colors. *Like a circle, somehow,* she thought. *Colorful, then white, then back to color.*

He led her into a particular chamber, and she saw what he'd told her to expect. Scribes crushed by the carpets that he'd awakened, bars ripped from their mountings, walls broken down. A ribbon shot from Susebron, turning over a body so that she wouldn't have to see its wound. She wasn't paying much attention. In the midst of the rubble were a pair of corpses. One was Blushweaver, bloody and red, facedown. The other was Lightsong, his entire body drained of color. As if he were a Lifeless.

His eyes were closed, and he seemed to sleep, as if at peace. A man sat next to him—Lightsong's high priest, holding the god's head in his lap.

The priest looked up. He smiled, though she could see tears in his eyes.

"I don't understand," she said, looking at Susebron.

"Lightsong gave his life to heal me," the God King said. "He somehow knew that my tongue had been removed."

"The Returned can heal one person," the priest said, looking down at his god. "It's their duty to decide who and when. They come back for this purpose, some say. To give life to one person who needs it."

"I never knew him," Susebron said.

"He was a very good person," Siri said.

"I realize that. Though I never spoke to him, somehow he was noble enough to die so that I might live."

The priest smiled down. "The amazing thing is," he said, "Lightsong did that twice."

He told me that I couldn't depend on him in the end, Siri thought, smiling slightly, though sorrowful at the same time. *I guess he lied about that. How very like him.*

"Come," Susebron said. "We must gather what is left of my priests. We have to find a way to stop our armies from destroying your people."

⁂

"THERE HAS TO be a way, Vasher," Vivenna said. She knelt next to him.

He tried to push down his rage, his anger at himself. He'd come to the city to stop a war. Once again, he'd been too late.

"Forty thousand Lifeless," he said, pounding his fist against the floor. "I can't stop that many. Not even with Nightblood and the Breaths of every person in the city. Even if I could somehow keep up with their marching, one would eventually get in a lucky strike and kill me."

"There *has* to be a way," Vivenna said.

Has to be a way.

"I thought the same thing before," he said, putting his head in his hands. "I wanted to stop it. But by the time I realized what was happening, it had gone too far. It had taken on a life of its own."

"What are you talking about?"

"The Manywar," Vasher whispered.

Silence.

"Who *are* you?"

He kept his eyes closed.

They used to call him Talaxin, Nightblood said.

"Talaxin," Vivenna said, amused. "Nightblood, that's one of the Five Scholars. He . . ."

She trailed off.

". . . he lived over three hundred years ago," she finally said.

"BioChroma can keep a man alive a long time," Vasher said, sighing and opening his eyes. She didn't argue.

They used to call him other things, too, Nightblood said.

"If you're really one of them," Vivenna said, "then you'll know how to stop the Lifeless."

"Sure," Vasher said wryly. "With other Lifeless."

"That's it?"

"The easiest. Barring that, we can chase them down and grab them one at a time, then break them and replace their Command phrases. But even if you had the Eighth Heightening to let you break Commands instinctively, changing so many would take weeks."

He shook his head. "We could have an army fight them, but they *are* our army. The Hallandren forces aren't large enough to fight the Lifeless on their own, and they wouldn't be able to get to Idris with any semblance of speed. The Lifeless will beat them by days. Lifeless don't sleep, don't eat, and can march tirelessly."

"Ichor-alcohol," Vivenna said. "They'll run out."

"It's not like food, Vivenna. It's like blood. They need a new supply if they get cut and drained or if it gets corrupted. A few will probably stop working without maintenance, but only a small number."

She fell silent. "Well then, we Awaken an army of our own to fight them."

He smiled wanly. He felt so light-headed. He'd bound his wounds—the bad ones, anyway—but he wouldn't be doing more fighting anytime soon. Vivenna didn't look much better, with that bloody stain on her shoulder.

"Awaken an army of our own?" he said. "First, where would we get the Breath? I used all of yours. Even if we find my clothing, which still has some in it, we'll only have a couple hundred. It takes one per Lifeless. We're severely overmatched."

"The God King," she said.

"Can't use his Breath," Vasher said. "The man's tongue was removed when he was a child."

"And you can't get it out of him somehow?"

Vasher shrugged. "The Tenth Heightening allows a man to Command mentally, without speaking, but it can take months of training to learn how to do that—even if you have someone to teach you. I think his priests must know how, so they can transfer that wealth of Breath from one king to another, but I doubt they've trained him yet. One of their duties is to keep him from using his Breaths in the first place."

"He's still our best option," Vivenna said.

"Oh? And you'll use his power how? Make Lifeless? Are you forgetting that we'll need to find *forty thousand* bodies?"

She sighed, resting back against the wall.

Vasher? Nightblood asked in his mind. *Didn't you leave an army behind here last time?*

He didn't reply. Vivenna opened her eyes, however. Apparently Nightblood had decided to include her in all of his thoughts now.

"What is this?" she asked.

"Nothing," Vasher said.

No, no it's not, Nightblood said. *I remember. You talked to that priest, told him to take care of your Breath for you, should you need it again. And you gave him your army. It stopped moving. You called it a gift for the city. Don't you remember? It was just yesterday.*

"Yesterday?" Vivenna asked.

When the Manywar stopped, Nightblood said. *When was that?*

"He doesn't understand time," Vasher said. "Don't listen to him."

"No," Vivenna said, studying him. "He knows something." She thought for a moment, then her eyes opened wide. "Kalad's army," she said, pointing at him. "His phantoms. You know where they are!"

He hesitated, then nodded reluctantly.

"Where?"

"Here, in the city."

"We have to use them!"

He eyed her. "You're asking me to give Hallandren a tool, Vivenna. A terrible tool. Something worse than what they have now."

"And if that army of theirs slaughters my people?" Vivenna asked. "Could what you're talking about give them more power than that?"

"Yes."

She fell silent.

"Do it anyway," she said.

He glanced at her.

"Please, Vasher."

He closed his eyes again, remembering the destruction he had caused. The wars that had started. All because of the things he'd learned to create. "You would give your enemies such power?"

"They're not my enemies," she said. "Even if I hate them."

He regarded her for a moment, then finally stood. "Let's find the God King. If he even still lives, then we shall see."

※

"My lord and lady," said the priest, bowing with his face down before them. "We heard rumors of a plot to attack the palace. That's why we locked you away. We wanted to protect you!"

Siri looked at the man, then glanced at Susebron. The God King rubbed his chin in thought. They both recognized this man as one of his actual priests, rather than an impostor. They'd only been able to determine that with certainty for a handful of them.

They imprisoned the others, sending for the city guard to come in and start cleaning up the wreckage of the palace. The breeze blew Siri's hair—red, to show her displeasure—as they stood atop the palace.

"There, my lord!" a guard said, pointing.

Susebron turned, walking over to the edge of the palace.

Most of his entourage of twisting cloths were no longer streaming about him, but they waited on his will in a pile on the rooftop. Siri joined him at the side of the palace, and in the distance, she could make out a smudge and what looked like smoke.

"The Lifeless army," the guard said. "Our scouts have confirmed that it's marching toward Idris. Almost everyone in the city saw it pass out through the gates."

"That smoke?" Siri asked.

"Dust of its passing, my lady," the guard said. "That's a lot of soldiers."

She looked up at Susebron. He frowned. "I could stop them." His voice was stronger than she had expected it to be. Deeper.

"My lord?" the guard asked.

"With this much Breath," Susebron said. "I could charge them, use these cloths to tie them up."

"My lord," the guard said hesitantly. "There are *forty thousand* of them. They would cut at the cloth, overwhelm you."

Susebron seemed resolute. "I have to try."

"No," Siri said, laying a hand on his chest.

"Your people . . ."

"We'll send messengers," she said, "explaining our regret. My people can withdraw, ambush the Lifeless. We can send troops to help."

"We don't have many," he said. "And they won't get there very quickly. Could your people really get away?"

No, she thought, heart wrenching. *You don't know that, though, and you're innocent enough to believe they can escape.*

Her people might survive as a whole, but many would die. Susebron getting himself killed fighting the creatures wouldn't be of much use, however. He had amazing power, but fighting so many Lifeless was well beyond the scope of whatever he could do.

He saw the look in her face, and surprisingly, he read it well. "You don't believe that they can get away," he said. "You're just trying to protect me."

Surprising how well he understands me already.

"My lord!" a voice said from behind.

Susebron turned, looking across the top of the palace. They'd come to the top partially to get a look at the Lifeless, but also because both Siri and Susebron were tired of being closed in tight quarters. They wanted to be in the open, where it would be harder to sneak up on them.

A guard came out of the stairwell, then walked over, hand on sword. He bowed. "My lord. There's someone here to see you."

"I don't want to see anyone," Susebron said. "Who are they?"

Amazing how well he can speak, she thought. *Never having had a tongue. What did Lightsong's Breath do? It healed more than his body. It gave him the capacity to use the regrown tongue.*

"My lord," the guard said. "The visitor—she has the Royal Locks!"

"What?" Siri asked with surprise.

The guard turned, and—shockingly—Vivenna stepped up onto the roof of the palace. Or Siri *thought* it was Vivenna. She wore trousers and a tunic, with a sword tied at her waist, and she appeared to have a bloody wound on one shoulder. She saw Siri, and smiled, her hair turning yellow with joy.

Vivenna's hair changing? Siri thought. *It can't be her.*

But it was. The woman laughed, dashing across the top of the roof. Some guards stopped her, but Siri waved for them to let the woman pass. She ran over, embracing Siri.

"Vivenna?"

The woman smiled ruefully. "Yes, mostly," she said. She glanced at Susebron. "I'm sorry," Vivenna said quietly. "I came to the city to try rescuing you."

"That was very kind of you," Siri said. "But I don't need rescuing."

Vivenna frowned more deeply.

"And who is this, Siri?" Susebron asked.

"My eldest sister."

"Ah," Susebron said, bowing his head cordially. "Siri has told me much about you, Princess Vivenna. I wish we could have met under better circumstances."

Vivenna stared at the man with shock.

"He's not really as bad as they say," Siri said, smiling. "Most of the time."

"That is sarcasm," Susebron said. "She is quite fond of it."

Vivenna turned from the God King. "Our homeland is under attack."

"I know," Siri said. "We're working on that. I'm preparing messengers to send to Father."

"I have a better way," Vivenna said. "But you'll have to trust me."

"Of course," Siri said.

"I have a friend who needs to speak with the God King," Vivenna said. "Where he can't be overheard by guards."

Siri hesitated. *Silly,* she thought. *This is Vivenna. I can trust her.*

She'd thought she could trust Bluefingers too. Vivenna regarded her with a curious expression.

"If this can help save Idris," Susebron said, "then I will do it. Who is this person?"

———— ∞ ————

MOMENTS LATER, VIVENNA stood quietly on the roof of the palace with the God King of Hallandren. Siri stood a short walk away, watching the Lifeless churn dust in the distance. All of them waited while the soldiers searched Vasher for weapons; he stood with arms upraised on the other side of the rooftop, surrounded by suspicious guards. He had wisely left Nightblood below and didn't have any other weapons on him. He didn't even have any Breath.

"Your sister is an amazing woman," the God King said.

Vivenna glanced at him. This was the man she was to have married. The terrible creature that she was supposed to have given herself to. She'd never expected to end up like this, pleasantly chatting with him.

She'd also never expected that she'd like him.

It was a quick judgment. She'd gotten over chastising herself for making those, though she had learned to leave them open for revision. She saw kindness in his fondness for Siri. How had a man like this ended up as God King of terrible Hallandren?

"Yes," she said. "She is."

"I love her," Susebron said. "I would have you know this."

Slowly, Vivenna nodded, glancing over at Siri. *She's changed so much*, Vivenna thought. *When did she become so regal, with that commanding bearing and ability to keep her hair black?* Her little sister, no longer quite as little, seemed to wear the expensive dress well. It fit her. Odd.

On the other end of the rooftop, the guards took Vasher behind a screen to change. They obviously wanted to be certain none of his clothing was Awakened. He left a few moments later, wearing a wrap around his waist, but nothing else. His chest was cut and bruised, and Vivenna thought it shameful that he should be forced to undergo such humiliation.

He suffered it, walking across the rooftop with an escort. As he did, Siri walked back, eyes watching him keenly. Vivenna had spoken with her sister briefly, but could already tell that Siri no longer took pride in being unimportant. Changed indeed.

Vasher arrived, and Susebron dismissed the guards. Behind him, the jungles extended to the north, toward Idris. Vasher glanced at Vivenna, and she thought he might tell her to go. However, he finally just turned away from her, looking resigned.

"Who are you?" Susebron asked.

"The one responsible for you getting your tongue cut out," Vasher said.

Susebron raised an eyebrow.

Vasher closed his eyes. He didn't speak, didn't use his Breath or make a Command. Yet suddenly, he started to glow. Not as a lantern would glow, not as the sun glowed, but with an aura that made colors brighter. Vivenna started as Vasher increased in size. He opened his eyes and adjusted the wrap at his waist, making room for his growth. His chest became more firm, the muscles bulging, and the scruffy beard on his face retreated, leaving him clean-shaven.

His hair turned golden. He still bore the cuts on his body, but they seemed inconsequential. He seemed . . . divine. The God King watched with interest. He was now faced by a fellow god, a man of his own stature.

"I don't care if you believe me or not," Vasher said, his voice sounding more noble. "But I will have you know that I left something here, long ago. A wealth of power that I promised to one day recover. I gave instructions for its care, and a charge that it should not be used. The priests, apparently, took this to heart."

Susebron, surprisingly, dropped to one knee. "My lord. Where have you been?"

"Paying for what I've done," Vasher said. "Or trying to. That is unimportant. Stand."

What is going on? Vivenna thought. Siri looked equally confused, and the sisters shared a look.

Susebron stood, though he kept his posture reverent.

"You have a group of rogue Lifeless," Vasher said. "You've lost control of them."

"I'm sorry, my lord," the God King said.

Vasher regarded him. Then he glanced at Vivenna. She nodded her head. "I trust him."

"It's not about trust," Vasher said, turning back to Susebron. "Either way, I am going to give you something."

"What?"

"My army," Vasher said.

Susebron frowned. "But, my lord. Our Lifeless just marched away, to attack Idris."

"No," Vasher said. "Not that army. I'm going to give you the one I left behind three hundred years ago. The people call them Kalad's Phantoms. They are the force by which I made Hallandren stop its war."

"Stop the Manywar, my lord?" Susebron said. "You did that by negotiation."

Vasher snorted. "You don't know much about war, do you?"

The God King paused, then shook his head. "No."

"Well, learn," Vasher said. "Because I charge you with command of my army. Use it to protect, not attack. Only use it in an emergency."

The God King nodded dumbly.

Vasher glanced at him, then sighed. "My sin be hidden."

"What?" Susebron asked.

"It's a Command phrase," Vasher said. "The one you can use to give new orders to the D'Denir statues I left in your city."

"But my lord!" Susebron said. "Stone cannot be awakened."

"The stone hasn't been Awakened," Vasher said. "There are human bones in those statues. They are Lifeless."

Human bones. Vivenna felt a chill. He'd told her that bones were usually a bad choice to awaken because it was hard to keep them in the shape of a man during the Awakening process. But what if those bones were encased in stone? Stone that held its shape, stone that would protect them from harm, make them nearly impossible to hurt or break? Awakened objects could be so much stronger than human muscles. If a Lifeless could be created from bones, made strong enough to move a rock body around it . . . You'd have soldiers unlike any that had ever existed.

Colors! she thought.

"There are some thousand original D'Denir in the city," Vasher said, "and most of them should still function, even still. I created them to last."

"But they have no ichor-alcohol," Vivenna said. "They don't even have *veins!*"

Vasher looked at her. It *was* him. The same look to the face, the same expressions. He hadn't changed shape to look like someone else. He just looked like a *Returned* version of himself. What was going on?

"We didn't always have ichor-alcohol," Vasher said. "It makes the Awakening easier and cheaper, but it isn't the only way. And, in the minds of many, I believe it has become a crutch." He glanced at the God King again. "You should be able to imprint them quickly with a new security phrase, then order them out to stop the other army. I think you'll find those phantoms of mine to be . . . very effective. Weapons are virtually useless against the stone."

Susebron nodded again.

"They are your responsibility now," Vasher said, turning away. "Do better with them than I did."

Epilogue

The next day, an army of a thousand stone soldiers charged from the gates of the city, running down the highway after the Lifeless who had left the day before.

Vivenna stood outside the city, leaning against the wall, watching them go.

How often did I stand under the gaze of those D'Denir, she thought, *never knowing they were alive, just waiting to be Commanded again?* Everyone said that Peacegiver had left the statues behind as a gift to the people, a symbol to remind them not to go to war. She'd always found it strange. A bunch of statues of soldiers, a gift to remind the people that war was terrible?

And yet, they *were* a gift. The gift that had ended the Manywar.

She turned toward Vasher. He, too, leaned against the city wall, Nightblood in one hand. His body had reverted to its mortal form, scraggly hair and all.

"What was that first thing you taught me about Awakening?" she asked.

"That we don't know much?" he asked. "That there are hundreds, perhaps thousands, of Commands that we haven't discovered yet?"

"That's the one," she said, turning to watch the Awakened statues charge into the distance. "I think you were right."

"You think?"

She smiled. "Will they really be able to stop the other army?"

"Probably," Vasher said, shrugging. "They'll be fast enough to catch up—the flesh Lifeless won't be able to march as quickly as ones with stone feet. I've seen those things fight before. They're *really* tough to beat."

She nodded. "So my people will be safe."

"Unless that God King decides to use the Lifeless statues to conquer them."

She snorted. "Has anyone ever told you that you're a grump, Vasher?"

Finally, Nightblood said. *Someone agrees with me!*

Vasher scowled. "I'm not a grump," he said. "I'm just bad with words."

She smiled.

"Well, that's it, then," he said, picking up his pack. "See you around." With that, he began to walk along the path away from the city.

Vivenna walked up next to him.

"What are you doing?" he asked.

"Going with you," she said.

"You're a princess," he said. "Stay with that girl who rules Hallandren or go back to Idris and be proclaimed as the heroine who saved them. Either way will give you a happy life."

"No," she said. "I don't think so. Even if my father *did* take me back, I doubt that I'll ever be able to live a happy life in either a plush palace or a quiet town."

"You'll think differently, after a little time on the road. It's a difficult life."

"I know," she said. "But . . . well, everything I've been—everything I was trained to do—has been a lie wrapped in hatred. I don't want to go back to it. I'm not that person. I don't want to be."

"Who are you, then?"

"I don't know," she said, nodding toward the horizon. "But I think I'll find the answer out there."

They walked for another short time.

"Your family will worry about you," Vasher said.

"They'll get over it," she replied.

Finally, he just shrugged. "All right. I don't really care."

She smiled. *It's true,* she thought. *I don't want to go back.* Princess Vivenna was dead. She'd died on the streets of T'Telir. Vivenna the Awakener had no desire to bring her back.

"So," she asked as they walked along the jungle road, "I can't figure it out. Which one are you? Kalad, who started the war, or Peacegiver, who ended it?"

He didn't answer immediately. "It's odd," he finally said, "what history does to a man. I guess people couldn't understand why I suddenly changed. Why I stopped fighting, and why I brought the Phantoms back to seize control of my own kingdom. So they decided I must have been two people. A man can get confused about his identity when things like that happen."

She grunted in assent. "You're still Returned, though."

"Of course I am," he said.

"Where did you get the Breath?" she asked. "The one a week you need to survive?"

"I carried them with me, on top of the one that makes me Returned. In a lot of ways, Returned aren't quite what people think they are. They don't automatically have hundreds or thousands of Breath."

"But—"

"They're of the Fifth Heightening," Vasher said, interrupting her. "But they don't get there by the number of Breaths, but by the quality. Returned have a single, powerful Breath. One that takes them all the way to the Fifth Heightening. It's a divine Breath, you might say. But their body feeds on Breath, like . . ."

"The sword."

Vasher nodded. "Nightblood only needs it when he's drawn. Returned feed off their Breath once a week. So if you don't give them one, they essentially eat themselves— devouring their one single Breath. Killing them. However, if you give them extra Breath, on top of their single divine one, they'll feed off those each week."

"So the Hallandren gods could be fed more than one," Vivenna said. "They could have a stock of Breaths, a buffer to keep them alive if one couldn't be provided."

Vasher nodded. "Wouldn't make them as dependent on their religion to care for them, though."

"That's a cynical way of looking at it."

He shrugged.

"So you're going to burn up a Breath every week," she said. "Reducing our stock?"

He nodded. "I used to have thousands of Breath. I ate all of those."

"Thousands? But it would take you years and years to . . ." She trailed off. He'd been alive for over three hundred years. If he absorbed fifty Breaths a year, that *was* thousands of Breaths. "You're an expensive guy to keep around," she noted. "How do you keep yourself from looking like a Returned? And why don't you die when you give away your Breaths?"

"Those are my secrets," he said, not looking at her. "Though you should have figured out that Returned can change their forms."

She raised an eyebrow.

"You've got Returned blood in you," he said. "The royal line. Where do you think that ability to change your hair color comes from?"

"Does that mean I can change more than just my hair?"

"Maybe," he said. "Takes time to learn. Go stroll around the Hallandren Court of Gods sometime, though. You'll find that the gods look exactly as they think they should.

The old ones look old, the heroic ones become strong, the ones who think a beautiful goddess should be well endowed become unnaturally voluptuous. It's all about how they perceive themselves."

And this is how you perceive yourself, Vasher? she thought, curious. *As the scraggly man, rough and unkempt?*

She said nothing of that; she just walked on, her life sense letting her feel the jungle around them. They'd recovered Vasher's cloak, shirt, and trousers—the ones that Denth had originally taken from him. There had been enough Breath in those to split between the two of them and get them each to the Second Heightening. It wasn't as much as she was used to, but it was a fair bit better than nothing.

"So where are we going, anyway?"

"Ever heard of Kuth and Huth?" he asked.

"Sure," she said. "They were your main rivals in the Manywar."

"Somebody's trying to restore them," he said. "A tyrant of some kind. He's apparently recruited an old friend of mine."

"Another one?" she asked.

He shrugged. "There were five of us. Me, Denth, Shashara, Arsteel, and Yesteel. It looks like Yesteel has resurfaced, finally."

"He's related to Arsteel?" Vivenna guessed.

"Brothers."

"Great."

"I know. He's the one who originally figured out how to make ichor-alcohol. I hear rumors that he's got a new form of it. More potent."

"Even better."

They walked in silence for a time longer.

I'm bored, Nightblood said. *Pay attention to me. Why doesn't anyone ever talk to me?*

"Because you're annoying," Vasher snapped.

The sword huffed.

"What's your real name?" Vivenna finally asked.

"My real name?" Vasher asked.

"Yes," she said. "Everyone calls you things. Peacegiver. Kalad. Vasher. Talaxin. Is that last one your real name, the name of the scholar?"

He shook his head. "No."

"Well, what is it, then?"

"I don't know," he said. "I can't remember the time before I Returned."

"Oh," she said.

"When I came back, however, I did get a name," he finally said. "The Cult of Returned—those who eventually founded the Hallandren Iridescent Tones—found me and kept me alive with Breaths. They gave me a name. I didn't like it much. Didn't seem to fit me."

"Well?" she asked. "What was it?"

"Warbreaker the Peaceful," he finally admitted.

She raised an eyebrow.

"What I can't figure out," he said, "is whether that was truly prophetic, or if I'm just trying to live up to it."

"Does it matter?" she asked.

He walked for a time in silence. "No," he finally said. "No, I guess it doesn't. I just wish I knew if there is really something spiritual about the Returns, or if it's all just cosmic happenstance."

"Probably not for us to know."

"Probably," he agreed.

Silence.

"Should have called you Wartlover the Ugly," she finally said.

"Very mature," he replied. "You really think those sorts of comments are proper for a princess?"

She smiled broadly. "I don't care," she said. "And I never have to again."

Ars Arcanum

TABLE OF THE HEIGHTENINGS

Heightening Number	Approximate Breaths Needed to Reach This Heightening	Effects of the Heightening
First	50	Aura Recognition
Second	200	Perfect Pitch
Third	600	Perfect Color Recognition
Fourth	1,000	Perfect Life Sense
Fifth	2,000	Agelessness
Sixth	3,500	Instinctive Awakening
Seventh	5,000	Invested Breath Recognition
Eighth	10,000	Command Breaking
Ninth	20,000	Greater Awakening, Audible Command
Tenth	50,000	Color Distortion, Perfect Invocation, ????

Note One: Reaching above the Sixth Heightening is incredibly rare, and therefore few people understand the powers of the Seventh Heightening and above. Very little research has been done. The only known people ever to reach the Eighth Heightening and above are the Hallandren God Kings.

Note Two: Returned appear to achieve the Fifth Heightening by virtue of their Breath. It is theorized that they do not actually receive two thousand Breaths when they Return, but instead receive a single, powerful Breath, which brings with it the powers of the first five Heightenings.

Note Three: The numbers given in the Table of the Heightenings are only estimates, as very little is known about the upper Heightenings. Indeed, even for the lower levels, fewer or more Breaths may be required to achieve a given Heightening, depending on circumstances and the strength of the Breath.

Note Four: Each additional Breath grants some things, no matter which Heightening an Awakener has achieved. The more breath one has, the more resistant to disease and aging a person is, the easier it is for them to distinguish colors, the more naturally they can learn to Awaken, and the stronger their life sense becomes.

HEIGHTENING POWERS

Aura Recognition: The First Heightening grants a person the ability to see the Breath auras of others instinctively. This allows them to judge roughly how many Breaths the person contains and the general health of that Breath. Persons without this Heightening have a much more difficult time judging auras directly, and must rely instead on how deeply the colors around a person change when they enter the aura. Without at least the First Heightening, it is impossible for the naked eye to notice an Awakener who has fewer than about thirty Breaths.

Perfect Pitch: The Second Heightening grants perfect pitch to those who achieve it.

Perfect Color Recognition: While each gained Breath leads a person to greater appreciation of colors, it isn't until one reaches the Third Heightening that one can instantly and instinctively determine exact shades of colors and their hue harmonics.

Perfect Life Sense: At the Fourth Heightening, an Awakener's life sense achieves its maximum strength.

Agelessness: At the Fifth Heightening, an Awakener's resistance to aging and disease reaches its maximum strength. These persons are immune to most toxins, including the effects of alcohol, and most physical ailments. (Such as headaches, diseases, and organ failure.) The person no longer ages, and becomes functionally immortal.

Instinctive Awakening: All persons of the Sixth Heightening and above immediately understand and can use basic Awakening Commands without training or practice. More difficult Commands are easier for them to master and to discover.

Breath Recognition: Those few persons who have reached the Seventh Heightening gain the ability to recognize the auras of objects, and can tell when something has been Invested with Breath via Awakening.

Command Breaking: Any persons of the Eighth Heightening or more gain the ability to override Commands in other Invested objects, including Lifeless. This requires concentration and leaves the Awakener exhausted.

Greater Awakening: Persons of the Ninth Heightening are reportedly able to Awaken stone and steel, though doing so requires large Investitures of Breath and specialized Commands. This ability has not been studied or confirmed.

Audible Command: Persons of the Ninth Heightening also gain the ability to Awaken objects that they are not physically touching, but that are within the sound of their voice.

Color Distortion: At the Tenth Heightening, an Awakener gains the natural and intrinsic ability to bend light around white objects, creating colors from them as if from a prism.

Perfect Invocation: Awakeners of the Tenth Heightening can draw more color from the objects they use to fuel their art. This leaves objects drained to white, rather than grey.

Other: There are rumors of other powers granted by the Tenth Heightening that are not understood or have not been made known by those who have achieved it.

Tor proudly presents Brandon Sanderson's
The Way of Kings, **the first novel in a
remarkable sequence that will be the
great new fantasy series of this decade.**

Book One of The Stormlight Archive

The Way of Kings

BRANDON SANDERSON

AN AUGUST 2010 HARDCOVER • 978-0-7653-2635-5

From the *New York Times* bestselling author chosen to complete Robert Jordan's internationally bestselling series, The Wheel of Time®, this is the first book of a monumental epic fantasy saga.

"Sanderson is clearly a master of large-scale stories, splendidly depicting worlds.... May the author write long and prosper."

—*Booklist*

**To learn more, sign up at TheStormlightArchive.com.
AND TURN THE PAGE FOR A SNEAK PEEK!**

The love of men is a frigid thing . . . a mountain stream only three steps from the ice. We are his. Oh Storm-father . . . we are his. It is but a thousand days, and the Last Desolation will come.

—Collected on the first day of the week Palah of the month Shash in the year 1171, thirty-one seconds before death. Subject was a darkeyed pregnant woman of middle years. The child did not survive.

Prologue: To Kill

Szeth-son-son-Vallano, Truthless of Shinovar, wore white on the day he was to kill a king. The white clothing was a Parshendi tradition, foreign to him. But he did as his masters required and did not ask for an explanation.

He sat in a large stone room, baked by enormous firepits that cast a garish light upon the revelers, causing beads of sweat to form on their skin as they danced, and drank, and yelled, and sang, and clapped. Some fell to the ground red-faced, the revelry too much for them, their stomachs proving to be inferior wineskins. They looked as if they were dead, at least until their friends carried them out of the feast hall to waiting beds.

Szeth did not sway to the drums, drink the sapphire wine, or stand to dance. He sat on a bench at the back, a still servant in white robes. Few at the treaty-signing celebration noticed him. He was just a servant, and Shin were easy to ignore. Mainlanders thought Szeth's kind were docile and harmless. They were generally right.

The drummers began a new rhythm. The beats shook Szeth like a quartet of thumping hearts, pumping waves of invisible blood through the room. Szeth's masters—the parshmen who were dismissed as savages by those in more civilized kingdoms—had brought the musicians. At first, the Alethi lighteyes had been hesitant. To them, drums were base instruments of the common, darkeyed people. But wine was the great assassin of both tradition and propriety, and now the Alethi elite danced with abandon.

Szeth stood and began to pick his way through the room. The revelry had lasted long; even the king had retired hours ago. But many still celebrated. As he walked, Szeth was forced to step around Dalinar Kholin—the king's own brother—who slumped drunkenly at a small table. The aging but powerfully built man kept waving away those who tried to encourage him to bed. Where was Jasnah, the king's daughter? Elhokar, the king's son and heir, sat at the high table, ruling the feast in his father's absence. He was in conversation with two men, a dark-skinned Azish man who had an odd patch of pale skin on his cheek and a thinner, Alethi-looking man who kept glancing over his shoulder.

The heir's feasting companions were unimportant. Szeth stayed far from the man, skirting the sides of the room, passing rows of unwavering azure lights that bulged out where wall met floor. Those held sapphires infused with Stormlight. Profane. How could the men of these lands use something so sacred for mere illumination? Worse, the Alethi stormwardens—the greatest scholars in the world— were learning to manipulate Stormlight for the creation of fabrials. Rumor had it they were close to being able to create new Shardblades. He hoped that was just wishful boasting. For if it *did* happen, the world would be changed. Likely in a way that ended with people in all countries—from distant Thalenah to towering Jah Keved—speaking Alethi to their children.

They were a grand people, these Alethi. Even drunk, there was a natural nobility to them. Tall and well made, the men dressed in dark silk coats that buttoned down the sides of the chest and were elaborately embroidered in silver or gold. Each one looked a general on the field.

The women were even more splendid. They wore grand silk dresses, tightly fitted, the bright colors a contrast to the dark tones favored by the men. The left sleeve of each dress was longer than the right one, covering the hand in the name of that strange Alethi sense of propriety. Their pure black hair was pinned up atop their heads, either in intricate weavings of braids or in loose piles. Often it was woven with gold ribbons or ornaments, along with gems that glowed with Stormlight. Beautiful. Profane, but beautiful.

Szeth left the feasting chamber behind. Just outside, he passed the doorway into the Beggars' Feast. It was an Alethi tradition, a room where some of the poorest men and women in the city were given a feast complementing that of the king and his guests. A man with a long, grey and black beard slumped in the doorway smiling foolishly—though whether from wine or a weak mind, Szeth could not tell.

"Have you seen me?" he slurred as Szeth passed, then began to speak in giggling gibberish, reaching for a wineskin. So it was drink after all. Szeth brushed by, continuing past a line of statues of the Ten Heralds. Or, at least, nine of them. One was conspicuously missing, though Szeth didn't know why Shalash's statue had been removed. The Alethi king was said to be very devout in his worship. Too devout, by some people's standards.

The hallway here curved to the right, running around the perimeter of the domed palace of Kholinar. They were on the king's floor, two levels up, surrounded by rock walls, ceiling, and floor. That was profane as well. Stone was not to be trod upon. But what was he to do? He was Truthless. He did as his masters demanded.

Szeth's white clothing swished. The loose trousers were tied at the waist with a white rope. Over them he wore a filmy white shirt with long sleeves, open at the front.

White clothing. A tradition among these wild parshmen who—defying all beliefs about their kind—had formed a nation out in the Unclaimed Hills. Although Szeth had not asked why he was told to wear white, his masters had explained anyway. White to be bold. White to not blend into the night. White to give warning.

For if you were going to assassinate a man, he was entitled to see you coming.

Szeth turned right, taking the hallway directly toward the king's chambers. Torches burned on the walls, their light unsatisfying to him, like a meal of thin broth after a long fast. Tiny flamespren danced around them like insects made solely of congealed light. They were useless to him. Fortunately, he saw more of the blue lights ahead: a pair of Stormlight lamps hanging on the wall, brilliant sapphires glowing at their hearts. Szeth walked up to one, holding out his hand to cup it around the glass-shrouded gemstone.

"You there!" a voice called in Alethi. There were two guards at the intersection. Double guard, for there were savages abroad in Kholinar this night. True, those savages were supposed to be allies now. But alliances could be shallow things indeed.

This one wouldn't last the night.

Szeth turned as the two guards approached. They carried spears; they weren't lighteyes, and were therefore forbidden the sword. Their painted red breastplates were ornate, however, as were their helms. They might be darkeyed, but they were high-ranking citizens with honored positions in the royal guard.

Stopping a few feet away, the guard in the lead gestured with his spear. "Go on, now. This is no place for you." He had tan skin and a thin mustache that ran all the way around his mouth, becoming a beard at the bottom.

Szeth didn't move.

"Well?" the guard said. "What are you waiting for?"

Szeth breathed in deeply, drawing forth the Stormlight. It

streamed into him, siphoned from the twin sapphire lamps on the walls, sucked in as if by his deep inhalation. The Stormlight raged inside of him, and the hallway suddenly grew darker, falling into shade like a hilltop cut off from the sun by a transient cloud.

Szeth could feel the Light's warmth, its fury, like a tempest that had been injected directly into his veins. The power of it was invigorating but dangerous. It pushed him to act. To move. To strike.

Holding his breath, he clung to the Stormlight. He could still feel it leaking out. Stormlight could be held for only a short time, a few minutes at most. It leaked away, the human body too porous a container. He had heard that the Voidbringers could hold it in perfectly. But, then, did they even exist? His punishment declared that they didn't. His honor demanded that they did.

Afire with holy energy, Szeth turned to the guards. They could see that he was leaking Stormlight, wisps of it faintly visible curling from his skin like luminescent smoke. The lead guard squinted, frowning. Szeth was sure the man had never seen anything like it before. As far as he knew, Szeth had killed every mainlander who had ever seen what he could do.

"What . . . what are you?" The guard's voice had lost its certainty. "Spirit or man?"

"What am I?" Szeth whispered, a bit of light leaking from his lips. "I'm . . . sorry."

Let it begin, he thought, looking past the man all the way down the long hallway.

Szeth blinked, Lashing himself to that distant point. Stormlight raged from him in a flash, chilling his skin. He lurched where he stood as the ground stopped pulling him downward. For a moment, he was instead yanked toward the far end of the hall.

No, *yanked* was the wrong word. He *fell* toward that distant point. Whatever force, spren, or god it was that held men to the ground had released its grip upon Szeth. From his perspective, the hallway was now a deep shaft down which he fell, with the two guards strangely managing to stand on the wall. This was a partial Lashing, the first of his three kinds of Lashings. It gave him the ability to bind himself, or other objects, to a selected point; he or his subject would then be pulled in that direction instead of toward the ground.

The guards were shocked when Szeth's feet hit them, one for each face, knocking them over. Szeth shifted his view and Lashed himself to the floor. Light leaked from him. The floor of the hallway again became *down*, and he landed between the two guards, clothes crackling and dropping flakes of frost. He rose, beginning the process of summoning his Shardblade.

One of the guards fumbled for his spear. Szeth snapped a hand to the side, touching the soldier's chest while looking up. He focused on a point above him while willing the Light out of his body and into the guard, Lashing the poor man to the ceiling.

The guard yelped in shock as *up* became *down* for him. Light trailing from his form, he fell upward and crashed into the ceiling. Knocked senseless, he dropped his spear. It was not Lashed, so it fell, clattering back to the floor near Szeth.

To kill. It was the greatest of sins. And yet here Szeth stood, Truthless, profanely walking on stones sinfully used for building. And it would not end. As Truthless, there was only one life he was forbidden to take.

And that was his own.

At the tenth beat of his heart, his Shardblade dropped into his waiting hand. It formed as if condensing from mist, beads of water forming along the metal length. His Shardblade was long and thin, edged on both sides, smaller than most others. Szeth swept it out, carving a line in the stone floor beneath him and shearing through the floor-bound guard's neck.

As always, the Shardblade worked oddly; though it cut easily through stone, steel, or anything inanimate, it made no mark on the guard's skin. The man's eyes, however, began to smoke and burn, blackening, shriveling up in his head. He slumped forward, dead. A Shardblade did not cut living flesh, but it killed just the same.

Above, the first guard gasped. He'd managed to get to his feet, even though they were planted on the ceiling of the hallway. "Shardbearer!" he shouted. "A Shardbearer assaults the king's hall! To arms!"

Finally, Szeth thought. Szeth's use of Stormlight was unfamiliar to the guards, but they knew a Shardblade when they saw one.

Szeth bent down and picked up the spear that had fallen from above. As he did so, he released the breath he'd been holding since drawing in the Stormlight. It had sustained him while he held it, but it was running out. The little remaining Light puffed away, dissipating.

Szeth set the spear's butt against the stone floor, then looked upward. The guard above stopped shouting, eyes opening wide as the tails of his shirt began to slip downward, falling toward the ground, the earth below reasserting its dominance. The Light streaming off his body dwindled.

He looked down at Szeth. Down at the spear tip pointing directly at his heart.

The Light ran out. The guard fell.

He screamed as he hit, the spear impaling him through the chest. Szeth let the spear fall away, carried to the ground with a muffled *thump* by the body twitching on its end. Shardblade in hand, he turned down a side corridor, following the map he'd memorized. He ducked around a corner and flattened himself against the wall, just as a troop of guards reached the dead men. The newcomers began shouting immediately, continuing the alarm.

His instructions were clear. Kill the king, but be seen doing it. Let the Alethi know you are coming and what you are doing. Why? Why did the Parshendi agree to this treaty, only to send an assassin the very night of its signing? Why did they insist that Szeth raise an uproar with the attacks?

More gemstones glowed on the walls of the hallway here. King Gavilar liked lavish display, and he couldn't know that he was leaving sources of power for Szeth to use in his Lashings. The things he did hadn't been seen for millennia. Histories from those times were all but nonexistent, and the legends were inaccurate.

Szeth peeked back out into the corridor and allowed himself to be seen. One of the guards at the intersection pointed and yelled. Szeth made sure they got a good look, then ducked away. He took a deep breath as he ran, drawing in the Stormlight. His body came alive with it, and his speed increased, his muscles bursting with energy. Light became a storm inside of him; his blood thundered in his ears. It was terrible and wonderful at the same time.

Two corridors down, one to the side. He threw open the door of a storage room for furniture. Szeth hesitated a moment—just long enough for a guard to round the corner and see him—then dashed into the room. Preparing for a full Lashing, he raised his arm and commanded the Stormlight to pool there, causing the skin to burst alight with its radiance. Then he flung his hand out toward the doorframe, spraying white luminescence across it like paint. He slammed the door just as the guards arrived.

The Stormlight held the door in the frame with the strength of a hundred arms. A full Lashing bound objects together solidly, holding them fast until the Stormlight ran out. It took longer to create—and drained Stormlight far more quickly—than a partial Lashing. The door handle shook, and then the wood began to crack as the guards threw their weight against it, one man calling for an axe.

Szeth crossed the room in rapid strides, weaving around the shrouded furniture. He reached the far wall and— preparing himself for yet another blasphemy—he raised his Shardblade and slashed horizontally through the dark grey stone. The rock sliced easily. Two vertical slashes followed, then one across the bottom, cutting a large square block. He pressed his hand against it, willing Stormlight into the stone. Behind him the room's door began to split.

Looking over his shoulder and focusing on the shaking door, he Lashed the block in that direction. Frost crystallized on his clothing—Lashing something so large drained a great deal of his Stormlight away. The tempest within him stilled, like a storm reduced to a drizzle.

He stepped aside. The large stone block shuddered, sliding outward. Normally, moving the block would have been impossible. Its own weight would have held it against the stones below. Yet now, that same weight pulled it free; for the block, the direction of the room's door was *down*. With a deep grinding sound, the block slid free of the wall and tumbled through the air. The soldiers finally broke through the door, staggering into the room.

And then the block crashed into them.

Szeth turned his back on the cries of agony and the terrible sound of the block crushing stone, wood, and bones. He ducked and stepped through his new hole, entering the hallway outside.

He walked slowly, drawing Stormlight from the lamps he passed, siphoning it to him and stoking anew the tempest within. As the lamps dimmed, the corridor was cast into shadow, like a tunnel. A thick wooden door stood at the end of the stone hallway, and as he approached, small fearspren—shaped like globs of purple goo—began to wriggle from the masonry, pointing toward the doorway. They were drawn by the terror being felt on the other side.

Szeth pushed the door open, entering the last corridor leading to the king's chambers. Interspersed among the tall, red ceramic vases lining it were nervous soldiers. They waited for him, flanking the long, narrow carpet. It was red, like a river of blood.

The two spearmen in front didn't wait for him to get close. They broke into a trot to gain momentum, lifting their spears. Szeth slammed his hand to the side, pushing Stormlight into the doorframe, using the third kind of his Lashings, a reverse Lashing. This one worked differently from the other two. The doorframe did not emit Stormlight; indeed, it seemed to pull nearby light *into* it, giving it a strange penumbra.

The spearmen threw, and Szeth stood still, hand on the doorframe. A reverse Lashing required his constant touch, but took comparatively little Stormlight. During one, anything that approached him was pulled toward the object he was touching. The spears veered in the air, splitting around him and slamming into the wooden frame. As he felt them hit, Szeth leaped into the air and Lashed himself to the right wall with a blink, his feet hitting the stone with a slap.

He reoriented himself immediately. *He* wasn't standing on the wall. The soldiers were, the bloodred carpet streaming behind them like a long tapestry. Szeth bolted down the hallway, striking with his Shardblade, shearing through the necks of the two men who had thrown spears at him. Their eyes burned, and they collapsed.

The other guards in the hallway began to panic. Some tried to attack him, others yelled for more help, still others cringed away from him. The attackers had trouble—they were disoriented by the oddity of striking at someone who hung on the wall. Szeth flipped into the air, tucked into a roll, and Lashed himself back to the floor. He hit the ground in the midst of the soldiers.

Completely surrounded, but holding a Shardblade.

According to legend, the Shardblades were first carried by the Knights Radiant uncounted ages ago, as gifts of their god. Only the Shardblades enabled them to fight the horrors of rock and flame, dozens of feet tall, foes whose eyes burned with hatred. The Voidbringers. When your foe had skin as hard as stone itself, steel was useless. Something supernal was required.

Szeth rose from his crouch, loose white clothes rippling, jaw clenched against his sins. He struck out, his weapon flashing with reflected torchlight. Elegant wide swings. Three of them, one after another. Much though he wished to, he could neither close his ears to the screams that followed, nor avoid seeing the men fall. They dropped around him like toys knocked over by a child's careless kick. If the Blade cut a man's spine, he died, eyes burning. If it cut through a limb, it killed that limb. One soldier stumbled away from him, arm flopping uselessly on his shoulder. He would never be able to feel it, or use it, again.

Szeth lowered his Shardblade, standing among the cinder-eyed corpses. Here, in Alethkar, men often spoke of the legends—of mankind's hard-won victory over the Void-bringers. But when weapons created to fight nightmares were turned against common soldiers, the lives of men became cheap things indeed.

Szeth turned and continued on his way, slippered feet falling silently on the soft red rug. The Shardblade, as always, glistened silver and clean. When one killed with a Blade, there was no blood. That seemed to Szeth to be a sign. The Shardblade was just a tool; it could not be blamed for the murders.

The door at the end of the hallway burst open. Szeth froze as another small group of soldiers rushed out, ushering away a man in regal robes, his head ducked down as if to avoid possible arrows. The soldiers wore deep blue, the color of the king's guard, and the sight of the corpses Szeth had left didn't make them stop and gawk. They were prepared for what a Shardbearer could do. They opened a side door and shoved their ward through, several leveling spears at Szeth as they backed out.

Another figure stepped out of the king's quarters; he

wore glistening blue armor made of smoothly interlocking plates. Unlike common plate armor, however, there was no leather or mail visible at the joints—just smaller plates, fitting together with intricate precision. He carried an enormous single-edged sword, a Blade designed to slay dark gods, a larger counterpart to the one Szeth carried.

Szeth hesitated. A Shardbearer would have to be dealt with before he chased the king; he could not leave such a foe behind.

Besides, perhaps a Shardbearer could defeat him, kill him and end his miserable life. His Lashings wouldn't work directly on someone in Shardplate, and the armor would enhance the man, strengthen him. It was also the only defense that would resist a Shardblade except for another Shardblade. Szeth's honor would not allow him to betray his mission or seek death. But if that death occurred, he *would* welcome it.

Once again, he Lashed himself to the side of the hallway, leaping into the air with a twist and landing on the wall. He dashed forward, Blade held at the ready. The Shardbearer fell into an aggressive posture, using one of the swordplay stances favored here in the east, and swept out with his Blade. He moved far more nimbly than one would expect for a man in such bulky armor. Shardplate was special, as ancient and magical as the Blades it complemented.

Szeth leaped again, skipping to the side and Lashing himself to the ceiling as the Shardbearer's Blade sliced into the wall. Chunks of mortar and stone fell free; Szeth landed and struck out at his opponent's head. The Shardbearer ducked, going down on one knee, letting Szeth's Blade cleave empty air.

Szeth dashed forward, running above the Shardbearer before Lashing himself to the floor again. He flipped to land on his feet and slammed his Blade into his opponent's armor.

Shardplate didn't bend or dent like common metal. It *cracked*. Where Szeth's Blade hit, the Plate on the Shardbearer's side sent out a web of glowing lines. Stormlight began to leak free.

Stormlight. It both gave durability to Shardplate and strengthened its wearer—without its infused gemstones, the armor was too heavy to move in, let alone fight in. Szeth danced out of range as the Shardbearer swung in anger, trying to cut at Szeth's knees. The tempest within Szeth gave him many advantages—including the ability to quickly recover from small wounds—but would not be able to restore limbs killed by a Shardblade.

He dashed forward. Briefly Lashing himself to the ceiling for lift, Szeth leaped over a swing from the Shardbearer, then immediately Lashed himself back to the floor and struck again. But the Shardbearer recovered just as quickly and reached out precisely with his backswing, coming dangerously close to hitting Szeth. The man was good, well trained. Many Shardbearers depended too much on the power of their weapon and armor. This man was different. In other circumstances, Szeth might have enjoyed the fight, but right now he was too concerned about the fleeing king.

He jumped to the wall and struck at the Shardbearer with quick, terse attacks, like a snapping eel. The Shardbearer fended him off with wide, sweeping counters, as necessitated by the size of his Blade. Its length kept Szeth at bay, and he was unable to get close enough to land any more blows.

This is taking too long! If the king slipped away into hiding, Szeth would fail in his mission no matter how many people he killed. He ducked in for another strike, but the Shardbearer forced him back. Each second this fight lasted was another for the king's escape.

It was time to be reckless. Szeth launched into the air, Lashing himself to the other end of the hallway, falling feetfirst toward his adversary. The Shardbearer didn't hesitate to swing, but Szeth Lashed himself down at an angle, dropping immediately. The Shardblade swished through the air above him as he landed in a crouch, using his momentum to throw himself forward.

He swung at the Shardbearer's side, where the Plate had cracked, and struck with a powerful blow. That piece of the Plate shattered, bits of molten metal streaking away. The Shardbearer grunted, dropping to one knee, raising a hand to his side. Szeth raised a foot to the man's shoulder and threw him backward with a Stormlight-enhanced shove.

The heavy Shardbearer crashed into the door of the king's quarters, smashing it and falling partway into the room beyond. Szeth left him, ducking instead through the doorway to the right through which the king had been taken. The hallway here had the same red carpet and was lined with carved reliefs on the walls. The Stormlight lamps between the reliefs gave Szeth a chance to recharge the tempest within, which was nearly gone.

Energy blazed within him again, and he sped up. If he could get far enough ahead, he could deal with the king first, then turn back to fight off the Shardbearer. It wouldn't be easy. A full Lashing on a doorway wouldn't stop a Shardbearer, and with that Plate he would be able to run supernaturally fast. Szeth glanced over his shoulder.

The Shardbearer wasn't following. The man sat up in his armor, looking dazed. Perhaps Szeth had wounded him more seriously than he'd thought.

Or maybe . . .

Szeth froze. He thought of the ducked head of the man who'd been rushed out, face obscured. The Shardbearer *still* wasn't following. He was so skilled. It was said that few men could rival Gavilar Kholin's swordsmanship. Could it be?

Szeth turned and dashed back the way he had come, trusting his instincts. As soon as the Shardbearer saw him, he climbed to his feet with alacrity. Szeth ran faster. What was the safest place for your king? In the hands of some guards, fleeing? Or protected in a suit of Shardplate, left behind, dismissed as a bodyguard?

Clever, Szeth thought as the formerly sluggish Shard-bearer fell into another battle stance. Szeth attacked with renewed vigor, swinging his Blade in a flurry of strikes. The Shardbearer—the king—aggressively struck out with broad, sweeping blows. Szeth pulled away from one of these, feeling the wind of the weapon passing just inches before him, then ducked and dashed underneath the follow-through, slipping past the Shardbearer and into the room. Szeth swung his Blade as he passed, cracking more of the Plate on the king's side.

The king spun around to follow, but Szeth ran through the lavishly furnished chamber, flinging out his hand, touching pieces of furniture he passed. He invested them with Stormlight, Lashing them to a point behind the king. The furniture tumbled as if the room had been turned on its side, couches, chairs, and tables dropping toward the surprised king. Gavilar made the mistake of chopping at them with his Shardblade. The weapon easily sheared through a large couch, but the furniture still crashed into him, making him stumble. A footstool hit him next, throwing him to the ground.

Unfortunately, Szeth couldn't Lash the furniture to a moving person—with a partial Lashing, you Lashed to a specific point, and that became *down* for the object. If he could get close enough, he could use a reverse Lashing on a person, causing objects—particularly those in motion—to be attracted to him. But the Shardplate would protect the king from that.

Gavilar rolled out of the way of the furniture and charged forward, Plate leaking streams of Light from the cracked sections. Szeth gathered himself, then leaped into the air, Lashing himself backward and to the right as the king arrived. He zipped out of the way of the king's blow, then Lashed himself forward with a double partial Lashing.

Stormlight flashed out of him, clothing freezing, as he was pulled toward the king at twice the speed of a normal fall.

The king's posture indicated surprise, and the maneuver got Szeth close enough to land a blow on his helm, cracking it. Szeth immediately Lashed himself to the ceiling and fell upward, slamming into the stone roof above. He'd Lashed himself in too many directions too quickly, and his body had lost track, making it difficult to land as gracefully as he had earlier. He stumbled back to his feet.

Below, the king stepped back, trying to get into position to swing up at him. The king used a one-handed swing, reaching for the ceiling, but Szeth Lashed himself downward, going for the helm again.

He'd underestimated his opponent. The king anticipated his move, and as Szeth hit the helm a second time, the Shardbearer struck with a prepared punch, slamming his gauntleted fist into Szeth's face.

Blinding light flashed in Szeth's eyes, a counterpoint to the sudden pain that crashed across his face. Everything blurred, his vision fading.

Pain. So much *pain*!

He screamed, Stormlight leaving him in a rush, and he hit something hard. The balcony doors. The blow had flung him backward into them; such an impact would have killed an ordinary man. More pain broke out across his back, like someone had stabbed him with a hundred daggers, and he rolled to a stop, everything trembling.

No time for pain. No time for pain. No time for pain!

He blinked, shaking his head, the world blurry and dark. Was he blind? No. It was dark outside. He was on the wooden balcony; the force of the blow had thrown him through the doors. Something was thumping. Heavy footfalls. The Shardbearer!

Szeth stumbled to his feet, vision swimming. Blood streamed from the side of his face, and Stormlight rose

from his skin, blinding his left eye. The Light. It would heal him, if it could, keeping him alive. His jaw felt unhinged. Broken? He'd dropped his Shardblade.

A lumbering shadow moved in front of him; the Shardbearer's armor had leaked enough Stormlight that the king was having trouble walking. But he was coming.

Szeth screamed, kneeling, pushing Stormlight into the wooden balcony, Investing it, Lashing it downward. The air frosted around him. The tempest roared, traveling down his arms into the wood. He Lashed the wood downward with another partial Lashing, then did it again. He Lashed a fourth time as Gavilar stepped onto the wood.

The balcony lurched under the extra weight. The wood cracked, straining. The Shardbearer hesitated.

Szeth Lashed the balcony downward a fifth time. The balcony supports shattered and the entire structure broke free from the building, tumbling in the air. Szeth screamed through a broken jaw and used the final bit of his Stormlight to Lash himself to the side of the building. He fell to the side, past the shocked Shardbearer, hitting the wall and rolling.

The balcony dropped away, the king looking up with shock as he lost his footing. The fall was brief. In the moonlight, Szeth watched solemnly—vision still fuzzy, blinded in one eye—as the structure crashed to the stone ground below. The wall of the palace shook with the blow, and the crash of broken wood echoed from the nearby buildings.

Still standing on the wall, Szeth groaned, climbing to his feet. He felt weak; he'd used his Stormlight too quickly, straining his body. He stumbled down the side of the building, approaching the wreckage, barely able to stand up.

The king was still moving. Shardplate would protect a man from such a fall, but both the helm and the second plate Szeth had cracked were now shattered. A large length of bloodied wood stuck up through Gavilar's side. Szeth knelt down, inspecting the man's pain-wracked face. Strong

features, square chin, black beard flecked with white. Gavilar Kholin.

"I . . . expected you . . . to come," the king said between gasps.

Szeth reached underneath the front of the man's breastplate, tapping the straps there. They unfastened, and he pulled the front of the breastplate free, exposing the gemstones on its interior. Two had been cracked and burned out. Three still glowed. Numb, Szeth breathed in sharply, absorbing the Light.

The storm began to rage again, and more Light rose from the side of his face, repairing his damaged skin and bones. The pain was still great; Stormlight healing was not instantaneous.

The king coughed. "You can tell . . . Thaidakar . . . that he's too late. . . ."

"I don't know who that is," Szeth said, standing, his words slurring from his broken jaw. Speaking hurt, but he was accustomed to pain. He held his hand to the side, resummoning his Shardblade.

The king frowned. "Then who . . . ? Restares? Sadeas? I never thought. . . ."

"My masters are the Parshendi," Szeth said. Ten heartbeats passed, and his Blade dropped into his hand, wet with condensation.

"The Parshendi? That makes no sense." Gavilar coughed, hand quivering, reaching toward his chest and fumbling at a pocket. He pulled out a small crystalline sphere tied to a chain. "You must take this. They must not get it." He seemed dazed. "Tell . . . tell my brother . . . he must find the most important words a man can say. . . ."

Gavilar fell still.

Szeth hesitated, then knelt down and took the sphere. It was odd, unlike any he'd seen before. Though it was completely dark, it seemed to glow somehow. With a light that was black.

The Parshendi? Gavilar had said. *That makes no sense.*

"Nothing makes sense anymore," Szeth whispered, tucking the strange sphere away. "It's all unraveling. Everything. I am sorry, King of the Alethi. I doubt that you care. Not anymore, at least." He stood up. "At least you won't have to watch the world ending with the rest of us."

Beside the king's body, his Shardblade materialized from mist, clattering to the stones now that its master was dead. It was worth a fortune; kingdoms had fallen as men vied to possess a single Shardblade.

Szeth glanced upward. Shouts of alarm came from inside the palace. He needed to go. But . . .

Tell my brother. . . .

To Szeth's people, a dying request was sacred and must always be honored. He took the king's hand, dipping it in the man's own blood, then used it to scrawl the words he had spoken on the wood beside him. *Brother. You must find the most important words a man can say.*

With that, Szeth escaped into the night. He left the king's Shardblade lying where it had fallen; he had no use for it.

The Blade Szeth already carried was curse enough.